THE FATEBOUND DUOLOGY OMNIBUS

THE FATEBOUND DUOLOGY OMNIBUS

Victoria Mier

Content Warnings

Pronunciation Guide

NAMES
Bedwyr: BED-weer
Blodeuwedd: bluh-DIE-weth
Bronwyn: brahn-WIN
Caledfwlch: KAL-led-fulk
Coblynau: COB-learn-eye
Danu: DA-noo
Emrys: EM-riss
Maelona: MY-lone-ah
Raegan: American pronunciation is RAY-gen, Irish is REE-gan

PLACES
Can Goedog: CARH-n koy-dog
Defynogg: DEV-in-no
Hiraeth: HERE-ayeth
Sgwd Yr Eira: skood uhr EAR-ah

MISC.
Cariad: KARR-ee-ayd (Cormac and Oberon would both slightly roll the "r")

Part One
Beyond the Aching Door

Book One
of the
FATEBOUND
DUOLOGY

BEYOND THE
ACHING
DOOR

a novel by

VICTORIA MIER

CHAPTER ONE

The September day dawned golden and glorious, ushering in a cool breeze, sunlight thick as molasses, and the third drowning in five days.

"Hey, Raegan," the barista—Sam, was it?—greeted as she approached. "The usual? Don't typically see you so early."

Four more text messages from her editor lit up Raegan's phone in rapid succession. She sighed. "No, I'm gonna do a sixteen-ounce drip today," she replied, digging her knuckles into still-sleepy eyes. "To go. The strong shit, please."

The barista rang her up, and Raegan paid, digging into the pockets of her long woolen overcoat for a crumpled dollar bill, which she dropped into the tip jar. She skirted the small crowd of customers awaiting their orders at the pick-up counter, instead moving to lean against one of the café's floor-to-ceiling windows. On the other side of the glass, the sidewalk teemed with morning rush-hour traffic: men in suits and screaming schoolchildren and people running late for their bus. All things she normally avoided by not waking up this fucking early.

Her order appeared on the counter, and Raegan snatched it, taking a large gulp that seared her tongue. She slammed on a travel lid and made her way to the side door. Outside, the remaining puddles and water droplets from last night's rainstorm shimmered in the sunlight, winking at her as if secrets sailed on their shallow depths.

She felt the buzz of more texts arriving and ignored it, though she lengthened her stride, suspicion curling in her belly. Her editor, Henry, trusted her the most out of his team of reporters, valuing her quick, ruthless mind, and unerring ability to connect the dots. And Raegan felt pretty sure Henry's early morning distress call, today's drowning, and the lead crime reporter's emergency gallbladder surgery were all going to tie up in a neat little bow. A bow that might very well knot itself around *her* neck.

When her phone rang half a block from the subway station, Raegan sighed, moving her coffee into her left hand and shifting the weight of her leather shoulder bag. She dug the phone out from her pocket, unsurprised by the name on her screen.

"I'm about to get on the subway," Raegan said after answering the call. "How many times are you going to call me, Henry? You could at least tell me why you want me in the newsroom right this second. I hate waking up early. Almost as much as I hate surprises."

"I'll explain everything when you get here," Henry replied, his voice even despite Raegan's venomous tone. "Sorry. It's a shitshow."

"Isn't it always?" Raegan drawled, making use of the last few seconds ticking down on the crosswalk display. She took a running step to clear the puddle around the curb, the heavy lug soles of her boots thudding on the sidewalk. Up ahead, the mouth of the subway station yawned wide.

"Look," Raegan said, interrupting something Henry was saying about a meeting with the managing editor of the paper. "I'm about to head into the station, so I'm gonna lose you. See you in a few, okay?"

"Yeah, sounds good," Henry replied, distracted. Raegan could make out what sounded like a loud conversation, or an argument, in the background. "See you in a minute."

Raegan hung up, shoved her phone into her pocket and then descended the stairs. The subterranean dimness was a welcome relief—the sun had been stabbing its yellow fingers into her eyes all morning. She wove through the station's bowels, arriving at her platform with only a light sheen of sweat dampening the small of her back.

Gray concrete hunched all around her, abandoned Styrofoam

containers and torn plastic bags scuttling across the tracks below. Other subway riders dotted the platform, mostly consumed by their phones, a few with their noses buried in books.

The screech of an incoming train shattered the air. She watched it approach, the dull silver of its mechanical hide glinting in the darkness of the subway tunnel. After boarding, she settled into a seat. The scratched orange fiberglass was slippery beneath her overcoat. She tilted her head back and drew a deep breath. The air smelled only faintly of piss at this hour, a pleasant surprise. As the train pulled away from the station, she tried her best to ignore the pop song blasting from someone's phone. Every day, Raegan got a little closer to strangling people who didn't think headphones were necessary in public spaces.

As her destination grew closer, a migraine thudded in her skull and irritation boiled poisonous in the pit of her stomach. God, it was only Wednesday. She sunk into her seat as the subway slowed to a halt, the sticky floor gluing the soles of her boots to the ground. Raegan scanned the busy platform through the windows in that way she usually did—always searching, just in case.

The outline of a tall figure leaning against the station's wall snagged Raegan's attention. The person read as masculine, clearly and aggressively so, at least a head taller than the other commuters milling about. He was dressed in nondescript but well-fitting black clothing; the way the fabric pulled at his broad shoulders spoke to hard-earned, coiled muscle. He carried no bag, and his casual stance—one hand in his pocket, weight evenly distributed—seemed deadly somehow.

As Raegan looked more closely, transfixed for a reason she could not place, she took in dark tumbles of wavy black hair, an unusually angular face, and a full, sculpted mouth that contrasted with the sharp jaw and knife-like cheekbones. The subway door slid open, and their gazes met for the barest of seconds. Even in the flickering underground light, she could see his eyes were a deep, unusual shade of gray, like the ocean in a storm.

All thoughts of the early morning and her frustration with Henry's weirdness and even the jarring chorus of the pop song melted away entirely. Raegan's heart leapt, familiarity crawling up her throat. A busker's violin music slipped through the subway car's open door like a silk scarf, the notes sweet as honeycomb. An entire sea swelled in her chest. Her breath caught, a broken-winged swallow in her throat, and desire crept up from between her legs. Pain bloomed in her fingers from how hard she was gripping the edge of her seat, nails scrabbling for purchase on the slippery surface.

And then the doors shut and the train rambled off. Raegan collapsed back, her breath coming in hard and fast. Her muscles flexed, ready to do whatever was necessary to get back to him. An alien thought rose in her mind: all she had *ever* done was try to get back to him. She squeezed her eyes shut, trying to breathe through the yearning unspooling in her chest. Dropping her head into her hands, Raegan fought hard to stay in the moment, in her body.

"Breathe," she murmured, suddenly incapable of remembering anything her therapist had told her to do when her mind scrambled to assign meaning to the meaningless. "Just breathe."

CHAPTER TWO

When the train's automated voice announced its arrival at Market East station, Raegan scrambled to her feet before the subway could even come to a halt, eager to leave the liminal space of an underground tunnel on the second to last day of September. This month always felt like a hinge, creaking open wider and wider until she had no choice but to face another October and another anniversary of the worst thing that had ever happened to her.

The subway spat her out into a huge indoor mall clad in tiles the color of dried blood and dotted with wells of dusty fake plants. All of it familiar, simple, real, which allowed Raegan to convince herself that nothing had happened at all. She'd seen an attractive stranger and had a little daydream. She'd been up early, functioning on only a few hours of sleep. Maybe the caffeine hadn't set in yet. As she trudged up the flight of stairs to the newsroom's back door, Raegan banished that odd, lilting yearning further and further away with each step.

At the landing, she scanned her keycard and pulled the door open. She was greeted by drab gray carpet, a sea of cubicles, and ridiculously tall ceilings, courtesy of the building's past as an industrial plant. Raegan released a long breath, her shoulders relaxing. The newsroom always soothed her. It was a monument to fact—a place where only the truth mattered.

People watched Raegan as she made her way to her desk. Even the sports guys stared. Her ease faltered. When she came around a sharp corner, nearly home free in the features section, the food critic stood up in his chair and gaped at her. Raegan lost her patience.

"Okay, what the fuck?" she demanded, dropping her bag onto her desk with a thud.

The food critic pulled a pen out of his pocket for no apparent reason. "Vince is laid up with the gallbladder surgery, so they're talking about making you lead on the drownings."

Raegan yanked her coat off, throwing it across the back of her chair. "That probably pissed some people off," she replied, looking over her shoulder with an arched brow. The copy editor across the aisle from her suddenly became very interested in his cell phone.

"Sure did." The food critic sniffed. "I mean, you're very young. With all due respect."

Raegan wanted to bat the words away like a stupid fly, but anger boiled in her stomach, red-hot against her insides. Warmth rose to her face, venom accumulating on her tongue. "I'm thirty, for fuck's sake." She massaged her temples as her migraine thundered louder in her skull. "And you write about food. With all due respect."

The food critic nudged his glasses farther down his nose in surprise, taking her in. "You're thirty? I thought you just graduated college."

Raegan gritted her teeth, reminding herself that there would be an uncomfortable number of witnesses were she to murder her colleague right here, right now.

"I hardly think Raegan's age matters," a cool voice said from behind her shoulder. She felt the surge of anger slow, more smoke than fire, at the arrival of Henry Washington. "You might recall, Colin, her excellent track record and multiple awards. Or maybe you don't, because as Raegan mentioned, you *do* write about food, which renders your opinion on investigative journalism a bit meaningless, doesn't it?"

Colin made a small noise and sat back down. In a mirror movement, Henry pulled a chair from a nearby cubicle and sat in it.

"So," Raegan said, leaning back against her desk, arms crossed. "You're putting me on the drownings?"

Henry's mouth twitched with amusement. "Yes," he replied, looking up at her. "The fact that you already figured it out makes me confident in my choice. Your appalling lack of a work-life balance also helps."

Raegan drummed her fingers across the peeling surface of her desk, emotions warring for dominance in her chest. Without glancing at Henry, she dragged a hand through her hair and squeezed her eyes shut.

"What? Did *he* get to you?" Henry asked in a low, incredulous tone. "Office politics have never seemed to bother you."

His words barely registered. With her eyes closed, the darkness loomed closer, and though Raegan knew she stood in the familiarity of the newsroom, she felt as though she could just as easily pitch herself into the void. Apprehension ate away at her excitement with sharp teeth that threatened to tear open old wounds.

"Unless it's not office politics you're worried about," Henry continued, clearly just as good at connecting the dots himself. "Does this hesitation I'm sensing have something to do with the fact it's almost October?"

At that, Raegan had no choice but to open her eyes. The return of the overhead lights sent her migraine into a howl, and she clenched her jaw, gaze meeting Henry's. She said nothing, daring her editor to keep going. He must have recognized something in her expression because he stared out the large windows instead of looking at her. Raegan glanced down at her hands, examining the raw, red cuticles.

"Look," Henry said, still gazing out the window. "There's whispers from the police department that this is a potential serial killer. I trust you to report this in a way that will keep people safe."

Raegan said nothing, lifting her coffee cup to her mouth even though she knew it was empty. The newsroom was quiet this time of the morning. She normally didn't arrive until closer to noon, typical for her section; a late start made it easier to cover events that didn't begin until eight PM or later. The soft hush made her feel exposed.

Glancing up, she found Henry looking at her. "It's been almost twenty years, Raegan," her editor said, concern and fondness creasing the skin around his brown eyes as he took her in. "Are you really going to do this every October for the rest of your life?"

She narrowed her gaze at him, opening her mouth to speak, but Henry held up a hand. "Actually, don't answer that," he said, leaning forward, elbows on his knees. "Take a day. I can hold the wolves back for a bit. Have your annual mope and then let me know tomorrow. Okay?"

Raegan chewed the inside of her lip. A war brewed within her. She wanted this opportunity. The desire to sink her teeth into whatever was going on in her city burned hot and bright. But she also wanted—*needed* —to follow her mourning practice. It didn't matter how many years it had been; Henry would understand that if he'd ever lost someone in the way she had.

"You made me get out of bed and rush here just to tell me I could have a day to think about it?" Raegan asked, arching a brow.

Her editor laughed, picking at a loose thread on his blazer. For a moment, he avoided answering her, but then his dark, warm eyes met hers. "Appearances, Raegan," Henry replied, gesturing to the offices ringing the outer corner of the newsroom—the ones that belonged to the managing editor, editor-in-chief, and head copyeditor. "I fought for you on this. Had to make it look like you wanted it bad, too."

"It's not that I don't—"

"I know," Henry said, cutting her off, scratching the side of his head. "But I wanted to buy you some time."

Raegan sank into her chair, one arm resting on her carefully organized desk. She crossed her ankle over her knee and stared her editor down. "You're going to tell them I said yes, aren't you?"

"I am," Henry replied solemnly, folding his arms. "People are *drowning* in the middle of a city, Raegan. They're drowning on the goddamn pavement. How in the hell is someone like you going to resist?"

Chapter Three

Henry was right, like he usually was. She couldn't ignore the buzz that started up in her skull when he suggested she have a look at the latest crime scene.

"If you tell me tomorrow you're not in a place to take the lead, fine, I'll handle it," Henry said, getting to his feet. "Besides, getting you to today's crime scene is mostly why I dared to awaken the beast from her slumber."

"It was a smart move." Raegan pulled her freshly charged voice recorder from a drawer, though she doubted anyone would let her get them on record. She shoved a notebook and two pens into her pockets before dry-swallowing some ibuprofen for her migraine. "You're thinking if you let me get a taste, I probably won't be able to let go."

"It's possibly the first serial around these parts in some time." Henry sounded amused despite the dark topic, skirting around her statement.

Raegan stood, searching for her press badge. She almost never used it—didn't usually need to with her work in features—but it might help her not get kicked out of an active crime scene. Or it would *definitely* get her kicked out, depending on which cops were at the location.

"It's a fucked up killing method," she said, trying to focus on the story, seeing if it would distract her from the other tale that she ached to tell this time of year. "They've been trying so hard to pass it off as a series of oddly similar accidents, I almost started to believe it. I mean, drowning? In puddles? And these men, yes, they're vulnerable due to being unhoused, but they're not small."

"The guy this morning was 6'2" apparently, well over two hundred pounds," Henry said, leaning against the half-wall of her cubicle. "Even if the victims were drugged or otherwise incapacitated, they shouldn't be drowning."

"I think the puddles are deeper when the attack occurs," Raegan said, reaching around to the back of her waistband to make sure her knife was there. "And then they dry up. Or something."

Raegan could feel her mind pivoting, less a dark sea and more a dagger, all her frantic energy finding something to settle on. She loved journalism because it could devour her completely and she wouldn't have to poke her head out into her personal life for days, maybe weeks. She'd more or less won awards for being obsessive and antisocial.

"I meant what I said," Henry began, breaking her train of thought. "If you can't take it on . . . I . . . I just know this time of year can be tough."

Raegan set her jaw. "Yeah." Her mind threatened to lose its focus on things that were not her life, the hard-won mask slipping for a moment. "Serial killer drownings will certainly lighten it up."

Henry hesitated, a pained look crossing his face. "Hey, I'm sorry—"

"No," Raegan said, waving her hand. "It's fine. That was supposed to be a joke."

He smiled. "Well, unfortunately, it wasn't very funny."

"Do you have the address of the newest crime scene?" she asked, shoving anything that wasn't work-related out of her head.

"Already emailed it to you." Henry beamed at her like he had just sent her a particularly cute video of a puppy, not the location of a dead body.

Raegan was already refreshing the email app on her phone. Despite her hesitation, the thrill of the hunt began to sing in her body like an old hymn.

"I'll see if they'll tell me anything real," she said, pulling her coat back on and grabbing her bag from the ground.

"You do have a way with people," Henry called after her. "It's kind of creepy but usually effective."

She looked over her shoulder and flashed a grin, a real one for once, before disappearing around the corner.

～

Raegan had known the second she saw the address that it was going to be weird. People who struggled with homelessness did turn up dead in her city but not usually in wealthy neighborhoods. The places that got their streets plowed first during blizzards for no reason other than median income could not be expected to bear the unsightliness of housing inequality, much less an actual crime scene.

In the slanting morning light, the alley off Delancey Place looked more like a European side street than a crime scene. Wisteria vines draped across whitewashed brick arches, and moss grew thick and lush between the mortar. But there was the crime scene tape all the same, and a man about her age in a medical examiner's jacket bent over a clipboard.

"Excuse me," Raegan said, turning on her smile. "I'm a reporter and was just wondering if you could tell me a little bit about what's going on."

"I'm sorry," the man replied without looking at her. "I'm not supposed to talk to the press."

Before she could reply, he threw a cursory glance over his shoulder. Only then did he turn, tucking away his pen and considering Raegan, eyes sliding down her frame. "It's not that I wouldn't want to help *you*, trust me."

Internally, Raegan shrugged. She could work with that, at least.

"Oh, I totally understand," she said, letting out a sigh and fiddling with her notebook as if she had never opened one before. "I'll go see who else I can speak with. I'm just hoping for some context, not a quote. And my editor said an experienced medical professional like yourself would be the best, since this is apparently . . . strange."

He considered her, and she let him look at whatever he wanted to. "If you're not quoting," he began, taking a step closer. "I can see why you wouldn't want a random officer giving you a rundown."

"No quotes," Raegan confirmed, smiling. Her face hurt.

"It's bizarre," the medical examiner murmured. "The guy drowned.

Like, lungs full of water, pulmonary distress, blue skin. But we found him in a puddle. A tiny, shallow puddle, and there's no indication the body was moved."

Raegan studied him carefully, wanting to make sure he wasn't bullshitting her.

"I'm dead serious," he told her, holding up his hands. "I'm out here because we need to collect about a million samples to figure out how this happened."

"Weird," Raegan conceded. "Thanks."

The medical examiner was digging in his pocket for his card, encouraging her to give him a call if she needed "anything at all" in a tone Raegan did not like, when two police officers rounded the corner. One of them was, of course, Detective Bartley.

"Shit," she exhaled through gritted teeth, the smile gone, her voice dropping an octave back to its natural tone.

"Miss Overhill? Is that you?" the detective called. "Raegan Overhill!"

His voice alone made her nauseous, the sound of it like a siren call for old memories to stir and sit on her shoulders, their weight heavy and taloned.

"Hey, Detective," Raegan replied even though her head swam. She walked over to where the detective stood closer to the sidewalk, leaving the medical examiner dangling his card.

"They got you doing crime?"

"They do," Raegan replied. "Vincent has to get his gallbladder taken out. I don't know how long I'll be on this. It's uh . . . something, isn't it?"

"You know I can't comment just yet," Bartley told her, "but yeah, it's weird. I can set you up with the press liaison for something more concrete."

Raegan considered. Some journalists would be relieved to know a member of the police who didn't think they were a vulture or a piece of shit, but nearly twenty years ago, Detective Winsome Bartley had been in charge of the case surrounding her father's disappearance.

He never found a goddamn trace of Cormac Overhill.

And so it seemed the detective felt he owed some kind of personal debt to Raegan. She was fine with working people and getting what she needed from them. But she didn't cross lines and she didn't want *anyone* to think a cop did her favors because she'd lost her daddy.

It didn't help that Raegan was staunchly of the opinion that if the cops liked her, she wasn't doing her job right.

"Oh, I can reach out for that later, but thank you," she replied, crossing her arms and looking at him a little harder. "I was hoping an officer on the scene might be willing to give me something short. I'm worried this is going to freak people out, you know, impossible drownings with Halloween coming up."

"How'd you know they were impossible?" Bartley asked, drawing himself up and staring down at her, the warmth seeping out of him like a cloud passing over the sun.

"I mean, I don't, technically," Raegan said, uncrossing her arms since he'd already given her the confirmation so easily. "But we're in an alley in Society Hill and there's a drowning. So. Impossible, yeah?"

Bartley relaxed then and let out a chuckle. "Okay, you've got me there. I guess it does seem pretty spooky, huh?"

"It sure does, Detective," she answered.

"Well, let me get you a brief statement," he said, motioning for Raegan to wait. While she did, she texted Henry that she was getting something—not very much, no more than a breaking news item, but something.

Another officer came by to tell her what she'd already suspected: the victim was unhoused. No one in the neighborhood recognized him, not the folks at the corner liquor stores or the outdoor cafés, so no ID yet. This was presumably not his usual haunt. His cause of death hadn't been determined yet.

"But a suspected drowning?" Raegan pushed.

"No," the cop told her. "I mean, there's some medical signs of that, but obviously that couldn't have happened, so we're not referring to it like that."

"No, of course not," Raegan said. "Hey, have you ever seen anything like this?"

The officer weighed her up, his bushy brows furrowed as she held his gaze. "No," he admitted slowly. "No, ma'am, I have not. But I'm sure there's a reasonable explanation."

"Sure," Raegan said with a noncommittal shrug. "Well, thank you for your time."

She double-checked the spelling of the officer's name, begrudgingly gave Bartley a wave, and then headed back to the subway. Her platform was oddly deserted despite the busy morning hour, and she dropped her weight into the cold fiberglass seat with a thud. The memory of the earlier subway ride—the ecstasy that had crept through her, the way her blood had hummed upon seeing the stranger—threatened to resurface, so Raegan kept her eyes trained on her phone. She scrolled through social media and was treated to photos of a high school acquaintance's wedding. Everyone looked happy and normal.

Raegan kept staring at her phone even when the reception cut out in the bowels of the tunnels, willing her own reflection in the small black square to not betray her. Someone across the car from her dropped their bag loudly on the ground. Another passenger at the other end was singing a song she thought she knew. Raegan focused on remembering the title, or maybe the artist, or even just conjuring an image of the album cover.

When her cell service returned and the subway pulled out of the deeper tunnels, a text from her ex-girlfriend appeared. Raegan inhaled and then exhaled so slowly that her vision swam for a minute. Swallowing, she tapped the text alert.

Hey, Layla had written. *Thinking of you. I know this time of year is hard.*

Raegan snorted, tried to run a hand through her hair, and got a ring caught in her curls for her trouble. Once she had painfully extracted her hair from the setting of the ring's stone, Raegan almost succeeded in telling herself to just say "thanks" to Layla and move on. She had almost succeeded in reminding herself that she didn't have to answer at all.

But Colin's reaction to her taking the lead on the drownings and the way the medical examiner suddenly wanted to help when she played a silly girl and the useless guilt that wracked Detective Bartley's face every fucking time he saw Raegan all came flooding back, buzzing in her skull like a thousand wasps that would only quiet once some venom was expressed.

How noble of you, Raegan typed back as the subway pulled into her station, *to check in on someone who is - how did you put it - so hard to love.*

Raegan banished her phone to the farthest recesses of her coat's deep pockets and exited the subway car. Despite her empty train, the station was packed and she was forced to file slowly toward the escalator. When Raegan finally stepped onto it, she pulled her notebook and a pen from her pocket, intending to scribble down some notes while the escalator moved at its glacial pace.

Instead of making notes, Raegan chewed on the top of her pen, apparently working her jaw too hard because the ink exploded everywhere. She cursed under her breath the entire way to the station's bathroom. As she did her best to scrub the ink off her mouth and neck, then off her hands, she caught a glance of herself in the dim lighting. Dark circles had invited their kin over for supper beneath her eyes. Black ink dripped from her mouth. It was familiar, somehow. Goosebumps rose across her skin as her mind keened. She choked on her next breath, hands flying to grip either side of the dirty sink.

Raegan held herself there for a moment, harsh coughs shaking her shoulders, eeriness coiling in her gut. For a second, she felt sure that if she looked at the mirror, she would not recognize her own face. A feverish chill traced its fingers up her spine.

But then the moment passed, quick as an autumn shadow. Raegan scrubbed the rest of the ink off her skin, and the thoughts of Layla and Bartley and her father from her mind. She would focus on the crime scene, on the story, on the *facts*.

There was probably a reasonable explanation why a six-foot-two man had drowned in a tiny puddle. That's what the officer had said. But the crime scene had felt just like that old story her father used to tell, and Raegan knew better than anyone that sometimes things just happened with no reasonable explanation. And sometimes, with no explanation at all.

Chapter Four

Her Wednesday did not improve—not that Raegan had been expecting such a boon. She buried herself in work, shirking off her promise to join a colleague for lunch at the pub down the street. In her defense, she was nearly finished with a long-form piece she'd been working on for almost four months and wanted to give the copy editors a good chance to review everything. Raegan had learned a long time ago that when you accuse the powerful of bad things, you better have all your ducks in a perfect fucking row.

Day dissolved into night, the approach of October waiting for her just beyond the building's door, grief and memory and shadow hanging in the eaves. When the newsroom quieted and her long-form piece was in Henry's inbox, she slipped out the back entrance and headed for the train station. But instead of the subway, Raegan boarded the commuter rail. Her destination was at the end of the line, deep in the suburbs. Over the years, her ritual had become refined, exact, and it was important to get as far away from her real life as possible. The few people she allowed to be close to her were tired of hearing it, her therapist had to have been exhausted by the tale, and what no one realized was that Raegan was sick of it herself.

But grief is a story, and it is one that demands to be told.

Which is how Raegan found herself in a cozy, if run-down, bar somewhere in New Jersey, signed up for an open mic night. The story was best presented to the unsuspecting as fiction. It seemed safer that way—like maybe it wouldn't worm itself into the listener's marrow if they thought of it as only an exercise of imagination.

She settled down on a stool at the bar and nursed a too-sweet cider, pretending to listen to the performer on stage. Despite the cool weather outside, the bar was unpleasantly warm and everything was sticky. After what felt like two years of spoken word poetry, Raegan had no choice but to peel off her overcoat and lay it across her lap. Condensation beaded on her bottle of cider. The story rattled inside of her like a caged thing, feathered wings beating against her ribs. Raegan reminded herself to sit like a regular person, to look normal and well-adjusted. In a place like this, only a few seconds of holding herself as if she were protecting an old wound could bring men sniffing—for daddy issues, for insecurities, for painful places they could poke and prod to get what they wanted.

But then the host called the pseudonym Raegan had signed up under, and she breathed a sigh of relief, quickly followed by an inhale sharpened with anticipation. She left her coat draped over the stool and pulled her mane of auburn curls off her damp neck as she approached the microphone. No one looked like they cared at all about the open mic, so Raegan didn't bother with the little introduction she sometimes had to give. Instead, she straightened her shoulders and looked out at the small bar: the mismatched chairs, the wobbly tables, the low ceiling, and orange-hued lights. Then, she took a deep breath and began.

"When my father was young, he met a man on a train platform. The man wore an old-fashioned three-piece suit. The sun was just beginning to set, the sky leaking spilled molasses.

"The man asked my father for a cigarette. He pronounced it 'cig-ah-*rette*,' stressing the last syllable instead of the first two. My father obliged, but when he offered a light, the man only stared down at the cigarette. He rolled it between the fingers of his left hand once, twice, three times, before tucking it into his pocket.

" 'Not even going to smoke it?' my father asked.

" 'No,' the man answered.

"My father fell silent, moving a step or two away from the man. He stamped his feet against the ground to ward off the winter chill. The platform remained empty. He couldn't see any trains in the distance. His gaze eventually drifted back toward the man.

" 'Aren't you cold?' my father wanted to know. My father was like that.

" 'No,' the man answered, his eyes roving down the tracks. He took out an old pocket watch from the folds of his tweed blazer. He rolled it between the fingers of his left hand once, twice, three times, before tucking it into his pocket.

"As my father watched, the train station began to change. The bricks became new, raw-red in the low light. The benches morphed into old-fashioned wrought iron, crisp and black. The colors of the sunset turned sepia.

"With a start, my father realized there was a train pulling into the platform, though he hadn't heard the engine. The man in tweed approached the door.

" 'Do not follow,' the man warned. My father noticed that despite the winter air, there was no puff of frosted breath when the man spoke.

" 'Who are you?' my father remembers asking, though perhaps he already knew the answer.

"The man stood in the doorway, pulled the cigarette back out of his pocket, and rolled it between his fingers. He lingered for a moment but did not answer, and then he disappeared into the darkness of the rickety train, its sides heaving like an exhausted animal.

"For so many years, my father remembered the man, the train platform, the sepia-colored sunset. All my life, he paused when we said the Apostle's Creed in church, right before the 'I believe' lines. It was just a small pause—

"one,

"two,

"three."

Raegan's mouth felt dry as paper, her heart a war drum. The story was true. Her father was gone, and this story was the only thing she had. And so, she would keep telling it, again and again and again. It was her way of looking for a door, a curtain to walk behind, a secret place she could go, and maybe her father would be there, waiting. If that kind of door existed, she told herself, she was the kind of person it would appear for. And she would walk through it without looking back.

Of course, no door appeared in the wall of the run-down tavern as she paid her tab and gathered up her coat. Nothing in the parking lot either, nor the train station, not even with its flickering lights and empty platform. No matter how many times Raegan begged for a door, no matter how hard she looked, nothing sprung its maw open with a creak that sounded like a lullaby. So, she kept telling the story because it was closer to a door than anything else she had ever known.

What she didn't know—couldn't know—was that the story was an invocation of sorts, a calling of the quarters, a setting of beacons, and when she told it, Fate herself swooped low from the never-places and listened to the story fall from Raegan's mouth like wine.

The next morning, the story still wrapped around her marrow, Raegan headed into the newsroom to tell Henry she'd take the lead. October drew closer now and her mind would still contort like a fish on dry land as it approached, but the desperation always settled after she told the story.

Thursday offered a cool, delicious gloom—the kind of early autumn chill that made the hair on the back of Raegan's neck stand up—the just-beginning-to-turn leaves emphasized by the backdrop of gray skies. She'd somehow beaten Henry to the newsroom, so she headed out to the front of the building to pay a visit to her favorite food truck.

Rich was stationed on his usual bench, stained duffle bag at his feet, feeding the pigeons from a crumpled seed packet. She hated running around behind the police and trying to do their work for them. But it was worth a shot.

"You need a cup of coffee or anything today?" she asked as she approached. Rich looked up at her, his salt-and-pepper hair catching the low, gray light. An already-emptied seed packet threatened to teeter out of the pocket of his faded coat. It had been blue once, maybe.

"Only if you would be so kind," the older man said, smiling up at her.

Raegan hated talking to strangers—a constant source of mockery in the newsroom, which she always admitted she deserved—but for some reason, when Rich had asked her for something to eat after one of her first days at the paper, she'd not only obliged but asked if he wanted company.

They had gotten to talking about the city—Rich knew more about its recent history off the top of his head than most people—and they'd been friendly ever since. She'd tried more than once to connect him with resources, but he always shrugged it off.

"You got it," she told him, heading across the wide expanse of pavement to the nearby food truck, the towering buildings casting weak shadows. A few minutes later, she walked back over with two steaming cups of coffee and handed one to Rich.

"I have a question that might be upsetting," Raegan said. "Is it okay if I ask you?"

Rich looked over the lid of the cup inquisitively, nodding.

"There was a murder or accidental death or something yesterday morning," Raegan said. "An unhoused man. He was found in an alley over by Delancey Place, but Rich, the thing is, all the physical evidence says he drowned. In a tiny puddle. In Society Hill. Have you heard anything about this?"

The moment she brought up the puddle, Rich's hands began to shake so hard he had to put his coffee down.

She felt a rare pang of guilt for possibly upsetting him. "We don't have to talk about it."

"No, no, it's fine," Rich said, smoothing out his pants with long strokes, again and again. "It's just . . . I think this has happened before."

Raegan immediately leaned in closer, her heart hammering. Rich was no official source, but he had never made up stories before, as far as she could tell. She didn't think he'd start now.

"Drownings? In puddles? You've seen this before?"

"I think so," Rich told her. He had picked his coffee back up but was still clearly uneasy. "Look, don't go quoting me—"

"No, Rich, I wouldn't, honest," Raegan said, fighting to keep her tone as even and soothing as possible. "I'm worried about your safety."

"Okay, okay, just don't get all news lady on me, that's all."

Biting back a smile at his wording, Raegan assured him she wouldn't. She settled her elbows on her knees, both hands around her coffee cup. The liquid burned through the thin blue-and-white patterned cup, searing her palms. Raegan breathed into the pain, telling herself to stay in her body no matter where Rich's story went.

"Back in the early '90s, I think, maybe the late '80s, I had some friends who drowned," Rich began, a little shaky, his gaze trained straight ahead. "Some friends like me, you know. There were people saying something was coming out of the puddles, out of the sewers. That all sounded like crazy talk to me. Something that was offering to take people to a better place, a nice place, with a warm bed and where you'd get a full belly."

For a moment, Raegan squeezed her eyes shut, trying to feel the breeze on her face. Her blood thrummed in her veins, mind curling around this lush impossibility.

"Lots of people said no," Rich said, sitting back on the bench, his gaze dipping toward Raegan. "I mean, something just pops out of a puddle and says, 'hey, youse, I'll give you a nice place to lay your head?' No, sir. That sounds suspicious, first of all, and second of all, how is something even popping out of a puddle in the first place?"

Rich's voice wavered, as if the fantastical bent of this tale made him self-conscious. Raegan turned to look at him, nodding for him to go on. She hoped the look in her eyes said that she believed him.

"Then I had some friends who said it kept coming back, every time it rained, every time there was water on the ground," Rich said, the words coming out in a jumbled exhale. "At first they'd see it in real deep puddles in potholes, you know, where it was maybe possible some maniac had climbed in there, but then it would be in just a little water gathered up on a bench, or in the reflection of wet glass."

One leg bouncing, Rich took a long sip of his coffee before continuing. "Sometimes it looked like a weird horse head and sometimes it looked like a beautiful lady," he said, glancing away as he spat the words out as quickly as possible, as if he didn't believe them himself. "In my opinion, the ones who said yes saw the beautiful lady. Think about it—a pretty lady offering a bed and a meal? Can't say I would've said no if I saw it, whatever it was."

At that, Raegan's eyes tracked to Rich. She tilted her head and raised one eyebrow, a question on her lips.

"And I never did see it, before you ask," Rich said, batting the air with one hand as if to swipe away the possibility. "Not once. But I watched people I knew see it over and over again, and they got . . . they got real strange, like it was wearing them down or something. I don't even know half their names—they were just friends, you know, pals that wouldn't take your shit if you walked away, people who knew which bench was yours. And then just—poof. Gone."

Rich hunched over for a moment, wrapping one arm around himself. Raegan let the silence stretch for a moment, not sure what to say.

"You're telling me a good number of people just disappeared?" Raegan eventually asked, her tone low. "No bodies, unlike this time?"

"I mean, I don't think so," Rich replied, looking over at her. "But, you know, the city was bad back then so dead homeless people . . . I don't know if anybody would have cared at all."

Raegan dropped her head into her hands for a second, her thoughts racing almost as quickly as her heart rate. Nausea unfolded in her stomach even though her blood sang with the thrill of it all. She'd have to corroborate this, of course. She'd dig into the archives, and if she had to, she'd reach out to Bartley. He was a senior detective. If he didn't know about these drownings, he was certainly friends with someone who would.

"People hardly care now," she admitted, her eyes softening as she turned to look at him. "Can't help but wonder whether, if the last victim had turned up somewhere less posh, maybe nobody would've noticed."

Rich shrugged and took a sip of his coffee. "Anyway, that's all I know," he said, seeming lighter now that he had released this story from wherever he'd been keeping it. "I can see if anyone else remembers anything, but it was a long time ago and a lot of people just go away one day."

"I'd appreciate that," Raegan replied, getting to her feet. "If you could bring it up when you see friends, that'd be great, but please don't stress yourself about it."

She slung her bag over her shoulder and considered Rich, looking for any part of the story that he might only be telling with his eyes.

"Will do," Rich replied. "You take care."

"You, too, Rich. Be safe." She pulled her coat closer against the incoming late September wind and grabbed the paper bag containing her breakfast from the food truck's counter, though her appetite was threatening to vanish entirely.

"Raegan!"

She turned, surprised, to see Rich standing a few feet from his bench, waving her down. For a moment, she paused, unsure, and then walked the steps back.

"Yes?" Raegan asked, hungry for another layer of this story.

"I just remembered something," he said, looking excited. "There was an Irish fella who used to hang around back then. I remember, he told everyone to stay away from the puddles. Called it a kelp, I think."

Something twisted in Raegan's gut, and her mouth went dry. "Rich," she breathed, trying to settle herself. Her mind keened, drunk on the poison of October and the way the world always bent strangely this time of year. "Do you . . . do you mean a *kelpie?*"

Chapter Five

"That's it!" Rich said, punching a finger in the air. "A kelpie. Does that mean anything to you?"

Of course it did. Her father had raised her on folklore and fairy tales the way other kids were raised on little league or the family business. Raegan's lungs tightened as she stood in a mundane place she knew so well, watching a folktale wander into the real world on damp, backwards hooves.

"Yes," she said slowly, trying to ration the air left in her lungs. "It's a mythological creature from Scottish folklore. They're usually not very nice. But they also don't usually show up in puddles."

"Maybe this is a puddle kelpie," Rich said, shrugging.

"Maybe, Rich," Raegan said, a forced, faint smile crossing her lips. "Hey, thanks for remembering that. It's really interesting. I appreciate it."

"No problem. I'll try to remember other stuff, too."

She needed to be back in the newsroom for two reasons: work, and the familiar tug to wilder, stranger things uncoiling in her chest. Raegan's mind was a vast, dark place, and like all places where shadows multiplied, she could not always trust it. Right now, her heart pounding, palms damp, Raegan found that her mind wanted to tell her many impossible things. She knew full well those things were large enough to devour her.

"Thank you," she said to Rich, her voice coming out shakier than she would've liked. Rich waved at her as she walked away. Raegan tried to breathe, in and out, in and out. Surely, some Irish guy who was struggling or just superstitious made the connection between the mythological water-horse that dragged people to their deaths and people dying of drowning in a city. It made sense, in a storytelling sort of way. That was all, wasn't it? She tried telling herself people turned to folk beliefs or myths when they were scared, but she couldn't make it stick. Not here. Not in a modern city in the Western world. She supposed a kelpie could be an explanation for a recent Irish immigrant, but even then . . . she was unconvinced.

When Raegan returned to the newsroom, that's exactly how she explained it to Henry. He agreed, of course, shrugging off the kelpie bit in its entirety. Raegan knew it was the logical thing to do, and she repeated that to herself about eighty times. And yet, there was that magnetic pull in her bones, the call and response whenever the world around her lilted off its axis.

"I'm more concerned that this has potentially happened before," Henry said, his arms crossed, looking up at Raegan from his seat. "Does this mean you're taking the lead?"

His cubicle and desk were, per usual, littered with sticky notes and marked-up proofreading flats. He called it "organized chaos," but it made Raegan's anxiety spike just looking at it. Three old coffee cups were stacked in the corner, and she was pretty sure something was growing in one of them.

"Shut up," Raegan said through a mouthful of bagel, tearing her eyes away from Henry's desk. "Obviously I'm taking the lead. Anyway. I don't disagree with you. That's the big thing here: has this happened before? But also, let's say these aren't explainable accidents. Let's say, for a second, it's a serial. Has someone been dormant all these years, or is this a copycat of a killer no one knew about? And is there going to be something enlightening in the kelpie myth that this killer is inspired by?"

Saanvi, another reporter, stopped her march to the kitchenette so suddenly that Raegan could've sworn her ballet flats skidded on the carpet. Saanvi walked backwards to Henry's desk, her pretty brown eyes going wide. "What did you just say?" she asked in a hushed tone, leaning toward Raegan.

Henry looked at Raegan, unwilling to answer Saanvi, probably because he considered it Raegan's story and thus her call. But Saanvi and Raegan were friends. Or as close as Raegan got to friendship. They texted. They had gone out for drinks a few times, including a few months ago when Layla broke up with Raegan out of nowhere.

"You heard right," Raegan replied, her tone grim.

"So the bodies *are* connected," Saanvi whispered, her eyebrows flying to her hairline. "I was really hoping they were just a series of unrelated accidents. I mean, what else could it be? It's not like we have any oceans nearby for Timingila to wander in from and have a feast."

Raegan and Henry looked at her blankly.

"Sorry," Saanvi said, waving an elegant hand, her gold bracelets jingling. "Big aquatic beast in Hindu myth. Can swallow a whole whale. What's a kelpie?"

"Oh, kelpies aren't that big," Raegan said, perking up at having someone to discuss folklore with, not surprised Saanvi was more interested in it than Henry. "A river horse, basically. People try to ride it or whatever and it carries them to their deaths."

"Shit," Saanvi said, dragging out the "i" between her teeth. "A kelpie-inspired killer. That's a new one."

"If that's what is even going on," Henry interjected. "They're good questions. Now you just have to answer them, Raegan."

It was normal for Raegan to pose the questions she had about a story to Henry to make sure she was on the right path. She never expected answers—that was *her* job. But this time, she was really hoping Henry would explain it to her. That he would assure her nothing supernatural was going on, that she was probably overreacting, and that there was no reason for the mention of a mythological creature to leave her feeling so untethered.

"You want to grab lunch with me?" Saanvi asked, sensing the editor-reporter chat had ended. "I have chai going on the stove."

Raegan wanted to bounce more ideas around with Henry, mostly for the sake of feeling less unhinged, but Saanvi's homemade chai was an absolute treat she was not willing to pass up. She told herself more caffeine was maybe not the best idea, but that didn't stop her from wrapping up the other half of her bagel and following Saanvi into the kitchenette.

"Besides serial killers," Saanvi said over her shoulder as she rummaged in the fridge, "how are you?"

"I've been better," Raegan conceded, grabbing two mugs from the cabinet. "I have a . . . personal thing. Anniversary of a death in the family. And Layla texted me that she was 'thinking of me' during 'this hard time.'"

Saanvi whipped her head around so fast she almost dropped the jug of milk. "Eww," she said, the disgust on her face so intense Raegan held back a laugh. "You've got your own shit to work out, but after what she said, she doesn't get to pretend she cares."

Unearned relief swept through Raegan. She had told Saanvi about the argument that led to the breakup, but she had excluded key elements. Because Raegan just needed someone on her side, even if it was only because of a selective retelling.

"Yeah, that's kind of what I thought," she replied, sliding the mugs toward Saanvi, not willing to say more.

"Like, who gets mad because you don't say the 'L'-word after four months? That's just not how dating works in America," Saanvi near-shouted, sloshing milk into the pot of chai and turning up the burner. "And then turns around and says it's too hard to try to love you?! No way." Saanvi turned to face Raegan, one hand on her hip.

"I think you're angrier about this than I am," Raegan said, a smile fighting its way onto her face because Saanvi was angry about the things she *had* depicted honestly.

"No," Saanvi replied, pointing a wooden spoon at Raegan. "You just keep everything pent up. Trust me. I know what that looks like."

Raegan settled onto a chair, pulling the sleeves of her sweater up and then back down, unwilling to discuss her own problems with the irritatingly perceptive reporter. "How are you?" she asked instead, looking up from the faux marble table.

"Since you've been thinking about murder all day, I will permit that little deflection," Saanvi said, raising a perfect eyebrow. The chai was boiling now, and Saanvi removed it from the heat, strained it and then ladled the tea into mugs, handing one to Raegan.

"Thanks," Raegan said, breathing in the aroma of spices and black tea.

"Thanks for appreciating my chai," Saanvi replied, wrapping her hands around the warm mug. "Your kind usually prefers weak-ass bagged tea." She made a retching sound and then took a long, luxurious sip.

Raegan laughed, trying to anchor herself to this: a hot cup of tea with a friend in the ugly but cozy newsroom lunchette. Simple, normal, natural.

"I keep forgetting to bring you some Glengettie," Raegan said. "It doesn't stand a chance against your chai, but it's pretty good."

Raegan took a swig from her mug, enjoying the familiar flavors made by her friend's hands. The pair sat in comfortable silence, the noise of the newsroom churning behind them. Then someone was calling Saanvi's name from across the room—it was Erin, one of the breaking news writers.

"Sorry," Erin called, jogging over. "Possible active shooter situation just came in on the scanner. We gotta get to University City."

"Shit," Saanvi said, jumping to her feet. "I guess you get two cups of chai, Raegan."

"I'm not complaining," Raegan replied, already reaching to grab Saanvi's mug. "Be safe, both of you. Text me if you need anything."

Saanvi waved at Raegan and then followed Erin, the pair already pulling out their phones and yelling something to their editor. Raegan sat back, staring at the empty chair across from her for longer than she realized. Her mind strayed to Rich's words and the crime scene and the knot in her stomach that sat as heavy as tar.

Raegan had almost wanted to, but she didn't even try to explain to Henry or Saanvi that she could feel something, a tiny seed that should be uncomfortable and scary. But it wasn't. The kelpie felt like hope, like proof that fantastical things could happen, that truth was stranger than fiction.

Gods, she was reaching. Some Irish guy probably got high or drunk and started blabbering about kelpies, and here she was, all these years later, taking it fucking seriously and slapping it onto her wounds like a bandage.

But the seed of the kelpie was deep in her lungs now, throbbing with every breath, filling up the empty places inside her ribcage—the places that had opened when her father disappeared completely and never came back. The parts of herself that Raegan had quieted over the years were awakening, beginning their choir of furtive whispers that there was more to this world, to herself, and to her father's disappearance. If she just looked hard enough, the hushed voices said, she'd find it.

So Raegan decided to look.

CHAPTER SIX

She spent two hours digging through the newspaper archives. Some reporters found the archives creepy, housed in the annex, an eerily quiet building blanketed in outdated hues of brown. The windows reminded Raegan of archers' windows in castles—arrowslits, she thought they might be called, though she couldn't remember where she had learned the term. Very little natural light leaked in, leaving the space reliant on yellow-tinted overhead fluorescents that hummed and blinked irregularly.

She was seated at a sticky-surfaced worktable with two cartons of back issues when she finally unearthed a possible mention of an uptick in "vagrant deaths." The wording alone made her blood boil. But the timeline was right. She pulled the issue and was planning to call Bartley until she saw it was already after 6 PM. Raegan closed the door to the archives and sighed. Her therapist had been encouraging her to have a better work-life balance, but now the two halves of herself had entwined themselves together, the disappearances and Rich's mention of the kelpie weaving separate fibers together. Raegan no longer knew how to unpick them or how to tell them apart.

That feeling, she supposed, was what drove her to leave the newsroom with a particular destination in mind, just as the sun began to slip behind the horizon. She did not get on the subway like she should've, and instead hopped on the commuter train. She sat on the old brown seat in silence, forehead against the cool glass, her breath fogging up the window. Outside, the darkness was blue-black and velvet, studded with traffic lights and streetlamps.

The ride took about fifteen minutes, all of which Raegan spent feeling as though she was exactly where she was meant to be, following some sort of trail, unwinding the fibers. But the moment she exited the train and stepped onto the platform that she once knew so well, all of the sureness went out of her. She walked down the stairs to the street level slowly, like she was in a trance, the heels of her boots clanging on the metal steps.

Raegan turned off the busy commercial corridor and into a quiet northeast neighborhood. The sidewalks were lined with streetlights that mostly worked. Leaves had already begun to dust the street, joining forces with the loose trash to clog the sewer grates. The houses were lit up on the inside, cars tucked away in their short driveways.

And then Raegan found herself standing in front of a pretty brick twin. The sycamore tree's leaves danced up and down the walkway like ghosts welcoming her back. She followed their tumbling path and rang the doorbell before she'd really thought about it. Raegan was almost surprised when someone answered. It was easier to imagine the house as torn down or abandoned, all the memories there locked away some-where unreachable.

A woman opened the door, her thick cream cardigan closed around her frame, the warmth of the house backlighting her into a nearly black silhouette. She said nothing for a long moment.

"Raegan? What are you doing here?" The surprise in Bronwyn Overhill's voice stung her daughter, though Raegan supposed she didn't have much of a right to feel that way.

"Hi, Mom," Raegan replied, her voice suddenly an unused hinge no one had bothered to oil. "Can I come in?"

"Of course. Is everything okay?" Raegan's mother asked, opening the door fully and ushering her inside. As much as she didn't want to, Raegan's walls came down just a little bit at the sound of her mother's weathered Welsh accent and the golden light trickling out of the house.

"Yeah," Raegan replied with a shrug. "I'm fine. Honest."

"It's just, you know, close to the anniversary, and you've had trouble before," Bronwyn said, shutting the door behind Raegan but not moving out of the small entry hallway. She scrutinized her daughter.

"I'm fine, Mom," Raegan replied, fingernails biting into her palm. "I just, uh, I'm covering a story and I wanted to see Dad's books. You know, the ones you didn't destroy."

Bronwyn stopped dead in the entryway for a moment, her mouth pressed into a firm line. "You know, your therapist said you shouldn't—"

"My children's therapist from fifteen years ago, Mom?" Raegan demanded. "We're still going off that?"

"Well, that's all the information I have because you don't tell me anything—"

"And this is exactly why," Raegan snapped, trying to ignore the way the house—her childhood home—pulled at her with soft, tiny, pleading hands.

Bronwyn let out a sigh, turning away from Raegan to walk into the kitchen. She couldn't help but notice the room was the same as ever: the compact swoop of counter and islands jutting out into the living room. All the wood was a distressed white with worn brass finishings. Teapots and tea boxes exploded from every corner, some obscured by the pothos vines Bronwyn loved so much. If Bronwyn had known a guest was coming, even just her own daughter, she would have cleaned and wiped the sink dry for reasons Raegan still didn't understand. Instead, a plate and a teacup sat in the metal basin.

The space was warm and cozy with lit candles everywhere. It smelled of cinnamon, like it always did, and Raegan could see the big, warm quilts on the couch in the next room. She wondered if her mother knew how desperately she wanted to just wrap herself up in one, how much she'd like to admit that she was not okay and she hadn't been for a long time and they should just put the kettle on and sit down.

She said nothing instead.

"I just want to know you're okay, Raegan," Bronwyn said, tears already welling in her eyes.

Raegan met her gaze, taking in the soft features and the waves of brown hair and the quivering lower lip.

"I know this time of year is hard, whether you want to admit it or not, and you know what," her mother continued, pulling her sweater tighter around her frame, "it's hard for *me* and you're the only person who understands. It was only ever the three of us, and now it's just the two of us."

Raegan recalled the weekend escapes Bronwyn used to plan when the anniversary got close. They would go apple-picking and shopping at TJ Maxx and out to dinner at a nicer chain restaurant, and they'd watch movies and cry and laugh and then cry again. The grief counselor said Raegan was adjusting well, all things considered.

Her heartbeat rising, Raegan remembered the day she found the books—or, at least, what remained of them. Occult tomes and folklore collections and cheap reprints of ancient texts, all marked up and dogeared by her father. Raegan had come home early from a friend's house to find Bronwyn in the process of burning a pile of Cormac's books in the firepit out back. *Burning* them. Like just throwing them out wasn't enough, like they had to be utterly destroyed, wiped from the face of the earth. Raegan begged her mother to stop and rescued what she could, but Bronwyn just yelled over and over again that it had to be like this because she couldn't lose her daughter, too. To *what*, Raegan did not know, and her mother didn't tell her.

After that, Bronwyn continued to avoid answering any of Raegan's questions. There were no more autumn nights spent making apple pies with their bounty from the orchard. They barely even spoke, and less than a year later, Raegan announced she was going to school in Boston. And that was that.

"I know it's hard for you, too. I know. I just . . . I don't know how to manage your feelings and mine all at once," Raegan said.

Bronwyn was softly crying, pretending to put dishes away. A spoon slipped out of her grasp, loudly clanging down onto the base of the drying rack.

"Mom. I just want to see the books," Raegan sighed. "We agreed you would keep them and I could come look at them. It's not for anything with Dad. It's for a story. The books are out of print and hard to find. They could help with the research I'm doing."

"What could they possibly have to do with an article you're writing? You're a goddamn newspaper reporter," Bronwyn demanded, wheeling on her daughter, a dish towel flying in the process.

Raegan considered her mother for a second, infuriated that Bronwyn was strong enough to allow her emotions to surface, to experience them and maybe move through them. If Raegan acknowledged all the grief clinging to the inside of her ribcage and the anger tucked between her lungs, she felt sure she would drown.

So she took a deep breath and tried to explain. "There's been some weird murders," Raegan began, immediately wishing she had lied instead, "and my editor and I think the killer may be influenced by a certain mythology."

Bronwyn's eyes went wide, her fingers digging into the dish towel in her grasp. "For god's sake, why the hell are you working on something like that?" she demanded. "That can't be good for you."

"Well, Mom, it's because this is my job and I'm not as delicate as you are," Raegan shot back. Immediately, remorse flooded her like a river, but she had never been very good at taking things back. Raegan watched as hurt unfolded on Bronwyn's face, but then her mother set her jaw and pointed down the hall.

"Everything is in his study like it has always been," she snapped. "Please just go look and then leave me alone."

"Yeah, okay," Raegan breathed, trying to walk out of the kitchen as quietly as possible. She tried to put her mother out of her mind as soon as she'd crossed the threshold—a weight she could not carry at the moment. Instead, she headed for her father's study. Raegan hated it as much as she loved it.

The small bonus room near the back of the house would have been a storage room for most people, but Cormac declared it his study, and that was that. The room had not changed: the big leather chair, small desk, ancient banker's lamp, and bookshelves packed to the gills. An old, knockoff William Morris-patterned paper adorned the walls. The faded green carpet was plush from disuse.

When she walked in, Raegan took a deep breath and wondered if it smelled like her father. She didn't really remember what he smelled like. She did remember the stories he'd tell and the hikes in Pennypack Park and this game they'd play where they'd have a tea party but she was a queen and he was her royal advisor. They'd stop wars and give secret support to the brave rebels and sometimes they'd just purchase more unicorns for the castle grounds. As she got older, Raegan always felt like she should stop playing, like she was too old for it, but she never did. They played it the day before he disappeared.

Trying to swallow the emotion gathering in the back of her throat, Raegan began looking through the books. She had a memory of the one she wanted: a big, old book on Celtic mythology. She didn't know for a fact if it was out of print—a lie invented for her mother—but all her Google searches had come up empty, so she assumed it was a rare edition or something along those lines. And it gave her an excuse to be back in the study.

She pulled each book out individually, even ones clearly labeled on their spines, looking for the right title. Ten minutes later, it hadn't appeared. But the big *Grimm's Fairy Tales* he used to read to her had. As had the old photo album that she didn't have the heart to crack open. And there was the pockmarked copy of the children's book about not being afraid of the dark. Raegan pulled it from the shelf, turning the wide hardcover over in her hands, feeling each little tear in the dust jacket.

"Look at this little boy—he's not afraid of the dark, either!" Raegan's father used to say, pointing at the characters on the pages.

He would read the text, but he loved to embellish, too, making up little side stories or pointing out details in the background of the illustrations. More than once, Raegan had wondered how she'd had such wonderful parents and still turned out the way she did. It seemed unfair to them, mostly, but also to her. Hers was a good childhood, spent in the woods with plenty of stories and bonfires in the little firepit out back, Saturday mornings at the flea market and summer days at the shore.

She should've been normal.

"So many of these brave kids aren't scared of the dark," Raegan's father would say. *"Do you think we should try to be more like them?"*

"I do!" Raegan would cheer, no longer afraid of the dark because her fictional friends had gone first.

The old lamp in the corner blinked, drawing Raegan out of the memory. The light fizzled again, and darkness yawned like a door. Raegan froze, her mind going blank with panic. A few heartbeats later, the light returned, but she was left shaken and caught in another memory: accidentally locking herself in the little dirt-floor basement almost twenty years ago.

She had been eleven. It was early spring—the spring before he disappeared—and both her parents were outside doing yard work. Raegan had thought she was no longer afraid of the dark, but when the door swung shut and locked behind her from the outside, the fear came quick and deep. She yelled but to no avail. She tried to remember the things her father had told her, but a primal instinct took root and she could do nothing but beat on the door. It could've been ten years or ten seconds, but at some point, her dad came inside and heard her.

He was quick to console her, scooping her up in his arms and making gentle shushing noises. But Raegan had worked herself into a hopeless terror, even if it was over something as simple as an accidental lock-in. Cormac found himself unable to calm her down. None of his old tricks worked. So he resorted to a new one.

"Do you want to know the old Welsh saying for when you're scared of the dark?" her father asked.

Raegan tried to slow the crying, now transforming into wet hiccups. *"There's a—a saying fo—for it?"*

"Oh yes, Rae-Rae, I can't believe I haven't told you before! It's a spell of sorts. Magic. It's a way of greeting the darkness, of saying hello. It goes like this: 'I greet you, Mrenin, as I walk within your shadow and your stead.'"

Raegan began to calm down, still hiccuping but standing on her own, skeptical as always. *"That sounds silly. How do—does it help?"*

"It helps, you see, because sometimes the darkness is simply a strange realm, and in all strange realms, you need a guide, do you not?" her father had told her. *"Think of this saying as a request for a guide to the darkness. Then it can be known and mapped, and once we know something, it can't be scary, can it? All you have to do is remember the phrasing and it will keep you safe. You have to remember it, though. By heart. It's very impor-tant to remember it."*

Raegan scrunched up her tear-stained face, unsure if she believed it made any sense, but her father always seemed to know what to do and what to say.

"Okay, so anytime you go into dark places, just say, 'I greet you, Mrenin, as I walk within your shadow and your stead.'"

He made her repeat it until he was sure she knew it, and even at eleven, Raegan felt this was more serious than her dad was letting on, so she made a note of it in her favorite notebook, which was decorated with at least ten unicorn stickers. She had a decent grasp on Welsh, being the child of two immigrants from Wales, but couldn't place *mrenin*. So later that night, after she was already supposed to be asleep, Raegan pulled out her flashlight that she kept stored away for late-night reading and took out her Welsh dictionary. She flipped through to the *M* section, bringing the flashlight closer to the small text.

mrenin - noun. **1)** meaning a monarch or leader, but usually, a king.

CHAPTER SEVEN

Raegan snapped the children's book shut. The hair on her arms stood on end. Something turned over in the depths of her being, and she could've sworn she physically felt another memory stirring inside of her head, though it did not reveal itself.

There was, she knew, only one thing to do.

Raegan shelved the book and strode out of the study, doubling back through the kitchen. Her mother was no longer there, much to her relief. Walking between the small island and the cabinets, she came to face the basement door. It hadn't changed—wide, white vertical planks and a black, iron flip latch. She took a deep breath, looked over her shoulder to make sure her mother was still in another part of the house, and opened the door. This time, she turned the flashlight on her phone to its brightest setting before closing the door behind her. No use in taking chances.

Working her way down the narrow, twisting stairs, Raegan came to stand on the dirt floor. There were a few storage containers, the rack by the stairs filled with pots and gardening tools. The air that met her nose was slightly damp, vegetal and cool. The space looked very normal, and smaller than she remembered.

Raegan felt silly, the electricity having evaporated from her skin. But she took a deep breath and turned off her phone flashlight anyway. And then she said it, her heart careening faster and faster with each word.

"I greet you, *mrenin*, as I walk within your shadow and your stead."

For a moment, the air thickened, the shadows growing oily and slippery. Something stretched, a door tried to open, and Raegan stopped breathing. The darkness around her turned to silk scarves, caressing her skin like a lover, so liquid and strange that she thought she might be going mad.

But then it dissipated, gone as quickly as it had come. Raegan was standing in her childhood basement, reciting weird Welsh sayings that she'd only just remembered she knew. Dirt scuffed the toes of her boots, and her breathing was heavy. She rubbed her forehead harshly, muttering to herself, and almost turned to leave.

All at once, she remembered the crawl space. Well, barely a crawl space—just an odd little spot near the front of the basement where the room crested the hill in the front yard. It was more like a dirt shelf, a small area between the ground and the slats of the subfloor above.

Just in case. She was down here already, wasn't she?

Turning her phone light back on, Raegan walked toward the crawl space. She couldn't remember the last time she'd come near it. She knew sometimes her dad would stash his favorite mead from Ireland there, using it like a shelf, but there were no mead bottles there now.

She peered over the ledge and there it was: a shadow, a lump, something that did not belong. Raegan dragged an old wooden step stool over, climbing the first few rungs to get a better look. The shadow turned out to be a little unicorn toy, definitely one of hers, from years ago. But how had it gotten up there? And why was it standing perfectly straight, its tail to her, the horn pointing upwards? She supposed she could have put it there, but why? When?

She twisted her phone around, trying to get a better look. And then she saw it: precisely where the unicorn's horn pointed, there was something resting on the beams. Something about the size of a large book, wrapped up in burlap.

Raegan froze. The object looked as though it had been purposely left there, the unicorn pointing an arrow toward its hiding place in the rafters, in a place few would ever think to look. Her mind reeled but her body, acting independently, reached for the package. It came free of the rafters easily, and she held it close, like a line to a drowning man.

"What the fuck," Raegan mumbled. "What the *fuck*."

She lowered herself to sit on the step stool, slowly unwrapping the burlap fabric from the object with shaking hands. It was a book. Adjusting her phone light, Raegan read the title out loud.

Celtic Mythology: Forgotten Tales, Old Stories, New Skins.

It was exactly the book that had popped into her mind: the old book on mythology with its green cover and embossed text. She flipped it open and was shocked to find it just as she'd remembered it with huge ink illustrations in grayscale and a gorgeous script title at the top of each new entry. The Banshee, the Spriggan, the Fey.

And there it was, The Kelpie.

The page showed a creature rearing its head out of a wave. The artist had chosen to depict it so the reader could see both above and beneath the water. On the top of the page, a horse's dark head broke the surface, black eyes situated strangely on its face. Beneath the surface, where its hind legs should've been, was a long, aquatic body, ending in a powerful, razor-sharp tail. Its gaze portrayed a deep, frightening intelligence. Even just looking into the illustration's eyes made Raegan's mouth go dry.

The text beneath identified kelpies as shape-shifting water creatures of Wales, Ireland, and Scotland. They were tricksters, dangerous and wily, often dragging people to their deaths. Sometimes they could be tamed with magical silver bridles, and sometimes they chose to live as mortals.

Raegan had known these aspects of the kelpie's mythology but the book continued with information she had never heard before. Setting it down on the stool and squatting in the dirt before it, Raegan adjusted her phone light, skimming over the words.

"Kelpies," the text read, "could see things that mortals couldn't. They lived in the Rivers, a vast system of water that extended well beyond bodies of water mapped by humans. They could be anywhere and everywhere, and though they mostly kept to their own kind, kelpies were occasionally called upon during wars or skirmishes, particularly by the Unseelie Fey."

The current that had begun to rush through Raegan earlier in the day strained against her dam of reason. She flipped through the pages again, discovering an envelope secured to the endpaper at the front of the book. It was crafted from thick, creamy paper, and written upon the flap was her name. In her father's handwriting.

Anticipation thrummed, her throat closing off, as Raegan dove her fingers into the envelope. It took her at least a full minute to realize it was empty, and only after she'd nearly torn the page in half by accident. Sorrow spiked dark and sour in her stomach; every place she searched for her father always came up empty, deserted, offering only a ghost.

Frustrated tears welled, and Raegan wiped them away harshly with the back of her hand, pawing through the book once, twice, three more times, her hands shaking. She held it aloft and shook it, hoping a wafer-thin letter might dislodge from its pages and suture her wounds closed after all these years.

Instead, her mother's voice came from behind her. "Raegan?" Bronwyn asked. "What are you doing?"

Startled, Raegan spun, forgetting to conceal the book in her panic. "Sorry," she replied, fruitlessly trying to slide the book under the front of her jacket. "Just lost in memory, I guess."

Bronwyn considered her daughter for a long moment, eyes narrowing in concern, but then she relented. "Lots of memories in this house," she sighed, folding her arms. "Did you find the book you were looking for?"

Raegan forced her face to remain neutral. Could her mom not see the giant book in her arms? Sure, it was dim in the basement, but light now flooded in from the open door at the top of the stairs.

"Uh, no," Raegan replied. "It's okay."

"Well, why don't we head upstairs?" Bronwyn asked, clearly unsettled by having found her daughter in the dark of an unlit basement.

"Sure," Raegan shrugged, taking a few steps to meet her mother. Even as they crested the stairs and emerged into the warm glow of the kitchen, Bronwyn did not seem to notice the book. At all.

"Sorry you couldn't find what you wanted," Bronwyn said, slipping her hand into a tea canister, not bothering to hide the sliver of relief in her voice.

"It's fine," Raegan said, fighting to sound even remotely normal, tracking every movement of her mom's eyes. "There's some information online. I just figured Dad had such a big folklore collection, so . . ."

"So you came all the way out here just to check? Without calling? Without making sure?" her mother asked, crossing her arms, forgetting the tea and leaning back against the counter.

"I was already in the neighborhood," Raegan replied. "I thought it might be nice to just drop by." Her words were automatic, rote, all her attention focused on the way her mother could not see the book she'd unearthed from the basement.

"Well, why don't you stay for some tea? Since you're here?" Bronwyn asked, lighting up. For a moment, Raegan's bones hummed with a desire to do exactly that. The scent of the black tea and her mother's preferred dish soap curled around her, gentle and comforting. But she couldn't stay. Not now. Not with the song of the kelpie in her blood. Not with a book on magical creatures no one else could see. Not with a missing letter from her father she dared not ask her mother about.

Her mother wouldn't understand. Her mother would say she was having an episode, raving about an invisible book and a missing letter from between its pages. Her mother would call people. Her mother couldn't fathom how Raegan needed to see this through before she did anything else.

"I'm sorry, I can't. I lost track of time. Just wanted to come home but forgot about how much work I have," Raegan said, a faux apology.

And then the warmth was gone, her daughter yanked back away from her as quickly as she had shown up, so Bronwyn sighed and went back to the sink. "Of course."

"Maybe sometime soon. You know, closer to the anniversary."

"Maybe, *cariad*. We'll see. You get home safe."

"I will," Raegan said, and then she was out the door and walking down the quiet street before the cinnamon and the tea and the quilts could get their claws into her.

She told herself not to cry, but a hitching sob came out of her ribcage all the same. Her father *had* left something for her. Right? The unicorn toy, the way the book had been hidden in the rafters, wrapped up in rough brown fabric, the letter her father had clearly penned to explain away all her pain.

It had been left for her. Which meant he hadn't wanted to leave. Which meant something had happened, maybe something with the train station and the man in tweed, and it was up to Raegan to figure it out. *Finally.*

CHAPTER EIGHT

Raegan unlocked her front door, still in a tear-choked daze from her discovery. The train ride home had been nothing more than a blur, her arms wrapped around the book so tightly her muscles had begun to shake.

She shoved old mail and last night's takeout to the side, laying the book on the kitchen table. She took a moment to run a hand across the beautiful cover, which seemed to shimmer beneath the warm kitchen light. Here, in a more ordinary space, it rang out so clearly as not belonging. The book's otherworldliness was harsh against the surrounding normality: the small café table, the dingy tile counters, the antique velvet wingback she hoped might be a nice spot for a cat to curl up on one day, when she got her shit together.

Before she knew it, Raegan's fingers were already turning to the page about the kelpie, hungry for more unusual things that did not fit with her apartment where there was only fifteen minutes of hot water and two dead philodendrons.

There it was—too faint to have been noticed in the basement, written in pencil by her father's hand. Beside the instructions for summoning a kelpie, which the book detailed but ultimately warned against, was a simple phrase:

"Particularly good for finding lost things. And of course, traveling between worlds".

Raegan sat back in her chair, feeling a little bit like she was having a mental breakdown, but mostly like she'd finally cracked the fucking code after more than ten years of depressive swings and angry outbursts and a broken family and crying on public transportation because she'd seen a man in tweed or the sunset skewed a certain sepia way.

She had always known that there was something different about her father, that he walked paths others didn't see, despite his normal appearance and job as a librarian. After all, he had told that story so frequently, so meaningfully, always beckoning Raegan close as if there was some secret hidden within it that she hadn't figured out yet. When she'd found her mother burning his books that fateful evening years ago, Raegan knew her father's disappearance was not as it seemed. It sounded crazy, of course, to her few high school friends and her therapist. And to her mother, who was still grieving and wanted to accept that her husband had simply walked out because then she could be angry, and anger was sustainable in a way that misery was not.

Raegan wanted so badly to believe that this was *something*. She knew it could be dangerous, but fuck, what did it matter if she entertained this for a few hours and left it alone when it yielded nothing? She did not want to lose the way she felt, like she was so close to something, like the air was thick, molasses-golden, enchanted and sparkling.

Her therapist's voice popped unbidden into her head, reminding her that she wouldn't leave it alone, that Raegan purposefully believed in impossible things to make what had happened easier. It was a coping mechanism, and it wasn't a healthy one, and someone like Raegan was not capable of *just* entertaining a thought like this one. It would become her entire reality, and she would drown in it. It had happened before, when she was in Boston, but she had buried that deep and told herself it wouldn't be like that again—the inpatient stay and the scratchy hospital gown and the fuzzy socks.

Raegan took a deep breath and really thought about whether she wanted to keep reading. She decided she did, but not before she put the kettle on. Somewhere between getting a mug and a teabag, the mug got filled with whiskey instead. When the kettle clicked, Raegan faithfully took it off its circular stand. But then she just stared at the little stainless steel kettle, unsure what to do with it now. She considered pouring the hot water over her hands to see if they would bloat and glisten like tea leaves, if that would make anything more or less real.

Instead, she found herself back at the table, mug of whiskey in her hand, a few gulps already downed, as she began to read the summoning. It called for a body of water, an offering, and a few words in Gaelic that she knew how to pronounce, but not much else. By the time she had read the passage multiple times, including the warning about how kelpies were dangerous, more than half the mug of whiskey was gone and her courage had exponentially increased.

Raegan thundered down the stairs to the front of her building, whiskey in hand, book tucked under her arm and a small folding knife shoved into her pocket. She rounded the corner into the alley, relieved to see the large puddle from the rain last night still intact in a pothole where a number of cobblestones had sunk down into the earth.

"Okay, this is insane," she muttered, and she told herself it was good she thought it was crazy, because that meant she was still sane, right?

For a moment, all held still. Raegan breathed in the car exhaust and that cool, rich scent indicating autumn had arrived. The skyline glimmered above the roof of her building, and a car speaker's bass thumped somewhere farther down the block.

And then Raegan did it. She made a small nick in her thumb, because she wasn't a fucking idiot about to slice open her entire palm, and dripped the required three droplets of her blood into the puddle. Then came the whiskey; she took a swig of her own and dumped the rest into the water, where it swam on the surface for a moment. It was supposed to be mead, but even Raegan didn't have mead at the ready, so whiskey would have to do. The streetlight flickered. She said the words.

Silence blanketed the alleyway, and Raegan could've sworn she felt her heartbeat in every fiber of her being.

Nothing.

Her vision swam with black dots because she didn't dare breathe.

Still nothing.

Raegan kicked at the water with one boot, shouting something incomprehensible. Suddenly, she was sober. Her hands tightened around the book, and for a moment, she considered chucking it into the puddle, but thought better of it—because honestly, what the fuck had she expected, anyway? She turned on her heel to make her way back to the door. Her eyes stung, anger catching at her throat like a clawed hand.

And then, just faintly, from over her shoulder: "You called."

Raegan turned, the hair on the back of her neck standing on end. There, from the puddle, rose a horse's head. It was inky black, the skin tar-like, the edges of its ears softly scalloped. Its forelock was little more than a piece of seaweed, murky green and bloated with water.

Disbelief bloomed in Raegan's mind. Her mouth went dry, and her hands, for some reason, curled into fists. She stared at the being that had emerged from the puddle, wishing with all her heart that it was real and that she hadn't just drank too much whiskey and passed out on the couch. It *looked* real. It looked realer than her, if she was honest, even with only its head and a short portion of its thick, arched neck above the surface. Puddle water ran down its muscles in rivulets, highlighting the odd nature of its flat, greenish-black coat.

"Did you summon me?" it demanded, more harshly this time, in a voice that sounded like crashing waves. "It is very rude to summon me and then walk away."

"I didn't think you were real," Raegan whispered, walking a few steps closer to the thing in the puddle.

The kelpie, having apparently heard her, made a scoffing noise. "We are of the same place," it told her. "I tasted it in your blood. Why would you, of all people, doubt a kelpie's existence?"

Now that this situation was real, or at least assumably real, or maybe realer than it should be, all the warnings in the book came rushing back to Raegan. Fear stirred in the pit of her stomach, a tenseness aching in the small of her back.

"Hey," Raegan said, not moving closer, planting her feet shoulder-width apart. "Don't drown me."

The kelpie met her gaze, eyes dark as river silt. "What *do* you want, then?"

Raegan was quite aware that the kelpie had not said it wasn't going to kill her. She thought of a million things to ask the supernatural creature in front of her, the thing that shouldn't be real and yet here it was, ripe with knowledge of worlds unseen and things she had thought impossible, but only one thing came out:

"Have you seen my dad?"

The kelpie held her gaze, dispassionate, like it couldn't believe she'd summoned a goddamn kelpie to ask such a basic question. "Who is your father?" it finally asked.

"Cor-Cormac Overhill," Raegan stuttered, pulling out her phone and scrolling to a photo of her father: her favorite one, the cropped portrait for the library, where he was smiling and happy.

"Overhill," the kelpie repeated, like it was gaining traction. The kelpie lifted its head out of the puddle, straining to look at the image Raegan displayed. In the back of her mind, she wondered what she would look like to someone passing by on the street, showing an iPhone to a dripping wet horse head in a puddle, or maybe to nothing at all.

"The name is familiar," the kelpie intoned, "but I cannot place it."

"He disappeared years ago," Raegan replied, hazarding another step which brought brackish water and the thick iron smell of blood to her nose. "He read me folklore, and he had all these books with notes. He had this experience at a train station with someone, something. He said you're good at finding lost things and for traveling between worlds." Her heart pounded and her breathing came so quick for someone just standing still.

The kelpie stared. "Child, what is your name?"

There were definitely rules about giving out true names, she knew, but fuck it to hell. "Raegan Maeve Overhill," she said, her blood pounding in her neck.

And after a long pause: "Now *that* means something to me. One moment, please." The kelpie's head sank below the surface, leaving only ripples in its wake. Raegan waited. She would wait for days, for years, because this was the only thing that mattered, the only thing that would ever matter.

She didn't know how long it took, but when the kelpie returned, it held something in its mouth: a tiny, silver key.

"This is for you, probably left some number of years ago," the kelpie said after spitting the key toward Raegan's feet, where it settled like a small fish, dripping with black water. "My kind experiences time differently, you see. All at once and nothing at all. Never in that straight line. We thought you would come sooner. Your kind does not live very long, marching your little line."

"What's it for?" Raegan demanded, breathless, aching to grab the key, but her instincts would not allow her to lean down so close to the creature and grab it.

"I do not know," the kelpie replied. "I only know it is for you."

"That's it?" Raegan asked, wondering if she had begun to push her luck. "You have no idea where I'm supposed to take this or what it opens?"

"No," the kelpie told her, its black eyes expressionless.

More questions crawled up Raegan's throat—it was, after all, her nature and her trade. "Did my father leave it?" she wanted to know, her gaze dropping to the key again.

"I cannot say," the kelpie said, its tone as final as a wave against rock, sounding to Raegan like an otherworldly, slightly Scottish version of John Malkovich, a comparison that might've made her laugh if not for the gravity of it all. "It is possible I have not yet experienced its arrival yet. Perhaps the Rivers spun whoever left it out of their little human line. I do not know. It is not my purview. I only know it is yours. It was lost, and now I have returned it."

Silence hung, tight as a drum, and Raegan forced herself to quell the other questions and thoughts spinning around in her mind. So far, she was not dead, and she should probably quit while she was ahead.

"Thank you," Raegan said, chewing the inside of her lip. "I'm sorry. I've been rude. I'm . . . I'm having a weird night."

The kelpie considered her from its puddle, tilting its large head to the side as if to get a better look. "I can see you are confused, indeed. I bid you a good night. Be more careful if you call the River Folk again," the kelpie said, beginning to slip beneath the slick water.

Raegan leapt forward to snatch the key from the ground and then took a large step back, not knowing how far out of the puddle the kelpie could climb if it wanted to do so.

"Wait!" she said, unable to pin the question down inside her. "Are you the one drowning people in puddles?"

It was a stupid question to ask, mostly because the answer was obvious—something she already knew, the reality of it like a harsh and sudden fever on her skin. And it was the kind of question that could get her killed. The kelpie sank a bit deeper into the water, obscuring everything but its eyes and ears. Its words came out clearly, despite its submerged mouth.

"I must consume."

"So," Raegan hazarded, her heart against her ribs, "that's a yes?"

The kelpie considered her with dark, oil-slick eyes. "Would you like to see?"

"Nope, no," Raegan backtracked. Her heart hammered as she stumbled another step back across the broken asphalt and cobblestones. "Definitely not. You are dismissed, I guess. If you remember anything about my father, send me a message in a bottle. Or something."

The kelpie continued its unblinking stare, eyes like a toad's. "Kelpies are not particularly good for answers. Only lost things. They are not the same. You have the key now, and the key will tell you where to go. I would not worry too much."

"Not to be rude, but that's pretty easy for you to say," Raegan said, gesturing at the kelpie's magnificent otherworldliness, its ancient eyes and riverstone skin.

"I suppose navigating the world is indeed much easier when you are an illustrious being like myself."

For a moment, Raegan thought the kelpie was making a joke, but its expression was serious, as far as she could judge. What she could not judge was whether it meant her any true harm. It said it didn't, but it was a being of half-truths and puddles as deep as oceans. She did not believe its words for a moment. Her father had taught her better than that.

"I appreciate that you, uhh, kept this key for me," Raegan said, trying hard not to stammer and failing. "You are released."

"I do not require your release," the kelpie replied. "I am under no power of yours. I can go when I please. You may summon me, or others like me, but after that, with no protective spells or sigils in place, we can do as we please."

Raegan blanched and realized that, of course, the supernatural creature she'd half-assedly summoned after half a mug of whiskey could have killed her.

"Of course, I would not drown *you*," the kelpie added in such a matter-of-fact tone that it startled her. "I dare say the King would not be pleased. We have a covenant, after all. Merry meet, Raegan Maeve Overhill, and merry part."

With that, before Raegan could ask anything about a king or a covenant, the kelpie slid back into the water, completely disappearing. After a long time—longer than she'd like to admit—Raegan worked up the courage to peer into the puddle. It was shallow, shallower than she remembered it being when she came outside. There was a beer bottle cap in the bottom. For a moment, she considered stepping in it, just to be sure, but nausea rose in her stomach at the idea of actually doing it, so she retreated.

The walk up the stairs to her apartment was long and strange, each step taking much more effort than it should have. By the time Raegan reached her door, she realized the coming dawn was already casting odd shadows outside, even though she could've sworn it couldn't be past midnight. Losing time, she knew, was no unusual thing when it came to encountering beings of myth. She told herself that all things considered, it was nearly normal.

Raegan locked the door behind her and pulled off her shoes. Her apartment had not changed. There was no mark of her encounter, of the step she had taken beyond the veil. She was utterly alone with the weight of otherworldliness on her shoulders. After seeing an actual mythological creature in the flesh, Raegan would've thought she'd be alive with energy, crackling with possibility. But she found she was exhausted, as if the summoning had drained her or retrieving the key had taken more than she realized.

There was always a price.

Raegan shuffled to her bedroom and began to undress slowly, almost in a trance. She made no attempt at brushing her teeth or anything of the sort because she did not think she could handle water. Not in a sink, not coming from a faucet, nothing, even though her mouth was dry after the gulps of whiskey. Thankfully, she was asleep the moment her head hit the pillow.

But this was not the inky-black nothingness she had always associated with deep exhaustion. Instead, this sleep was thickly webbed with dreams. They marched in, unstoppable and all at once, unfolding like new, sticky wings fresh from the cocoon.

She walked across an autumn meadow, the fur cloak on her shoulders nearly as heavy as the sense of duty and purpose that filled her ribcage. The skies hung low and gray. Her destination, she knew, was the river in the distance—wide and rough-currented, winding along the foothills of the mountains that rose to touch the bleak gray. The air spun thick with woodsmoke. To her left, just beyond her vision, walked a companion—no, much more than a companion. She knew the person walking with her through that meadow would follow her into the depths of hell if she asked. Hesitating, she turned to look at them.

But then the dream cracked down the middle, darkening as if to signal the end of one scene before another began.

Her vision was blurred, blinking in and out of blackness. The remains of a fire, barely more than embers, and the haze of dusk lingered in the distance. Wherever she was, night was coming, and it was coming soon.

Then the world tilted, seemingly of its own accord. No, she realized, it was not the world—just her. She was being carried, slung over a rough shoulder like a carcass. Her mouth was dry and metallic-tasting. Something uncomfortable pressed into her skin, cold and sharp. It took her some time to pull her reeling mind together, but she eventually understood it was the chainmail of the man who carried her.

There were more men, moving in a pack around her. They all smelled of blood and metal and sweat. They moved up a hill at a quick pace, headed for a stone structure. She could not get a good look at it, but it was familiar, she knew.

The man carrying her readjusted her weight across his shoulder, sending a quick jolt of searing pain through her body. Her vision spiraled into black again.

When she awoke, it was only because someone was screaming. For a long, dim second, she wondered if maybe it was her—her final song, her last resistance, but she knew only a few moments later that the sound could not be coming from her.

It was no scream. It was a howl, a horrible sound, long and low and full of rage and despair all at once. It sounded like retribution. It was not human, and it rang through the space as if the stone hallways would always carry a memory of it.

She blinked—or at least, she thought she had only blinked; the darkness was terribly soft and inviting—and the men were gone. The smell of damp earth and woodsmoke and black pepper overtook her. Then there were strong arms around her, and she knew suddenly that she was dying. She did not understand why she hadn't realized it earlier. It was obvious that her body hurt, that it hurt so very badly. Life was seeping out of her like syrup, clinging to everything but her.

Whoever held her, she loved them. She understood that more than anything else. She knew it fiercely. Hot tears trailed down her face, more of relief than sadness. She had been so afraid she was going to die alone, laid out on a rough wooden table like an offering.

But the arms were tight and strong and she was not alone. A voice like heather on the hills and dusk over the lake spoke to her, over and over again in her ear. Like a chant. A ritual. A prayer, maybe. It stopped the pain.

"Outlive me. Please outlive me. I love you too much." She strained, trying to see the face of the person whom she knew she loved, to take it in one last time. But then her vision slipped away and there was only a curl of black smoke and the smell of things long dead.

CHAPTER NINE

Raegan jolted awake, the sheets glued to her sweat-slicked skin. The darkness of the room swam and snaked around her as she fought to make out any familiar shapes: the fake fern in the corner, the overstuffed reading chair by the window. For a long, looping moment, nothing came to her. There was only the same infinite blackness she had seen in the dream when life trickled out of her body.

The dream. She sat straight up, unease digging cold fingers into her stomach. Groping around the nightstand, Raegan found her phone and unlocked the screen. It was 3:33 AM on a Friday in October and the dream was back.

The night terror of being a near-dead body hauled around like a sack had haunted her since childhood. When she was younger, before her father had disappeared, it had come to her nearly every night. Some of her earliest memories were running as fast as she could to her parents' bedroom on unsteady toddler legs, trying to use her limited vocabulary to explain what had happened in her dreaming mind.

As she got older, the dream filled her less with terror and more with a sense of longing that far outpaced her age. Raegan was absolutely sure that all she needed to know was the identity of whomever held her as she breathed her last. Then everything would fall into place. The world would be set back on its axis. She so often peered into the faces of

crowds at intersections and examined every commuter on a train platform because she was always looking. Searching. Hoping. Her father
had told her she was probably missing someone from a past life. When
he'd disappeared, the dreams had stopped abruptly, another finite
ending.

And now here the dream was, resurrected and realer than ever.
Raegan could not recall tasting blood in a dream before, nor the intensity
of the scents that had surrounded her. She swallowed, her mouth dry, a
metallic tang still present on her tongue.

Why, she wondered, lifting her damp braid off her neck with one
hand, had the dream returned now?

The events of the evening came rushing back to her at all once, like a
levy let loose, and she remembered: the book and the kelpie and the
summoning and the key. Raegan lunged for the nightstand, open hands
hunting for the key, hungry for it, desperate and wild and aching like she
had never ached before. A cruel voice in her head chided that it was just
a dream—or worse, a full mental breakdown—and that there were no
books left by her father, no tiny silver keys made from pure molten
hope.

Then the cool pang of metal met her hot hand and she clutched the
key to her chest, feeling its contours with her fingers, convincing herself
everything had to be real because here it was, pressed against her skin.
She waited until the metal warmed to her touch before she flicked her
phone light on. The key was still there, resting in the palm of her hand,
winking silver in the light.

More awake now, Raegan conceded that she could have halluci-
nated the kelpie part. Maybe the key had been in a puddle or on a
doorstep somewhere. Maybe she'd just snatched it up and concocted the
rest, desperate for the world to slant strangely in her favor. She should
probably call her therapist.

Raegan lay back down, flat on her back, stiff as a board. She rested
the key on her breastbone and forced herself to breathe in and out, soft
and slow. Knowledge settled deep in her marrow: this—whatever it was
—was her door.

And goddammit, she was going to walk through it.

For the first time in her career, Raegan relished her Sunday-to-
Thursday work schedule. She set an alarm and resolved to attempt a few

more hours of sleep. She would need to be fresh to follow through with this. The key was only a small token. She would need more to get wherever she was going. The key grasped fiercely between her fingers, Raegan turned onto her side and closed her eyes. Sleep, she told herself. And then: she would walk into another place, another time.

The screen read 8:32 AM when she woke up next—a far more reasonable hour. She rolled over and buried her face in the pillow, wondering if she still had a single foothold in reality, then wondering if she even cared about the answer.

She decided not to dwell on the question of her sanity. For now, she would assume she'd summoned a kelpie and it had given her a key, because there was nothing else to be done. She would not question what she had seen and heard with her own eyes and ears. In the old stories, that's how throats were slit and bad deals were agreed to, Raegan knew. She'd stay diligent. Stay sharp. Treat this like any other story, journalistic or folkloric or otherwise.

Of course, she conceded to herself as she threw her legs over the side of the bed and sat up, she had never wanted any other story to be true quite so badly before.

The face that greeted her in the bathroom mirror looked older. Avoiding her reflection entirely would've been preferred, but it felt necessary to look into her eyes and see if she still saw herself staring back. Her freckled skin was sallow, and her cheeks looked gaunt. Her hazel eyes were dark, and they glittered strangely in the light. All in all, the only thing looking back was an exhausted, sleep-deprived Raegan Maeve Overhill. For now, it seemed, she was still wearing her own skin.

She brushed her teeth using the smallest amount of water she possibly could, re-braided her hair, and then headed into the kitchen. Glorious autumn light greeted her, the suncatchers on her window spinning out rainbows across her apartment. The antique keys on their threadbare velvet ribbons greeted her knowingly. A crow cawed loudly outside. Raegan felt suspended in the moment, held aloft by molten light and fate-threaded keys and black feathers. She knew deep within her bones that something was happening, just the way she had always wanted, and she vowed to not let it slip through her grasp.

The crow cawed again as it took off from its perch, sending a silky black shadow gliding across her window that made the suncatchers wink at her. Elation bucked in Raegan's chest, and she forced herself steady, focusing on the tiny silver key in her palm.

She set the key on her little café table and filled the electric kettle with water, not daring to look into the depths of the small container. It was a worthwhile risk. She needed caffeine—her body felt like it did after an election night or when edits on a longform stretched until 4 AM. But she'd bet her brain had produced more serotonin in the past twenty-four hours than it had in the last ten years.

"I didn't need SSRIs, just a quest," Raegan joked softly to herself as she spooned sugar into her mug. While the water reached a boil, she took her medications anyway and then returned to the table to examine the key more closely in the better light of the kitchen.

On one side, the key read "Property of First United Bank." On the other, three digits protruded from the silver flesh: "333."

Chills spread like frost along her neck as she remembered the hour she had awoken. Or perhaps she had misremembered, conflating the two numbers to add an extra punch of meaning to all of this. Raegan let out a sigh, forcing herself to focus on the concrete information in front of her.

The key had to be for a safe deposit box, didn't it? She sank into the chair, pulling out her phone and ignoring the kettle on the counter when it clicked. After a few furious Google searches, Raegan confirmed her theory. A few more well-phrased searches led her to the conclusion that the bank was one she was familiar with—and just a few blocks from her mother's house. Her father's good friend had managed it years ago, and perhaps still did.

Raegan rose, heeding the siren call of caffeine, and poured not-quite-hot-enough water into her mug. Standing at the counter, she chewed on her lip until it bled. There had been no safe deposit box when the police helped Bronwyn settle things after her father disappeared. There could be an easy explanation, like her mother lying—which she had done before—or some bureaucratic thing.

Taking her mug with her to the table, Raegan sat back down and turned the key over in her hands. She knew there was only one way to see this through. But myth-making was often the most delicate at the beginning: doors you missed the first time weren't there when you doubled back for them, and fast-growing vines obscured the path you thought you had sighted from the other end of the meadow. If she was going to pull the curtain back and attempt to see beyond it with her mortal eyes, she would have to act hard and fast.

Raegan sipped her tea, ignoring the way the heat stung the raw spot on her lower lip. She told herself to contact her therapist. She told herself to let a friend know where she was going, maybe even share a significantly pared-down account of the last few hours. She told herself that her medications could sometimes cause hallucinations, though she'd never had them in the five or more years she'd been on the same regimen. She told herself to count to ten before she made any decisions.

On the count of four, Raegan was on her feet, sprinting to her bedroom to pull on an old, worn jeans that clung to her curves and a loose t-shirt. She darted to the door, yanking on boots and jamming her arms into her favorite leather jacket. As she swiped her keys from the catchall bowl, the framed portrait of her father on a nearby bookshelf caught her eye. Their gazes met.

"There better be a reason for all this shit," Raegan said out loud, surprising herself with how calm her voice sounded. "Or I swear to god, when I find you, I'm going to be so pissed off."

And then she was out the door, thudding down the steps. If she made the next train, she could be in the northeast in less than twenty minutes, the bank only a few minutes' walk beyond the station. She silently thanked the newspaper for the monthly train passes it bestowed upon all its journalists—the good ones, too, with no zone restrictions.

The early morning sun turned everything to molten bronze, even rusted-out chain-link fences looking more like the chainmail of a hero. The city was just beginning to wake, sparrow-song still discernible over the hum and bleat of traffic and humanity. The air was cool against her face, tipped with the coming seasons of frost and chill.

She told herself not to sprint to the station but then conceded that a jog would be reasonable. After a nail-biting, foot-tapping, obsessive-phone-checking train ride and a concerted effort to not look absolutely unhinged as she bounded out onto the sidewalk, Raegan was standing in front of the First United Bank in Fox Chase.

The bank occupied a squat brick building that was typical of the neighborhood. The busy boulevard whizzed behind her, horns blaring and pedestrians scurrying like beetles. A cream cornice crowned the building's roof, marred with bird feces and debris. Raegan lingered on the sidewalk, eyeing the tinted glass doors, feeling like what waited beyond could save her or destroy her.

She gripped the key tighter, forcing herself to take a deep breath.

"Hey," a gruff male voice called from behind her. "Hey there, baby! Looking mighty fine in those jeans this morning!"

Raegan narrowed her eyes and glanced over her shoulder, clocking a middle-aged man making his way across the cracked sidewalk toward her. Anger surging, she slipped her hand toward her waistband, where she always kept her knife.

"Hey," Raegan replied, timing the visible unfolding of her knife with her words. "Fuck off. *Now.*"

The man blanched and then snarled something half-heartedly at her, waving his hand in the air as if she were a fly he wanted to bat away. His complaints were lost to the roar of traffic just behind him. Raegan gritted her teeth and turned back to the bank, trying to find her footing again, fighting to remain in the current of the book and the kelpie and the key.

Setting her jaw, she tucked the knife back onto her waistband and took the last few steps across the sidewalk and into the bank. The air-conditioning, too cold for the morning hour, hit her in a rush of chill. The space was carpeted in a worn-out navy. A phone rang in the distance, and a photocopier droned down a hallway to her left. Though someone was using the ATM in the lobby, no one else was in line for the tellers.

Raegan wavered a few paces from the counter, wishing she had answered a million questions before walking in. What had been the name of her father's friend? How did you ask to see a safe deposit box? What was she going to do when they denied her, or when there was no safe deposit box at all, or when the only thing inside the box was empty space that she could not fill, no matter how hard she tried?

Myths, Raegan reminded herself, were rife with messy beginnings. She set her jaw, gripped the key so hard in her pocket that its teeth bit into her palm, and walked up to the teller.

"Hey, good morning," Raegan said, leaning casually against the counter. The teller was older, male-presenting, and she made a snap decision to play a damsel in distress. "Um, I've gotten myself into a bit of a situation. I hope you might be able to help me out?"

She was about to pull the key from her pocket when someone walked out from the back offices—a tall, balding man with a kind face. Their gazes met, and recognition turned over in Raegan's mind.

"Well, my goodness!" the man called, making his way over. Raegan noticed that he dressed like her father—worn-in slacks, a buttoned cardigan, reading glasses tucked into a breast pocket. She also noticed he was not American—Scottish, she thought.

"Could that really be Raegan Overhill?" the man asked as he drew closer. Was it possible to get so lucky that her father's friend not only still worked at the bank but walked out right when she arrived?

"Oh, hi. It's me!" Raegan said, taking her hand out of her pocket. "I'm sorry—you were friends with my dad, weren't you? I'm embarrassed. I'm totally blanking on your name." She smiled then, the kind of smile she saved up for situations like this: dazzling, disarming.

"I thought it was you," the man said, clearly delighted, coming to stand on her side of the counter. "And please, don't fret about my name —it's David. Your father and I met at the book club he ran at the library. I miss him very much. And aren't you just the spitting image with that hair!"

"I miss him, too," Raegan told David, surprising herself with how much she liked his deep, warm voice and the way he hunched his shoulders a bit to make his height less intimidating. "I stopped by to get myself out of a pickle. Maybe I could see what you think and catch up a little?" She resisted the urge to bite the inside of her cheek while she awaited his response, every muscle in her body tense.

"Of course," David replied easily, waving her deeper into the building with one hand. "Why don't you come into my office and sit down? We can have a cuppa, if you'd like."

"I would like that very much," Raegan said, following him down the carpeted hallway.

He stopped at the third door on the left and gestured her inside. She stepped into the bland office, sweeping her gaze over the low bookshelf, filing cabinets, and two chairs in front of a big desk. There were no windows and the overhead light was too bright. She did not sit, instead hovering in the blank space between the two chairs.

"So, tell me about this problem you're having," David asked, sitting down at his desk. He pulled his glasses from the pocket of his cardigan and put them on, like he was ready to solve the issue at that very moment. Raegan silently pleaded to whatever goddess would listen that this would go the way she needed it to.

"Look," Raegan started, rubbing her temple for a moment, "I found a key in my dad's study. I think it's for a safe deposit box here. I know he's been gone a long time and it's probably silly I'm even checking in on this. I just miss him."

David sat back in his chair, some of the joviality seeping out of his face as he visibly paled. He looked like he was trying to find the right words, and Raegan waited, letting the silence blanket the room.

"Your father . . ." David began, immediately trailing off. He readjusted his glasses. "Your father was a bit odd. It was endearing. Everyone liked him, you know that—I'm sure you remember. About a year before . . . before it happened, he asked me to set him up with a safe deposit box. I did. I didn't particularly think anything of it—both of your parents, like me, are immigrants, and we have papers and documents that need to be kept safe."

Raegan lowered herself into the left chair. She could hear her heart thudding in her ears. For some reason, her eyes tracked to the carpet between her boots. It was stained. An old coffee spill, she thought, before she fought off the dissociation, pulling herself back to the present.

"But then he made a stranger request," David continued. "He asked me to keep the safe deposit box here, no matter what happened, and that if one day you turned up with a key, to make sure you got access."

"That's not usually how this sort of thing works, is it?" Raegan asked, looking up at David. Suspicion pricked her, but she didn't know if she was simply being unfair. Her father always had a way of gently shrugging off the regular rules, no matter where he was.

"No," David admitted, steepling his fingers. "No, it's not, but it seemed harmless enough and he had never asked me for anything in our many years of friendship. He had done so much for me—he was there for me when my wife left, and he essentially introduced me to my whole social circle. It was the only thing he had ever asked of me. I told the police when he went missing, but they never followed up. I probably should have told your mother—your poor Mum—but Cormac had been so . . . serious about it, and serious about it being for you. Frankly, I haven't thought of it in years. But now . . ."

"Now here I am," Raegan said, her tone low and soft. They considered each other across the expanse of David's desk, where folders were piled up and a mug emblazoned with "FEARLESS READER" sat abandoned off to the side.

"I'm sorry," David said suddenly, rubbing the back of his head as he looked away from her. "I never thought your dad was in danger. I just thought he was being his usual odd self."

Raegan folded her hands on her knee, waiting for David to look at her again. When he did, she saw guilt in his gaze, as if he thought her father requesting the safe deposit box was some sort of harbinger he should've identified. She saw sorrow, a deep sadness that his friend was gone, disappeared, and he hadn't been able to do a damn thing about it.

Straightening her spine, Raegan took a deep breath. "David," she said, her tone sharpening.

He sat up, leaning forward onto his desk as if her next words would be some of the most important he'd ever hear.

"I need to see the box."

CHAPTER TEN

Time suspended itself within the four walls of the First United Bank, all the ordinary workings of such a mundane place cast aside for something greater.

David moved first, drumming his fingers on the desk. "Right. Of course you do. Come with me." With that, he stood and took a few long strides across the room, checking at the doorway to see if Raegan was behind him. She hadn't gotten out of her chair, her fingernails digging into the upholstered arms.

"It's right this way," David said, gently gesturing down the hallway. Something in his gaze had softened, and embarrassment swirled in Raegan's gut. Did she look like a deer in the headlights? Did she look like a lost child, hoping her daddy had left something behind for her?

Raegan forced herself to her feet, the soles of her boots quiet on the carpet as she followed David down a long hallway. When it came to a T, David veered to the left into a shadowy corridor. They marched in silence until a large gray door loomed at the end of the hallway.

"This is the safe deposit room," he said, pulling out a key ring and flipping through a number of keys. "We'll go inside, I'll show you to the box, and then you'll be able to view it privately. You can let me know if you'd like to leave the contents here or if you'd like to withdraw them."

"Okay," Raegan said, surprised at how hoarse her voice was.

Darkness greeted them before David took a step inside and motion lights kicked on, illuminating a modest room with a table in the center. The walls were covered with safe deposit boxes, all neatly numbered. It reminded Raegan of a mausoleum.

She followed David inside, stopping at the table. She was pretty sure that's what people did in movies and wondered how accurate those depictions were, though now was not a particularly useful time to be curious about it.

"What's the number?" David asked, pushing his glasses back up his nose.

"333," Raegan said, not daring to reach for the key in her pocket just yet. David nodded and set off for a section of the boxes, clicking his tongue as he scanned the numbers. She could see from across the room that all the boxes in the row started with three.

"Ah," David said, pulling a small silver box from its place on the wall. "Here you are." He placed the box on the table. It looked normal as far as Raegan could tell. The earth did not seem to shift on its axis. No ancient knowledge bubbled to the forefront of Raegan's mind.

"Right," she exhaled.

"I'll be just outside," David said, tucking the key ring back into his pocket. "Come on out whenever you're ready."

Raegan nodded, turning back to gaze at the box. When David closed the door behind him, it felt like the entire universe disappeared. It was only her and whatever was inside the box. Or whatever wasn't.

"Just open it," Raegan told herself between gritted teeth. She clutched the key in her pocket. Her heart raced and her stomach flipped. She swallowed hard, squeezing her eyes shut for a second.

Then she stepped forward and inserted the key into the tiny lock. It turned over with a quiet click. A drawer slid out. Before she could stop and think, before she could even allow a single feeling to raise its head in her body, Raegan pulled it open.

Inside were thick sheets of paper, folded in on themselves letter-style. She reached in and plucked them from the metal case. Inhaling shakily, she unfolded them and laid them flat on the table, one by one.

There were seven papers in all. They were large and the material was substantial, bringing parchment and vellum and ancient libraries to mind. On Raegan's first glance, the writing upon them appeared to be scribbles. Endless loops and mad lettering, all amounting to nothing.

She narrowed her eyes and looked closer, leaning over the table. Madness unfolded in front of her, presenting instead furious notes and graphics and circles and half-sentences, unusual drawings in miniature and things crossed out and reworked. There was complicated math that far surpassed Raegan's abilities and instructions for what looked like hand positions or symbols. One page was full of notes about the appropriate accommodations for different moon phases and the positions of certain planets. The last two pages were just illustrations: a large set of ornately wrought, towering gates and a circle with complicated symbols around it.

Her mouth dry, Raegan smoothed the papers against the table again, straining her eyes to look at the minute details in the margins of the pages, often trailing off onto the next sheet. She could not make head or tail of it—some of it didn't even seem to be in English. Even places where she could understand some of the individual words proved too esoteric overall for her to riddle out.

The circle with the symbols, though . . . She had no idea what it meant and certainly had little knowledge of the symbols themselves, but it was a pentacle. Raegan was sure of it. A casting or summoning circle, a magical fetish of some kind, though she had no idea of its purpose.

She dragged a hand through her hair, clenching her jaw. All the logical parts in her were saying that her father had simply suffered some kind of mental health crisis that led to his disappearance. But with each breath, each heartbeat, Raegan became surer and surer that this was real, whatever it was.

"Magic," she admitted to herself, barely more than an exhale in the quiet space. She suddenly became aware of how much time had passed since David had exited the room. Moving quietly, Raegan folded the papers back up and gingerly placed them inside her pocket, tucking the key beside them. She rubbed her eyes hard, trying to mimic the appearance of having just been crying. Then she pulled herself together and walked out. At the threshold, silence yawned wide and hungry, the space at her back feeling infinite and full of dangers.

Then David appeared in the ordinary hallway with its ordinary carpet and ordinary overhead lighting. "Oh, Raegan, are you alright?" he asked once he'd taken a look at her face.

She swallowed. "It's just some original copies of my dual citizenship papers," Raegan said, pushing her voice out low and hoarse. She swiped at her cheek as if wiping away a tear. "I don't know why I thought there would be something more fantastical in there."

David looked at her, startled, and opened his mouth to say something. Then he seemed to remember he was speaking to the daughter of the man who'd disappeared without a trace and closed it again. "I think we both worked ourselves into a bit of a tizzy," he said, ushering her down the hallway. "We both miss your father very much. It would be nice for there to be some magic to it all, wouldn't there? You can have a seat in my office and take a breath."

"Thank you," Raegan said as they rounded the corner, a woman in a tan pantsuit breezing past them. "I think I just need to go home and cry for like an hour." The papers sang a quiet chorus of rustling sighs from deep within her pocket.

"Is there anyone you can call?" David asked, stopping in front of his office, discomfort settling across his face. "Anyone I can call for you?"

"No, no," Raegan said, straightening and taking a deep breath. She raised her gaze to David's and gave him a grim little smile. "I'm fine, I promise. Well, okay, I'm not. But I will be. I'll be fine to get myself home."

David wavered, looking unsure. "Alright," he finally said. "Please be safe. Don't hesitate if you need anything. I'm sorry it's all turned out this way."

Raegan shrugged, taking another step down the hallway and away from David. "That's life, isn't it?" she said.

David sighed, leaning against the doorframe. "That's life," he echoed. "Be safe, Raegan."

"I always am," Raegan replied, walking backwards toward the bank lobby. "Thank you again." Then she turned and strode across the lobby, out through the doors, and into the crisp morning. She stood for a moment on the pavement, squinting at the bright sunlight. Triumph surged through her body like a tidal wave, and she slipped a hand into her pocket, a thrill running down her spine when her fingers met the thick folds of parchment.

Raegan took a deep, ragged breath, her mind racing. "Okay," she said to herself. "Okay." And then she walked down the block at a reasonable pace, looking for all the world a somewhat morose woman who'd just had another hope dashed. She turned at the corner, casting her gaze back at the bank. It sat squat on its lot, unmoving. No one came out of its dark-eyed doors. No one made frantic phone calls on the pavement outside. No one seemed to give a single shit about what had just transpired.

She took a deep breath, zipped her pocket closed, and broke into a run.

CHAPTER ELEVEN

Raegan took her apartment's steep stairs at a full-out sprint, bursting through the door for the second time in less than twenty-four hours. She removed the papers from her pocket with careful, shaking hands, placing them on the café table next to the book.

"Okay," she murmured. "You can figure this out." She peeled her leather jacket off her damp skin, pulled her hair into a bun, and grabbed her laptop from her work bag. Her stomach growled for food, but she ignored it, logging into her computer instead and bringing up the old faithful: Google.

It wasn't long before she found herself with about a million tabs up at once, attempting to decipher individual symbols, taking copious notes the entire time. She quickly realized the contents of the papers made no sense together, which didn't surprise her, but she was doing her best to parse out each symbol's meaning in the hopes of discovering a broader intent or message.

Raegan knew a lot of this was way over her head—most of her search results were concerned with high ceremonial magic, the kind associated with secret societies and dusty old white men. After a few hours of research, she came to the realization that the contents of her father's safe deposit box would be a challenge for a lifelong occultist to understand.

She was good at figuring new things out—it went with the journalist territory—but every time Raegan thought she had a grasp on a symbol or a tiny part of a note, she'd find another piece of information that contradicted it. She tried casting her net a bit wider, but all she found were spells for making a straying boyfriend come back and a large group effort to hex the government that she briefly admired.

Raegan shoved her chair back, face hot with frustration. She chewed on a hangnail. She thought about making a cup of tea. She considered visiting the occult bookshop tucked into the city's northwest hills to ask the bookseller with a thousand-yard stare and a tattoo of a door on their shoulder about her father's papers, but decided she didn't want to risk another person knowing about what she'd discovered. She ignored more rumbles from her stomach. She stared at the sheets of thick, creamy paper, willing them to divulge their secrets.

And then it dawned on her: she had recently gained the ability to summon an actual magical creature. Embarrassment flushed her chest for not thinking of it sooner. Summoning the kelpie again would be dangerous, no doubt, but she felt out of options. Raegan knew herself well enough to know she wouldn't sleep, wouldn't eat, wouldn't do anything else except focus all of her energy on the contents of her father's safe deposit box. So really, she reasoned, summoning the kelpie was the less dangerous option.

Raegan quickly searched for some basic protective sigils to use and scribbled them into a notebook. She doubted their efficacy against the creature with oil-slick eyes and riverstone skin. But she supposed it was better than nothing.

Tucking the notebook into her back pocket, Raegan pulled a bottle of whiskey off the shelf, wishing she had taken some time to figure out where the hell to get mead. She checked her waistband for her knife and skimmed the ritual for summoning the kelpie again, though it felt etched in her brain or maybe like it had always been there and the book had only helped her remember.

Then Raegan opened the door, abandoning her jacket on the couch, and walked down the stairs to summon an ancient being from a puddle. More time had passed during her research than she'd realized. The glorious day was fading into early evening, dusk hunched on the horizon like a bat's wing clinging to a branch. Her neighborhood was busy with the thrum of Friday happenings, so Raegan followed the alley to the back of her building, where it tucked itself into another structure. A chain-link fence stretched to her left, encircling a dumpster and a large tree stump. A dog barked in the distance. She felt the hum of the subway from the metal grates lining the street as she searched for a suitable puddle on the blistered blacktop.

The only puddle was quite shallow, and an old paper plate sat at its bottom, but it would have to do. She hoped the kelpie would not be offended by her choice of water source as she scraped protective sigils into the asphalt using a piece of chalk she'd improbably found in her kitchen junk drawer. Then she poured the whisky, squeezed the small incision on her thumb to produce blood droplets, and spoke the summoning.

A preternatural hush fell around Raegan as she said the final phrase, like the rest of the world had been silenced. This time, sober and sharp-eyed, she noticed something change in the atmosphere; it was not unlike the process of putting in contacts. A slippery, shiny film overlaying something else, only noticeable for a moment before disappearing completely.

The dumpster and the tree stump and the chain-link fence faded away. Her heartbeat was loud in her ears, and she could've sworn that for a long, stretched moment there was nothing at all in the world but the drumming of her own blood.

Then the puddle water went black. The paper plate slunk from view, and there, right before her, was the kelpie: oil-slick skin, eyes wide and expansive, bulging from its head like a toad's, the seaweed forelock, the deep primal feeling unfolding in Raegan's gut that told her she was in the presence of an ancient thing.

"Hello," she said, involuntarily taking a step back. "I drew some sigils this time. To be more careful. Like you said."

The kelpie rose out of the water, rivulets of black running down its thickly muscled shoulders, its eyes trained on the ground around the puddle. Raegan held her breath as it studied her handiwork.

"I already said I would not harm you," the kelpie intoned, raising its eyes to hers. "But you do understand I could simply wipe those away? With the water? In the puddle? That you summoned me from?"

Raegan sucked in air, her stomach dropping out like she was on a rollercoaster. Fear pricked her skin, a thousand hot needles. "Oh. Yeah. Not my best work. Um, but you're still not going to drown me, right?"

"No, I shall not," the kelpie replied, slinking back into the puddle until only its head was exposed. "You are lucky I've already arrived at that decision. Otherwise, it would be simple to drag you into the depths."

Raegan wiped her damp palms on her jeans, resisting the way her entire body told her to run and to keep running. "Lucky, indeed, thanks to your benevolence," she said, bowing her head to the ancient creature. "I . . . I had a question I was hoping you'd be able to answer, if you would consider extending your kindness again."

"Do you plan on disturbing me every time you seek knowledge? I am no Questing Beast," the kelpie replied, shaking water out of its mane.

"Um, I'm not planning to," Raegan said, edging farther away from the puddle. "Honestly. I've just hit a very unexpected roadblock and I did not think anyone else would be able to tackle this problem. There are few, if any, that hold your wisdom."

The kelpie held her gaze with its black eyes, working its heavy jaw. She couldn't read its expressions, but she hazarded a guess that it was considering. "This is the last favor, Raegan from Over The Hill," the kelpie said. "I hope it is worth it."

She hoped it was worth it, too. "My father, the one who went missing, he left me these papers in a safe deposit box. The key you gave me— that's where it led me." She caught herself, wondering if the kelpie knew what a safe deposit box was, so she added, "The key you gave me opened a box with these papers in it."

"Yes," the kelpie replied, its tone flat. "I understand how safe deposit boxes operate."

"Sure, okay," Raegan said, nodding, thinking it was not unreasonable to assume a mythological creature was unfamiliar with banking. "I suppose I should understand there is no limit to your knowledge."

The kelpie shifted in the puddle, the arch of its heavy neck cresting. "You may stop with the flattery. It has become exhausting and hollow," it said, sounding bored. "Show me the papers of which you speak."

Raegan hesitated. So far, this interaction was going in her favor, but keeping a healthy distance between herself and the kelpie's strange, fathomless eyes seemed wise. To show her father's papers to it, she would have to step right up to the edge of the puddle.

Gritting her teeth, she told herself there was no point in any of this if she wasn't willing to be brave. She gathered the papers in her hands and took small steps toward the puddle, her eyes trained on the kelpie.

"Here," Raegan said, slowly shuffling through the pages, holding them up like a picture book for a child. "Tell me if there's any you want to have a closer look at."

The kelpie let out an exasperated sigh and then raised itself a bit farther out of the puddle. When it leaned in to look, it suddenly paid sharp attention, as if it had been expecting a crude cartoon and had instead gotten a Monet. "*This* is from your father?" the kelpie demanded, its eyes flicking to hers. Her palms damp, Raegan reminded herself not to stare into the endless blackness of its pupils.

"I believe so," she replied, her voice shaking. "At the very least, it was in a safe deposit box that he owned."

"Raegan from Over the Hill," the kelpie said, its voice authoritative and booming, the kind of voice she could imagine commanding armies, "what you hold in your hands is an incredibly complex spell, the likes of which your kind rarely attempts."

Silence cloaked the alley, as downy and hushed as the first snowfall of winter. Raegan fought the faintness growing at her knees and the black dots that threatened to crowd her vision. If her heart beat any faster, she thought, she might faint.

"A spell," she repeated, her mouth dry. "A spell . . . to do *what?*"

The kelpie pulled away, settling back into the puddle, the arch of its neck disappearing beneath the water. "That I cannot say," the kelpie answered. "You see, your kind *practices* magic. To do so, you need spells for channeling and harnessing power, as you are too simple for anything else. The greater creatures of this place, such as myself—we *are* magic. We do not use the spells or incantations of lower beings. I have seen enough of human spellery to recognize that this was a complex, intense effort, but no more. It is beneath me, you see. Wolves need not grasp the workings of an anthill."

Raegan's throat felt like it was closing off, and her head threatened to explode. She wondered if her world was collapsing or finally coming together.

"Right," she said, placing the spell carefully into her pocket and then beginning to pace in front of the puddle. "So how do I find out what the spell was intended for? Like, is there a local witch or something I can speak to? I'll pay."

"That spell far surpasses a local hedgewitch," the kelpie replied, its black eyes narrowing in concentration. "Allowing another human to view it will be dangerous on a number of levels."

Raegan waited as the kelpie's jaw worked back and forth.

"You must take this to the King," the kelpie decided, once again raising its pitch-black gaze to hers. "He is less friendly and charming than I, but no one else can be trusted. Tell him Rainer sent you. My name shall grant you safe passage."

Raegan narrowed her eyes at the kelpie. "I appreciate your help," she said slowly, choosing her words carefully. "But why are you allowing me to use your name? What's the price for such a thing? You already bestowed your last favor on me."

The kelpie shot her an appraising look and said nothing for a long moment. Its mane dripped river water onto the puddle's surface, the soft plops the only noise in the space. The smell of brackish water and decaying bones in deep, dark places flooded the alley.

"There is no price."

"I very much doubt that," Raegan laughed, putting one hand on her hip. "I mean, come on. Do you expect me to believe that?"

The kelpie closed its eyes and sighed, sending ripples out through the puddle. She pulled her hand off her hip, hoping she hadn't annoyed the creature so much that it'd decided to take back its promises not to harm her. Historically, she had that sort of effect on people.

But then the kelpie opened its mouth, closed it again, and Raegan realized it was simply searching for the right words.

"All that has passed," the kelpie began, sounding each word out, "between you and I feels familiar, and more so, important. Both times we have met, I have heard the hum of a Fatesong and felt my Threads plucked by an invisible hand. Which can only mean that you and this spellcraft are Fate-kissed. Gods-touched."

The world threatened to fade entirely to black, the ground trembling beneath her feet. Of all the things that Raegan yearned to be, the most sacred of them was this: Fate-kissed. Important. Worthy of a quest.

Allowed a peek behind the curtain. Permitted to steal a glance through the worn spot in the tapestry.

"Gods-touched," she breathed numbly, her entire body humming.

"Yes," the kelpie said. "There is no doubt Fate has Her hand in whatever is unfolding, so you must go to the King. He and Fate often travel the same narrow Threads. He knows much in the way of your human magic."

"So this king, he's . . . human, too?" Raegan asked, clutching the spell papers tightly.

"Do not be absurd," the kelpie snapped, snorting through its long, equine nose. "Of course he is not."

"Right. Of course not. Does he have a full name?" she asked, trying to retain the tone and body language of a supplicant. "Or an address?"

"I am not sure what name he goes by these days," the kelpie replied. "But go to the place I tell you to and he will be there."

The kelpie told her an address without asking if she was ready, and she almost dropped her notebook from whipping it out of her pocket so quickly to take the information down. Raegan's hands shook wildly, her handwriting taking up a whole page with its overblown loops and unsteady lines. Before she could say or do anything else, the kelpie was slipping beneath the water, just his eyes remaining, two midnight jewels.

"Wait," she pleaded, feeling like a child who understood nothing. "What do I even say to him?"

"You are Gods-touched, Raegan from Over the Hill. You already know the words. Just say them." In the space of a blink, the kelpie was gone and the puddle was just a puddle. Raegan clutched the notebook with the address to her chest. She couldn't decide if she felt more like the loneliest or the luckiest person on the planet. Settling on both—they were not mutually exclusive, she thought—she began the climb up the stairs to her apartment.

Raegan locked the door behind her and laid her father's papers out on her coffee table, where she thought they would be safest. Stepping into the kitchen, she rummaged through a cabinet and plucked a protein bar from a box. She collapsed on her couch, pulling the green knit blanket around her like armor. Her mouth dry, she forced herself to eat at least half of the protein bar before she did anything else.

Mid-chew, Raegan realized that the kelpie had told her his name.

Rainer. She shot to her feet, tripping when the blanket snagged at one leg, darting toward her laptop. Snatching it off the bistro table, she returned to the couch. She knew from her father that creatures like kelpies almost never revealed their names—names were sacred. Names were a form of control, and things like the kelpie never gave up control.

Curious, she searched "Rainer" on Google. There was nothing about kelpies—which she had expected—but a few of those sites for naming babies informed her that the name had Germanic origins. It was formed of two words: "advice" and "army." She scrolled a little farther and saw another entry; this one claimed the name meant "warrior from the gods."

Raegan thought of the kelpie and its river-green skin and its self-importance, and wondered why her very first call had summoned not just any kelpie, but an important one. A warrior, a source of wisdom, one that could feel Fate's tendrils down its back.

A being that could look at Raegan and say, definitively, clearly, without a shred of doubt in its lucid black eyes, that she was Gods-touched.

Chapter Twelve

Raegan slammed the laptop shut, catching crumbs from the protein bar between the screen and the keyboard. She cursed under her breath and cracked the laptop open just far enough to sweep them into her hand. Getting to her feet, she threw the crumbs in the garbage can under the sink. Then she paced back and forth in her small kitchen. She stopped at the window above the sink. In the sweep of nightfall, it was more like an obsidian mirror, reflecting her face and the lights from her living room.

"Am I losing my mind?" Raegan asked herself in a low whisper. Before her reflection could contort or give her an answer she didn't like, she poured herself a glass of water and meandered back to the couch. On her way, she saw the notebook with the address sitting open and sat down to look it up.

As she had suspected from the street name, the address was in Old City, tucked away in the far corner near the river. Raegan toggled to Street View. The building was typical of the neighborhood: a lovely antique row house, made from brick and adorned with well-maintained details like shutters and a decorative cornice. The carved front door was painted a deep shade of black. A glass insert in the middle of it read "ARAWN ANTIQUES" in gold-gilt lettering.

Raegan bit the inside of her cheek, pulling up another tab to search for the antique shop. She paged to the Google Maps listing. The hours were by appointment only. It looked like the shop had been there for at least a year or more, but there were no reviews and no website.

"Who doesn't have a goddamn website these days?" she muttered, grabbing her phone to see if there was any trace of the business on social media.

She got nothing, so decided to call the listed number. Unsurprisingly, it went to voicemail, though she held her breath the entire time it rang. The voicemail was an electronic recording. It informed Raegan that the shop was open by appointment only, encouraged her to leave a detailed message about what she was looking for, and that the owner would contact her if any current inventory matched her request.

Raegan briefly considered making something up, but then the voicemail beeped and she panicked and just hung up instead. She toggled back to the Google Maps listing and looked at the name again.

"Arawn," she muttered, narrowing her eyes. It rang a bell. She plugged it into Google. The top hit was a Wikipedia page, which informed her why the name sounded so familiar. In the *Mabinogion*, a collection of Welsh mythological stories, the king of the Otherworld was called Arawn.

The King.

"You cheeky little shits," Raegan said between gritted teeth, addressing every supernatural creature in existence.

It was too late to go to the address now, partially because of the late hour—it seemed she'd once again lost time by summoning Rainer—but also because Raegan wasn't keen to confront the possible king of the Otherworld at night. That activity, she reasoned, was better saved for a bright morning.

She closed the laptop—more gently this time—and tucked her legs up on the couch, pulling the blanket around her. She stared at the wall and chewed her lip, trying to get her head around what was happening, or maybe what *wasn't* happening outside of her head. With a sigh, Raegan concluded that constantly debating whether or not she had completely lost her mind was probably not helpful. Occasional check-ins on her sanity seemed normal, but sitting on the couch and torturing herself over it was useless.

With that decision made, she untangled herself from the blanket and got to her feet. She stretched, a few spots in her back cracking, her neck complaining about all the tension it had been holding. A hot shower would probably help. Water still made her feel weird given the whole kelpie thing, but Rainer probably couldn't crawl out of a showerhead, she reasoned.

Raegan immediately wished that thought had not popped into her head as she turned the water on, checking the back of the door for a fresh towel. Then she closed and locked the bathroom door and undressed, the clothes and the body of a woman who knows magic exists feeling entirely new to her. Like she had been reborn.

The bathroom steaming up broke her reverie; it was the cue that her fifteen minutes of hot water had started. She stepped into the shower, trying to ignore the water pooling around the drain, tying her hair up because wash day wasn't until tomorrow.

A little while later, Raegan exited the shower, wrapping herself in a soft towel. She savored the simple power of hot water and the smell of her favorite soap: spicy peppercorn and bergamot with just a hint of oakmoss. Taking a deep breath, she conceded she felt marginally better and somewhat saner.

By the time Raegan had brushed her teeth and gotten ready for bed, the soothing effects of the shower had worn away. Even with the lights off and the weighted blanket positioned perfectly, she found herself just staring at the ceiling, her muscles humming with anxiety.

She told herself to sleep. Tomorrow she would go to the person Rainer called "the king," who would immediately interpret her father's spellwork. Then she would somehow use the spell to find her father and everything would be okay again. Her mother would stop looking at her like somehow, vaguely, this had been Raegan's fault all along. She could stop scanning the face of every stranger on the street. She wouldn't get the breath knocked out of her in those rare moments that she heard another Welsh accent. She and her mom and her dad would all go to their favorite pub in Old City, the one that her parents swore looked just like one in Wales, and they'd drink all night and repair all the old wounds and make up for lost time.

And then of course, magic—*magic*—would still be real, and it'd be thanks to her father that anyone knew at all. She and her father would explore the limits of it and tell the whole mundane world about it. How many systems of oppression could be toppled, she wondered, with magic?

What was meant to be a comforting series of thoughts to lead her into slumber quickly spiraled out of control, and Raegan found herself riddled with even more anxiety, trying to contend with the idea that something as beautiful as magic could exist in the horrible world she knew.

Seeing no other useful remedy to the situation, she flopped on her side and pulled open her bedside drawer, retrieving her vibrator. Sex, particularly casual encounters, had always been a relatively safe place for Raegan—all the intimacy with none of the attachment, none of the personal backstory. But she was not particularly interested in dealing with another human being tonight, so she'd have to make do on her own. Besides, her bed *was* getting more comfortable by the moment, and an orgasm would probably only make her sleepier.

It did, though that stranger from the subway—all obsidian waves and oceanic eyes and ivory muscle—rose into her mind unbidden before she could push the thought away. A little embarrassed, she curled onto her side. Raegan closed her eyes, and exhaustion began to weave its way into her mind, quieting the thoughts and pulling her gently into a softer, darker world. As she drifted into sleep, she could've sworn that for a moment, she felt the weight of a muscular arm on her waist and the smell of woodsmoke in her nose, though it was gone the moment she focused on it, sleep tugging at her again.

But Raegan was not permitted to enjoy a peaceful rest. Instead, Fate leaned down and sang of older places, of different times, of wilder dreams.

Raegan was herself in the dream, she was fairly sure. The braid over her shoulder was thick and long and auburn, and her body felt the way it always did. She wore a dress with a belt, and she was happy, she realized —within the confines of this dreamworld, at least. She stooped over, pulling a plant from the ground, shaking the dirt from it, and tucking it into a pouch at her waist. The sun warmed her back and the cool breeze blew gently and everything felt right with the world. Distantly, Raegan recognized that this was a new dream, or at least as far as she could remember. She fought to stay with it. Of course, that was the exact moment it burst like an irate bubble.

The next image unfolded slowly—she was walking down a sidewalk on a pretty spring day. It was London, she thought, or someplace similar. A line of schoolchildren came marching around the corner, and old-fashioned cars drove by. The women in the park she passed by were perfectly made-up, chasing after children in three-inch heels. Startled, Raegan looked down at her own clothing and saw a smart, buttoned blouse tucked into wide-legged pants.

It had to be the 1930s, maybe 1940s, she thought. Her body marched down the sidewalk of its own volition, and she turned the corner to enter a café. She stepped inside, her eyes adjusting to the dim interior. As they did, a man turned away from the counter and walked toward her. For some reason, something that she couldn't place, her heart stopped and she felt sure that she knew him, that she had been looking for him for so very long. He kept walking toward her, and when he caught her gaze, she knew without a doubt that she had seen those ocean eyes before. Elation rose in her chest, as sharp and sweet as a glass rose.

"Excuse me, I'm so sorry to interrupt," Raegan said, her voice coming out accented and unfamiliar, thick with emotion. "Do I know you? I have to know you. I think I've been looking for you."

The man was so close now, and she took him in with a greedy gaze, savoring his well-cut suit, his broad shoulders, the dark hair swept away from his forehead, the brows that knit together as he searched her face. Raegan glanced down, embarrassed at her fervor, and noticed his hands were shaking.

"No," he said hoarsely, as if choking out that single word was all he could manage. Then he straightened, his face relaxing. "No, miss, I am sorry. I do not think we are acquainted." His voice was deep and lush and dark; she could have sworn she heard a bit of Welsh peeking through the harsher London accent. "In fact, I am sure we are not," he added.

Raegan could be wrong, could have seen incorrectly in the low light, but his sharp jaw clenched when he spoke, like he was trying to swallow traitorous words crawling up his throat. For a moment, she swore his eyes shone with something she could not identify.

Before she could say anything else, he was out the door and walking briskly away. She watched him go, watched the way he moved with an unusual, lithe sort of grace, his long strides devouring the ground beneath his feet.

When he was out of sight, Raegan found herself choking down a harsh sob. For no reason at all, she felt that she had lost everything. Those brief moments in the presence of that startling man felt like watching a passing comet—the sudden awareness that so much heat and light and warmth and wonder existed just out of her reach. But then the comet sailed by and she was left to reckon with the cold, dead darkness of her own universe.

Grief unhinged its jaws and threatened to devour her whole.

Raegan awoke with a start, her fingers gripping her sheets so hard it hurt. With a shaky breath, she released the fabric, raising one hand to her face. Her cheeks were damp with tears. She sat in the darkness trying to regulate her breath, trying to grasp the dream—a café, a man, someone she knew, someone she had always known, someone she needed to find. All feelings she was already well familiar with.

Rolling to her side, Raegan massaged her temples and wondered why her dreams couldn't be about normal shit. Or better yet, she thought, she'd like to be one of those people who didn't remember their dreams at all.

Knowing that normality had never really been in the cards for her, Raegan reached over to check the time on her phone. The light from the screen washed the room in shades of deep blue and gray. Her phone screen read 6:33 AM. It was a reasonable time to get up, she told herself, a time in the morning many regular, functioning adults awoke on a regular basis. She knew sleep would not return to her.

Raegan stood and stretched, her body protesting movement at such an early hour. She shuffled her way to the kitchen, filling the electric kettle and clicking it on. Her gaze went to the papers from her father's lockbox, gathered safely on the coffee table. She only knew a precious amount more than she did yesterday, but that was going to change. She was going to get dressed, she was going to go to the address from Rainer, and then—

Her phone rang shrilly, and she knew based on the hour that it had to be important.

"Raegan? It's Henry," came her editor's voice through the speaker.

"Henry. It is Saturday."

"I know, I know, I'm sorry—there's been another drowning," Henry replied, his voice still tinged with sleep. "You should go to the scene."

Fury simmered in Raegan's stomach, sending spikes of heat through the rest of her body. She clenched her jaw, extraordinarily pissed for a number of reasons: for forgetting the kelpie had not denied killing people, for taking the lead on a possible serial killer right before discovering that magic was fucking real, and lastly, for having to talk to another person before 8 AM.

"I can't today," Raegan found herself saying, which was not something she had ever said before.

Henry's sharp inhale of surprise made her uneasy. Silence greeted her from the other end. Her heart hammered, and she felt herself begrudgingly caving before Henry even said another word.

"Where is it?" Raegan asked, defeated. "I'm sorry. It's just . . . the anniversary's coming up . . . I saw my mom yesterday . . . It's pretty early —I'm just kind of out of it. I'll go."

"Look, Raegan, you're one of our best reporters. I don't think you've ever missed a deadline. If you're having a shit day, you're having a shit day, and I can get someone else to cover it. It's just, you know, if someone else gets something breaking—"

"Yeah, I know, I might not be lead anymore," Raegan said, but she already didn't feel like the lead, because she hadn't done an ounce of research after finding the book in her parents' basement, and that was going to show very, very quickly. "Look, I'll do it. Today is just rough, and obviously I wasn't expecting to work. What's the address?"

"You *are* off on Saturdays," Henry said, and she could hear him doing that thing where he pulled his glasses off and rubbed his eyes, deep in thought. "I'll cover it. If anyone asks, you were puking. Stomach bug. If I get anything wild, you'll still stay on lead."

Raegan wanted to tell him it did not matter to her at all if she stayed on this story, but that would be a dramatic departure from the person she had been just a day and half ago when she'd seen Henry last, and she knew she had to keep that close, stuffed away in her ribcage.

"Thank you, Henry, seriously. I really appreciate it. I'm sorry."

"You don't need to be sorry. Just send me updates tomorrow."

"I will," Raegan promised. "Seriously, thank you."

Henry told her to take care, and then she was alone in her kitchen, the tea kettle puffing steam and her mind running in a million directions. Though she was grateful to Henry, she was still *angry*—angry that anything would dare distract her from the path she was walking. Most of all, Raegan was angry that Rainer—her Virgil, essentially—had to be a goddamn murderer.

Muttering under her breath, she turned sharply and filled her sink up with water. She had no idea if it would work, but she grabbed the whiskey bottle and her knife because she was going to summon the kelpie again, right here in her fucking kitchen, and she was going to tell him to stop running around and murdering people.

Her fury should have cooled by the time she finished the incantation. She should've realized her mistake when the tips of Rainer's scalloped ears rose from the sink water. And she certainly should've turned back when the kelpie's black eyes met hers.

"I thought," the kelpie said, its tone flat and deadly, "we agreed we would not be speaking like this again."

"I would appreciate it if you stopped murdering people! I have other things to do!" Raegan shouted, slamming her fist on the countertop.

The kelpie looked taken aback, blinking at her silently for a heartbeat. "It is the way of things," the kelpie replied, pulling itself up, the entirety of its head rising out of the water. "I spread out the death. I do not plague one location for too long. I take only those who wish to go. But as I told you, I must consume."

Raegan realized, not for the first time, that the creature was *very* large—but in her kitchen, it seemed even more obvious. The kelpie's massive head obscured nearly all the morning sun from the window behind the sink, casting it in an ominous backlight.

"And *I'm* telling you to stop murdering innocent people and making it so goddamn obvious!" she shouted. "Why don't you kill a bad person? There's so many fucking bad people in this city. But you're killing vulnerable folks, people who haven't hurt anyone, and then you're leaving the bodies behind like a fucking amateur?"

Rainer tilted its head down, like a warhorse about to charge, and then it held Raegan's gaze. She narrowed her eyes at the kelpie, crossing her arms. They stayed like that for a few moments, neither moving, Raegan barely breathing, the only sound the echo of the water cascading off Rainer.

Right when she was losing her resolve, the kelpie sighed and looked away. "You are not wholly incorrect," the kelpie said, its tone low and quiet. "I will consider your input. Do not summon me again."

The kelpie began to sink back down into the water, but not before Raegan drew herself up, all her anger and sadness boiling over, and leaned into the kelpie's long face.

"Rainer," Raegan said, "I command you to stop killing."

"It does not work like that," the kelpie sneered, but Raegan thought she saw the whites of its eyes, so she tried again.

"Rainer, by the power of your name freely given, I bind you and I command you to preferably stop killing people, or at the very least only kill objectively shitty people, hide the goddamn bodies, and *stop making more work for me.*"

The kelpie shrank back then, moving from side to side in the sink, frothing water everywhere with its distress. "Where," Rainer began, the words ground between its many teeth, "did you learn such words?"

Realizing the kelpie's reaction probably meant it had worked, Raegan stood a little taller. "I'm Gods-touched, Rainer," she spat.

She watched as the kelpie took a long, shuddering inhale, sending waves of ripples out into the sink. Tiny waves lapped at the counter.

"Very well, Raegan Maeve Overhill," Rainer said, as if to demonstrate it had her name, too. "I will stop feasting in your city. For now. As long as you walk your silly little line. Which will not be long, and I am only bound for as long as you breathe."

"Sounds great," Raegan sneered. "Now go."

The kelpie blinked its black toad-eyes at her. "It would do you well, Raegan from Over the Hill," Rainer said, "to be wiser in this dangerous world. It is dark and terrible. You know little of it and even less of yourself."

And then the creature was gone from her sink as if it had never been there at all.

Chapter Thirteen

The water drained away of its own volition, clear and a little soapy, not the opaque black-green it had been just moments ago. Raegan stared at the bottom of the deep sink for a long time, begging the drain not to elongate its jaws and release a monster into her apartment.

When the hairs on the back of her neck stopped standing on end and she noticed the sounds of morning traffic returning, Raegan set about getting her first cup of tea prepared, trying to push all thoughts of the furious—and terrifying—kelpie aside now that her adrenaline had receded. But when her tea was fully steeped, she found herself frozen, the milk carton hovering above the cup. She stared into the black liquid, wondering exactly how much water the kelpie needed to reappear. As she kept a steady eye on the mug, something about the way the steam reached up in elegant plumes, sly and curled at the tip, was achingly familiar.

Rolling her shoulders, Raegan poured the milk into the tea, giving it a quick stir and downing it while staring out the window above her sink. There were still a few gulps left when she slammed her mug down on the counter and went to get dressed. She had no idea what to wear for a rendezvous with someone—something?—called "the king," but she eventually settled on fitted black pants, lace-up leather combat boots that came up to just below her knee, and a long, dark overcoat. After a lingering look in the bathroom mirror, Raegan elected to leave her hair down; the wild, dark auburn curls tumbled over her shoulders like armor.

Gathering her keys and phone, she cast a glance at her father's papers laid out on the coffee table. Raegan collected them carefully, gathered them in a manila folder, and then slid them into her work bag, which she then stowed beneath the coffee table. There was no chance in hell she was taking the spellwork straight to this king. She would decide when—and if—the time was right for such a thing. This king would have to prove themselves worthy of such trust.

With a long inhale, her heart pounding much faster than she would ever admit, Raegan opened her door and exited her apartment, thudding down the three flights of stairs to the ground level. The day greeted her overcast and damp, the street stickered with wet leaves. She took a deep breath of the air, smelling woodsmoke somewhere. And then she stepped out onto the sidewalk, the breeze catching at her hair. She felt as if the world turned ever-so-slightly on its axis, like a strong headwind had filled her sails for the first time in years. She was sure, so sure, that the soft gray breeze was singing her name. What had the kelpie called it? Threads. She felt like her Threads were being pulled, a strange song played across her skin. Raegan stood for a moment, admiring the sensation, the vastness of it, the way she felt as if she were an entire ocean.

And then she put her hands in her pockets and headed for the subway station.

"Raegan." The voice came from behind her, not on the wind but a tongue, and it was one she did not recognize. She did not know if it was the strangeness of her morning or simply a wish, but Raegan thought that the voice had a heavy North Welsh accent. Just like her father's.

Her stride faltered, but she kept going. Ignoring it, she thought, would be a good test.

"Raegan!" More insistent this time, barked from a hoarse throat. Otherworldly or not was another question, but there was no mistake that something had spoken. Raegan froze. Squaring her shoulders, her jaw clenched tightly, she turned on her heel and looked down the sidewalk.

A few paces from the door to her building stood a woman. She had dark, curly hair streaked with steel and green-gray eyes. Her complexion was pale, lightly dusted with freckles, and she wore a loose button-down and jacket over dark pants. She stood off to the side, a lit cigarette in her hand, as if only moments before, she had been leaning against Raegan's building, just waiting for her to come down the stairs.

The woman was undeniably familiar in a way that made the back of Raegan's throat close off. "Do I know you?" Raegan called, crossing her arms over her chest.

The woman took one slow step closer, her boots making no noise on the sidewalk. Raegan mirrored the step in reverse, keeping a solid distance between them.

"Yes and no," the woman replied. Her voice was low and raspy. "It's a long story."

"Most stories are," Raegan said, locking gazes with the stranger.

"Could we maybe go inside and talk?" the woman asked, gesturing to Raegan's apartment building.

Raegan let out a scoff. "Fuck no. I don't invite strangers into my home." That was categorically untrue. She had a long history of inviting strangers into her home—more specifically, her bed—but she figured the lie would go over just fine, considering she had never seen this woman before in her life. She hadn't, *had* she? The more Raegan looked at her face, the more her thoughts clouded.

The woman stared back, taking a long drag on her cigarette. And then finally: "That's wise," she said with a sharp nod. "Maybe somewhere more public?"

The woman walked closer, and Raegan allowed it this time, studying her features: the large green-gray eyes, the square chin, the delicate hands, the tight curls. Suddenly, she realized: except for the hair, this woman looked like her father. But that wasn't possible. Her father had no siblings. No family, really—dead parents and an estranged uncle.

"Why do you . . ." Raegan asked, her voice trailing off when the woman came within a few steps of her.

At this distance, the resemblance was uncanny, though dark circles clung beneath the woman's eyes. She looked ragged. Raegan always remembered her father as being full of life, but nostalgia was a hell of a drug.

"Why do I look like Cormac?" the woman asked, one sharp brow arching. "Because he was my brother. I'm your aunt. And before you say anything—I imagine your father never brought me up. He may have even said he was an only child."

Raegan's mind swam, her eyes becoming unfocused for a moment before locking in, unreasonably, on a yellow oak leaf, its fingers stained brown by the cold snap. Then she brought her gaze up to the woman, who had returned to her cigarette.

"What are you doing in the States?" Raegan demanded, ignoring the rest of the situation for now. If she had an aunt that her father had never told her about, there was likely a good reason, possibly a dangerous one, so she'd start easy.

The woman stared her down, eyes gone gray as the wind kicked up, tugging at both of their jackets. A muscle in her jaw jumped before she exhaled. "Because you did magic," she replied simply, as if it were the most obvious answer in the world. "I'm here because you did magic. I felt it. And I got here as fast as I could. Because if I felt it, then . . ." The woman's voice trailed off, the wind gobbling it up. Raegan tilted her head at the stranger's words.

"Then . . . what?" Raegan asked, confused.

The woman's eyes widened, surprise—and fear, Raegan wagered— was clear across her face. It was the first time in their conversation that the stranger had not guarded her expression. "Hell," the woman spat out. "You don't know?"

"I don't know . . . *what*, exactly?" Raegan asked.

The woman grimaced. Raegan noticed the other hand that held the cigarette by her side was shaking.

"Gods, I don't know how to make you believe me," the woman said, taking another step toward Raegan, her eyebrows pulled together. "But if you don't even know what impact doing magic could have, you and I must talk *now*."

Raegan studied the woman. Her distress and fear seemed genuine. Only one of her pant legs was tucked into her boots. Raegan was fairly sure a bit of mascara was smudged beneath her eyes. Fear was hard to fake. When people attempted it, they usually forgot that most folks don't like showing fear and kept it in their expression for too long. In reality, almost everyone did their best to wipe it off their face immediately— which was exactly what the woman had done.

"There's . . . there's a café a few blocks from here," Raegan said, the words climbing out of her throat before she could stop herself. "It has some quiet nooks. We could talk. If you tell me your name?"

Unexpectedly, the woman looked at her and grinned—dazzling, utterly disarming, and Raegan recognized her own smile on a stranger's face. "Maelona," the woman replied. "My name's Maelona Overhill."

"Okay, Maelona," Raegan said, shifting her body weight in the direction of the café. "Let's go talk."

Raegan turned and headed down the street without checking if Maelona was following her. After a few steps, she sensed the woman slightly behind her and she could smell the cigarette smoke. She appreciated the space, and that Maelona didn't try to talk as they walked because Raegan needed that time to get her head on straight. Her heart was pounding nearly out of her chest, and her fingers itched to call her mother. She thought better of it after a few moments; even if Bronwyn had information about Maelona, Raegan would likely have to wade through a large emotional reaction before getting to it.

And if her father had lied about having living family members . . . ? That thought sunk like a stone to the bottom of Raegan's stomach. If that were true, Raegan absolutely did not want to hurt her mother with the idea that her husband had been lying to her. There was already enough grief.

Above, the skies roiled and darkened, mist eventually working its way down from the heavens and onto Raegan's shoulders. Despite herself, she sighed. Wearing her hair down was essentially a guarantee of precipitation.

The café was just up ahead when Maelona spoke suddenly, jarring her. "It reminds me of home, sort of."

When Raegan turned to look at her, brow furrowed, Maelona gestured to the street around them. "I've never been to Philadelphia before. I thought it would be like other big cities in the States. It's not, not really. I like it."

"Dad always said that," Raegan replied. "I was born and raised here, but I still think Philly feels very different from other major cities."

"Phil-ee," Maelona echoed. "Is that a nickname? For such a short word?"

Raegan laughed, despite herself, pulling the café's door open. "Five syllables is long in English," she replied. "It's a term of endearment, I suppose."

"Right," Maelona said, forcing a smile that looked more like a grimace. "Can I smoke in here?"

"Nah," Raegan said with a shake of her head. "Feel free to finish up, though. I can go get us a table?"

"Yeah, that would be great," Maelona said before taking another long drag. Up close, she was taller than Raegan but thinner. Raegan would wager that beneath her loose-fitting clothing, Maelona was almost skeletal, at least based on the bones that jutted out of her wrist just below her sleeve cuff. She watched the woman for a moment longer before someone came through the door and thanked her for holding it open. Raegan mumbled a response and walked inside.

Ray's Café and Tea House was one of her haunts when she couldn't stand to be alone in her apartment but only had the tolerance for strangers. Its awning was stained, and the red neon letters in the window always flickered. The interior hadn't been updated in years—no big glass windows or cold white walls with minimal black lettering. Unlike most cafés in the area, it was warm and cozy and friendly.

Raegan chose a table tucked into a corner, taking the seat that allowed her to see the majority of the café and the door. Just in case. Outside, Maelona crushed the butt of her cigarette under her boot's heel in a practiced maneuver. Then she put her hands in her pockets and walked inside. Her gait was slightly hitched, like she was covering for an old injury. Raegan noticed that the woman walked with her head down, shoulders hunched, as if she were perpetually trying to avoid being seen.

When Maelona reached the table, she didn't quite sit down; it was more like all her joints finally gave up and she just fell into the seat. She said nothing to Raegan, taking in the surroundings.

"I like this place," Maelona said eventually, her fingers tapping an anxious melody on the tabletop.

"Good," Raegan replied. "Because you're paying." With that, she pulled up the laminated menu like a shield, perusing the offerings that she already knew very well. When a waiter arrived to take their tea order, Maelona asked for the strongest siphon coffee and Raegan got her usual Earl Gray.

"Would you like to put in any food orders?" the waiter asked, tucking their pad back into their apron.

"Maybe in a few minutes," Raegan replied. "I think my aunt still needs to decide." The waiter nodded and headed for the counter, leaving Raegan alone with the woman who claimed to be family.

Silence fell over the table. Maelona was chewing the inside of her cheek, looking out the window. In this light, Raegan could see the lines that etched her skin. If this woman was actually her aunt, Maelona shouldn't be much older than her late fifties. There were parts of her that made her seem younger—the frantic energy, the wild mane of hair, her choice in clothing. But the deep exhaustion in her features spoke of someone at the end of their life, not a little past the halfway point.

"We should get the pork and leek dumplings. They're good," Raegan announced, for once being the one to break the silence. She relinquished her menu-shield, placing it on the table.

"It's seven in the morning," Maelona replied, arching a brow.

"I said they're good," Raegan repeated, more sharply this time.

"Fine," Maelona agreed, immediately deflating like Raegan had a feeling she would. The woman's fingers danced on the tabletop again, and she stole glances at Raegan periodically until their drinks arrived.

When they did, Maelona peeled back the lid on Raegan's teapot as if something might be hiding within its white ceramic belly, but she looked appeased and put the lid back with a soft clink. Then she grabbed her coffee cup with shaking hands and took a long drink. Maelona placed it back on the table, misjudging the saucer and sending a black tidal wave over the lip of the mug, eliciting a quiet curse. Raegan wordlessly handed her a wad of napkins.

"So," Raegan said eventually, folding her hands on the table, looking expectantly at Maelona. "Apparently we have very important things to discuss."

Under the harsh indoor lighting, Raegan saw Maelona's face pinch, the movement outlining the worry and stress that seemed to be permanently sculpted into her skin. For a moment, the only sound in the café was the quiet chatter up front and a low, lilting melody that slunk in the front door from a passing car. It was orchestral and full of hurt and want, as delicate as a curl of smoke, reaching into the space like a column of fog.

Then a long sigh left Maelona's body, seeming to rattle her bones. She dug the heel of her palm into one eye; Raegan noticed that her long, spindly fingers shook.

"What's important," Maelona finally said, raising her gaze to meet Raegan's, "is that magic is real and it's dangerous. You know that, though. Because you've done it."

Raegan clenched her jaw, waiting, but then she saw Maelona was not making an accusation, only a statement. Her heart leapt against her breastbone. How could Maelona possibly know she'd summoned the kelpie? And from across an entire ocean, nonetheless?

"By doing magic," Maelona continued, searching Raegan's face, "you've thrown away the protection we sacrificed *everything* to give you."

Unease swept through Raegan's body, a brackish tide teeming with sharp-toothed mouths. Questions speared her thoughts—what kind of protection was Maelona referring to and who exactly was the "we" that had sacrificed so much. She squeezed her eyes shut for a moment, willing her mind to quiet. When she opened them, Maelona had leaned her upper body across the table, so close—too close—to Raegan, something half-mad gleaming in her gray-green eyes.

"You have made yourself known," Maelona said, her voice edged with a rough rasp. "And the Protectorate have seen something that looks like one of theirs—unoathed, untrained, and thought long-lost."

The older woman paused again, her brows coming together in a heavy V, looking like the weight of the world rested squarely on her shoulders.

"So they're going to come for you."

Chapter Fourteen

"Who?" Raegan asked, holding Maelona's gaze. "Who is coming for me?"

At that, Maelona reeled back as though she'd been struck, something like outraged horror shadowing her expression. Raegan could feel her heartbeat in her throat.

"You don't even *know?*" Maelona hissed, eyes wide, face pinched. Her shaking hands curled into fists on the tabletop.

"What do I not know, Maelona?" Raegan replied, trying to keep her voice calm and level. "Help me out. That's what you're here for, right?"

Maelona leaned back in her chair, looking stricken with despair. Her jaw worked, gaze darting to the sidewalk. The moment stretched taut as a bowstring. Raegan waited, turning over the information she had from the book and the kelpie. She had a sharp, sinking feeling that it would not be even close to enough.

"This is worse than I thought," Maelona finally said, her tone quiet and hoarse.

"If things are so bad, *help* me," Raegan implored, throwing everything she had into the words. But Maelona only fell silent again, her mouth settling into a firm line, eyes trained on the sidewalk beyond the window. Raegan watched, confused, until she realized with a queasy, feverish jolt that Maelona was searching the block outside. Almost as if she were looking for someone.

"You know nothing, and we're nearly out of time," Maelona mumbled, sounding dazed, her eyes appearing to follow the slow track of a large raindrop traveling down the windowpane.

"Hey. Who the fuck is going to come for me, Maelona?" Raegan demanded again, switching tactics, going back on the offensive.

Maelona did not even register that Raegan had spoken. Instead, she turned in her seat and examined every single patron of the café, lingering on a mundane-looking man in a navy suit who sat at the counter. Raegan fought away rising panic. While she felt certain Maelona had answers, she was *not* sure if Maelona was sane, or her real aunt, or actually here to help.

When Maelona turned back, her gaze fell heavy as a millstone on Raegan. "Do you even know about the Protectorate?" she demanded, her eyes wild. "Do you know about the Fey? The Gates? The Time-keeper? Do you know the fucking *King* is here, in the States?"

The king again. First from the kelpie, and now from Maelona. She almost caught a memory, something deep in the recesses of her mind, but it slipped out of her grasp, leaving her feeling adrift.

"Where is my father?" Raegan asked, voice strained, finding herself unable to summon any other words. She wished she were less predictable, but anytime she felt unmoored, her compass pointed due north—right to that aching hole in her chest.

"He's dead, Raegan," Maelona snapped, but there was no venom in it. She looked drained. "If you're holding on to some idiotic hope, let it go. He risked everything to have a normal life with you and your mother, but the Gates called too sweetly in the end."

Raegan's breath caught and she studied Maelona carefully. She certainly seemed to believe what she'd said—that Cormac was gone. Raegan wound her hands into fists, ignoring the nausea rising like a tide in her stomach. No. She'd know; she would've felt the warm, bright light of him leave this plane. She would *know*. But all Raegan knew for sure was that her father's story wasn't finished, no matter what Maelona said.

Besides, throwing out that her missing father was actually dead was a good tactic. The resulting emotions could make Raegan weak, pliable. She grit her teeth. She would be neither of those things. She would cling to hope, not sorrow. Hopelessness had never done much for her, anyway.

"Is that what you were trying to do when you broke the protective warding?" Maelona asked, weariness shadowing her face. "Scrying for your father, just in case he wasn't really gone?"

Raegan inhaled, still steeling herself against the idea of her father being dead. The thought, she knew, was parasitic—it would latch its teeth into her and lay claim to her mind if she allowed it access. So she shut it out, pressing her lips together and letting her gaze drift away, hoping Maelona would see whatever she wanted in the non-verbal response and keep talking.

"Unlike you, Raegan, I am inducted and oathed," Maelona laughed, sharp as porcelain shards. "I'm trained to deal with the Fey. I'll only accept a clear 'yes' or 'no.' "

"Yes," Raegan gambled, wiping damp palms on her thighs beneath the table. It wasn't technically untrue. "I was looking for him."

Maelona choked out a scoff, glancing away to search the crowds on the sidewalk again. "He and I sacrificed so much for you," she said, words thick with exhaustion. "And you've fucked it all up looking for someone who's been dead more than a decade."

Silence hung between the two of them, the sounds of the café all but faded away entirely from Raegan's ears. She wanted to scream that her father wasn't dead—couldn't be. But she clamped her jaw shut instead.

"And I suppose you're looking at a dead woman as we speak," Maelona added with a humorless laugh, throwing one hand up in the air as if she didn't have a care in the world, as if death had always been lingering on the threshold. "If—or more likely when—the Protectorate learns I've been helping you all these years, and your father before that, there will be hell to pay."

Raegan took a few seconds—one long inhale, one long exhale. Then she sharpened her words to see where Maelona might bleed.

"I find it difficult to believe you put your life on the line for *me*, someone you hardly know," she said, her tone harsh and unbelieving, one eyebrow raised haughtily. She braced herself for a reaction, and Maelona did not disappoint—with a wordless snarl, she slammed a fist on the table, rattling the porcelain.

"I couldn't save my own fucking brother," she hissed, her eyes flashing, all of her tension and anxiety unfolding into rage instead. "Let me at least save *you*."Maelona stared Raegan down for a long, skittering heartbeat or two before she deflated, shoulders sagging beneath her coat. "The Protectorate wants you," she continued, sounding weary again, though her hand on the tabletop was still curled into a fist. "But I'm not going to let them have you. I owe Cormac that, at least."

Raegan clenched her teeth, trying and failing to slow her heartbeat. She needed to be clever and quick. She had to keep Maelona talking; she needed every bit of information the woman had to offer.

"Why would they even want me?" Raegan countered. "Like you said, I know so little." But hearing that name again—the Protectorate—rattled her. Something almost like a memory slithered in the dark recesses of her mind. The sensation was formless and wordless, but she could feel it against her skin, a gossamer touch of another world.

Before she could catch the fleeting thing inside her head, or even open her mouth to ask another question, the chimes on the door to the café rang, announcing another patron. Maelona's head snapped up to look, her shoulders hitching with tension. Raegan peered beyond Maelona, catching sight of a mountainous man in a pinstripe suit of a murky, indeterminate color. She felt quite sure she'd never seen the man before in her life, and yet her chest constricted sharply, dread dragging cool fingers up her neck.

Maelona moved so fast Raegan could hardly track it. She shot out of her chair and bent low over the table, her body obscuring Raegan's view of the man at the door. Then her hand wrapped around Raegan's forearm and pulled with surprising strength. Without a chance to brace herself, Raegan was yanked halfway out of her seat.

"Come with me," Maelona hissed. "*Now*."

Raegan's initial response was resistance—she planted herself beside the table, feet set shoulder-width apart. Instead of pulling harder, Maelona stepped in close.

"What could you possibly know of the Protectorate's reach and power, Raegan?" she asked in a low, dangerous voice. "Of the things they will do to reclaim what they believe to be theirs—*you*?"

At that, Raegan relented, mostly out of shock. She raised her eyes to meet Maelona's. "Not enough," she admitted quietly.

From the front of the café, she heard a voice—rough around the edges, clipped with faux politeness, thick with an English accent. Revulsion bloomed in the back of her throat. Suddenly and fiercely, Raegan needed to be away from here—away from that mountain of a man in the pinstripe suit. Her life, she was sure, depended on it.

So she let Maelona drag her by the wrist to the back of the café. The long, narrow space ended in a small hallway, the fronds of twin palm trees draping across the entry like a curtain. Raegan opened her mouth to tell Maelona she'd only ever been back here for the restroom and had no idea if there even *was* an exit. But the older woman spoke instead.

"When your father disappeared," Maelona said, her voice low, fingertips like a vice around Raegan's forearm. "The Protectorate didn't consider for a moment that he'd been killed in action, even though that's usually how we meet our end. No—Cormac had sown so much doubt and discord with all his starry-eyed ideals about magic that we were told to hunt him as a deserter."

Maelona yanked Raegan along, picking up the pace as they passed the door to the bathroom. The rest of the hallway was a dim, unknown space. Raegan had nearly managed to find some semblance of calm when Maelona's grip on her arm tightened. Then the taller woman swung Raegan against the wall, a strong hand wrapping around each of her biceps.

"They made me *hunt* my own brother like a fucking dog," Maelona hissed, her face inches from Raegan's, eyes wild in the gloom. "And if I found him, I was to kill him—and you and your mother."

Raegan's mouth went dry, adrenaline seeping hot into her veins. So Maelona was trying to scare her—that much was clear. She quieted her thoughts and searched Maelona's face. All she found was ragged dedication and the kind of rabid gleam she imagined was not unlike a wounded animal's eyes when backed into a corner.

As if she were confident she had made her point, Maelona relaxed her grip on Raegan, continuing down the hallway. Up ahead, the wall curved, culminating in a large metal door. An exit into the alley, Raegan hoped.

"But you're not here to kill me," she said, forced to break into a jog to match Maelona's long, purposeful strides.

"Neither is the Protectorate," Maelona replied without looking at her. "Not anymore. You're too useful. War is coming. And all good little soldiers must report for duty."

Maelona shoved Raegan toward the door, releasing the grip on her arm. The force of her fingers might've left bruises, but Raegan felt no pain—only the blood pounding in her veins.

"You need to run, Raegan. Get as far away from this as you can. You're unoathed, which means you're still free," Maelona said, almost imploringly. "Give me your phone."

Again, Raegan hesitated, her heart thudding so hard her chest hurt. Going off gut instinct and not much else, she handed her phone to Maelona, unable to hide how hard her hands were shaking. Maelona took it and began to type with unsteady fingers.

"I will contact you," Maelona said, stealing another furtive glance over her shoulder before handing Raegan's phone back to her. "Do not trust anyone and do not do more magic. Not now, not ever. That's the price of your freedom, and if I were you, I'd pay it."

Raegan hesitated, a cold hand slipping over her heart. To give up magic—the thing she had always been searching for and had *finally* found—was too steep a price.

"But wait—"

Maelona shook her head, reaching behind Raegan to push the door open. "It's not real magic, anyway," she said. "It's poison loaned to us by the Timekeeper to do his bidding in places he can't reach." With that, Maelona grabbed Raegan by the shoulders and shoved her out into the damp mist, slamming the door shut behind her.

Raegan stumbled backwards over a set of concrete steps, bumping her hip hard into a large dumpster. The pain barely registered. She caught her balance just as frustration swept through her. Charging back up the steps, she banged the heel of her palm against the metal door. When Maelona didn't answer, she yanked the handle, but to no avail—it was locked.

Raegan bit down on her tongue, resisting a childish urge to throw her head back and scream. Instead, she ducked deeper into the rain-sodden alley behind the café. Pulling her jacket shut, she navigated the maze of overfilled dumpsters and broken glass to the mouth of the alley. She edged along the building's wall, her heart a war drum in her chest.

"They're coming from the front, love."

Raegan's stomach dropped out, a wave of panicked nausea rushing through her. She spun, nearly tripping on a torn trash bag, to face whoever had just spoken. There, swathed in the gloom of the alley, stood a woman. She was taller than Raegan, built in an elegant way that reminded her of someone, something, somewhere.

The woman smiled, the lines around her mouth creasing. Raegan found it impossible to tell how old she was—the stained gray hoodie, grime-caked sneakers and patched jeans gave little away.

"Yes," the woman said with a sharp laugh, gesturing to herself, her voice reminding Raegan of old-time starlets with transatlantic accents. "I'm not what I used to be. Surely not what you remember. But they're coming from the front. You're safe out here for a few more moments."

Raegan's mouth was impossibly dry, her heart thudding so hard in her chest it had begun to hurt. Her palms were slick. Apparently, this moment was the breaking point at which her brain refused to take in more new information. She stood dumbly, unable to take her eyes off the woman. Beneath the dirty hood, the woman's face was full of sharp planes and odd angles, bronze skin and unusual golden eyes.

"You best be going, *brenhines pennaf*," the woman said, her voice firmer this time. "Before they see. Shoo. Out you go."

A sorrow too heavy for any one person to hold fell over Raegan's shoulders like a winter pelt. "Where am I supposed to go?" she asked, surprised by the sound of her own voice—thin, hoarse, utterly lost.

The woman stepped closer, hollow-eyed wistfulness dancing across the ancient planes of her face. "Oh, love," she replied. "Where else? To the King, of course."

CHAPTER FIFTEEN

Raegan hovered at the mouth of the alley, her gaze locked on the hooded woman, wondering if she should run. Her muscles quivered—she felt every inch a deer standing at the edge of a meadow, wondering if the hunter's arrow was nocked.

Yes, Raegan decided. She should run. With one last look at the woman, she turned onto the sidewalk away from the café, her boots thudding hard on the pavement. But she was not going to run away.

No. Raegan was going to run *toward* whatever this was—toward magic, toward her father's secrets, toward the king. The remnants of rush hour parted like the Red Sea for her. She sliced through the neighborhood, reaching the threshold of the city's oldest section. She slowed at a busy intersection, her breath rattling in her chest, throat raw.

When the light changed, she took off again, not minding the way she had to gulp air in painful gasps or how her calves began to protest. Transformation was never easy. The blocks passed in a blur—pavement giving way to cobblestone, glass and steel architecture melting into neat, squat, brick and stone houses lined up like teeth, their wooden shutters creaking in the wind.

When Raegan reached the cross street she was looking for, she paused on the corner, her skin a wildfire. Her eyes tracked down the block in search of the address given to her by the kelpie. The thought sent a shard of ice into her chest. The sureness she had worn like armor only moments ago, faltered.

Raegan set her jaw and squeezed her eyes shut, letting out a long breath. She would be insane to barrel into this, wouldn't she? She should go back to her apartment, lock up tight, and wait for Maelona to contact her. She should not waste everything her father had put into motion, no more than she should squander whatever Maelona had suffered to keep her safe.

Absent-mindedly, Raegan reached into her coat pocket. Her fingertips hit the tiny silver key of the lockbox. She pulled it out, turning the object around in her palm. Its metallic surface caught the weak sun, sparkling like a coin at the bottom of a fountain. She wrapped her hand around it tightly, allowing the teeth of the key to dig into her skin.

Despite everything, it was not in her nature to let this go.

Raegan stepped off the street corner and onto the block where Arawn Antiques should reside. Her strides were long and slow now, her eyes hunting, wanting to spot the building before she dared walk closer. Perhaps the structure itself could tell her something, some story in its window-eyes, a tale scarred into its brick.

And then Raegan found it, standing at the far end of the block: a handsome row house thick with decorative wood accents, all painted a deep, shiny black. The front door was set to the left, adorned with a large silver knocker. Two windows were to its right, both with the shades drawn. Satisfied, she took a deep breath, shoved her hands in her pockets, and headed toward it.

And then she felt it: Fate playing her like a violin, her Threads taut, singing a melody that almost brought her to her knees. The air was thick with woodsmoke, which made no sense this deep in the city, and the gray, gloomy sun was steady on her back. Everything seemed to slow down, sticky as molasses, steady and purposeful and gilded like amber. Only a few more paces, and then Raegan would be standing directly across the street from this place that called to her with the gravitational pull of a black hole.

Movement at the end of the block, just past Arawn Antiques, caught her attention. Raegan jogged around a café's outdoor tables that blocked her view. And then—from around the corner, on the other side of the street, out of the mist—there he was: the stranger she had seen on the subway platform.

Tall and muscular with his dark tumbles of wavy black hair, unusually angular face, full, sculpted mouth, and knife-like cheekbones. He was dressed differently than when Raegan had seen him from the train; instead of casual black clothing, he wore a white button-down shirt cuffed at his elbows, dark pants, and Chelsea boots. He moved down the block with a strange, lithe grace that swallowed Raegan's attention.

"Please," she begged to no particular deity, her mouth dry, her eyes tracking his movement down the street, her heart pounding louder, and her hands shaking more and more with each step he took closer to the door of Arawn Antiques.

A symphony as sweet as honey wine slipped through the air, swelling like the sweep of a rolling hill as Raegan watched the man scale the steps to the front door, his long legs devouring the distance as though he were merely stepping over the curb. When he reached for the door knob, Raegan did not question the instinct that told her to move.

She gathered each fragile hope she had ever dared to allow into existence in her unsteady hands like glass eggs, and then, without hesitation, she sprinted across the narrow cobblestone street with wild abandon as he disappeared behind the door.

Scrambling up the steps, Raegan felt a thrill run through her when she realized the shining black door with its ornate silver finishings had not yet fully closed. Before she could think about it, before she could do anything but allow the oldest and deepest ache in her chest to pull her forward, Raegan pushed through the door and collapsed into whatever waited beyond it.

The door shut behind her. Darkness crowded in. It was as if her ears had been stuffed with cotton and she had been blindfolded. The space she had boldly entered was nothing but darkness. She drew herself up, waiting for her eyes to adjust, but the moment never came. The only thing she noticed was the faint smell of woodsmoke and black pepper.

Terror slid a cold hand onto her neck, but Raegan forced it away. "Hello?" she called. Her voice rang out much louder than she thought possible or logical. "Rainer sent me."

Nothing for a heartbeat, but then something stirred, maybe, in a far corner. The darkness beneath her feet seemed to slide, to move of its own accord, inky black and curled at the tips, like elegant plumes of steam drifting from a cup of tea.

The shadows closed around her, suffocating. The misty autumn morning felt a thousand years away. In her head, Raegan heard Maelona's warnings. She felt like a kid again, trapped in the damp dark of that childhood basement, except this time her father would not come to her rescue.

Oh. Of course.

Raegan straightened her spine and planted her feet firmly on the floor. She swallowed hard, just once, and then she opened her mouth to speak. "I greet thee, *mrenin*, as I walk within your shadow and your stead."

A beat, a moment of hesitation, and then Raegan's mind turned over like a serpent, sending words to her tongue that she could've sworn she did not know.

"This darkness is your dominion, and to you I surrender," she recited. "Do me no harm."

The shadows subsided, slipping away like tendrils, and as they did, Raegan was forced to accept how unnaturally dark it had been only moments ago. She understood that it was never a matter of her eyes adjusting. This darkness was no mundane thing. It was a different kind of shadow entirely, slippery like silk and soft as velvet.

"No harm shall be done."

The voice came from the center of the shadows. The sound of it was like rain on wet stone, or heather on the hills, or dusk over the lake. The voice was low and deep and regal, and god, for some reason, she thought it sounded like home. The shadows slunk away farther, as if pushed aside like a curtain. Raegan found herself facing the stranger from the subway platform, and she was transfixed.

He was even taller up close, all spring-loaded muscle beneath porcelain skin. His black hair fell in elegant waves. And his eyes. Eyes that Raegan somehow knew, had known from even before the subway platform—ocean eyes, gray and fathomless. Something emanated from him, pulsing out from his being, and it made her head swim. *Power*, she realized. It was power. Pure, raw, unadulterated power.

She stood stock still as he approached her slowly, leaving space between them. It wasn't space he would have any trouble closing in a heartbeat, Raegan knew, but she appreciated the courtesy. Closer now, the scent of woodsmoke and rain and black pepper was strong and unbearably gorgeous.

"Rainer sent me," Raegan breathed. She was repeating herself. Her heart was in her throat.

He appeared to be looking at her too intently for the words to register anyway, those impossible eyes searching her face, as if he didn't trust that it actually belonged to her. His dark eyebrows drew together, something like disbelief came across his features. Then he clenched his jaw, a muscle jumping.

For a moment, Raegan thought his full lips might part and he would utter something like, *"Welcome home, I have been waiting for you. I have always been waiting for you. Like the heather returns to the hills every year, so I have hoped you would return to me."*

He did not. Instead, he steadied his expression, all cold grace, and gathered himself. "It is always a pleasure to meet an acquaintance of Rainer's," he said, his tone cool and professional.

The way he reached his hand out to hers was not. It was tentative, delicate, unsure, like it was a dry winter day and he was afraid of shocking her. Meeting his gaze, Raegan pressed her palm into his and found that he had been right to worry about a spark. Electricity flooded her body, and outside a birdsong crescendoed, like everything the bards used to sing about had fallen into place, like this was the very moment the gods had been waiting for all along.

"Have we met before?" Raegan asked, the words tumbling from her mouth before she could scoop them up and put them back where they belonged.

"I do not believe so," he told her, his expression inscrutable. An accent she could not place hung heavy on his words, though she did not think she'd be remiss to equate it to Welsh.

"Who are you?" Raegan asked, the smell of black pepper and woodsmoke and rain, that torrential kind of rain during autumn, making her head swim. She wondered distantly if her question was one that could even be answered in full.

"I am known as the King," he told her, and even though it came as no surprise, her heart still raced wildly in her chest.

Up close, the planes of his face were not human. Too symmetrical, yet too feral. The aquiline nose was too perfect, the features too angular and too sharp. He was beautiful in the way all deadly things are.

"What may I call you?" the King asked. His careful words neatly sidestepped the long history of trickery between their people. *If* he was what she thought—though she had little doubt she was standing in the presence of the Fey.

"Raegan. Raegan Maeve Overhill," she replied once she found the strength to look up at him and meet his gaze again.

The King arched a dark brow at her, the corner of his mouth curving up into something unkind. "You should not give a full name to things like me."

The words on their own were only a warning, but the twist of his mouth and the cold gleam in his eyes was a taunt. Raegan leveled her gaze at the King, though her heart was pounding against her ribs.

"You would have learned it from the kelpie if not from me," she replied, lifting her chin. "If you are going to take from me what is not yours, at least have the decency to take it directly."

Something akin to amusement rolled across the King's angular face like a heat wave. His gaze slid down from the crown of her head to her shoes, then back up to her eyes. "Why are you here, Ms. Overhill?" The words were lazy, looping, something about them reminding her of the Cheshire cat.

"Do you conduct all business in a poorly lit lobby? Or do you have somewhere more comfortable to sit?" Raegan demanded, letting steel slip into her tone.

Hospitality, she knew, was important to the old things, and playing that card gave her a tiny shred of control over the situation. Surely it would lead her deeper into the King's space, but she did not feel it wise to continue this conversation in a shadow-filled room. For a long, stretched moment, the King simply watched her appraisingly. Raegan's heart thudded louder and louder until she was sure he could hear it, too, but she held her ground.

"Please, do follow me," the King said in a dry tone, gesturing with a lithe, powerful hand.

Raegan clenched her jaw and took a tentative step toward the King as he turned on his heel. He moved through the darkness, and she maintained as great a distance from him as she dared. The King had not agreed to her request verbally, only asked her to follow him, and she had not missed the technicality.

Surprise flooded Raegan when she emerged from the shadows into a small side room. Lit by mundane electricity, the space was much cozier than she had anticipated—like something she'd create for herself, given a much larger budget.

An ornately carved Victorian couch upholstered in meadow green velvet stretched along one wall. To Raegan's right, ferns and vines hung around the large, high windows she had seen from the street. A gorgeous, neatly arranged desk sat in the far corner. In the middle of the space, a circular table with two chairs waited. Books were piled on one side of the table's well-worn surface. She snuck a glance at the spines, but the gold lettering there did not appear to be either of the two languages she could read.

With a jolt, Raegan cut her survey of the space short, realizing she had lost track of the King. She whipped her head to the left, dismayed to find he had been standing just off to the side, arms folded across his broad chest, watching her the entire time. The stance caused the shirt's fabric to pull at the King's shoulders, outlining his lithe, muscular build. Despite everything about the situation, heat pooled in Raegan's belly.

"Didn't expect something so cozy," she sneered, trying to recover.

"Most people do not get this far," the King countered, unfolding his arms. He waved toward the table with one hand—an impossibly elegant, long-fingered hand. Raegan could not imagine those hands shaking or jostling a coffee cup. "Please have a seat."

It was not a request. Unsurprisingly, the King spoke with the quiet, cool authority of someone used to being obeyed. Raegan had been planning to sit anyway, so she meandered over to the table, trying to make it clear with her slow pace that his command had little to do with her choice. She sank into the chair with its back to the window, giving her the most open view of the doorway and the rest of the room. The chair was hard and uncomfortable, which she imagined was intentional.

Only once Raegan was seated did the King close the distance with one long stride. He lowered himself into the chair across from her and crossed his ankle over his knee. Here in brighter light, the King's inhuman beauty only grew more apparent. She knew it was embarrassing and she wanted to stop, but all Raegan could do was gape at him.

He shouldn't be real. He was only meant to be some attractive stranger she met on subway stations and in dreams. He was not supposed to be made of such gorgeous alabaster flesh and strong, powerful bone.

Raegan caught his gaze inadvertently, and immediately found herself nearly lost in his eyes: an impossible shade of gray, the color of an ocean in a storm. She swallowed down the familiarity that crawled its way up her throat, a déjà vu so violent she had to shake her head to clear it.

For the barest of moments—probably when he thought she would not notice—the King's expression softened and Raegan saw something other than cool detachment. There was a haunted sort of longing in his gaze, as if he desperately wanted something he knew he could not have.

Raegan suddenly wished to weep, like she might at the conclusion of a very long and arduous journey, but any emotion the King had perhaps shown was entirely gone. He folded his hands on the table silently, waiting for her to speak, and she watched him carefully, wondering if her gut feeling could be trusted.

It seemed too improbable: that she had always been looking for him and now, finally, here he was.

CHAPTER SIXTEEN

Raegan drew a shaky inhale and turned as if to examine the Victorian couch, trying to pull her mind back to herself. Whatever strange feelings surfaced from deep within her marrow were irrelevant. She was meeting with a faerie king, who was likely older than castles and mountains and countries. Leaving in one piece, let alone with what she needed, would take every ounce of her wit. She shifted her gaze back to the King, who took it as an opening.

"Whatever you seek my assistance with," he said, tilting his head to the side and watching her closely, "must be very important for you to choose such a perilous path."

Raegan held her tongue. A car horn sounded outside, which she couldn't quite reconcile with the otherworldly being in front of her. "Yes," she said eventually, steepling her fingers as she rested her wrists on the table. "But considering the gravity of the situation, Rainer insisted upon involving you. I chose to honor the kelpie's counsel, despite an audience with the King being far from my first choice."

She would do what she always did. Be in control. Know more. Have more aces up her sleeve. Or at least she'd try.

"Nor should it be," the King returned, one elegant eyebrow arching up for a moment. "Particularly not for your kind. We owe each other no allegiance."

It was a very polished way of saying that Raegan's race and the King's people had been warring for a thousand years, but she was admittedly more focused on how the arch of the King's brow sent warmth to her core. For an instant, she would've sworn beyond all reason that she'd seen him arch that brow a million times before.

"There is an artifact I'm hoping you might be willing to examine," Raegan explained, her tongue heavy, trying to navigate the situation at hand despite her confused tangle of emotions. She knew she should focus on how terrifying the planes of the King's face were. On finding her father, who she refused to accept was dead until she could confirm it herself. A basic tenet of journalism—believe nothing, trust no one. "But it is a delicate situation," she continued, "and I'm hoping to establish some basis of trust before permitting access to the artifact."

He looked at her with dark, heavy-lidded amusement, his expression gone wolfish. He glanced away for a second and then back at her, head tilted again, the gray eyes now nearly entirely black. "I cannot begin to imagine," the King said, his voice sharp as a sword, "what would cause a human to trust *me*."

One of his impossibly powerful-looking hands reached across the table to emphasize his words. The veil of politeness was gone. The creature in the room with her was all wolf, all snake, all predator.

And then he drew back, the aggression gone from his broad shoulders, his weight shifting back into his seat. Raegan studied him, her heart racing, the chair's back pressing painfully into her skin.

"Overhill," he said, his tone measured again. "I imagine this will frustrate you, but this is not something I wish to entangle myself with."

"What?" Raegan demanded before she thought better of it, as if she had already forgotten his politeness was only a mask. "I've barely told you anything at all. How can you decide so quickly?"

"I cannot help you," the King repeated, shifting so his body was now angled toward the door. "Please give my regards to Rainer."

Raegan's face grew hot, her mind reeling at this dead end. Where could she even go next if the literal Fey king failed her? She had thought coming here might spell an early death or that she'd have to promise him her firstborn. But she'd never thought that her audience with the King would be so brief. It'd never even crossed her mind. Granted, Raegan had not stopped to think about much more than going beyond the shining black door that had called to her so sweetly.

"No," she spat, leaning forward onto the table. "No. I refuse to accept that."

The King stared at her. Raegan stared at the King. For several long seconds, she felt the entire world condense to this building, this room, and the startlingly beautiful gray eyes of the ancient being across from her.

"You must accept it," the King said, his words long and low, drawn out, dark and deadly. *Or else*, he did not say, though Raegan supposed something as dangerous as the King never needed to tack on the extra words. The threat was implied. Always. Her mind raced to grab onto anything, anything at all, even if she was just stalling. Her fingernails bit half-moons into her palms, and she was entirely too warm in her leather jacket. It did not help that the longer she shared this space with the King, the more she felt something unfolding in her chest that she did not understand.

"I know you," Raegan spat like an accusation, like it was a reason to so openly disobey a being clearly used to commanding others.

"No," he responded, his face blank. "You do not, and I must ask you to leave."

Raegan did not understand what drove her to it, what madness possessed her to make the choice, but she reached across the table and seized the King's hand with her own. "Why are you lying to me?" She intended the words to come out angry, demanding.

Instead, that strange thing in her chest unfolded sticky, cocoon-fresh wings, and her words were half-strangled with grief, an ocean of tears breaking the levy behind her eyes.

She watched as the King's long fingers curled reflexively around hers, as if their palms were two sides of a locket. The rigid line of his shoulders relaxed. With their skin laid flush against each other's, Raegan was struck by how the map of his tendons and veins was more familiar than anything else she had ever known. A peculiar feeling hung in the air: Threads were plucked and pulled, and Fate sang a very old song, soft as a lullaby and treacherous as the jaws of a wolf.

As it did whenever Fate sang this particular tune, time slid its scales out of order, a snake latching fangs onto its own tail, a river flowing backward and sideways and not at all.

Raegan no longer sat in a small room in Old City. Instead, she found herself on a heathered hill at sunset, August in all its glory around her, two strong hands tangled in her auburn curls, her body pressed against one much harder and larger than her own.

Then the hill was gone, and instead she walked alongside someone through an autumnal meadow, woodsmoke heavy on the air, a rushing river before them. The feeling of finality was thick in her marrow, as weighted as the wool cloak upon her shoulders. She knew without a shred of doubt that whoever walked beside her, silent and resolute, would unwaveringly be with her until the very end.

The meadow collapsed into a bonfire, surrounded on all sides by deep and ancient woods. She could feel the warmth of liquor in her veins and the exhaustion thick in her body. The side of her cheek rested on someone's powerful shoulder. The firelight danced, revealing no one else seated around it. She lifted her head, took a breath, and kissed the person next to her before either one of them could think better of it.

The bonfire simmered and snuffed out, the darkness of a dim, stone-walled room swallowing it whole. A single candle burned in one corner, a wide pool of wax beneath it, the flame almost spent. Silvered pre-dawn light slunk in through the window. Her mouth was against someone else's, desperate and keen, her lips swollen from the intensity of the exchange. And then her own voice, whispering, "I am yours until they come."

The stone-walled room pitched, and a voice penetrated the very edge of her consciousness. "Overhill."

The voice was low and deep and masculine, richly accented with a lilting roll that sounded like home. The stone room pulled away, fading out into nothing.

And then she was panicking. She had no idea where she was, who she was, what the gray light leaking in from the window meant, what the cacophony of sounds just beyond the walls could possibly be—a thousand footfalls and the blow of a hundred horns.

"Overhill," the voice came again, calm and steady. "Could you picture your home for me, in your head? What color is the door?"

She fought against the river of her own mind, peppered with

meadows jeweled in dew and banquet halls hung with silken dressings, the lightest breath of a kiss against the nape of her neck, her heavy waves lifted to one side by a lithe hand.

"Overhill," the voice repeated, still just as calm. "Where do you keep your tea?"

"In the cabinet," she mumbled, fighting to stay with the voice, to not be swept away by the feeling of a gray warhorse charging beneath her, the sensation of her hand on the pommel of a sword.

"Which cabinet?" that beautiful voice wanted to know. "Picture it for me. Please."

And then she saw her small kitchen with its deep sink and scuffed white cabinets and the tiny window overlooking the street and the brown leather couch waiting just beyond it and the little bistro set she had dug out of a restaurant's dumpster.

A heartbeat, and then powerful arms closed around her and everything else was gone.

～

The world faded back in slowly. Warmth first. Next the brush of a hand on her cheek. Finally, words murmured low and gentle against her ear, spoken in a darkly melodic tone: *Let it wane. We cannot keep singing the same song.*

And then Raegan fully awakened, sitting straight up, feeling as though she had come spiraling out of complete and utter darkness. The door of the void closed behind her as she frantically took in her surroundings. She was wrapped in her green knit blanket upon her familiar couch. Her head was woozy. Had she fallen asleep while researching? While writing? Should she be at work? Day and time slipped away from her entirely, a cool river running between her fingers.

She turned her head and looked to her left. A glass of water sat on her coffee table. Curious, Raegan reached her hand out and touched the glass. It was still cold. She couldn't have been asleep that long. With a groan, she swung her legs over the side of the couch and sat up.

Relief sang through her veins when she caught sight of her father's spell papers, still neatly stowed in her work bag. Her phone was on the coffee table, sitting on the book she'd pulled from the rafters. The date on the screen read Saturday, as she'd expected.

Raegan gulped down half the glass of water, wiping her mouth with the back of her hand. She didn't usually nap for this reason—she never felt refreshed when she woke up, just foggy and completely out of it. She reached for another drink of water and nearly choked on it when the happenings of the day came flooding back all at once, as if some door had been opened within her.

Raegan remembered Maelona and her warnings. She remembered her fruitless visit to the King. She remembered that she had left the mundane world behind just like she had always wanted to. And beyond that, deeper, lurking beneath the surface, she remembered heathered hills and charging warhorses and blazing bonfires.

What Raegan did *not* remember was how she'd gotten from the King's space to her apartment. She did not remember walking up the stairs and coming through her door. She didn't remember throwing her keys in the bowl or taking off her jacket or wrapping the blanket around herself. Granted, it was cocooned around her in just the way she liked, so it was impossible that someone else could have done it. But why couldn't she *remember?*

"What the fuck did he do to me?" Raegan muttered, fear settling into her bones.

She had gone into the territory of an actual fucking Fey king and demanded something of him. And he had refused. Raegan bit the inside of her lip, her palms gone clammy. Even a refusal was not free. There would have been a price for the audience alone.

She lunged for her father's Celtic mythology book, clutching it to her chest for a moment before flipping through the pages to find the long entry about the Tylwyth Teg. The illustrations that had captivated her as a child depicted beautiful creatures in clothing spun from thunderstorms and necklaces strung with broken promises. Their faces were shadowed, but from what Raegan could pick out, they *did* resemble the King: knife-sharp cheekbones and elegant necks and shapely mouths.

The beginning of the entry told her the things she already knew: Wales, Ireland, Scotland, and England all had names for and tales of the Fair Folk. Later mythologies in other lands had gentled them into tiny, flitting things in gardens or jovial red-haired men with pots of gold, but there were still those who knew the old ways and hushed the tourists who spoke of the Fey in crowded pubs. They avoided certain hills at twilight. They did not obstruct the way of fairy roads.

Raegan began skimming, pausing briefly over the words "Seelie" and "Unseelie," but the text more or less reflected her existing knowledge. She flipped the page, her clammy fingers sticking to the paper for a moment.

Tilting the book toward the window to get better light, Raegan hunted for her father's spidery handwriting somewhere in the margins. She nearly jumped when she saw his bracketing in pencil around a section of the book's text.

The Age of the Gentry fell and the Age of Man began at the Battle of Camlann. Despite their many eyes, the Unseelie Court could not predict humanity's willingness to unleash the Timekeeper, for in many ways, such a choice was a simple exchange of one eldritch terror for another. The Timekeeper, of course, is order and law and rule, while the Fair Folk are chaos and magic and mayhem. The tenuous alliance between the Timekeeper and the early league of men, now known as the Protectorate, was based nearly entirely on a shared hatred of the Fair Folk. The Tuatha De Danann[1] had imprisoned the Timekeeper beneath the Isles, and men likewise sought to be rid of what they perceived as the Fair Folk's rule.

In return for his release, the Timekeeper granted the men power to wield magic, as well as weapons for their armies. Now often called holy or sainted iron[2], this set of weaponry was imbued with the Timekeeper's power, and as such, had an unprecedented ability to dispatch the Gentry. When the Unseelie Court[3] was defeated, the Timekeeper erected the Gates.

The Gates have transformed over the years under the Timekeeper's influence. First, they merely divided the world in two, providing a dedicated space for humanity to flourish. But the Fair Folk, particularly the Unseelie Court and its most well-known King[4], were displeased both with the Gates' impact on magic and the way men viewed Earth as their possession. Conflicts between the Unseelie Court and mankind resulted in more and more restrictive versions of the Gates, until arriving at the state of affairs today: no passage between the Gates and no magic flow to the human realm.

There is a little-known Third Place that is said to exist between the Realms, a space purely under the Timekeeper's dominion. The purpose and shape of this In-Between is unknown, though this author posits it is simply a no-man's-land that functions as an easy killing ground for anyone foolish enough to attempt dismantling the Gates.

----

1 - The Fair Folk have gone by many names for millennia, but this author uses the Tylwyth Teg and the Tuatha De Danann interchangeably to reference the first generation of the Gentry, the children of Danu.

2 - It is often thought that Excalibur, the fabled sword, was one of these weapons, but all evidence reveals that Arthur had the blade before the Timekeeper's release, though it, too, was forged with the intention of spilling the blood of magical beings. But that is another story entirely.

3 - Nearly all oral tradition and historical texts indicate that the Seelie Court did not fight. If they had, this author supposes the tide of the war would have almost certainly been turned and the Age of Man would never have been.

4 - This author, of course, speaks of the Exiled Unseelie King. He took the throne from Ragrshydan the Cruel not long after the Gates were erected. Oral accounts and Feyish historical texts indicate that, in a stunning departure from tradition, he was asked by the Unseelie subjects to take the throne and had little personal interest in the acquisition of power. Though the throne was still obtained by the traditional method of slaying its current occupant, this occurrence was the unusual beginning to a very unusual—and powerful—rule. It is rumored he has no true name—part of what makes him so incredibly dangerous—but he has been called Gwyn ap Nudd, Obe'ryn, Annwfyn, and other names throughout time. In modernity, he is most often referred to simply as the King. His bloodlines and history are completely unknown, which is strange considering his immense power and capability. Noble houses of

the Unseelie should be clamoring to claim him, but he belongs to no one. The prevailing myth is that the King is one of the Tuatha De Danann—a child of the gods. Of course, this myth is heavily disputed, as all of the Tuatha De Danann are thought to have left this plane with the goddess Danu long before the Battle of Camlann.

Raegan let her head fall to meet the back of her couch, unfocused gaze directed somewhere toward the ceiling. So she had not just met *a* Fey king, but *the* Fey king. The Unseelie King, to boot—though she had little doubt that the reality was much more complicated, the Unseelie Court tended to be the most antagonistic and sadistic toward humans in folklore. What was he doing in *Philadelphia*, for fuck's sake?

And the Protectorate—the organization she should have been born into—was as ancient as Camelot and presumably just as powerful as Maelona had said. She'd also spoken of the Gates and the Timekeeper, but with essentially no context; at least Raegan had *something* now.

But fuck. This entire situation was a chess match that everyone else had been playing for a thousand years before Raegan had even realized she was a pawn on the board at all. She bit the inside of her cheek. There were parts that she could swallow—the parts that felt more like folklore, like sucking the marrow out of bone and recognizing the taste of the inner story. The Fey-mankind conflict, a god getting involved, and some epic battle were all like ambrosia on her tongue.

The King and the Protectorate and the Gates were different because she had interacted with two of them, and her father had—at the very least—tried to touch the third, which Maelona clearly considered a death sentence. The book that Raegan's father had purposefully left for her—that had led her to the kelpie and to Maelona and to the King—seemed to agree.

Which left Raegan wondering, for the millionth time, why her father had done what he had done.

She cast the knit blanket off her shoulders, stood and stretched, a vertebra in her back cracking. She chewed on her lower lip until she tasted blood.

Her phone lit up on the table. With a strange urgency, she reached out and snatched it. There was one new text message from an unknown number.

It's Maelona. Call me as soon as you see this.

CHAPTER SEVENTEEN

The phone rang and rang, the sound looping in on itself until Raegan started to think that maybe an eternity had passed since she'd tapped the call button next to Maelona's name.

"Pick up, pick up," Raegan hissed, pacing back and forth in front of her couch. "You just fucking texted me."

Then the line finally clicked. "Raegan," Maelona greeted, her voice thick with a hedged kind of hope. "Are you safe?"

"I'm fine," Raegan breathed, dragging a hand through her hair. Words tangled themselves in the back of her throat.

"I can get you out of this," Maelona said, sure and determined. "I've prepared a safe place for us to meet. Soon—it needs to be soon."

"Okay," Raegan said, her pacing slowed for a moment. "Thank you. But I need you to tell me more about my father. Can you do that?"

Silence yawned wide at the other end of the line. She thought her heart might explode through her chest as she waited, biting her tongue.

"It's not a good idea." Maelona's voice was as heavy and suffocating as damp leaves. "It's safer for you to know less. I'd rather focus on preparing you to leave."

"I summoned a fucking kelpie," Raegan shot back, her pacing turning into stomping. "I think it's a bit late for that, don't you? Besides, I need to know, Maelona. I have a goddamn right to know."

"No," Maelona replied, grounding the words between her teeth. "The wolves are already at our fucking door. It will only make everything harder."

"Then *let it* be harder," Raegan snarled, pouring all her fervent need for closure into those five words.

She heard Maelona let out a long, low sigh on the other end, but then the woman didn't speak again. Raegan caught what she thought was a fumbling noise, followed by nothing. She almost began to panic before she heard the clink of a lighter through the speaker.

"Only your father," Maelona finally said, her accent thicker as she spoke with a cigarette between her lips. "We will *only* talk about your father. And I don't even know how much closure I can give you. I sure as hell don't have any."

"Fine," Raegan replied, clutching the sides of her phone violently with anticipation. "Only my father. I promise."

"Right," Maelona said, her tone curt. "Meet me at the Green Line Café. Baltimore and 43rd. I've set a number of wards, and it's safer in public. At least, it should be. I don't know anymore. This is a risk, Raegan. I need you to know that."

Raegan could not stop to think about the risks. She held the phone to her ear with her shoulder as she darted toward the entryway to pull her boots back on. She noticed for a fleeting moment that they were tucked neatly against the wall, toes pressed into the baseboard, laces stowed in the shaft—so unlike the way she normally kicked them off in any random direction. But then Maelona was saying her name, asking if the coffee shop would work as a meeting place, so she just shoved her feet into her shoes without further investigation.

"You're going to have to give me like forty minutes," Raegan said, almost dropping the phone as she began to lace up her boots. "You're all the way over in Spruce Hill."

"Yeah, that's fine," Maelona replied. "But I'm going to ask you again to let this go. Let *him* go."

"No," Raegan said. "See you." She hung up before Maelona could say anything else.

She pulled the phone away from her ear, releasing her cramping shoulder. For a moment, she stared at the black screen, wondering if perhaps the tiny, rectangular darkness held some sort of an answer or a sign for her.

It did not, so Raegan finished lacing up her boots and reached for her favorite leather jacket, adorned with silver hardware, buttery soft padded-leather paneling the shoulders and sleeves. She shoved her keys and wallet inside its pockets. Then she cast a glance over at her work bag and her father's spell. Despite herself, Raegan ached to tell someone. Part of her was still paranoid that the lockbox and the papers were just cruel delusions. She wanted someone else to touch the thick parchment where it curled at the edges and tell her, "Yes, *this is real, this is so very real.*"

She swallowed, her jaw clenched. Maelona would not—could not—do that for her. Maelona would be more likely to set the spell aflame with her cigarette lighter, telling Raegan in that hoarse voice of hers that it was for the best.

Pulling on her jacket, she decided that her father's spell and the King should be tucked away and kept from her aunt. She would go to Maelona *only* for answers about her father and the Protectorate. Pulling the door closed behind her, Raegan stampeded down the stairs and broke out into the autumnal mist. Afternoon brought darkness closer to the city's horizon, smudging soot around all the edges. Raegan scanned the block, eyes sharp for anyone suspicious. Seeing nothing, she shoved her hands in her pockets and began the journey.

After a subway ride that seemed to last forever, she emerged back into the aboveground world and found that the clouds and fog had burned off, allowing autumn sunshine to turn everything bronzen. She half-wished to be angry at the bright, slanting light, but this side of the city was gloriously draped in the season, rows of sycamore trees festooned with reds and yellows. As Raegan walked south, the commercial buildings melted into Victorian townhomes wreathed in creaking wooden porches dusted with leaves, kids' bikes, and boxes of books free to a good home.

She rounded the corner onto Baltimore Avenue, the painted green façade of the café like a beacon in the distance. Her pulse thrummed against her skin. She would be careful and clever, and she would get answers about her father. Then, and only then, would she decide what to do next.

Raegan slipped through the door, taking stock of the airy café, which was characteristically busy. She hadn't seen Maelona at the outdoor tables—not that she had imagined she would. Quickly scanning the room, she noted that one of the coveted seats by the large bay window was open, and considered grabbing it and forcing Maelona to join her. But then Raegan's skin crawled at the thought of being visible to any passersby. She felt like a bug under a rock lifted, high and sudden, into the air by an overly curious child.

Weaving through the tables, she finally found Maelona tucked away in the back corner and made her way toward the older woman, who was doing a decent job of acting as though she had not spotted Raegan the second she'd walked through the doors.

"Hi," Raegan greeted, peeling off her leather jacket, which had become much too warm in the autumn sun.

Maelona looked up from the mass-market paperback she had been pretending to read. An untouched almond croissant sat on a plate before her, but Raegan saw Maelona's coffee cup was already drained.

"A *kelpie*, Raegan? Seriously?" Maelona said in the way of a greeting, running her eyes down Raegan's form, almost like she was checking for wounds or extra appendages. When she did not reply, Maelona narrowed her eyes and added, "Took you long enough."

"This café, while lovely, is very far from my apartment," Raegan said, sitting down across from her. She put her elbows on the table and propped her chin on her hands. "And I don't drive."

Maelona waved the words away with one hand, the other sliding the croissant toward Raegan. "All yours if you want it," Maelona said, looking away for a moment. "Can't get my stomach to settle."

Raegan tore off the end of the croissant and popped it into her mouth, as if to prove she was of a stronger constitution, capable of eating even under extreme duress, though she couldn't remember her last real, full meal. She noted that internally, the way her therapist always told her to. Raegan loved food, and this decrease in appetite could be a warning sign.

"You might want to lay off the coffee if your stomach is giving you trouble," Raegan said pointedly, her gaze shooting to Maelona's mug. Her aunt scowled, but her hands fidgeted with the edge of the saucer.

"Are we safe here? Who showed up earlier at Ray's?"

Maelona looked away, tonguing the inside of her cheek. "We *should* be," she answered, eyes sliding back to Raegan. "But nothing's completely safe. I told you that." A long sigh and then, "A higher-ranking member of the Protectorate showed up earlier. Like I said, they're very interested in finding out who exactly you are. I've concealed you, for now. But—"

Someone dropped a plate nearby, and Maelona cut off whatever else she was going to say, her entire body swinging in the direction of the noise, every muscle tense and ready. Raegan watched—it was like seeing a dog's hackles go up. When Maelona found the source of the noise, she relaxed, turning back to Raegan, who wondered what it would be like to live her life so reactive to every sound, every quick movement, every stir of the shadows. She supposed she might know soon enough.

The thought turned her stomach, and she pushed the croissant a few inches back toward Maelona.

"Right," Raegan said, taking advantage of the pause. "You said my dad risked so much for a normal life, but then . . . the Gates. Why would he go to them?"

A muscle in Maelona's jaw jumped, and she twisted her coffee cup around. "Not going to start with any softballs, I see," the older woman grumbled.

"That's not my style," Raegan replied sweetly. She tucked her hands beneath the table, resting them on her thighs so Maelona could not see the way they shook like leaves tumbling into gutters.

Maelona sighed, the tension in her shoulders rising. "I've asked myself the same question a million times," she finally told Raegan. "I have no good answers."

"He had to have a reason," Raegan pushed, narrowing her eyes. "He was pretty fucking smart."

"About *some* things," Maelona snapped. "Okay, about most things. But not magic. Real magic; not the parlor tricks we now have courtesy of the Timekeeper. The real shit, from way back when. The things the Gentry knew. He was obsessed, and that made him foolish."

A few tables away a toddler suddenly burst into shrieks, cutting off whatever Maelona was going to say. Raegan's head ached. She wished fervently for the notebook and good pen she'd left at home, unsure of how Maelona would react to note-taking. Her aunt wouldn't be the first to freeze or clam up at the sight of a reporter's notebook on the table. But Raegan needed her process, her way of making sense of things, the clarity she only found at the end of scribbled notes and meandering arrows and three crossed-out conclusions.

The toddler's cries quieted as a man in a brown wool sweater lifted them from their seat, cradling the child in his arms, all sorts of soothing words falling from his mouth as he made for the door. Unexpectedly, emotion swelled in Raegan's throat. She thought of autumns past and long-burned-out bonfires and the smell of her father's cologne permeating a red scarf—

"Raegan." Maelona's sharp tone cut into her thoughts. She turned back to her aunt, heat rising to her face at having drifted away over such a silly thing. Her aunt was watching her closely, and Raegan saw there was no use pretending. Maelona seemed to know exactly what she had just witnessed.

"Raegan," Maelona said again, this time much gentler, something in her expression crumbling. "I've bought us a little time. I'll answer your questions. But . . ."

The woman sighed, squeezing her eyes shut for a moment. When she opened them, there was more sadness and fear in Maelona's gaze than Raegan knew what to do with.

"But Raegan, I need to get you out. I need to keep you safe," Maelona said, steel creeping back into her tone. "Your father's gone. I might as well be, after all these years of hunting one moment and running like prey the next. Let's break the cycle together, yeah? Let's not give the Protectorate another Overhill to devour."

With those last few words, Maelona was the most terrifying Raegan had seen her—the late afternoon light slanting off the silver threads of hair around the crown of her head, the jawline set, spindly fingers quietly resting, the wiry muscle in her forearms coiled and ready.

Surprising the both of them, Raegan reached one hand across the table to grip Maelona's palm tightly. Her aunt's flesh was hot and dry beneath her fingers.

"Thank you for giving a fuck," Raegan said simply, meaning it. The pair exchanged sheepish smiles, faces flushed with the intensity of the moment, before Raegan pulled away.

Maelona cleared her throat and then plucked her paperback from where it had been discarded beside her coffee cup, paging through it to retrieve a slim sheet of folded paper. Raegan thought there might have been some handwritten words on it—phrases, mostly, it seemed—but then Maelona smoothed it down flat on the table, obscuring it from her view.

"I pulled a few ideas of where you might go and the paths you might safely take," Maelona said, her eyes jumping as she scanned the sheet before her. Then she looked up at Raegan, the hollows under her eyes a bit brighter, the deep crease between her brows not quite as sharp.

It only lasted a moment, because then Maelona's gaze skipped just to the left, out into the café over Raegan's shoulder. The air around their table changed completely, Raegan sensed, her stomach plummeting.

"Listen to me very carefully," Maelona said, her tone like ice as she tucked the paper back into the pages of her book, gaze locked with whatever threat loomed behind Raegan. "If you only listen to one thing I ever say to you, please, let it be this."

Raegan sat stock-still in her seat, her pulse howling in every crevice of her body, muscles tensed and ready.

"Raegan," Maelona continued, voice as flat and cold as a frozen lake. "*Run.*"

CHAPTER EIGHTEEN

Nothing else had changed inside the café. Raegan could still hear the hum of the espresso machine and the clink of mugs on saucers. The college students studying in the corner had barely moved an inch, and the tiny dog sheltering beneath the table next to her hadn't awoken from its nap. The ambient chatter and soft lull of the indie rock music playing over the speakers all remained the same, the smell of fresh coffee and sweet syrup filling the air.

And so Raegan hesitated. By the time she had actually managed to fling herself from her seat and in the general direction of an exit, Maelona shouted something, holding up one hand to send what Raegan could only describe as a shockwave through the air. Maelona's other hand reached over to grab Raegan by the scruff of her sweater, swinging her around so that Maelona stood between her and whatever had appeared at the door.

"Get down!" Maelona yelled, turning toward Raegan to flip their table on its side, creating a small spot of cover.

Adrenaline thick in her veins, Raegan scrambled behind the table, pushing her back against it, trying to make herself as small as possible. Her mind was racing to keep up; no gunshots or explosions or even the calmly-delivered news of a bomb threat had preceded the chaos. Whatever was going on, Raegan was not wired for it.

Something shook the café hard—not an earthquake, something else —and she hazarded a look to her left, wondering if there was fuck-all she could do for everyone else in the building. If they were in danger, it was certainly her fault.

To Raegan's shock, the once-bustling café was absolutely empty, entirely devoid of the people and the lipstick-stained coffee cups and sugared pastries it had held only moments ago. Before she could process such a development, something tore through the air, whistling past her. Raegan tried to track its movement, but there was nothing to see, only something to be felt, and it raised the hair on the back of her neck and made her teeth vibrate.

Magic, Raegan realized, near-delirious. Magic that her bloodline could work on this half of a world that had been broken into two.

"Overhill!" The voice thundered from behind Raegan, unnaturally loud and coarse. Something bloomed sour in her stomach at the sound of it. She almost answered, spat back a curse or insult reflexively, but Maelona spoke first, and Raegan realized she was not the Overhill being addressed.

"I told you I had this handled!" Maelona snarled. Her aunt's words sent distrust spiraling through Raegan's chest, but she told herself to hold steady. "Why are you storming in here like this?"

"Handled?!" came the scoffing response. "I think you had little intention of bringing your brother's whelp into the fold."

Raegan clenched her jaw and forced herself to detach as much as she could from the shouted words. For now, the explosions of magic had stopped. She should take the opening.

Rocking back onto her heels, still concealed behind the table but ready to spring from a crouch, Raegan scanned the back of the room for any exits. Her heart raced faster as she saw none, but then her gaze landed on the wraparound café counter. Surely there had to be an exit in the kitchen just beyond it. She hoped it wasn't a dead-end alley, but Raegan didn't see any other egress point besides throwing a chair through a window, which she imagined was harder than it looked in the movies.

She wiped her damp palms on her pants, locking her gaze with the counter. Her body felt like a car trying to turn over—as if her muscles knew exactly what to do in this scenario, as if she had handled it a million times before, but she just couldn't get the process started.

Taking a deep inhale, Raegan prepared herself to run for the counter, but not before she caught movement out of the corner of her eye. Maelona was losing ground, it seemed; her aunt now stood abreast with the overturned table instead of three strides in front. Whoever had come for them was fanning out like a pack of wolves around the café: a nondescript man in an even more nondescript suit of an indeterminate color was slinking along the far wall. Raegan could see another—taller, thinner, but strangely homogenous—picking his way through the café to her immediate right.

Regret landed heavy in the pit of Raegan's stomach. There would be no vaulting over the café counter to freedom. Maelona had told her to run, and she had hesitated. Now here they were, everything wasted.

"Could we please handle this in a civilized fashion?" the heavy, guttural voice from before asked, suddenly so much closer.

Raegan heard Maelona's sardonic snarl of a laugh in response. "You stormed a building filled with civilians," she snapped, "and used battle magic against your own kind. We're well past that point."

"Some might argue we passed that point when your traitor of a brother defected and you *watched him go*," came the response, like a machete through the dull, unnaturally still air.

Raegan felt stupid and childish continuing to cower behind a small, overturned café table, so she slowly rose to her feet, turning to face whoever was confronting her aunt. The man who had showed up at Ray's only a few hours ago now stood just inches from Maelona's face, though he towered over her, dressed in that dusty pinstripe suit. His light eyes, straight, noble nose, and heavy, mountain-like build rang a thousand bells of familiarity in Raegan's brain, but none sang in a timbre she could comprehend.

"There she is," the man snarled, turning his gaze toward Raegan. "The prodigal child returns."

"Bedwyr," Maelona said, putting one arm out in front of Raegan. "Leave her out of this. She is not fit for the role we play."

The man—Bedwyr, Raegan knew, had maybe already known—hardened his expression, eyes boring into hers, like he was searching her for something she did not even know she possessed. Panic rose with Raegan's pulse—the disappeared people, and the men spreading out like wolves, and the chaos, all forgotten. She knew this man. And she absolutely despised him. She did not think she had ever been so certain of anything in her life.

Bedwyr's gaze snapped back to Maelona for a moment. "I'll be the judge of her fitness to serve," he said, and then the man reached out and grabbed Raegan by the forearm.

The moment his fingers brushed the sleeve of her sweater, she felt something deep within her snap. Her father had given up everything to create a life for her away from the Protectorate. Maelona had taken a number of risks that Raegan doubted she could even begin to comprehend. And here the Protectorate was, rearing their ugly, pinstriped heads and taking what they wanted anyway— the most exhausted trope played out again and again in human history.

Raegan was not a thing or a whelp or a jewel to be snatched. Above all, she knew with a strange and absolute certainty that this man Bedwyr had dared to lay his hands on her before, and she would burn herself to ash before he did it again.

Something within her gave way, like a valve or a dam or perhaps a levy, and before she knew it, Raegan was screaming—screaming like there was nothing to do but scream, her head thrown back, her hands contorted into claws, heeding the blackened waters' call. Her own voice fell alien in her ears, less a human cry and more the thunder of a swollen river overtaking everything in its path.

The sounds of pipes bursting, metal turning in on itself, water rushing free and unbidden, filled the room, and there was, somehow, what looked like a tsunami of river water—brackish, strangely woven with silver threads—sweeping in from the kitchen.

Everything moved in slow motion, frame by frame. Bedwyr saw the wave and looked back at Raegan in surprised confusion and— unless she was flattering herself—fear. He yanked his hand away from her, instead snatching Maelona by the wrist. The two disappeared in a blink, as if the café had folded in on itself and devoured them whole.

Raegan noticed a few other besuited Protectorate blink out of existence like Maelona and Bedwyr had. The ones closer to the kitchen—the ones who were not fast enough—were instead swallowed by the rush and swell of black water.

It was not the darkly quiet peace Raegan had always equated with drowning. Instead, the water slipped a thousand hands around their limbs, dragging them down, forcing tendrils into eyes and mouths and lungs. She found herself frozen to the spot, facing the towering wall of water, knowing she could never outrun it.

For a moment, the wave crested and took the shape of a woman with many arms, each fist grasping a Protectorate body. The watery hands brought four men to its gaping mouth, devouring them one by one, crushing bodies into the damp darkness that hungrily awaited.

Then the wave-woman collapsed into a silvery stream that swept the café, rushing toward Raegan. She remembered reading that even ankle-high water moving fast enough could knock a person off their feet, so she braced herself for impact. But when the water reached her, it seemed to split around her boots, flooding everything but her. She watched it dance around her, wondering what such a thing could possibly mean.

Eventually, some of the floodwater slipped through the door or down through cracks in the floor, leaving only a few inches that shone silver in the low light.

Raegan wasn't sure how long she stood there, taking it all in: the broken chairs and shattered pastry case, the soaking wet antique rug balled up against the door. The only sound in the space was her quick breathing and a few irregular pitter-patter drips of water.

She clenched her fists, begging for the sharp bite of her nails in her palms, hoping it would be enough to tell her what was real and what was not. She pressed in until the pain was quite real, but the destroyed café and dripping water did not change. Panic climbed her throat. Her aunt, her only lifeline, was gone. She had utterly fucked any escape plan—the Protectorate knew she existed, knew Maelona had tried to hide her, and Bedwyr seemed intent on harvesting her like an overgrown orchard.

"Breathe," Raegan told herself, but her body hardly obeyed. She was breathing, yes, but the gasps were short and hard, certainly not conducive to soothing.

Shouldn't there be sirens? Horrified pedestrians peering in? Anything? The street outside was empty, the wind blowing gusts of gray, dried leaves against the café's doors.

"Steady," Raegan murmured, closing her eyes for a moment, half-daring to hope that when she opened them, she'd find herself waking up in bed from a bad dream.

No such luck—the same scene greeted her and the wrongness of it all mounted quickly, fanning the flames of panic. And then, somewhere in the haze of her thickly thudding heart and racing mind, Raegan felt eyes upon her.

CHAPTER NINETEEN

She spun on her heel, almost slipping on the damp hardwood. Emerging from the gloom of a far corner, draped in shadow, was the King. She noticed his impeccably tailored black suit for a heartbeat before she caught the expression on his face: eyes wide as he searched the wreckage, long-legged strides quick and urgent. For a brief moment, the King seemed to be cloaked in panic instead of deadly authority.

And then his gaze met hers and the eyes turned hard, a muscle in his jaw leaping. The King said nothing, looking at her with an expression Raegan thought might actually be loathing.

"Where the fuck did you even come from?" she sputtered, her heart rate spiking, her hands clammy.

Though he offered no reply, the tall Fey creature moved forward with terrifying grace, picking his way through shattered plates and broken chairs. Raegan watched him, breathless, until he came to a halt a few feet away from her. She told herself there was absolutely no point in noticing how beautiful his hands were—vascular, powerful, and long-fingered.

"Do you know what happened here?" the King asked, looking down at her, his tone armored in the cold authority she'd been expecting.

"Uhh, me, apparently," Raegan stammered, leaning against a still-upright table, only for it to give under her weight.

She caught herself with a jolt, the movement splashing water on her pants. The King watched her silently. When she said nothing more, one of his dark brows arched up expectantly.

"The Protectorate," Raegan began, to which the King nodded grimly, as if she were just confirming what he already knew. "They came for me. A man tried to grab me. I . . . I got mad, I guess. Something just sort of snapped. I think it was me? I was so angry, I screamed, and then all this water rushed in from nowhere."

The King tilted his head to the side, looking at her with more interest. "You did this?" he asked, gesturing with one sweeping hand at the destroyed, water-logged café.

Raegan nodded, swallowing hard. "I think so?" she replied, assuming it unwise to lie to such a being. "They still took my aunt, though, and she was the only source of information I had. A lot more helpful than you, by the way."

Nothing on the King's face registered her small jab, though something outside the café caught his attention and he narrowed his eyes. "We should go," he said, not taking his gaze off whatever he saw. Raegan tried to follow his sight line, but she didn't see anything at all in that general direction which would be a cause for alarm.

"Oh, it's *we* now, is it?" Raegan demanded, not quite capable of stopping herself.

The King's eyes tracked to her, and one side of his mouth curved up for a split second. "Do you want to leave this place alive or not?" he asked, voice low and cool.

"I suppose when you put it that way . . ." Raegan conceded, trying to fish her soaked leather jacket from the ground. When she looked back up, the King was closer—much closer. The scent of black pepper and damp stone and autumn rain washed over her, dispelling the brackishness that had been sitting in her nose.

To her surprise, he extended his hand to her. She eyed it like a snake in her boot.

"Why are you helping me?" she demanded, holding her ground, her fist tightly wound around the damp collar of her jacket.

The King considered her question. Raegan had a strong sense that he was not thoughtfully reviewing her request, but instead deciding whether to answer at all, and how much truth to reveal if he did. She wondered if it was true that the Fair Folk couldn't lie. She wondered if the King got around that by just not saying very much.

"At this exact moment, it is advantageous to me," he finally replied, distant and professional, as if they were discussing a real estate deal.

"Temporary allyship works for me," Raegan conceded with a shrug, reaching out to take his hand. The moment their skin touched, she stiffened and nearly blacked out; it was as if a tidal wave of every human emotion slammed into her all at once.

The King made a low sound of frustration and released her hand, hooking his arm through hers instead. The fabric of his suit jacket and her sweater dulled the tidal wave considerably, and Raegan straightened.

"Come," the King commanded, turning toward what was most certainly not an exit, but for once in her life, Raegan hardly felt she was in a place to question anything.

Besides, to her chagrin, she was more focused on how deep and velvet-cloaked the King's voice became when he issued a command. Raegan began to imagine him uttering the same word under very different circumstances, but then he yanked her roughly over a pile of obliterated furniture.

"Jesus fucking Christ," Raegan snapped, grabbing his arm with both hands to avoid losing her balance entirely. "I am half your goddamn size."

Instead of an apology, the King merely gazed down at her from between infuriatingly long, dark lashes. "Less than half," he observed in a detached tone, and then he scrutinized a section of wall. "You will not like this."

Raegan opened her mouth to protest, but then the entire world collapsed inward, darkness closing all around her. She felt like a rubber band pulled all the way to its breaking point, stretched and stretched and stretched until all she knew was the inevitability of her entire being snapping in two.

And then she stumbled out into a very normal alley. The sun was bright and thick in her eyes. Raegan wasn't immediately sure where she was, but she could hear the hiss of a bus coming to a stop and the chatter of people going about their everyday, mundane, utterly human lives.

More importantly, she felt incredibly ill, worse than she'd felt in a while—like she'd developed a bad hangover in thirty seconds. She doubled over and choked back a dry heave. The King no longer had his arm hooked through hers. Instead, having grabbed the back of her sweater in one large hand as if she were a naughty kitten, he dragged her toward a line of trash cans tucked against the opposite brick wall. He flipped open one lid with his free hand just in time for Raegan to throw up the contents of her stomach. She wasn't sure how her body had so much to regurgitate; she'd had, what, a few cups of tea and a bite of Maelona's croissant?

Raegan wiped her mouth with the back of her hand, beginning to straighten before another intense wave of nausea hit her. She doubled over again, her stomach finding more to expel. Somewhere through the nausea and the bone-deep exhaustion, she realized the King was holding her hair back, the tips of his fingers brushing the nape of her neck. The sensation sent a jolt of longing through her that she didn't understand.

When she finally felt as though there was nothing left in her stomach, Raegan stood up straight. The King's fingers lingered in her hair for a second too long, tracing the spirals of her curls. She should have responded with a barbed comment, but was preoccupied with stopping herself from leaning into his touch. Yearning rose unbidden and thick in her ribcage, dark and sweet as molasses.

The King released her, taking a step back. She fought to find her balance, her sanity, her dignity, standing for a moment or two, woozy and exhausted, the light too bright and the world too loud and the King too achingly familiar.

She blinked. The King extended a hand, offering her a handkerchief, because of course he just carried those around. Raegan took it, taking care not to brush against his skin as she did. She glanced down at the square of fabric before wiping it across her lips. It was a dark gray, subtly shimmery like a pearl.

"Appreciated," Raegan said, stuffing the handkerchief in her pocket. She pivoted to lean against the brick wall, shielding her eyes with one hand to look over at the King.

In the late afternoon light, his unusual features were even more prominent—the aquiline nose, the full mouth, the sharp jaw, the ivory skin, the black hair falling in waves to the base of his neck, where it curled up against his skin. His beauty was dangerous, sharply edged, and like Bedwyr, the King felt familiar in a completely impossible way. Unlike Bedwyr, who had looked at her with an emotion Raegan couldn't decipher, the King was gazing down at her with a very obvious expression. It was the way one might look at the bug in their apartment they thought they had already successfully squashed.

But he was quiet, no icy words dripping from his sculpted lips, so Raegan pounced. "Why are you following me?" she asked, her voice like a knife.

It could have been the slanting sun in the alley, the way shadow and light sliced his face in half, but Raegan swore the King rolled his eyes. "Do not flatter yourself," he replied, leaning back against the alley's opposite wall, infuriatingly casual. "A large contingency of my sworn enemy appeared. Battle magic was exchanged. Old elemental magic reared its head. An unstable pocket realm flared into existence. Naturally, I came to investigate."

"Yeah?" Raegan asked, her stomach still queasy. "And what did your investigation yield?"

He watched her, not unlike a wolf wondering if its prey could still be played with or if it was better to bring teeth to throat and end it. "That you have caused an impressive amount of problems in a short period of time," the King replied, gray eyes cold as winter.

"Thanks," Raegan replied, batting her eyelashes at him and twirling the end of one curl for emphasis. "Causing problems is my specialty."

One side of the King's mouth curved up again, and amusement simmered in his expression. He pushed off the opposite wall with no warning, closing the distance between them. One long stride carried him so close to Raegan that she was forced to tilt her chin up, the crown of her head meeting the rough brick wall behind her.

"You are not afraid of me," the King observed, his tone low, eyes searching hers.

"No," Raegan replied—not a lie but not a truth, either. Her heart beat wildly, and every primal instinct in her body told her to run. "I'm not."

"Draw the attention of the Protectorate or meddle in the affairs of the Unseelie Court again," the King began, his mouth only inches from hers, his voice soft and deadly, "and it will be the last time you do anything at all."

Raegan's body was panicking, sending adrenaline careening through her veins. Her muscles itched to fight or run or maybe both. And yet the King's physical closeness felt as natural as the return of spring, and it strengthened her resolve.

She tilted her head, gaze dropping to the King's parted lips. "Tragically, meddling is my profession," Raegan returned, matching his tone. "If you'd like me to stop, I'm afraid you'll need to offer me a deal."

Chapter Twenty

The air around her seemed to drop twenty degrees in temperature as silence stretched taut across the space. Raegan did her best to hold her ground, but her back was pressed roughly against brick and the King of the Unseelie Court was looming over her, his eyes nearly black in the shadow of the alley.

And then, just like that, the spell broke. The King stepped back a few inches, and autumnal warmth returned to the air. Raegan permitted herself one shaky exhale. She knew this dance was far from over.

"You," the King began, voice low, though no expression moved across his features, "are a *fool*."

For the first time, true fear swam in Raegan's chest, its long fingers reaching up her throat.

"Was my offer of your life in exchange for ceasing to interfere not a deal?" he demanded. "And perhaps the kindest one I have offered in centuries. Yet you wish to renegotiate."

The King stepped toward her again, lithe as a panther and twice as dangerous. Looking at him now, Raegan was without a single doubt that he was ancient and deadly and beyond anything she had ever encountered before. She did her best to hold his gaze, every muscle fiber in her body shaking.

When the King swooped down into her space, she resisted the urge to shrink back. He was so close that she felt his breath dance past her cheek.

"Name your desire," he murmured, his head tilted to the side, eyes sliding to hers. The amusement had returned, but it was soured now, all the heat wrung out of it, nothing left but cruelty beneath its veneer.

Raegan sucked in as deep a breath as she could muster. It was now or never, it seemed. She forced herself to wait a moment, to review her wording. Precision had never mattered more, but thank the gods she was good with words.

"Assist me truthfully in locating and rescuing my father," Raegan began, forcing herself to meet the King's gaze, "with no trickery or malice, and with no adverse impact on my physical and mental well-being. Once my father is found and safely returned here, to Philadelphia, in this timeline and this year, I will cease any interference with your court and the Protectorate."

Moving quicker than her eye could track, the King planted his palms on either side of Raegan's head, boxing her in against the brick wall. Her stomach bottomed out, and fear landed a thousand hot pinpricks across her skin.

"I could just kill you," he stated, as casually as one might take notice of the weather or a new café opening down the block. His gaze bored into hers, and she bit down on her tongue.

"And yet, you have not," Raegan said, imitating his cocky tilt of the head, searching his expression for something she could identify. "Which tells me that you won't."

It was a hell of a gamble. Fear melted into terror, slippery and insidious as it wound its way through her body.

For a long moment that stretched into a small eternity, the King simply held her gaze, his eyes black as the night sky, expression unwavering. For all Raegan knew, she might already be dead, the last thing she ever saw imprinted on her mind as the final bursts of life and electricity gave way to nothingness.

But then a muscle in the King's jaw leapt and he pushed off the wall, dropping his arms to his sides. Raegan watched his chest rise and fall. She made a decision, hoped to god she was right, and then opened her mouth to speak.

"If you don't want to help me, I could certainly draw the attention of the Protectorate again," she said, crossing her arms. "I'm sure they would be very interested to know the Unseelie King himself is in this city."

The King shot a powerful hand toward Raegan, and for a moment, she was absolutely certain he was going to kill her. Instead, he gently caught her jaw between long, curled fingers, tilting it up as he leaned in closer to her, so close that a passerby might think a kiss was imminent.

"*That,*" he said, amusement simmering across his features like a heat mirage, "is much better leverage."

Raegan's body keened at his touch, begging for more, a stark betrayal. She gritted her teeth and exhaled sharply through her nose. "So we have a deal?"

"Yes, Raegan Maeve Overhill. You have a covenant with the Unseelie Court, and I will act in its stead."

The King slipped away from her and made his way down the alley, long legs devouring the distance. Raegan felt frozen to the spot, her body trembling, using every ounce of her mental capacity just to keep up with everything that had occurred in such a short period of time. She wondered if she could help Maelona. She wondered how she could possibly keep herself safe long enough to have a chance at seeing her father again.

For the first time, leaning against the rough brick wall, her breathing harsh and shallow, a nervous sweat ghosting her skin like a film, Raegan dared to wonder about the thread between her dreams and her father and the Protectorate and the King.

The answers were large and formless, obscured by an ominous fog, and she squeezed her eyes shut. She told herself to count to ten and reached eight before she was interrupted.

"Come along," the King called from the mouth of the alley, his voice velveted in authority. "I hardly have all day."

His words deepened the thudding of Raegan's heart, and she forced her eyes open. She feverishly wished for a few moments, just a few, to think over her options, to make a list in a quiet space, but she knew that chance was gone.

She had made a deal with the Unseelie King, and there was nothing to do but see it through. So Raegan gathered herself up and pushed off the wall, walking down the alley as though it were the entry to a labyrinth. Luckily, she had a sight line on the Minotaur, though he hid his beastly half well.

The King waited for her on the sidewalk, standing off to the side, cloaked in the shade of a tree. Raegan almost expected him to be invisible to any other humans, but in the three seconds she paused at the mouth of the alley, it was quite clear that the rest of the world had no issue perceiving the King. Two college girls stole not-so-secret looks at the lithe being in the three-piece suit, whispering to each other approvingly, and a gorgeous passerby with a shaved head and an impeccable overcoat dared to make eye contact and smile flirtatiously.

To Raegan's surprise, the King returned the flirtation with a sly smile of his own—at least before he realized Raegan was watching. Then cool impassivity slid across his features again. "You've finally managed to walk a few meters," he observed archly, his tone so dry it cracked in the air like a whip.

Raegan settled for a scowl she hoped was formidable, though she doubted it. Autumn had swept clouds back across the sky like cream in coffee, and with the sun's retreat, the seasonal chill had returned. The damp leather jacket she still stubbornly carried in one hand would be of no use.

Her lament over her outerwear was cut short as the King's shadow fell over her. Wordlessly, he offered her his arm, even though there were no broken bits of furniture or pools of water. A fanciful thought reared its head in Raegan's mind, but she cut it short, trying to ignore his heady scent of rain and woodsmoke.

She took the King's arm—friends close and enemies closer, after all— and tried to prepare herself for whatever awaited. For now, there was just the sidewalk beneath her feet, though it felt so much more like a rushing river or an impossibly thin thread of Fate. Déjà vu cloaked her; it was as if their steps had been rehearsed and choreographed a thousand times before.

"Where are you taking me?" Raegan inquired, instead of asking if he felt that strange, lilting sensation, too.

"Back to Old City," the King replied. "To my office. I have an object there that should be able to locate your father."

Hope stirred defiantly in Raegan's chest, and she fought to temper it. There were miles to go, she knew, as finding her father was one thing. If he was alive—because there *was* a possibility that Maelona was correct, though she roughly pushed that thought aside—then retrieving him would be another quest entirely. For now, she allowed herself to walk along this narrow Thread beside the Unseelie King.

Moving together, they slipped past a large group of students in high school uniforms, coming to a pause at the curb. Raegan busied herself with the cars that rumbled through the intersection: black, gray, black, blue, blue, yellow.

"We will have to use another portico," the King said, pulling her attention back. She turned to find him looking down at her, dark eyebrows drawn together in what Raegan would almost call concern, if she were a fool. She liked to think she was not.

"It is an established one," he continued, "so you should not be as ill, but you will likely still feel unwell."

The light changed and the traffic halted, and they moved through the crosswalk, passing a food truck on the other corner. Ordinarily, the smell would make Raegan's mouth water, but in her current state, her stomach only churned uncomfortably in response.

"I hope you have a trash can in your office," she replied, lengthening her stride to keep up with the King as they rounded a corner, moving away from the busier corridor of the neighborhood. "A portico is a portal, right? Like what we did earlier?"

"More or less," the King said with a shrug of his broad shoulders.

Raegan waited for him to elaborate or explain how a fucking portal even worked, but of course, he remained silent, guiding them through a calm, leaf-strewn section of the neighborhood until they arrived at an overgrown community garden. A fence stretched across the lot, brown leaves gathered in heaps around its posts. A gap in the fence's line served as an entry point. Trash from the street had tumbled into the front of the garden, plastic bags stuck on branches and flying like flags, takeout containers caught in the tall grass. The rest of the garden fell into darkness, blanketed in the shadows of the row houses on either side of the double-wide lot.

As they approached the threshold, the King hesitated, casting a glance over at Raegan. "Stay close," he instructed, his expression unreadable. "There is more than one door in this place. Some are hungry."

Before Raegan could respond, the King plunged into the gloom of the overgrown garden, their arms still linked together. As she passed through the gap in the fence, the smell of rotting leaves and damp earth overtook her. She could almost believe she had left the entire city behind —the exhaust and grease and steam erased, replaced with the smashed flesh of gourds and soil gone too long untended.

Desiccated leaves crunched underfoot as the King led her through a surprisingly maze-like space. Broken trellises loomed on either side of their path, and garden gates hung askew, chicken wire rusted and peeling.

"Doesn't your kind love beauty?" Raegan wondered aloud, looking around at the rot and decay, surprised the Fair Folk would use this garden as a space for their magic.

To her surprise, the King stopped dead in his tracks, turning to look down at her, inquisitive. He held her gaze for a moment longer than Raegan could handle, and she looked away.

"Is this not beauty?" the King asked, his tone genuine, at least as far as she could tell. "Old roots were cut to the bone here, and yet they reemerge, defiant. Is there anything more beautiful than defiance, than survival? It is the most ancient song and perhaps the sweetest."

The King did not give her a chance to respond; he simply returned to whatever path he had chosen and began to walk. Intrigued by the seemingly open way in which he answered, Raegan tried to watch him more closely in her peripheral vision as they traversed the garden. And she was rewarded for her careful attention: she caught the moment when his free hand reached out to a vine of morning glories, fingers brushing the trumpeted buds.

Silence fell again. Raegan could only hear the soft whisper of the wind in the dead leaves and her own footsteps; the King appeared to move soundlessly through the space. The garden defied logic—they should've hit another building, or a cross street, or anything, by now and yet there was only the unfolding of tall brown grass.

The King slowed to a halt, sliding his arm out of Raegan's. She suddenly noticed a large wooden archway before them—the kind that usually had thick ivy or flowering vines wrapped around it, reserved for places like botanical gardens and fancy spring weddings. This one had no green at all—just a weathered, almost-gray tinge. The wind whistled through it gently, and its legs swayed as though unsteady. She had no idea how she hadn't noticed it as they approached.

The King's voice interrupted her thoughts. "Wait here for a moment," he said, tone low. Then he stepped forward, his hair and suit a harsh black in the drab earth tones surrounding them. He slowed when he reached the archway.

Raegan's vision condensed to the King's shoulders and the fine black cloth that covered them, framed on either side by the sagging wood arch. She thought he said something, though it was hard to tell over the rustle of so many dead things in the wind, and then there was a low pop. It was as though a film had been removed from her eyes and suddenly the garden was riotous with life and color and green. Two elegant trees stood on either side of the arch, their boughs laden with white petals.

The King glanced back at her, as if perhaps she would've taken the moment to bolt, but Raegan only gazed on, spellbound as the trees' petals fell around him like snow. She almost laughed; a creature with such feral beauty, so clearly a predator, dusted with petals as downy as the wings of a dove.

And then the laughter dried up in her throat as she watched him: the petals, the arch, the black cloth, the snow, the door, the black cloak. She had seen this before, a thousand times before, endlessly rooted in this same spot, no snow or petal touching her skin, no door opening at her touch, forever abandoned in the desiccated garden like a rotted-out husk.

"Oberon," she murmured, the name tumbling out of her mouth like a stolen jewel. The ancient thing in the three-piece suit tilted his head, his features stark, and then something in the line of his powerful shoulders softened.

"Steady," he told her, his voice calm and gentle in a way she hadn't thought he would be capable of. "Steady."

She nodded, wiping clammy hands on her thighs. She shook her head to dispel whatever odd feeling had come over her, returning to this place of parched grass and half-dead shrubs. Raegan watched as the King reached forward with an elegant hand, long fingers outstretched, and tapped at the center of the archway. The air rippled like the surface of a pond, moving with an oil-spill shimmer.

She squinted and yearned to take a step forward, to examine and to understand, because watching whatever the King was doing rang so familiar in her bones. But before she could, he pivoted and stalked the three steps back toward her.

He reached over, one hand poised in the air above her upper arm. "May I?" the King asked, looking at her with those ocean eyes in a way that made her very aware of her pulse.

"Sure," Raegan replied, desperately trying to sound nonchalant. She braced herself for whatever feelings would arise at the King's touch, but he had looked away, displeasure coming across his features.

She froze, her heart a rabbit in her chest, wondering what horrors had entered the garden, armed with that vicious, teeth-rattling magic, ready to snatch her up as if she were the only thing worth harvesting in a blighted orchard.

"Your jacket," the King said, sending Raegan's mind reeling. "It is wet."

"What?" she asked thickly, her eyes darting about the space until she realized her damp coat was the source of his irritation. "Oh, this old thing? It's not a big deal. I'm not even sure why I'm still carrying it."

To demonstrate how little her favorite jacket apparently mattered, Raegan mimed throwing it away, accidentally slapping herself hard in the thigh with heavy, wet leather.

"You should have told me," the King replied, leaning across Raegan to brush his fingers on the jacket's sleeve. As he did so, she felt the material dry in her grasp. She pulled it against her chest to inspect it, running her hands over the material. It was supple and clean and good as new.

"Oh, thank—I mean, that was . . . very kind of you and I am happy my jacket is repaired," Raegan stuttered, nearly thanking an ancient Fey king like a goddamn amateur.

His gaze slid to hers, and something like mischief played at the corners of his mouth. The autumn breeze rattled through the dried-up leaves of a nearby climbing vine, reaching over to tug at his dark waves of hair. To Raegan, the entire effect was dangerous—it made him much less feral-looking, removing a reminder of what he was.

"You may thank me, if you so desire," the King told her. "We have a covenant."

"Just to be safe, I'd rather not," Raegan beamed, pulling her jacket back on, feeling a bit like she was putting on armor.

She knew it was silly, but having the touchstone on her was a relief—the garment had been with her since college and had seen her through more than one sketchy situation. She had come to think of it as her lucky jacket, and she knew the power of such things.

"One cannot be too careful," the King agreed, one eyebrow arched. Then the breeze halted and the mischief drained away, like it took him too much energy to keep it going. Cool indifference settled back across his features as he gently laid a large hand on Raegan's upper arm, meeting her gaze and inclining his head, asking for permission.

"That's fine," Raegan said with a nod, her heart in her throat as she looked beyond the King to the portico's shimmering arch.

The King gave her no warning, no countdown, and certainly did not ask for further permission—instead, he seized Raegan and pulled her along with him into the mouth of the portico, straight into whatever darkness awaited on the other side of its oil-spill skin.

Chapter Twenty-One

Raegan emerged from the shimmering darkness sputtering and nauseous, her legs unsteady beneath her. Though she couldn't be sure with her head so woozy, she was fairly certain she had stepped out into another alley, this one narrower and gloomier. An overturned trash can had spilled its litter onto the ground, and browned weeds crawled through cracks in the concrete. She bit down on the inside of her cheek, staring at her shoes, willing her stomach to settle.

"Are you ill?" came an accented, dark and lovely voice. Raegan forced herself to look up and meet the King's gray eyes. He stood only a foot from her, leaning down to examine her current state of affairs.

"It's not as bad as the first time," she said weakly, swallowing back nausea.

"Can you walk?" he asked, brushing nonexistent lint from his impeccable suit with one hand.

"Of course I can," Raegan sputtered, as if the mere suggestion were ridiculous. She took one step and immediately swayed hard to the left, her shoulder clipping the wall. She heard the King grumble something under his breath.

"May I take your arm to guide you?" he asked, irritation creeping into his voice as if Raegan should absolutely have magical travel down pat by the second try.

Reacting to his snide tone, she spat, "No. I said I'm *fine*. God, humans aren't as fragile as you think."

As Raegan straightened, trying to find her balance, she heard the King let out a long, low sigh, as though he were absolutely beleaguered by her presence. Which she supposed he was. He didn't *have* to make the deal, though. He could have just killed her, which he seemed very comfortable doing. In fact, he looked like he was born to commit violence, all that coiled muscle and towering height and capable hands and—

"You presume to know what I think?" the King asked, his tone verging on mocking. "Amusing. I have walked this earth for a thousand years. Your kind cannot even *fathom* such a span of time. Come along."

Irritation grated inside her as Raegan shoved off the wall and kicked an empty can toward the King. It didn't hit him, of course—it just ricocheted off the opposite wall, clattering all the way. The King's gaze tracked the can and then slid to her, eyes narrowed.

"Is it enshrined somewhere in Fey code that you have to be an absolute dick all the time?" Raegan demanded, taking a few stumbling steps toward him.

Again, the shadows fell in just the right way so she couldn't be sure, but she thought the King rolled his eyes in response. It didn't seem like something ancient Unseelie kings would do, but she supposed she wasn't the foremost expert. At least not yet.

Raegan reached the King and moved to sweep past him, though she had no idea where they were headed. Just as she drew even with him, the King caught her by the elbow and leaned low, his lips brushing her ear.

"Take care that I do not tire of your amusements," he warned, fingers gripping her elbow like a vice. The delivery of his words, coupled with his physical proximity, sent a delicate chill spiraling down her spine, but it was not *only* fear she felt—that would be entirely too simple. Then the King straightened, his free hand reaching to take Raegan's other elbow. He pulled her to face him, chest to chest, in the gloom of the alley.

As he examined her, impossibly beautiful and impossibly cold eyes searching her face, Raegan held her breath, trying to summon the courage to break his grasp and run. She was not going down without a fight, no way, nohow. Her knife was on her waistband, but she wasn't sure if she could reach for it and run at the same time, and besides, she didn't think a folding knife would be much use against the King of the Unseelie Court.

But then he spoke a short string of words she didn't understand. Raegan immediately felt warm, as if someone had thrown a heated blanket around her, and the fogginess in her head and sickness in her stomach disappeared. The warmth seeped out of her as the King released her, stepping back. She felt good as new.

"What did you do?" Raegan asked, her tone thick with suspicion, eyes narrowed in distrust.

"Abated your portico-related illness," the King replied. "You are welcome."

"Why the fuck didn't you do that the first time when I was vomiting in a random trash can?" she spat, anger bubbling over inside her.

The King shrugged his broad shoulders. "I did not wish it." He pulled Raegan along by her elbow, exiting the alley and taking a sharp left onto the sidewalk.

"You guys are *just* like all the folklore says you are," she snapped, trying to pull her elbow out of his grasp but finding he was much larger and much stronger than her, which she supposed she already knew, but she found it annoying and wished it were not so.

At her statement, the King laughed. It took her by surprise—the sound of it was like an autumn bell in an afternoon meadow, as bright and tart as biting into a Honeycrisp apple. "Those stories, which most of your kind are not even clever enough to bother reading," the King began, softening his grip on her but not releasing, "were your fair warnings. And yet here you are."

"Yeah, well, being clever never got me very far," Raegan grumbled in response, dodging a middle-aged man who could not be bothered to look up from his phone as he walked. The King did not answer her, so she took a moment to observe her surroundings.

Antique buildings sat squarely on opposite sides of cobblestone streets. Cars trickled by, rattling on the uneven surface. Across the street, a minivan was trying—and failing—to parallel park. She spotted a familiar café up ahead. Relief flooded through Raegan as she recognized the neighborhood; they were indeed returning to the King's office in Old City. When he'd pulled her through the portico, she hadn't been sure where they were actually going to end up. She was pleasantly surprised the King had told the truth. Though, she supposed he couldn't lie. Or was that pure myth?

"That place makes great lavender lemonade," Raegan announced, desperate for something she knew for sure, pointing across the street. The King followed the trajectory of her hand with his gaze. "And excellent pastries."

"Can your kind go any time at all without thinking of food?" he inquired, only a little unkindly.

"I haven't eaten very much today," Raegan replied, meaning it to come out as a simple statement, but instead it sounded a bit like she was a Victorian orphan begging for just a bit more soup.

The King slowed his step, a muscle in his jaw leaping. "Do you require a meal?" he asked, voice dripping in so much condescension she longed to punch him.

"Not at this time but probably later," she replied, sickly-sweet, quickening her pace to keep up with him as he crossed the street, not seeming to heed the oncoming traffic very much.

"Your people require much nourishment," the King observed. "Is it exhausting? It appears exhausting."

"What, having to eat three meals a day?" Raegan asked, half her question getting cut off by the blare of a car horn. "Honestly yeah, maintaining a human body is a stupid amount of work."

The King laughed again, deep and bell-like, and warmth pooled in Raegan's core. She scolded herself internally, but it was too late: she liked making him laugh, and she was probably going to try to do it again, despite her better judgment.

The King swung around another turn, coming onto a busy, popular street. It was thick with tourists, the historical attractions thronged with lines, the Starbucks on the corner packed to the brim.

"This way is better," Raegan said, slipping her arm through his and tugging. "You avoid all the mayhem of this block."

The King looked at her, eyebrows drawing together as if he thought perhaps this time the human would trick the Fair Folk, but he acquiesced, and in a few moments, they emerged from a tiny, winding side street, only a few footsteps from his office.

"I was not aware of this shortcut," the King said, shooing off someone who was trying very hard to hand Raegan a flier advertising a furniture store.

"You're welcome," she replied as they approached his office. It seemed more ordinary now—just a pretty building in a row of pretty buildings. The black door no longer seemed to yawn wide like an invitation. It was just a door. Strange things, she supposed, would become ordinary to her the farther she waded into the depths of this world behind the world.

The King pushed the door open. Raegan noticed he used no keys, but she had a feeling the entrance would be locked for anyone else who tried to enter. She focused, bracing herself for that infinite darkness that had greeted her the first time. But as she crossed the threshold, Raegan found only a small vestibule, attractively clad in vintage black-and-white honeycomb tile and a muted dark floral wallpaper.

"Where did all those terrifying, endless shadows go?" she inquired as the King closed the door behind them.

He moved past her, sliding out of his suit jacket, looking at her inquisitively, like he did not understand.

"You know," Raegan continued, making a swirling motion with her hands. "It was pretty dark and spooky the first time I walked in here."

"Yes," the King replied, hanging his suit jacket on a coat rack. "The first time, you were uninvited."

Raegan waited for more information, but it was clear the King considered his response a full explanation because he turned on his heel and walked down the short hallway. Though she certainly wanted to understand the breadth of his power, that wasn't the question she was interested in pressing him on at this exact moment, so she followed him mutely into his office.

It was the same as it had been earlier, though Raegan thought perhaps the stack of books on the table had changed, and there was an envelope with a dark green wax seal placed upon the topmost book. The King flipped a switch on the wall as he walked in, lighting an antique lamp that would've been at home in some dark-academia-wet-dream library.

Raegan wavered at the threshold as the King plucked the letter from the table, turning his back on her and stalking to his desk at the other end of the room. Feeling safer without his eyes on her, she took a deep, shaking inhale, remembering that she was here to find out if her father was alive or dead or something else entirely. Permitting herself a moment of weakness, Raegan closed her eyes on the exhale. She breathed in again, noticing the scent of the space: warm and spicy, orange flower and vanilla and clove.

Feeling a hair more settled, she opened her eyes to find the King pulling a wicked-looking dagger from his desk. Her heart immediately leapt into her throat, hands clammy, fear shooting stakes into her chest. But then he sliced into the green-wax-sealed envelope, and she realized the dagger was only an unnecessarily terrifying letter opener. Or the King simply used a dagger as a letter opener, which seemed both possible and also on-brand.

As she also realized he was going to make her wait while he read the letter, Raegan coaxed her heart rate into a more normal pace. The task was made more difficult by the way she had to fight to look at anything but the King's broad shoulders and his ass, now very much exposed with the removal of his suit jacket.

With his back still to her, eyes on the contents of the letter, the King said, "Stop looking upon me like that."

Raegan's face burned with a blaze of heat, and her mind went white with panic. "Like *what?*" she scoffed unconvincingly.

The King turned to face her, folding the letter with slow movements and placing it back on the desk. "Like you are . . . imagining," he said, sounding out each word as his eyes met hers. No amusement simmered on his expression as it had on other occasions, but Raegan noticed that the skin around his eyes had crinkled just a bit, and she wondered what that might mean.

"Presumptuous," she replied, voice thick with condescension, having recovered herself. She crossed her arms and arched a brow at him, the very picture of scorn.

One stride carried the King to the front of his desk, where he also folded his arms, leaning back against the antique piece of furniture. He crossed one long leg over the other and cocked his head at her. "Are you ill again?" he asked in a tone so perfectly innocent Raegan had trouble believing it was leaving his lips. "Your face is quite red."

"Would you like to continue wasting your precious time flirting with me, or do you want to fulfill your half of the deal and get this over with?" she inquired archly, taking a step toward him.

For a moment, the weight of the King's full attention fell onto Raegan's shoulders like a heavy silk cloak. He considered her, his lips slightly parted, apparently feeling no shame in running his gaze down her frame and then back up to meet her eyes. Her heart beat wildly, and anticipation knitted itself thickly in her chest. The longer he looked at her in that way, the farther her pulse slipped down her body—from her breast to her ribs and then her stomach and then lower, lower, lower.

"Of course," the King replied, pushing off the desk and moving toward a filing cabinet against the wall. All the heat fizzled out of the room, leaving Raegan with a physical chill. She pulled her leather jacket tighter around her body and tried to get her thoughts marching straight again. She was here for her *father*, for fuck's sake. She had a chance to dispel the oldest thing that haunted her late at night. And more than that: a quest unfolded itself before her, rich as ruby and sweet as sin.

Raegan forced herself to look around the King's office; collecting facts and context always made her brain kick into gear. There was so much she hadn't seen the first time—whether that was due to her heightened state of fear and anxiety, or some kind of Fey fuckery, she wasn't sure. A door—slim, iron-latched—stood behind his desk. On the wall diagonal from her hung two swords, a shield, and an enormous battle ax. Raegan didn't know shit about antique weaponry, but she had a feeling all four were very, very old. In the corner, a large fern draped itself elegantly over the edges of its planter, lusher than it had any right to be.

"Antiques dealer, huh?" she asked, incapable of not poking and prodding. "Weird occupation for an ancient king of unimaginable power."

She felt his eyes on her for a heartbeat, but by the time she looked over, his gaze was trained on whatever he was looking through in the cabinet.

"I would have thought it obvious this is what your people call a front," the King replied, gesturing with one elegant hand to the space. "It is harder to slip through unseen these days. A more plausible costume helps."

He had a way of speaking as though he would rather be swallowing broken glass than having a conversation with her, which Raegan secretly admired. In retaliation, she said nothing, pulling her phone from her pocket as if he could not be more boring. Two hours ago, Henry had texted her to ask if she was doing okay. And then, more in character, his text from forty minutes ago wanted an update on any background research she had unearthed.

Raegan ignored it, switching apps to check her email, finding ordinary newsroom chatter, including some edits back from Henry on a long-form piece. She stared at the email with what she supposed could best be called disbelief. Just a few hours ago, there was almost nothing Raegan cared about more than her work. Now she wasn't even interested enough to open up Henry's email. She slipped her phone back into her pocket and stared at the scuffed toes of her boots, telling herself that three deep breaths would be helpful right about now.

The sound of a door creaking open rang out in the space, and Raegan jumped, looking up in panic. But it was just the King, pushing open that mysterious door behind his desk.

He wavered on the threshold, gaze locked on her. "Ordinally, I would simply request that you wait here," the King began, his eyes narrowing. "But I imagine you would be incapable of stopping yourself from rifling through my correspondence and belongings."

"That is incredibly rude," Raegan replied, offended, crossing her arms, "and entirely correct."

"I thought as much," he said, leaning against the doorframe. "And so I will ask that you follow me."

Raegan reminded herself that just beyond the window at her back lay the world she knew, where her colleagues were filing stories and yelling at politicians on the phone. Where the 48 bus was almost certainly late. Where Rich sat on his bench and Aleksey, the Polish guy who ran her favorite food truck, knew her breakfast order: bacon, egg, and cheese on a toasted everything bagel.

All she had to do was choose. "You want me to follow you where?" Raegan asked, her heartbeat increasing.

"Into my archive," the King replied, gesturing to the shadow-spun, cavernous space behind him.

"Right," she said, thoughts of the mundane slipping away as she moved toward the door and the King, albeit slowly. "Is this some kind of a trick?"

He looked at her long and hard; she could read nothing in his expression.

"I imagine I would not tell you if it were," he finally answered.

"Reassuring," Raegan replied, coming to a halt on the other side of the desk, still a good pace or two from the King and the door.

"Must I again remind you that I do not have all day?" he inquired, one brow arching.

She shot him a look full of long-suffering irritation, once again wishing to pummel his impossibly beautiful, terrifyingly feral face. "After you," Raegan said, gesturing for the King to lead the way.

The tall, dark-haired creature in the black suit nodded, turned, and then disappeared through the doorway.

Chapter Twenty-Two

Raegan wavered. The space beyond the door seemed impossibly dark, blanketed in shadows too thick for daytime. She recalled how the darkness had coiled at the King's call and wondered if the gloom eagerly awaited her footfall, poised to strangle and suffocate. Her agreement with the King had hardly been ironclad, and she knew it. But it should hold.

Still, it felt like placing all of her hopes on a silken thread balanced high above an abyss. She paced in front of the doorway, wishing to god that she had at least tucked a little iron in her pockets before she'd left her apartment earlier that morning. But now here she was, trapped in an enclosed space with a deadly creature, utterly defenseless.

"Overhill." Her surname echoed through the darkness as if spoken at the opposite end of a long, tiled corridor. The voice was unmistakably the King's—she would know that voice anywhere, like heather on the hill and dusk over the lake. For a moment, something about his voice saying her name stirred a memory in the very back of her mind, like the fragment of a dream, but it withered nearly as soon as it had bloomed.

Forcing herself to stay in the moment, in her body, Raegan took a deep breath and walked over the threshold. To her relief, it was not nearly as terrifying or deadly as she had imagined—more like walking through a bit of mist. Only a few steps carried her to the other side, where the King awaited her.

It was the space and not the Fey king that claimed Raegan's attention. Though she hadn't exactly had enough time to formulate what she might've expected out of something the King called his archive, she supposed this wasn't far off. The ceiling was high and vaulted, dark-stained wooden beams arching across the space. Flickering sconces studded the walls in even increments, casting shifting shadows over the stone-clad floor.

A few paces from her, two leather chairs with high, curved backs sat poised on either side of a reading table, the area marked out by a well-worn antique rug. Just beyond the seating area, a long, gleaming work-table stretched across the room. And beyond that stood endless rows of cabinets and storage; Raegan suspected everything was meticulously tagged and arranged. The space smelled of something soft and lemony floating above a base of the pleasing, musty scent of old books, powdery and almost sweet in her nose.

"This is magnificent," she breathed, turning on her heel in a full circle to take it all in. "Are there books here, too?"

"We are here for one item alone," the King replied, much to her disappointment. "If you would follow me. Stay close."

He began to walk down the center aisle, and Raegan trailed close behind, her footfalls oddly muffled on the stone floor. She tried to peer down rows as they passed, wildly intrigued by what might be housed in this place. Her treasure hunt was cut short when the King slowed and then took a sharp left, having apparently found the row he was looking for.

They walked maybe ten feet into the aisle, single file, until he halted in front of a large curio cabinet. Raegan stood just off to the side, the weight of what she was here to do settling on her shoulders again. She wished with all her might that she were simply here to look at magical things and read strange books, not to answer a question that would wound her no matter the answer.

The King's voice broke the silence: low, hushed words in a language she could not identify. A ball of light appeared above them, illuminating the area they occupied. Between the brightness and the proximity,

Raegan could not stop her attention from straying to the King. Something like him should be less real under close examination. As he turned his focus toward the cabinet's lock, she took the opportunity to scrutinize him.

He was impossibly real, the porcelain skin more marked than she had noticed at first. An old scar, barely more than an indentation on the skin, bisected the outer corner of his right eye. And another just above the collar of his shirt, a faint, white line encircling his neck. Raegan shifted uncomfortably at the thought of what could've produced such a scar. She told herself to stop looking at him, but the King seemed absorbed in carefully removing something wrapped in silk cloth from the cabinet, so she figured another moment or two wouldn't hurt. As he moved to stand straight again, the object safely cradled in his hands, she caught just the barest hint of silver around his temples, a stark contrast to the rest of his raven black hair. But still—no one would ever look at the King and think he was more than forty, though thirty-five seemed a safer bet. And yet he had walked this earth longer than Raegan could even wrap her mind around.

The King turned to his right, toward the mouth of the aisle and Raegan. The overhead light disappeared, leaving only the soft, flickering warmth of the sconces. Something about the darkness of the space and the way he faced her, some precious object in his hands, his full mouth set in a determined line, was painstakingly familiar.

"We've been here before," Raegan said before she could stop herself, jarred by the prospect of such a thought.

The King met her gaze as he glowered down at her. His brows drew together, face tight with clear distaste. "No," he replied, shaking his head. "We have only just become acquainted."

"You're wrong," she protested, panic rising in her throat. "Why would you say such a thing?"

His eyes, that impossible shade of gray, held hers. His strong jaw, backlit by the warm glow of the sconces, seemed as familiar as if she had spent a thousand years tracing her fingertips along its curve. The cold, dark intensity of his expression held a casual, unhurried sort of hatred. And yet heat stirred unreasonably in her core.

"Overhill," the King intoned, steel creeping into his voice. "If you would return to the reading area, please. We have the object we require."

Whatever had possessed Raegan slipped away like a shed skin, leaving her heart pounding and her mouth dry. She pressed a palm to her forehead, surprised to notice her hand was shaking. "Right," she said, fighting a wave of dizziness. "I'm sorry. I don't—"

"No need," the King interjected. "But let us exit the stacks."

"Oh," Raegan replied with a start, realizing that she was blocking his path. Mumbling something she couldn't even process herself, despite it leaving her own mouth, she turned and marched to the end of the row and then down the main aisle without stopping to see if the King was behind her.

Raegan slowed to a halt by the reading area, and he breezed past her, placing the object on the table. Though the silk cloth still covered it, she estimated that whatever it was couldn't be much wider than a dinner plate. It stood about two hardcover books in height. Based on the way the cloth fell around the object, it seemed rounded.

"I think it would be best for you to sit," the King said, gesturing toward one of the comfortable-looking, whiskey-colored leather chairs. Raegan nodded, mute, and sank into the closest one. The King, to her surprise, lowered his tall frame into the one beside her. He kept his gaze on the object, moving to unbutton his sleeve cuffs. He began to roll up his sleeves to the elbow, revealing powerful forearms roped in coiled muscle.

Raegan set her jaw and sent a plea for temperance to the Christian god her parents had adopted when they came to this country. Not quite willing to pull her eyes away, she noticed the King's forearms were littered with scars. Many of them had faded to white, almost entirely unnoticeable except for their sheen in the flickering light, but a few stood out more clearly.

"Are you prepared to begin?" he asked, causing her to jump. She yanked her gaze away from his forearms and to his eyes, but he had already been looking at her and she knew without a doubt he had noticed.

Raegan rubbed clammy palms on her thighs. "Begin what, exactly?"

"We are going to scry for your father," the King explained. "Most scrying, even by a talented seer, is not capable of seeing into different realms or through enchantments."

He leaned forward and pulled away the silk cloth, revealing a shallow dish made of a material so black that it seemed to devour the dim light of the space.

"This is Nyx's scrying glass," he continued, folding the cloth neatly and tucking it into his pocket. "It will permit a longer view."

"Nyx?" Raegan asked, disbelief—despite everything—sneaking into her voice. "As in the goddess of the night? We're talking about *that* Nyx?"

"Yes," the King said, his tone measured, as if having a primordial goddess's personal object was an everyday occurrence. Raegan longed to ask a thousand questions about the object's provenance and the King's relationship with Nyx, but all the words died in her throat. None of it mattered. Her father was close now, her quest reaching a pivotal point.

"What do we need to do?" she asked, tone solemn, eyes darting between the bowl and the King.

He raised a few fingers, and the reading table grew in height, bringing it level with her waist. He shifted his chair slightly to face the table more directly, and she mirrored him.

"This object was spun from the fiber of the night sky," the King told her. "It is powerful, and as such, it has teeth. It will take something from you. Dreams. Sleep. Nightmares. I know not—it exacts a different toll from everyone. Do you consent?"

Raegan inhaled, her breath shaky. She had expected a price. There was always a price, but she preferred to know the cost up front. What if it took her recurring dreams? None of them were pleasant, and she didn't know why she felt she must keep them—would she not sleep easier without them? And yet she hoped feverishly that the scrying glass spun from the night sky would not take them from her.

"This is the best option?" Raegan asked, raising her eyes from the bowl to meet the King's gaze.

"Yes," he replied. "To my knowledge. I am not infallible."

Raegan nodded, gripping the arms of the chair tightly, her nails digging into the soft leather. "Okay. I consent to the glass's toll," she said. A thought crossed her mind. "Will it cost you something as well?"

"Of course," the King replied, leaning forward. "It does not play favorites. A toll is a toll."

She thought it made sense that something created by a primordial goddess would demand a price from a random mortal as readily as from the Unseelie King. She respected that.

"Please place your hands, palms up, on either side of Nyx's glass," he instructed. "I will guide you through the process. You may find it helpful to close your eyes."

Raegan moved her hands as the King instructed as soon as the words left his mouth, but closing her eyes seemed out of the question. She was alone in a cavernous place with an ancient, powerful being.

As if he knew her thoughts, the King caught her gaze. "I will not harm you," he said. "Besides, if I wanted to, I would. Your eyes being open or closed would hold little sway."

Raegan grumbled something under her breath about the King's bedside manner that he certainly heard but chose to ignore. Then he dimmed the sconces with another slight movement of his hand. Her mouth went dry, and she tried to focus on centering herself. She closed her eyes. One breath in, the vanilla-y smell of old books thick in her nose. Exhale. Another breath, this time the woodsmoke and black pepper and rain that clung to the King suddenly in her senses. Exhale. One more inhale, and somehow, the smell of her father's wool sweaters.

When she opened her eyes, two candles—beeswax tapers, slender and non-uniform—floated on either side of the scrying glass. The warm, dancing light across the King's face hit some part of Raegan's mind hard, again that intense déjà vu feeling.

"May we begin?" he asked, his voice low, tinted with reverence like a stained-glass window.

"Yes," she said, nodding, her blood thrumming in her veins.

The King wasted no time—the second the "yes" left Raegan's lips, he began to speak in a language that made her marrow thrum. A few seconds in, she could tell it was an incantation. It could be nothing else, not with the rhythm of it, like a drum beating over and over again, circling back around to devour its own tail. The language did not feel completely alien; it was almost like she had studied it once, long ago.

The King stopped speaking, and then he reached out and tapped the center of the glass, like the motion he had done earlier to open the portico. Suddenly, he looked taxed—the strong line of his shoulders slumped, his perfect posture gone, hands moving to grip the sides of the table. She wondered what power it took to say that incantation, to pluck magic from this half of the world that had none.

"Picture your father," the King said, his breathing a bit too heavy for someone sitting still. "His face, his clothes, the sound of his voice, the way he walked, the color of his eyes, the smell of his soap. Every memory you have. Allow the glass to see."

Raegan nodded, letting out a long exhale and, despite her better judgment, closing her eyes. She recalled everything she could: the stories he would tell, his favorite green cardigan, his round tortoise-shell glasses, his hair—even redder than hers—and the sound of his voice, accent lessened by his years in the States. She remembered how he'd taught her to sew a button back on, and when they'd found a hagstone in the nearby park's creek, and how they'd look at his wedding photos together. She remembered that he'd taught her to spill salt or seeds in front of the door and to always carry iron. She remembered the scent of his cologne: oakmoss and cedar and hay.

Raegan was not sure if it was simply the situation or if the scrying glass was influencing her in some way, but she felt a few hot tears slide down her face. A cry was building at the back of her throat—all the old anguish, the not-knowing, the fear of *never* knowing, the grief with no coffin to bury, the mourning with no wake—but she pushed it back, holding herself steady.

She opened her eyes, the world blurred and watery. She nodded at the King, and he reached forward, lightly placing his fingertips on the outside of her wrists and turning her hands over to cup either side of the scrying glass. As seemed to always be the case, his touch elicited a wave of emotion in her deepest recesses, but she swallowed it down, sharply focused on the task at hand.

"Do you permit me to see with you?" the King asked, reverence still clinging to his tone. "I do not wish to intrude, but the glass knows me well and I can guide its gaze."

Raegan balked. She knew he was asking, and there was no pressure in his voice or his body language, but she had expected to be the only one to see whatever the glass held. But she had also never scried before, and it seemed foolish to turn down the assistance of something like the King.

"Alright," she agreed, her voice shaky, trembling around the edges.

"I will need to lay my hands over yours," he told her. "If you permit it."

Raegan realized she would have to keep whatever the King stirred in her at bay, but she thought she could handle it. She supposed any being of the King's power likely summoned such a reaction when touching a mere mortal.

She set her jaw. "Yes. I permit it."

The King inclined his head and reached out with his powerful hands. For a moment, just when his palms were almost touching the back of her hands, she could've sworn he hesitated or steeled himself or something—which she furiously tried to file away for later questioning. But then the King's hands—cool, heavy, calloused—were on hers, and her mind tilted and keened.

Her father. His favorite cardigan and the way he'd perch his glasses on his nose and the sound of his voice, warm and lilting. Her father and wherever he had gone, leaving this empty place in Raegan's chest that could not be filled with anything, no matter how hard she tried.

"Look into the glass," the King instructed, his voice seeming to surround her from all angles. "Look and see."

Raegan shifted forward, her hands still gripping the sides of the glass, and leaned over the reflective black surface. She was surprised when the King did the same, the crowns of their heads almost touching. For a heartbeat, both of their reflections appeared in the dark glass, until the King spoke another word that made Raegan's bones hum. The surface shifted, a hundred shadows twisting like limbs.

And then, there in the devouring black of Nyx's scrying bowl, was her father.

The view was framed on either side by gray metal, and it took Raegan a few beats to realize she was looking at her father through a window. He seemed to be seated next to it. Salt tinged his deep red hair. His face, more lined than she recalled, seemed relaxed, at ease, as if he were simply gazing out a window at a lovely view.

Anger and hurt boiled in Raegan's stomach, but then her thoughts latched on to something peculiar—her father was wearing the exact same clothing he had on when he'd disappeared. It could be a coincidence, but it was odd to see the same tweed blazer over the cream sweater, the dark green pocket square tucked against the brown fabric. Raegan tried to push closer, to look for more answers.

The moment she strained, leaning closer to the glass, a split second of unreasonable foreboding bloomed in Raegan's mind. Then, a sensation like being slammed into a brick wall, and next, nothing at all.

Chapter Twenty-Three

Raegan bolted upright. Her head rewarded her for it with a sharp ache and pinpricks swarming her vision. She ripped the blanket off and pushed herself painfully to her feet. Black spots crawled across her eyes, a thousand flies, and she swayed, her balance slipping away.

Two large hands caught her by the waist. "I recommend you lie back down," said a cool, dark voice from just behind her.

"Fuck your recommendation," Raegan spat at the King. "What happened?"

"Sit down," he replied, venom creeping into his tone, "and I will enlighten you."

Raegan ground her teeth, annoyed to have met someone apparently resistant to her communication style, which seemed to work on almost everyone else, even if they didn't enjoy it. She tried to think for a moment, her mind still woozy and heat rising to her face at the feeling of the King's hands on her waist. His touch had no right to be so intoxicating. Every fiber in her being yearned to lean back against his chest. God, she hated the Fey.

"Fine," she snapped, groping for the chair's arm and lowering herself onto the seat. An ottoman had been pushed up against the front of the chair, creating enough space for someone her height to recline. As her vision cleared, Raegan noticed a still-steaming cup of tea on the table where the scrying glass had been. Her gaze flicked to the crumpled woolen blanket on the floor.

"Did you tuck me in and make me tea?" she demanded incredulously, glancing up at the King, who had moved to stand in front of her. "What the fuck?"

In response, he shot her such a withering look that she actually shrank back a bit. "You collapsed on a stone floor," the King began, steepling his fingers, one brow raised. "Your shoulder hit the ground first, your head in quick succession. You did not wake for several minutes and then began to shiver uncontrollably. Considering our agreement, no, I did not leave you unconscious on the floor. Have I done something in violation of our covenant?"

With each word, the King's tone grew icier and icier until his expression turned so hard and full of hatred that Raegan averted her gaze, choosing instead to look down at her hands. Silence stretched between them.

"What happened?" she asked, raising her head to look at the King again.

"Drink," he said, pointing to the teacup.

"You said if I sat down, you would tell me," Raegan replied, slamming a fist on the chair's arm. "So fucking tell me."

Moving as quickly as a serpent's strike, the King reached across her, snatched the teacup from the table, and shoved it into her face, all without spilling a drop. "Drink," he repeated, as if dealing with a bratty child. "The tea contains herbs—expensive and difficult to obtain, mind you—that will assist your recovery."

Feeling as though she'd been hit by four large trucks consecutively and also having dealt poorly with the enormous emotional turmoil of what the scrying glass had shown her, Raegan grabbed the teacup from him and hurled it at the opposite wall. It shattered spectacularly, the hot liquid seeping into the stone.

She did not even have a moment to shakily consider the consequences of her actions before the King's hands were gripping either arm of the chair, his body lowered over hers.

"My people do not take kindly to such a repudiation of hospitality," he hissed, their faces only inches apart.

Raegan forced herself to look up and meet his gaze, finding ice-cold rage in his gray eyes. Before she could quell it, a twin flame sparked in her chest—her trauma was being freshly sliced out of her, and he was angry about *hospitality?*

"I will ask nicely one more time," Raegan snarled, leaning forward, her nose nearly brushing his. *"Give me what I want.* Tell me what happened."

The King tilted his head slightly to the side, and she no longer saw anger in his expression; instead, something dangerously close to desire slithered onto his features. One side of his impossibly beautiful mouth curved, sending a shower of sparks through her chest.

Suddenly and uncontrollably, she craved to be devoured by this creature of silken shadow and impossible power. Her heart beat like a hymn, louder and louder, some half-forgotten, broken-winged hope pulling air into its lungs for the first time in a millennium. She knew against all reason that his kiss was a key, the feel of his skin a portal, and that his body against hers would be her final absolution and her greatest sin.

And then the spell broke. The King yanked himself away from her, staggering a few steps back before his usual grace returned. Raegan dug her fingertips into the leather arms of the chair, her breath coming in unreasonably ragged gasps. When she finally dared to, she tilted her gaze up to look at him. Shock skittered through her when she noticed a wave of his hair had come out of place, falling across his forehead. The moment she saw it, the King raised an elegant hand to tame the black lock.

"Tell me what happened with the scrying," Raegan said, her voice an octave higher than it should be, "and then tell me what the fuck *that* was about."

For once, the King did not protest or try to slip out of responding to her request. Instead, he addressed her in a flat voice, not making eye contact. "Our scrying was successful," he said, slipping his hands into the pockets of his pants. "But something was capable of pushing away our gaze so violently that the action had a physical impact on us both. Even Nyx's glass will certainly gain us no further insight, and now there is something quite powerful that knows we are looking. How that intersects with your father, a mortal, is beyond me."

"Alive, though," Raegan croaked, looking down at her hands. "He's alive? That couldn't have been the past or something?"

The King considered. "Nyx's glass is difficult to fool. I am hesitant to claim anything is impossible, but I would be surprised if we did not see your father alive just now."

Elation rose in her, battling with the wooziness and weakness. Raegan moved forward to sit on the edge of the armchair. "What do we do next, then?"

The King's gaze shot to hers, and the identity he wore so convincingly had locked back into place: sly, cold, slick as a waxed bar top. "We cannot scry again," he replied, crossing his arms.

Raegan did not even attempt to resist the urge to roll her eyes. "Why are you dragging this out?" she demanded, leaning forward, her elbows on her knees. "I know the game you're playing. Okay, let me ask this a different way to satisfy your Fey fuckery: if you can't find my father, who can, and when can we see them?"

The King let out a low sound of displeasure, his eyes closing as a muscle in his jaw tensed. "I would not ask anyone but an Oracle to inspect this further," he replied.

"Great," she said, getting to her feet. Her balance pitched to the left and her eardrums howled, but she held steady. "Let's go. On our way, you can tell me about . . . the other . . . thing . . . that happened." As good as she was with language, even Raegan wasn't sure how to word it, and she was certainly not willing to admit the depth of what had transpired. Intellectually, she imagined it was another by-product of being around the Fair Folk, but the intensity of what she'd felt in her body made her want to throw sense and caution to the wind.

"You desire me," the King said, suddenly beside her, his voice like a silk scarf sliding around her neck. "Given what I am, my instinct is to use that desire to my advantage. But our covenant is quite clear."

"Men are not usually my thing, so that sounds like bullshit," Raegan said, her face red, mortified that her emotions and thoughts were apparently splattered across a canvas for all to see instead of properly bottled up and stored out of sight.

She turned to look at him, summoning as much disdain as she could. But the King met her gaze evenly, with no judgment or mocking in his eyes.

"And I am not a man," he replied.

Raegan could plainly see his words were true. She could see that the angles of his face were too sharp, the cheekbones like knives beneath the porcelain skin. Here in this impossible space that held knowledge beyond her comprehension, the King towered over her, gowned in shadow, a beast that had walked straight out of the oldest, darkest folklore. To think such a thing would feel anything but amusement at her desire seemed ridiculous now.

"No," Raegan agreed, her voice firm because she desperately needed this reminder herself. "No, you are not."

The King's face seemed to soften at her tone, though she was not foolish enough to think it was anything but an imitation of kindness. "You need not feel shame," he told her, gaze drifting to the door that led to his office. "You are neither the first nor the last mortal to feel what you do."

Raegan wanted to shoot back a comment about his arrogance, but the King's tone was clinical, no cockiness or pride laced through his voice; he was simply making a statement he knew to be true. So instead, she zipped her leather jacket closed and shoved her hands in her pockets, mirroring the King's stance.

"How do we get to the Oracle?" Raegan asked, anxiety crowding her throat. "I'd like to at least know my father's location by the end of the day. I don't exactly enjoy your company, so let's not drag this out."

Unlike nearly everyone in her life, the King refused to take the bait. Instead, he inclined his head, elegant as always, and held out his arm for her to take.

"I can walk on my own," she spat, stomping two steps toward the door before he caught her by the elbow.

"It is neither a courtesy nor chivalry," he told her, his expression dead and cold. "I must shield us from the Protectorate's attention, particularly with the blood you carry in your veins. It is less taxing to conceal you from their view if we maintain physical contact."

Raegan gritted her teeth, furious with herself as disappointment sang through her body. She should have known. Of course something like the King relied on mortals finding themselves carried away by his power, his beauty, his magic. And to think she'd considered herself above that.

She took his arm roughly, and the King led them back through his office. He slipped on his suit jacket, and then they were out the front door. They walked several blocks in silence, her teeth grinding the whole way as she refused to even spare a glance in his direction. Too many things swam and spun in Raegan's stomach for her to attempt to name them, so she focused on putting one foot in front of the other.

She needed a hot shower and at least ten minutes to cry her eyes out over the sight of her father, living and breathing all these years later, but instead, the King pulled her into an alley. A towering chain-link fence at the opposite end featured a door-shaped cut, the top section of metal twisting into a now-familiar shape.

"I feel like shit," Raegan announced, "so it would be great if you didn't let me suffer again when we go through." Even to her own ears, her voice sounded weary, weighted, torn at the edges like an old sweatshirt put through the washing machine too many times.

The King turned to her, faux-concern etching his features for a moment before he simply nodded. "You will feel no discomfort," he promised before leading her through the trash-strewn alley, a nearby dumpster contaminating the air with the stench of rot. Up above them on a fire escape, a woman was yelling at someone on the phone, her voice shattering the still air.

The King paused in front of the portico, speaking a series of words that curled around Raegan's senses, blocking out the yelling woman and the smell of rotted food and the traffic in the distance. Then, like before, he raised his hand and tapped the air, turning the space before them into a shimmering, oil-slick surface, thin as the skin on overheated milk.

He turned to look at her, one brow arching. Raegan nodded her permission, and then the King swept them into the portico, the world tumbling and twisting all around them. When they emerged from the formless in-between, she waited for the nausea to strike her, but it never came—and neither did any source of light. Whatever space they had entered yawned wide and shapeless, devouring her in its pitch blackness.

Despite herself, Raegan clutched the King's arm tighter, panic rising in her chest.

"We are safe." His voice came from just above her ear, as if he had leaned down to speak to her. "Please stay close. We will be out in the open air momentarily."

Raegan had never thought she was claustrophobic. She'd endured packed elevators and airplanes and tunnels with no issue. But here—wherever they were—the darkness was absolute and pressing, as suffocating as a thick blanket on a summer's day. Fear slunk through her. Had the King found some loophole in their deal? Was this consuming darkness to be the last sensation she felt?

"Steady," the King murmured, his voice gliding through the dark. "We are nearly there."

Raegan forced a deep breath into her lungs. The air was damp, slightly vegetal, almost as if the scent of petrichor had been bottled and left to age. The King guided her around what felt like a sharp corner, and then she noticed weak light in the distance. She thought she could make out a steep set of stairs. Questions lingered on her tongue, but she kept quiet, focusing on navigating the terrain.

The King reached the top of the stairwell first, waving his hand over the lock of a heavy metal grate. It clicked, and then he pushed the grate open, leading Raegan through before closing it behind them. She watched as the grate shimmered and then disappeared entirely, melting into ordinary parched grass, complete with the tattered remains of a plastic bag.

"Let us move with haste," the King said, beginning to walk at a pace meant for legs of his length, not hers. "There are always eyes."

He led them across a busy highway and then beneath the overpass, its cement belly humming with the sound of traffic. The neighborhood quickly shifted into something more residential, row houses lined up shoulder to shoulder, interrupted only by corner stores and bakeries and dental offices. She stayed silent, watching every alley for a portico or the river-black eyes of a kelpie peering from a sewer gate, for any sign that this place held magic she had been too blind to notice before.

When the King turned into a large shopping center—Raegan had definitely been to the Home Depot here more than once—confusion swam in her mind. They made their way across the parking lot to the end of the strip mall, where a nondescript, one-story brick building squatted on the pavement. A door stood in the middle, sealed up tightly behind safety bars. Two square windows bookended the door without ceremony or elegance. Dusty blinds obscured any view inside, except for the admittedly lush plants that dominated the windowsills. A few glass ornaments hung from the larger stalks, but Raegan didn't see anything she recognized in their sly, slinking shapes.

The King slowed, and then after one sideways glance at her, he reached for the door's handle. Somewhere behind her in the parking lot, perhaps from the window of a car or a passing boom box, Raegan heard a beautiful song soar through the air, the notes moving in a fiercely triumphant crescendo so powerful that tears pricked the back of her eyes.

And then the King opened the door.

CHAPTER TWENTY-FOUR

The feeling in Raegan's body was not dissimilar to passing through a portico, but slower—more of a gentle pull through a long space than the violent squeeze of the portal. This time, she stuck the landing, appearing on the other side with her arm still entwined with the King's, not even a little off-balance.

The surroundings that greeted her could not possibly have existed in the same shopping center as a Home Depot and the DMV. The dark blue ceiling, painted with gold leaf depictions of stars and planets, was at least thirty feet high. Creamy marble floors stretched across the space, covered in a few places with plush rugs in cool jewel tones. Flowering plants filled every corner and crevice, fairy lights twinkling between their stems. The space seemed to be lit entirely by the chandeliers that hung from the ceiling, appearing to be nothing more than shallow, engraved gold bowls emanating a soft glow. The air carried the scent of thunderstorms and cold vanilla and Italian lilac—chilly and fresh and floral.

Raegan pulled her attention away from the grandeur of the setting when she felt the King slip his arm out of hers. She turned toward him to see he was already walking a few paces to a long, gleaming marble counter that ran along the left side of the room. A stunning mosaic portrait of a woman devoured the upper portion of the wall behind the counter. Her skin was rendered in what looked like abalone shells, her long dark hair falling in twists, her hands holding a shallow dish and a sprig of a leafy plant.

"My liege, it is a pleasure," a voice called out, jarring Raegan from her admiration of the mural.

From a hallway she hadn't noticed, a short, nondescript man with deep olive skin and horn-rimmed glasses, dressed elegantly in a tailcoat, appeared. His attention was focused entirely on the King, and at least to Raegan, he seemed genuinely happy to see the ancient being.

"I did not realize you were coming," the man said, walking to stand beside the curve of the counter closest to them, a slow smile on his face. "Have I made an error? I ask only because the Oracle is currently absent."

"What?" Raegan asked, her tone sharper than she meant it to come out.

The man's gaze swung to her. They made eye contact, and the man tilted his head, brow furrowing. His expression stirred something in the back of Raegan's mind—something about the tailcoat and the olive skin and unremarkable features made her think they'd met before.

"Do you know when the Oracle will return, Keeper?" the King asked, leaning on the counter with one elbow. He was always so sure of himself in every room he entered, his power and authority a given, and it firmed Raegan's resolve to outsmart him. Somehow. At some point. Maybe.

"I know not, my lord," said the tailcoat man—the Keeper, Raegan supposed, growing increasingly frustrated with the lack of actual names —bowing his head to the King. "I understand she is dealing with an important situation involving the Seelie Court's accusations against one of her Sister Oracles."

"Ah," the King scoffed, shaking his head. "I imagine they will keep even Octavia occupied for some time."

"Unfortunately, you are likely correct," the Keeper replied, pulling a heavy leather journal from beneath the counter. "I have no interest in rushing you out—in fact, I have more of that whiskey you enjoyed so much last time. But if your visit is purely for business, I am happy to note that you stopped by and ensure you are one of the first the Oracle sees upon her return."

Frustration simmered in Raegan's stomach. Was all of this a game—the scrying glass and the Oracle and whatever was going to come next? Just a way of wasting the stupid mortal's time until the King figured out some way to dispatch her or until she gave up?

"I'm looking for my dad," Raegan asked, stepping up to the counter. "Can't imagine it would be hard for you people to find a random mortal."

In her peripheral vision, Raegan saw the King press his mouth into a firm line. "There are complications," he said after a beat or two. "I attempted to locate the man using Nyx's glass, and something quite powerful shattered our divination. I feel only the Oracle can safely explore this situation further."

As soon as the King started talking, the Keeper leaned forward onto the counter, listening to every word raptly, his eyes occasionally darting to Raegan. In the moments she met his dark brown gaze, she felt sure she was dealing with a creature more complex and ancient than it appeared; something in his eyes betrayed a deep, calculating intelligence. She reminded herself of whose side the Keeper was likely on, and the fact that it was certainly not hers.

"I do not wish to press a sensitive issue," the Keeper said, drawing back, crossing his arms over his tailcoat, looking between the King and Raegan, "but our Apprentice here is nearly an Anointed Oracle. Though you should share your concerns and allow her to make the final decision, I do think it is worth consulting her, if you would like."

To Raegan's surprise, the King looked toward her. The soft overhead light cast shadows onto his face, underscoring how out of place he looked in these surroundings of jeweled opulence. He belonged on the page of an ancient book, rendered in shaking charcoal. Or on a battle-field, the earth rent beneath his feet.

"Any Apprentice to an Oracle is a talented, experienced seer," the King told her, "and an Apprentice close to her anointment is nearly an Oracle's equal, though there are certain talents she cannot access. Those abilities are not ones that should impact your search, but I cannot say for sure."

"Seems like it's certainly worth a shot, right?" Raegan asked, surprised that he'd bothered to explain anything to her. Then distrust climbed up the back of her neck and she looked at the Keeper. "Is what he just said true?" she wanted to know, narrowing her eyes at the Keeper. He and the King were clearly friends, at least judging from the whiskey offer, but if the finely clothed being was Fey, she imagined he could not outright lie.

"It is a true and accurate summation," the Keeper said with a nod. "I assure you."

"Then fine," Raegan said, shrugging out of her leather jacket to signal she was settling in and following this through. "I'd like to see the Oracle's Apprentice."

The Keeper nodded, exchanging the heavy, bound parchment for a few looser sheets and an ink quill. He placed them on the marble surface, offering the quill to Raegan. "Please sign in," he told her, gesturing to the parchment. "Just your name."

As she glanced down, a line appeared. There were names above it, she could see, but they blurred when she tried to look at them directly.

"*Just* my name," Raegan scoffed, looking back up at the Keeper. "Are you kidding me? You're the goddamn Fair Folk."

To her left, she heard the King let out a soft sound that could've just been an exhale but sounded suspiciously like a laugh.

"Your caution is wise and warranted," the King said, leaning over her to pluck the pen from her hand. When his fingers brushed hers, Raegan's entire body trembled, images blooming at the back of her mind, just as blurred as the names on the paper. "But I assure you, it is simply standard practice." He slid the parchment a few inches down the marble counter, then he leaned over the thick paper and wrote on its creamy surface. Realizing this was a chance at his true name, Raegan darted a step over, eyes hungry.

Upon the parchment, in elegant, looping writing, the King had written: "Oberon, High King of the Unseelie Fey."

Oberon. She had already known that, she thought. She had maybe always known that. She'd said it herself earlier, hadn't she? Seeing his name and title written out made Raegan's vision blur, sleeping things stirring deep within her, snippets and flashes dappling her mind. She gripped the edge of the counter, the stone cool beneath her fingertips, and yanked herself back to the present through sheer force.

"Is Oberon your true name?" she demanded, attempting to take the offensive stance, but the way his name fell from her mouth felt as sacred as sacrament.

When she turned to glance at him, the King was already watching her. There was an intensity in his gaze, thick as wildfire smoke, that sent a lightning strike of desire down her chest. She might have held his gaze for an eternity had the Keeper's voice, bold and sure, not come from behind the counter.

" 'Tis the truest name he's ever had," the Keeper said, "though that is hardly a polite question for our people."

Raegan turned to give the Keeper a dirty look, but when she met his gaze, she saw humor twinkling in his brown eyes.

"It is enough to bind me to the rules of this place," the King replied, sliding the parchment back toward Raegan. His expression had returned to neutral, the smoke cleared.

"Oh, so I *am* agreeing to something," she snapped, throwing a hand up in the air with annoyance.

"By entering the sacred space of the Oracle, you agree to the laws of the Keeper," the King said. "It is certainly no more than what your kind signs away regularly for medical treatment and such."

Raegan wondered what the High King of the Unseelie Court knew about medical consent and intake forms, and also *why*, but she turned her attention toward the Keeper instead. "What are the laws that I'm agreeing to?" she asked him.

Without saying a word, the Keeper reached a hand forward and flipped the parchment. As Raegan looked at it, words appeared on the back. She sharpened her mind, ready to disentangle complicated, meandering language meant to confuse. Surprise jolted her when she saw the rules essentially boiled down to: payment was due at the time services were rendered; Oracles and Apprentices and all other seers were to be treated with the utmost respect at all times; service could be refused for any and all reasons or revoked at any time; and finally, entry and service were subject to the discretion of the Keeper.

"This feels deceptively simple," Raegan admitted, reaching for the quill. She did not want to fall for a basic con. She also did not want to miss an incredible opportunity to search for her father, available to her because she had somehow managed to force a Fey king into a deal. That didn't exactly seem like a situation that came around frequently, so

Raegan sighed and, before she could torture herself with further thoughts, put pen to paper and wrote down her name.

"Excellent," the Keeper said, his shoulders squared. "I will summon Seer Cordelia. I believe you are already acquainted with her, my liege. In the meantime, please, have a seat."

The Keeper gestured to a luxurious seating area across from the counter with a stately, wide sweep of his hand, and then he turned to disappear back down the hallway, which was too dimly lit for Raegan to see very far into its depths. She did, however, notice that from between the split of his tweed coat sprang a long, curling tail covered with downy brown fur.

Despite herself, she stared wide-eyed for a moment before following the King to the seating area. He had settled onto the far end of an emerald velvet couch. A wingback clothed in impossibly pearlescent, creamy leather sat on the other side, and nearest to Raegan was a graceful rattan chair with a tall, curved back. On closer inspection, she saw the material seemed to be living tree branches, slender as her finger, woven delicately into the desired shape.

In the end, Raegan chose the other end of the velvet sofa. The marble-topped coffee table before her was adorned with a vase of fresh flowers so spectacular that she thought a number of the species may not even exist in her world. A bowl that looked more like a giant silver shell held oranges, pomegranates, and pink apples; a note in spidery font indicated they were quite real and to please, help yourself. Glossy hardcover books were stacked high, their spines inscribed with gold gilt lettering. Her fingers itched to slide one out from the pile.

"Cordelia Iravani is a talented diviner." The King's words came from beside her, at the other end of the couch. She looked up from the pile of books to find his gaze locked on hers, something heavy in his expression. "But she may not be able to reach what you are seeking," he continued, crossing his arms and studying her.

Raegan assumed this was some sort of test of her resolve, so she met his gaze and held it, one hand reaching to pluck a pink-skinned apple from the bowl. She gave it a little toss and then took a large bite from its flesh, a satisfying crunch echoing in the air. "Then you are gonna be stuck with me until you find someone who can," Raegan told him, her voice as sweet as the fruit's flesh. She smiled at him as she chewed, then almost choked as a thought dawned on her. "*Fuck*, did I just eat faerie food?" she demanded of the King, her eyes surely as wide as the silver fruit bowl.

To her surprise and horror, the King threw his head back and laughed, the sound of it like a deep silver bell echoing through the space. Dread stirred in Raegan's stomach. She had come so far just to fall for a trick so simple.

"I apologize," the King told her, his laughter ceasing, "for laughing at you. I found your expression very amusing."

"I'm delighted to have entertained you with my terror," Raegan snapped, the apple sitting uselessly in her hand, juice running down her fingers. "But answer the fucking question."

The King's gaze slid to hers, lazy and sly as a curl of smoke. "No, Overhill," he replied, "it is not faerie food. We are not in Faerie. You are not trapped here forevermore."

He lifted his chin to look out around the space, and Raegan followed his gaze to the gleaming marble floors, the inky blue celestial ceiling, the rich jewel tone fabrics and the ever-present sound of softly falling water.

"Though I suppose it would not be such a curse, would it?" he asked, his tone brightened with a blush of levity.

"There's worse places, but I've been described as 'fiercely independent' since I was four years old, so I don't take well to confinement," Raegan replied. To show how quickly she had recovered from her admittedly very real moment of fear, she took another bite of the apple. She chewed and then—crossing one ankle over the other and leaning back against the plush velvet of the sofa—asked, "Can I call you Oberon? I'm certainly not going to run around referring to you as 'my liege' or 'your highness' or any of that shit."

For a moment, the King—the most collected, terrifying, and even-keeled person she had ever met—resembled a deer in the headlights. But like every other time Raegan had thought she'd caught something beyond his cool, deadly demeanor, it was gone in half a heartbeat.

"That is acceptable," the King said with a slight incline of his head.

Footsteps echoed on the marble, and Raegan looked past the King to see the Keeper and a tall woman clothed in sweeping robes of blue velvet approaching them.

Getting to her feet, a half-eaten apple clutched in one hand, Raegan tried to steel herself, anxiety churning in the pit of her stomach. The King stood as well, brushing out slight wrinkles in the sleeve of his suit jacket with the back of one hand.

With all her might, Raegan fought to calm the panic rising in her throat, begging every deity she knew for two things: to find her father safe and unharmed, and to squash the small, strange part of her that ached unreasonably for the King.

CHAPTER TWENTY-FIVE

Raegan had shoved as much of the panic back down into her stomach as she possibly could by the time the Keeper and the seer reached the seating area. Tucking her leather jacket under her arm, she strode toward the pair, meeting them a few feet past the couch, out in the sea of creamy marble. Shadows fell to her left, and she knew without looking that the King had come to stand beside her.

"May I humbly introduce Seer Cordelia Iravani, Apprentice of the Third Oracle," the Keeper said, sweeping into an elegant little bow.

The seer beside him was tall—not just an optical illusion from standing near the short-statured Keeper—and impossibly graceful. Her black hair fell in perfect waves that Raegan strongly suspected were perfumed with scents like jasmine and neroli and bergamot. Every visible inch of her deep bronze skin was perfect. Her dark amber eyes were expertly lined in kohl, cheekbones highlighted with a shade like molten gold. The lush blue velvet of her robes—chic and alluring on her, when they would surely look costume-ish on someone else—highlighted her white teeth and inviting smile.

Raegan bemoaned the continued attractiveness of the Fey, watching in confusion as Cordelia stepped forward, her arms open to embrace the King. Shock nearly drove Raegan a full step back, and snideness danced at her mouth as she awaited the King rebuking the seer.

But the King returned Cordelia's embrace, holding her tightly against his chest for a moment. Raegan's character assessment of the King apparently consisted of multiple blind spots, which she begrudgingly noted as she watched the interaction with rapt attention, hoping to fill the blanks.

"Cordelia," the King said warmly, continuing to lightly hold the seer by her shoulders as the Fey woman stepped back. "What a pleasure to see you."

"The feeling is mutual, my liege," Cordelia replied, smiling up at the High King of the Unseelie Court like he was an old college friend. "I don't think we've seen each other since you first arrived in this city, have we? Are you well?"

"I have been better," the King replied, releasing the seer. "But I suppose it comes with the territory."

"Heavy is the head that wears the crown," Cordelia replied, a hint of sarcasm creeping into her tone. Raegan delightedly realized the seer was mocking the King.

"No court, no crown," he replied, one ink-black eyebrow arching. "I am king in name only, and we both know that."

Cordelia swatted at the King's bicep, a devilish grin spreading across her face. "Well, you maintain my fealty," she said, ducking into a mock curtsey. "For what it's worth."

"More than an entire legion," the King answered, confusing Raegan to her core when he winked.

Were they flirting? Were they close friends? Was this some sort of weird Fey social dance? Had Raegan read him completely wrong—an unheard-of occurrence? She stood mute, rooted to the marble floor, wondering how this darkly charming, gregarious person had managed to snatch the King's body without anyone noticing.

And wondering why she felt *jealousy*, of all things.

"Hardly. But I appreciate the confidence," Cordelia replied, her gaze trailing to Raegan for the first time. "And who do we have here?"

"This is Raegan Overhill," the King said. "We are hoping you might be able to locate her father, though there are some complications."

"Yes," Cordelia said, nodding, clasping her hands together. "The Keeper briefed me. Why don't we head to a more private area, and you can fill me in on how you got mixed up with a mortal looking for her father."

With that, the seer turned on her heel and strode toward a tall, arched doorway at the back of the cavernous room. Raegan made a face at Cordelia's back but began to follow her anyway—begrudgingly, of course. She turned in surprise when she felt the King gently brush her shoulder as he kept pace beside her.

"There is little need for such condescension, Cordelia," the King said, his tone somehow both charming and deadly at once. "You know I have lived much of my life beside humans."

Cordelia turned to look at him, walking backwards in her high heels, which Raegan admittedly found impressive. "Maybe that's why you're so fucked up," the seer suggested wryly, sliding her hands into the folds of her velvet kaftan. Her amber gaze slid to Raegan. "No offense."

Raegan decided to play nice, telling herself that it had everything to do with finding her father and nothing to do with how gorgeous Cordelia was. "None taken," she replied. "Humans *are* very fucked up. Granted, you lot don't seem much better, but I'll take responsibility where it's due."

"You're funny," Cordelia said, though she wrinkled her nose as if she had smelled something bad. She turned back around on her heel, crossing beneath the large archway. "Follow me to the right, please."

Raegan trailed the seer, noticing that beyond the archway, plush rugs ran down the middle of the marble floors, devouring the sound of their footfalls. A long, dim hallway stretched out before them, lit by flickering torches. The ceiling was the same as within the parlor, but the blue was inkier, as if the sun were lower in the sky. The gold leaf constellations had taken on a pearly hue.

Both sides of the hallway were lined with smaller archways, their openings obscured by sumptuous velvet curtains. Raegan stifled the burning desire to pull some of them back, to see how this place worked and what was going on beneath the surface. Instead, she continued walking, concerned about the way she felt reassured by the King's dark, silent presence at her side. She tossed the core of her apple into a tall silver container that she belatedly realized may, in fact, not be a trash can at all.

Cordelia reached an archway that looked no different from the rest and paused, pulling the curtain aside and stepping within; it seemed clear that they were to follow. Raegan wavered at the threshold.

"She's a peach," Raegan said in a low tone to the King once Cordelia had melted into the darkness. "Hopefully she can at least find my father."

"My apologies," the King replied, surprising her. "She is not overly fond of your kind. She will get her barbs in—she is young—and then she will be professional and complete the tasks we require of her."

"Speaking of that," Raegan said, aware that they were likely lingering in the hallway for too long. "What will this cost? Another thing like the scrying glass?"

The King shook his head. "It is a monetary cost," he replied. "I will handle it."

Raegan looked at him in disbelief, her voice rising. "And then what will I owe *you*? Do you think I'm an idiot?"

The King let out an exasperated sigh, looking at her with exhaustion. "Do you happen to have twelve Feyrish silver coins on you?" he asked, one brow arched.

Raegan made a frustrated noise, tossing one hand in the air. "You know the answer to that."

"Then allow me to take care of it," he replied, reaching forward to pull the velvet fabric back. "I consider it part of our deal."

She crossed her arms, fixing him with her best "don't bullshit me" stare, but likely on account of being more than a thousand years old, he just stared back at her, utterly unfazed.

"Fine," Raegan snapped, ducking past the section of curtain the King held open for her. Gloom greeted her on the other side, punctuated by several small candle flames. She paused, waiting for her eyes to adjust, and when they did, Raegan could hardly absorb all of the magic within the space.

The ceiling was made of the familiar velvet fabric, but it was tented and pointed like the top of a circus tent. The fabric hung down in rippling waves, flashing different colors in the warm candlelight. At the far end, Cordelia sat at a round table that could have been made entirely from moonstone—it was near-translucent, rich with a pearly shimmer, a deep blue dancing in its depths. The air within the space was cool and refreshing. Beautifully illustrated charts covered the walls—moon phases and astrological constellations and maps and things that Raegan had never seen before in her life, including a diagram of a nautilus shell marked with instructions to be followed at each turn of its labyrinthine insides.

Most importantly, the room *hummed*. The space seemed to throb with the ebb and flow of something she strongly suspected was magic. Being on this side of the curtain felt like what Raegan imagined pure oxygen might feel like in her lungs.

"How is this possible?" she asked, turning to the King as she tried to reconcile what she saw before her with the information she had gleaned. "Don't the Gates completely bar magic from our side of the world? And wouldn't the Protectorate be able to smell all this like blood in the water?"

The King did not look at her, but she saw the corner of his mouth curve up into something dangerous. "It is advantageous," he said slowly, "for some to believe those things. The truth, as it usually does, lies somewhere in between."

Raegan opened her mouth to ask more, but then Cordelia's voice interrupted them. "Come," she called. "Sit. Tell me how I can be of assistance."

The seer looked impossibly powerful and beautiful seated on the other side of the moonstone table, her palms placed flat on its surface, her form backlit. When she tossed some of her dark, heavy hair over her shoulder, exposing the skin of her neck and her collarbone, Raegan was admittedly distracted.

"I need to find my father," she managed to say, coming to stand at the edge of the table, ignoring the two soft-looking chairs. "Oberon helped me scry for him in Nyx's scrying glass, but something very powerful pushed us out. We were hoping you could help."

Cordelia looked from Raegan to the King, who had come to stand at Raegan's side, in disbelief. "The Unseelie King let you use Nyx's glass?" the seer demanded, her eyes widening. "And permits you to address him so informally?"

The King lowered himself into one of the chairs with a heavy, near-theatrical sigh. "Yes, Cordelia," he replied, his tone becoming arch. "I have never been one for formalities. Additionally, you may be familiar with deals. Overhill had something I wanted, so I bartered for it."

"You must have wanted it quite badly," Cordelia said, her gaze falling on Raegan, as if to decipher what the King desired from such a small, unremarkable mortal. In her peripheral vision, Raegan saw him hold up a hand.

"I did not come here to discuss my dealmaking with you, seer," he said, expression gone cold. "I came to see if you could assist with finding the location of a mortal."

For a long moment, Cordelia looked between Raegan and the King as if there was some invisible thread between them that could explain the situation at hand. Suspicion still on her face, the seer shrugged and reached for a silver box on the bookshelf behind her. She laid it carefully on the table, removing the lid gently. Raegan watched, her heart hammering in her throat. Cordelia moved with a reverence that made her hair stand on end. She was close. She had to be. She wondered if her father knew she was coming.

Cordelia slipped a sheet of paper—no, not paper, too translucent— from the box and placed it in front of Raegan. She lowered her gaze to examine it, but it gave away no secrets, looking for all the world to be just a sheet of vellum, but with more flash and shimmer.

Then Cordelia placed a quill and ink in front of Raegan. The feather was silver, almost metallic in appearance, and the little pot of ink was a similar shade of pearlescent gray. She raised her gaze, looking at the seer for instruction.

"I will do a simple scrying first to get a feel for the complexity of this situation," Cordelia said, calm and collected. "Based on your concerns and earlier trouble, I want to take this slow. Raegan, if you would please, write down your father's full name and date of birth. As you do so, try to visualize him—actual memories help as opposed to trying to conjure a stagnant image. Anything you can recall clearly works. It need not be significant."

Raegan sank into the chair, feeling like she was underwater, her movements dulled and slowed by the weight of an entire ocean. But she forced herself to nod and do as Cordelia instructed. She reached for the quill and picked it up, finding it to be much lighter than she'd expected. With her other hand, Raegan slid the pot of ink closer and dipped the quill's nub into it, automatically scraping the excess ink off on the side of the jar, though she could not recall having ever used a quill before.

Raegan hesitated only for a moment, and then she began to write her father's name and birthdate, her mind running thick—for the second time that day—with memories. She moved deliberately, breaking each letter down into the lines and half-circles that formed his name, driving the quill deep into the strange vellum paper, as if doing so could make the material absorb more of her father. By the time she finished, tears pushed hotly at the back of her throat. Raegan put the quill down and slid the paper toward Cordelia, bringing the back of her left hand to her eyes and squeezing them shut. She gritted her teeth and told herself not to cry, not here, not now.

Letting out a shaky exhale, she opened her eyes. Her vision still a bit blurry, she watched as Cordelia folded the paper with her father's name upon it. The seer's elegant hands moved with lithe grace, creasing the paper again and again, as if she planned to make origami from it. When Cordelia had created a small, star-like shape from the vellum, the seer opened her mouth, placed the paper on her tongue and promptly swallowed it whole.

Raegan's gaze darted to the King, but his expression held no reaction —not even that slight furrowing of the brows, which she had gotten fairly good at recognizing—so she assumed this was standard practice. Then Cordelia closed her eyes and spoke. The words were in no language Raegan knew, yet they made her bones tremble all the same. Something—magic, power, gods, demons, perhaps all four—fell over the space, whisper-soft, like the feathered wings of some ancient creature.

Next, Cordelia opened her eyes and pushed the silver box to the side. Placing both of her hands flat on the table's surface, thumb-to-thumb, the seer swept her fingers across the glimmering stone. Lines lit up across the table—a map, Raegan thought, though not like any map she had ever seen before.

She bit down hard on the inside of her cheek, blood blooming in her mouth. Her fingers gripped the sides of her chair's seat, nails slicing into the fabric. Her stomach lurched, queasy with anticipation.

Cordelia lifted one hand high above the table's surface and the glittering lines transposed upon it. She loosened her fingers slightly, and a rounded, triangle-shaped stone tumbled from her grasp, stopping sharply just a few inches above the table. The seer spoke another word that made Raegan's teeth vibrate and then leaned forward to breathe on the stone, the way one might to create condensation on a cold window.

When Cordelia sat back in her chair, the stone began to sway back and forth. Raegan watched it, realizing this pendulum had no chain and no feasible, logical way to be moving the way it was.

The pendulum picked up speed, its side-to-side sashay transforming into slow, looping ellipses across the table and its maze of golden lines. Raegan glanced at Cordelia to see if anything could be deciphered about the progress so far, but the seer's eyes were closed. Her face was almost entirely relaxed, except for the erratic way her eyes moved beneath her lids, like moths swarming a sole light source on a dark night.

The moment stretched long and thin, Raegan's heart hammering with anticipation. Just as she was about to look at the King and search for any sign of concern, Cordelia's eyes snapped open. Her irises had turned pale silver, flat as two coins laid over her lids. The seer did not appear to be breathing, though the power Raegan had felt upon entering thrummed louder and louder.

Cordelia leaned forward, palms flat on the table's surface, clear of the glittering lines. Then she straightened, furrowed her brow, and spoke one single, sharp word that felt like a thunderclap.

The pendulum tumbled from the air, clattering uselessly onto the moonstone surface, rolling to the left before lolling into a circle. The seer gasped, pulling her hands away from the table, the silver gone from her eyes as she watched the pendulum slow to a halt just beyond the reach of the golden lines.

For a long moment, no one moved or spoke. Raegan was fairly sure she had stopped breathing, her entire world consisting of the unmoving pendulum and the seer's blatant mixture of surprise and horror.

"That," the King said, breaking the silence, his words like a low-lying storm cloud, "is impossible."

Chapter Twenty-Six

"Yes," Cordelia said, her gaze locked on the pendulum stone. "Even if his location were cloaked or he were in a pocket realm or between planes, the scrying would still show *something*. This . . . Whatever happened, my sight was completely rejected."

Beside her, the King sighed heavily, dragging one hand through his hair in the most human-like gesture Raegan had seen him make.

Cordelia raised her eyes for the first time, looking at the King. "I will attempt a few less obtrusive means," she said, her eyebrows drawn together. "But I hope you understand that you are dealing with something . . ."

"Primordial," the King finished for her with a sharp nod of his head. "Yes."

"What the fuck does that mean?" Raegan demanded, twisting in her chair to address the King.

He considered her, a weariness creasing his expression. "It means, as we suspected earlier, that something powerful and likely very, very old is interested in obscuring the location of your father. Or perhaps more realistically, your father is within the realm of a very powerful, very old thing that does not wish to be found," he told her.

"Hold on," Raegan said, just barely stopping herself from leaping out of her chair. "Does that mean he's definitely alive? Like, for sure?"

She swung to face Cordelia, her teeth dug into her tongue, watching the seer closely.

The seer tilted her head slightly to the side, eyes narrowed, in a vaguely animalistic way that mirrored what Raegan had seen the King do more than once. "You mean you are not sure if the focus of these efforts is even alive?" Cordelia asked, her tone short, eyes darting between the King and Raegan.

"Well, no," Raegan said, the words stretched. "I thought you knew that. I mean, we saw him, but it was only for a moment."

"Seeing an image of someone in a scrying glass does not always mean they are alive," Cordelia said, her words barbed and intended solely for the King.

"I may have forgotten that part," the King said, almost apologetically but not quite.

"For Olwyn's sake," Cordelia spat, rolling her eyes. "We should have started there."

Raegan almost opened her mouth to say the words that clung to the back of her throat, but she pressed her lips together instead. She knew deeply, truly, and absolutely that her father was alive. She had always known and had never doubted, no matter how many years went by, no matter the funeral with the empty casket, or the way her mother's endless, gnawing anger finally left her one autumn and she put Cormac's photo on the ancestor shelf, his features lit up by the flicker of the candles. Even Maelona's insistence hadn't swayed her because Raegan had never questioned whether her father lived or not. She'd only ever asked herself why he had gone and to where and if he might ever come back.

"We're going to start from the top," Cordelia announced, pushing a stray lock of molasses-thick hair behind her ear. "This is going to take a while, and I need you to do exactly as I say."

Despite herself, Raegan glanced toward the King for a heartbeat, long enough for him to meet her eyes and give a small nod. Unreasonably calmed by his response, she turned her gaze back toward Cordelia. "Okay," Raegan said, folding her hands on her lap. "Just tell me what to do."

Taking charge did not appear to be an issue for Cordelia. Over the course of the next few hours, the seer valiantly attempted to determine whether Cormac was alive. She did some weird thing with two eggs—one black as night with iridescent speckles, the other the color of an oil spill—that the King seemed very delighted to be witnessing. She cast lots. She heated wax in an ornate tin cup and poured it into a bowl of cold water, studying the shapes the hot wax formed. She cleaved a silky black chicken in half upon a stone altar and studied its entrails for forty minutes.

Finally, Cordelia insisted upon scrying for Cormac in her own glass, despite both Raegan and the King's protests. The attempt ended in a broken eight-hundred-year-old heirloom divining glass, two black eyes for Cordelia, and a wicked migraine for Raegan.

"Cordelia," the King said, beginning to sound strained for the first time all afternoon. "I think it is best we wait for the Oracle. No more of this."

The seer made a vague, noncommittal sound from the chaise lounge where she was sprawled out, a cold compress laid across her eyes.

"He's probably alive," Cordelia mumbled a few moments later, hoarse and exhausted. "That's all I can give you. The Oracle will know more."

The seer pulled herself into a seated position with a low groan, discarding the compress. The back of her hair was mussed from being pressed against the arm of the chaise. A bit of kohl had migrated to her temple, and though her black eyes had decreased in overall darkness and puffiness, the seer still looked as though she had been through the wringer. "Allow me to walk you out," she said, swinging her legs over the edge of the chaise. "I'm alright, I promise."

"Cordelia," the King said, his low, rich voice firm. "You look the very opposite of alright."

"Fuck you, my High King," Cordelia replied, though there was no venom in it. "I look incredible as always."

The King laughed, clear as a silver bell, the sound of it uncoiling a spool of longing deep in Raegan's core. She ignored it, getting to her feet, unsteady with exhaustion. The King mirrored her, extending a hand to help Cordelia off the couch. Instead of daintily taking it and getting to her feet all on her own as Raegan expected, the seer grappled the King's wrist with both hands and hauled herself off the chaise. Raegan watched the King's tendons flex in his forearm—he had removed his jacket and rolled his sleeves up at some point—and averted her hungry gaze.

"Well, thank you for the entertaining afternoon," Cordelia said, her smile thin. "I suppose it's good to be humbled now and again."

"Thank you for your heroic efforts," the King replied, rolling his sleeves back down and buttoning them at the wrist. He took a few steps toward Raegan, leaning forward to pull his suit jacket off the back of the chair beside her.

"I'd say to call on me whenever you wish, but please don't do this to me anytime soon," Cordelia said, her voice wrung dry, shoulders defeated. Underscoring her words, she gestured for the King and Raegan to follow the Keeper, who had appeared at the mouth of the room.

Raegan fell into step beside the King, picking at the skin around her cuticles, her mind already racing. Securing an audience with the Oracle was imperative. Raegan could only hope the prophetess would not be gone for much longer.

"The Keeper will take care of everything up front," Cordelia said, her voice cutting into Raegan's thoughts. "Oberon, if you were anyone else, you'd be getting surcharged to death."

The King paused in the doorway, turning toward Cordelia. Raegan stopped beside him, her shoulder brushing his upper arm. "I am always happy to pay what is owed," he told the seer with a regal incline of his head. "Your efforts will be rewarded with more than coin."

Cordelia took a step closer and grinned; it was dazzling, all molten bronze sunshine and autumn glory. "Favors from the Unseelie Court are the best kind of payment," the seer replied. "Take care, both of you."

Then Cordelia raised her hands to touch the King and Raegan on their shoulders at the same time, a gentle goodbye between three people who had peered a bit too deeply into the void together. But the moment her fingers brushed both the King and Raegan at once, Cordelia's head snapped back as if dealt a violent blow. A low, pained wail escaped her lips, and she dropped like a stone, her legs cut out from beneath her.

Raegan reacted more to the sound than anything else. She spun and jumped to the side, her heart pounding with sudden adrenaline. Thanks to his much quicker reflexes, the King caught Cordelia by the forearm and then the waist, steadying the seer just before her knees could meet the cold marble floor. Everything else happened in slow motion, all noises dulled and softly echoing, as if someone had stuffed Raegan's ears full of cotton.

The Keeper, who had gone out into the hallway ahead of them, came rushing back in, crouching at Cordelia's side. He turned to Raegan and asked her a question, but something—more than adrenaline, more than fear, more than confusion—was building inside of her, and she just stared at him mutely. She knew on a logical level that he was speaking words, but she could not understand any of them.

The King had taken a knee beside Cordelia, holding her waist and supporting the back of her head with his other hand as she shook violently, her eyes having turned that same silver shade from before, when she'd scried for Raegan's father. Pressure continued to build inside Raegan, a sweeping, soaring feeling, like an orchestra escalating to an overture's climax. It was as if every part of her body were built of strings, crosshatched and woven together, and a god was trailing their fingers against them, playing an old, sweet song. Her bones reverberated with the swoop and shape of it, her migraine evaporating.

From behind her, somewhere in the hallway, she caught just a snippet of a melody—grand and aching, its valleys low and dark, its peaks as joyous as a hero's return. It sent shivers across her skin, this song —honeyed with Fate and heavy with Sorrow. She felt Time slip out of tune, scales sliding past her skin, a snake devouring its own tail.

It was the seer's voice that broke through the melody, her tremors having apparently abated, her eyes still that eternal, silver-slicked shade.

"Exactly who—or *what*—have you brought into The Temple of the Pythia, High King?"

Chapter Twenty-Seven

The Seer's words hung as heavy as smoke in the air, though Raegan could barely process anything with the notes of that melody still so thick in her ears. She could nearly taste it: sweet like mead, metallic like blood, damp like rain. It sounded, she realized, like Fate.

"Our business is our own," the King replied, dark and regal and terrifyingly cold. He pulled his hands from the seer without much concern for whether she could support herself, straightening to his full height. "I have shared the information necessary for the requested—"

The King's words cut off suddenly as the spun-gold song slunk in from the hallway, louder now, undeniable. Raegan watched as the rest of the statement died in the King's throat, his attention focused entirely on the gilded notes slipping through the velvet curtains.

The Keeper, still crouched beside Cordelia, was awestruck—as if he were seeing something he thought long dead, entombed a thousand miles away, never again to rise and walk among the living. "It cannot be," he murmured as he helped Cordelia to her feet.

Upon standing, the seer clasped her hands together, reverent as a sinner rising from the confessional. "It is," Cordelia whispered, her eyes glimmering with tears. "It's a Fatesong."

Chills cascaded across Raegan's body. A tide roared inside her head, moving with the same swell and swoop as the sacred melody that circled her. She saw jeweled meadows and blackened battlefields and rushing rivers and cities aflame. She tasted mead and ash and blood on her tongue, her throat aching. Fingers digging into the cuffs of her leather jacket, Raegan fought hard to stay in the moment, reminding herself of the marble floor beneath her, breathing in the creamy, aquatic scent of the space—anything to not be swept away in the rush and roar of the song. It sang to her so sweetly, and she knew she would allow it to consume her entirely.

She let out a shaking breath, the melody still wrapped thickly around her. She saw the Keeper take off his glasses and fold them in his hands, the way a gentleman might remove his hat before entering a church. Cordelia had thrown her head back, nostrils flaring, as if to let the golden thrum of the song fill her entire being.

The King, though—looking upon him nearly broke Raegan's heart in half. Somehow, the melody made the shadows hang more heavily on him, the gloom a cloak upon his shoulders. When his gaze met hers, the song swelled, and Raegan found herself looking into an ocean's worth of grief—the King's sorrow and torment so jagged and raw that she thought she could cut herself upon its sharp edges.

And then, as quickly as it had arrived, the melody slunk away like the sun slipping over the horizon at sunset. A soft silence filled the space, punctuated only by the sound of breathing—sharp, quick inhales, impossible to tell from which of the four bodies they originated.

"Oh, and what a song it is," Cordelia breathed. "I heard *Prophecy*. Grand, ancient, eternal . . . inevitable."

Anything Raegan wanted to say withered on her tongue—and there was *so* much she wished to say; it was as if everything was unfolding just how she'd planned it, but of course she had not planned anything at all, had she? So silence cloaked the space again, and how silent it all felt without that song in her ears, without its thrum filling up the empty spaces in her chest.

"I have heard it before," the King said, each word spoken like an iron stake being driven into the ground. The shadows of the space gathered dark around him, his eyes like black water. "It lies."

"My liege," Cordelia pleaded, her hands reaching out for the King before she snatched them back, as if she thought better of it. "No one has heard a Fatesong in nearly a millennium. We thought them extinct, or more likely, mere myth."

The King's expression grew darker, and he seemed tall, taller than ever, the shadows knitting themselves around him, as if he had perhaps never been flesh and bone at all. "That Fatesong," he began, his gaze trailing to Raegan for a heartbeat, "is rooted in violence and death. When its Threads are followed, when its melody is sung, it brings nothing but destruction."

His words hit Raegan like a pile of large stones. She felt the truth of it in her marrow, the seas of her mind throwing snippets of shattered bodies and slit throats and burning villages onto her shores like broken, battered driftwood.

And yet Cordelia barely hesitated when she reached out to grab Raegan's hands with her own, the seer's entire body radiating with pure, unadulterated hope. "It is *you*," she whispered to Raegan, her eyes flitting between amber and silver, mead and mist. "It sings for *you*."

Raegan let out a shaking breath. The understory had become the overstory, the way had opened, and the door yawned hungry and aching. Before any words could come to her mind—it didn't seem like an event to be trapped by language, anyway—Cordelia folded her fingers into Raegan's and pulled.

"To the Vaults," the seer said, addressing Raegan alone, though her gaze flitted to the Keeper. "There is a Prophecy to be read."

And with that, Cordelia pulled Raegan out through the velvet curtain and back into the hallway. Raegan did not resist. She knew a Fatewind when she felt one, and she would sail this tiny vessel, laden heavy with hope, for as long as it would carry her weight.

Raegan pulled closer to Cordelia, matching her pace, only for the seer to surge ahead, breaking into a run down the wide, softly lit marble hallway. For a moment, Raegan hesitated, throwing a look over her shoulder—where was the King? Instead, she found only the Keeper, standing a few paces from the archway they'd departed from.

"Cordelia!" The Keeper's voice careened through the corridor, his tone sharp.

The seer slowed her pace and turned but did not stop, her hand gripping Raegan's tighter and tighter. "Keeper," Cordelia replied, her rich voice magnificent, like the heroine of an ancient fable. "I heard it. In that Fatesong. I heard the Gates fall."

Even from this distance, Raegan could see the Keeper stop breathing, could see the way his heart leapt into his throat.

"Seer," the Keeper called, his voice lower than Raegan had heard it before, thick as honey. "Truly? You heard them fall?"

In response, Cordelia simply threw her head back and laughed, the sound of it so wild and free and endless that Raegan found herself joining in, electricity buzzing in her marrow like a thousand bees.

"Yes," the seer replied, gripping Raegan's hand, her skin hot and feverish. "The Vaults. Take me to the Vaults, Keeper."

The small man—who was not a man, who had never been a man, who could not be contained within a plain face and a tailcoat—drew closer to them, only a few of his walking steps somehow bringing him to stand right before them. "It is highly irregular," the Keeper said, though his voice betrayed something else entirely. "You are not anointed as the Oracle. And yet you have offered Fatespeak and now you dare to request access to the Vaults."

Cordelia let go of Raegan's hand and closed the distance that separated her from the Keeper, placing her hands upon the shorter being's shoulders, gazing into his eyes. "The Gates," she breathed before bringing her forehead to his and letting out a laugh that sounded like every wish ever made.

Raegan found herself transfixed by the interaction. She thought it might be like watching two prisoners of war find out someone was finally, *finally*, after all this time, coming for them.

The Keeper gently shook his head, pulling away from Cordelia, who was whispering quiet pleas, one of her hands gripping his. "A Prophecy is not a promise," he said, soft as a dove feather on the breeze. "It is the furthest thing from a promise."

"It is not a promise," Cordelia agreed. "But it is a door. And how long we have been battering ourselves against a wall. How long we have yearned for a door."

Cordelia's words let loose a sob at the back of Raegan's throat. She tried to push it down, pressing one hand to her mouth, but the cry untethered itself anyway, and tears fell softly down her face. The

Keeper watched her, as if her reaction were evidence or proof that could sway him, though she knew not which way.

"The Oracle," the Keeper began, hesitant, "would not, I believe, wish us to wait on such a revelation due to her absence. We will investigate the Prophecy this Fatesong has spoken to you, Cordelia, but nothing more until she returns."

Upon speaking the last few words, the Keeper pulled a large iron ring from somewhere on his person. From it hung too many keys to count, some of them positively ancient-looking, the others as mundane as Raegan's own apartment key. With a delighted whoop, Cordelia turned, grabbed Raegan's hand again, and then took off down the hallway, nearly pulling her shoulder out of its socket. But Raegan did not mind the pain; more so, she almost did not feel it, as if even her body knew nothing had ever mattered more than this moment, a moment scaffolded upon every insane choice and wild leap that had brought her here.

As she ran with the dark-haired seer down the velvet-lined hallway, Raegan understood that there was absolutely nothing rational about whatever was happening all around her. She couldn't even be quite sure that this was not some sort of fever dream. But was it possible to feel so alive in a dream? To taste mead and blood and hope so clearly? She did not think her body would sing like this for but a dream.

The light of the flickering sconces grew dimmer the farther she ran headlong by Cordelia's side. Her heart pounding, her lungs aching, Raegan slowed without regard for the seer's desire to sprint ahead. This was her path to walk, yes—but she had never done it alone before, had she? She threw another glance over her shoulder, searching the dim hallway for the King. They had come so far together—would he not see this through? And more importantly, could she see it through without that silent, unwavering presence at her side? She felt as though she were going into battle having just lost a limb.

Cordelia finally slowed to a brisk walk, and Raegan turned to find a door just a few strides ahead. It was not a regular sort of door. It was crafted from wood, yes, but laden with impossibly detailed ironwork. Metal stars studded the wood grain. The top of the door was arched, coming to an elegant point. A large, ornate iron keyhole was set into the door's right side.

Before she could stop herself, Raegan reached her hand out and laid her palm against the door. It felt alive—warm to the touch, softer than wood should be. She felt a heartbeat pulse beneath her fingers.

"Oooh," Cordelia cooed. "The door likes you. Of course it likes you."

Raegan turned to the seer, her mouth half-opened to ask exactly what that meant, but the Keeper was approaching, and Cordelia's attention locked on to his ring of keys. The Keeper's eyes strayed to Raegan, and then he held her gaze. Raegan hadn't taken her hand off the door.

The Keeper's movements slowed, almost like everything was underwater, as his fingertips brushed a large iron skeleton key. Age had blackened its patina. Even from where she stood, Raegan could see it contained none of the fine craftsmanship of the door, no matching arches or stars or scrolls. The key was simply a key.

Beside her, Cordelia seemed to be holding her breath as the Keeper's footfalls brought him to the door's mouth. Time moved strangely, too slow and too fast at once, like a river unsure of which way it was meant to flow. The moment the Keeper inserted the key into the door's lock, a golden melody trilled from above their heads. All three of them looked up at once, but of course all they saw was the celestial ceiling, the heavens painted upon it now a brighter silver, the rich blue background nearly black.

The Fatesong looped long and low, soft as silk, and then the Keeper pushed the door open. Pure, unadulterated darkness waited beyond the threshold—not like the King's, which felt alive with magic. It was dead nothingness, like the empty galaxies before stars blinked their eyes open.

The Keeper waited, holding the door open, his grip firm, almost as if it were an untamed thing that might decide at any time to remember its wildness and devour them all whole.

"Follow me," Cordelia said, her fingers still intertwined with Raegan's. She looked at the seer, her heart pounding, hesitation lacing itself through her euphoria for the first time. "It's safe," Cordelia added, her amber eyes imploring. "I promise. There will be light once the Vaults allow us in."

But the seer had misjudged Raegan's hesitation. She was not afraid; in fact, she had never felt calmer. But her very essence called out for him, just as it always had and likely always would. Now that she had finally found her dark and terrible king once more, she had no desire to let him go.

Besides, were the shadows not his dominion?

"Where is Oberon?" Raegan asked, her heartbeat spidery and skittering in her chest. Cordelia's expression folded in, the space between her eyebrows wrinkling—it was clear to Raegan that the seer had just now noticed the King was not with them.

The Keeper, however, did not register the King's absence as new, though he did heave a sigh at Raegan's line of questioning. "Our King," the Keeper began, leaning his shoulder against the door, looking as though he was searching for the right words, "will not hear this Fatesong out. That being the case, it is not right for him to accompany us into the Vaults. He cannot help us locate a Prophecy that he rejects."

Doubt simmered in Raegan's stomach, anxiety climbing the walls of her chest. It was not so much that she did not trust the Keeper and Cordelia. As distrusting as Raegan was by nature, she knew something much larger than herself was going on here, and trust was simply not a relevant factor. It was more that she could not imagine going into a dark place without her King.

Tears pricked her eyes, and she forced down a dry swallow to stem the emotion rising in her throat. "But he will be waiting for us?" she asked, looking between Cordelia and the Keeper, trying to keep her tone even. "When we return from the Vaults?"

The Keeper looked genuinely surprised at Raegan's question, his eyebrows shooting up. "Oh, of course," he said. "Despite his bluster, I hardly believe him capable of leaving you behind."

From beside her, Cordelia let out a little laugh, like she and the Keeper were in on something that Raegan was not. She opened her mouth to ask what the Keeper could possibly mean, but Cordelia tightened her grip on Raegan's hand, took a running step across the threshold, and dragged Raegan into the waiting darkness with her.

Chapter Twenty-Eight

Beyond the door there was nothing—a complete and utter absence of anything at all. Primordial darkness, Raegan hazarded, the black matter that made up space, just waiting to be formed by cosmic upheaval or the sweep of Fate or perhaps the hands of bored gods. It closed in on her, hungry and stifling, everything an inherent dichotomy: her living, breathing flesh, and the darkness's great, glorious nothingness.

Then there was a low, shuddering sound—almost mechanical, but too ethereal, like machinery imagined by elves—and suddenly Cordelia's face came into Raegan's view, lit by a lantern the seer held aloft.

"Here," Cordelia said, handing Raegan the lantern, which she accepted wordlessly. "The Vaults are massive, you see, so when you first enter, it takes a moment for it to know which section to spit you out into."

Raegan steadied herself, fighting for some sense of cool composure. She wrapped her fingers tightly around the ring at the top of the lantern, grateful for the way its flickering flame drove away the oppressive dark. "Which section are we in?" she asked, knowing damn well the answer wouldn't mean anything to her. But asking questions calmed her, and more knowledge was rarely a bad thing.

"I cannot believe it," the Keeper said from farther ahead, standing on the edge of the platform that floated in the darkness.

Raegan moved forward to get a better look, and her stomach dropped. The three of them appeared to be standing on a large slice of rock jutting out over a massive archival library. A spiral staircase, crafted from intricately carved wood, wound a dizzyingly long way down to the bottom.

Cordelia rushed to the edge to stand next to the Keeper, the hem of her robes a whisper against the rock. When she reached the edge, she gasped softly. "Unrequited," she murmured.

Steeling herself, Raegan raised her lantern and walked slowly to the edge, taking her time to ensure there were no other drop-off points.

"I suppose it makes sense," the Keeper was saying as Raegan came to stand beside the two Fey beings. "What else could it be but Unrequited? Any Prophecy that mentions the King has surely been pored over a thousand times."

"The Fatesong spoke of them both," Cordelia said, the lantern light casting stark shadows across her face, accentuating her strong features. She looked positively otherworldly. "It sang for her. But I am sure it spoke of them both."

Raegan attempted to digest that piece of information—it was rude, but admittedly useful, that the Fey seemed very content to talk about mortals like they weren't in the room—when Cordelia turned toward the Keeper, her lantern swinging wildly.

"The Fatesong sounded old. *Very* old," the seer said, her words heavy with implied meaning.

"He was not King yet," Raegan said without realizing she was speaking aloud, simply sliding the most logical puzzle piece into place. Cordelia's eyes flitted to her, the seer's expression approving, and the Keeper turned to her, nodding in agreement.

"That makes our task easier," the Keeper said. "Let us examine the sections containing Prophecies made in the span of time between the King's creation and his rise to the Unseelie Throne."

Cordelia nodded, letting out a shaky exhale before gathering up her robes and making for the staircase. Raegan watched her go, wanting to see the path the seer took before she risked further steps upon this rocky ledge that hung in the shadows.

To her surprise, the Keeper caught her gaze and offered his arm to her. She froze, considering, but then walked forward to accept. When Raegan slipped her arm into his, she felt a buzz of power, like a low electrical hum, but it was nothing, of course, like touching the King.

"This must all be overwhelming, I imagine," the Keeper said, his tone diplomatic, as he began to usher them forward toward the staircase. Raegan had lost track of Cordelia, who must have begun to descend the staircase already.

"For a mere mortal," she said, hoping her sarcasm translated. "It most certainly is."

As they approached the edge, Raegan gripped the Keeper's sleeve a bit harder, trying to focus on taking one step at a time. She had never been afraid of heights before, but this was something else entirely. The staircase seemed unending from her vantage point, and darkness clung to every corner. She had the impression the ceiling was very, very high—hundreds of feet or more—but the lack of defined walls made her head spin.

The Keeper began to descend the staircase slowly, halting after a few steps to ensure she was alright. "You are not precisely mortal," he said, deep in thought, "but the Vaults have an impact on everyone when viewed for the first time."

"Not precisely mortal?" Raegan demanded, edging forward a few more steps, wishing she could put down the lantern to grip the railing but not wanting to relinquish the light.

The Keeper made a disappointed noise like she was a child with her hand in the cookie jar, coming to an abrupt halt. "I should not have spoken so freely," he finally said, looking up at her from a few steps down. In the half-light, he looked simultaneously ancient and impossibly young. He could have been eighteen or fifty; he seemed to exist entirely outside of time.

"It's fine," Raegan said, stepping closer, taking advantage of the few extra inches that the higher step she was perched on gave her. "I have that effect on people. I'd love for you to keep speaking freely. Very interested in your previous statement."

The Keeper smiled at her then, a secret little smile, as if this was some sort of running joke between them. "Let us not keep Cordelia waiting," he said. "This is her first Prophecy. She must be quite excited."

Raegan held his gaze for a long moment, again struck by the positively inhuman slant of his features, wondering if his façade would crack. But the Keeper merely bowed his head politely, almost meekly, and then continued his descent down the stairs.

"What makes it Unrequited?" Raegan asked, thinking she could sidestep the discussion of her 'not precisely mortal' status for now and loop back around when the Keeper had gotten comfortable talking about safer topics.

"Unrequited," the Keeper said, his usual elegance back, his voice rising in volume as if he were performing for a crowd, "refers to a Prophecy that has not yet come to pass and has not been seen by other Oracles. Many prophecies with no merit are made by charlatans every day; Unrequited Prophecies are not like that. They are in every way real —Threads shake and Fate sings for them. But then they don't happen, or perhaps, we do not realize they are happening, or they do not happen when we think they will. Even with Prophecies very far in the future, there are normally touchstones that allow us to match them up with some possible future Thread. Unrequited Prophecies have no touchstones, no matches."

Raegan made the mistake of looking down while the Keeper was speaking, hoping they were close to the bottom, but their progress was slower than Cordelia's, and they were still a horrifying distance from the last stair. Her stomach flipped, and she gritted her teeth together so hard her jaw cracked. "Right," she said, fighting to focus on the Keeper. "If there is indeed an Unrequited Prophecy that names the King and me, and it's Unrequited because no one's realized it was talking about *us*, how old would it need to be?"

The Keeper considered, his lantern swinging as he picked up the pace slightly, as if talk of Prophecies without being near them made his hands itch. "At least a thousand years, I'd imagine," he said finally, ducking into another tight twist of the staircase.

Raegan's eyebrows shot up involuntarily as she attempted to wrap her head around the Keeper's answer. "That feels like a long time," she eventually said, sounding out each word. "Is it actually? Like, for a Prophecy? For your kind?"

The Keeper chuckled, glancing back at her for a moment. "A millennium is a long time, even for us," he replied. "A sharp-eyed, long-sighted

Oracle could certainly see that far along the Threads, but it would be a very good reason for it to end up in the Unrequited section."

A thousand years. Someone, from all that time ago, had seen Raegan and thought that whatever she might do was worth recording, worth keeping tucked away in the Vaults for all this time. Someone had thought Raegan might brush up against Fate. Someone other than the kelpie she'd summoned from a puddle believed she was Gods-touched. The thought was dizzying, even more so than the fucking staircase they were somehow *still* on.

Raegan said nothing as they turned into another of the staircase's twists, preparing to face the sheer drop into nothing again, but relief flooded her when she saw solid ground awaited her. Ahead, a dark stone floor—solid, not inlaid with tile—spread out for what seemed like miles. Hundreds, if not thousands, of large carved shelves were lined up like dominoes, spiraling in on themselves in some sort of labyrinth. It was not unlike an immense library—the ends of the shelves seemed to denote some kind of filing system, though it was not in any language Raegan could read.

She followed the Keeper into the soft hush of the place, releasing his arm. He set his lantern down at the base of the staircase. Raegan did as well, and saw that Cordelia must have done the same with hers. Then she set off beside the Keeper down the outer curve of shelving. To her right, the shelves rose like trees, massive and towering, and to her left, the sheer cliff face climbed out of her vision. Down on the floor level, the Vaults were lit with a soft, diffused glow that she could not decipher the source of, much like the lobby. The cliff face seemed to shimmer and wink in the light, like it was made of obsidian or another smooth, shining rock.

A series of antique-looking rugs formed a walkway along the shelving, quieting their footsteps. The Keeper passed by a number of rows without a second glance, and Raegan realized he must be working his way back a thousand years, to the time when the King was not yet the King. She tried to remind herself to see how many shelves came *before* the earliest possible date of this Prophecy. Curiosity had always been one of Raegan's gifts—and flaws—and she ached to know how long the Fey had presumably walked this planet.

"I think I've found a good section to start with." Cordelia's voice from up ahead broke the soft silence. The seer stood three spirals in from Raegan and the Keeper, half her body obscured by the shelves.

Without answering, the Keeper picked up his pace, strides lengthening as he cut through the labyrinthine shelves. Raegan followed, her heart suddenly remembering to thud anxiously in her throat. Reaching Cordelia felt like it took all of eternity. Every step seemed to set her back two, like she was battling waves to swim past the break. A heaviness settled across her chest, the burden of all the things she had dared to hope for unfurling weighted wings.

When Raegan finally turned into the curve of shelving, she took one look at the contents of the dark, carved bookcases and glanced at Cordelia in shock. Instead of books or perhaps scrolls or maybe even unfamiliar artifacts, the shelves were heavy with glass containers. Some were nothing more than slim, etched perfume vials. Others were massive, glimmering domes. Most fell somewhere in the middle: apothecary jars and fluted cloches.

Raegan stepped closer to the nearest shelf, her mouth opening in awe as she examined the contents of the containers. Within each curve of glass was some kind of winged creature, seemingly born from paper. In a large dome above Raegan's head stood a raven made from thick parchment. Inside a tiny glass box crouched a dragonfly, its wings painstakingly cut from what she thought might be vellum. She moved a few steps down the tunnel of shelves, her steps slow, utterly spellbound.

Her gaze fell on a bat made from heavily ink-stained paper suspended in a bell jar. Everything about it was so real, down to the thinness of the skin on its wings. Raegan approached, raising one shaking hand to the glass. She half-expected it to crack its eyes open and swivel its ears, though it did not—the paper bat remained mute and still behind the elegantly curved glass.

Raegan continued walking down the aisle, lost entirely to the sparrows and damselflies and griffins and other winged creatures she could not name, all housed behind shimmering glass. She stopped at a dove perched in a stained-glass box before she realized the Keeper and Cordelia wavered a few steps behind her, watching her every move.

She turned to examine them as she had the paper creatures. "How do I find it?" Raegan asked, already knowing, somehow, that she was the only one who could.

"Keep walking," Cordelia said, her voice hushed and reverent. "You will know when you do."

Raegan nodded and then, like a woman in a trance, continued to make her way down the slowly-curving aisle. The carved shelves soared high on each side—so high that she wondered how she could possibly know if the right Prophecy were yards above her head, far out of her sight. But she was deep in the world behind the world, and she knew such mundane concerns had little place here. So, she walked a perfect, swooping line in the center of the shelves, her gaze slipping from side to side, trying to believe as much as the Keeper and Cordelia did, that she would know the right winged thing when she saw it.

Time passed. Raegan was fairly sure of it, though it also could have been but seconds since she'd walked through that arched wooden door. All the things she understood about the world seemed to fall away here in the Vaults; everything real, everything true, balanced on paper wings. The rest did not matter. So she kept walking, her gaze falling on birds and insects and dragons.

She was almost about to turn to the two Fey beings at her back and say that perhaps she was not, after all, who they thought she was. But then, a luna moth housed in a small apothecary jar caught her eye. The sharp curves of its wings were rendered in age-spotted paper so thin she could see right through it. Despite its delicacy, the moth was larger than her hand. Two ink stains on the bottom of its wings formed eyes, or maybe moons. She recalled suddenly that once reaching adulthood, luna moths only lived about seven days. They weren't necessarily rare, only sparingly sighted. Alive, magnificent beyond compare, and then gone.

Something like grief unmoored in her chest, and she raised her hand to the glass. She allowed a few shaking fingers to make contact with the cool surface. As she did, Raegan thought she saw the moth's wings flutter. She yanked her hand back, shocked, staring at the paper moth to see if it might reveal its secrets to her.

"Again." The Keeper's voice came from behind her; he only spoke one word, but it conveyed everything: some kind of honeyed, weighted sorrow, like there was only one option and they were all doomed to keep choosing it, over and over. As if there was nothing else he could do but tell her to raise her hand once more to the glass jar and the paper moth that slept within.

Without turning to look at him, urged only by the single spoken word, Raegan nodded and touched the glass again. She was not surprised when the moth's wings gave a small shake. This time, she kept her fingers there, hot against the cool, smooth surface of the glass. In a few more moments, the moth beat its wings as though coasting on some invisible current. The eye-moons blinked in and out of existence, somehow holding Raegan's gaze all the while.

Eventually, the moth took flight, rising above the base of the jar, its large, curved wings holding its small, down-covered body aloft. It hung there, suspended in the air, glorious wings dipping up and down, up and down.

From behind her, Raegan heard Cordelia let out a gasp, or perhaps more like a breath the seer had been holding for a hundred years. As the moth continued to beat its wings, the Fatesong looped again above them, golden-bright and rich as good soil.

"What now?" Raegan asked, not removing her eyes from the paper creature.

"Take it into your hands," the Keeper said. "Hold it close. To your heart. And then we begin our ascent."

Raegan let out a shaky breath and rested her palms against either side of the jar. The moth responded, its wings beating faster, so she carefully removed the glass dome from the shelf, pulling it close to her chest as the Keeper had instructed. Then she turned—a small, mortal woman in a leather jacket holding a Prophecy spun by an Oracle more than a thousand years ago between her hands.

In a silent procession—Keeper, Seer, Fated—the three began to once more walk the labyrinth, taking the path to return to the surface where the Unseelie King awaited them.

CHAPTER TWENTY-NINE

Raegan's heartbeat kept time with her footsteps, damp palms leaving misty imprints on the jar she clutched to her chest. Blue fell in sweeps of velvet all around her, the seer and the Keeper at her back. The hallway felt longer than it had with her forearm in Cordelia's grasp. She resisted the urge to run once more—the paper moth was so fragile and broken glass so sharp—even though something primal in the pit of her belly demanded a sprint.

The two Fey creatures behind her posed no immediate threat, Raegan knew, and even if they did, fleeing on her human legs would hardly make any difference. She tried to shove the urge away, but it only pulsed stronger, overwhelming every fiber of her being with one thought: *run*.

And then understanding swept through Raegan like a tide, and she shot into a sprint, tucking the jar into the crook of one elbow, palm flat against the glass. She was not running from anything. She was running *toward* something.

Toward someone.

Up ahead, a shadow cut through all the blue, tall and angular and waiting, as always. Tears pricked her eyes, and she ran faster, the sound of her heavy boots devoured by the cavernous hallway. By the time the King's face—brow knit, jaw clenched—came into view, Raegan was nearly upon him. She slowed but did not stop, snatching at his suit sleeve to pull him into Cordelia's workspace behind her. Something about a moth and an apothecary jar and a Prophecy meant they needed to be alone, even if only for a few moments.

Raegan eyed the seer's moonstone desk in the far corner, and instead, gingerly placed the jar on a low coffee table made from an unfinished slab of wood. She tried to force her thoughts into an orderly line, but her legs were weary, leather jacket plastered to her skin from her sprint. Breathing hard, she perched on the end of a chaise lounge—blue velvet, predictably—and turned to look at the King.

Everything slowed as his ocean gaze examined her and then the Prophecy on the table. Raegan waited to see elation or wonder in his expression, but instead, bone-deep weariness was all she found.

"We have done this so many times," the King said, gaze meeting hers, long strides carrying him closer. "No more."

He spoke the words in a low, hoarse tone, intended only for her. She suddenly had the strangest feeling that her skeleton had once belonged to a thousand other people—that her body was barely more than a grave for someone she used to be.

"But this is everything," Raegan said, eyes darting to the doorway, not wanting to waste this small moment. "This is everything I've ever wanted. Magic. Fate. Purpose."

She waited for more of his casual cruelty, for another dose of dark-eyed hatred. But it did not come. Instead, the King closed the distance, standing between her and the Prophecy. The tips of his elegant fingers grazed the underside of her chin. "It is your choice. Know that I will follow you to the ends of the Earth," the King murmured, head tilted as his eyes searched hers. "But we have done this a thousand times, and I never like the ending."

The heat from running and the closeness of the unearthly being sent a flush racing across her face. The King released her, straightening but not looking away.

"Cordelia said she heard the Gates fall," Raegan said, clawing at her jacket as more sweat pooled at the base of her spine. "Isn't that exactly what you want?"

The King ignored the query, moving behind her in a sweep of black cloth and predatory grace, extending his hands to help her out of her jacket. Black pepper and damp stone and woodsmoke rolled over Raegan's senses, conjuring more unnecessary heat in her body. She yanked herself away from the King, rising from the chaise lounge and sending one elbow flying back toward him.

He dodged the attempt so neatly it infuriated her.

"Fuck off," Raegan snapped. "I know how to take off a goddamn jacket."

She waited for rage or offense or distaste, but the King only raised one eyebrow, amusement rippling in his dark eyes.

"Of course I want the Gates to fall," he said after a heartbeat, looking out into the hallway. "But Prophecies come with steep prices. Once you release a winged thing, you cannot cage it again."

Raegan took a deep breath, thinking about the enormous marble-clad lobby of this place and how much it felt like a chessboard. How much she felt like a pawn around these ancient Fey creatures. She opened her mouth to say something but then closed it, peeling the rest of her jacket from her damp skin.

"You came here for your father," the King said, jarring her, his tone regal and authoritative again, edged in thorns. "Finding him is your desire. Everything else—the Gates, a Prophecy, the predicament of my people—has nothing to do with you. Not anymore."

She squeezed her eyes shut, fighting to conjure an image of her father, battling for the King's words to be true. But she knew—and suspected he did, too—that everything was tangled together, a snake devouring its own tail.

When Raegan opened her eyes, Cordelia entered the doorway, velvet robes swishing with her movements. The seer paused for a moment, gaze falling upon the Prophecy. She looked at the paper moth like it held every hope and every promise and every wish ever made. "Our salvation is at hand," Cordelia said, breathless, as she began to circle the coffee table.

In her peripheral vision, Raegan saw the King blanche.

"You cannot mean you intend to release it?" he demanded, watching Cordelia with an expression sharp as a dagger. "You are no Oracle."

"I'm the closest thing you've got," Cordelia snapped, meeting the King's eyes for a split second. "We cannot wait for her return. We cannot waste another moment. The *Gates*, my King. Even from behind the glass, this Prophecy sings so sweetly of freedom."

Any softness Raegan thought she might have seen in the King disappeared entirely at Cordelia's words. Razored shadows slid across his features and his eyes narrowed. But he said nothing—he didn't need to, not with the way he wore authority like a cloak.

"Cordelia," came the Keeper's voice from the mouth of the room. He said the seer's name evenly but with a hint of warning, as if the dark, feral glint in the King's gaze did not suffice.

"Do you want to keep rotting away in a dying land?" Cordelia demanded, her voice distant and watery, like she was speaking from a thousand miles away.

Nothing but the domed Prophecy and the King seemed real to Raegan. Paper body and dark waves and whisper-wings and black cloth. Something that might have been her blood thundered in her ears.

"You are not Anointed, Cordelia," someone—the Keeper, she thought—was saying. "You had no right to offer Fatespeak earlier, and now you seek to do it again? Releasing the Prophecy *must* wait until the Oracle returns. You know this. We've tested enough boundaries by simply retrieving it."

The moth's wings beat up and down, the sails of a ship billowing in the wind. It was the most beautiful thing Raegan had ever seen, delicate and powerful at once. Its song threatened to break her heart and mend every wound she'd ever suffered. The sound was faint, but as she focused on the moth, the golden slip of it filled her ears and her head and her heart again, effervescent with magic, buoyant with promise, heavy with Fate.

Just there, beyond a thin curve of glass, was everything she'd ever wanted.

So she reached out and lifted the lid from the jar.

All that followed happened in slow motion, almost like she was not really in the room at all. The King's powerful hands reached for her wrists a fraction of a second too late, followed by a low sound of sorrow slipping from his parted mouth. The Keeper shouted in protest, grappling for the apothecary glass, but it was of no use.

The Seer, though, looked lit from within—triumph gathering around her like an impending storm. Her eyes, usually a rich brown, turned gold entirely: no pupils, no iris, just gleaming, glinting gold that tracked the moth fluttering above her head in a spiral. Then it banked, landing on the seer's chest. The moth's body rested against her sternum, its wings flattened on either side. The air hung sacred and thick, as if all of Time and Fate had always been waiting on this moment.

Then the Seer began to speak—her voice amplified, booming, louder than it had any right to be, ringing out through the space.

"WHEN THE WORLD IS SPLIT IN TWO, THE MAEVE OF THIRTEEN FROM O'ER THE HILL—NOT FROM BENEATH— WILL MEND WHAT IS SHATTERED. SHE WILL COMPLETE THE WORK OF THE ONE WHO CAME BEFORE. SHE WILL WALK THE IN-BETWEEN BESIDE THE EXILED KING. SHE WILL TURN BACK THE TIMEKEEPER."

The Seer paused, her robes flowing around her on some invisible wind, looking not unlike a long-lost goddess only now returned to her rightful divinity.

"AND SO THE GATES SHALL FALL."

Chapter Thirty

The words floated on the air like a pair of paper wings, translucent and beating with life. A golden swell of purpose gathered in Raegan's chest. Perhaps all the sorrow that marked her like an ink stain was not meaningless. Perhaps all roads had always led here, into a marble room with three ancient beings who spoke of Fate and Gates and magic.

"You have no idea what you have done, child," the Keeper said, shattering the silence. His voice sounded hollow, scooped out and empty.

The Keeper strode farther into the space from the doorway, and Raegan braced herself for further rebuke. But beyond a ragged sigh, the Keeper remained silent. He snatched the Prophecy's jar from the table and held his hand out to Raegan. Mutely, she placed the glass lid into his hands, gaze straying back to Cordelia. The velvet-draped seer's eyes were still flat, golden discs, but no wind fluttered her robes any longer. Raegan dared not look at the King.

But he stepped into her sight line anyway, moving toward Cordelia, his steps stilted and stiff, lacking their usual grace. He reached out two cupped hands—his fingers were shaking, Raegan noticed—toward the seer. With a soft beat of its wings, the luna moth left its perch on Cordelia's chest, and moved toward the King's palms with an eagerness Raegan felt in her own body. Together, the Keeper and the King returned the moth to the glass jar with startling ease. There was no question in Raegan's mind that the pair had done this before.

The King set the jar down onto the coffee table, resuming his stance beside her. Raegan craned her neck around his large frame, feverish for another look at the moth. When her eyes landed upon it, she saw with a start that it was just a paper thing. No life shimmered along its wings. It looked sad and flat and lonely inside the glass.

"The Oracle will understand," Cordelia said, breaking Raegan's thoughts. When she looked up, she noticed the seer's eyes had returned to their normal brown hue. "We had no choice, and really, we are just in time. I thought I was about to see the last of magic on this side of the Gates wither away entirely."

Confusion spiked Raegan. She narrowed her eyes, arms crossing on her chest before she realized she had moved at all. "Is *that* what's happening?" she asked, though she felt she already knew the answer, an understanding beginning to unfold in her mind. Such an idea, though, seemed impossible with all that she had seen—the kelpie and the King and the portico and all those divination rituals and the absolute terror and wonder of the Vaults.

The Keeper collapsed into one of the chairs by the moonstone desk, rubbing his temples with one hand. "In short, yes," he said, not meeting Raegan's gaze. "When the Timekeeper sealed the Gates, we were cut off from the Otherlands and left with only the residual magic already here. Magic is bleeding from this world—or perhaps it is better to say it is being choked out like a weed."

A delirious laugh clawed its way up Raegan's throat. These impossibly powerful beings needed *her*.

"Why wouldn't the Protectorate allow you to return to the Otherlands?" Raegan inquired. She turned briefly toward the King. "Not you, obviously. But the rest of your people. The ones who just got stuck on the wrong side of the Gates. Wouldn't they rather that you be far away from humans?"

"How would the Protectorate ensure my own people hated me if they were simply allowed to cross the Gates?" the King asked her, one eyebrow arched, his tone turned rueful. "If I ever manage to return, reclaiming my throne will be nearly impossible. I am the reason the world was cleaved in two. I am the reason the remains of my court wander this half of the planet in exile, constantly pursued by the Protectorate with no hope of making a home. I am why lineages were ripped in half. Only some of us can survive so far from the Source."

"The Source?" Raegan inquired, her legs suddenly zapped of strength. She sank back onto the velvet chaise. "What, like a fountain or a Hill of Tara-esque place? Somewhere that all magic originates from?"

Cordelia's sharp gaze shot to Raegan, amusement playing on the seer's features. "You are taking to all of this with little issue," she said, her mouth curving into a dagger of a smile.

"I read a lot of books," Raegan replied, deadpan, leaning back on the chaise and crossing an ankle over her knee.

"It's an oversimplification," the Keeper said eventually, his brow furrowed. "But yes. Essentially."

She nodded and picked at a cuticle, wishing fervently for a printer, a corkboard, and a massive amount of thumbtacks. Everything happening around her, despite being mystical and absolutely beyond her wildest imagination, should still follow some kind of logic. She wanted to write it all out and pin it up on a wall until she found the connections.

Realizing there was a loose end, she looked up at the King and cocked her head. "How *did* you get exiled, anyway?" she demanded, her eyes narrowed. "The Protectorate would've had to capture you, right? How the fuck did they manage that?"

For a long time, the King simply searched her gaze. And again, he looked at her like he could see right into her, like he already knew all of her deepest secrets and oldest yearnings. Historically, Raegan was not a fan of being perceived. But she fervently hoped to be *seen*. She rarely was. And yet here was an impossible creature, ripped right from the pages of folklore, who looked at her like he knew her as well as the back of his hand.

She said nothing but held his gaze, wondering if she might be able to peer into him as easily he did into her.

"You truly do not remember?" the King asked, lowering himself onto the other end of the chaise in a way that made his suit jacket stretch tight across his broad, muscled shoulders. Something low in Raegan's belly thrummed.

"What could I possibly have to remember?" she demanded, the words stumbling and unconvincing, even to her own ears.

"The Protectorate managed to capture me," the King said, drawing out each word like an arrow from a quiver, "because of you."

Confusion swam thickly in Raegan's mind. She was distantly aware of Cordelia's attention suddenly snapping to her, the seer's gaze intense and hot.

"*Me?*" Raegan asked, her mouth dry. The question managed to leave her mouth despite how, the longer she looked at the King, the more she did not believe her own doubt. Too many conflicting images rose up from the silken depths within her.

A battlefield on a high hill, black smoke rising into the air. Someone who looked remarkably like the King but younger, his hair longer, looking over his shoulder at her, smiling in a way that exposed dimples. A river coursing madly before her, its waters darkened with rage and despair. A low-lit room, a fireplace sputtering in the corner, skirts hitched around her waist, the gnarled wood of the table rough against the backs of her exposed thighs, the mouth of a raven-haired knight kneeling between her open legs softer than sin. Battlements built from uneven blocks of gray stone drenched in rain, her own voice cursing as she snatched a bow from a dead archer's body, and prayed to every god she knew that she could recall how to string an arrow.

By the time Raegan's mind was her own again and the undeniably vibrant memories—if that's what they were—cleared from her vision, she found herself back in the seer's workspace, the King kneeling before her in a way that was entirely too similar to what she had just seen. She scrambled away from him, her fingers clawing for purchase on the velvet chaise. She fought an urge to pull her feet up and hug them to her chest.

"Steady," the King murmured. "You were gone for some time."

Raegan bit on her tongue until she tasted blood, and did everything in her power to banish the image of the low-lit room with the sputtering fire. She tried to focus on the coursing river and the death and the black smoke. Somehow it was easier.

Dragging the heels of her palms across her eyes, she looked to one side to see the Keeper standing in front of the coffee table, lips pressed together as he watched her. A tray of tea sat on the table, steam curling up cozily from it. Cordelia had taken up residence by the doorway, her gaze trained on Raegan, eyes wide and arms crossed.

Panic eased a hand over her throat. Her skin crawled with a thousand hot pinpricks, and her stomach lurched, sweat gathering at the back of her neck and the base of her spine.

"Tea?" the Keeper asked unhelpfully, extending a cup to Raegan. She eyed him with what was probably best described as unbridled contempt, which she supposed was not precisely fair, seeing as he'd taken the time to make her tea while she tumbled uselessly through her own mind.

But the simple words to politely decline did not seem to exist in her brain. The King, still kneeling before her, raised a hand to gently push the Keeper's offered teacup away.

"Can you tell me your name?" the King asked, his voice costumed in a deep, warm tone. Perhaps it was meant to be soothing. It did not soothe her. Instead, it unspooled threads of heat in her core, a gentle throb erupting.

"Raegan," she replied, shoving a handful of curls off her damp forehead. "You want the year and the current US president too?"

Something entirely too playful pulled at the edges of the King's mouth before he stood, retrieving her leather jacket from the back of the chaise. She noticed another hitch in his movements; a rough spot in the endless grace.

"Though I appreciate your continued offer of hospitality," the King said to the Keeper with a regal bow of his head, "I think it is apparent that Overhill and I have much to discuss. We will take our leave."

Cordelia leapt forward at his words, frowning. "You don't get to shut us out," she said. "There is much to be deciphered about the Prophecy and so much we can do before the Oracle has even had a chance to return. This mortal is the key we've been searching for. I'm begging you —let me see what doors she can unlock."

Irritation spiked hot in Raegan's chest, and she watched, gratified, as the King's jaw clenched, his gaze falling heavy on Cordelia.

"Overhill is not a *key*," the King replied, his voice a thunderstorm rolling across the horizon. "She is a person. I will not have you speak of her as if she is some tool to be tinkered with."

Cordelia took a step toward the King and Raegan, planting herself in front of the doorway. Though she said nothing, her brows drew together and the pinch around her mouth promised unpleasantries.

"Regardless," the King continued, "before anything else, I believe Overhill needs rest."

Relief coursed through Raegan. She felt like she hadn't slept in days. She wanted fresh clothes. She wanted to be alone and *think*. She looked away from Cordelia for a heartbeat and found the King's eyes, heavy as an entire ocean, already upon her.

"And answers," he added, his tone gentler. "I believe some answers are owed. I would have rather avoided this entirely, but that moment has passed."

Then the King extended a hand down to her. Despite every story she had ever read about his kind, she took it. He helped Raegan to her feet, his larger hand engulfing her palm and part of her wrist. His touch sent her swimming in dark, electrifying currents. She fought to stay steady.

"We will be in contact," the King said, handing Raegan her jacket, which she accepted a beat too late. "The finer workings of this Prophecy need attention but in due time."

"They need attention *now*," Cordelia countered, looking toward the Keeper for support as her voice rose. "Are you going to place the needs of a mortal vessel over your own people? If she's really the reason you were exiled, why do you not seek revenge? How far does our once-mighty King plan to fall?"

Faster than Raegan's eyes could track, the King closed the distance to Cordelia, backing the seer into a corner. His broad frame engulfed hers entirely. In her peripheral vision, Raegan saw the Keeper's gaze widen as he rose from his chair in slow, deliberate movements. Quite suddenly, she recalled a childhood afternoon at the zoo when a toddler tipped over the fence of the panther enclosure. The zookeeper had moved just like the strange, neat man in his tidy suit did now: as if his calmness was all that stood between tender flesh and dismemberment.

"Do you want," the King asked of the seer in a tone that scattered chills down Raegan's spine, "to see *exactly* how far I can sink?"

As he spoke, all the shadows in the room unfurled from their hiding places. The diffused, warm light that seemed to emanate from the very core of the Oracle's Temple dissipated, as if snuffed out by the single breath of some forgotten beast's unhinged jaws.

"Cordelia," the Keeper warned, though his veneer of calm was shaken, arms held up in a stiff attempt at soothing. "He is our High King."

"Precisely," the seer seethed. "Which is why he should be willing to dissect this human piece by piece if that's what it takes to return our people to their home."

The King threw his head back and laughed. The sound of it was all wrong in Raegan's ears—none of that autumnal bell she'd heard earlier, only wolfish darkness heavy with warning.

"Child of barely two hundred summers," the King began, his voice thrumming as if every Unseelie regent had risen from their resting places to lend authority to his words, "you see so far but understand so little. Recall that I am Gwyn ap Nudd, the Render of Worlds, the King in Shadow. Do not make the mistake of threatening what is mine."

Something feral and sharp-toothed uncoiled in Raegan's core, a wildfire igniting deep in her core. A secret part of her yearned to see the King rip Cordelia and the Keeper limb from limb. Not for the sake of empty violence but because she was his and he was hers and any blood spilled would be in her name.

She tried not to be disappointed when Cordelia instead stepped to the side of the doorway, features pale with poorly masked fear. Raegan heard the Keeper let out a long, shaky breath as he shifted his weight back, arms dropping to his sides.

Pleased, the King turned to Raegan and offered his arm like they were about to stroll along a grassy promenade. She took it, desire sweeping through her body. He guided them under the archway and into the hall without a backwards glance at Cordelia or the Keeper.

In silence, they strode down the velvet-draped corridor, arriving once again in the marble lobby. Raegan focused on the sound of her boots on the stone floors, fighting the urge to check over her shoulder for a wild-eyed seer in pursuit. The thought did not frighten her, as perhaps it should have; she felt only prickly annoyance. Instead, what bid her heart to race and her head to spin was the King disentangling his arm from hers to place an open palm against the small of her back.

Raegan was no fool. She had an idea of what the misplaced memories and the strange feelings and the Keeper's words and Cordelia's reaction might mean. After all, she *did* read a lot of books.

Brows knit together, Raegan turned toward the King to find he was already looking down at her. Though she saw no cruelty in his expression, none of the tenderness she thought she had caught earlier remained, either. In a sudden rush, doubt replaced the desire.

"Let us depart before Cordelia has any more foolish ideas," the King said, gesturing toward the doorway.

She nodded, wanting to return to the part of the city she knew better, where she had an advantage, where she might be safe. Her mind turned over like an engine in the cold, suddenly calculating and sharp again.

Outside the Oracle's Temple, everything was human and mundane, just as Raegan had left it. Perhaps only she had changed. The yellow light of the setting sun was near-blinding. She shaded her eyes with her hand, trying to get her bearings now that they were back on mortal sidewalk, the familiar sounds of a neighborhood shopping center falling in around her.

The King lingered beneath the tattered awning above the storefront that somehow held endless wonders. A regular person in a green hoodie walked by, a plastic shopping bag dangling from their forearm as they replied to a text. With a start, Raegan dug into her pocket to retrieve her own phone.

Her screen lit up with a missed call and two texts from Henry, a voice memo from Saanvi, and sixteen new emails. Henry wanted to know if she had gotten anything on the story and had grown impatient in the hours since he'd first contacted her. The real world—*if* her world was still the real one—crashed down hard.

And with it came the suspicion of things that seemed too good, too storybook-slick, to be true.

Chapter Thirty-One

"Are you fucking with my head?" Raegan demanded, wheeling on the King. Behind him, the Oracle's Temple had disappeared, replaced with the nondescript storefront. "These memories, these feelings, this sense that something bigger is going on—you could make me feel all of it, couldn't you?"

The King watched her with a guarded expression but said nothing.

"Answer me," Raegan hissed, taking an aggressive step toward him. "Could you?"

"It is within my power, yes," he replied, something she could not place flashing across his expression. "But it would take a considerable amount of energy, and I do not view it as a worthy expenditure."

She stomped a few steps down the sidewalk and then halted, remembering the King's words about physical proximity allowing him to better conceal them from the Protectorate. She clenched her jaw and wondered if that was even true or if it was just another way to pull her barriers down.

Dragging a hand through her hair, Raegan leaned back against the storefront's grimy windows. She squeezed her eyes shut. Her instincts were adrift; *nothing* felt real anymore. Everything had taken on a fairy-tale hue, edges rimmed with thorns and mist. She had no due north.

After a heavy exhale, she forced her eyes back open to find the King standing in front of her, watching her carefully, brows drawn together. She raised her gaze to meet his and hated that, in the ocean of his eyes, she found the only thing that felt real.

"It's smart," she admitted, rueful. "If you threaten your fellow Fey and storm out of there with me by your side, of course I'll think you care about me. You'll build on that trust, and then when the time comes, you'll cash in on it. And I'll probably be dead, but the Gates will be open and you'll have your throne back, won't you?" Raegan held her ground, back pressed against the window, arms crossed over her chest.

The King tilted his head as she spoke, mouth parting. Then he held her gaze for a long, skittering moment before stepping in close, his body mere inches from hers. "It would be so much easier," the King said, his head bowed like a sinner, voice low and reverent, "if that were true."

"Fuck you," Raegan snapped without half the venom she'd hoped to muster.

He smiled then, the curve of his full mouth sensual and the ocean in his eyes turned to slinking smoke. Her body pushed off the window of its own accord, pitching her into his realm of expensive black cloth and coiled muscle and damp stone. Tentatively, filled with as much desire as terror, Raegan laid the flat of her hand against the King's chest, right where his heart should be. He permitted it, watching her with that guarded expression again, though something like hope flickered in his gaze for a split second.

Heartbeats—probably even Fey ones—were practically indistinguishable without biomedical equipment, Raegan knew. And yet the slow, strong waves that pulsed through the cloth and into her palm felt like a song she'd forgotten she knew the words to, devoured by time and circumstance.

But then a shrill note sounded, shattering the moment. Her mind churned and she stepped back, the window meeting her spine. Moments passed thickly before she realized the sound was just her phone ringing in her pocket. Only three people's numbers were set to audibly ring with an incoming call: Henry, her mom, and . . .

Hands shaking, Raegan yanked her phone out, seized with a sureness that the person on the other end of the line was her father, resurrected by her actions, by her fierceness, by her quest. She answered the call without so much as glancing at the screen.

"Hello?" Raegan said with so much desperation that alarm rolled over the King's face.

"Raegan?" came the response. "You alive? I know it's your day off, but it's unusual to not hear from you for this long. And you are reporting on a possible serial killer, so . . ."

The hope she'd harbored in those precious moments spoiled and turned sour in her stomach. Bile rose in Raegan's throat—hardly a fair reaction to the voice of the best editor she'd ever worked for.

"Yeah, Henry, I'm fine," she replied, sagging back against the shop window. "Sorry. I managed to track down what could be a pretty incredible source, if they'll talk to me. I was hoping you were them, returning my call." She squeezed her eyes shut and prayed Henry accepted the lie.

"Well, I'll let you go, then," her editor said, sounding satisfied. "Looking forward to hearing about whatever you've found."

"I'll tell you all about it when I know more," Raegan assured him, trying to sound like the obsessed, workaholic journalist she'd always been. Anxiety gripped her insides and squeezed. She was supposed to be in the newsroom tomorrow, doing her job as if absolutely everything hadn't changed.

Henry hung up, leaving her with two halves that did not fit together —the career she had fought so hard for, and the quest she'd rather die than ignore. Her father had been the same, hadn't he? She did not seem entirely to blame for this glittering madness; it clearly ran in the family.

"Oh, fuck," Raegan realized suddenly, her tone loud and sharp as she looked up at the King. "Will the Protectorate go after my mom?"

He considered her question, head tilting slightly to one side. "Remind me how you remained undetected previously as we walk," the King said, offering Raegan his arm. She took it and hated that she immediately felt safer.

The King directed them north of the Oracle's Temple, a different path than they had approached it from. Raegan appreciated the precaution. As they walked, the neighborhood now punctuated with yellow school buses and children in uniforms exiting corner stores, she explained to him what little she knew of her father's protective warding —via Maelona, of course, who was hopefully still alive—that kept the family hidden.

"I think your mother is safe," he said, solemn. "Your father sounds proficient. I imagine your summoning of Rainer was the only reason the Protectorate detected you. Nothing ever occurred previously, correct?"

"As far as I know," Raegan said, kicking a piece of trash out of her way. The neighborhood smelled heavily of diesel exhaust from all the school buses. A cacophony of songs blaring from car windows, and the sound of storm doors creaking open and shut, filled the air.

"It is unlikely your mother also carries Protectorate blood," the King continued thoughtfully. "There are only a few original families left, and they do not intermarry; most already share some lineage. Your ability to do magic on this side of the Gates is thanks to the Protectorate's oath to the Timekeeper. It makes you much more easily discoverable. I would hazard that your father's working cloaked you entirely, but summoning Rainer shattered the illusion he had placed on you, making your magic as good as a beacon for the Protectorate."

Raegan's eyes went so blurry with the implication of that statement that she had to fight to keep the pavement in view ahead of her. "That means . . ." She trailed off, her tongue thick in her mouth.

It meant she would never know the rush of calling to the waters like she had in the coffee shop again. It meant whatever fantasies she had of being taught magic by a Fey king—unlikely, Raegan realized, but she was also far closer than the vast majority of people—seeped out of her. A tangle knotted itself in her stomach.

"Yes," the King replied, clipped, professional. "As long as the Protectorate reigns, you cannot do magic without inviting them to find you. But your mother should be safe. The Protectorate may be interested in her as leverage, if they can even find her beneath your father's spellwork, which I doubt."

Quite suddenly, Raegan wanted to sit down on the nearest stoop and cry. With all the ongoing turmoil, she hadn't even realized that she'd been holding the possibility of doing magic—real, actual, terrifying magic—tightly against her chest like a consolation prize. A promise to herself that no matter how fucked up everything got—no matter how dead, or maybe just uncaring, her father turned out to be—she had a chance at magic. A rosy-hued, delicately constructed chance, like something out of a storybook or a middle-schooler's daydream.

But now that hope fled, and she felt all the emptier for it. She reminded herself that at least her mother was safe. When she could think a bit more clearly again, hopefully after food and sleep and a shower, Raegan vowed to investigate that topic further.

She tried to bring her attention back to her body—the heaviness in her limbs, the broken glass winking in the street, the weed-choked alleyway the King had turned down. Up ahead, a brick wall sealed off the path. She hesitated, but then she caught sight of the now-familiar archway painted onto the wall.

"My archives have long operated as a safehouse," the King said as they came to a pause before the portico. He turned, gauging her reaction. "It is unwise for you to reside anywhere that lacks magical protection."

"Right," Raegan said, her voice sticking to the sides of her throat as the realization settled over her shoulders.

She'd known this was coming. She'd passed the point of no return, and now she couldn't have her old life back. Tipping her chin up, Raegan gazed at the strip of sky visible between the surrounding buildings. To her embarrassment, her eyes blurred with tears again.

"Do you know what you need right now?" the King asked. "It is understandable if you do not. We can return to my archives, and you may rest until you are more clear-headed."

"I'll need my meds and clothes and probably a few other things from my apartment," Raegan managed to get out, not looking at him, hating how pathetic she sounded. "But for now, I would really like a shower and to lie down."

"Of course," the King said and then gestured to the portico. "Are you ready to depart?"

A strange part of Raegan whispered—or, pleaded, really—that no, she was not. She turned to look at the entrance of the alleyway and watched another school bus putter by. Could this be the last time she belonged to the same world as the children on that bus and its driver seated at the wheel, in full control of where they drove next?

It was not that normalcy suddenly held any appeal. It was that she'd always imagined taking charge of how the stranger worlds bled into her own. Foolishly, she'd never thought that the wilder things would wrap themselves around her like marionette strings. But here Raegan was, crisscrossed in vines and threads and shadows.

Not having the will to speak aloud, she simply nodded her head. Then she allowed the King to sweep her into the ink-spill mouth of the portico and whatever awaited them beyond.

CHAPTER THIRTY-TWO

"And you're just going to let me stay *here*?" Raegan asked, annoyed that a hint of awe made its way into her voice.

But it was hard not to appreciate the space around her, and besides, it certainly felt less dangerous than appreciating the King himself. Instead of admiring ocean eyes and powerful shoulders, Raegan looked around the room again, taking in the stone walls and large fireplace, then the soaring ceiling studded with exposed beams. Ancient tapestries adorned the far wall, depicting decadent feasts and sprawling forests. A corner bookshelf towered a few paces from the fireplace, heavy with leatherbound volumes.

"Yes," the King replied evenly from where he stood at the entryway, leaning against the doorframe. "These are the safehouse quarters I offered."

It seemed impossible that the archives had been hiding so much during her first visit, but upon their return from the Oracle's Temple, Raegan discovered that the long wall beside the reading area concealed a door. When the right words were spoken, the door opened and led to a corridor housing a number of guest chambers.

"What's the toll? Will I owe something in return?" Raegan asked, fatigue seeping into her voice. The soft-looking bed dressed in cozy flannels across the room seemed at odds with what the Fey usually offered mortals in all the stories she'd ever read.

"I said I would ensure your safety," the King replied, pushing off the doorframe to stand straight as an arrow. "You cannot return to your home. I offer this freely in its stead."

She told herself she'd imagined the tiny flicker of hurt that crossed his features for a moment, or that he had engineered it. She was dealing with the Sidhe, after all, which made her want to examine every loophole and contort her thinking to keep up with the wily, ancient beings. But right now, she just couldn't. The day had been too long, her body was too weary, and even her tongue felt heavy. Her jaw hurt, surely from grinding her teeth all day.

"I appreciate it," she said eventually, looking down at her shoes, looking anywhere but at him.

"I will remain in the archive portion," the King replied. "If you should require anything, or want to discuss something, you may seek me."

And then he was gone, slipping away into the shadows of the stone hallway. Raegan was left with a door slowly creaking closed and the silence of the space around her. She took a deep breath. The air carried the same scent as the King's office—warm smoke, shimmering chestnut and a deep, bitter vanilla.

Raegan chewed the inside of her cheek, considering her options. She could chase after him and demand answers. But she couldn't form the questions no matter how many times she practiced them in her head. An unearthly beautiful, unimaginably powerful, and terribly ancient Fey king showed up and was not only willing to help her, but also *knew* her, felt something for her, brought memories rushing to the surface . . .

If someone asked Raegan for her opinion on such a situation, she'd laugh in their face and say they were being tricked by the Fair Folk—a tale as old as time. It didn't matter how real any of it felt or how badly she wanted him. Believing any of it was a fool's game, and she'd never been a fucking fool.

So she took three deep breaths, pulled off her boots, and went to investigate the bathroom instead.

"Holy shit," Raegan murmured, looking around the space with wide eyes.

Like so much of the archives and the King's office, it felt like she could've designed it herself. Light from two sconces danced over the stone walls and floors. A large claw-foot tub lounged in the far corner, and a rainfall showerhead sprouted from the wall above it. Beside the tub, fluffy towels were piled high on an antique chair, a bar of soap in pretty paper wrapping balanced on top.

She didn't bother looking at the rest of the room. Raegan marched to the edge of the tub, cranked the spigot until the water was almost too hot, and then stripped, discarding her clothes on the floor without a second glance.

The bliss of the hot water sliding around her skin pulled a long sigh from her mouth. Her eyes closed in a matter of seconds. For the first time all day, her shoulders sagged and her jaw relaxed.

Raegan told herself she'd get out when the water cooled off. But the minutes slipped away from her on silken strands and by the time she was feeling a bit better—and had become rather pruney, too—the water temperature hadn't dropped. In fact, sweat began to cling to the back of her neck and her hairline.

"Magic," she muttered, frustrated at herself for thinking a bathtub in a Fey king's accommodations would do something so mundane as get cold.

She gathered her hair up with one hand and stood, a groan escaping her at the pull of muscles and catching of joints. After washing up, she rinsed off and pulled a towel from the chair. Then Raegan stepped out of the tub, confused to find her clothes were no longer in their unceremonious pile on the floor. Instead, a quick glance around the bathroom revealed her garments neatly folded on the vanity, nestled between two porcelain sinks. She distantly wondered if there was some kind of tidying enchantment at work, but when she approached the vanity to dress, something else entirely caught her attention.

A small piece of paper, folded over more than once, sat atop her sweater. Raegan frowned and darted for the note, as if it might change its mind and flutter away. She stood there, naked and damp, water droplets still adorning her collarbone and the soft slopes of her belly, and unfolded the paper.

Typed upon it was a list of locations, pros and cons noted beneath each place in an indented paragraph. Raegan furrowed her brow, trying to understand and failing—until she saw the scribbled, handwritten message at the bottom.

Don't contact Bronwyn. Will break Cormac's cloaking. She's safe.

And then it all came flooding back to her—the piece of paper Maelona had unfolded at the café, talking about places Raegan might live a life away from the Protectorate, the Fey, and everything else that she was now firmly steeped in. She traced damp, shaking fingers over the words Maelona had somehow managed to write in all of the mayhem. And then she sighed, letting the note flutter onto the vanity.

At least her mother was safe. Both Maelona and the King seemed to think so, which she supposed was the best evaluation she'd ever get. But she had not considered that even contacting her mom would break the spellwork her father had so painstakingly set to keep their family safe. She didn't know why her father would leave the book in the basement and the spell in the lockbox if the simple act of her doing magic could endanger everyone. With a heavy sigh, Raegan let her head fall back, tilting her chin toward the ceiling.

Oh. Of course. Whatever her dad had done was segmented, designed to keep working on one side even if the other broke—as if he knew Raegan would never be able to resist the siren song, or at least he didn't wish to risk it. She thought back to the way her mom couldn't even see the book he'd left for her, and she wondered if he'd concealed it from Bronwyn, leaving it visible only to Raegan's eyes. Because her father had *known* her, had recognized that same glinting strangeness in his daughter.

Fresh grief rolled through Raegan's chest, but she told herself to focus on dressing instead of dissolving into tears. Gingerly moving the note to the side, she unfolded her sweater. When she pulled it over her head, it smelled like she had just gotten it out of the dryer. She lifted the hem and took a deep inhale of the fabric. Yes—definitely laundered, definitely accomplished by whatever enchantment was woven over the bathroom.

The simple gift of clean clothing on clean skin helped Raegan refocus, shoving the torment down for at least a little bit longer. Plucking Maelona's note from the vanity, she walked out of the bathroom and searched the room for writing paper and a pen. After a few minutes, several curses, and at least fifty percent more drama than necessary,

Raegan emerged triumphant with a cracked leather notebook and a 1960s-era pack of sharpened pencils.

She darted for the worn-in leather couch in front of the fireplace. Curling her legs up underneath her, she began to write down everything she knew. It only filled up about half a page, which was depressing to look at. She drew a line beneath the information and, in the new section below, wrote out what she remembered of the Prophecy.

"When the world is split in two," she muttered under her breath, the words she scribbled keeping pace with her voice, "the Maeve of thirteen from over the hill—not beneath—will complete the work of the one who came before. She will walk beside the exiled King and turn back the Timekeeper. And so the Gates shall open."

Or something like that. It was close enough to try to dissect each line.

"World split in two"—current state of affairs, the Gates separating the world with magic and the world without.

"Maeve of thirteen"—me, it seems. My middle name is Maeve. Born January 13th.

"From over the hill"—a human; not someone from beneath the hill, i.e. the Fey. Also, my last name, obviously.

"Work of the one who came before"—

Raegan froze. Information crystallized quickly in her mind, connections jumping together now that she had finally been able to follow her process of putting words to paper.

"Fuck," she said to no one, drawing out the word. Adrenaline shot through her veins, hot and energizing. God, she hoped she was right about this.

Raegan stood, her breathing hard and quick as she tucked the notebook into her pocket. She willed her heart rate to slow down, but it only climbed higher, thumping louder and louder in her chest and then her throat. She made for the door, ignoring her discarded boots, and sprinted down the corridor that led back to the archives.

She was almost surprised when she found the King there, exactly where he'd said he would be, standing at the worktable and examining a large piece of parchment. He had removed his suit jacket and rolled his sleeves to the elbow, exposing the coiled muscles of his forearms. A few buttons were loosened at the top of his shirt as well, she noticed.

Raegan forced herself to focus as the King looked over at her. He said nothing, eyes shadowed in the low, warm light of the archives.

With one last deep breath, she stepped forward from the threshold, arms at her sides, shoulders back and spine straight. "I am in possession of something the Prophecy needs to come true," she said. "And if you want to see it, we need to renegotiate our deal."

CHAPTER THIRTY-THREE

Adrenaline pounded loudly in her eardrums. Her heart climbed another inch in her throat every second the King said nothing at all. He only watched her, not even shifting from his stance: palms flat and shoulder-width apart, supporting his weight as he leaned over the table.

For what felt like the thousandth time in only a few hours, Raegan told herself not to look away from his infinite, ice-gray eyes.

"If any other mortal claimed to be in possession of something so earth-shattering," the King finally said, one brow arching, "I would likely disregard it entirely."

Raegan permitted herself a tiny smile and walked closer, clasping her hands behind her back. "But I'm not just any mortal, am I?" she asked, stopping a few paces from him. With a sigh, she hinged at the hips to lean over the worktable. Then she rested her elbow on the well-worn surface, propping her chin up on her hand. "So you can't just disregard it, I suppose."

The King's gaze dripped from her eyes to her mouth, from her mouth to her collarbones, and then lower still. He blinked slowly before meeting her gaze once more, head tilted and sculptural lips parted. Something dangerously close to a challenge flickered across his expression.

"Oh, I certainly can," he replied with a shrug of his powerful shoulders. Then the King returned to studying the manuscript unrolled in front of him.

Normally, being so easily dismissed would infuriate Raegan. But from the King, it wasn't just a simple dismissal. Instead, it felt like a gauntlet drop. But more than that—as loath as she was to trust this particular instinct of hers—it felt a hell of a lot like flirting.

And so, with a confidence instilled solely by the fact that the Unseelie King had not only refrained from killing her but also possibly flirted with her, Raegan slid closer. Then she reached over and tapped the middle of the manuscript he was inspecting with one hand. "Hey," she said, her voice lower now. "I was not done speaking with you."

Without raising his head, the King looked at her sidelong, his lips parting again. A thrumming uncurled in the center of Raegan's body, the beat of it so thick and sweet that it took all of her willpower to ignore the sensation. She wanted to blame it on the King's magic, on some kind of thrall or enchantment, but she knew without a single doubt that the desire she felt for the dark-eyed, lithe, and dangerous creature belonged to her alone.

"Nice try," she said, lifting her eyebrows appreciatively, her hand still splayed over the manuscript, "but it will take more than some pretty eyes to distract me."

To his credit, the King hit her with the most sensual half-smile she had probably ever seen, the curve of his mouth saying more than words ever could. Open desire claimed the cavity of her chest, sending daggers of heat into her flesh.

"You find my eyes pretty?" he murmured, mirroring her stance now, dropping his weight to his elbows and propping his chin up on one large hand.

Raegan watched him, eyes narrowed, trying to decide how she wanted to proceed. If she played too far into his response, she'd get caught up in it all and probably attempt to climb the High King of the Unseelie Court like a particularly broad tree.

So she moved to diffuse instead, even though the fire kindling in her belly begged for the opposite. "I'm trying to speak *seriously* at the moment," Raegan continued, removing her hand from the manuscript, looking at the ancient Fey as if he were a very naughty little boy. "I know what a certain section of the Prophecy is referring to. I would wager it's the part you haven't been able to puzzle out."

The King immediately stood up to his full height, crossing his arms. Raegan had to hand it to him—the cool, slick composure was back so quickly it was hard not to be impressed, though she preferred the molten core that lingered beneath.

"A bold wager," he told her, reaching for a steaming teacup set off at the end of the table and taking a drink. Raegan did her best not to notice how deft his hands were despite their size—how a bone china teacup, its construction so thin and delicate that light shone through it, was not reduced to ash between his fingers. She wondered how she would fare there.

"I've been called bold before," Raegan replied with a dazzling grin, standing up straight and sliding her hands into her pockets. In the background, a fireplace she hadn't noticed before popped and sputtered, scattering molasses-colored light into the imposing space. "My request is simple."

"And yet I still do not know what you can offer me," the King said, one dark brow arching, his voice dripping from his mouth like honey.

"The work of the one who came before," was all Raegan said.

It was all she needed to say. This was the moment she had been building toward, trying her best during all the foreplay to not directly mention it, studying the King's expression the entire time, wagering that she just might be able to catch enough of a glimpse to know if she was correct.

And catch it she did—there and gone in his eyes, quick as a comet, but Raegan saw what she was looking for. Just the tiniest flash of interest, barely more than a glint that could've been attributed to the light of the nearby fire. But she also noticed the way the King's eyes narrowed ever so slightly, as if he had found something worth studying further. Raegan had absolutely no idea why she felt she could read him this clearly, but she did.

"You can save your protests," she said with a wave of her hand. "I *know* you, and I know you haven't the foggiest what that part of the Prophecy means."

The words tumbled out before she could stop them, leaving Raegan and the King regarding each other in the golden, softly wavering light. A wave of emotion crested at the back of her throat, thick with a longing so bottomless that for a heartbeat Raegan was not sure if she had ever felt anything else.

Against all odds, the King saved her. "Let us say I *am* stumbling over that section of the Prophecy," he said, diplomatic and regal, steepling his fingers. "And let us say that you, a mortal who only discovered all of this existed a few hours ago, somehow holds the answer. What do you desire in return?"

Raegan's breath caught in her throat. Oh, what a loaded word—*desire.* There was much she desired, so many things she hungered for that had never been hers to taste.

"I desire," she managed, willing herself to finish the sentence in the way she knew she must, "for you to be on my side. Through all of this. I don't want simply your agreement to act in specific ways I must painstakingly hash out. I want you. On my side."

Those had not been the words she'd meant to use. She had no desire to reveal the depths of the ferocious hunger uncoiling low in her belly.

The King took too long to answer. She watched his chest rise and fall, his breath harder and faster than the situation called for.

"I am the High King of the Unseelie Court," he said, the words correct but the tone all wrong, a pale imitation of the cool, unaffected Fey being she'd first met. "I cannot act against the interests of my court. Not even if I desired your offering. Which I . . . which I do not."

Raegan did everything in her power to bite back a grin as she watched the fairy king stumble over his words. She had him. Triumph and lust mingled in her veins, thick as ambrosia.

"I thought you might say that," she replied with a shrug, fighting to display indifference. "I don't blame you. I would simply show you if I could, but the necessary object is at my apartment, where I believe you were quite insistent I do *not* go."

And then the King moved—faster, so much hopelessly faster than she could track—to stand right before her, mere inches separating them. Autumn rain and woodsmoke rolled over her senses. "Overhill," the King said, looking down at her, his head cocked in a way that brought to mind large predatory birds. "Are you attempting to lure me to a location the Protectorate is also familiar with?"

Fuck. She hadn't considered that part, which she supposed was exactly what she deserved for thinking this idea through for all of thirty seconds. Raegan's mind raced, trying to find the right words to smooth this misunderstanding over. Apparently, she did not speak fast enough, because suddenly the King caught her jaw between his long fingers and leaned down so their eyes were level.

"Do not," he said, his voice a low murmur, "become more trouble than you are worth."

Her flight or fight should have been screaming. It wasn't. The King's touch was, against all sense, gentle. Considering the situation, she'd expect his fingers to dig into her flesh, for the King to force her to look directly at him. None of those things were happening. She had the sudden, distinct impression that if she only took a single step back, he would release her entirely.

And yet she stayed exactly where she was. "Precisely how much trouble *am* I worth?" Raegan asked, raising her eyes to meet his oceanic gaze.

The King's breath caught in his throat, and she fought the urge to slam her mouth against his. The keening in her core erupted into a howl. He held her gaze, the muscles in his jaw catching. She pressed the advantage, grabbing the wrist of the hand he had on her chin. Beneath her fingers, she felt his cool skin, and beneath that, his racing pulse.

"Answer me," Raegan demanded.

The King studied her but did not release his grasp—nor Raegan hers —and she watched as something like a forest fire rolled over his features. All at once, she became aware that her skin was touching the King's in two separate places, mostly on account of the way her mind bucked and boiled like a sudden squall.

Just before her vision clouded over completely, the King let go of her, straightening. "Get your shoes," he told her.

"What?" Raegan asked despite herself, the word coming out in a high-pitched, bewildered tone.

The King rolled up the manuscript on the table and slid it into a leather case before reaching for his teacup and draining the remaining liquid. "We are going to see if you are telling the truth," he replied, making eye contact with her as he began to roll his shirt sleeves back down, "or if you are going to die tonight."

CHAPTER THIRTY-FOUR

Out on the sidewalk, beneath the dark sweeps of the autumnal evening, the King offered Raegan his arm. She took it despite the very credible death threat he'd made no more than five minutes prior. Mostly because—if she was being honest—he looked very good in his charcoal wool overcoat and black three-piece suit.

"You people take your manners so seriously one moment," Raegan grumbled, falling in step beside him, "and then threaten to kill people the next. It's absurd."

She told herself she'd imagined the way one corner of his mouth curved up, a trick of the neighborhood's nighttime dress of murky street-light, cigarette smoke and antique shadows.

"I have always found it polite," the King replied, looking over at her, "to be clear about one's intentions."

"Oh, yes, you're extremely clear-cut and straightforward," Raegan snorted in reply, rolling her eyes.

He said nothing, and for a moment she thought she'd offended him—goddamn fairy kings—but then she actually thought about it.

"Fine," she added, quickening her step to match his much longer ones as they crossed the street. "I'm not *aware* of any misdirection. But I guess you all can't lie, or whatever. Right?"

The King made a low sound of consideration from somewhere deep in his chest that did not help dissuade Raegan from wanting him to slam her into a wall and fuck her as hard as he could. She swallowed and looked down, trying to focus on avoiding cracks in the sidewalk.

"Your people think we cannot," the King eventually offered, sounding amused with himself.

Raegan swatted at his shoulder in response, releasing a dramatic, exasperated sigh. Again, she told herself that it was only the skittering light of the streetlamps that made her think he had smiled. She shook her head and slid her free hand into her pocket, fingers meeting the cool surface of her phone. All the levity of the moment swept out like a tidal wave. Her real life still existed somewhere. Steeling herself, she checked her home screen.

Predictably, more texts from Henry. Another voice memo from Saanvi, then an hour later, a simple text that read, *you okay?* A missed call from her mother. No text follow-up, though, so there wasn't an emergency.

Anxiety knotted in her stomach as she stared at her screen, trying to decide what to do and what was real. Her steps became more like stomps, and she saw the King tilt his gaze in her direction, though he said nothing. Raegan gritted her teeth. She was finally, *finally*, on a quest. Why couldn't everyone leave her the hell alone?

"Is everything alright?" the King asked, his voice coming from close to her ear, like he had leaned toward her to speak.

In response, Raegan let out a derisive laugh. "Obviously not," she replied, biting down on the inside of her cheek. "But it's all dumb mortal stuff. I doubt you'd care."

In the passing glow of the streetlight, she watched the King's expression stiffen. "Per our bargain, I am required to care about your well-being," he replied, some of the previous languor seeping out of his tone. "That being the case, if something is troubling you, I will do my best to assist."

Raegan told herself to breathe for a few seconds, but sorrow had been brewing inside her all day, and now it had fermented into anger. "Fuck off," she spat at the King, tilting her chin up at him. "You could probably fix every problem in the world with a wave of your fancy fucking faerie hand, and yet you haven't, have you? You're here because you want the Gates open. Let's not pretend otherwise, yeah?"

Her words were as much a reminder for herself as they were barbs for the King. It didn't matter that just now, as they walked arm-in-arm, their bodies slotted together perfectly, like they'd been made from the same stardust. It didn't matter that, against all reason, the King seemed capable of seeing the truth of her beyond all the layers of bluster and misdirection. And it certainly didn't matter that Raegan was probably more attracted to him than she had ever been to anyone else in her entire life.

The King slammed to a standstill in the middle of the sidewalk, so abrupt that Raegan tripped a little. She looked up at him, ready to spit venom, but the expression on his face cut off the words in her throat. His eyes were an ocean in a storm, the muscles of his jaw standing out harshly beneath his pale skin, dark brows drawn together.

"Do not mistake me, Overhill," the King replied, his voice like black ice. "I have done everything in my power—and more—to remedy the plight my people face. It consumes me. If our liberation were so simple an exercise, understand I would have done it, no matter the cost, a millennium ago."

Raegan realized with a shaking breath that she'd actually made him angry, possibly for the first time. For once, nothing about the King was slick or calculated or cunning. Of all places, it was here in the glow of a French café to her left, among its outdoor bistro tables, that he had drawn himself up like a snake about to strike. And of all things, it was over the idea that he had not done everything he could.

Interesting.

"Look, I didn't mean to offend you," Raegan attempted, but one look from the King cut her off.

"And for *you?*" he continued, glowering down at her, the intensity of his gaze palpable on her skin. "For you, I have—"

He halted, swallowing the words, looking away from her, sharp profile glowing against the dusk sky. Before Raegan could say anything, he began to walk again, pulling her along with him. She followed a few steps in silence, glancing over to see the storm still brewing across the King's features. How she wanted to poke and prod, to see what would make the thunder rumble and the lightning strike.

But she had the strangest feeling she would be pouring salt in her own wounds somehow, like maybe she and the King shared the same tender, aching places. She spent the next block clenching her jaw, telling herself that the idea was not only infinitely stupid but also impossible.

And yet it did not leave her.

"We will be taking the underground," the King said, his tone again clipped and professional. "I would like to engage in as little magic as possible."

Raegan nodded but did not reply, reaching her free hand out to trail her fingers along the iron fence of a church courtyard to her right. Up ahead, a sycamore tree draped over the gate, dappling the sidewalk with scraps of red and yellow silk, an autumnal fairy carpet. She took a deep breath and then another, the familiar scent of cigarettes and car exhaust and cool air soothing her a bit.

They slipped past a rowdy group of bar goers wearing matching t-shirts, and then the King led Raegan to the mouth of the subway entrance. She slipped her arm tighter into his, a response to the evening bustle of the station and the threat of the Protectorate, and absolutely nothing else.

Jogging down the stairs to keep time with the King's long strides, Raegan asked, "Does doing less magic make it harder to find us?"

"Precisely," the King replied, casting a wary eye out around the belly of the subway station. The daily commuter traffic was over, but the night had descended cool and crisp, so the city would surely be bulging at the seams.

Raegan tracked his gaze, understanding that the time of day actually made it harder to see who didn't belong. Restaurant workers mixed with corporate professionals headed home from happy hour, night shift nurses stepping off subway cars behind fresh-to-the-city college students. At least during rush hour, miserable as it may have been, the Protectorate would've been easier to spot.

"This way," she said, gesturing toward the correct platform to return to her apartment. They walked through the turnstiles, Raegan amused to find that instead of tapping a pass, the King simply waved his hand over the scanner. Forced to shuffle through side-by-side to maintain physical contact, she wondered if they looked like two people so in love that they couldn't bear to forgo touch for even a moment. She wondered what that might feel like.

When they reached the platform, which was blessedly quiet and relatively empty, the memory of seeing the King for the first time from the subway car lodged itself between Raegan's ribs. A wave of emotion caught at the back of her throat, and despite the layers of fabric between them, she suddenly felt overwhelmed by the King's proximity.

An express train flew through the station, all screeching metal and howling wind. When it passed, Raegan busied herself with reading the flier that had settled like a strewn leaf at her feet. For a few seconds, she was convinced the text was in a language she could not read. But bewilderingly, she realized the flier was very much printed in English, advertising a flea market.

"Did you see me, too?" Raegan asked, having no idea where the courage to say the words came from. "A few days ago, on the train? At the City Hall station?"

She was not in the habit of asking questions she did not already know—or at least suspect—the answers to, but this hushed inquiry made in the dim, gray-walled cavern of the subway platform shattered that rule. She had no idea how the Unseelie King might answer her, and even more so, Raegan had no idea what the implications of that answer would be.

He turned to her, his brow creased, looking impossibly lonely and tired. His gaze met hers and then drifted away, only to return again. "Yes," he replied, the word coming out hoarse and empty, a dried-out husk.

Raegan's heart was beating faster, and time seemed to have slowed down, as if it were moving around her in a circle instead of dragging her forward on its usual current. At least twenty words tried to climb her dry, aching throat before she thought of the right ones.

"What is going on here?" she asked, her voice low and reverent even though they were now alone on the platform. "Beyond the rest. What is going on underneath?"

His perfect alabaster skin nearly sallow in the green-hued lighting, a phantom wind kicking up the ends of his overcoat, the King almost looked familiar. Something surfaced from the depths of his gray eyes that Raegan thought she might have seen a thousand times before. And then it blinked out of existence.

"Let us stay focused on what is to come, not what has already passed," he replied, cool but not unkind, straightening the line of his shoulders.

Raegan's every instinct was, of course, to push and pry. But instead, she was overcome with a bone-deep exhaustion. Time felt strange again. Hadn't they been on this platform for at least a hundred years? Everything she did felt like a repeat—the way civilizations are built on top of the bones of the ones that came before, just for those cities to fall, too, and provide stable footing for the next swell of humanity.

So instead, she simply fixed her eyes on the track and waited for the train to come.

CHAPTER THIRTY-FIVE

Raegan and the King boarded the subway without speaking to each other. The car was barely half-full, and she pulled him toward the open seats at the back, away from the other riders. They settled onto the worn vinyl, Raegan's left arm and shoulder pressed up against him. She told herself some degree of physical contact eased his burden of hiding them away from prying eyes, but there was absolutely no reason to lean into his warm, sturdy mass.

The subway lurched into motion, sending an empty coffee cup skittering across the floor. Something hung between the two of them—something they had been talking about on the platform, Raegan thought. Though she couldn't get her head around exactly *what*. She dragged her right hand through her hair. It had been a long day. Of course she felt a bit scrambled.

In a completely different world, the sway of the subway car might lull her into drowsiness, and she might rest her head against the King's substantial shoulder.

Instead, she straightened and cleared her throat. "What should I expect?" Raegan asked, as if that would quell the anxiety twisting her insides.

"It is likely your living quarters have already been disturbed," the King replied, looking over at her. "If that is so, you will feel violated and angry—a normal response. Beyond that, I doubt we will get through this evening without a Protectorate interaction."

A chill seared its way down her spine. Why had she been thinking they'd just take a friendly jaunt to her apartment and back? Of course this was going to be unpleasant, and she chided herself for imagining otherwise.

"Stay close, follow my instructions," the King added, his voice low and intense, "and no harm will come to you."

She sucked on her teeth and slunk farther down in the slippery seat. How badly she wanted to trust him. It would be so much easier to stop fighting the tide that pulled her toward him, telling her they had always kept each other safe. But he was an immortal Fey king and she was a mere mortal woman, and she'd read that story often enough to know where it usually ended.

So Raegan just nodded, letting the back of her head rest on the top of the seat. She stretched her legs out in front of her, crossed at the ankles, and watched another passenger farther up in the car who was busy knitting. The needles moved back and forth, weaving smaller, separate strands into one singular, grander thing.

"This is it," Raegan said to the King when the subway slowed a few minutes later, pulling into her station. She sat up and slid her arm through his without a word. Together, they walked onto the platform and then up the stairs, avoiding the debris that always seemed to line every crevice and corner in her city.

Anxiety coiled thick and sour in her stomach with every step. She couldn't shake the feeling that she was abandoning the safety of her nest for the terrors of the wide world outside. But letting the King go alone wasn't an option—her father's spell was her only foothold, and it was a weak one at that. How hard would it be for an ancient Fey being to simply take the sheets of parchment from her, if he wanted?

As they reached the top of the subway stairs, Raegan turned to examine the King in the glow of the evening. Above him, the moon—a slim, elegant crescent—had emerged into the sky. Two otherworldly things side-by-side that she could see but not fully comprehend.

"This way," she said, trying to pull him across the street. But the King didn't budge against her weight. She looked over her shoulder at him, eyes narrowed.

"We cannot march in down the sidewalk," he told her, one eyebrow arched. Then he gestured to the side, where the worn awning of a closed deli created a velvety swathe of darkness on the walkway.

Raegan followed him with skeptical, tender steps, a hidden part of her wishing they were ducking into the shadows for another reason entirely.

Once the dimness had swallowed them, the King spoke again. "If you permit it, I would like for you to show me the way to your home," he said. "To remain less noticeable, I will be employing a cruder method that requires me to touch you. Do I have your consent?"

Raegan had to bite her tongue to stop the word "yes" from leaving her mouth immediately. Because of *course* he had her consent—the dark-haired, lithe-limbed creature knew her body better than anyone, had touched every inch of her a thousand times before.

She let out a long exhale, looking down at her shoes, barely distinguishable from the sidewalk in the awning's shadow. Regardless of how she felt, Raegan would be damned before she gave any Fey blanket consent like that.

"You have my consent to touch me for this specific situation and only to aid your knowledge of reaching my apartment in the safest way possible considering the threat of the Protectorate," Raegan finally replied, raising her gaze to his. Even in the dark, she found his storm-gray eyes with ease. "But I retain the right to revoke that consent at any time."

A flash of white—a smile, she realized—and then she felt the King step in closer to her. "Well done," he murmured, a rumble in his chest. Then his large, powerful hands were upon her.

Raegan suppressed the roll of pleasure that moved through her body as the King's fingers brushed the place where her jaw met her neck. Both of his hands moved upward in a gentle swoop, coming to cradle the back of her head. She swallowed hard and tried to think of anything but the way their bodies pressed together, all her soft curves against his hard angles.

"Please picture the route to your home," the King commanded, though there was a slight hitch in his voice. Raegan furiously told herself it was only because he was concentrating and not because of her.

Biting down on the inside of her cheek, she walked the first few blocks in her mind's eye with minimal issue, carefully mapping every turn and footstep. As she drew closer to her front door, she no longer walked the path alone; instead, the presence of the King became undeniable. Heavy, dark, certain, and relentless, half a step behind her, so like her dream in the autumn meadow with the river in the distance—

The King pulled back suddenly, one hand falling to her shoulder, the other pinching the bridge of his nose. Though the dimness made it difficult to be certain, she thought his eyes might be squeezed shut, hard.

"Sorry," Raegan murmured, heat rising to her cheeks.

"It is alright," the King replied, not looking at her. "What are the remaining directions?"

She told him the final two turns and then gave a description of her building. He nodded, looking out from beneath the awning and into the night.

"Are you ready?" the King asked, his tone solemn now.

"I mean, I guess," Raegan replied with a shrug. "I have no real idea what I'm getting myself into. So fuck it."

He turned back, gaze meeting hers again. A cold steel lingered in his expression. "I will not allow any harm to come to you," the King said, the line of his shoulders and the clench of his jaw so fierce that she had no choice but to believe him.

Before Raegan could say anything, he slipped his arm back through hers and swept them out into the night. The first few blocks passed slow and tense. The King moved methodically, sticking to the shadows, doubling back, stopping and waiting at odd intervals.

"There is only one entrance, yes?" he asked a block from her apartment.

"Yeah," Raegan replied with a nod, distracted. It was hard not to see every pedestrian they passed as possible Protectorate. Even the pack of overgrown frat boys on the last street felt suspect to her—it'd be a damn good disguise, wouldn't it?

Beside her, the King grumbled something about fire hazards. Any other time she'd demand how in god's name an Unseelie regent had an opinion on human safety codes, but at the moment, her heart was in her throat, and it took every ounce of her willpower to keep walking. She felt violated. The idea that the familiar comforts of her neighborhood—the soaring alleyways and imposing industrial buildings and overgrown weeds woven into chain-link fences like a patchwork quilt—could all suddenly become a threat was terrifying. And infuriating. How much more did the Protectorate plan to take from her?

"Steady," the King murmured beside her, as if he had continued access to her thoughts.

She hated how much the scant syllables spoken in his low, melodic voice actually did soothe her. *Steady*. All she had to do was stay the course. Raegan skirted a piece of free furniture left out on the sidewalk, feeling some of her anger solidifying into determination. Though mortal, she was still a force to be reckoned with, and she had a literal Fey king at her side.

Approximately three seconds later, the King dragged her into an alleyway, shattering the veneer she'd been constructing. Raegan didn't even have a moment to catch her breath before he pulled her into his chest, his back against the stucco wall.

"Be silent," the King said between his teeth, the words just barely audible. She nodded, wondering how loudly her heart was beating. Whether it was in response to the potential threat or to the way the front of her body was flush against the King, one of his strong arms tightly wound around her waist, was anyone's guess. Black pepper and autumn leaves filled her senses, banishing the alley's scent of damp rot.

Too soon, the King released her and pushed off the wall. Backlit by the streetlamp, his strong features stood out against the night, his eyes nearly black, chin tilted up as if he could catch the Protectorate's scent in the air.

"We must be quick," he said after a few moments, looking over at her. "Your neighborhood is infested."

"Protectorate?" Raegan asked, just to be sure, in a near-whisper.

The King nodded, impossibly regal even in an alleyway filled with trash and knee-high weeds. "I will offer them a distraction," he told her. "And then we will move."

He reached deep into his pocket and retrieved a long, elegant vial—not dissimilar to an antique perfume bottle. From the vial, he pulled something so gossamer-thin that Raegan could barely make it out in the dim light. Then he cupped it in his hand and blew on it gently, sending the object spinning into the air like a wish made on a dandelion.

Raegan opened her mouth to ask if an ancient organization dedicated to fighting the Fair Folk would really fall for something so simple as a distraction. But then the ground shivered beneath her, like someone had run their fingers along the back of an attention-hungry feline. She felt *something* stretch, claws experimentally flexed.

In the distance, beyond the ever-present murmur of sirens and car radios and the hum of the subway below, a roar shattered the night. The sound of it cut right into Raegan's body, like a cold wind through a flimsy shirt.

"What the fuck," she muttered despite herself.

"*Cath Palug*," the King replied, his voice cool and even, like she'd asked about the weather. "She gifted me three of her whiskers some time ago. A debt paid."

Raegan's head snapped toward the King so fast she thought she might've given herself whiplash. "The giant cat?" she demanded. "Didn't Sir Kay kill it, like, hundreds of years ago?"

The King tipped his head back and laughed as if the idea of a human knight killing a monstrous faerie cat was the most amusing thing he'd ever heard. And then, without answering, he grabbed Raegan by the wrist and pulled her headlong into the night.

CHAPTER THIRTY-SIX

As Raegan yanked the door to her apartment building closed behind her, another roar cleaved the night in two. She wavered for a moment at the bottom of the stairs, breathing hard, holding one hand up to the King in a request to wait. Of course, he appeared entirely unfazed by their sprint across multiple blocks.

"Okay," she wheezed, gesturing toward the long, steep flight of stairs before her.

His hand still locked around her wrist, the King plunged toward the stairs. She imagined he would've made it to her door in half the time without his mortal baggage in tow. On the landing, she tried to slow her breathing as she dug into her pocket for her keys.

But then the King pressed a few fingertips to her door, and it creaked open.

"Did you . . .?" Raegan breathed, fear shooting through her chest.

"No," he replied with a grim shake of his head. "The Protectorate has already been here."

Raegan set her jaw, following the King into her apartment. He closed the door behind her, running his hands along the frame and speaking in low, monotonous tones—magic, surely, she thought. She told herself she was safe enough to process what she saw before her for at least a few seconds.

Her coffee table was overturned, the underside cut into as if she could've hidden secrets within the particle board. Her couch was gutted, all the stuffing yanked out and sorted through before being left in a heap. The bookshelves had fared no better, nor had the books upon them. Raegan looked away before the sight of her books treated so roughly brought tears to her eyes.

All the cabinets in her kitchen were wide open, some of her vintage plates scattered on the countertops. Strange symbols shimmered on the little window above the sink. She forced herself to take one long breath in through her nose and out through her mouth. It got caught somewhere halfway up her lungs and came out instead as a sputtering huff of anger.

And then she remembered—of course, her father's spellwork. Raegan spun on her heel, her skin pricked by a thousand white-hot needles, and dove for her work bag. Its contents had been rifled through, her belongings strewn across the floor. She turned in a few fruitless circles before spotting the manila folder poking out from a pile of books. With the King still at work by her door, she half-ran, half-fell toward the folder.

"Thank fucking god," Raegan muttered upon examining the spell-craft papers. Everything seemed to be intact, so she clutched it to her chest, her body filled with utter relief that she hadn't failed her father.

Swiping at the tears that spilled hotly onto her cheekbones, Raegan examined the pile of books the manila folder had been sorted into— modern fiction and memoir, investigative crime, drier journalistic texts. She let out a sharp exhale, hoping that meant somehow, against all reason, the Protectorate had ruled her father's spellpapers as being insignificant.

"I see you have found that which you seek," the King said from behind her.

Raegan rocked back on her heels, wrapping her arms around her chest, the papers pinned against her. "Why didn't the Protectorate take them?" she asked, the question posed mostly at herself.

Behind her, the King remained silent, though she could've sworn she felt his gaze on her for a few intense seconds. She squeezed her eyes shut, her mind racing. What a crossroads she faced—if she was wrong to show the King her father's spellwork, everything would be over. She'd be left behind as the stronger, older, better beings went on their quest. Perhaps he'd be kind enough to wipe her memory. Or perhaps the cruel faerie king would leave her with the knowledge that she had been so, *so* close but the door had closed in her face and she would never again feel the winds of myth in her sails.

Raegan counted to three, letting her gut decide for her. Every muscle in her body tense and coiled, she stood and turned to face the King, offering him the folder. Time stood still as he reached forward—delicate, gentle, as if the spellpapers might turn to dust—and flipped the folder open without removing it from Raegan's grasp.

He examined the first page, brow furrowing. Then his gaze slowly met hers. For a long, harrowing moment, Raegan didn't understand the expression on his face—until her stomach dropped, and she realized it was rage.

"Overhill," he said, "I do not understand. You are showing me a blank piece of parchment, are you not?"

For some reason doubting herself, Raegan glanced down at the paper, half-surprised to find the ornately detailed illustration of the Gates still there, the scrawled notes still littering the margins.

"No?" she asked, her hands beginning to shake. "It's not blank to me. It wasn't blank to Rainer."

Her next thought—standing there in a ransacked apartment, a manila folder clutched in her hands like a lifeline—was that she'd gone absolutely fucking insane. So insane that her own delusions were incapable of perceiving what she plainly saw before her.

Terrified, Raegan raised her gaze back to the King and instead found amusement, of all things, simmering across his features.

"Your father is in a class of his own," he said with a slight shake of his head, the corners of his mouth curving upward. "You will need to permit me to see what is contained within this parchment. Kelpies are oathed to different rules and less constrained than those who sit upon a court throne or those who are sworn to the Timekeeper."

Her head spun. If her dad had laid a spell on the papers to conceal their contents, *should* she give a goddamn Fey lord the ability to view them? Her mouth went dry, her throat aching. The world condensed to the folder she held in her hands and the King standing before her.

A clamor split the air, closer this time, the windows in the apartment shaking. Her teeth rattled, and then the moment shattered like broken glass, scattering in glimmering pieces on the floor.

Reflexively, Raegan closed the folder and pulled the papers tight against her chest, taking one large step back from the King. "Tell me what the fuck is going on here," she said, her voice choked with a thousand emotions she could not begin to identify. "Not the Protectorate, not my father. Tell me what is going on between *us*. The truth."

She expected the King to draw himself up, to examine her with cold eyes, for his mouth to curl into a snarl.

Instead, his shoulders sagged and he dragged a hand through his dark hair. "Overhill, we do not have the time," the King replied, exasperated, gesturing toward the door and all the horrors that clearly lay beyond it. "And besides, that was not the deal."

"Well, I'm changing the fucking deal," Raegan near-shouted, holding the folder aloft and shaking it for good measure. "You want what's in this folder? You want me to let you see it? Amend the fucking deal! I want you on my side, protecting me, protecting this quest, without having to watch my language every goddamn second to satisfy your Fey bullshit. And I want you to tell me why I've had these weird dreams all my life and these inexplicable feelings and why when *you* showed up, everything went fucking insane."

She paused for a deep breath, and the King only watched her, his expression careful and guarded. So she kept going.

"And all you have to do is touch me and I lose my mind, like there's too many thoughts and emotions inside of me and I'm going to burst!" she shouted, a bit louder than intended. "Not to mention all the crazy shit Cordelia and the Keeper were saying, like you and I have some sort of past, but of course that *should* be completely impossible. It doesn't feel that way, though—and sometimes I even think I remember. It's right there, so clear, if only I could say it out loud. And then two seconds later, it's gone, just sand falling between my fingers. Am I losing my mind, or is something happening?"

Raegan pressed her lips together, breathing hard, staring up at the King. She could keep going—part of her wanted to—but she'd asked the question that had been stuck in her throat for too long now. She'd gotten it out of herself, like a particularly stubborn weed with deep, deep roots.

"Your sanity is sound," the King told her, his voice gone into that soft, silvered tone he had used back at the Temple of the Oracle. "There are other powers at work. Though I would prefer to leave the past buried, I am willing to discuss all of it with you further, but *not* here—we are not safe."

He shifted his weight, glancing over his shoulder for another moment, as if something outside had uncoiled or intensified. She hesitated, pulling the folder tighter against her chest.

"Show me one page," the King suggested, beginning to look exasperated, the cruel gleam returning to his eyes. "Only one. I understand that you believe if you show me everything, I will no longer need you."

Raegan opened her mouth and closed it again. The windows of her apartment shook hard again, the dirty silverware in her sink rattling. Every second she squandered standing here was one less they could use to escape the Protectorate, and this did not seem like a good time to test the King's limitations. Besides, Maelona—or perhaps the shell of what had once been Maelona—seemed testament enough to the Protectorate's power, and frankly, that horrified Raegan.

"Fine," she snapped, opening the folder again and taking a step forward. She paused, looking for the right words, only half-surprised when they came to her easily, like she already knew them. "High King of the Unseelie Court, I invite you to view one—and *only* one—of these cloaked pages to judge whether you wish to alter our agreement. Any additional pages will remain obscured from your eyes until I permit otherwise, and only after said agreement alterations are sealed."

For a split second, the King looked at her as if she might be the sun. Then he stepped forward, hands clasped behind his back, towering and imposing in the low-ceilinged space of her apartment. Raegan's entire world held still as she watched his eyes rove over the page. Like the kelpie, his cold composure held steady for a few moments, her heart thumping noisily in her chest all the while. Then his dark brows drew together and something like confused awe flooded his expression.

The Unseelie King looked up and considered her, the darkness clinging to his shoulders like a cloak, looking for all the world like he had just stepped out of a nightmare.

"I accept your offering," he said, inhuman and ageless as the shadows whispered around him. "While I remain ever faithful to my court and the Unseelie Throne, I align myself with you, Raegan Maeve Overhill, in pursuit of your interests."

Blood pounded in Raegan's ears. For a halting moment, she wondered—far too late—about the consequences of putting her father's spellcraft in the hands of such an ancient and terrifying power.

But then instinct flared in Raegan, bright as the first fireflies after a long winter. She was Gods-touched, Fate-kissed, a Prophecy running wild within her. A sense of rightness fell onto her shoulders like armor. For the first time in her life, she felt she was exactly where she was supposed to be.

CHAPTER THIRTY-SEVEN

Raegan might have lived in that moment—spun from pure gold, honeyed and mythic—for an entire age, were it not for the series of explosions that echoed from outside.

"We need to depart," the King said as their eyes met. "*Now*."

She nodded hurriedly, grabbing her laptop and notebooks from the coffee table and stuffing them into her bag, followed by her father's mythology book, his spellwork tucked between its pages. Then she darted into the kitchen, opening the cabinet by the sink and grabbing her medications.

"You know, no one's going to believe that's just fireworks," Raegan said as she ran into her bedroom. "Someone's gonna call the cops."

The King followed her, wavering at the doorway. In the corner of her eye, she thought she might have caught discomfort in his expression. "Mortals are not privy to what is occurring," he replied, his voice tight.

"That's convenient," Raegan replied, reaching under her bed for her duffle bag, which seemed to have either caught on something or was heavier than she remembered. "Could you be useful instead of just standing there?" She chucked her duffle onto her bed, standing to find the King's imperious look had returned, arched eyebrow and all.

"Could you pack slightly faster than your current glacial pace?" the King returned.

Raegan rolled her eyes at him and pulled her nightstand open with too much force, shaking the lamp and photo frames that sat atop its surface. She grabbed socks and underwear by the fistful and shoved them into her duffle. "Has anyone told you that you're incredibly annoying?" she demanded, moving onto the next drawer. She paused, wondering what bras were best for an entire quest. Her tits hurt just going down the fucking stairs. "I would *love* to punch you in the face right now." She didn't dare sneak a glance at him, though she didn't think he had moved.

"You would be unable to reach," the King replied, ice-cold.

"Fuck you," Raegan said out of reflex, this sharp-tongued banter with him dangerously natural. She awaited his response but heard nothing, so with a huff, she grabbed a few different bras—underwired, heavy-duty athletic, comfort—and turned to face him.

The King no longer stood at the doorway; instead, he had stepped into her room without making a sound. His gaze connected with a framed art print on her wall, one she'd thrifted a number of years ago. A maiden with Pre-Raphaelite waves of red hair leaned over a small balcony, offering her token to a dark-haired knight astride a powerful black destrier.

As she watched him consider the art, something unfolded inside Raegan like an old letter opened for the first time in decades. A heartbeat later, the King seemed to startle, as if he hadn't realized she was looking at him. His regal exterior and metal exoskeleton materialized a few seconds too late, and for the briefest of moments, Raegan saw past it all.

And beneath, there was only pain. Pain so bottomless and suffering so endless that the color of his eyes no longer seemed like an ocean or a storm but instead, the grayed-out hue of misery itself.

"Oberon," she murmured, her hands falling useless at her sides.

He examined her, sculptural mouth parting. For a moment, she was so sure whatever he said next would change everything, bring all the pieces together, and send her to her knees, weeping with relief.

But instead, the entire building shook and the King's expression closed. "Hurry," he said, raw and urgent. "Let me keep you safe. Please."

Something about his tone made Raegan shut her mouth and nod.

She shoved jeans, sweaters, joggers, and tees into the duffle, then grabbed toiletries from the bathroom. When she returned, the King had left her bedroom, lingering in the small living room. She stepped toward him gingerly, having the strangest feeling that even such a powerful creature could—at some point—break.

He turned, holding out his hand—elegant, long-fingered, lightly calloused. A wave of foreign emotion slammed against Raegan and she almost reached out to place her hand in his. But then she understood, hefting her duffle from the ground and handing it over to the King. His fingers closed around the handle as if the bag carried no weight at all.

"Do you have everything you need?" the King asked, like he was trying to be careful, perhaps even gentle.

Her brows drew together, and then she grasped his meaning, sweeping a glance around the apartment: the suncatchers and keys in the window, the tucked-away kitchen, the dead houseplants, her quiet sanctum. "I won't be able to come back, will I?" Raegan asked.

"No," the King replied with a slow shake of his head. "No, I think it is best you do not."

"Right," she said, a hoarse echo. She grabbed two undisturbed photo frames from the bookshelf—her favorite portrait of her father and one at her college graduation with her mother—and slid them into her work bag before handing that to the King as well. "Yeah. I have everything."

At her confirmation, the King did something with his lithe hands. Her eyes tried and failed to track the movement as both her bags shrank down into something smaller. Not in a funny kids' movie kind of way—it was like the fabric came alive and knitted itself into something else, a mass of snakes writhing about. But the event was over before Raegan could analyze it further, and he handed her a leather luggage tag with her initials on it.

She took the tag and tucked it into her pocket, trying to take a deep breath. The attempt was interrupted by the King reaching over and engulfing her hand in his much larger one. The feeling of his skin on hers threatened to capsize Raegan's sanity, but there was also a deep-seated, worn-in comfort beneath the chaos.

"Stay close," he murmured, "and please do as I say. You will be safe. I promise."

Outside, the air soured around her, that teeth-rattling feeling coming from nearly every direction. The block was empty save for the moths crowding around the streetlights. She thought the King would direct them from shadowy corner to dark nook, but instead, he strode directly down the sidewalk. His movements were haughty, no hiding or sneaking, muscular shoulders back, strides long and languid. She tried to match his confidence, but her heart hammered in her chest, so she wrapped one hand around her knife, pulling it from her waistband and sliding it into her pocket.

"You are familiar with the viaduct, yes?" the King asked, his voice low and serious.

"Yes," she replied, the raw wind nearly taking her words.

"When I tell you to run," the King said, his eyes narrowing in concentration as he scanned their surroundings, "go there."

Raegan nodded, gritting her teeth, surprised to find no distrust clawing up from the pit of her stomach. A voice in her head insisted with absolute certainty that the raven-haired Fey would never harm her. With a sharp inhale, she pushed that thought aside and focused on what she knew for sure—their covenant was real, concrete, and it should hold.

Any additional time to consider her next move was cut short when a man in a rumpled suit appeared on the sidewalk ahead of them, his form backlit by the streetlamp. Her entire body tensed.

"Not yet," the King murmured into her hair, just loud enough that she could hear it. Raegan could only hope she had bet on the right eldritch terror.

Something invisible rocketed past them, tearing the air apart as it went, releasing a horrible screeching sound like nature itself could not bear the wrongness of its existence. She had to tell herself not to flee with each step.

"Steady," the King said. "Not yet. Let me give you more cover."

Her blood pounded. The air smelled of burnt hair and rusted metal, her world condensing to this one city block lined with a developer's chain-link fence and crumbling old row houses, broken glass winking in the streetlights.

The man in the suit bellowed something, and Raegan was surprised to find it was her own name. "We only want to help," he continued, his London accent crisp. "We do not want you to bring more shame on your family."

The King did not stop, nor did he speak, until they were only a few paces from the man in the suit. Up close, he had lank blond hair, long limbs, and a pointed, hawk-like face. He also looked, at least to Raegan, like he was trying very hard to disguise his deep-seated terror. His brow pinched together and then released, fear flooding his eyes like a tide, in and out, in and out.

"While it is always a delight to spill *Gwarcheidwad* blood," the King said, slick as an eel, "we have pre-existing commitments for the evening."

The man said nothing, his lips pressed together. On some instinct, Raegan swept her gaze out and around the area, seeing what the King must've been waiting for: more Protectorate emerging from the mist. Though many of their suits looked for all the world like off-the-rack Brooks Brothers, their accouterments were anything but. Chainmail and chest plates sat atop navy wool blazers, gloved but ordinary human hands wrapped around brutal axes, maces, spears, and swords—all iron, she had little doubt.

And then she felt the King slide his hand from hers. Raegan's entire body seized, knowing what word was going to leave his mouth next, and hoping to god she would actually be able to do it. Time stretched long, far too elastic, entire lifetimes fitting into each of her breaths.

The King splayed his hand on her back and spoke a series of words that she knew to be an incantation; she could feel the hum of the magic in her bones.

"Where did she go?" the man in the suit demanded, nearly jumping out of his skin, eyes darting to and fro. "What did you do to her?"

And then the King's voice in her ear: "*Run.*"

To her absolute shock, Raegan did. Her body took off, bolting for the viaduct, which was not far. Farther than she'd like to run, sure, but the adrenaline made her feel as though she could cover any distance.

Behind her, Raegan heard what sounded like a small explosion, a bone-rending scream, and then laughter.

The King's laughter.

She kept going, rounding the corner and diving into an alley she knew cut through to the cross street she was headed for. The nighttime autumn air was blessedly cool on her face, and she felt like the city was opening up for her, guiding her through its streets to safety. Raegan blew past someone in a yellow puffer coat walking a bunch of small dogs and then cut off a bus pulling away from a stop, doing whatever she could to cross the busy street faster.

Her short, heavy breaths fell in time with the sound of her boots hitting the pavement until she turned down the street that held her destination and finally slowed, winded. She hazarded a look over her shoulder but saw nothing. Ahead, the abandoned High Line railway soared above her, a weed-devoured ramp rising up to connect it to the street level. A chain-link fence surrounded the entrance, but she was sure another denizen of her city had freshly taken bolt cutters to it, like always.

She jogged along the fence line, trying to find an opening with only the weak moonlight as a guide. Growing frustrated, she ran her hand along the chain-link instead and finally found a cut. She crouched down, preparing to wiggle through. The tall grasses and weeds on the viaduct would provide better cover, she thought, and the height of the ramp would give her a good view of what might be coming.

Raegan was halfway through when two hands roughly grabbed her —not the King's, she knew instantly. Digging her heels into the loose, rocky soil, she tried to get leverage, but with nothing to hold onto, she was yanked back through the fence and deposited onto the uneven pavement below.

She rolled, banged her knee hard, and then staggered to her feet. In the weak, murky light, she could make out a mountain of a man before her—brown hair cropped close, pockmarked skin, a heavy brow and deep-set eyes. He'd been at the café, too. Unlike the others, he wore no chainmail, though Raegan felt fiercely sure he always did. He was familiar in a way that made her stomach lurch.

Bedwyr. Something buried deep inside of her seethed with rage, like she'd waited lifetimes for revenge.

The man took one look at her and spat on the ground. Then he lunged. Raegan tried to use his size against him, but he was far, far faster than he should've been. He got an arm around her neck in less than a second. She raised her heel and stomped hard on one of his feet, but he merely grunted and yanked her back against his chest. Raegan hissed threats of violence, trying to kick his groin, but he simply lifted her off the ground so her legs flailed uselessly. But even with her arms pinned to her sides, she thought she might still be able to reach her knife in her pocket. Raegan centered herself.

"Let me go, you fucking asshole," she screamed, slamming the back of her head into his nose. He spat a curse this time, revealing a thick British accent. She shouted an insult in response, struggling hard against him, doing anything she could to conceal the movement of her hand into her pocket.

Then, slinking out of the darkness, came a voice as low and dark as the night itself. "If you dare to harm her, I will slit your belly open and invite the *Cŵn Annwn* to feast upon your entrails."

Chapter Thirty-Eight

The man did not release Raegan, but his grip slackened, some kind of involuntary response to a threat from the Unseelie throne itself. She sucked air into her lungs, feeling a surge of adrenaline return as she looked up and saw the King.

Really, entirely, truly saw *him*, not the guise he had been wearing. The being just a few steps from her and her captor was exactly as her father's book had described: the last of his kind, a destroyer of worlds. Pitch-black shadows knitted themselves into armor over the King's body, obscuring his clothing entirely. Despite the impossibility of it, Raegan could make out arm bracers that came to viciously sharp points, a longsword with a heavy hilt, and a dark sweep of chainmail across his shoulders. All made of slinking, slippery shadows, plumes of black ink humming with deadly energy.

She felt her captor's breath hitch.

"Haven't seen this version in a while," the man said, jiggling Raegan like he was showing off the keys to a brand-new car. "Always been my favorite. Maybe it's just nostalgia."

She watched the King readjust his grip on the shadow-blade and realized very quickly that he was not the type to trade insults back and forth with the enemy. Well, she certainly wasn't going to wait around either, then. With her captor's attention understandably focused on the ancient being of nightmares standing before him, Raegan finally got a good grasp on her folding knife. She slid it from her pocket, flipped it open, gathered all the backward momentum she could and then slammed the blade into the man's stomach.

He let loose a horrible scream and dropped her, much like a child does when the animal they picked up unexpectedly sinks fangs into flesh. Despite her best efforts, Raegan was not prepared for such a definitive response, and she stumbled forward, her face about to meet the chewed-up pavement.

The King caught her by the upper arm with his free hand. All the forward-moving energy sent her straight into his chest, where she discovered that his armor felt just like cold metal, despite its unearthly origins.

He steadied her, his arm sliding around her waist. "Did you *stab* him?" the King wanted to know. Having caught her breath, Raegan turned to look at her would-be captor, who was still standing but barely, blood flowing freely from a wound in his gut.

"Yes," Raegan replied, holding up her soiled knife with all the glee of a kindergartener at show-and-tell. Somewhere through the man's anguished moans and her own breathing, so loud that it seemed fundamentally impossible, she noticed the King's powerful arm was still around her waist.

Raegan looked up at him in the gloom of the alley, his features illuminated by the wan, steel-gray moonlight. His mouth curved into the no-man's-land between a smirk and a smile. She ached for nothing but to drag his lips down to hers.

"Beautiful," the King said, only just louder than a murmur, and Raegan had no idea if he was speaking about her assault on the Protectorate man or . . . *her*. Heart racing with fear and adrenaline and desire all at once, she said nothing, for once in her life not wanting to disturb the moment.

But that familiar teeth-rattling wail made its way up the alley, followed closely by shouts. Whatever had slipped onto the King's features drained away, his mask of cool composure sliding back into place.

"We must move," he told her. "Are you unhurt? I am sorry my concealment on you did not hold for longer."

"Yeah, I'm fine," Raegan said, still breathless.

In response, the King nodded, grabbed her hand, and began to stride toward the viaduct's ramp. As they passed the Protectorate man bleeding out on the pavement, the King reached down in one fluid motion, brushing his fingers against the man's forehead. Raegan felt something push or maybe pulse, and then the King kept walking, having barely broken his stride.

When they reached the chain-link fence, he spoke a word and the barrier tore down the center like old wallpaper splitting at the seam. He stepped through the gap and turned to assist Raegan through the shorn metal edges. Then they began to walk up the incline, the King's firm grip still on her hand. She almost wanted to say she disliked it. But she could not.

As they walked, the grass and weeds grew taller, approaching Raegan's chest and then growing even higher. For a moment, she was worried about navigating the terrain, but then she saw how the plants bowed to the King as he went by—and by extension, cleared a path for her as well.

Ten thousand things fought to leap from her tongue, mind running too quickly for her mouth to keep up. Her hands were maybe shaking, she realized, and her knees felt a bit like goo. Even after a few more steps, her body didn't seem to have realized they were out of imminent danger—her heart still thundered madly in her chest.

"D-did you heal that man?" Raegan asked, reverting to her place of calm: acquiring knowledge.

"Certainly not," the King replied, looking at her sideways. "I made him forget that he had witnessed either of us, only our friend *Cath Palug*. If I was successful with the others, no Protectorate operative will remember sighting us tonight, though I cannot be sure."

Raegan did not know how to respond to that, not exactly. In a way, she was glad the King had not healed the man. But she supposed she had only been so willing to stab him because she had assumed magic would make even a dangerous wound heal easily.

A closer shout went up from behind them, and Raegan glanced over her shoulder, thoughts broken as fear skittered through her body.

"We are fine," the King replied, slowing his pace for a moment to look at her. "We should not be fools, of course, and we must continue to make haste. But this is a wild place. And wild places are still mine."

Nodding, Raegan bit down on her lip. There was no denying the feral nature of the viaduct, even in the middle of a densely populated neighborhood so close to Center City. Nature had taken over every inch of the man-made structure. Vines coiled like elegant tattoos around patinated steel, and up ahead even an oak tree had taken root. As clouds shifted away from the moon above them, Raegan noticed the fluttering wings of moths and other creatures. The tiny insects created a halo around the King's head, paying homage with each beat of their crystalline wings.

When the ramp leveled out and they reached the main High Line, the flying things dispersed, disappearing back into the gray velvet of the night.

"Just through here," the King said.

His grip on her hand softening, he led Raegan diagonally across the High Line to the ruins of an old storage building. Graffiti adorned the walls in jewel tones. She admired a huge loop of blood-red cursive as they slipped around the corner of the structure. Shock vibrated through her as she caught sight of a black crown with seven points on a wall they passed. The rendering was far from ornate, but the synchronicity of it made her reach out her hand and trail her fingers along it. If the King noticed, he said nothing.

When Raegan set her sights ahead of her again, she found a familiar shape. A series of huge, old-growth wisteria vines knotted themselves into a pointed arch, using two interior columns of the abandoned building for support. Distantly, she heard a soft drip of condensation. Despite the cool air outside, the atmosphere inside was warmer, damper, bringing to mind reptilian enclosures.

"I may not be able to shield you from as much portal sickness as before," the King said, leading the way around a giant crumble of cement and rebar. He came to a halt before the wisteria portico.

"I'll live," Raegan grumbled, though she glanced over at him, eyes narrowed, looking for signs that the King was taxed. In truth, she expected to find none, but his posture had slackened and he appeared to be keeping as much weight off one leg as possible.

"Were you injured?" she asked, having not even thought it possible. She ran her eyes up and down the King's form. The shadow-armor had dispersed, and she imaged that a wound should be obvious through his assortment of fine wools.

The King looked at her, something that was both a grimace and a playful smile moving across his mouth. "Just now?" he asked, arching a brow. "No. I was not injured. But in earlier battles? Yes, many times."

"I suppose," Raegan mused, watching him closely, "that it's easy to forget you have worn the same body all these years. I didn't think of a cumulative toll."

Something flashed in his eyes that she did not understand, though it hardly seemed to matter as the King looked away and moved toward the portico. Raegan stayed beside him, her hand still in his as a tremor ran down her spine. She twisted, gazing over her shoulder. She did not like the feel of the vast expanse at her back, the weed-choked railroad and open black sky. At the precise moment that the itch of being watched turned into sheer foreboding, Raegan saw the King freeze, his free hand mere inches from the middle of the portico.

"Something is wrong," he told her in a low tone, tilting his head back, as if to catch a scent of the enemy in the air.

"Look!" Raegan exclaimed, pointing to her discovery at the base of the wisteria vines. Hidden by the weeds and crumbled concrete, the bottom of the vines was blackened, sickly with disease. Now that she looked closer, she could see the upper reaches were parched and dry.

The King said something under his breath in a language she suspected was ancient and long-dead, though she knew without a doubt his words were a curse.

"Come," he said, turning on his heel and taking a large stride back toward the way they'd come. Raegan leapt over a pile of rebar to keep up, her heart beginning to thump around in her chest again, a wet towel in a washing machine.

He paused at the threshold of the structure, scanning the horizon. Beyond the tallest weeds on the viaduct, Raegan could see the familiar skyline lit up against inky darkness. Looking at the view had always comforted her, but tonight it felt distant, like a homeland she had once known but could no longer return to.

"Did they do something to it? To the portal?" Raegan asked, keeping her voice low.

The King did not look at her, but he nodded. "I did not think they could enter such a place," he murmured, his body like an arrow nocked and ready to fly.

"It used to be a railroad," she said, looking up at him, brow creased. "Doesn't it matter what things used to be just as much as what they are now?"

At that, he swung his gaze to meet hers, eyes black in the gloom. "Yes," the King answered. "I suppose it does."

With that, he slid into the waiting shadows, pulling Raegan along with him. The King set a fair pace, she thought, almost as if he was finally accommodating for her much shorter legs. They moved through the crumbling structures and high grass of the viaduct, doubling back around to the large area by the ramp.

The King moved slower then, shooting Raegan a terrible look when she accidentally sent a few rocks skipping across the ground. He pulled her a few more paces forward and then, out of nowhere, spun her into his arms as if they were dancers and not fugitives. Raegan found herself crushed between the corroded metal wall of a storage shed and the imposing, muscled frame of the King, her nose bumping into his chest.

"Make no sound," he advised, barely more than a whisper, easily mistaken for a rustle of the tall grass in the night breeze. Raegan nodded, trying to stop her hands from shaking. In an effort to stay calm, she took in a long, slow breath, heavy with the smell of rotted leaves and condensation and rusted things.

Her heart ran away in her chest at the sound of two voices just outside the shed. Looking up, she saw the King's attention snap to the location of the voices, so much like a predator sighting its prey. Raegan swallowed hard and told herself to breathe. She was in the company of the Unseelie King. He could handle whatever the Protectorate wished to throw at them.

But she couldn't forget the way he kept weight off his left knee or how tired he looked. It made sense. The King was doing magic in a world that had none. Raegan wondered, not easing the growing panic in her chest at all, how much he had left in him.

A twig snapped close—much too close—and the King stepped in even closer. Raegan's panic momentarily abated at the sensation of his long, powerful leg sliding between her own. She found herself caught at the crossroads of desire and terror.

The King raised his free hand—the one not holding hers—and made a small movement. Farther down the viaduct, a loud, metallic clang sounded. Though she could not see anything, her sight line blocked by the King's body, Raegan heard two sets of footsteps barrel out of the shed, chasing the phantom noise.

Without a moment of hesitation, the King pulled away from the wall, nearly dragging her behind him as he slipped around the opposite corner, keeping to the outer ring of five-foot tall weeds. With a jolt, Raegan saw that there were other Protectorate people up on the viaduct. She had only emotionally prepared herself for the two, but she could see at least four more gathered around like a hunting party, iron spears gripped hard in gloved hands. She tried to remind herself they were likely looking for the faerie cat, not the Unseelie King and his mortal companion.

But then one turned in their direction and Raegan froze, as if she had suddenly grown roots instead of legs. The King had size and weight to his advantage, and so he merely yanked her off balance until she followed him. Fear gripped her—she was so sure they had been sighted. But as the King led her through the grass, she realized the Protectorate woman had in fact not seen them at all; it was simply a terrifying coincidence.

Instead of taking the ramp to the sidewalk, the King led Raegan to an access ladder that ended significantly far from the ground. Its surface was chewed over with rust, and Raegan was fairly certain she saw it sway in the breeze.

"Are you fucking insane?" she hissed at him.

The King looked at her and nodded, almost gleefully. Then he pulled her into his arms and leapt.

CHAPTER THIRTY-NINE

"Jesus fucking *Christ*," Raegan hissed the moment her feet were solidly on the ground. "Was that necessary?"

The King looked down at her. "There were at least six Protectorate operatives," he replied. "Yes, it was necessary."

Raegan glanced up, expecting menacing faces peering over the edge of the viaduct's hulking iron mass. But only the underbelly of the trestle greeted her: ever-damp, decorated with graffiti. She let out a long breath.

"We will have to walk back," the King told her, gesturing to the broken sidewalk and litter-lined gutter across the street. "I do not wish to risk attracting any additional attention."

Raegan nodded, moving automatically to entwine her arm with his—certainly a more natural pose than trotting around a busy neighborhood with his hand clamped around hers. They moved off into the night, walking in silence. Best to focus on their surroundings, Raegan thought, and keep a sharp eye out for anything suspicious, any change in the atmosphere that spoke of that terrible, air-shattering magic. To call it magic felt wrong entirely. Whatever powers the Protectorate wielded seemed more like an abomination to her.

An abomination that she hoped she was free from for the evening as they crossed back into the King's neighborhood some time later, having taken any would-be followers on a merry and exhausting jaunt through the commercial district. Now they strolled down a popular series of blocks lined with restaurants and bars, the kind of place that had twinkling lights strung up in the trees and live music slinking out into the night.

And yet it was exactly there that Raegan felt the hairs on the back of her neck rise up. She saw no one out of the ordinary and certainly did not feel that teeth-hammering magic. But a spike of white-hot fear pierced her chest all the same, her hands suddenly clammy.

"We need to get off the street now," the King said, his voice low and intense, dark eyes examining the block.

"There's a bookstore up ahead," Raegan said, trying to stay focused. "It's big on the inside. Lots of places to hide."

"Of course," he replied, nodding. "The one with the cats."

That described at least half the bookstores in the city, but Raegan could not bring the correction to her lips. She felt like a tiny mouse rushing through a field, hoping to reach safety before an owl's talons sunk into her flesh. The remaining distance to the bookshop stretched comically in her mind, a horrible funhouse mirror that turned half a block into ten miles.

But they reached the front doors, which the King pulled open, ushering Raegan inside. Relief sang hymns in her chest. The friendly mess of the shop welcomed her back with open arms. Bookcases reached high toward the ceiling, packed full of titles in haphazard organization. The fat orange cat snoozed upon his usual chair tucked away in the corner, a piece of sheet music beneath his paws as if he had been examining the composition before drifting into sleep.

"There's a second floor," Raegan said, taking the lead and pulling the King along behind her.

For a moment, she worried about how the King would fare with his size trying to navigate the narrow, winding rows of shelves. Then she remembered he was a big boy, more than a thousand years old in fact, and plunged into the maze of towering bookcases. By the time they reached the stairs to the second floor, she had tripped over two piles of books and almost run into another browser, while the King had disturbed a grand total of nothing.

At the top of the stairs, the second floor greeted the pair gently, enveloping them in a quiet, dusty, book-scented hug. The lower level had been dotted with other customers, but up here, silence hung in the antique eaves of the old building. The hair on the back of her neck was still raised, foreboding thick in her ribcage.

"Over here," she said, sticking to the outer ring of the shelves as she navigated to the small room of vinyls at the very back of the shop.

When they crossed the threshold, she loosened her grip on the King's arm, trying to slip into the feeling of safety she had so often felt within the confines of a bookshop. But she could not muster it now, her mouth dry, her heart pounding. Not with the Protectorate prowling the street outside, not with all that lay before her—and not with the King.

He certainly did not make her feel safe. He made her blood race and her pulse throb and her heart ask questions her mind did not know how to even begin answering. In the dim, dusty light of the shop, she turned to look at him, only to find the King's gaze was trained out through the doorway, reminding her of hunting dogs catching scent of their prey.

"They are nearly here," was all he said.

Time skittered strangely, the dark walls lined with CDs replaced by cold gray stone. Words hung off the tip of Raegan's tongue like the last drop of tea, *I am yours until they come.* She shook her head to chase the thought away.

"I need you close," the King said, his powerful arms wrapping around her waist as he stepped back behind a towering display rack. "I need to conceal us, but I am in pain and tiring."

Raegan nodded, mute, her heart careening for another reason entirely, as the King pulled her against his chest for the third time that evening. She fit into his arms like a lost key, and the temptation to place her cheek against his chest and hear his familiar heartbeat was unbearable.

"Why do I know you?" she asked the King, the words leaving her mouth in a hoarse whisper. It was the question she had wanted to ask since the moment she saw him, the words that had pounded against the back of her throat in that subway car.

The King inhaled, a muscle in his jaw jumping as he watched her. She hated the way he said nothing. She wanted to scream at him or maybe shake him until she understood, until this slinking, dark howl within her stopped its raw keening.

"I imagine you already know," the King said, his words surfacing slowly. "Or that at the very least, you have begun to suspect."

Raegan didn't feel like she knew anything. Or rather, she felt like she knew things—knew everything, knew too much—and yet *understood* nothing. Actually recalling what she might know would require digging through endless, unlabeled filing cabinets in her mind. Feeling raw and tired beyond belief, she let her forehead drop against the King's chest. She felt him freeze, all hard, unyielding muscle. But then one of his hands alighted on her hair, gentle as a butterfly.

The framed illustration in her room he'd been looking at sprung back into her mind. She remembered when she'd found it at the thrift store, some alien feeling rising in her as she had traced over the woman and the horse with her fingertips. The knight's face was not visible in the piece, his back to the viewer, and he wore no colors or a shield that would perhaps give more hint to his identity. It mattered not—the artwork was compelling either way. Raegan had nearly been able to taste the dust rising from the street, and smell the horses and the flowers trampled underfoot when she'd first seen it.

She looked up at the King, no words leaving her mouth, but a question forming all the same—not one that she was sure she could even put into words. Whatever she wished to ask was formless, fathomless, as unknowable as the anonymous knight upon his black horse.

The King's hand slid from her hair, brushing her jawline. Her heart skidded to a halt, breathing terse and quick, as an unfathomably old longing uncoiled in her belly. With a weathered sigh, the King cupped the side of her face in his powerful palm, fingertips skimming her temple. But still, he said nothing.

"Tell me," she begged, her voice quivering. She was both mortified and astonished to find she could taste the wet, bitter salt of tears upon her lips when she spoke.

To her surprise, the King closed his eyes and complied, exhaustion as heavy as a mantle on his shoulders. When he spoke, his voice reminded Raegan of torn velvet. "You keep coming back," he said, as if that explained anything. "Always mortal. Always doomed. And yet you will not cease."

The words hit her with a palpable weight and her body wavered into the nearest display case. A million voices screamed inside her head, each vying to be louder than the rest. Raegan heard nothing but noise: the clash of ancient battles and the thundering of hooves and the swell of a symphony and the lap of river waters upon sandy shores.

She looked back up at the King, wanting more—*needing* more, knowing despite all reason that the being before her held the keys to everything she yearned for. There had always been a door in Raegan's heart, and she had spent her life trying to fill it with things that were not door-shaped.

Just as she opened her mouth to speak, two other browsers entered the room, chatting amicably. The King yanked his hand away from her, placing it against the wall to brace himself instead, shifting weight off his left leg. One of the browsers—tall, lean, wearing a patched denim jacket—looked over at Raegan and the King, somehow aware in the way only strangers are that a moment had been broken, dropped like an egg onto tile floors.

"Come," the King said, his tone low. "The Protectorate has moved on, and this is no conversation for public spaces."

Aware that tears were still streaming down her face, Raegan nodded, mute, and slipped her arm into the King's. She didn't know if it was because of the unholy, impossible thing hidden deep inside her, or simply because of the length and difficulty of the day she had just survived, but she had to fight the urge to turn toward the King, bury her face in his chest, and weep. But the fear of such vulnerability churned sour in her stomach, so she kept moving, letting her body remember to walk and breathe on its own.

Somehow, they returned to the King's archives and safehouse without incident, though he was insistent about sticking to alleys and shadowy side streets just in case. They walked in silence through the front door, the vestibule, the office, and then through that strange corridor that spat them out into the huge room full of books and shelves and hidden things.

"Please, sit," the King said, gesturing to a pair of worn-in leather chairs perched at the edge of the fireplace.

Raegan stared at the cozy scene for a moment, dumbfounded— apparently, the archives kept much of itself concealed unless the King permitted otherwise. She lowered herself into a chair and stared at the fire, aware that he was moving around the space behind her. It took all of her willpower not to turn and watch him. Instead, she gritted her teeth and examined what else the archives had decided to reveal: a kitchenette in the far corner, equipped with a tea kettle, espresso machine, mismatched mugs and saucers, as well as a mini fridge beneath the counter.

She realized that the King seemed to intentionally glamour away any parts of his space a visitor might find too cozy. Like he didn't want anyone getting too close. Like it was easier to keep everyone at arm's length. Raegan sighed. She could understand that.

Movement stirred in her peripheral vision as the King settled into the chair beside her. In the firelight, the hollows of his face were sharp and deep, as if he hadn't slept in many, many years. He'd removed his suit jacket and waistcoat, leaving only his dark shirt, sleeves rolled to the elbows. Her blood pounding, she watched the tendons in his forearm tighten and release as he stared into the fireplace. Then, gazing straight ahead, almost as if he could not bear to look at her, the King began to speak.

"You and I, Overhill, have known each other for a millennium."

Chapter Forty

The King's voice was flat and even, as if he were reciting words from a teleprompter or reading aloud from a memorized script. Raegan dared not speak—she found herself trying to limit even her breathing.

"Sometimes we pass by each other with hardly a ripple," he continued. "Other times, like the situation we have found ourselves in now, we are hopelessly entwined at the root."

Raegan felt as though someone had simultaneously poured cold water all over her and pricked her with a million hot needles. Her mouth was painfully dry. Something about her heart seemed brittle all of a sudden. For once in her life, she had nothing to say.

The King crossed his ankle over his knee, still not looking at her, the firelight dancing up and down the feral places of his face. Raegan preferred it this way, too. The words leaving his mouth were difficult enough; she was not sure she could also look into his eyes while he said them.

"The closest concept your people have is reincarnation," the King said, a hint of condescension creeping into his voice. "It is exceedingly rare, despite the casual way mortals speak of it. For most, including the Fey, death is the final door. But not for you. Death cannot seem to hold you down. It can barely get its hands around you for more than a moment or two."

This was the most Raegan had heard the King speak without further prompting, and she became surer and surer with each passing moment that this speech had etched itself onto his bones.

"We have broken vows for one another," he continued, listless. "We have fought beside one another. We have crossed oceans for one another."

Raegan's heart hammered so furiously in her chest that it frightened her. The King's words explained *everything*. Not just the strange, intense way he made her feel but also what she had experienced since childhood—the recurring dreams, the strange memories, the way sometimes she'd know things she should not, or reach to grab at skirts that were not there as she began to ascend a set of stairs. His words explained what she had always known to be true, the fantasy she'd harbored deep in her marrow even when she became too old to believe such things.

She swallowed hard as she felt the King's eyes fall upon her. Dampness gathered on her palms. Steeling herself, she turned to meet his gaze and found a sea of simmering cruelty, hewn over a thousand years of torment.

"In dozens of lifetimes, I allowed you to consume too much of me. I suppose it is only human to attempt to taste the divine," the King said, his voice a dagger, the line of his shoulders turning predatory.

Raegan held his gaze, alien things clamoring in her chest, no words materializing. So she said nothing, and instead let him fill the firelight-soaked space that hung between them.

The King took a sharp inhale before he turned away from her. "The Protectorate captured me because of you. You wished to play the hero, and foolishly, I went after you. I thought I could not live without you," he said, his tone hollow. "I know better now."

The chill of his words settled over Raegan like a frost. She needed warmth; she craved something that was not caustic and over-brewed by time.

Beside her, the King raked a hand through his dark hair, jaw tense. "We lost the war. You were executed. The Protectorate kept me. I am unsure how long. They tried every way they could come up with to kill me. When they saw they would be unsuccessful and it would only give my court time to retaliate, they exiled me, closed the Gates forever, and invited the Timekeeper to devour this half of the world."

The King stretched, panther-like, his hands coming to rest on the arms on his chair. He dug into the leather, long fingers flexing.

"In the two hundred years since, you have occasionally returned to destroy any chance I have at reclaiming my throne," he said. The fire sputtered low, one log reduced to embers, and he stood, moving to collect more kindling from beside the hearth. "I have to hope you will not poison everything this time, too."

Raegan's stomach dropped, sourness gathering at the back of her throat. The King crouched to feed the fire, his large frame nearly blocking out all the light. Then he straightened and turned to face her, silhouetted by the flames.

"And more so," he continued, crossing his arms, "I have to hope I will not *allow* you to. I am a better king when I do not know your touch, when my flesh does not crave yours."

Raegan knew all of it to be true the same way she knew her middle name was Maeve and the sky was blue and her mother was from Caernarfon. But the way he said it, so accusingly, looming over her, backlit by flame, was infuriating.

She crossed her arms, mirroring him. "Your flesh is safe, Oberon," she sneered, pouring all the venom she could into the few short words. "All I want is to find my father. I'll use you to that end and nothing else."

It was a lie and she knew it, but she said it anyway, because if finding her dad was no longer her north star, then what was? *Who* was? This ancient thing before her, all sharp angles and jagged edges? He'd cut her just now, so deep that far too much of her anger had been replaced with hurt. In fact, she felt like she could choke on it.

"You know," Raegan said, leaning back in her chair, examining her nails as if she had not just been scraped raw, "I'm going to need you to prove what you're saying. Because I think I'd feel something more for you if all this were true. Sure, I might fuck you, but you're talking about a lot more than that—you're talking star-crossed *love*."

She let out a haughty laugh instead of a tearstained scream, eyes sliding toward the King as he settled back into his chair. The impassivity on his features stoked her anger, and she relished it.

"Fairy magic is quite a drug, I hear," she continued, watching him closely for any sign her knives had hit their mark. "Making a human believe they've been entangled with you for a thousand years is a touch romantic for your kind, but it's awfully clever, and it'd be careless of me to let such a wild statement go unverified. I mean, you *are* a monster, after all."

The King tried to hide it, but he flinched. She slunk back in her chair again, mouth twisting into some dark shadow of a victorious smile. Tilting her head, she looked over at him, eyebrows raised expectantly, wondering if she'd have to deliver another barb to prod him into speaking.

But the King cleared his throat. "What process do you require?" he asked, cold and professional, steepling his fingers.

The Fey could not read minds. Raegan was sure of it because she remembered asking her father one afternoon, wondering what god-like power the Fair Folk did not have. It was obvious, too, in a way—all that guile would hardly be worth the effort if one could simply peer into another's mind.

Okay, she was *pretty* sure.

Raegan glanced at the King and saw he was waiting for her to speak. She told herself it was a deeply inconvenient time to like that about him.

"I have a recurring dream," she began, the tip of her tongue darting out to moisten her dry lips. Her idea was sound, but there was something in speaking about her dream that suddenly felt like uncovering a fresh wound. "It's autumn. I'm walking across a field. I smell woodsmoke. Someone's walking beside me, just out of sight. If anything of this is true, then I imagine it's *you*. Tell me, Unseelie King, which side of me are you walking on, and what are we walking toward?"

The King leaned across his seat toward her, propping one elbow on the arm of his chair. She tried not to let the few additional inches of closeness have its intended impact, but now she could smell him, the damp stone and black pepper and swirling woodsmoke.

"I am on your left," he replied, his gaze unwavering, "and we are walking toward a winding river. Its shores are narrow and sandy. The mountains rise up just beyond it in the distance. The forest begins on the far bank."

Raegan thought she had braced herself for it, but hearing the King describe the landscape of her recurring dream—so private she had never told anyone but her parents about it—made everything else he had said become blisteringly and irrevocably real.

"What are we doing there?" she asked, softening her tone, hoping that he wouldn't shut down completely now that she wanted something. "It feels so . . . important. Dreadful. Grim. But important." It had felt like the purpose she'd been searching for her entire life, but Raegan wouldn't give him that.

The King considered her and then shook his head, turning back to the hearth. "There is only so much that it is safe to tell you," he said, the words flat and trodden-upon, like he'd already said them a million times. "After you were executed and I exiled, you had a Seal placed on your magic and your memory during your next return. I know not if it was out of selflessness—to keep my people's secrets safe—or simply your own weakness. Too much knowledge of your memories risks the integrity of the Seal. For it to break on its own, instead of being removed, would almost certainly induce madness, rendering you useless to me."

Raegan spoke before even thinking, lurching forward in her chair, her heart pounding. "So remove it. *Now*."

Again, the King shook his head, leaning on his knees, staring into the fire. "Only the one who placed it can remove it," he replied. "And no one has heard from her in at least a hundred years. Seals are one of the few magics that remain even after the creator's death, so it is possible it cannot be removed at all. Even the way magic is leaving this side of the world will not degrade its integrity."

Raegan nearly threw herself out of her chair in frustration. A thousand years of knowledge, of memory, of magic, and most importantly of *herself*—of all the pieces she had always known she was missing, locked away by her own doing and now right here at the tips of her fingers, yet still unreachable.

"Who was it?" Raegan hissed. "At least tell me her name."

The King glanced at her sideways, evaluating her, a look in his eyes like he did not think she could handle whatever came next.

Then he sighed and said, "Baba Yaga."

Chapter Forty-One

He had to be lying, Raegan thought. Some kind of cruel trick on the stupid little mortal foolish enough to get in his way.

"Baba Yaga," she echoed, the last syllable choked by an incredulous laugh. "Right. Of course."

She waited for a sly knife between the ribs. But the King said nothing. He looked more statue than living thing, gaze directed at the fire, all the unnaturally sharp points of his frame—the shoulders, the jaw, the cheekbones—etched in the shadows of the wide, dark space. He was not something anyone could hold or caress or, god forbid, attempt to love.

He was no longer the man from her dreamscape's café or the knight walking beside her toward the river or the lithe, dark-haired lover tangled in her bedsheets. He was not her once-in-a-hundred-lifetimes, and she was not his.

Not anymore.

A bottomless sorrow enveloped her, the edges folding in on themselves, and Raegan felt something deep inside her fracture. She had managed to lose a grand and beautiful impossibility—a love that haunted her from one life to the next, echoing across space and time. Her throat closed off, and she dropped her head into her hands, fingers digging into her scalp. Emptiness lurched from the corners of the room. Her vision blurred.

It was just like Layla had said when they'd broken up. Raegan was too hard to love. Even for the person who had done so for centuries, until he just couldn't take it any longer. She bit down hard on the inside of her cheek, willing herself not to cry. Not here. Not in front of him.

Somewhere beyond the furious beating of her own wounded heart and the low blaze of the fire, bells sounded—soft, ethereal, like dappled light on the forest floor. Beside her, the King rose. She did not look up, twisting away from him as if she couldn't stand the mere sight of him. She heard him exhale.

"Excuse me," the King said, clipped. "I am receiving an urgent call."

Raegan said nothing, gratitude and grief mingling in her ribcage as the King strode across the room, disappearing into the shadowy hallway. When she was sure he was gone, she raised her head, dragging the backs of her hands across her eyes. She fought to prepare something to say when he'd return—anything at all that wasn't about what had transpired between them across the millennium. Self-disgust roiled in her stomach at the thought, but Raegan knew she was not strong enough to continue this line of discussion without breaking down.

"It's a fucking trick," she whispered to herself, surprised at the raw, desperate tone of her own voice. "A faerie trick. Nothing more."

She said it again and again, hoping the shape of those words might become more familiar in her mouth than anything else involving the Unseelie King. By the time she heard his footfall, she almost believed her own lies.

"If you would like to remain under the protection of the Unseelie Court," he said, breaking the silence, his mask firmly back in place, "I need to examine your father's spellcraft."

Raegan turned to him, movements sharp, her mind racing. "What is that supposed to mean?" she demanded, springing to her feet, grateful for a different reason to be angry. "What about our agreement?"

The King folded his arms in a way that made his powerful shoulders seem all the more apparent. He looked down at her as if she were the most tiresome toddler on the entire planet. "Keep up, Overhill," he said, one hand making sharp, elegant articulations in the air beside him. "You have my aid, my protection, my word. Not my Court's."

"I didn't realize that Fey courts were fucking democracies," Raegan scoffed, rolling her eyes at the very idea that the King did not rule with an iron fist.

To her surprise and discomfort, the King smiled, the expression made all the more unsettling by the way the firelight sent shadows slinking across his face. "There is undoubtedly much you do not understand about the Unseelie Court," he murmured, his voice low and soft, somehow more dangerous for it. "Do you wish to experience the darkness of our depths, or would you prefer to deliver on your promise?"

Despite herself, a delicate chill traced cold fingers up Raegan's back. She swallowed hard, a primal instinct woven deep into her marrow urging her to run and never look back. But she stood her ground, hands balling into fists at her side, her skin gone clammy. "Fine," she replied. "Let me put my things away, and then I'll show you. It'll only take a minute."

The King examined Raegan, hawkish, his weight shifting toward her, as if he had sensed her body's desire to run. For a long, simmering moment, they held each other's gazes. Fear and heat uncoiled in Raegan's belly, the combination both unreasonable and delicious.

"A moment to settle in," the King agreed, dragging his gaze from her eyes all the way down to the bottom of her feet. Then he turned on his heel and stalked to his worktable.

Not willing to push her luck, Raegan turned and disappeared into the guest quarters. Once she was safely behind the door to her chambers, she pulled the luggage tag from her pocket. She turned it over in her hands, suspicious, before deciding to just lay it on the couch and see what happened. Before her eyes, the small leather item twisted and morphed back into her duffle and work bag.

Raegan let out a tired sigh, incapable of thinking about the mechanics further. She pulled her father's spellwork from her work bag and held it against her chest for a long moment. Then she reached into her bag to begin unpacking her things. But a thought hit her violently—what was the point? When would she next have to flee?

So instead, Raegan zipped her bag back up and hesitantly returned to the archives. When she arrived, the King was placing two coffee cups and saucers onto the long, gleaming worktable. He had switched on a row of old-fashioned reading lamps, the green glass and brass frames glinting in the firelight.

Raegan paused for a moment at the edge of the table, her father's spellcraft clutched in her arms. She inhaled, taking in the arched bookcases behind the King, crafted from a gorgeous dark brown wood that almost appeared black in the low light. The Art Nouveau-patterned rug beneath the worktable unfurled in leafy scrolls of deep emerald green. The rich smell of espresso perfected the scene. In so many ways, these surroundings seemed handpicked to soothe her. But of course, Raegan felt no peace. She was not sure she had felt peace in many, many years.

The King cleared his throat, and she shook off the thoughts that had settled onto her shoulders, pulling the nearest ceramic mug closer. It looked like a latte, but she didn't care. As long as there was plenty of caffeine, she'd be happy.

"Here," Raegan said, placing the spellcraft sheets onto the table without ceremony. Her eyes trained on the King, she brought the mug to her mouth, savoring the flavor.

He pushed his own coffee aside, leaning over the table toward the spellcraft. "May I?" he asked, looking up at her, his hand hovering over the closed folder. She furrowed her brow, not understanding—the spellcraft had been part of their deal, and yet he still requested permission to touch it.

"Yes," Raegan confirmed, ignoring the deft movements of his powerful hands, taking another long pull from her coffee. "And you are permitted to view all of it this time."

By the time she settled the cup back onto its saucer, the King had laid out all seven pages on the table. Raegan watched silently as he shuffled them a few times, changing the order, peering closer at certain elements. After a few moments, he reached for a nearby storage shelf, plucking a leather-bound notebook and fountain pen from it. Then he studied each page in turn, making notes as he went. Raegan was struck by how similar his process of understanding and unraveling seemed to her own. She shoved that thought aside. He was a tool to find her father; nothing more.

But she drew closer all the same, peeking around the King. He seemed absorbed in deciphering a symbol etched in the margins of one page. She took another step, leaning over his arm, so close—too close—that their hips almost brushed. The King's concentration seemed to snap, and without moving the rest of his body, he turned his head to face her. The intensity of his gaze made Raegan's heart pulsate, warmth rebelliously pooling in her belly.

"What can I do? To help, I mean?" she asked, shifting back and taking another sip of her coffee, struggling to remain focused and unaffected by the Fey being beside her. A task was a necessary distraction, and besides, anything could be another step closer to finding her father.

"Remind me of your occupation?" the King requested, his full attention settled on her, as electrifying as it was disconcerting.

"I'm a journalist," she replied, trying to keep her tone steady.

He made a low noise of approval that sent the heat in Raegan's core roaring through her body. Then he reached across the table, pulled a book from a pile he must have gathered earlier, and offered it to her. Eyes narrowed, she took it, careful not to allow their fingertips to brush.

"Could you research this symbol?" he asked, gesturing to a glyph in the margins. "It may be incidental. I do not want to waste too much time on it, but ignoring it entirely would be foolish."

Raegan looked down at the clothbound book he had handed her, turning it over in her hands. It was a collection of symbols, glyphs and runes commonly and not-so-commonly used in spellcraft.

"Sure," she replied with a shrug, tucking the book under her arm. "Do you have more paper and pens?"

Already back to the spell papers, his attention gone from her as quickly as it had arrived, the King gestured to a nearby shelf. Raegan let out a breath and dug around for a pen she liked, snatching a spiral-bound notebook from a small cache of writing pads. Then she leaned in toward the King again, hoping to copy the symbol for ease of researching.

"You are quite close despite ample workspace," he snapped at her, none of that heady softness in his voice, only sharp irritation.

"Oh, fuck off," she grumbled, casting him a sideways look. "You're hogging all the spell papers. I'm trying to copy the symbol down so I can, you know, actually research it."

The King straightened, one hand flat on the table to support his weight, the other reaching up to pinch the bridge of his nose. Raegan found the mannerism sharply familiar, the ache of it seeping deep into her heart.

"I am sorry," he said, eyes meeting hers. "I am in a good deal of pain.

I prefer my physical space when it reaches this intensity, which only occurred recently. You had no way of knowing."

Raegan was taken aback by both the admission and the honesty. She looked at him for a moment, wondering if this was some kind of play or ploy. But the crease in his brow was as real as anything, and she'd already caught the way he moved with occasional discomfort more than once.

"It's okay," she said, holding his gaze. "Thanks for telling me. Does this happen a lot? Being in this much pain?"

The moment the words left her mouth, she realized she already knew the answer. The King looked away, a rueful, bitter half-smile sliding across his angular features. He drummed his fingers on the table as if he were making a decision. Raegan waited, letting the silence settle in around them, only the fireplace crackling and popping in the distance, the smell of old books and gleaming woods and tanned leathers dancing on the edges of her senses.

"Yes, it does," he replied finally, looking at her again. "I am always in some degree of pain, often severe. I would appreciate you not mentioning this to anyone. Many would see it as weakness."

"Sure," she murmured. "Of course."

She felt so keenly then the gap between them. The King had survived all these years, no rest, no fresh starts, no new bodies; she had slept and awoken anew again and again. Before she could voice this feeling, or even say anything else at all, the openness on his face dissipated like morning fog, gone in an instant. It stung. But it was a useful reminder to sharpen herself against their shared past, to bring her walls up higher.

"See what you can find on the symbol," the King said, looking back down at the spellcraft again.

Raegan didn't need to be told. She'd already opened the book, skimming the table of contents, grateful for anything to look at that wasn't him. She didn't mind the work, even at the late hour. It was a foothold, a familiarity, a place where her body might not sing his name.

She wasn't sure how long it had been—only that she was eight notations and a page of theory notes deep—when she saw the King wave his hand in her peripheral vision. A chair appeared at her side, as well as his, both the perfect height to sit at the worktable. She settled into hers gratefully.

Another half-page of notes later, the words of the book began to blur. She sat back and stretched her arms above her head, not able to hide her yawn.

The King caught her gaze, sidelong. "It is nearly three in the morning," he said, examining her. "Perhaps you should retire to your room to rest."

Frustration skittered through her body; neither of them appeared to have found anything earth-shattering so far. Raegan clenched her jaw, about to spit back that she wasn't done just yet, but then the opportunity to be away from him washed over her with a bitter kind of relief.

Infuriatingly, the King read her as easily as the three books he'd been paging through. "Rest," he urged, sitting back in his chair. "Join me here tomorrow morning when you awaken?"

"Sure," she said with a shrug, getting to her feet, body stiff. She snatched the notebook she'd been using from the table, wondering if she should also take her father's spellwork, when a thought hit her. "Wait. Where do *you* live?"

"Not here," the King replied blandly. "You will require a morning meal, yes?"

Raegan rolled her eyes, pushing her chair in and taking a few steps toward the guest chambers before answering. "Humans need three meals a day," she replied, looking at him over her shoulder. "Not sure how you can't keep that straight. Oh, and tea. I'll need a lot of tea."

Without another glance, Raegan slipped through the door to the living quarters and padded down the hall to her room. She undressed as she walked to the bed—socks, sweater, pants, bra—and rooted through her bag for the first comfy things she could find.

She knew she should use the time away from the King to plot and plan and be ready for all that was to come, but the moment she was curled beneath the soft flannel sheets, sleep overcame her. Lost somewhere in the drowsy twilight, she thanked whatever god oversaw this small mercy. To stay awake, she knew, was to weep for all that she had lost, and she did not know if she would ever be able to stop once she began.

So she tumbled headfirst into oblivion, hoping to find a gentle, quiet darkness. But she found nothing gentle, nothing quiet. Only darkness.

CHAPTER FORTY-TWO

It was a familiar landscape that awaited her: the wide, deep river, craggy mountains, and gray skies of her recurring dream. A deep sense of dread laced with iron-willed purpose coiled in her stomach like a snake. She knew this dream, knew it as well as she knew anything at all. But something was different this time, like a rock had been overturned to show what slept beneath.

An autumn breeze blew, heavy with the scent of woodsmoke. Leaves crunched underfoot, and she had the sense of a cloak over her shoulders. Someone walked next to her, trailing a bit behind, but she knew them. She never doubted for a moment that they would remain at her side no matter the cost.

When she reached the riverbank, a lucid part of her reeled, recognizing that the dream had never allowed her to plumb its depths before. But the tide of the dream was stronger than that tiny lucid spark, and all she heard was her companion pleading for her to leave it be, that what she was doing would never be worth the price.

She ignored them, dropping to her knees at the riverbank, carving strange spirals deep into the mud, whispering something under her breath. Time stretched and dilated—an eternity could've passed—but then she was covered in mud and a scintillating spiral overtook the bank before her, its curves sinuous and strange.

"This will take far too much from you," the voice behind her said, and that lucid part of her froze because she knew that voice—would know it anywhere.

Of course, of course, it was the King's.

She wanted to turn around, to ensure her hearing had not deceived her, but the dream had its own life and sway, and before she knew it, her dream-body was shedding her cloak, and then her skirts and kirtle before unbuckling a belt and pulling off her boots. Only when she wore nothing at all, free of the weight of the mud-soaked cloth, did she wade into the river. It should have been cold. But she felt nothing.

When she reached the middle of the river, she threw her head back and screamed, all unbridled rage and half-mad desperation. The sound was a summoning, something that reached beyond words, something old and deep and lonely. It strained at her vocal cords, like it might tear her throat in two. But she was strong—more than strong enough to command this darkling cry.

Her hands were open, she realized, held perpendicular to her torso, the river's current lapping over her palms. Suddenly, there was a foreign weight in her grasp. She looked down.

It was a shield made of the most peculiar material, so brown it was almost black, slick like river silt, sharp like old magick, and heavy as folklore. It had no seams or thin spots, as if it had been carved from one solid piece. The shield was formidable, heavy, uncleavable. She kissed its surface and bowed to the river. Then her dream-body turned toward the shore.

And there he was, without a doubt. The King stood there on the banks.

Younger, the lucid-her realized, with no lines around the eyes, no hint of silver in his inky black hair. He should, she thought, look terrified of the woman whose body she was in, naked and covered in river silt, emerging from the water with a conjured shield the color of dried blood.

The King did not. He was looking at her like he had never seen anything so magnificent in his entire life, like perhaps he never would again.

She reached the bank, strides carrying her to the King. He did not throw a cloak over her shoulders, did not pull her shivering body close, because she was not cold and she did not need him to keep her warm. She spoke his name—but that name wasn't Oberon, she noticed, too late to catch what she had said—and handed him the shield, her muscles beginning to falter under its weight.

He took it, their eyes locked, and the second his fingers touched the shield, she felt it—the Fatesong in her chest, the knowledge that she would see this to the end. Together, they could try to change the ending.

The King-with-a-different-name slid the shield over his arm, holding it across his chest like a knight already in his mausoleum. She reached for him, her mouth meeting his, the cool surface of the shield between them coming to rest on her breastbone. He tasted, she thought, of mead and judgment and Fate. For the briefest of moments, the shield shone like wet blood before he let it rest against his side.

She fit her body against his, her bare skin pressed to the rough cloth of his garments, his hard muscle just beneath. Only then did he pull her close, arm sliding around her waist, palm open on her soft belly, bowing his head to bring his brow to her shoulder.

She parted her lips to remind him, mouth moving against his ear,

"You will be the one to end this."

And then a strange series of gentle booms resounded in the dreamscape, melting away the river and the King and the shield.

Raegan awoke, sitting straight up, her heart racing quick as a current. She found herself back in the guest chambers of the archives, flannel sheets tangled around her legs. The sound was much more mundane than it had seemed in her dream—just someone knocking on the door to her room. It had to be the King. She could probably pretend she was still asleep.

But the Seal and the Protectorate and the dream and her father's spellcraft . . . all the strange and terrible things that pulled at her with pleading hands, a labyrinth waiting to be walked.

Groggy, Raegan forced herself to her feet, shuffling toward the door and pulling it open. She found the King on the other side of the threshold, much as she had expected.

"Is everything okay?" she asked, pushing auburn curls away from her face. Her heart hammered mercilessly in her chest at the sight of him.

The King took her in with his usual cool, calm demeanor. He was dressed in an impeccable three-piece suit, its shade a deep, dark green. It did wonders for his pale complexion. He looked infuriatingly well-rested and unspeakably attractive.

Raegan, by contrast, surely had an entire rat's nest on her head, as she hadn't even remembered to braid her hair before sleeping. Her joggers were covered with a downy layer of lint from the flannel sheets and her thin camisole was intended for sleep only. She wished she had grabbed a sweatshirt or told him she'd be there in a moment. She wished she had done anything but obey the part of her that wished to see him as quickly as possible.

"I am sorry to disturb you," the King said. "You have slept for the entire day. It is nearly nine in the evening. I only wanted to ensure you were alright."

Dumbfounded, Raegan said nothing for a long moment. She could not remember the last time she'd slept for so long, not even when her depression was at its worst and leaving her bed felt like an impossible task.

"Shit," she eventually said. "I guess I was tired."

"As long as you are alive and well," the King replied, like it would only be mildly inconvenient if he had found her corpse instead. "When you have rested adequately, we have a number of items to discuss." His words should have been generous, but his voice had a sour undertone, lips curling mockingly.

"I did flood an entire café and discover the world is nothing like it seems," Raegan said in defense of herself, leaning against the doorframe. Her mind moved more slowly than she liked, the dream haunting the corners of her vision like a double exposure.

"Yes," the King replied, amusement sliding across his features. "The result of pent-up abilities. It would take you another thirty years to do something similar again."

He said it back-handedly, as if it were of no great interest. But Raegan noticed that the mention of what she had done made the King look at her differently, like he was remembering who she had once been. She caught his gaze tracking down her frame for a heartbeat. The way her body reacted—heart surging, desire kindling low in her belly—was as strong as if he had physically touched her.

"I will be in the reading room," the King said, his tone clipped now, weight shifted away from her. "Please continue to rest if that is what you require."

Then he turned and continued down the hallway, gait as effortless and graceful as Raegan had ever seen it. She closed the door, pressing her back against it for a long moment, eyes squeezed shut, lips pressed together. Her body yearned for the King in a way she had never experienced before—like there was a tightly-locked chest inside her and he was the only one with the key. And god, she wanted him to open her wide, to feel those powerful hands run down her body and then slide inside . . .

Raegan opened her eyes and forced a long inhale. A quest yawned wide and hungry. She couldn't allow something as simple as lust to distract her. Not even for the person she defied death for again and again.

She dragged herself across the room to root through her bag for something to wear, doing her best not to think about whatever it was that she and the King had once had together. Love had always been a tricky thing for her. She had found out very early that people could disappear at any time, gone forever without a trace. Love was like opening a door, and Raegan was worried that if she stepped through, she'd only find another empty grave.

She abandoned that sharp-edged thought, dressing in soft, oversized clothing before heading into the bathroom to take her meds and brush her teeth. Even though the King claimed she'd slept for nearly an entire day, the face in the mirror did not look any less exhausted. Dark circles curved like bruises beneath her eyes.

She leaned forward, meeting her reflection's eyes in the mirror. As of this moment, she was unchanged. Raegan supposed that, at some point, this journey might mark her. No one escaped a fairytale unaltered. Perhaps, she considered, she would know she was approaching the end when her reflection held something beyond herself.

"More things you don't have the bandwidth to consider right now," she chided herself, trudging over to the coffee table to retrieve her notebook and pen.

When she arrived at the archives, the King was awaiting her, seated at the long, gleaming worktable. "There is hot water in the kettle," he told her, not looking up from the book he was reading.

Raegan, as always, went where the caffeine was. Along the kitchenette's counter, she found not only a freshly boiled kettle but also a platter with pastries and fruit. She prepared a cup of tea and a plate for herself, then went to sit with the King. For the briefest of moments, the scent of woodsmoke and black pepper and rain nearly pulled her back into the dream entirely, and she found herself standing on the riverbank with the shield and the long, hard length of his body pressed against hers.

"Had some pretty intense dreams last night," she said, trying to keep her tone level. "I think that's why I slept so long."

The King didn't bother to look up. "It is good you were able to rest."

Annoyed for a reason she couldn't quite place, Raegan reached for her tea. The bergamot and Ceylon covered up any lingering scent she associated with the King, which she was grateful for. But the dream still clung to her, digging fingers into her flesh, and she could not release it from the waking world.

"It . . . finished, I guess, for the first time I can remember," she said, staring straight ahead, tracing her fingers along the teacup's mouth. "There was the river, and I conjured a shield and . . . you. You were there. Younger. Different name."

At that, the King finally looked up, but there was no surprise or confusion in his features. Raegan was no fool and had picked up that he was not particularly emotive, but she would have expected at least a trace of *something*.

Then the King released a breath, the line of his shoulders sagging. "I know," he said, holding her gaze in a way that once again made her realize how ancient he was, his gray eyes fathomless. "I know, Overhill. I too had the dream last night."

Chapter Forty-Three

A hush settled over the vast, dim space, broken only by the hitch in Raegan's breathing. She didn't think she had even gotten her mind around the experience yet, and now she had to wonder if the King had been there, too. The same lucid splinter caught in the skin of his dreaming body.

"It is unusual that you can recall such an early memory," the King said, closing his book, the weight of his full attention now on Raegan's shoulders, not unlike a heavy fur cloak.

"It's a memory, then?" she managed to ask, her late breakfast and hot cup of tea forgotten.

He nodded, watching her so closely that it almost made Raegan shrink away—his searching eyes an abyss gazing back at her, hungry and endless. A thought came to her, quick as a bead of blood after a thorn's prick.

"Are you looking for *her*?" she asked in a raw whisper.

For a moment, the enormity of the King's sorrow was so plain that she wondered how he could possibly carry its weight. His grief called to her own, and the immense loss she had felt last night swept onto her shores again. She wanted to throw herself on the ground and weep, to beg and bargain, to forgo everything and forsake everyone if only she could have him back.

Instead, Raegan looked away from the King, wishing she had never said anything about the dream at all, wishing she had forgotten it the moment she opened her eyes, wishing Death would just fucking keep her next time.

"My father's spell," she mumbled, gesturing toward it. "What does it do? And will it help me find him?"

The King took a long pull of tea, looking almost grateful for her redirection. His mask of cool composure had returned. "It is an attempt to reach the Gates," he replied, as if the past few moments hadn't happened at all, "unlike any others I have seen before, which is no short list. If this is the 'work of the one who came before,' and if that refers to your father, then finding him and fulfilling the Prophecy could be one and the same."

Raegan chewed on the inside of her cheek, happy to be lost in thought. She opened her notebook and asked him to continue. He complied, explaining that the spellcraft was dangerous, as the Gates existed on the far side of the In-Between, ruled by the Timekeeper. There was no guarantee of destroying the Gates themselves, or even staying alive long enough to do anything at all.

"Hold on," she said, a massive headache blooming behind her eyes. She drained what was left in her teacup. "I've heard the Timekeeper mentioned a few times. Who is that, exactly?"

For a moment, surprise flickered on the King's face, but then he seemed to recall the nature of Raegan's memory. "An old god," he told her, choosing his words slowly. "He demanded worship and sacrifice from the early mortals in Cymru, so my people imprisoned him beneath the Isles. Years later, the men that would become the Protectorate freed him in exchange for defeating the Tylwyth Teg and creating the Gates."

Raegan nodded, scribbling a few lines in her notebook, desperately trying to ignore the way the King had shifted in his seat to face her, his eyes tracking her movements. She set her jaw and forced herself to be a reporter right now—nothing more. "Why would the Protectorate free him?" she asked, tapping her pen against the worktable. "If the Fey felt imprisoning him was necessary, it seems like he would be bad news for us humans."

A rueful expression moved across the King's face as he pushed his teacup away. "Time," he said, as if that explained everything. "He is the god of time. My people are exceedingly long-lived, if not immortal. What need do we have to bargain for more years? Mortals, though—oh, the deals and sacrifices they will make for just a little more time. Particularly during the days when the Fair Folk walked ageless among them."

Raegan's headache all but exploded, and she squeezed her eyes shut, her pen falling limp against her notepad. *Everything* was about time, was it not? Her own life revolved around how fast she could file a story, how quickly the mayor's office would call her back, who got the scoop on the latest scandal first. Wasn't everyone just selling their precious, sacred time for wages because it was the only way to survive?

"Wait," she said, her mind turning over in her aching skull. "Are you saying that men were mad the Fey were more powerful than them, so they released Kronos, and now we have fucking *capitalism*?"

Amusement sparked in the King's gaze, making Raegan's stomach flip. He leaned forward onto the table on his forearms, startlingly close to her hands. "More or less," he replied, eyes dropping to her notebook for a moment.

"Okay," Raegan said, scribbling down more and then flipping to a new page. "Thanks. So back to my father's spell. Why is it so interesting to you? Because of the Prophecy? You didn't seem particularly happy about that."

The King sighed, unfolding to stand. Then he turned his back to the worktable, staring out into the cavernous space. In the silence, Raegan noticed slinking notes of classical music floating above the ever-present murmur of the fireplace.

"I have been named in Prophecies before," he finally said, crossing his arms. "I find I do not like the loss of agency. No, the Prophecy is not why. Though I admit it lends weight."

Raegan opened her mouth to ask more, but he kept speaking, his gaze falling to the large, yellowed pieces of parchment spread out like a door on the table.

"This," he continued, gesturing to her father's spellcraft, "is different because it calls for an anchor already placed within the Timekeeper's realm. Completing this spellcraft requires two people who share blood or an oath of some kind. The first is a sacrifice; they make a bargain with the Timekeeper. When he comes to collect his due, he takes them to the In-Between to slowly feast upon whatever years they have left. That establishes a tether—or perhaps a lighthouse, if you will."

The King paused, and Raegan wondered if it was because of how furiously she was writing. She wished she had thought to bring a recorder; her hand was cramping.

"Sort of like selling your soul to the devil?" she asked, putting her pen down for a minute to massage the base of her thumb. "You make a bargain to be, let's say, a great musician for ten years, but then your soul goes to hell."

"Yes," the King said, rearranging a stack of beautiful leather-bound books on the end of the table. "The Devil is a fascinating figure in human folklore. There is little doubt a large part of his behavior and character are directly lifted from the Timekeeper."

"Okay," Raegan said, tucking one leg underneath her as she turned to a fresh page. "And then the second person uses the tether to locate and enter the Timekeeper's realm, I'm guessing?"

The King said nothing, looking over at her with a guarded expression. She gazed back blankly, confusion swarming about in her mind. And then it came to her, heavy as laced boots on a drowning man.

"Oh," she murmured, her heart plummeting to the bottom of her stomach. "My dad is the tether."

The way he disappeared without a trace. The way even Nyx's scrying glass could not afford them more than the barest of glances: her father's face behind a window. The way the King and Cordelia both thought he was within a primordial being's realm. The way the spell-craft had been waiting for her all these years—for its second dance partner.

Raegan dropped her head into her hands, only the soft mustiness of the books and the crackle of the fireplace still perceivable. And then she lost herself in the memory of her father's encounter with the tweed-suited man on the train platform. She recalled his obsession with it in aching detail—the way the tale had haunted her, always just on the edge of her vision. Squeezing her eyes shut, she staved off tears as she remembered how insistently her father always told that story.

Like she would need to know every detail because the entirety of magic hung in the balance. "Fuck," Raegan huffed into her clammy palms.

"I am suspicious of why a mortal would go to these extremes," the King said from somewhere in her periphery. "And I am always suspicious of a Prophecy. But this spellcraft is a true chance, and I have given far more for far lesser hopes. Of course, you will be unable to complete the spell without your Seal removed, and even then, it remains to be seen how quickly your capabilities will return. Make no mistake: this venture is dangerous."

She raised her head, propping her chin with her hands and staring out into the vastness of the archives. The center pathway twisted and then disappeared into shadows, the sconces along the walls shimmering like orange jewels. And yet among all these nameless and unknown treasures, the seven pieces of parchment on the table might be the most precious of them all.

If she was strong enough to follow the trail her father had left behind. A few days ago, Raegan would've never doubted that. But now she'd existed in this darker, stranger world for barely any time at all and had needed to sleep for an absurd amount of time to recover—almost an entire goddamn day.

And then, just like that, a thought of the more mundane variety paralyzed her. "Wait," she said, her voice hoarse as she turned to look at the King. "You said I slept for almost a day. What day of the week is today? It's not Sunday, right?"

"Yes," he answered, sharp and sure. "It is Sunday."

Raegan leaned back in her chair, both hands coming up to cover her face again. Nausea swirled in her abdomen, and damp, prickly anxiety swept through her. "I should've gone to work," she moaned from behind her hands. "Fuck me."

"Did you not handle your affairs?" the King asked, the condescending calm of his voice among the calamity of her realization making her furious.

"No, Oberon!" Raegan shouted, slamming her hands on the table. "No, weirdly enough, I wasn't exactly thinking about the future, considering the kelpie and my dad and the Protectorate and the Prophecy and you! I was sort of playing it by ear for a bit there! How could I *possibly* forget about my fucking *job* when I've spent the last twenty-four hours thinking I was going to die or be abducted or tricked into some terrible agreement with a faerie king?"

She stared at him, breathing hard, feeling the anger seep red across her face and chest.

"I suppose that is reasonable," the King conceded after a moment's pause, seemingly not at all fazed by her outburst.

Raegan dug into her pocket for her phone, letting out a furious, half-strangled shriek when she realized it was back in the living quarters. She stood, her chair scraping discordantly against the stone floor.

"Can I be of assistance?" the King asked in such a polite voice that she wanted to throw something at him.

"I need my phone so I can . . ." she spat in reply, trailing off, trying to think, "say I've been tremendously sick, I guess?"

He straightened and took a step forward in one long, fluid movement, more shadow than flesh. "Please follow me to my office. It is impossible to receive service here due to the wards."

Raegan trailed behind the King as he headed for the hallway leading away from the reading room, muttering about wards under her breath. Of course, her phone didn't work here. How else could she have slept so long without Henry, and probably Saanvi, calling her about eighty times?

When they arrived at his office, the King gestured toward an old-fashioned landline telephone set atop a filing cabinet. She stared at it, the realization that there was no point calling in sick for the day crashing down around her.

Raegan knew that she'd be gone much longer than that. She knew she might not even come back at all. What to say, she wondered, to the people she planned to leave behind in a world broken in half?

And all those years ago, had her father wondered the exact same thing?

Chapter Forty-Four

Raegan set the telephone handset back in its cradle, her hands trembling. She'd been so distraught when speaking with Henry that he'd had virtually no choice but to believe her—to believe that the old darkness had returned again, and now one of his best reporters faced inpatient hospitalization at a mental health facility. Just for a few weeks, she'd sworn a number of times, as if speaking the timeline into existence would make it come true. As if locating an ancient folkloric witch, regaining her lost memory, and then marching into an unknown realm to fight a god would take but a few weeks.

The reading room stood empty when Raegan returned, and she sank into one of the chairs that faced the fireplace, pulling her knees to her chest. Its warmth did not seem to reach her. The realization that following this thread of Fate required leaving people behind sent a palpable chill over her skin. Henry had promised he'd contact Bronwyn after Raegan made up some lie about only being granted so much time on the phone. But still, she'd be the second person her mother loved to leave in this way.

A soft stirring to her right—like that feeling in the air just before a thunderstorm rolls in—pulled her from her thoughts. Raising her head, she found the King standing a few feet away.

He met her gaze and then lowered himself into the chair beside her.

"I have arranged a meeting with an informant offering details on Baba Yaga's whereabouts," he said, the firelight flickering across his high cheekbones and aquiline nose.

"Okay," she breathed, twisting in her seat to face him. "And? Feels like there's a catch here."

His eyes slid to hers, broad chest rising with a deep inhale. A log crashed against the grate in the fireplace, making her jump. "The informant is a member of the Seelie Court," the King said, a wry amusement pulling at the sides of his mouth. "They will only meet on neutral ground, and they specifically want to see *you*."

Something unfolded inside her, light as a moth's wing, beaded in dew. Then it dissipated as quickly as it had arrived, a dove-colored wisp of smoke. She tongued the inside of her cheek, focusing on the King's words. "Fine," she said, meeting his gaze. "So we go. I assume it's within your abilities to keep me safe from any nonsense the Seelie Court might have in mind?"

As she spoke, Raegan remembered one of the footnotes in her father's mythology book—that the Seelie Court had not fought at Camlann, and if they had, the battle may have turned out entirely differently. She had a feeling that the past thousand years had done little to erase any contention.

The King scoffed in response, getting to his feet. Her mouth went hopelessly dry as she watched him re-button his jacket as he stood, the deft movement of his powerful hands kindling desire in her core.

"It matters not," he said, striding toward the worktable, where he picked up a stack of books. "You are not going. There are too many variables at a place like Gossamer—too much delicate politics."

He placed the stack of books on the table beside her, bringing his body close to hers—almost as if he hoped to distract her from the dismissal. It nearly worked, the fire in Raegan's belly building to an inferno, black pepper and damp stone slinking into her senses. But her anger was just as quick to spark.

"What?" she demanded, looking up at him, settling clenched fists on each side of the chair's arms. "Of course I'm coming. The Seelie Court wants to see *me*. Handle the fucking politics, Oberon. Aren't you a goddamn king?"

There was something about speaking those words aloud that tugged at her—a silken rope wrapped around her wrist, as if to pull her back when she wandered too far away. Briefly, a vision of an impossibly long table in a forest laden high with fruits and golden goblets and a million lit candles sprang to her mind. Before she could examine it, the moment danced away.

Beside her, the King let out a low sigh, plucking the top book—a pretty volume with gold gilt lettering and dark floral cloth—from the pile. He ran his hand over it, his gaze meeting hers again. "You will be safe here," he said, his authoritative tone displaying how accustomed he was to being obeyed. "For all my power and influence, Gossamer is neutral ground and the Protectorate has your scent. I would be a fool to promise I can absolutely guarantee your safety."

He cut himself off, something shifting in his expression. Then the King stepped in toward Raegan, gently pulling on her wrist until her clenched palm faced upward toward the ceiling. He slipped his long fingers beneath her tightly-curled ones, prying with a light touch until she unfurled them. Despite everything, the brush of his skin against hers was a cool breeze after a thousand scorching summers.

The King pressed the gold gilt-lettered book into her open palm. His much larger hand engulfed hers as he closed her fingers around the volume before reaching for her other wrist. All the while, Raegan's heart throbbed dangerously beneath the delicate skin of her throat. Her eyes were level with the King's broad shoulders, and there was nothing she could do to stop her mind from imagining the corded muscles beneath the deep green cloth.

She could have tried to look away, but Raegan was afraid that if she did, her gaze would drift upwards, past the King's strong jaw and to his full, beautiful mouth. Then she would have no choice but to imagine the feel of his lips against hers, and she was not sure she could survive that.

The King's powerful hand slid around her wrist, his touch gentle but indecently firm, fingertips brushing the sensitive softness on the underside of her forearm. He brought her other hand to the book—though she desired so desperately instead for him to pin her hands above her head and lower the hard expanse of his body against hers, to draw all the forgotten things out of her by sheer, unrelenting force alone.

"Stay here," the King commanded, and for once in her life, Raegan wanted nothing more than to yield and to be rewarded for her obedience. "Read. Sleep. I will return with information about Baba Yaga."

Intoxicated by his touch, her skin yearning for his, the low thrum of his voice spreading fire through her core, she almost listened. Almost.

"No," she said, raising her eyes to his, their noses mere inches apart. "This is about me, too."

His expression darkened, the beautiful eyes narrowing, a muscle in his jaw clenching. "You will stay here," he repeated, his hands now applying pressure on hers, as if he could physically press her into doing what he wished. "You are *safe* here."

"I said I'm coming," she snapped, leaning forward and sliding her legs off the seat, knees brushing his legs.

"I am the High King of the Unseelie Court," he countered, his voice as low and dark as she'd ever heard it. He seemed to welcome her physical aggression, removing his hands from hers to grip the chair's arms, pinning her in on every side. "And I said you will stay here."

As the King spoke, he drew closer, lowering the weight and power of his immortal body toward her much softer, weaker, mortal one. Raegan could feel the heat of his skin through the layers of clothing that separated them. She wondered if he could sense how mercilessly her blood pounded for him, a siren song that begged with each breath to simply give in.

But then the tidal wave of anger broke upon Raegan's shores, all white-hot and indignant, fueled by a feeling of complete and utter helplessness. Any words she could conjure died on her tongue—and so without another single intelligent thought, she tightened her grip on the book the King had pressed into her hands and chucked it over his shoulder at the opposite wall. It made a soft thud on impact, the pages crinkling against the stone, spine crumpling as it landed in a heap on the ground below.

"Get a grip, High King!" Raegan shouted, surprised at how loudly her voice rang out in the space. "Do you honestly think I'm going to stay behind to read and knit or what-fucking-ever because you can't handle your own shit? Because that's what this is. I'm finally back, and you can't handle the idea that something might happen to me. Guess what? Something *always* happens to me. You're always going to lose me. Get used to the goddamn pain."

Her voice broke on the last sentence, the air in her lungs depleted. But the King didn't even flinch. No matter what she flung at him, he never retreated like everyone else always did. Instead, he held himself in exactly the same place, his body hovering above hers, arms caging her in.

"*Fine*," the King spat at her, his lip curling with fury.

Raegan hadn't even processed that she had bent the Unseelie King to her will before he caught her jaw between the fingers of one hand, holding her gaze with those deep gray eyes.

"Get dressed," he snarled, the planes of his face growing increasingly feral in a way that should have sent fear skittering through Raegan's body, though she only felt heat and need, coiled so tightly she thought she might explode. "I hope you have something in that bag appropriate for the finest Fey club on this continent."

She held his gaze. "And if I don't?"

He offered her a dagger of a smile. "I could make you a beautiful gown from a handful of oak leaves, but personal enchantments aren't permitted at Gossamer, so the moment you step through the doors, you'd be quite . . . exposed."

The challenge sang across Raegan's skin, and she shoved off the chair. Only at the last moment did the King release his grasp, stepping just to the side, allowing her to slip by.

She took a few strides toward the living quarters and then turned to examine him over her shoulder. "I can see what you've been thinking about in your spare time," she said with a dangerous grin before heading to the passage into the guest chambers.

Reaching her room, Raegan slammed her shoulder into the door, barging inside. For obvious reasons, she hadn't thought to pack any formal clothing that would come even close to matching the King's perfect suiting. Anger and damp hot lust swirled through her body as she began to dig into her overnight bag. Frustratingly, her best options appeared to be leggings with tumbled leather panels and a long, sheer sweater.

But then her hand hit an unfamiliar textile at the bottom of the bag. Curious, Raegan pulled it from the depths, gasping out loud when she saw her favorite dress: a tight, black, midi-length piece with a low neckline, corset-style bodice and a long-sleeved, closely-fitted sheer shrug that cut away from the bust. It was wrinkled, and she had absolutely no idea how it had gotten in there—not until she dug deeper and found a pair of pointed-toe heels with long leather ties that wound up the leg. And then it hit her: she'd visited a college friend last month to see his new apartment in New York, and he had insisted they go out to a club his colleague had been promoting. She'd probably just shoved the bag under her bed after the trip without unpacking.

Feeling powerful, Raegan ducked into the bathroom and began to sort through her haphazardly packed bag of toiletries. At the bottom, she found an ancient kohl pencil she'd thought she'd thrown out a long time ago. It would do. She was elated to find that a tube of mascara and a bottle of ibuprofen had made its way into the random assortment as well.

She downed three pills for her headache and then turned to examine the bathroom floor, remembering how the room had appeared to clean and fold her clothing the night before. Skeptical, she gently put her dress on the ground and then turned back to the mirror.

There, she scrutinized her complexion, taking in the redness around her eyes and the unusually pale shade her golden-hued, freckled skin had taken on. Leaning toward the mirror, Raegan traced the kohl in a sideways V-shape from the outward corner of her eye, smudging it with her fingers until it created a dark, grunge-y cat-eye effect. She applied mascara and then used a tube of lip gloss, both for its intended purpose and also to add a little highlight and dimension to her cheekbones.

"Not bad," Raegan said appraisingly, dampening her hands under the faucet to lightly reshape her long curls. When she looked back up, her dress was hanging by a hook on the back of the door, perfectly pressed.

She found a black lace thong that sort of matched the nicest bra she'd brought with her, and then she was pulling on the dress and stepping into her heels. She stopped to appraise herself in the mirror: hot and deadly, all curves and contrast. A few years ago, she would have lamented the way her stomach was far from flat beneath the tight dress and second-guessed the amount of cleavage on display. But now that she had a Fey king's life to ruin, it all felt perfectly right.

Her blood hummed as she exited the room and strode down the hallway. When Raegan emerged into the reading room, she found the King sitting in front of the fire, the book she had thrown against the wall between his hands. He did not acknowledge her, his gaze directed at the dancing shapes of the hearth. But as she drew closer, Raegan saw the King's gray eyes slide to her, and then down her frame—pausing for a heartbeat in all the right places. His right hand clenched for the barest of moments.

Nothing sensible or wise won out. None of Raegan's street smarts or even a basic regard for her physical safety was able to overcome the thick, beating desire that consumed every inch of her body. So she prowled to the King, planting one hand on either side of the chair, just as he'd done to her. For good measure, she slid her knee onto the chair's seat, right between his thighs.

"Is this good enough?" Raegan asked him, one eyebrow arched, staring down at him.

The King took his time, as he always seemed to, and she tried not to be consumed by thoughts of what else he might do slowly, achingly. His face was impassive as he dragged his eyes from her generous thighs to her soft waist before lingering tauntingly at her bust, and then finally meeting her gaze. "It will do," he replied, bored, unaffected, but his grip on the book she'd thrown tightened. "Do leave my books out of your tantrums in the future."

Without a second thought, Raegan pounced. "Oh, I'm so sorry about your book," she replied, tilting her head to one side, heavy auburn curls falling over her shoulder. "I suppose they are your only company, aren't they?"

Apparently she would have to cut deeper, because the King only sighed, trailing a few fingers down the book's spine. She said nothing, watching him, lips slightly parted. Raegan was rewarded for her efforts when she saw the King's control slip, just a hair, his eyes greedily dipping to her body for a moment or two.

"This title is quite rare," he replied, gaze holding hers again, molten amusement in his expression. "It should be treated with more care. There are some things, Overhill, that demand a finer, more experienced touch."

Heat swept through Raegan. She needed to hike up her dress and wrap her legs around him. She needed to feel the flex of his hard muscle against her body, to remember where the scars etched his skin and to place her mouth on every single one.

She leaned closer, pressing her leg against the King's inner thigh. "I'm not used to being gentle," she breathed. "You'll have to show me what you mean."

His beautiful mouth curved up ever so slightly, and Raegan could've sworn she saw his breath hitch, the rhythm of his broad chest interrupted for a split second. The King removed one hand from his book, reaching over to slide his fingers up the inside of her arm. The rest of the room faded, all of her attention on two things: the memories sparking in her mind, and the frenzied hunger with which she desired the being before her.

But then the King unfolded, rising to his feet like a shadow peeling off a wall, leaving Raegan unbalanced, her leg still between his, dizzy and half-mad with want. One arm sliding around her waist, his palm open against the small of her back, the King steadied Raegan as if it were simply the gentlemanly thing to do. "Come," he said, looking down at her, knowing exactly what he was doing, as always. "We are due at Gossamer."

CHAPTER FORTY-FIVE

Just outside the King's archives, the moon hung heavy and silver in the sky. A breeze swept down the cobblestones, bringing a tiny tornado of leaves along for the ride. The coffee shop across the street was closed up tightly, and a BYO café farther down the block glowed with warm fairy lights, tiny tables spilled out onto the street, the sounds of wine-drunk patrons just barely reaching Raegan's ears.

"My court's security councilor, the Lady Andronica, will not forgive me if we step outside of the highest wards," the King said, his voice rich as honey in the autumn night, "so she has approved a compromise."

Raegan followed his gaze to what appeared to be a normal taxi idling at the curb. No one occupied the driver's seat, at least not any kind of being that was visible to her eyes. She took a deep breath, filling her lungs with the woodsmoke-rain scent of the King and the crispness of autumn air. At least five questions about the compromise and Lady Andronica sprang to her mind, but she found she hardly cared about the answers, her attention firmly placed elsewhere.

The King opened the passenger door for her, and she ducked inside, preparing to slide across the leather seats like she would have done with any of her friends. But the High King of the Unseelie Court was not her friend or anything even remotely close to it, and he closed the door behind her before coming around to the other side and joining her in the backseat.

Shortly thereafter, the taxi ambled away from the curb, still no driver in sight. Getting into the car had hiked the slit on Raegan's dress higher, and she was pleased to see the King immediately take notice. It was as if he had been trying to avoid seeing her as a flesh-and-blood being this entire time, and now she had given him no choice in the matter. Raegan leaned toward him, enjoying the power such a thought gave her.

"Tell me about what to expect," she requested, smoothing her dress across her thighs.

The shadowy weight of the King's attention draped across her shoulders. "The Seelie Court is useful when it wants to be," he replied, studying her. "A warning, their informants tend to be twice as flirtatious as they are helpful."

"That seems to be your type," she said, narrowing her eyes, twisting her torso toward him. In this confined space, Raegan's desire threatened to consume her entirely. "What exactly *is* your type?"

The King's sculpted lips parted then, an exhale escaping before he looked away. She waited for him to say something, but no response came, so Raegan pressed her thigh against his. At that, he turned back to her, a playfulness moving across his mouth that would've made her lightheaded if not for the sadness shadowing it.

"I imagine," he began, the words a low rumble in his chest as his long-limbed body began to bow around hers, "you already know the answer. Do you intend to make me say it aloud?"

How many times had someone panted in her ear that they wanted to fuck her or would make her scream or whatever bullshit so many men seemed to think was even remotely stimulating? But here *he* was, using language that was hardly profane in any way, and yet the heat and tension between her legs was building to a sheer torment.

"After all these years?" she asked, fighting for control. "I've ruined your life how many times and you *still* want me that badly? A little pathetic, honestly."

For a moment, Raegan felt his muscles stiffen against her, like he had been struck by a blow. She bit down on the inside of her cheek, watching him, wondering if she had gone too far. It wouldn't be the first time she had dug a bit too deep, claws too sharp for play.

But then the King slackened, the pressure and weight of his heavy muscle back against her build again, and she saw the corner of his mouth curve upward. Relief flooded her. No, not too far. And, some distant memory reminded Raegan that he had always been able to withstand her edges, jagged as broken glass.

The cab slowed to a stop, and she studied the view out the window to see if anything looked familiar. She had been sure it would—after all, she knew the city so well—but the landscape that greeted her looked nothing like anything she'd ever seen. Raegan found echoes of her city in the sparkling schist-stone walls and the elegant turrets, but there was something otherworldly about whatever waited for her beyond the taxi doors, something dark and slinking that reminded her of the King.

She felt the heat of him leave her side before she noticed that he had exited the cab, looping around to, once again, open the door. The King helped her out, every touch lingering for half a heartbeat longer than necessary. When she stood on the sidewalk, Raegan could see a long stone pathway leading to a large black door, the top of its expanse swooping into a sharp curve.

Above it, she was surprised to see neon lettering that spelled out "Gossamer" in a looping, archaic-looking script. Either side of the pathway was closed in by the neighboring buildings' towering walls.

All her thoughts swept away when the King slipped his arm around her waist, fingers splayed across the curves of her belly. With their bodies fitted together like lost puzzle pieces, they walked to Gossamer's entrance. Raegan fought to stay alert, to keep her wits about her and her distrust sharpened, but every passing moment bracketed by the King's hard wall of muscle made it harder and harder.

The large, arched doors opened easily at the King's touch, which she could understand. Raegan found herself surprised that the entrance to a heavily warded Fey club was so simple, but things made more sense when she found herself in a vestibule. Another set of doors waited at the far end, a hulking Fey, larger than even the King, stood guard. Their features had that sharp, feral look Raegan had come to recognize. Dark locs gathered at the base of their skull. In the dim halfway space, lit only by rows of candles that lined the alcoves high above, the guard's obsidian skin gleamed like a midnight eclipse.

"My liege," the Fey said, bowing their head at the King.

"Kamau," the King replied, something like humor seeping into his tone. "Andronica pulled many strings for tonight, it seems."

At that, Kamau burst into a deep, golden, belly laugh, crossing their massive arms. Raegan noticed their skin was adorned with tattoos, details hard to make out in the low light.

"You know Andronica," Kamau replied. "She's mad you left the safehouse at all. But Baba Yaga must be found. So I am here if you need anything."

Raegan looked up at the King and was surprised to see him actually smile—bright, disarming, and utterly dangerous.

"There is no one else I would rather have at my side," he replied, before turning toward Raegan and introducing her to Kamau, who turned out to be one of the Unseelie Court's most formidable knights.

Raegan's interest was piqued; the good-natured gleam in Kamau's deep brown eyes did not exactly square with war and murder. But that quick assessment was about as far as she got before the King pulled her even closer and stepped through the second set of doors into Gossamer.

Considering that the entirety of their short ride had been spent trying not to do something ridiculous like climb on top of him, Raegan had not taken sufficient time to prepare herself for what a hidden, magically warded Fey club might look like.

"If you do not close your mouth," the King murmured in her ear, "you will look quite unsophisticated, which is decidedly *not* my type."

Raegan wished his sentence had ended in something a bit different, but she still tried to look less awed by the grand space. It was no easy task. The ceiling sprang away from her, reaching up into an inky black abyss. Vines and branches climbed the walls in effortlessly beautiful patterns, the leafier limbs creating a forest canopy above. Soft pinpricks of light, alarmingly similar to a spray of stars on a clear night, reached through the leaves. Intricate chandeliers of wild brambles were suspended throughout the club, the molasses glow of candlelight flickering from within.

"Fuck," Raegan said under her breath, allowing the King to pull her into the deeper recesses of the beautifully impossible place. "How is this even possible with the Gates?"

"Pocket realms," the King replied, his tone breezy as they made their way through the crowd. "A number of them existed here before the Gates—including my archives. They were created with the old magic, and so they remain. For now. If the residual magic leaves this world entirely, it is likely they will collapse into nothing."

Despite her general obsession with fact-finding, Raegan was only half listening. Yes, this place was a stunning mystery, but . . . the patrons themselves had grabbed her attention. Some were like Oberon and Cordelia and Kamau—sharp-featured, their beauty hard and feral, with graceful limbs and dark eyes. Others sported skin the color of tide pools or iridescent, beetle-like wings. Unlike human clubs, the din was not unbearable. Raegan imagined there had to be magic at work. She could hear the King murmur in her ear, but the space still held the echo and vibration of a packed bar—all the excitement and atmosphere with none of the frustrating inability to flirt or tell someone to fuck off.

The King had no trouble weaving through the throng of Fey to his intended destination. The moment anyone sighted him, heads bowed and conversation slowed. Raegan even caught a few curtseys. She did not escape attention, either—eyes slid over her, a probing kind of interest, not malicious but not kind, either. She was hardly bothered amongst all the wonder. Every fabric she brushed by felt divine. Everyone smelled positively delicious in different ways: a silver-haired slip of a being in a gown made of petals wore lily of the valley, whereas a dark-skinned Fey with a dazzling smile in a shimmering, golden suit smelled of amber, spiced wine and honey.

In a few moments, Raegan caught sight of what she presumed to be their destination: a long, curving bar that seemed to be made of living trees, their trunks meticulously wound together. The bar top itself shimmered like labradorite or an abalone shell. Beyond the busy hustling of the bartenders, a wall of quicksilver—endlessly more magnificent than a mundane mirror—stretched up to the ceiling. Decadent, beautiful bottles lined the elegant metal shelves, filled with liquids that Raegan couldn't even begin to identify.

The King chose two open seats toward the end of the bar, where curving branches tucked into a velvety wall before beginning the climb upwards to meet their brethren. She was sure nearly anyone here would have volunteered their seat for the Unseelie King, but it did not seem to be his style to accept.

She slid onto a stool made of the same twisting limbs as the bar, its flat seat topped with a velvet pillow in one of the jewel tones the Fey seemed to favor. The King sat beside her, raising a hand to a bartender who had already noticed them despite the packed space. Someone on the King's other side greeted him exuberantly, and he turned to respond. In the meantime, Raegan swept her gaze around the room, noticing the alcoves along the walls where more candles burned with a flickering, golden light. A few hallways led off from the main room, but darkness cloaked their depths like a velvet curtain, leaving only the initial bramble arch visible.

She was just turning back to the bar when she abruptly came face-to-face with a tanned Fey to her left, standing much too close. His corn silk hair was swept up and away from his forehead, and his eyes were a disconcerting absinthe green. Just like all the other Fey she'd encountered, his features were nearly human, but not—that strange, skittering otherness so clearly marking them as something else.

The shit-stirring grin on the Fey's face, though, was completely mundane. She'd seen it a hundred other times in a hundred other places, and it was not something that usually went away by being ignored. So Raegan rested one arm on the bar, her back to the King, who was still engaged with someone, and cocked an eyebrow at the blond.

In response, the Fey also placed his hand on the bar top, angling his body around her, a poor attempt at boxing her in. "You here with anyone, Red?" the blond asked, as if he was the first person to ever nickname a redhead in such a way. Raegan wondered if he was relatively young or if he had somehow squandered immortality by remaining so stupid.

At the precise moment that she opened her mouth to reply, the blond's entire face crashed—the grin wiped off as if it had never been there. She watched the Fey swallow hard as his green-eyed gaze shifted to look over Raegan's shoulder. As if fear had prevented him from remembering the existence of his limbs, the blond snatched his hand off the bar top a few beats too late.

"Fuck," the Fey stranger stammered. "I—I didn't know she was here with y-you, High King. I do m-most humbly b-beg you and your lady's pardon."

Raegan had little doubt about what was going on behind her. Her mental image was more or less confirmed when the King's voice, low and dark as dusk, came from just over her shoulder.

"So then *beg*."

Despite the deadly chill in his voice, or perhaps because of it, desire dug its claws deeper into her flesh. She leveled her gaze at the stranger, pleased to see naked terror in his expression as he began to fumble through a series of strained apologies and pleas. His voice shook harder with each sentence.

Then the King's hands slid around Raegan's waist, and every nerve ending she possessed liquified. Hunger drummed in her core. His mouth brushed her ear, and there was nothing she could do to contain the shiver that ran down her body.

"Is he forgiven?" the King asked, the words thick as honey.

Raegan thought about saying no, about seeing how much violence the Unseelie King would enact on her behalf and if the blood would make her desire grow tighter and sweeter. With effort, she pushed the temptation down. "Yes," she said, narrowing her eyes at the blond. "For now. You should go before I change my mind."

The offending Fey melted into the throng of bodies, gone in seconds, leaving Raegan at the King's mercy. His large hands still engulfed her waist, and she could feel his chest at her back. She clamped her jaw so tight she thought a tooth might crack.

The King pulled one hand away, which was enough for Raegan's mind to clear a little. But such clarity lasted only a moment, as he used his free hand to reach for the lip of her stool and pull it closer to his. Trying and failing to push the thrumming of her unmet hunger to the side, Raegan turned to face the bar—and the King.

"I apologize," he said with a small shake of his head. "Seelie scum."

The entire lengths of their thighs were pressed together, the curves of Raegan's hip meeting the sharp, muscled points of the King. She could hardly breathe. "I sort of wanted to ask you to kill him," she found herself saying. "But I thought that might complicate the situation, considering what we're here for. Also would've seemed generally uncool of me, I guess."

His eyes slid to her, the ghost of a smile moving across his mouth. But before he could say anything, two drinks were placed on the bar before them.

"Did you order for me?" she asked, indignant, turning to look at him full-on.

"I would never dream of it," he replied, pushing one glass closer to her. "It is a Fey bar, Overhill. The bartenders know what you want."

She offered only an arch laugh in response, picking up the old-fashioned glass offered to her and examining the molasses-brown liquid within. It looked like a negroni—and a well-made one at that—which was exactly what she had planned to order.

But she could not stop her eyes from slipping to the dark-eyed, raven-haired being beside her. Because at this moment, all Raegan really wanted was the King.

Chapter Forty-Six

She forced herself to take a sip of her drink anyway, though alcohol was sure to only make matters worse. The flavors fell on her tongue in a way she had never experienced before. Brows furrowed, Raegan held the glass up in front of her as if she could stare at the drink until it told her its secrets. When it did not, she shrugged and took another sip. And then another much longer one for good measure.

"Now what?" she asked, looking at the King in her peripheral vision.

"We wait," he replied in a hushed tone, twisting on the stool to face her. "And we pretend that we are having a wonderful time, certainly not here for any ulterior motives, like clandestine meetings."

"Ahh," she said with a smile. "I suppose no one has a bad time out with you, do they?"

The King smirked, making no attempt to hide it, and the way his mouth moved into the expression made Raegan even more desperate to feel his lips against her skin. Maybe she could get someone to punch her in the face or throw a drink at her. Maybe that would reduce the absolute frenzy her body had worked itself into during the past hour.

"I think not," he said, taking a sip of his own drink, a stormy-colored liquid in a lowball glass. "But I would encourage you to share your thoughts."

"I should've grabbed my notepad," Raegan teased, looking at him sideways, all the questions she'd jotted down rushing into her mind. "Oh, that reminds me, does iron not impact you the way basically every folktale implies it will?"

Maybe treating the King like an interview subject would make this easier. If she could only focus on the facts, on rooting out information and finding the patterns that were sure to exist, perhaps she would be able to avoid the unyielding temptation to fuck him.

"That sort of information," the King replied, tracing a line in his glass's condensation with a fingertip, "is quite privileged."

"We came here in a car, and we've been on the subway together," Raegan deadpanned in response, her body turning to face him before she even realized what was happening.

The King sighed as if she had caught him in some elaborate lie he'd spent months planning, raising his gaze to meet hers. "Yes, technically it does," he replied, his expression open. "But nearly all Fey born on this side of the Gates are immune. We are a resilient people."

Raegan propped her elbow on the bar, resting her chin on her hand. This information was interesting, and more importantly, it was an excellent distraction from how close the King's body was to hers. "But you?" she asked. "And other older Fey who weren't born here?"

The King raised his glass in a mock toast, one eyebrow arched. "We have grown accustomed to the pain," he told her, downing a large portion of his drink. The King handling something with dark humor seemed a bit jovial by his usual standards, which made Raegan even more curious.

"In addition to your existing pain?" she asked, not able to stop the pity that seeped into her tone.

He stiffened at the slight change in her voice, forcing Raegan to wonder exactly how attuned he was to her. She put *that* question away for later, a few loud shrieks momentarily distracting her. Over the King's shoulder, she saw a group of pretty, green-skinned girls who did not even look to be of drinking age dancing beside the bar. She reasoned that they were all probably older than the city she had been raised in.

"Pain has been my constant companion since I was very young," the King said sharply, though the admission surprised Raegan. "It is of little concern."

She shrugged, taking another sip of her drink. "Sure."

And just like that, a chasm opened between them. The levity evaporated and the King did not lean into her any longer, though he hadn't exactly pulled away, either. Raegan wondered how difficult it was to explain the same things to the same person over and over. To feel for a moment that something lost had finally been regained, only for one question to destroy the illusion.

"Hey," Raegan tried, leaning her shoulder into his for a moment. "I was wondering. It's fine if you don't want to talk about it. But uh, I was curious what I looked like, the first time we met? And what was I like in general?"

He turned to look at her, his features more guarded, the line of his shoulders returning to that familiar predatory stance. But then his gaze softened, eyes drifting across her frame—not leering or hungry, simply taking stock. Perhaps counting the freckles on her cheeks or examining the precise shape of her collarbones. "Like this," he said, a muscle in his jaw leaping as the words left his mouth. One powerful hand gestured noncommittally toward her.

She tilted her head, lifting an eyebrow, not wanting to push him too far but still hungry for more. His dark eyes drifted back to her, heat slinking into his expression. Her body responded immediately: heart increasing its pace, stomach flipping, desire uncoiling.

"You were this," Oberon repeated, the words soft. "You were . . . *just like this.*"

A gentle ache spread across her chest as the implications of his response unfolded. Something other than lust awoke within her, alighting on soft wings. It was old and so very tender, laced through with grief. She reached her hand toward his, yearning for the familiar map of veins and tendons. But she could not bear to meet his eyes—the feeling that bloomed within her was crystalline, and one mistake would shatter it into a million pieces. She did not think she could endure its shards lodged forevermore in her chest.

A heartbeat before her skin brushed his, a bartender appeared, reaching across the shimmering surface for their empty glasses. The moment burst. Raegan dropped her hand into her lap, her heart thudding thickly. She pressed her lips together, looking down, trying to get her shit together. In her peripheral vision she saw the bartender buff a damp spot, and the King shift his weight forward as if to obscure something. An old instinct raised its head, and the moment the interaction ended, she lifted her gaze to the King's, inquiring wordlessly.

Leaning toward her, his broad shoulders blocking her line of sight, the King held his closed fist between them. As his long fingers unfurled, Raegan knew what would be waiting in his palm even before her eyes registered the object in the dim, scintillating candlelight.

In the King's open hand was a velvety, downy wisp of an owl feather. She inhaled, some alien meaning settling over her shoulders, like her body could feel the importance even as her mind scrambled for concrete answers.

Then the King closed his fingers, sliding his hand—elegant, natural—into his pocket instead, leaning toward her. "It would be best," he said, speaking in a low tone, "if this looked as natural as possible. Please forgive any liberties I take."

Raegan tried to nod as imperceptibly as possible, thoughts racing. Beside her, the King unfolded to his full height, a shadow elongated by dusk. She turned to face him, tilting her head back to meet his eyes.

The King gazed down at her with heavy-lidded desire, the feral planes of his features shifting the expression into something ravenous and dangerous. Raegan's heart rate spiked, her arousal hot and swift. Then his fingertips were at her chin. This time, she didn't even bother trying to resist the urge to lean into his touch—after all, she was only doing her part to convince any onlookers of their ploy. His long fingers slipped into her hair, warm palm against her cheek.

And then his dark eyes met hers, a question lingering there. She shifted her weight toward him, placing one hand on his chest. *Yes,* she wanted to scream—of course he could kiss her. For show or sincerity, she didn't care. Her entire body burned for him, the heat between her legs damp and torturous. A hundred heartbeats in the space of one, and then the King swept low to bring his mouth to hers, hand cradling the back of her skull as if their bodies had met in this way a thousand times before.

His kiss was cavalier and urgent at once, conveying both cold indifference and heated desire. He tasted like mead and folklore and darkness. Snippets of memories exploded behind Raegan's eyes. She returned his kiss like it might save her from drowning, or awaken her from an enchanted slumber. Her blood turned to fire in her veins when she felt his other hand slide around her waist, fingers clutching at the fabric of her dress.

And then because it meant nothing at all, the King pulled away, though he slid his hand into hers and tugged gently. Raegan gave in as she suspected she always had, following the path he carved through the silken rush of Fey bodies. For a moment or two, she wondered if perhaps they were too obvious, too conspicuous, but then she realized just how much she had been utterly absorbed in him. Banquette seating lined the back walls, occupied by what appeared to be mostly tangles of mismatched limbs. More than one couple or group out on the floor had moved far beyond talking or dancing. A Fey club, Raegan realized, was sure to be about sex or violence—perhaps both—and in this case, she was grateful it was only the former. At least at the moment.

The dark hallway was a cool relief from the throb of bodies on the floor. They walked side-by-side, hands still entwined, through the labyrinth of hallways. Beeswax pillars provided flickering light from tiny, rounded alcoves. The low sounds spilling from behind closed doors on either side of the hall revealed the nature of the tucked-away spaces.

Up ahead, the King slowed at a door, leaning over to snuff the candle beside it, sending smoke coiling into the air. Then he led Raegan over the threshold. She found the interior was not unlike the rest of Gossamer—candles burned in alcoves, heavy with dripping wax. The branches that climbed the walls were laden with pale pink flowers. One corner offered a rather excessive pile of fresh silken sheets and pillows, while the other was taken up entirely by an open water closet crafted from shimmery tiles. It featured multiple showerheads and an enormous claw-foot tub. Just to Raegan's right was a long velvet chaise and a darkly lacquered side table.

It was all very beautiful and impressive, lightly scented with jasmine and oud, though she thought a dispossessed people might be better off putting such effort into things like revenge. But then she realized creating such a stunning space just for the sake of joy and pleasure was, in a lot of ways, an enormous and glorious "fuck you."

When she returned her attention to the King, he had stepped away from her, his hand slipping out of her grasp. She watched without a word as he strode over to the side table. From an elegant pitcher, he poured two glasses of what Raegan desperately hoped was water. When the King handed a glass to her, he did not meet her gaze and seemed to do everything in his power to stop their fingers from brushing.

And just like that, all of the heat and desire evaporated from the room as Raegan wondered if every flirtatious touch and lingering look this entire evening—even *before* arriving at Gossamer—had only been to manufacture the charade that would conceal their movements and intentions. Her stomach plummeted, the cool condensation of the glass jarring against her warm fingers. Was the thick and honeyed lust she felt for the King entirely one-sided? Why hadn't she bothered to ask herself before if this ancient Fey being was playing her like a fiddle again and again and again, across time and space and eternity?

And worst of all, Raegan wondered if the strange feeling that had unfolded in her chest for a moment back at the bar could be crushed now that she recalled the sweetness of its bloom.

Chapter Forty-Seven

A gentle knock sounded on the door before Raegan could tumble any deeper into that bittersweet tenderness. With a sideways glance, the King strode to the door, opening it only a small margin. A few low words were exchanged—not in a language she could understand—and then he stepped back, ushering someone inside.

A tall female-presenting person with closely cropped silvery-blonde hair stood silent before her, golden eyes meeting Raegan's. Their frame was somehow sinewy and soft at once, the duality beautifully showcased by a short silk dress in a rich cream color. The keyhole neckline offered a flash of bronze skin, and the attached cape cascading down their back was trimmed in sashaying rows of fringe, something about the movement reminiscent of an owl's wings.

With a start, Raegan realized she was looking at the woman from the alley, the one she'd seen just after Maelona had shoved her out the back door. The woman with the owl-like gaze and familiar voice. The woman who had turned a key in Raegan's chest and unlocked something old and slumbering.

"Overhill," the King said, his voice deep and rich, though his expression was guarded. "You may recall—"

"Blodeuwedd," Raegan breathed, the syllables catching in the middle. Tears stung at her eyes, longing climbing up her throat with sharp talons.

The woman's impassive, elegant features burst open, a flower in bloom, and she plunged toward Raegan. Though no tangible memories revealed themselves, Raegan found herself falling into the embrace all the same. Within Blodeuwedd's arms, she found the feeling of wholeness—crisp as an autumn afternoon and twice as golden. Sobs untangled from her ribcage, saturating the gorgeous fabric of the woman's dress.

"*Renhines pennaf,*" Blodeuwedd said in a tear-choked whisper, tucking the crown of Raegan's head beneath her chin. "My queen is returned. After all these years."

All at once, Raegan remembered an injured owl in the sacred oak glade, and the surprise when the snowy-feathered bird with a bandaged wing became an unconscious woman in her arms. Not during that first life with the river and the shield and the younger King, but a different one, many years later. Something more pushed at the membrane of her Seal, so tangible that she could feel the sensation on her skin. But the locks held, leaving her with a vast ocean of nameless emotion.

Blodeuwedd pulled back, her strong hands coming to cup either side of Raegan's face. "I like this hair," she murmured, sniffling. "Though I am less confident in my ability to help you care for it. I'll learn."

Behind Blodeuwedd, the King said something in that lilting language—almost Welsh, but not quite—and took a step forward. "Please be mindful of the Seal," he added in English, gaze falling onto Raegan.

Blodeuwedd looked back at him over her shoulder, nodding through the tears that cascaded down her face. And then she drew away, pulling the warmth of her hands from Raegan's face, leaving behind a sensation of clouds passing over the spring sun, obscuring the first real radiance after a long winter. "I understand," she said, dragging the heels of her palms across her face to wipe stray tears, "that you seek Baba Yaga."

The King moved then, peeling away from the shadows that clung to him, coming to stand beside Raegan. He leaned his weight against the tall, lacquered side table. She wondered if it was an attempt to appear casual about the information, or if the pain stitched into his skin had heightened its cacophony. "Does she live?" the King asked, direct.

Raegan glanced over to find that the predatory line in his shoulders wasn't present, and she hoped that it meant he trusted Blodeuwedd. Raegan certainly did, absolutely and irrevocably, the intensity of their connection so deep that she could not conjure a shred of doubt.

Blodeuwedd looked between them, her gaze turning hard for a moment. "Is this truly what the two of you wish?" she murmured, her voice like a May breeze through a thicket of yellow broom flowers. "You don't have to take up this mantle over and over again."

The King met her offering with a harsh laugh, though he made no attempt to hide the exhaustion it exposed. "When have the three of us ever been afforded wishes?" he asked, sounding wistful, wrung out. The words settled like stones at the bottom of Raegan's stomach.

Blodeuwedd winced, looking down at her feet for a moment. She let out a long breath and then tilted her chin up, lovely round face like a moon in the dim candlelight. "I can direct you to Baba Yaga," she continued, looking between Raegan and the King. "This is an eventuality she and I once prepared for, but the years have passed and she has grown more reclusive. I think she buried her hope long ago. But you may yet be able to reach her."

With those last words, Blodeuwedd's gaze landed on Raegan. She understood the meaning innately; it was Raegan who would have to remind the folkloric witch of the hope she had once harbored. Perhaps it was still there, an ember in a forgotten hearth.

In the silence, Blodeuwedd examined her, the golden eyes gone owlish, hunting for something hidden behind Raegan's expression.

"This is what I want," Raegan assured her. "This is what I've always wanted. Let me mend what has been broken."

"Then you must go very soon," Blodeuwedd replied. "The Protectorate is inflamed, hungry. Even with your great power, Oberon, you'll need assistance to leave the city safely. My court cannot know I've consulted with you, nor can anyone become aware of the other likeminded Seelie souls who have aided this effort."

Beside her, the King bowed his head in agreement, as noble and regal as anything Raegan had ever seen. Anticipation and terror, and the slick, bravehearted thrill of a quest galloped through her veins.

"You have my gratitude, Blodeuwedd," the King said, holding the woman's gaze. "Anything you require, know that you need only ask."

Pride and pleasure at the King's words flushed Blodeuwedd's skin.

She said something in that lilting, musical language, reaching out for Raegan. Emotion curled thickly in her chest as she accepted Blodeuwedd's hand, the woman's skin pleasantly cool in her feverish grasp.

"You and I were both flowers plucked by greedy hands," Blodeuwedd said, her words fervent, eyes holding Raegan's. "They thought they might contain us in pretty vases or breed us for more blooms. But the plucking turned us into something else, didn't it? Something with wings and talons. Do not forget that."

Blodeuwedd pressed an object into Raegan's palm—a dry, bundled softness of some sort—and then stepped forward. With a long, swooping sigh reminiscent of feathered wings in the air, she bowed her head to rest her forehead against Raegan's. Something in the very fiber of her being released a breath for the first time in hundreds of years.

"Do not forget," the woman murmured again.

"I won't," Raegan promised, the words wobbling on her tongue. "Thank you. For everything."

At that, Blodeuwedd pulled away, looking at Raegan for another moment, eyes brimming over with tears. "I will arrange with Andronica," she said, her gaze lifting to the King. "Rest. Prepare. The less you tax yourselves before this, the better."

With that, Blodeuwedd turned on her heel, the silken cream cape swooping out behind her as two long strides carried her to the threshold. She opened the door and slipped out into the hallway. The King closed the door behind her, waving his hand over the latch. Something in the air shimmered like an oil spill before disappearing completely.

Raegan looked down, examining what Blodeuwedd had given her: seven short sprigs of a green-stemmed plant with halos of small, white flowers. Meadowsweet, she realized. Something pushed against her Seal, and she raised the blooms to her nose. Images danced in her mind: a sun-drenched courtyard and the sound of a woman's laugh; a dagger encrusted with sapphires, a garnet bead of blood on its tip; rolling hills veiled in meadowsweet lace; the weight of a great bird on her shoulder, talons gripping the velvet of her gown. Again, that feeling of softly spun wholeness washed over her, golden and sacred.

Memories tugged at her with pleading hands, and her body pitched with vertigo. Raegan tucked the meadowsweet bundle into her sleeve and looked up, trying to anchor herself back into the stone-clad room with wisteria vines climbing the walls.

Instead, she found only the dark, heavy, ravenous gaze of the King. He had turned back toward her and was now leaning against the door. The realization that she was alone with him—truly alone, and freshly cursed with the knowledge of what his kiss felt like—blazed across her skin like wildfire.

"What now?" she asked, hoping for any direction that would distract her from the incessant thrum in her belly.

"We wait here briefly until our safe passage is prepared," the King replied, his eyes narrowed, scrutinizing her from across the room. "And then we return to the archives to ready ourselves for the road that awaits."

Frustration at his vague response flared in her, a welcome bitterness to cut the saccharine bloom. Raegan turned away from him, trying to take inventory like her therapist always suggested. She noted the tiredness in her limbs, and the confusion, and the complex web of emotions. She leaned onto the table, her feet and ankles beginning to protest the pain inflicted by her high-heeled shoes. With a short, harsh exhale, she glanced over her shoulder at the velvet chaise lounge. It was the only place to recline in the room that did not feel so blatant about its purpose.

Raegan straightened and took a step toward it, only for her heel to catch on the uneven stone floor. She tripped. Maybe in different shoes she would've caught herself on the edge of the side table, but in the lace-up pumps, she rolled one ankle. Pain shot through her leg, and she cursed, the sound coming out louder than she'd meant it to. Teeth gritted, she attempted to adapt, shifting her weight to her good side and reaching down to unwrap the many loops of the leather ties that crisscrossed her ankle and her calf. If she could just yank the damn things off, she'd limp away to the chaise.

Raegan caught the King in her peripheral vision—the glorious sweep of him, his skin like moonlight against the dark green suit, his movements all strange grace—and cursed for another reason entirely. She tried not to look like she was struggling. She did not succeed.

"May I be of assistance?" the King asked, his shadow falling over her.

Raegan braced herself and looked up, wild tangles of hair falling into her face. And then those oceanic eyes met hers and a thousand winged-things began to buzz in her chest.

"I'm fine," she said, the words coming out strangled. "I just tripped."

"Your shoes seem oddly designed to impede movement," the King told her, his voice dry. She could just make out one arched eyebrow from her uncomfortable, doubled-over stance.

"Yeah, but they look hot," Raegan replied without thinking. "And, uh, you are stupidly tall. If I hadn't worn heels tonight, you would've had to squat every time you wanted to say something to me."

As she loosened the top knot of the leather ties, she heard the King laugh—a low rumble from his chest, husky around the edges. She tried not to pay attention to the way her body responded: all uncoiling heat. The King said nothing else, though Raegan didn't think he had walked away. Besides, woodsmoke slunk into her senses now, heady with rain-damp stone.

Pain provided a useful distraction, the ankle she hadn't rolled now screaming out in protest from bearing all of her weight. Raegan prayed for her blood to rush in any other direction as she yanked at the leather knot, which was not coming undone.

"Overhill," came the King's voice again, even drier this time. "You appear to be struggling."

"Yeah," Raegan snapped, though not unkindly. "I think I rolled my ankle, and I want to get this goddamn shoe off, but I need to sit like *right now* because it fucking hurts."

And then he was close, so close—she could've just leaned to the side and found herself pressed against him.

"May I?"

She straightened, attempting to push hair out of her face, but a number of curls stubbornly curtailed her vision. "Sure," Raegan replied, thinking that some help would get her safely to the other side of the room quicker.

Both of the King's large, powerful hands slid around her waist. The gentle pressure of his fingertips against her curves unspooled the thick lengths of desire that she had tried her best to shove in a box and drown in a lake. The King lifted her as if she weighed nothing—Raegan did *not* weigh nothing—and placed her on the side table. Between the immediate alleviation in pain and the sensation of his touch, she let out a low sigh before she could restrain the sound.

At least the King possessed the decency to take a step to the side, remaining nearby in case she continued to require assistance, but not so close that Raegan lost her mind entirely.

"Thanks," she mumbled, not daring to look at him. Instead, she scooted farther back on the table with her palms and then drew the pained ankle up and onto her knee. The hem of her tight dress traveled with the movement, sliding up from her mid-calf to her thigh. She continued to work on the knot of leather she had tied herself only a few hours ago to no avail, feeling like a giant idiot. And also, like she came closer and closer to doing something stupid with each passing breath. "Sorry," she said, letting her eyes slide to the King.

He stood a few feet away, his arms crossed in a way that made her wonder, yet again, about the muscular build of his shoulders hidden beneath the suit. And he *watched* her, every bit the faerie lord conde-scendingly examining a mortal and their silly little habits.

"The knot," she explained, pulling the leather ties away from the swell of her calf. "It's stuck. I promise I know how to take a shoe off."

The King's full mouth moved at that sentence, lips parting slightly, as if he were picking his best barb. Under the glow of the candles lining alcoves in the walls, his eyes were endless pools in which Raegan would happily drown. Her hands went still on the ties, and she remembered all over again that she was alone with him, his very real body only inches away, and hers already conveniently placed on a piece of furniture at the correct height for a multitude of activities.

A shimmer in the shadows and the King moved toward Raegan, as if he had been thinking the very same thing.

"It is excruciating," he said in a low voice, "to watch you."

And the King reached for her.

Chapter Forty-Eight

Raegan's breath caught in her throat, all the slinking, swollen pressure in her unwinding. But then the King's hand met only the leather tie at her calf, his fingers—god, she needed to stop watching them so closely—deftly separating the strands. He held his arms straight out, keeping his body as far away from her as possible. His skin never brushed hers as he untied the knot. Raegan wondered if he was trying just as hard to keep his desire under control as she was. The thought manifested like a flare of heat, but the King moved away immediately, retreating a few steps back, shoving his hands in his pockets as if he could not trust them uncaged.

She swallowed, her mouth dry. "Thanks," she said, high, wispy. And then, before she could stop herself—the ache in her bones far too much to withstand—she added, "Probably won't be able to get the other one undone, either."

Raegan watched the King cycle through his next choice, every thought so clear on his face. For a moment, she felt acutely that she knew him, that she had always known him. That a room full of people would see nothing in his expression while she could read a hundred stories laid bare on those high, sharp cheekbones and oceanic eyes and feral brow.

Without a word, the King approached her, and Raegan's core curled in on itself. Something dark and lovely simmered across his features. His movements were sharp and predatory, and god, how she wished to be devoured. He said nothing, though she may not have heard it over the sound of her heart careening in her chest, and began to untie her other shoe. Perhaps she was imagining it, fulfilling her own wishes even as reality unfolded differently, but the King took less care this time. The back of his hand brushed the bare skin of her calf, sending goosebumps racing up her leg. He stood closer, facing her now, bowed over her frame instead of approaching from the side.

Raegan fought it, she truly did, but the instinct to part her legs for him was too strong, an ancient and unyielding urge that had followed her senselessly across time and space. The King released the knot, this time unwinding the thin leather ties from her leg as opposed to just letting the shoe clatter to the floor. The lightest brush—so easily accidental—of his touch sent Raegan's heart leaping into her throat, the ache buried deep within her singing louder and louder.

Beneath the high, shadowed ceiling, spirited away from the world she knew, little felt real to her except for the King. Suddenly, she was enveloped in him, a door opening within her that allowed the past to slip out, gowned in black velvet:

A wild look in his eyes and blood on his jaw, striding toward her across the ruins of some empty stone hall. Then the glint of firelight against the dark swoop of a forest, her bare back arched into a woolen blanket, powerful hands wrapped around her thighs, her own fingers grasping at silken threads of familiar raven hair. A sunset turning his pale skin golden, tall stalks of heather crushed beneath her boots as she caught up to him atop a light-soaked hill, grabbing a fistful of his loose, linen shirt and pulling his larger body toward hers.

And now here: the pain in her feet dulled, the surface of the table warming beneath her skin, the heat of him just an arm's reach away, an infinite need spreading everywhere he had not yet touched her in this life.

A name bloomed on Raegan's tongue, old and dead everywhere except for within this room, and she watched him look at her as if he were seeing her for the first time. His body gave into hers, eyes searching her face for something she thought she may finally be able to give him. Blistering desire erupted within her, and she reached out, filling her fist with the fabric of his suit jacket, a poor replacement for his flesh. There, in a place that was not a place, in a time outside of time, the King gazed down at Raegan.

He gazed down at her as if he would sacrifice everything for her and hate himself all the while. All these years spent trapped in the same spiral, tirelessly mapping the labyrinth but never finding its exit, having no one but himself to blame, and yet and yet *and yet* . . .

So Raegan did the only thing she could, which was to clutch both sides of his jacket and pull herself to him. Her mouth crashed against the King's in desperate, keening want. He met her with bottomless need, wrapping his hands around her waist as she threaded her fingers into his hair. Every place her body met his form came alive with yearning aware-ness, as if she had never quite understood what it meant to be flesh and blood until this moment.

All Raegan's unmet desires turned molten within her as she wrapped her legs around the King's hips, pulling him closer. Even in the maddening way they both hungered for each other—as if they had only ever known starvation—his movements were impossibly elegant. The sensation of his hands sliding up her legs and bringing the fabric of her dress along with him was nothing short of divine.

The King's mouth trailed to her jaw and then her throat, hands wrapped around the tops of her thighs. She tipped her head back, a soft moan escaping her parted lips. The sound deepened as he slid a hand beneath her knee, pulling her closer to the edge of the table. Her legs opened wider for him, the fabric of his suit scraping deliciously along the delicate skin of her inner thighs.

Their hips slotted together, her aching softness pressed against his hard desire, as Raegan fumbled with the buttons on his dress shirt. She released another breathless moan as the King's hand moved to cup her heavy breast, his lips trailing down from her collarbone. Arching her back with anticipation, her need for him crescendoed beyond reason, all of her weak and throbbing.

And then it was gone. The heat of him retreated, his larger frame no longer pressing into hers. More dazed than she wanted to admit, Raegan watched him slide out from between her legs, gently pulling her dress back into place as he went.

Her heart hammered as she watched the King step away, his eyes shut. The hand that had just touched her with so much hunger moved, instead, to pinch the bridge of his nose.

"I am sorry," the King said in a strained, hoarse tone. "You have done nothing wrong. It is me. I—I cannot."

Raegan curled her hands together, fingernails biting into her flesh as she watched him.

Eventually, the King's dark eyes met hers. "Not again," he said softly, shaking his head. "Never again."

She opened her mouth and closed it when no words came out. She could not decide what she wanted: to hurl venom, to beg, to ask for more ways to understand. So she said nothing, her heart in her throat.

"I want you," he murmured. "I always do. But you make me weak. There is no other way to say it." At least he had the decency to look at her when he said it. But it did little to assuage the way Raegan's anger turned over in her stomach, sour and sharp.

"I make you weak?" she scoffed. "It seems like I'm the only way to make you *whole* again."

More than anything, she wanted him to correct himself, to elaborate with rose-colored sentences. If only the King explained his words correctly, she thought, then she could keep her rising wave of rage under control. She waited, picking at her cuticles until she produced a single drop of crimson.

"Perhaps," the King replied, leveling a cool gaze at her. "Perhaps in this life, things could be different. But I have little reason to believe so. You have always made me feel too deeply—in ways that my people are not meant to feel. I was created for a purpose. You get in the way of that purpose."

Raegan tasted blood and bile, and she stared across the few feet that separated them, her heartbeat thundering in her ears. "And yet you keep coming back to me," she snarled, lacing her words with as much poison as possible. "Like a beaten little dog, you come back to be made weaker again and again."

The King sighed, dragging a hand down his face. He looked nowhere near as upset as Raegan would've liked. She wanted him to feel as she did, like she'd been gutted.

"This time is the first in many years," he told her, beginning to pace, though his tone was measured, as if he were presenting at some corporate function. "I have made it a habit to stay far away from you."

The implications of his words sunk into Raegan like a knife. The only person that could make any sense of the alien feelings and the ancient yearning and the incoherent longing had stayed away—and on purpose? The King had made it a habit to abandon her to polluted half-lives where all she did was ache, always looking for an answer to the older things that lived inside her?

"*What?*" Raegan spat, anger covering up the hurt, hoping to god she could muster enough rage to hide how much she needed him. She sat up straighter, her hands curling inward, nails cutting into her flesh. "For how long, Oberon? How long have you been discarding me?"

"Since the Gates closed fully," the King replied, holding her gaze. "Since I was exiled."

She thought it might've been easier if he'd sounded guilty when he said it, or if he'd spoken the words with some kind of haughty pleasure at injuring her. But the King had not. He'd told her the simple truth when she'd asked for it, and somehow it hurt all the more for that.

"That's . . ." Raegan began, mortified to feel a sob clawing its way up her throat. "That's like hundreds of years. Hundreds of years you just . . . abandoned me. To this. Do you have any idea what it is to ache and ache and ache for something and not even know *what* it is?"

Her fingers raked at her own throat, as if she could tear out all that she had endured and throw it into his arms for him to contend with instead.

"I wake up from dreams I can't remember with strange names in my mouth," Raegan continued, her voice weary. "I know deep in my marrow that I have walked other worlds but no longer possess the keys to their doors. It's like I have loneliness stitched into my skin and you're the only person who knows how to remove it."

The King still watched her, not looking away for a moment, his chest rising faster with each word she said. He slid his hands from his pockets but only held them at his side, making none of the placating gestures she thought he might. "Please understand," the King began, moving like he might take a step toward her but thought better of it, "I know you. I have known you for more than a thousand years. I know your ache, for it is lodged just as deeply within me. And every time I lose you, the darkness inside me grows vaster. I cannot be with you again only to light your funeral pyre. I am sorry I am not strong enough."

Raegan bit down on her cheek, hoping for anything that would stop her from digging claws into the softness the King had offered her. But no iron tainted her tongue, and wouldn't all of this be easier if she were not consumed by that strange, gentle feeling that only he had ever conjured within her?

"I didn't realize how seriously you were taking this," she laughed, the sound of it harsh even to her ears. "I'm stressed out and I wanted someone to fuck me. You were here. Don't flatter yourself. You are a means to an end, Oberon. I'll be delighted to discard you as soon as I possibly can."

Raegan wanted to take the words back as soon as they left her mouth, but pride soured in her stomach. The King only nodded, his features closing off as if he had shut a physical door. He looked away from her, his gaze falling somewhere near the far corner of the room.

"If I come back again, after this," Raegan continued before she realized she had even opened her mouth, "I hope I'll find someone else on the Unseelie throne, for the sake of your people. Someone who isn't made weak by a few kisses from a mortal woman."

In all truth, she had thought the Unseelie King would ignore her words. She'd thought he had surely heard worse, and would again, that such a low jab from her would hardly mean anything at all. But he turned back to her, his face contorted in rage. In hardly two steps, the King closed the distance between them, slamming his hands down on either side of her legs so hard that cracks appeared in the table's wooden surface.

The King's eyes were dark and wild, his features feral, everything about him the stuff of myth and nightmare. "*You* are the weakness," he snarled, so close to her that she could still feel the heat of him. "An infestation, a sickness, and how quickly you spread. Look at you—three decades you have squandered accepting that the world was what you were told it was, despite the ache in your chest that so clearly said otherwise."

He relented, only slightly, granting her no more than breathing room, his muscled frame still an impassable wall between her and a quiet place where she could tell herself that nothing he said was true.

"You admit that I am hardly more than a fleeting memory, a means to an end," he spat, cruel and appraising. "And yet you will happily forget about your supposedly beloved father long enough to share my bed. How very *weak*."

With that, he finally pushed off the table and away from her, taking several long strides until he stood by the door. Raegan watched the shadows stretch toward him, rolling like the front of a thunderstorm to their King's feet.

She waited a heartbeat for him to turn or to say anything at all, but then her throat closed off and she knew tears would be close to follow. And Raegan refused to cry in front of him. He had been willing to show her his soft undersides, but that was his error, not hers.

Gathering herself up, Raegan shifted her weight, trying to slowly lower herself to the floor, stretching her good ankle down first. Her bare foot met cold stone. She leaned into the movement experimentally, pleased to only find the usual kind of soreness from a night out in uncomfortable heels.

Then Raegan braced herself and placed the ankle she thought she'd rolled onto the ground. Surprise drew her eyebrows together when she felt no pain.

With his back to her, the King spoke again, his voice hard and even. "I addressed your injury," he said, not turning around. "Andronica will arrive shortly. Perhaps you would like to pull yourself together."

Anger swept through Raegan again, blind and white hot. She stomped forward and reached out to grab his arm. He moved at a terrifying speed, pulling his arm out of her reach as he swung to tower over her. The shadows tore themselves from the walls at his command, constricting and stretching into horrible shapes, demonic and ungodly things creeping in the gloom.

"Do not," the Unseelie King commanded, his voice ringing out from every inch of the room, "*ever* touch me again."

CHAPTER FORTY-NINE

Raegan wasn't afraid of him, though maybe she should have been. But it was not fear that moved through her chest. Instead, embittered sorrow pierced her breastbone. She spat something in return, not even sure of the words she spoke, and turned her back to him, desperately scanning the room for an escape.

By some small grace—either of Gossamer's or perhaps the King's—the water closet had grown walls, crafted from matching fish-scale tiles. A tall, elegant door with a wavy glass insert marked the entrance. She threw herself through it, slamming the door behind her. On the other side, a small seating area and vanity rendered in rich, shimmering ocean hues awaited her. With a ragged, tear-soaked sigh, Raegan lowered herself onto one of the seafoam velvet chairs.

"What a stupid choice for a fucking bathroom," she choked out, clawing at the fabric with her nails.

She pulled her legs to her chest, resting her forehead on her knees. Was this how it always was between them? Her hardheadedness running quick and hot, his cold-blooded nature just as inescapable as his sense of duty?

Wrapping her arms around herself, Raegan's levy broke and she began to cry. She tried with all her might to be as quiet as possible, the idea of the King overhearing her too mortifying to even consider. When a headache began to thunder in her skull, she made herself stop. She got to her feet, feeling like a wrung-out dishrag.

Upon examination in the mirror, she found she didn't look much better. Her face was red and puffy, her eyelids ballooned to about twice their usual size, the kohl eyeliner she'd applied streaked. Raegan sighed, running the faucet—shaped like a golden swan, of course—until the water was pleasantly cool. She splashed her face and scrubbed at the kohl, trying not to drench her hair in the process.

A knock sounded at the door, sending her heart racing. She blotted her skin dry with an impossibly soft towel, trying to decide if she wanted to answer. Anger was still wrapped around her midsection, sorrow like a weight in the pit of her stomach. Would he expect an apology? Would he offer one? Could she make her mouth say, "I'm sorry," even if she wanted to? Or would it catch in her throat the same way "I love you" always did?

And yet the pull was still stronger than the push, so Raegan took a deep breath and opened the door.

It took her a few moments to realize that the person standing there was in fact not the King. Instead, a Fey woman stood there with the duffle bag Raegan had left at the archives, her arms crossed. A thick braid of gleaming black hair was draped over the shoulder of her fitted, nondescript black jacket. She was quite slender but powerfully built, an unpleasant expression on her sharp-featured face.

"Goddess's sake," she said in a velvety, deep-pitched voice. "Is it really you?"

Familiarity crept down Raegan's spine. She glanced at her bag, feeling a strong urge to simply grab her belongings and slam the door. "Sorry," she said instead. "I'm sure we know each other, but you may have heard my memory's sort of shit."

The Fey woman's expression pinched further, and she looked at Raegan with dead-eyed displeasure. "The situation has degraded, as it tends to when you are involved," the woman replied, almost certainly instead of a quip about how more than Raegan's memory was lacking. "It would be helpful if you could get changed into something more practical."

At that, Raegan snatched her bag from the faerie's feet, straightening to meet her gaze with an expressive display of distaste. "My apologies.

Some of us don't attend formal affairs in our gym clothes," Raegan said, letting her eyes linger purposefully on the Fey woman's outfit.

In response, the woman openly sneered at her, so full of hostility that Raegan felt begrudging respect. "Seeing as your memory is as lacking as your insults," the woman replied, flipping her shining braid over her shoulder, "I'll remind you that I'm Andronica, security councilor and high knight of the Unseelie Court. We've met before, namely when you went against years of careful planning to play hero and got captured in the process, which led to the taking of our King, the closure of the Gates, and my exile into this hellscape."

Discomfort stirred in Raegan's stomach, and she swallowed. "Oh," was her only reply.

"Oh *indeed*," Andronica said, narrowing her dark eyes. "We'll talk in a few moments."

Then the Fey warrior turned on her heel, graceful as a ballerina and ten times as deadly, and stalked away. Raegan scanned the room quickly but didn't see the King. Gritting her teeth, she closed the door. She tossed her bag onto the stupid seafoam chair and unzipped it. Everything seemed to be in place—clothes, medications, notebook, and laptop, her work bag and its contents packed neatly inside the duffle. Heart pounding, she checked the side pocket. Relief rocketed through her when she found her father's spellpapers tucked safely inside.

For a moment, Raegan squeezed her eyes shut, pressing her lips together. She could do this. Her feelings were just as irrelevant as whatever scraps of romance she had with the King. All that mattered was her father and her fate.

A few moments later, she was dressed in high-waisted, tapered black jeans, a long-sleeved tee with thumbholes, and her knee-high, lace-up boots. At the vanity, Raegan braided her hair, starting at the crown of her head.

"Right," she said to her own reflection. "Good enough."

Her duffle slung over her shoulder, Raegan exited the water closet, closing the door softly behind her. The room was empty of other living beings, though it had reconfigured itself. The velvet chaise and corner piled with silk sheets were gone; instead, a long table stretched down the middle of the space. A platter of bread, cheese, and fruit—all infinitely better-looking than any food she'd ever seen in her life—sat on its surface.

She ate ravenously, suddenly realizing exactly how hungry she was. When she'd finished, she stood and pulled out a chair. Placing her duffle into it, she leaned her forearms onto the chair's back. The universe afforded Raegan a few more moments of silence before the door opened.

Andronica arrived first, not even sparing Raegan a glance. Close behind her was Kamau, whose greeting was almost too cheery considering all that had transpired. Tension swelled in the room like an incoming wave, and then Blodeuwedd slipped inside, in the middle of a conversation with the King, who entered the space at her heels.

Raegan set her jaw and told herself to look literally anywhere else, but in the end, she could not. The King pulled the door closed, replying to Blodeuwedd—something about wards—but his ocean eyes slid to Raegan all the same. He held her gaze, his sentence trailing off, full mouth moving into a firm line.

She swallowed but did not avert her eyes. Her palms felt hot and damp, her heart thudding ferociously.

"Are you alright?" the King asked, looking at her in that way of his—like no one else in the room existed at all. Her mouth went dry, and Raegan told herself that it was as much of an olive branch as anyone could possibly hope for from an ancient sovereign with god-like powers.

And yet her pride puffed its chest out like a preening lion, and she sneered. "Why wouldn't I be?" Raegan scoffed, arching an eyebrow.

He held her gaze for a moment longer, dark lashes dipping like a raven's wing. But she gave him nothing, crossing her arms. At that, the King relented, and with a shrug of his shoulders, he looked toward the table and moved for it. Andronica, Blodeuwedd, and Kamau had already taken a seat, so Raegan did, too.

The King did not sit. Instead, he came to the head of the table and rested his folded hands on the back of the chair. "Everything has gone to hell," he announced, some sly trace of dark humor ghosting his lips. "The Protectorate attacked an Unseelie sentry post for the first time since we came to this city last year, Blodeuwedd's faction has a turncoat, and apparently Baba Yaga's pocket realm will move halfway across the globe in six hours."

Raegan looked around the table, trying to gauge the temperature. Andronica looked pissed, but that didn't seem unusual. Kamau appeared troubled, their large hands tapping out a nervous staccato on the table's surface. Blodeuwedd hadn't stopped chewing on her lower lip since she'd walked through the door.

"If you are willing," he continued, his eyes falling on Raegan, "the recommendation from my most trusted advisors is to leave immediately."

Panic crowded out the air in her lungs. "Now?" she asked weakly, hating the sound of her own voice. "We're going to find Baba Yaga and try to remove my Seal right *now*?"

Across the table, Andronica snickered, not bothering to conceal the sound, though everyone ignored her.

"You can either leave now," Blodeuwedd added, her voice kind, "or go deep into hiding until things calm down, which could take a very long time."

Raegan tried to force a deep breath, dragging a hand through her hair. She felt feverish, anxiety gripping her shoulders with heavy hands. But she wanted this, didn't she?

"Why has the pace . . . accelerated?" she asked, doing her best to focus on information-gathering and not the intense pressure across her chest. "What happened?"

Andronica's eyes shot to Raegan, her expression full of long-held distrust. "*You* happened," she said, blunt and harsh, leaning across the table on her forearms. "The Protectorate is swarming this city, and our people might be exposed because of you."

"Now," Blodeuwedd began, "that's not entirely—"

The room rocked, as if some great beast had slammed into it. Candle soot dislodged from the alcoves and floated down to the floor like black snow. Kamau got to their feet in the same way a volcano erupts, launching themselves toward the doorway.

"Fuck," Andronica spat, rising to stand like a panther bored of sunbathing and ready to seek blood instead.

Blodeuwedd's eyes had gone wide, her fingers curling into her palms. Raegan looked to her for a cue, her muscles locked, but the golden-eyed woman's attention was settled on the King. He had leaned his head back, exposing the long expanse of his ivory neck, a deep breath pulling at his chest in an even stride. Then his chin was parallel to the ground again, and there was nothing in his expression but cold, brutal composure. "Overhill," he said, meeting her gaze, "we depart now for Baba Yaga."

It was a command, and Raegan balked instinctually, but the King had already turned to Kamau to address the Fey knight in that musical, lilting language. Andronica barked something in response, standing in front of the King as if she planned to physically stop him from leaving.

"Andronica," the King replied, switching back to English. "Caledfwlch did not end me. Neither did all the Protectorate's attempts. I have not diminished on this side of the Gates. I will be fine."

Andronica did not relinquish a single inch of space as Raegan watched the interaction closely, sliding the strap of her duffle over her shoulder and rising to stand. "How are you going to hold the wards *and* protect her?" Andronica demanded, her attention swinging away from the King to land squarely on Raegan. "You are unrestored, correct?"

Raegan seriously considered a smartass response, but she was intelligent enough to realize the Fey knight could realistically behead her before the King could do anything about it.

"Yes," Raegan replied, bracing herself.

Andronica's dark eyes flashed in the low light, her shoulders climbing closer to her ears with frustration. "Fate wastes all Her precious energy," she snarled, "to bring back something so *useless—*"

"Andronica," Kamau interrupted from their post by the door. "Maybe this is not helping?"

By the time Andronica had turned back to the King, he had laid a powerful hand on her shoulder, his expression gone serious, tenderness flitting about the edges. "You will hold the wards in my stead," he said, his voice heavy. "I know it is a burden."

Raegan watched Andronica's rich complexion pale as she looked up at the King with something that was not far off from fear.

"Before you protest," he continued, one dark brow arching, "do you believe I would ask for such a thing from you if you were not capable?"

Andronica ground her jaw as the Unseelie warrior recognized her king had just trapped her effortlessly. "Am I, though?" she asked, her words coming out in a long sigh. "You have trained me well. I have successfully held them when we've practiced. But *only* in practice, my liege, and with nothing else required of me. What if I'm not ready? If I fail, Gossamer will fall, the archives will become discoverable, and all our people's home warding will cease to exist."

"I am not tasking you with continuing your responsibilities *and* holding our people's wards," the King replied. "Kamau can oversee your work. Unless you do not believe they can?"

Raegan recognized that the King's words formed a genuine question. He had backed off from the pressure he'd put on Andronica, giving her a spot of leeway to exert her own influence, while also providing an escape route if she truly had doubts about her own abilities. Impressive.

"Yes, they can," she said so fiercely that a knot of admiration twinged in Raegan's chest. "Just as I can hold the wards. Go. Do what you must for all of us."

The King bowed his head to Andronica, bringing his brow to hers—much in the way Blodeuwedd had done earlier—as his powerful hand held the base of her skull. The knight and her liege stayed like that for a long moment. When they pulled apart, Andronica's shoulders were as straight and deadly as an arrow.

"Overhill," the King said, looking her way again. "Though I have little right, I will once again request that you follow me into the darker places of this world to see if we can find salvation there."

Raegan could say no. She could see what was salvageable of her little mundane life. She could try to find someone else to help search for her father. She could visit those places Maelona had written down and see if the Protectorate would leave her alone.

She could beg Fate to release her, petition Death to return her to the void, be done with magic and the gods and the Fey and all the wild, feral-hearted feelings this Unseelie King summoned from deep within her.

And yet, and yet, and yet . . .

Raegan took a few tentative steps toward the King, her blood beating like a war drum in her veins.

"To salvation, then."

CHAPTER FIFTY

Raegan had not imagined that their transportation to Baba Yaga would be an ordinary sedan in a middling blue color. The underground garage at Gossamer held carriages crafted from orchid petals, and purring automobiles sleek as cheetahs, but the King had, for some reason, chosen an utterly mundane car. She slowed her pace as he unlocked the doors and tossed his bag onto the backseat.

"I want to remind you," the King said, looking at her over the frame of the vehicle, the weight of his attention pulling her from her thoughts, "that I will not force you to do this."

The statement surprised Raegan. For a moment, she only studied him, carefully considering what to say next. "What would you do?" she asked, crossing her arms. "If you were me?"

The King let out a low, humorless laugh, the sound of it absorbed almost immediately by the high, earthen walls that surrounded them. "If I were you," he echoed, "I would run."

She stared at him, ignoring the fear that crept along her spine. And then she scoffed. It was the last thing any sane mortal would do in the face of an ancient faerie king—but she was at least half-mad, and not precisely mortal, either.

"I don't want to run, Oberon," Raegan said, putting as much force into the words as she could. "I want to restore my memory, and then I want to hunt the Protectorate down and take back *everything* they stole from me."

The King's oceanic gaze consumed her for a long, skittering moment. And then he smiled, wolf-like and ravenous, the sight of it sending a bolt of exhilaration and desire into her chest. Before she could change her mind, Raegan yanked open the back door and threw her bag inside. She didn't dare look at him as she settled herself into the passenger seat, picking at her cuticles. The balance of the car shifted as he slid into the driver's side. The green numbers on the dashboard indicated midnight was approaching.

"Doesn't being in a car hurt?" Raegan asked as he reversed out of the parking spot. "You know, essentially an iron box?"

"Cars are made of steel and fiberglass these days," the King said, his tone distant. "Steel is iron mixed with carbon, rendering it less potent."

She nodded mutely and then sat in silence as he pulled out of the underground parking garage and onto a side street. The familiar city's shadows seemed to leer at her through the window. Raegan imagined the gloom of each alleyway filled with swarms of Protectorate, their soot-colored suits blending into the surroundings.

"You need not respond," the King began, flicking the windshield wipers on as rain suddenly spattered the windshield, "but I am sorry for what I said earlier. It was cruel, which I admit is not out of character for me. I often find it simpler to make you hate me. Then you leave, and I need only summon the strength to resist following."

Raegan let out a long breath, turning to rest her forehead on the cool, rain-streaked window. She'd rather stay angry at him. She'd rather put her Olympic-level grudge-holding to good use. She'd rather do anything than what every fiber of her body ached for—to accept his apology, offer her own, and maybe feel the hard, muscled weight of him once again.

Her stubborn pride, that red rash of rotting anger, won out in the end. Raegan said nothing, instead gazing out the window. She watched familiarity melt away as they took the bridge across the river. On the other side of the Delaware, the land was flat. The evening seemed to devour the end of the road somewhere in the distance, like they were driving straight into the mouth of some ancient beast cloaked in midnight.

A beast that may very well devour her whole.

~

An hour or more passed in silence. She would've preferred it strung tight with tension, but the quiet quickly became companionable and she could not find the desire to fight it.

"We have nearly arrived," the King said, jarring her. "Once we do, we will need to move quickly. Baba Yaga's pocket realm is currently in the Pine Barrens, but in only a few short hours, it will relocate to a remote Russian forest that would be significantly more difficult to reach."

Raegan had seen enough road signs to be pretty sure of their location, but she still felt faint amusement at the confirmation. Baba Yaga spending time in the Pine Barrens made almost too much sense. She'd love to tell her dad. One day, hopefully, she might.

"Stay close, stay sharp, and use your knife if you must," the King continued, turning to look at her for a moment. "Together we will see it through."

He spoke as if they were war-toughened comrades who had fought at each other's sides a hundred times before—which, of course, Raegan realized, they were. Their shared history, even if impossible to recall presently, steadied her.

"What's going to happen to me when the Seal is removed?" she asked, looking down to see her hands were shaking. She settled them onto her thighs.

The King said nothing, as if the darkness had gobbled up her words. They'd passed through a few small towns, and the last one had long since turned into another winding two-lane road cutting straight through the heart of a forest.

"I do not know," he replied eventually. "Baba Yaga will be in a better position to answer this inquiry."

"Will I still . . ." Raegan set her jaw. ". . . still be me, I guess?"

At that, she felt the King's eyes fall on her for a stretched moment before he had to return his gaze to the road. "From what I understand," he said, "there are risks. You could go completely mad. You could fracture, developing alters for each life you lived, losing the interconnected nature of what you are. One of your lives could take over, erasing the rest. Ideally, the Seal will be peeled back and you will slowly integrate your memories over a period of time."

"And in that ideal scenario," she asked, resting her temple against the cool window, "I would be me but . . . more?"

"Yes," the King answered, drumming his fingers on the steering wheel. "You would have some degree of access to all your memories and knowledge, but you would remain."

"Right," Raegan murmured, closing her eyes against the thoughts buzzing in her skull. She hadn't expected to have so little time to wrap her mind around accepting that—if they even made it to Baba Yaga's doorstep—the removal of the Seal might be the end of Raegan Maeve Overhill. What chance did she stand against something infinitely older and more powerful awakening within her?

Of course doubt would creep in here, beyond the streets of her beloved city, beneath a vast canopy of rain-black trees and cloudy skies. She had cast herself entirely to the winds of Fate. There were a thousand questions she should ask. If her Seal was safely removed and they made it to the Gates, how would the world change with magic's release? What would become of mortals? How exactly had the Timekeeper tricked her ancestors in the first place? And were the Fey tricking her right now to get what they desired?

But all Raegan wanted to think about was her magic and her father, so her mouth stayed shut. Better to not know. Better to think only of the things that she had too long been denied.

The King pulled off the main road onto a meandering sandy lane that led deeper into the forest. Loose soil crunched under the tires. Pine trees loomed from all sides. In a few minutes, they reached a small parking lot that Raegan thought could be for a hiking trailhead, but she couldn't make out any signage. She sat motionless, trying to remind herself that she wanted this. She *did*. And yet . . .

"I'm terrified," she admitted to the King without meaning to, the realization leaving her mouth at the same moment as it clarified in her mind.

He looked toward her as he switched off the car's headlights. The moon broke through the cloud cover, illuminating his angular features. "You would be a fool if you were not," he said.

With that, the King turned the engine off and slid from the driver's seat. The smell of damp, sandy soil, resinous pine, and cold rain slunk in through the open door. Raegan let out a heavy breath, zipped up her leather jacket, and got out of the car.

"Here," the King said, handing her a luggage tag.

"Like from before?" she asked, thinking of the way he'd reduced the size of her overnight bag when she'd packed up her apartment.

The King nodded a confirmation, looking absolutely otherworldly and deadly beneath the moon's silver glow. He tucked a second luggage tag into the pocket of his own jacket, which matched the rest of his clothing—black, sleek, tactical. "I would like to enchant your vision so you do not have to rely on me for sight in the darkness," he told her. "May I hold my hand over your eyes?"

"Yes," she replied, the word coming out a croak.

"Please keep your eyes open," he instructed, cupping one large hand over her vision, plunging her into darkness.

Raegan heard his deep voice move in a low, guttural cadence, and then his hand fell away. The world suddenly looked as if she had put on night vision goggles, but with more shades of gray than green. She swept her gaze through the forest clearing, amazed at how she could see individual rocks in the sand and the pine needles dusting the ground.

Raegan looked up at the King to say thanks and saw him—horrifying, cruel, unfathomably powerful, beyond ancient—looking over her shoulder with something that she thought might be fear. She blinked, forcing a sharp inhale. Could the Protectorate have found them already? How much could the King weather if they were to be hunted the entire path to Baba Yaga's door?

She had just about worked up the courage to turn around and face whatever made even the King react in such a way when his expression shifted, deep-seated hatred surfacing. She felt him wrap his fingers around her upper arm, pulling her close. He moved in a long, elegant step, placing himself between her and whatever lay ahead.

At the other end of the clearing, haloed in moonlight, stood something celestial. The stars themselves—just barely visible through gaps in the cloud cover—seemed to toss their shine down like flowers at the being's feet. Long silver hair flowed in a waterfall down their back, more tresses plaited like a crown around their head. Above their slender shoulders rose twin arches of snowy, downy feathers. Wings, Raegan realized in awe, like a swan's but much, much larger.

"Aranrhod," the King said, a picture of threadbare civility.

"My children," the being replied. Her voice was starfall, turning wheels of silver, and everything that has been and everything that is yet to come. The sound of it seemed to shake the air around Her.

"Fate," Raegan breathed.

The being took a step closer to them, though She did not so much walk as glide. "I pulled your Threads," Fate said, "and you answered my call."

Raegan said nothing, her breath caught in her chest, blood pounding. The King's grip on her upper arm tightened.

"I have come," Fate said, standing just before them now, though Raegan never saw Her close the distance, "to offer you my blessing, for it is my path upon which you walk."

Up close, Raegan was startled to find echoes of the King's features in Fate's face. Not in a way that denoted relation so much as lineage—a shared otherworldliness that set them both far apart from humans.

"We receive your blessing," the King said after a moment's pause, though his tone was blank and hardened.

Fate inclined Her head, trails of silver hair running across Her shoulders like liquid metal. The world, it seemed, held still, all eyes turned to this forgotten clearing at the end of a rain-slick road.

"Good luck," Fate murmured, Her thin lips barely moving. "May you see this through. Seek the door Cormac Overhill left ajar."

Something like fire roared through Raegan's body at the mention of her father as Fate looked between the two of them with nearly colorless eyes, Her mouth moving into an austere smile. The being turned, the swoop of Her feathered wings lifting away from Her shoulders as if She were about to disappear back into the misty evening, leaving all the suffering and the terrible, never-ending ache to the smaller creatures crawling across the planet's surface like ants.

"Wait!" Raegan called, pushing the word out.

Though he said nothing, the King's fingers suddenly dug into her flesh. Fate did not turn, but She gazed over one shoulder, the planes of Her face taking on that cold, feral look Raegan knew so well.

"What do you know about my father?" Raegan shouted, ripping her arm out of the King's grasp. "Tell me. Please."

"That is not for a little thing like you to know," Fate replied, Her tone cool. "He made his bargain, played his part."

A cold, horrible realization settled over her. "You put him on this path, didn't you?" Raegan demanded, her voice hoarse with fury and sorrow. "He just wanted magic back—*real* magic. And you used that against him to set all of this into motion."

Anger boiled in her stomach as she finally fit the pieces together. She knew she should stop. But a thousand years of anger was seeping into her bloodstream, and she thought it might poison her to death if she did not let it out.

"Do you enjoy watching us suffer?" Raegan screamed. Fate did not answer, the wind beginning to whip around the clearing. "Have you enjoyed spending the past thousand years grinding the two of us down into nothing but rage and indifference?"

"Little one," Fate said, though Her tone belied no kindness, "I do not expect a creature such as yourself to understand the grander workings, but you must have faith in the forces larger than you. This path is yours to walk. Any suffering is the result of your own failures."

"*Our* fucking failures?" Raegan yelled back, stepping toward the celestial being, the King forgotten behind her. "You are the architect. If we're failing, don't you think maybe it's because of you? Why don't you *do* something?"

At that, Fate's face darkened, silvered light shifting into the black of an eclipse. The feathers of Her wings shook and sharpened, downy white becoming jagged gray. "You've lived so long yet understand so little," Fate snarled, growing larger, the trees bending away from Her. "I am a function of the universe, essential to the fabric of the world. Imagine the enormous shock waves I would create if I were to interfere directly. No. Lower creatures such as yourself are the avatars by which I accomplish my great work."

To her surprise—and Fate's—Raegan threw her head back and laughed, the sound harsh and full of derision. "From the bottom of my heart, fuck you. I hate you."

It was true, and the realization of it almost broke Raegan. She had bent toward Fate all her life, begging for scraps, hoping to find that narrow Thread and walk upon it, a dutiful disciple. Something soured in her stomach, and standing here in the mist and the gloom, Raegan wondered if she had spent all these lives catering to the whims of a being that did not even have the decency to let her be unmade when the time came.

Fate said nothing, though She loomed over Raegan now, the smell of tarnished silver and sea winds thick on the breeze. Her pupils looked blown out, black seeping into Her colorless irises. The sight of it all should have stopped Raegan. But it did not.

"And what gave you the right to do what you've done to him?" Raegan demanded, gesturing back to the King, her voice loud and rough around the edges. "Look at *him*. He has kept to the path all these years, forced to watch his people fade if he does not play your game. Is that all you have to offer your chosen ones? An endless exhaustion we carry around our necks like a millstone? If that's the case, have the decency to end it. At least in death we will not have to feel your filthy fingers on our Threads."

Raegan's throat felt ragged, like she had swallowed broken glass, as she stared up into the face of Fate, the being's features as wide as the moon. Something caught the dim starlight, and she realized it was Her teeth—too many to count, gleaming like mother-of-pearl daggers.

"The Nameless One I cannot replace," Fate said, the force of Her voice shattering the air, the earth quaking beneath Raegan's feet, the trees cowering in the distance. "But you, child? I could devour you whole and put another where you stand. You are far from special, hardly even Fate-touched. You were simply convenient and so eager, so very *desperate*, to serve me."

The being reached for Raegan with spidery hands wrapped in miles and miles of Threads, woven through Her crooked fingers like a web. That made Raegan the fly, it seemed, and she was tired of being the fly— her legs crumpled up and her wings crushed, all for the sake of fitting neatly into someone else's mouth. Raegan summoned every ounce of her bottomless rage. Then she threw her head back and screamed.

Fate could choke on her this time.

Chapter Fifty-One

Everything happened at once.

Fate, Her Thread-bound hands at Raegan's neck. Water pulling in from the sky and the ground and the trees, forming a wave that looked more like a wall. The King at Raegan's side, his shadows interlacing with the streams of water. A voice, screaming—her voice, she realized, bloodcurdling and vast, the sound of something that has died a hundred times and can no longer summon fear for the inevitable.

And then nearly everything was gone, drained out of her like an emptied tidal pool, and Raegan thought that perhaps Fate had devoured her whole, unspun her Threads and put her back in the dark.

But she would not be so damp, Raegan thought, if that were true, and she did not think her throat would hurt in the void or that she would hear the beating of great snowy wings upon the air. Her vision returned in broken pieces: an empty clearing, a pool of thrashing water, a single white feather spiraling in the air.

Raegan stumbled back from the edge of the pool, the treads of her boots dragging in the wet sand. Her entire body tingled and buzzed, as if newly-discovered nerve endings were firing for the first time. Unsteady, she risked another step in retreat, only for her knees to buckle. But her back hit hard, solid warmth, and then arms closed around her.

"What have you done?" a voice demanded in her ear, thick and intense with barely contained anger. The warmth at her back disappeared as Raegan's world spun. She found herself face-to-face with a different eldritch terror: the exiled High King of the Unseelie Fey. His eyes were near-black in the gloom, face mere inches from hers. Rage sharpened his expression, the planes of his features gone feral and hungry.

The King pinned her against the cold steel of the car, his powerful hands gripping her by the shoulders. Raegan strained against his hold, her breathing ragged. But he did not relent. Instead, the King dug long, elegant fingers deeper into her skin. Her head swam. She should be terrified. But Raegan's heart skittered like a wild thing in her chest for an entirely different reason. Good sense always seemed to abandon her when it came to him.

"I did what I should've done a thousand fucking years ago," she responded, tilting her head back to meet his gaze. "Fuck her. Fuck destiny. Fuck all of it, Oberon. I'm so *angry*."

The King studied her with the ferocity of a predator searching for the tenderest morsel of flesh. She flinched when he moved suddenly— his hands left her shoulders, diving into her hair instead, the heat of his palms searing against her face. Raegan's breath caught, long-unmet hunger burning low in her belly even as part of her wondered if he planned to just snap her neck and be done with it all.

"With no training and your Seal still intact, you managed to reach past your Protectorate magic and use your true power to turn back a primordial being," the King said, his voice hoarse and uneven, his usual composure forsaken. His eyes were wild, broad chest rising with sharp, quick breaths. "You leave me no choice. You never do."

And then, against all reason, the King bent low and kissed her beneath the rain-shook sky. He met her mouth like a creature half-starved, his intensity pulling a soft gasp from Raegan. She returned the King's kiss without hesitation, reaching for him with the same hunger. But the King caught her wrist the moment she raised her arm, pinning it above her head, coaxing a moan from deep within her. Undeterred, she curled a few fingers into his waistband and yanked him closer with all her might. The ancient creature of shadow obliged, crushing his hips against hers before snatching her free hand in his and pinning that, too, against the cool metal of the car, their fingers intertwined.

His mouth trailed to her throat. Thick, heavy desire drummed loud between Raegan's legs, and she arched into him, desperate for more. The King released her hands, his own sliding to the slopes of her hips. His teeth grazed the sensitive skin of her neck, and she said his name in a low, breathy tone she hardly recognized as her own.

"I have spent so long trying to live without you," Oberon panted against her throat, the curve of her waist caught between his palms. "No more."

Before she could say anything, his mouth was on hers again, the intense heat of his kiss pulling all the breath from Raegan's body. His hands slipped beneath her shirt, fingertips brushing her bare skin. Goosebumps careened across her flesh. Of course a quest always sang to her so sweetly—she had spent a millennium traversing the alabaster valleys and sinewy mountains of this otherworldly being. Distantly, Raegan wondered what exaltation or purpose she might find in Baba Yaga's realm, or beyond, that could be greater than this dark, propulsive, eternal thing between her and the faerie king.

At that moment, he broke the kiss, his breathing ragged and unsteady. But the King did not move away from her; instead, he cradled her jaw in his lithe hands. When his eyes met hers, there was a storm there, as sharp-toothed as lightning.

"I am yours," the King murmured, each syllable dripping with gravity and something not unlike devotion, "and I will happily burn in the fires of your rage. You need only command me."

Raegan held his gaze for a long moment, the rest of the world forgotten. And then, finding no words to suffice, she grabbed the front of his jacket in her fists and dragged his mouth back to hers.

Some time later, the King spoke, his lips moving softly against her skin. "She will return. We have only delayed our punishment. We must go."

"Yeah," Raegan agreed, straightening, still a bit breathless. "Are you going to be alright? When the Protectorate comes, I mean?"

Something dangerous slipped across the King's features. He disentangled himself from her and began to walk toward the mouth of the woods, his footsteps hardly making a sound despite his size. Without a word, Raegan followed him, anxiety piercing her lungs.

"You may have noticed," he began, looking sideways at her, "that I have not needed to hold physical proximity in order to conceal our movements."

"Oh," she said. Because, with all the other shit that had been going on, no, she truly hadn't noticed. She was losing her touch.

The King paused for a moment at the place where the clearing turned into forest, placing one hand against the trunk of a large pine tree. Raegan heard a low hum that echoed out like a ripple, deeper and deeper into the woods beyond.

"I am, like all of my kind, limited by the lack of magic in this half of the world," he continued, beginning to navigate between the towering pines, following some direction or sense that she did not have. "But more than anything, I am limited by my commitments. At all times, I have held my people's protective wards. A great burden and a great honor."

Raegan kept pace with his longer strides, the forest closing in around them. The thick canopy above created a murky gloom that she imagined remained even on the brightest of days. Beneath her feet, the ground was spongy and blanketed with pine needles.

"But now," the King said, his voice huskier, as if the surroundings brought the wild out in him, "I am unburdened."

A delicate, delicious chill crept up Raegan's neck. In the perpetual dim of this barren forest, she was watching the Unseelie King unfold. It felt like witnessing a holy rite, or perhaps undertaking one. The darkness clung heavily to him, glorious and horrific, trees bowing as he walked by, raindrops not daring to land upon his shoulders. Maybe even Mother Nature herself preferred not to offend this particular faerie regent.

Raegan was not sure how long she followed the Unseelie King into the dark of the wood. She worried that she might be willing to follow him anywhere, his ferocity sweet as blackberry wine upon her tongue. Gone was the being who favored three-piece suits in fine wools and held his court within shadowed libraries smelling of citrus and vanilla dust. Instead, before Raegan was something positively feral, moving through the forest as though he were part of it—a predator finally released back into the wild.

Somewhere in the distance, a twig snapped. Raegan froze, her pulse thudding thickly in her veins.

The King slowed, pivoting in the direction of the sound, dark eyes roving. "Our quarry has joined us," he told her, voice drenched in blood-lust and years of unspent rage, "and Baba Yaga's door is nearby. She does not obscure the way."

Another muffled sound—a scuffle of a boot through the thicket of pine needles—drew the King's attention. He turned toward it hungrily. Raegan would have almost pitied the Protectorate had they not taken everything from her. She prayed his violence might alleviate her grief.

The King moved forward again, his pace faster now, long legs devouring the ground. Raegan realized he was leading the Protectorate deeper and deeper into the forest, making them think they were tracking a wounded animal—when in reality, they were walking right into the jaws of a beast. After a few more steps, he turned toward her, catching her gently by the arm. Raegan looked up at him, awaiting instructions. But for a moment he only studied her, almost as if he could not quite believe she was flesh and blood before him.

"Baba Yaga's door is ahead," the King told her, shaking off whatever had come over him. "The twisted black pine. You will know when you see it. Knock thrice and then enter. She is, in all likelihood, expecting you."

"Aren't we going together?" Raegan asked, pushing down the panic that arose at the idea of navigating Baba Yaga's realm alone.

"I will be right behind you," the King replied.

The great, impossible thing before her brought his forehead to hers, one hand sliding around her waist. She lived a thousand lives in that moment—nothing but the muted rainfall echoing around them. Then he pulled away, taking a few steps back from her. Shadows swept in from all directions, gathering at his feet like a pack of wolves.

"Go," the King said, solemn.

She nodded, her breath shaky. She swallowed hard and told herself not to say anything at all, unable to trust her tongue. With one last look at him, Raegan turned on her heel and made her way deeper into the forest. It did not take long to spot the twisted black pine: taller than the other trees, twice as thick, bent double with what could be rage or grief or hunger. Its trunk looped in a thick serpentine shape, branches reaching down instead of up. She stepped toward it, reverent.

And then that terrible sound of Protectorate magic shattered the air, a teeth-rattling wrongness. Despite herself, Raegan turned. Through the narrow hall of pines, she could see the King and at least twenty—if not more—soot-suited humans crawling out of the surrounding forest. She couldn't help it. She *had* to wait a few moments and make sure he would truly be alright.

One hand curled with knuckles already resting upon the tree's trunk, she bit down on her lower lip and waited. Blood bloomed on her tongue. The King held his ground as she'd thought he might, allowing the Protectorate to get so close that her heart lurched.

One of the Protectorate—a man at the front, built like a mountain—said something. The King threw his head back and laughed, the sound of it twisted and terrible. She realized the Protectorate man was the same one that had grabbed her by the viaduct. Something that Raegan didn't think was hers rose its head inside her sternum, hungry and eager. Time moved at half-pace. Her world condensed to the King in the distance and all the Protectorate—too many, surrounding him like flies.

And then: a crack, a split, and the sodden, pine-needle-strewn earth at the King's feet opened wide as a wound. Exposed roots roiled and rioted, reaching out like tentacles with their newfound freedom. The roots wrapped themselves around those frail human bodies, pulling a sizable amount of the Protectorate's force toward a gaping maw in the earth. They fought, Raegan could see—some throwing magic at the roots, others drawing more conventional weapons—but in the end it was all futile. With shouts and screams and a few pitiful, begging cries, they disappeared beneath the ground, the dark, shifting soil closing over their heads. The roots reached back out again, writhing with hunger.

"I do not wish to kill your people," the King said, and when he did, all the roots stopped their slithering, holding still as if they had never been anything so horrific in the first place.

The Protectorate, too, held still. Even from her position by the twisted pine, Raegan could see the suits exchanging looks, faces pinched, fear clouding their expressions. They had never before seen the King unburdened, and now only a taste had left them willing to listen to the words of a faerie lord.

One of the Protectorate stepped forward, hands moving into what looked like an appeasing gesture. Their air-shattering magic stopped. Raegan held her breath.

"But I have done many things I did not wish to," the King said, and then the ground opened wider, the trees grew hungrier, and there was nothing in the air but the rending of flesh and cloth.

Chapter Fifty-Two

Little could have prepared Raegan for witnessing the full capacity of the Unseelie King. Violence came as easily to him as breathing. Roots snatched at ankles, slithering across damp soil with startling speed. When a smaller pine failed to snag the leg of one Protectorate, it simply bowed its head and impaled the man with its trunk.

She told herself to leave. She told herself to crush the triumphant bloodlust and throbbing arousal that bloomed within her as she watched the King tear the Protectorate operatives limb from limb. She gritted her teeth, running her gaze through the forest, trying to determine how many more from the Protectorate remained. Her fear for the King's well-being had diminished, trepidation of traversing Baba Yaga's realm alone rising to the forefront.

Perhaps if she held on for just a few more moments, she would not have to face whatever waited there by herself. The twisted black pine was so clearly a delineating marker. It was a place where anything left of who she had thought she was would fall away, and she'd be forced to see if her new skin could fit over her skeleton. So Raegan waited.

Until a flash of pinstripe caught her eye. With horror, she found at least five Protectorate flanking her about a hundred feet off into the woods. She had hesitated, too fragile to enter Baba Yaga's realm alone, and now she had endangered both herself *and* the King. Reflex made her reach for the knife in her pocket. Old memories sparked, and she tried to dig for whatever she had summoned earlier against Fate, but nothing answered her call.

Heart pounding, a thousand ice-cold needles of dread pricking her skin, she shrank a step back against the twisted pine. Dread and indecision coiled in her stomach. She did not want to leave the King behind. But she was going to get herself killed if she stayed. Raegan told herself to stop being a coward and do the only thing she could. She knocked thrice on the twisted black pine, held utterly still for a moment, and then threw herself into the open space made by its contorted trunk. For a long, terrible moment, she only saw damp, pine-needle-strewn soil rushing at her, and all felt lost.

But then something stretched or snapped, and Raegan felt a harsh tug on her limbs. She slammed her eyes shut against the pain, and the world went black.

❧

When she opened her eyes, the light was different: brighter, warmer. The tugging sensation had retreated, replaced by a sharp, sudden pain in her ribs. She coughed, raising her head to find the source of the discomfort.

As her eyes focused, Raegan saw a pair of worn leather boots and what she thought was the hem of a skirt the color of old blood. Bones were sewn into it. Then the pain again, sharper this time. She tried to climb to her feet but only managed to weakly roll over. The movement sloshed the bile in her stomach, and she vomited onto the ground, pine needles clinging painfully to her hands. When her sickness faded to a few dry heaves, she rocked onto her heels and wiped her mouth with the back of her hand.

"Why do you all always get sick?" someone asked. Their voice was heavily accented. Something Slavic, Raegan thought, but older and darker, thick as molasses. "Impressive, though. Fastest I've seen a mortal overcome realm illness. Though I suppose you're not *all* mortal, now, are you?"

Slowly pulling herself to her feet, Raegan turned to find the source of the voice: a ferocious-looking woman, her features gnarled and wrinkled, her nose beaked, the eyes black and sharp, bright as glass beads. Her sparse gray hair was in an intricate knot at the top of her head. A ragged black blouse was tucked into the bone-hemmed skirt beneath a wide leather belt. In her hands, the woman held a thick walking stick as gnarled as she was, which Raegan suspected had been the source of the stabbing pain in her ribs.

The woman was large, belly hanging over her belt and skin melting off her chin. Raegan found herself jealous of how this woman, if that's what she was, took up space. Jealous of the way she could enchant an entire realm into existence but did not bother or desire to turn herself into something slim and shiny.

Supporting herself with one hand on a nearby tree trunk, Raegan stood and made eye contact with the taller woman. "You're Baba Yaga, aren't you?" She supposed there was not really any point in asking. The being before her radiated power and smelled of acrid smoked bone, dried mugwort, and open flame.

"You know," the old witch said, her brow creasing in a way that almost read as concern, "I thought you'd come much sooner."

"Sooner?" Raegan echoed, her mouth dry. Something slinking and old—something that did not feel as though it properly belonged to her—appeared in the back of her mind, only to retreat into shadow before she could get a good hold on it. "Oh," she said. "Yeah. I was supposed to do that, wasn't I?"

Baba Yaga fixed her with a disappointed gaze that Raegan shrank under, just a little. Then the witch turned away, looking over her shoulder. "Come on," she said. "It's this way."

Wordlessly, Raegan followed the woman down a thin, packed dirt path that she hadn't noticed before. It snaked through the forest, vanishing almost entirely behind its own bends before reappearing again. The forest that surrounded the path was not the Jersey Pine Barrens. The trees towered much higher, many of their trunks too large for Raegan to wrap her arms around. Swamps ringed in thick, dark vegetation lingered to the right of the path, their waters black and murky. Heavy mist clung to the horizon. It felt primeval in the truest sense, untouched by perhaps anyone but Baba Yaga.

The air carried the scent of a distant bonfire, but beneath the smoke, the forest smelled richly of conifers, damp leaves, green ferns, and fungi. Raegan could've spent all day on this winding trail, marveling at the strange mushrooms and enormous oaks and knife-sharp swamp grasses. But instead, she kept her eyes on the back of the ancient witch leading the way. She marched, one foot in front of the other, until she lost track of how long she'd been walking the well-trodden dirt path.

Up head, something large materialized from the mist. She barely managed to hold back a gasp—it was Baba Yaga's hut. The structure was *exactly* like the illustrations Raegan had seen a million times—a simple, four-walled hut with a pitched roof perched on top of chicken legs. The legs were enormous, looking more like dinosaur claws than anything to do with a mundane farm animal.

A laugh bubbled out from the back of her throat, something between disbelief and triumph. Baba Yaga glanced at Raegan with a sharp eye but ultimately ignored her as they continued walking. The forest began to clear in a gradual, natural way, the larger trees tapering off into slender birches and then downy beds of ferns. The hut crouched in the center of the clearing, surrounded by a fence made of bone. At the top of each post, just as Raegan had imagined, sat a skull. She wondered if lights would flicker within the hollow bones once the man in the black clothing on the black horse rode past. Folklore settled onto her shoulders, heavy and imperfect and lovely.

"You are very late," Baba Yaga said, cutting Raegan's moment of awe short as she halted beside one of the hut's scaled legs. "Which complicates everything."

Raegan's gaze slid to the gray-haired witch, who'd crossed her arms over her patched black blouse, leaning onto the walking stick she had jammed into Raegan's ribs. "I know," Raegan murmured, things stirring in her belly, memories rising up unbidden. "I've tried before, you know. More than once."

Baba Yaga offered up only a scoffing noise, looking down her nose at Raegan. "So I heard," the witch replied. "I stay out of most things these days. I'm tired."

Raegan opened her mouth to say she was tired, too, but something sharp and gleaming in Baba Yaga's black eyes warned her away from making such a statement. So she closed her mouth and nodded, trying to look understanding.

Baba Yaga's mouth twisted, not unkindly, and she turned away from Raegan. Then the witch slammed the bottom of her walking stick into the soil three times. A moment later, the hut's legs folded, lowering the structure to the ground. Without looking back at Raegan, Baba Yaga ascended the rickety wooden steps to the door.

Raegan wavered, not daring to glance at the dark and wild wood behind her, but also understanding the implications of passing over a witch's threshold. There was only one reason to follow Baba Yaga through the burgundy-stained door, and that was to be unmade.

"Well," the witch called, looking at Raegan over her shoulder. "Are you coming or not?"

Raegan glanced up, setting her mouth into a firm line. For a moment, the world hung still. Then she nodded at Baba Yaga and followed the witch up the stairs, over the threshold, and into the darkness that hung from the eaves of the hut.

The inside was much larger than the outside. A fire roared in the massive stone-hewn hearth. A long table ran down the space to Raegan's right, a few mismatched chairs tucked beneath it. The air was thick with burnt herbs and strange rituals.

"Sit," Baba Yaga commanded, pointing one finger, curved with age, at the table.

Raegan, vaguely unsure if anything was even real anymore, slunk across the hut toward the table. The wide-plank floor creaked beneath her feet. She chose a chair with a wedge-shaped seat, three legs, and arms that were carved to look like two twin axes. The back of the chair rose up in a half-oval, decorated with ornate engravings. Raegan sank her body into it, realizing all at once how much her feet and knees hurt.

She turned and found Baba Yaga at the hearth, pulling a kettle away from the open fire. The witch placed an iron trivet on the table and set the kettle atop it before walking past Raegan into an open kitchen area. Mismatched shelves were affixed to the wall, and a narrow wooden counter held ceramic bowls and a large assortment of knives. She watched Baba Yaga retrieve two chipped teacups and saucers from a shelf.

Then the witch returned to the table, pouring dark, rich tea from the kettle. She slid one cup toward Raegan. She wrapped her hands around the mug, grateful for the comfort. The brew smelled of winter bonfires and crackling, smoky warmth, mellowed by a smooth, full-bodied richness.

"Remind me," Raegan began, her voice hoarse, "if it's alright. How did we meet?"

Baba Yaga came to a halt, the chair she had been sliding out for herself grating on the hardwood floor. Her black, stony eyes met Raegan's gaze. "Do you not remember?" the witch asked. Suspicion crept into her tone.

Raegan tilted her head, prodding at that dark softness inside her. Something surfaced. "It's hazy," she said, speaking slowly. "You were looking for a way out of something. An agreement? An arrangement? Not one you had made—one you had been bartered into."

Raegan had little idea if she were simply pulling from folklore or her actual memory, but for a split second, she saw Baba Yaga: a young woman striding up the path to a fence line, cloaked in a velvet cape marred with mud, her blonde hair in an intricate braid.

The witch said nothing for a long moment, sinking into the chair and stirring her tea. Raegan's heart began to pound at the thought of what something like Baba Yaga might do if she did not believe her.

But then the witch spoke. "It was a marriage," Baba Yaga said dryly. "*You* were the old Witch in the Wood then. I was a princess—hard to believe now—and I did not want the union. I had no use for a husband. You taught me the other ways, out there on your island I'd traveled so far to find, years ago. I did not marry, and I've never done another thing I did not wish since that day. I owed you a great debt."

Raegan noted the past tense, staring into her teacup for a moment before looking back across the table at Baba Yaga. "I imagine I already called that debt in with the Seal's placement," she said, running the tip of her tongue over her dry, chapped lips.

Baba Yaga's expression became grim, gaze drifting toward the window across from the table. "They hunted me, you know," the witch said, her tone far away. "The Round Table or the Protectorate or whatever they're called now. They've always hunted you through all your lives, and when they discovered your connection to the Białowieża Forest, they found me, too."

Guilt slipped pale, cold fingers between Raegan's ribs. It seemed that everyone foolish enough to entangle their lives with one of hers was never better off for it. "I'm sorry," Raegan said, but she was apologizing for someone she had once been, and that was a difficult thing to do, so her words came out hollow.

Baba Yaga shrugged, taking a long slurp of her tea. "A debt was owed," the witch said, her eyes meeting Raegan's again, "and I paid it. Now we are even, and I have lived long enough to discover my actions also concealed a budding Prophecy. Yes, girl, do not look at me like that. I heard it when the half-Oracle read it. Witches hear everything. And *real* magic—not this halfway, barely-there lie—is worth any risk. I remember this world before the Gates were closed all the way. It shimmered back then. Now it just fades away, farther and farther into the gray. You're supposed to fix it."

Raegan held the witch's gaze, her mouth going dry as her heart thudded, the sensation of her pulse thick in her throat. "So I'm told," she settled on saying, trying for a rueful smile.

But Baba Yaga only stared back, stone-faced, her small eyes like two pits.

Raegan sat up straight, sobering. "I only hope," she said, her voice hoarse now, "that I'm worth it."

"Hmmph," was all Baba Yaga said in reply, reaching for her teacup. She shifted her weight in the large chair she occupied, gaze returning to the window.

Raegan found herself looking, too, suddenly worried a threat may have appeared, but all she saw was the sprawling primeval forest. A hawk swooped by the window, a mouse writhing in its claws.

"You have returned to the King, yes?" Baba Yaga asked. "I cannot imagine another reason he would be so close to my door."

Despite herself, Raegan's heart leapt in her throat, her fingers curling tighter around the chipped ceramic mug. "He's here?" she asked, the words coming out in a terse whisper.

The witch stared at her with those coal-black eyes, something not unlike disgust moving across her harsh features. "I have loved many strange and terrible things in my time," Baba Yaga said slowly, sounding out each word as though it were poison. "And even I have never understood how you managed to love him."

CHAPTER FIFTY-THREE

The words hung in the air, heavy as overripe fruit and rotting with accusation. Baba Yaga examined Raegan as she spoke. Maybe the witch expected her to look stung or even lash out in anger. But Raegan only sighed, pressing one hand to her forehead. Her skin felt clammy.

"Love is a bit strong," she replied, weary. "Only met him—or re-met, I guess—a few days ago, though it feels more like a year. Do you know if he's through your door yet, or just near it? The Protectorate came after us, of course, but . . . Fate also showed up."

At that, Baba Yaga reeled, her hands flying away from her mug, moving as if she might stand up and storm to the door. But then the witch appeared to collect herself, though her pockmarked hands curled into fists. "Aranrhod?" Baba Yaga demanded, keeping her voice low as if the downy-winged being could hear. "In the Pine Barrens? Near *my* door?"

Raegan nodded. The witch leaned back, tipping her head to look at the ceiling like it might hold some answers.

"How is She even here?" Raegan asked, watching Baba Yaga. "Aren't all the gods on the other side of the Gates?"

"That beast," Baba Yaga said eventually, her fingertips drumming on the table, "is one of the First. Not a goddess—much, much more.

Nothing could contain Her, and I doubt even the Timekeeper would try. There are certain forces that keep this planet spinning on its axis, and Fate is one of them. She will slow the King down. I don't want to remove your Seal without him here, though it pains me to invite such an unnatural thing onto my lands."

Raegan added those bits of knowledge to her puzzle and took a sip of her tea. It was hot and bitter and exactly what she needed. Then she waited for Baba Yaga to speak. Her exhaustion sent her to the instincts built up over her years in journalism, and perhaps that wasn't a bad thing, even here, in the house of a famed and ancient witch.

"He is your tether," Baba Yaga said, her mouth forming around the words as if she'd eaten something vile. "The only similarity across all your lives. Already risky business removing a Seal that old. I'm not about to do it without a tether."

Raegan took another sip of her tea, setting the cup down on its saucer when Baba Yaga's eyes returned to examine her. "Then I suppose we wait," she said with a shrug. "What do you mean about him being unnatural?"

Baba Yaga's mouth turned downwards, sour. She sucked her teeth before replying. "He was made, not born," the witch answered, scrutinizing Raegan. "Two goddesses, an ancient Fey sword, the blood of the Unseelie Court's best warriors. That's why he has no true name."

Raegan desperately tried to file away these precious bits of information. She ached for her notepad and a pen, not trusting her exhausted mind.

"How did you find him, anyway?" Baba Yaga asked, as if her curiosity had gotten the better of her. "I heard he was doing his best to stay away from you."

Raegan met the witch's eyes and smirked, leaning back in her chair for a luxurious stretch. "I'm relentless," she replied, crossing her arms.

At that Baba Yaga shifted again, almost like she saw something she recognized. Raegan took that as a sign to keep going. "It's a long story," she continued, stifling a yawn. "But I cornered him into a deal. And then we found out about the Prophecy, and I renegotiated. In my favor, of course."

Baba Yaga's eyes were appraising now instead of coldly examining, the set of her mouth not so hard. The witch's tongue darted out to moisten her lips. "I hope you hold the plait," she grumbled.

Raegan had no idea what she was talking about. Normally, that was something she'd withhold from showing on her face, but she'd been awake for too long with too little caffeine, and her poker face was not exactly at its best.

Baba Yaga, of course, pounced. "You do not hold it?" the witch wanted to know, leaning across the table toward her, the eyes dark and glimmering again. "*Never* let the faerie hold the bargain plait."

Raegan, beginning to see that something was very wrong here, brought her teacup to her mouth. She hoped the few seconds it took to have another sip would buy her some time. But it was hard to think clearly with the actual, real-life Baba Yaga staring her down from across the table. And Raegan very much wanted to know the information she was clearly missing. So she set her teacup back down and sighed.

"If you would be so kind," Raegan said, rubbing her temples, "what is a bargain plait? It seems I have fucked something up quite tremendously."

In response, Baba Yaga threw her head back and laughed—the sound like crows taking flight, old trees creaking in the wind, the first roar of a fresh bonfire. Any other time, Raegan's temper would have surely flared. But her exhaustion overpowered nearly everything, except for the gnawing worry she felt for the King.

"You fool," Baba Yaga said, wiping a tear from her eye as if Raegan's idiocy was the funniest thing she'd heard of in ages. "You have made no binding deal at all. Any bargain made with a faerie should end in a lock of their hair and a lock of yours being braided together. Otherwise, a bargain has no power. Faeries often try to maintain control over the bargain plait so they can destroy it, for the deal only holds as long as the plait does. But you did not even plait your hair together in the first place?"

Raegan considered this information, tracing the lip of her saucer with one finger. "They've done a really great job of keeping that bit out of human folklore accounts," she said eventually, eyes sliding to Baba Yaga.

The witch grinned at that, showing off blackened teeth. "Of course they have," Baba Yaga snorted. "Human folklore also says faeries can't lie. What a load of horseshit. Faeries lie as often as they damn well breathe. But now nearly everybody who even bothers to know a fuckin' thing about faeries believes it. Madness."

Raegan drained her tea, looking at the constellation of tiny tea leaf fragments scattered along the bottom of her cup. If Baba Yaga were telling the truth—and the witch did not strike Raegan as someone who needed to lie to trick or outsmart someone—that meant she'd never had a deal with the King at all. Not once was he sworn by any bargain to not harm her or act in her best interests.

And yet . . .

She chewed on the inside of her lip. She needed to sleep. She had no idea why the King would do such a thing. She had no idea how it was only twilight here in Baba Yaga's realm but had been well past midnight in New Jersey. She had no idea whether she was strong enough to withstand the removal of her Seal. She had no idea if her father awaited her at the end of this.

"Yeah," Raegan said eventually, dragging a hand through her curls. "I'm kind of surprised he didn't just kill me. I mean, before we found out about the Prophecy, of course. Then, obviously, I became very useful to him."

Propping her chin on her hand, Raegan looked over at Baba Yaga, wondering what new level of scorn she'd receive from the witch based on that tidbit of information. But Baba Yaga hardly reacted, though one of her thin, nearly translucent eyebrows arched.

"You are the only living creature I could ever say this to with any degree of certainty," Baba Yaga said, leveling her gaze at Raegan, "but the Unseelie King would never harm you."

The words hit Raegan hard, an arrow to the weak spot in her armor. She had already known this to be true. She realized that maybe she had known it from the first time she'd met the King in this life. But hearing it said so matter-of-factly by a being who did not shy away from putting people's skulls on pikes was another thing entirely.

Raegan said nothing, holding Baba Yaga's black eyes, her breathing shallow.

"What an odd thing it must be," the witch continued, "to have something like him belong to you."

At that, Raegan bit down on her tongue so hard her eyes watered.

She had no idea what game Baba Yaga was playing—if the witch was even playing a game at all—so she pushed her teacup to the side and folded her hands on the table. "I hardly think," she said slowly, "that either of us belongs to the other."

"No," Baba Yaga said, setting her mug down on its saucer with a clatter, a storm blowing over her face. "That is not what I said. In your marrow, before all the rest, you are like me. You are a witch. And we are the darkest parts of the forest and the woodsmoke on the wind when October comes roaring in. We belong to no one. We don't even belong to ourselves, not all of the time, and certainly not the way everyone thinks we do. We belong to the older curves, the deeper shadows, the quiet things that no man dares to know. But the King?"

The old witch cast her eyes to the window beside the door, her silhouette carved out by the hearth's light. "The King belongs to you. It is a strange thing, indeed."

Raegan, quite unsure of what else to do, looked out the window with the witch. She sat there in silence, only the sound of Baba Yaga's breathing and the fire crackling across the room filling the space. Sleep pulled at her with heavy hands and her eyelids drooped. Raegan was so tired that when she saw a black-cloaked rider on a black horse ride across the clearing below Baba Yaga's hut, she did not know whether it was real or not. At least, not until the witch spoke.

"Night has come," Baba Yaga said, getting to her feet, "and your King is not yet here. Let me show you to the bathhouse. You can sleep there. You stink too much of human cities for me to tolerate sharing my home with you for another second."

Raegan used all her effort to pull herself out of the chair, not even offended by Baba Yaga's comment. She wasn't sure how she was going to sleep in a bathroom, but frankly she would've accepted any place where she could lie down. A bathtub softened with some of the sweaters she'd packed would do.

Pulling herself to her feet, Raegan stood and followed the witch to the door. Upon reaching it, vertigo hit Raegan hard. She hadn't noticed, nor felt, the legs supporting the house stand up straight. The view out the window while sitting suddenly made sense, but her brain scrambled to process it all. When Baba Yaga plucked her walking stick from beside the door and tapped the hardwood floor three times, sending the massive legs back down to the ground, Raegan thought for a moment she might puke right on Baba Yaga's shoes.

She did not. The night outside was mercifully cool and fresh, the moon high above the trees, stars and galaxies twinkling. In any other place and any other time, Raegan might have lingered outside to enjoy a perfect autumnal evening. But her heart was too sick with worry and her head heavy and tired, so she trudged behind Baba Yaga down the hut's stairs and across the clearing.

Woodsmoke curled in the air—but not *his* woodsmoke—as Raegan walked. She took in the low, eerie light glimmering inside the skulls mounted on the fence—another thing she would have liked to stop and examine. But the darkness was thick and swift, and even Raegan was not sure she had the heart to navigate this place alone in the night.

Baba Yaga led her across the clearing and through a small grove of trees. At the end of the leafy hallway stood what looked to be a log cabin. Not exactly, Raegan could see in the dim light—or at least not what she'd usually call a log cabin in America. The roof rose in a sharp, pointed peak, much like Baba Yaga's hut, and the logs had been stripped of their bark and brined in age and fire soot. A chimney rose from one side, and a small door with an iron latch stood at the entrance.

"Here," Baba Yaga said, yanking the door open. "I'll send over supper. Don't expect anything fancy."

Raegan hadn't been expecting to be fed at all, and her stomach rumbled in pleasure. She peered into the bathhouse, not crossing the threshold. All she could see of the interior was firelight glinting off tile and age-worn logs. "Thank you," she said, turning to face the taller woman.

"I'll send the King when he arrives," Baba Yaga said, her tone appearing to curdle at the mere idea of having to speak with him. "And then we can go about removing your Seal. I said it's dangerous, and I meant it. You should know what you're risking: yourself. Madness is not only possible but likely. I can remove it, but I do not know who will wake up inside your body when I'm done."

The night stretched between them, a hundred emotions crawling up Raegan's throat. Her eyes blurred, and her stomach burned. She swallowed hard, looking up at the witch. "Baba," she whispered in the same way one might say "grandmother" or "please" or perhaps both.

Nothing in Baba Yaga's face changed, her shoulders still unrelenting, but she reached out and pressed Raegan's hands between her calloused palms. Emotion filled her dark, shining gaze. The witch's grip was tight—too tight—and Raegan was forced to wonder if this ancient, folkloric thing was afraid, too.

"Something feels different this time," Baba Yaga said eventually, sounding younger than what seemed possible. "So maybe it will be alright. Maybe."

Her hands squeezed Raegan's in a tight, warm embrace, and then she released the shorter woman from her grasp. Without another word, Baba Yaga turned on her heel and strode back through the grove of trees into the darkness that waited beyond. Raegan let out a long, shuddering breath, looking in through the open door of the bathhouse. There was no other option, she supposed.

Raegan entered carefully, waiting for her eyes to adjust to the dim light. The King's enchantment on her vision seemed to have worn off. Once inside, she raised her eyebrows in surprise. It seemed a great diminishment to call this space something as simple as the bathhouse. A long corridor ran parallel with the front of the building, white tile floors gleaming. Large bundles of dried plants hung at even intervals along the wall. Raegan took a deep breath. Something sharp, woodsy, and camphor-like met her nose—eucalyptus, she thought. She stepped through the hallway, pulling off her muddy boots and tucking them under a wooden bench built into the wall.

The main room offered a large stone fireplace that was already crackling with a beautiful flame—warm, bright, impossibly cozy. Two wooden lounge chairs were placed in front of the fire, each draped in blankets and furs. Candles lined the fireplace mantle. On the far end of the space was a pile of furs not dissimilar to the one in Baba Yaga's hut. The furs rested on a raised wooden platform, and Raegan imagined how quickly she could fall into slumber in a place like this, despite everything.

She moved to stand alongside the wall across from the fireplace and pulled her luggage tag from her pocket, placing it on another built-in wooden bench beside a stack of fluffy towels. While she waited for whatever magic was wound up in the object to release, she wandered toward the fireplace, noticing a large, open archway to its left. She stepped through, thinking she'd find a more traditional bathroom waiting for her.

Instead, an expansive room with gleaming tiles the color of smoke stretched out before her. The walls were crafted from the same stacked logs as the rest of the structure. Steam drifted lazily from the shimmering surface of a huge bath cut into the ground—accessed by a set of ornate, brightly colored tile stairs—ringed with lit pillar candles. Decorative tapestries hung from the walls, featuring scenes Raegan half-remembered from Slavic mythology and folklore. Plants exploded from every corner, turning what might have been a sterile, spa-like environment into something absolutely extraordinary. The room was somehow half-greenhouse, half-bathhouse, smelling of rich eucalyptus with glimmering water and mist-covered leaves. Raegan fell in love immediately.

She returned to the main room to find her suitcase on the bench and rifled through it to produce toiletries and some sleepwear. Then she stripped off her damp clothing, not having the energy to do more than leave it in a pile in front of the bench, grabbed a towel, and headed for the bath. She stepped in slowly, unsure of the temperature, but the water that met her skin was blissfully silky and perfectly hot. With a long sigh, Raegan walked down the remaining stairs and submerged herself up to her neck.

Finding a tiled bench built into the wall, she settled onto it, resting the back of her head against the lip of the bath. With only the sound of the fire crackling in the other room and the gentle ripple of the water, some of the more immediate stress seemed to slip away from her body. For now, she was at least physically safe.

A few minutes of peace, then guilt. Here she was, seeing the other side of the curtain, soaking in a divine bath, while her mother and her co-workers were no doubt worrying about her. The King was on a battlefield. Baba Yaga had a trial ahead of her that Raegan had brought directly to her door. Maelona could already be dead as a result of her attempts to help. Andronica could be crushed beneath the weight of holding the wards, pulling Kamau down with her. Blodeuwedd might endure punishment for treason if the Seelie Court became aware of her movements.

A ragged sigh escaped Raegan's mouth, ending in something more like a wounded cry. She squeezed her eyes shut and then forced herself to focus on scrubbing the evening from her body. Everyone had made their choices. Worlds were not repaired without carnage and consequences. Hadn't Raegan given up plenty, too? When the King reached Baba Yaga's realm—Raegan would not allow herself to start that thought with an "if"—she might lose herself entirely. Having a nice bath before possibly going completely mad didn't seem too selfish or luxurious.

Raegan held on to this halfway place of water, the main room just barely visible through the steam. So much life exploded in the bathhouse—from the tiles in bright hues of red and blue and yellow to the climbing vines and dark, waxy leaves of the plants. It felt like a place away from everything else. A place that Prophecies and owl-winged weavers of Fate and power-drunk mortal men could not touch. In her heart, Raegan knew that no such place existed, but blind hope had gotten her this far, so she held onto the idea and let it plant seeds within her.

CHAPTER FIFTY-FOUR

Raegan stayed in the bath until sweat began to bead on her forehead and the back of her neck. The thought of the King appearing when her clothes were already shed, her collarbones anointed in bathwater and firelight, was intoxicating, and she flirted with overheating before admitting defeat and sloshing up the stairs.

She grabbed a fluffy towel and wrapped herself in it, though she hardly needed the warmth. As she reached down to dry off her legs before walking into the main room, Raegan heard movement at the front of the bathhouse. Thinking it might be the meal Baba Yaga had promised, she padded toward the archway that divided the two main rooms.

The moment she approached the threshold, Raegan watched the door all but rip open. She froze, clutching her towel closer, wishing she had her knife on her and wondering if she could reach it in time. For a long, harrowing moment, there was only darkness on the other side of the door, complete and absolute. Her heart thudded hard in her chest. Then, materializing out of the night as if he were made of the same substance, came the King.

He stepped into the bathhouse like he had scented his prey, eyes blackened with a feral gloom. Blood marred the left side of his jacket, and Raegan felt quite sure it was not his. Her breath caught in her throat. The King was horrifying and magnificent, not a stitch of humanity clinging to him.

His gaze roved to Raegan, and when he sighted her, he closed his eyes for a moment, inhaling like it was the first deep breath he'd taken in a long time. He stepped through the door, pulling it shut behind him. "I was not sure if you had made it through," the King said, his voice low and raw. Raegan watched his hand clench at his side. "Are you unharmed?"

"I'm fine," she said, blood drumming in her veins. "Didn't Baba Yaga tell you? I'm completely fine. It's you I've been worried about. Are you alright?"

The King took another step into the room and brought himself to a harsh halt, as if he were not fully in control of his body. Then he seemed to process her words and shook his head. "I did not speak with Baba Yaga."

Raegan's brows knit in confusion, and she tilted her head. "You didn't?" she inquired, wondering how he'd made it through the door without getting a solid stab in the ribs from Baba Yaga's stick.

"No," the King said, peeling off his jacket, which appeared to be damp with rain in addition to the blood. "I came straight to find you."

Raegan's breath hitched. She looked the King up and down, suddenly aware of what all his tightly coiled tension might've been about.

With a deep inhale, he came toward her, but only to hang his jacket by the roaring fire. Then he kneeled to unlace his boots, a muscle in his jaw leaping. "Did you learn anything when you spoke to Baba Yaga?" the King wanted to know, not looking at her. "You are, of course, not required to share it with me."

Raegan let out a long breath, leaning against the archway, trying not to think about the level of undress both of them were approaching. "She said the Seal wasn't meant to stay on this long," Raegan answered, watching his lithe movements, which made something as mundane as unlacing a shoe graceful. "So removing it is going to be dicey. But she'll do it. She wants to do it."

The King pulled off his boots and placed them by the fire before standing to look at her. His eyes were dark, bottomless pools in the dancing light of the hearth, his sharp features carved deeper by the shadows. Desire smoldered in Raegan's belly.

"What do *you* want?" he asked, gazing at her like nothing else existed in the world, sending her heart skittering faster.

Raegan should have wanted to demand answers about the false bargains he'd struck with her, or ask if Fate was coming for them, or do anything at all that was logical and smart and brave. All the things she'd thought she'd be if the world ever parted the veil for her. But she did not. She wanted the King to fuck her until the howling ache in her core finally subsided. And then, she wanted to tear apart every single person who had twisted magic and turned this once-beautiful world into a ruinous piece of cruel rock floating in dead space.

"With regard to the Seal?" Raegan asked, trying to keep her voice level. She forced herself to take a deep breath before answering, doing her best to shove aside the thick coil of lust wrapping itself around her midsection.

The King nodded and then pulled his damp sweater over his head, exposing a fitted gray t-shirt. Raegan lost track of her thoughts. Her eyes roamed across his sinful slopes of muscle, the sleeves of his shirt clinging tightly to the swell of his upper arms. She forced her gaze away, to the window on the other side of the room.

The King waited for her to answer. He did not prod her with more questions. He did not insert his thoughts. He did not rush her. And so, Raegan took a moment to think about the risks of removing the Seal, about the demands of Fate, about the tender bud that had pushed through her soil at Gossamer, and about the endless pit of rage burning in her chest.

It was, predictably, the rage that broke the surface, and the realization that came with it—one that had been unfolding in her for some time —stained everything in furious shades of red.

"I don't want to give a fuck about Fate anymore," Raegan said suddenly, fiercely, her fists curling as she met his gaze. "What do I actually want? I want to take everything back. I want my father. I want magic. I want *revenge*."

The King said nothing, again watching her like there was nothing else in the world. He prowled another step closer, his beautiful mouth parting slightly as he took her in. She became deeply aware that she wore nothing beneath the towel and that they were alone, tucked away from the world, and that tomorrow Raegan Maeve Overhill may cease to exist.

"And I want you, Oberon," she said, unable and unwilling to stop herself. "I want you as I always have: completely. Not in spite of what you are and not because of it, either. And I want you before the Seal is removed, before I might become someone else. Just once. Just once in this body, in this life, as *me*, I want you."

Immediately after speaking the words, she collapsed back against the archway. Her blood thrummed so loudly in her ears that the crackle and pop of the fireplace vanished. Time hung still as she waited for the King to say something—to say *anything*. Raegan felt as if she had sliced herself down the middle, displaying her still-glistening insides. She could only hope he would not choose to gut her again.

The King closed the distance between them in a heartbeat, reaching up above her head to rest one hand on the wall, looking down at Raegan in a way that made all the feelings she'd tried to smother throb and uncoil within her. With his other hand, the King reached out and took her jaw between his fingertips. His touch felt like a promise, and her body keened.

"You are my deepest wound," Oberon murmured, his eyes searching hers. "And yet I cannot live without the taste of blood in my mouth."

And then he kissed her, hard and unrelenting, his much larger body crushing hers against the wall. Raegan grabbed the front of his shirt, clawing her fingers into the fabric. Heat and need and a thousand years of longing exploded inside her, the gentle throbbing in her belly turning fast and wild.

Oberon's hand slid to her throat, fingers splayed, and she moaned, arching her body into his as she raked her nails down his chest. The rough groan he let out in response threatened to undo her entirely.

"Deny me," he rasped, his mouth moving against the delicate skin where her neck and jaw met. "It will hurt so much less in the end."

The husky timbre of the words sent a shiver across Raegan's skin. She had no intention of obeying. Instead, she let go of her towel, allowing it to pool around her feet, and then slid her hands to the hem of his shirt, yanking it upward with all her might.

"Make me remember you," she gasped as he pulled the garment over his head. "Whatever comes next, whoever I wake up as, make me *remember* you, Oberon."

A low, deep sound escaped from the back of his throat, and he gripped her waist so hard it hurt—beautiful, delicious pain. Raegan moaned as he lifted her from the ground, pinning her hips against the wall with his own. She dug into his shoulders with both hands, kissing him harder, as if her life depended on it.

Oberon slid his hand into her hair, his touch turning sensual and gentle.

She pulled back, breathing hard. "I don't want tenderness," she panted, wrapping her legs tighter around him. "I want *you*, Exiled King of the Unseelie Court. Give me your inhumanity and your cruelty. Leave your mark on me like a bloodstain."

His chest rose and fell against hers, his head tilted to the side as he examined her. Raegan watched something move across his face that both terrified and aroused her. Slick heat slid through her core. With a sound that could have just as easily come from a predator prowling the forest outside, the King tore her from the wall, his powerful arms wound around her so tightly she couldn't breathe.

He threw Raegan down on the bed of furs on the other side of the room, his body pinning hers against the soft bedding in an instant. She wanted him to leave handprints and bruises and any manner of ways to remember him. Oberon slid his arm beneath her leg, pulling hard to wrap it around his hips. Raegan obliged with her other limb, closing her thighs around him. The movement drew a low, strangled sound from his chest that immediately seared itself on her memory.

Oberon lifted himself up, arms bracketing either side of her head as he crushed his hips against hers, devouring the sound of her resulting moan with his kiss. Desperate and half-mad with need, she slipped one hand down his scarred torso, tracing the silken dusting of hair that led from his chest to his abdominals and then lower, lower.

The King's hand wrapped around her wrist with crushing, bruising power. She panted his name in a feverish murmur as he pinned her hand above her head, reaching to capture her other arm to do the same. "You said you wanted me," he said, mouth moving against her throat. "You already have me. You always did."

The King pulled away, pressing down harder on her wrists. Then he held her gaze, driving Raegan nearly out of her mind, the howl inside of her building like a blaze.

"But you do not belong to me," he continued, bringing his mouth back down to her throat, lips grazing her skin. "So you leave me no choice but to ruin you for any other lover you might take."

With tongue and teeth, the King mapped a trail down her body from her jaw to her breasts to her stomach—somehow both ferocious and languid at once—touching her in all the places she wanted to be touched. When he reached the apex of her legs, he released her wrists, drawing back to wrap his hands around the soft flesh of her generous thighs. The harsh pressure of his fingertips alone pulled another long, low moan from Raegan, her back arching with anticipation, blood drumming hard with desire.

As she looked down at him, the King's eyes found hers again. His lips moved along the inside of her thigh, gaze locked with hers. Then his mouth met the damp heat at her center, and she said his name like a prayer or a wish or a confession, her breath strangled in her throat.

"You will remember me whenever you are with anyone else," the King said, bringing his long, deft fingers to her core in the absence of his mouth. "When you pleasure yourself, you will remember me. No one will fill you or devour you or take you the way I do."

Raegan moaned again, louder this time, her heart pounding faster than she thought possible. When Oberon returned his mouth to her core, she grappled for him with blind hands, needing more. In response, he dug his fingers into her thighs, his capable tongue bringing her blisteringly close to orgasm in mere moments.

"Raegan," he said, his voice curling possessively around her name, "I want you to come for me."

"No," she panted, trying to sit up, reaching wildly for him. "Not without you inside me."

For a second, there was nothing but his hands around her thighs and the sound of her own breathing. Then Oberon straightened and dragged her toward him, his upper body coming to meet hers. One arm supporting his weight, he grabbed her by the jaw and kissed her as if it might save them both. Distantly, Raegan was surprised when he tasted only of himself—folklore, smoke, and mead. But she was more focused on winding her hands into his hair, begging and pleading for more against his mouth in a way she had never done before. She reached for his waistband, making quick work of stripping the cloth away from his body.

"Now," she implored, dragging her hands across his back. "Please. Oberon, *please.*"

The King pressed her into the furs with the heavy weight of his muscled body, lining up their hips in exactly the way Raegan so desperately wanted. Then his hard length met her soft, wet heat, and her back arched against her will, pleasure and pain filling her entire body. Her mouth fell open at the same time she heard a strangled groan escape from Oberon. Then the feeling of his kiss returned, coupled with the full, thick intensity of him at her center, their bodies moving in the same rhythm.

Oberon allowed her to wrap her arms around his neck as he slid one hand into the juncture where their hips met. The careful movement of his fingers in exactly the right spot made Raegan's vision go white.

"More," she moaned, digging her nails into the top of his heavily muscled shoulder.

The King complied, pulling another ragged gasp from her mouth. "Raegan," he said, his voice low and raw and thick with need. "Come for me harder than you will for anyone else."

She did as he commanded, the pressure within her finally snapping, an orgasm shattering her—making her his, as much as he was hers. She said his name more times than she could count as he tangled his hands in her hair.

Once Raegan thought she might be able to feel her bones again, he rolled them over in one quick, sharp move of muscle, placing her on top. She missed the near-suffocating weight of his body immediately, but every inch of her was red-hot and she needed to breathe.

So she collapsed against his chest. Oberon slid both arms around her, one hand massaging the back of her neck. After a few long, gorgeous moments that Raegan tried to live in—their breathing in sync, her flushed cheek against his chest, her thighs still wrapped around him— she sat up halfway, meeting his gaze.

Again, as if he knew what she wanted just from the look in her eyes, Oberon gripped her hips hard, ravenously taking in her collarbone and soft stomach and generous curves. When he dragged his eyes back up to hers, Raegan's core pulsed wildly. He reached out and grabbed her wrists, placing her hands onto his chest, palms down. His touch trailed up her body until he reached her breast. There, Oberon teased her until she whimpered, rolling her hips against his.

She ran her eyes across his body—the elegant collarbones, deft sweep of powerful muscle, the dusting of raven hair across his chest, narrowing and darkening as it trailed down to the sharp cut of his hip bones, which formed a hard V. With all her might, she tried to memorize it.

Then she met his gaze again, finding his mouth slightly parted.

"Raegan," he said, both hands returning to her hips, a question tilting his low, deep voice upwards.

She would've done anything he asked. He possessed her completely and entirely.

"I want you," the King told her, "to give me your rage."

Fire roared through her body, and Raegan did as he bid.

CHAPTER FIFTY-FIVE

Much later, he carried her to the bath, not releasing her from his arms. As he settled onto the tiled bench, Oberon pulled her onto his lap, her back against his chest. Raegan sighed, low and long, resting her head against his shoulder. For once in her life, she was completely and utterly satisfied—no ache fluttered against her sternum, no yearning unfolding in her marrow. Raegan knew it wouldn't last, but she tried to savor it all the same.

She tucked her head under his chin, laying her cheek against his collarbone. The angle brought Oberon's shoulder into view—and more noticeably, the red marks her nails had left. She raised a hand, brushing the scratches with her fingertips. "I didn't hurt you, did I?" she murmured, though she knew it was probably a ridiculous question.

"No," he said into her hair, his hand tracing a set of bruises on her thigh she hadn't noticed yet. "Did I hurt *you*?"

"If you did, I liked it," Raegan replied, looking up at him to smirk. "Very much."

He lifted his hand to her jaw, brushing her lips with his thumb before leaning in to kiss her. It was soft, slow, sensual, his fingers sliding into her hair. The sensation of it awakened an entirely different feeling in Raegan, one she was not familiar with and did not wish to explore right at this very moment. But she kissed him back all the same, twisting to press herself against him.

And then Oberon just held her. He said nothing. He didn't have to. The feeling of him—real, corporeal, here—was all she needed. At some point, he unwrapped his arms from her waist to massage up her neck and into the base of her skull. Raegan melted into his touch, her eyelids growing heavy.

She'd never admit it, but she felt like a stray cat finally being offered a few scratches and a bowl of milk. Oberon had fucked her hard and relentlessly, exactly what she'd asked for and precisely what she'd needed. But as much as it confused her, Raegan also desperately wanted this aftercare. The feeling scared her. It had been something she was happy to administer, most of the time, but was ambivalent about receiving. The sex itself—the rush and the chase and the orgasms—was the part she liked.

And yet whatever was happening now, the way it seemed like Oberon encircled her completely with his larger frame—how could he be so fierce one moment, and so gentle the next—was just as good. Maybe even better.

Raegan shoved that thought aside. It was too confusing, and it might not even matter this time tomorrow.

"Would you like to get into bed?" Oberon asked in a low voice, providing a much-needed distraction.

"With you?" Raegan asked, stretching to sit up straight. "Absolutely."

He carried her out of the bath even though she reminded him twice that her legs did, in fact, still work and that it was very presumptuous of him to assume they didn't. But she still let him help her dry off, and she leaned on him for balance as she stepped into a pair of soft sleep joggers. He lay down with her, and she curled into his chest, his scent and his skin and his voice all so painfully familiar.

"Was it ever just like this?" Raegan asked, her voice thick with sleepiness. She felt his powerful hand alight softly on her hair. "You know. None of the rest. Just this?"

"I wish I could tell you the answer you want to hear," the King replied. A pang smarted inside her chest, but she hadn't been expecting anything else. "For now," he continued, wrapping an arm around her waist, "it can be, if you wish."

Emotion swelled in Raegan's throat, tears pricking her eyes. "For now," she echoed, "I would like that."

~

When she awoke the next morning, sunlight floated in gently from a nearby window. She was pleasantly sore in places that had not been sore in some time. The previous evening came back to her in a flood, and she shifted to roll over. As she did, a muscled arm snaked around her waist. Raegan smiled, trying to hide the expression in the pile of furs as Oberon pulled her against him, her back to his chest.

The smell of woodsmoke and damp stone enveloped her. For a lilting moment, she had little idea who she was or what century it might be. All she knew was the fragile feeling in her chest and the impossibly beautiful creature with his arm around her.

"If I had known telling Fate to fuck off got you so turned on, I would've done it a while ago," she murmured.

She waited for the sound of his laugh, but when she heard nothing, she twisted in his grasp, turning to face him. As she did, Raegan found only the kind of sorrow that would've drowned most people.

"You did, once before," Oberon told her as he brushed hair away from her face, his touch gentler than it had any right to be. "The first time we met, I was the doomed one. And you refused to accept the path Fate had placed me upon."

Raegan's breath hitched. She opened her mouth to ask a question but realized she'd know soon enough and probably shouldn't risk further corrosion to the Seal. Long-dead things rattled their cages in her mind, but the locks held. For now.

"How did everything get so fucked up?" she wondered out loud, letting her head fall back onto the furs.

He did not answer—could not, she knew—but he held her tighter, as if to show Fate and Time and all the rest that he had little intention of letting her go. Raegan breathed in his scent, trying to memorize the scars across his chest. Each of them had a story and once upon a time, she had been able to read them like constellations.

Raegan traced one scar with a light touch, following its swoop to the top of Oberon's chest, just below his collarbone. There she saw the deep mauve slash she remembered noticing the night before. He flinched when she touched it, surprising her.

"Sorry," Raegan murmured into his skin. "What the hell did that to you?"

His hand landed on her hair again, somehow soft as a butterfly's wings. Another question he couldn't answer for the sake of her Seal. But something surfaced as she stared at the harsh puncture wound that had clearly just missed his heart.

Excalibur, whispered a voice from deep inside her. She examined the scar again, sleeping things stirring. For no reason at all, Raegan felt positive that this particular injury had been dealt by Excalibur. One of the world's most famous swords, made immortal by myth and legend. And still not capable of killing him.

"It is nearly time for us to meet Baba Yaga," Oberon murmured, his remorse-laced words breaking her thoughts.

"Right," she replied, not moving. She wanted whatever this was with him. She also wanted her power back, and more importantly, she wanted the ability to do something about her broken world. She reminded herself that removing the Seal could give her those things. If she didn't lose her mind, of course.

Raegan sat up when Oberon did, wrapping herself in a fur pelt. The fire still smoldered in the hearth, but she found the bathhouse colder this morning. When Oberon placed a plate of bread and fruit in front of her, she ate automatically. She tasted nothing. She stood and dressed, choosing comfortable clothes: tapered wool pants and a large, oversized sweater.

She found the King standing by the fire awaiting her, looking composed and deadly in well-tailored black clothing. But when her gaze met his, Oberon faltered, a muscle in his jaw leaping.

Raegan moved to stand beside him, her shoulder brushing his arm. "Why did you lie about the bargains?" she asked, staring into the fire, feeling so strangely sure that it didn't really matter all that much, even though she knew she should be furious.

The King sighed. "Because something felt different this time," he said, sliding his hands into his pockets, his words echoing Baba Yaga's, even if he didn't know it. "I wanted to keep you close, but I do not make decisions based on feelings. So when you offered me a reason, I took it. That said, I could not bind myself to you, considering our history and the Seal. I did give you my word, though, and I always honor my word."

Raegan's gaze slid to his again, her eyes narrowed.

"I *usually* honor my word," Oberon amended, a sly, cruel smile creeping onto his face. Then he shrugged. "I am what I am."

"Did you do something to me when I first came to see you?" she asked, trying to fill in all the remaining blanks, before she possibly became a blank herself.

"I took you home and eased your memory," he replied. "I apologize for the intrusion. You touched me without warning, and your mind reacted quite strongly. I was worried your Seal was at risk."

Raegan shifted her weight, pulling at a loose thread on her sweater. "You told me that we can't keep singing the same song or something," she mumbled, her eyes falling to the soot that ringed the hearth.

"And yet here I am, reminding you of its melody," Oberon said bitterly. "I am sorry I am not stronger. I did warn you. You make me weak."

Raegan stiffened at his words, remembering the way they'd cut into each other at Gossamer. But his tone was different, she realized, and a degree of awe laced it. Excalibur could not kill him. Nor could the Protectorate. Exile into a land without magic had hardly diminished him. But *she* did. In the worst way, the statement was a compliment—that she had the power to weaken a being molded by primordial forces, torn from the night sky itself.

In the distance, Raegan heard a bell tolling, low and lonely, more at home over a windswept moor than Baba Yaga's tangled green realm. But she knew the sound was for her all the same, a summoning of sorts, and she raised her gaze to the King.

"Please kiss me," she said. "Just once more. Before I go."

He did as she requested. It was the kind of kiss that spoke of extinguished flames and unyielding loss, a goodbye that stretched across eternities. Raegan kissed him back desperately, as if her rage and heat could keep both of them warm.

Oberon exhaled and rested his forehead against hers, hands still in her hair. She tried to memorize the feel of it all—hungry, as always, for everything she could not have. She closed her eyes against the weight of the sorrows she laid at his feet time and time again.

Then he murmured two words that sent light cascading into all her darkest places, locks falling away and doors flying open.

"Outlive me."

Suddenly, she was no longer in Baba Yaga's bathhouse but a wide, verdant field at the edge of the forest. She turned away from the woods, pointing at a tree and explaining something about its bark. A few feet behind her stood the King, resplendent with youth, his porcelain skin marked only by a few slight lines around his eyes, courtesy of riding in the sun all his life.

Then she stood at the mouth of a grand stone citadel, a large wooden door swinging open to allow her to walk through.

A clearing and a swan-winged woman and blackberry-stained lips.

A lightning-streaked sky, red as blood, a vast and terrible army at her side.

A man with pale eyes and pale hair, a sword on his belt that hummed with power.

A cottage with a thatched roof, her dried herbs lined up just the way she liked.

A feverish kiss from a towering, beautifully inhuman creature in black armor. His low, rich voice—like heather on the hills or dusk over the lake—murmuring against her skin, "Outlive me. I love you too much."

A feast, colorful banners hanging from the ceiling of a great stone hall, tables laden with food and wine. She stood in the corner beside a tall, gray-haired man, nervous but trying not to show it.

"Don't fret," the man was saying, looking at her with what she thought might be fondness. "It took many years for the nobles to acknowledge me at a feast, or even out in the market, despite me having spent the night ensuring their child did not succumb to fever."

The man took a long pull from his goblet, gaze darting over her shoulder. His thick brows rose in pleasant surprise, eyes mischievous when they returned to hers.

"At the very least," the man began, a smile tugging at his mouth, "you

have someone's attention that no one else seems able to obtain, try as they might."

She looked at him, confused, and turned to glance behind her. And there he was, dressed in deep tones of steel blue that looked beautiful against his moonlight skin. His dark waves of raven hair were swept away from his face, tumbling down his neck. He wore a sword at his waist, and even from a few paces away, she knew he smelled of woodsmoke and black pepper and damp stone.

He said her name, and she demurred politely, trying not to drown in his ocean eyes. Just behind him, the other people gathered in the hall looked on with a rapt sort of curiosity, as if this absurdly handsome knight did not always pay attention to the unmarried young ladies at feasts.

Then she returned the greeting, his name filling her mouth.

And suddenly, she remembered all of it—how it was the same name she'd said in the dream at the river, how there had been a changeling in King Arthur's court and almost none of it had happened like the stories said. She should know. She'd been there.

And so had he.

She raised her eyes to his, that same oceanic gray after all these years. And then, she said his name. Not a true name, no, but his first.

"Mordred."

Chapter Fifty-Six

Everything that happened next was chaos. Her vision blinked in and out, and even though there was ground beneath her feet, it felt like she was constantly plummeting. Someone had been kind enough to lay her down on something soft, and then someone else was yelling, while the first person's voice kept getting lower and lower.

"How is it even possible?"

"It's *not*."

"Clearly, it is."

"I placed the goddamn Seal myself! Two little words shouldn't corrode it. Neither would fucking. Don't look at me like that. I'm no fool. You know as well as I do that she'd need extensive, specific knowledge of multiple lives. Despite my general distaste for you, I very much doubt you sat her down and walked her through everyone she's ever goddamn been. I certainly didn't say very much."

Then silence stretched long, except for the buzzing in her head, like a thousand bees ramming into her skull.

"If you do not salvage this, I will rip your little realm apart while you watch. Only once I have crushed the last of it between my teeth will I allow you to die."

More silence, then a wolfish whistle. *"Ебать.* I get threats all the time, but that's the first one I've taken seriously in a while. Well done. Now hush and let me save our girl."

Soft shuffling sounds, her chest caving in, her mind jumping and fracturing, mixing childhood memories with places she did not know, jumbling movies she'd seen with images of stone halls and brutal battles.

"Raegan, if you can hear me, we've hit a spot of trouble. I'm going to peel away your Seal, but it's corroded quite badly. To be frank with you, old friend, this is going to be brutal. Remember the old stories and look for the doors."

And then Raegan was Raegan again, at least a little, but she was also falling. Sort of. There was no up or down in this space, just blackness and a distinct sensation of rushing movement before her consciousness failed her, blinking out.

When Raegan woke, antiseptic lingered in the air, conjuring images of linoleum floors and watery light. She blinked her eyes open slowly. She was alone in a bare, quiet room. White sheets were pulled up to her waist, and a pale yellow blanket, wooly with pilling, stretched across her calves.

Shakily, she swung her legs off the edge of the bed and sat up. Her feet were encased in fuzzy socks with grippy pads on the bottom. Panic crowded her throat. Jaw clenched, she stared down at her lap, horrified to discover a plastic bracelet around her wrist, spelling out "RAEGAN OVERHILL, NO ALLERGIES."

No, no, no. Not again. Not like this.

The door across the room opened softly, and she snapped to attention.

"Oh, good, you're up," a kindly older man chimed from the doorway, backlit by overhead fluorescents. "I hope your head is feeling better. Your mother is here for a visit, but she said she could come back if your migraine is still an issue."

Raegan's tongue felt too thick in her mouth. "No," she said after a long pause. "No, I'm feeling better. I can see my mom."

"She's waiting for you out in the garden," said the man who she was trying to tell herself was not an orderly. She waited for him to walk away, but it became clear he would be escorting her. So she stood up, slid her feet into the slippers she knew would be next to the nightstand, and pulled the long cardigan off the edge of the bed frame.

And then Raegan followed the man out the door and down a hall-way. She took in every sign, every person—anything and everything she could—to gain any kind of information. None of it made any sense at all. She had just been in Baba Yaga's bathhouse with an ancient Fey king.

As soon as that thought fully formed in her mind, Raegan burned with shame at how absurd it sounded. She tried to remember the feeling of the thick furs against her skin and the smell of the eucalyptus bundles and the taste of Oberon's kiss.

Before she could untangle anything further in her mind, the orderly led her into a small courtyard. Garden was a generous name for the space, which consisted of a few potted plants and an algae-choked fountain. Large gray cement walls surrounded it on all sides. She couldn't even smell plants or rocks out here—just antiseptic.

"I'll be back in a half an hour," said the orderly who she'd forgotten was there. And then he was gone, leaving Raegan to walk the remaining few yards to her mother, who was seated at a small café table that had seen better days.

"Hi, Mom," Raegan said, sliding onto the chair, finding her voice higher than she remembered, her heart hammering in her chest.

"Raegan," Bronwyn greeted. It was definitely her mother, Raegan was sure, the silver rings on her fingers and the worn mulberry sweater coat so familiar. She caught a whiff of her mom's perfume and calmed just a little.

"Nice to hear you call me mom," Bronwyn added, her tone harsh, confusing Raegan.

"Uh, right," Raegan said. "How are you?"

"Wow," Bronwyn replied, raising her eyebrows. "Maybe this is finally helping you. I'm doing okay. How are you?"

"I've been better," Raegan said, her throat closing off as tears threatened to descend upon her. "Mom, um, could I ask you some questions? There's some things I don't quite remember."

"Maybe you should talk to your doctor about that," Bronwyn said, looking concerned, which at least stung a little less.

"Oh, um, I'm on a new medication," Raegan ventured. "Some foggi-ness and memory loss might happen at first. And I just woke up. I had a bad migraine. So I was hoping it would be okay to bother you rather than take up time in my sessions?"

It sort of addled her that even now, riddled with confusion and fear, she could still lie that easily.

"Sure," Bronwyn said, her tone less guarded. "What do you not remember?"

"Uh, this sounds really bad, but how long have I been here?"

Her gut twisted as she watched the expression on her mother's face move into something that looked like sweet, sickly pity.

"Raegan, that's concerning," Bronwyn returned, looking toward the orderly by the courtyard entrance like she might run screaming to him because her daughter was unraveling again.

"I know," Raegan said, forcing a laugh. "I'm going to talk to my doctor as soon as you leave. I didn't want to miss your visit. I'm sure it's just the medicine." She forced a smile onto her face, feeling like her own puppeteer.

"You've been here almost a year, Raegan," her mother said, eyes boring into hers. Bronwyn said each word slowly and deliberately, as if Raegan were either too stupid or too insane to understand. Her stomach flipped, and nausea threatened to overtake her. "It's almost November. You came here last October," Bronwyn continued, her eyes darting back to the orderly at the courtyard's entrance. "Do you remember? You, um, you were not feeling too well."

Raegan could not remember anything, a white wall of nothingness hitting her when she tried to recall anything from before waking up in that bed just a few moments ago.

"I think you should talk to your doctor," Bronwyn said finally when Raegan offered her nothing. "I don't want to upset you, and I'm not trained . . . I'm not trained to deal with this."

"Okay," Raegan breathed, her hands curling into fists so hard that her fingers hurt. "Uh, how's the house? Are you decorated for Halloween?" She would be clever and unafraid. She would poke and prod at this reality, testing its realness in exactly the same way it seemed to be testing her.

"Raegan, I don't decorate for Halloween, you know that," Bronwyn said, narrowing her eyes. "Are you okay?"

"I don't know, Mom," Raegan said hoarsely. "I really don't know. Um, have you talked to anyone at the paper?"

"The paper?" Bronwyn echoed, confusion crossing her features.

"You know, where I work," Raegan offered, her brows knitting together.

"Work?" her mother repeated. "Raegan, that's a bit strong for freelancing a few stories now and again. You haven't been well enough to work full-time since college."

Raegan's stomach dropped out from beneath her, and nausea swept over her in larger waves. With all her strength, she suppressed the rising panic. "Right," she said, drumming her fingers on the table, thinking. None of this was real. It couldn't be. "Uh, how are you doing?"

"You already asked me that," Bronwyn said, her tone flat.

"I mean, with the anniversary coming up."

Bronwyn waved Raegan's suggestion away with a swat of her hand through the still air. Her throat constricted as she resisted the urge to look up. Would she find some heinously painted ceiling depicting the open sky because she was not deemed sane enough to gaze upon the real one?

"That's a dramatic way of phrasing it," Bronwyn said after a pause. "I don't assign much meaning to the day your dad decided to leave us for someone else."

"Dad didn't leave . . . He's *missing*," Raegan said, her mouth dry. The iron grip she had on the panic faltered. It slid into her veins, hot and hungry.

"I think you need to talk to your doctor immediately. We've been through all of this before," Bronwyn said, closing the front of her sweater coat across her chest in that familiar way. "Cormac left us for another woman. You see him a couple of times a year. He hasn't visited you here because he can't handle it, but he's not missing. He's just an absolute asshole."

All of Raegan's control shattered, and her eyes welled with tears. A heavy weight settled on her chest, and breathing suddenly required all of her strength. Bronwyn watched her struggle, worry etching her features.

"I think I do need to talk to my doctor," Raegan sputtered. "I don't remember any of this, and I'm scared." Her voice hitched because now she *was* afraid—terrified, even.

Bronwyn softened for just a moment, reaching over to put a hand on her daughter's shoulder. "It's going to be okay," Bronwyn whispered, though Raegan wasn't sure which one of them she was saying it for. "Stay right here."

Raegan numbly watched her mom get up and walk toward the large glass doors, where a few orderlies were waiting. Two immediately walked over with her, and Raegan caught the edge of the conversation: "She doesn't remember anything. It's like all the work of the past year just went away."

Bronwyn's brown eyes were wide and shiny when Raegan stood. "They're going to take you to see your doctor," she confirmed.

"Okay, that's probably for the best," Raegan mumbled. "I guess I'll see you later?"

"I'll be back next month," Bronwyn confirmed, which sent a little dagger into Raegan's heart. A visit once a month? That's all her mom could spare?

The orderlies were gently guiding her away, so Raegan took a deep breath and asked, "Hey, um, where am I?"

"The Pines Center," the woman on her left said. "You're part of an inpatient program so you can feel better."

Raegan turned the name over in her head. "Where is it, like, physically?"

"You're in New Jersey," the male orderly said. He was the same one from before, she realized. "Just on the edge of the Pine Barrens."

Raegan bit down on the inside of her cheek, hoping for blood, hoping for pain, hoping for anything but what was in front of her. Fear crept up her spine, sly and slinking. Her mind had hidden the truth from her before. Otherwise, all of this would be so easy to dismiss. She'd been hospitalized in Boston during college. Not for a year, though. It was barely more than a week. In and out. She was fine, more or less.

Wasn't she?

Before Raegan could wrap her head around the situation, she arrived at the doors to her doctor's office. The male orderly ushered her inside. She dragged herself across the scuffed linoleum. Sitting there at the desk, shuffling some papers and calm as could be, was her editor, Henry Washington.

"Sit down, Raegan, sit down," he called in a gentle voice. "It sounds like you may not be feeling well today. I rearranged my schedule so we could talk."

It was too much for her to take, her body running cold like someone had dumped a bucket of ice water over her head. "Henry?" Raegan sputtered, sinking into the chair.

"Dr. Henry," he corrected, not unkindly. "Dr. Arman Henry. But I know in that story you're writing, I inspired . . . Henry Washington, isn't it?"

"I'm not that kind of writer," Raegan said, her mouth dry.

"What are you, then, Raegan?" Henry asked. "Do you remember why you're here?"

She spent a few precious moments trying to push past that blank white wall, or find a way to tear down this convincing reality built all around her. But then she looked at him again, and god, he looked so much like *her* Henry, and the pain of that realization snuffed out the last stitch of willpower.

"No," she finally said, quiet and small. "I have no idea at all."

CHAPTER FIFTY-SEVEN

Henry—Dr. Arman Henry, apparently—spent a few minutes explaining what Raegan had already assumed. She had been admitted to The Pines nearly a year ago following an episode that involved a complete split from reality, including lots of ranting and raving about the Fey and magic and the Gates. Henry didn't say it like that, but she got the point.

He was sorry to hear she was having trouble remembering and made a suggestion with an impressive amount of tact that the real Henry never would've had. Well, if her Henry was the real one. In all truth, Raegan did not know for sure.

"Maybe, because it's around the time of year your family changed in your youth *and* when you more recently joined us here, some of that old pain is being dredged up," he said, steepling his fingers. "And that's okay. Darkest before the dawn and all that. I think we should look at this as an opportunity to dig a little deeper."

Raegan kept alternating between obsessively listening to every word he was saying and trying to scan the room, looking for clues that this was made up. She didn't find any. It even smelled like an inpatient facility—the bleach and the fake floral air freshener and the aura of misery carefully scrubbed away. She looked down at her feet. If this was fake, they got the socks right too, down to the little grippy beads on the bottom.

So maybe this was real?

Suddenly, Raegan snapped back to attention because Henry had just said a name she had not expected to hear in this place. "I'm sorry—what did you say?"

"Oh, it's alright, Raegan," Henry said, unfolding his hands. "I brought up Oberon. The King."

Raegan's mouth went completely dry. "Oberon," she repeated, hollow.

"Yes, we've discussed before how he's essentially a stand-in for or a daydream of your perfect partner," Henry replied. "Unrealistic but aspirational in a lot of ways. Too good to even be human. He holds hallmarks of what we would identify as masculinity but isn't a man in the way we understand it, which sidesteps your issues with real, human men."

Her insides twisted. She thought she might be sick. "What?" Raegan settled on, the word coming out choked.

Henry sat back in his chair, examining her. Raegan tried to pull her thoughts together, tried to formulate something that felt close to logic. She reminded herself that the real Henry would've been familiar with her jokes about being attracted to all women and, like, four men, so the idea of someone male-presenting being her perfect partner would seem absurd to him.

Raegan rubbed her forehead. "Why are we talking about this?" she wanted to know.

"Does talking about it in this way make you feel defensive?" the doctor asked. "That he's imagined? Sometimes our imaginations can help us out, but it's important you realize no romantic partner has ever come to visit you. So we need to start deconstructing what's real to everyone else and what's only real to you. That doesn't make you bad or crazy. It only means we need to be sure we can both agree on what parts are real, and what parts are just for you."

The man seemed less and less like Henry, his tone descending into something Raegan found hard not to equate with open condescension.

"How much does this place cost a week?" she demanded, pleasantly surprised by the amount of venom she'd summoned. "It better be cheap if this is the extent of your psychoanalytic skills."

"Okay, Raegan," Henry said, placing his hands on the desk. "I think we should take a break and maybe revisit this tomorrow. I know you were pretty confused earlier."

Henry got up from behind his desk to guide her by the elbow to the door. Raegan lifted her arm, not wanting whatever this thing actually was to touch her. She looked desperately around the office for anything at all that might indicate he was a fraud. Her eyes fell on a framed picture on the wall. It had a gold plate inscribed in looping calligraphy that read "our honeymoon." It still had a price sticker in the top right-hand corner and the photo inside was of a smiling couple. Maybe Henry just hadn't changed the stock photo yet, but it didn't look like one of those grayscale inserts. The couple was blonde, white, maybe in their thirties, standing in front of what looked like a vineyard. They weren't airbrushed or retouched.

And neither one of them was Henry. Because Henry was a single Black guy in his fifties.

He was rushing her through the door and into the hands of the orderlies, almost like he knew she was looking for something to break this construct. But Raegan's teeth had sunk in this now, and she twisted around. Her eyes locked onto the diploma hanging over his desk. It wasn't made out to anyone. All it said at the top was "The University."

Raegan threw her head back and laughed so hard that the orderlies exchanged glances. All of this was fucking fake. All of it. She didn't know why it was happening or what in the hell she could do about it. But she knew that everything around her was fake, and that meant the bathhouse and Baba Yaga and the quest and the King belonged to the real world. Her world.

The orderlies deposited Raegan in her room. In the lonely silence, she began to panic. What if she was just hallucinating to support her delusion? What if her mind was lying to her, showing her breadcrumbs where everyone else just saw regular photos and diplomas?

Raegan sat down on her bed, forcing herself to breathe, terrified by how fake everything looked, like cardboard cutouts. If this *was* the real world, she would never, ever be happy again. Panic and horror and that deep well of sorrow rose up her throat like a tidal wave.

"Okay, so then think, you dumb bitch," Raegan snarled at herself under her breath, running her hands through her hair so hard she yanked out a few strands.

Her mind remained horribly blank, as pale and stale as the space around her. She pulled her cardigan around her body, hoping that if she cocooned herself, she might emerge stronger and braver. As the fabric moved, something rustled in her left pocket.

All of Raegan's attention zeroed in, sharp as the point of a knife. Hand shaking, she delicately prodded her fingertips beneath the seam of the pocket. Something brushed her skin—soft, dry. Hope surged in her chest as Raegan pulled her hand away, cupping a bundle of meadowsweet in her palm.

Blodeuwedd.

Do not forget.

Raegan was on a quest. All quest-goers were tested, and this particular test was a classic. She'd seen it in a hundred stories, on the pages of her favorite books and on the screen of her parents' battered TV. She clutched the meadowsweet in her hand, the antiseptic smell banished by its springtime scent—green and fresh and full of life instead of this muted, quiet death.

She shot to her feet, beginning to pace. What had Baba Yaga said? To remember the old stories, to look for the doors. If she were trapped in some gray, shallow alternative world, what was the way out? What was the common thread through all of fantasy and folklore and old country stories? What was the escape hatch? The door?

And then, just like that, she knew. In a mad dash, her hands shaking, Raegan yanked off her sweater, pulling the arms inside out. She laid it on the bed and pulled off the white t-shirt next, turning it inside out as well. Then the flannel pants, then the socks, and for good measure, the sports bra and the underwear.

Feeling like a madwoman and standing naked in the small, dim room, Raegan began to re-dress with her clothing turned inside-out, starting at her feet and working her way up. When she reached the final piece of clothing, the long sweater, she gritted her teeth.

This had to work, or she would kill herself, she realized. If this world was real, she could not exist within its hollow margins, could not do its plain and simple bidding. Not after what she had touched, not after what she'd almost had. No matter whether it had been real or not. Raegan could not—would not—go back to a life without magic.

She stared at the sweater for a long time, longer than she'd care to admit, and then she bit her tongue so hard it almost bled and pulled the garment on, right arm first. As it settled over her shoulders, her heart pounded.

Steady, steady, steady, the meadowsweet clutched against her chest.

Nothing changed. Raegan fell into complete and utter despair. Nothing was real, nothing mattered, she was just sick and deluded and amounted to nothing. She was not some chosen hero. She had made it all up in her head to contend with her mediocrity, to apply a balm to the wound her father had left her with.

Her throat was closing off when she heard it.

A rumbling, or something akin to it, a low roll far off in the distance. It could've been thunder, except that it was October in the northeast. And besides, she could feel it in her bones, reverberating and humming.

And then suddenly, a crack began to form in the ground, right between her feet. It splintered and grew, climbing up the wall directly across from her and sliding onto the ceiling, tiny bits of plaster and drywall beginning to fall down like snow.

Fuck. She hoped she was not making this up, too.

There was no time to hesitate, Raegan knew, so she turned and fled for the door. It opened at her touch. Outside, the hallway was empty, the lights flickering strangely, the smell of acrid bone and herbs and damp stone thick in her nose. Without thinking twice, she sprinted down the hallway, down to the big double doors, and then, breathless and half-strangled by what might be, she threw them open and fell into the sunlight.

Chapter Fifty-Eight

Everything she had ever been began to fall around her like stardust and ash and confetti. A sunset on a heathered hill. The view out of the top of a turret. A younger Oberon lifting his eyes to hers in a candlelit room. The hum and pulse of a battlefield. The familiar weight of a blade in her hands. The smell of smoking bone. A small room with a tarot reader. The green hills of an Earth that man had not dared to carve into just yet. The top of a battle-blackened hill, her scream raw in her throat. A river roaring and then parting around her, water rising high on either side. A gray courser beneath her, galloping hard through a forest.

Something, a film or a veil, peeled away from her. And then all the parts of her collided and her body felt like it was being split into a thousand pieces.

She saw the life where everything had begun, and the years when the snake had developed a taste for its own tail.

The ocean-eyed, raven-haired changeling created by two goddesses who feared that the old ways and magic were in danger. They implanted him in the court of a king who wished to unite the mortals of the Isles under one banner—the banner with a dragon rampart. The banner with a blade of iron forged specifically to shed Fey blood. The banner that posed a genuine threat to the Fair Folk and the gods and magic itself for the first time in history.

The hazel-eyed, fire-haired girl raised by the Druids deep in the woods after her parents cast her out for her magic, who'd shed her minor nobility in favor of the stranger, wilder things—only to be tasked with embedding herself in that same court to see if there would truly be war between the mortals and the Fey, and if so, how the Druids could survive it.

They were never on the same side, were never meant to be, and yet the changeling and the Druid girl subverted Fate, shifting the tides and nearly preventing the war that would tear the world in two.

They had failed, and now time slipped off the changeling entirely, while the soil called the Druid girl's name twice a century only to spit her back out.

She saw her first death and understood why the mountain of a man named Bedwyr made her stomach turn. That recurring dream, her body carried and dumped like refuse, was at his hands, ordered by his king. When men are afraid, they always kill the witches first. One day, when she was good and ready and more pressing matters had been attended to, she would ask the King to hold Bedwyr down while she carved out his insides.

The thought released something inside her, and then she saw everything else, too. The crows of war when they came cawing, leaving feathers outside her dwelling and pulling at her hair when she walked too deep into the forest.

The fierceness of the Fair Folk's resistance to the Protectorate rule of the Otherlands—humans infused with unnatural magic they should not have by a god who wanted dominion of a world that had never been his.

The weight of her own body as life left her, again and again and again.

The King, his shoulders draped in a black cloak, standing before a dead door that once linked the realms together, snow falling all around him.

The rebellions and the dark places and the sunsets and the quiet moments in between. The way the King had been there for it all. The way his shadows had become a refuge for her.

Time, she could see, was not so much a straight line as it was snow falling everywhere all at once, gathering on treelines and weighing down the mountains. Here, she was as much Raegan as she was Nyneve as she was Titania as she was the Lady of the Rivers and the Deathless One and the Witch in the Wood. Everything seemed to bend and refract, reflecting right back at her and then out. A snake devouring its own tail.

She was infinite, maybe.

And then the light changed—directly overhead, casting no shadows. She was reaching her way across an endless dream, walking a tundra of a thousand lives, seeking the warmth of the one she now lived.

"It's this way," a voice called out.

Raegan turned on her heel, heart beating, and faced herself. Well, this woman didn't look anything like her—she had weathered skin and gray hair in a loose braid, leaning on a rough-hewn staff—but Raegan knew.

"Witch in the Wood," Raegan greeted.

"It is nice to see you again," the old woman answered. "I can lead you through this. Please don't be afraid. You're not stuck or trapped. You're just in between. You and I, we are very good at being in between."

"I fear I do need to get back," Raegan said, taking a step toward her.

"Oh, I know, I know," the old woman tutted. "I'll get you back. Come along."

So Raegan began to follow the Witch in the Wood through this frozen place, tracking her footsteps, the sun too bright for her eyes. She felt as though she should still be panicking, but she was calm, smooth as a still lake. She would see this through.

"You know, Raegan," the Witch of the Wood said, "time, it's not quite a straight line."

"I've noticed," Raegan said, her voice dry.

The Witch laughed. "I should've suspected you did," she replied. "Well, I'm only reminding you, I suppose. If I know, then you know. It's an important thing to remember. Time is happening all around us, all at once, never-ending. Where I once walked, so do you, and where you go, I will follow. Doors I have opened remain open, even if they do not appear so."

"I'll remember that," Raegan told her.

"Good," the old woman said. "It's very important you remember." The woman came to a stop for a moment. "How is he?"

Raegan did not need to ask. "He's tired."

"Ah. I suppose I can't blame him for that."

"No," Raegan agreed. "He knew who you were, by the way. When he found you in the woods, when the villagers wanted to burn you at the stake. I don't know if he ever told us directly, but he knew."

"I had a feeling," the Witch of the Wood said. "He remained with me for a touch too long to not have known." She began her procession again, somehow knowing where to go in this blank land. "I miss him."

"Where I go, you follow," Raegan reminded her.

The old woman turned and smiled at her. "Say hello to Baba Yaga for me," she said.

Suddenly, there was a door. It was ancient and wooden, curved at the top, with ornate iron details. Raegan could've sworn she had seen it before. Probably because she had. She had seen it a million times. In dreams, in museums, in photography books, in paintings. Always. Everywhere.

"What is this?" she wanted to know.

"A door," the old woman told her.

"I can see that. I mean . . . well, you know."

The Witch in the Wood shrugged. "Some things have no true name. Some things are too powerful."

Raegan did not have a chance to press her, a moment to ask more, because then the Witch in the Wood swung the door open and, before she could even think, she was walking through it. Walking back to her body and her revenge and her magic.

Raegan inhaled deeply, bringing the scent of a fire and fur pelts into her nose. She wiggled her fingers. They all worked. Her toes, too. There was still a pleasant, familiar soreness in her body. Her head hurt. Her lips were chapped, and her throat ached.

She took another deep breath and opened her eyes. A fire smoldered in a large stone hearth. She looked down at herself and saw she had been tucked into a pile of heavy pelts. Raegan reflexively identified the animals from which they'd come.

Realization dawned on her, heavy and bewildering. "Oh," she murmured, her eyes widening, wondering what else she might know, and also realizing that she was still very much herself.

With a soft groan, she rolled over. In less than a heartbeat, oceanic gray eyes met hers. The King leapt from his chair and knelt beside her, but he said nothing. Raegan heard Baba Yaga grunt as she rose from the other chair.

The witch loomed over Raegan, looking at her quizzically. "And who might you be?" Baba Yaga asked, her gaze slipping to the King for a heartbeat.

"Raegan Maeve Overhill," she replied, lifting her chin, surprised by the strength of her voice considering how sore her throat was. "And everyone else, I guess. But falling around me like snow or confetti or ash. It's all happening at once anyway, isn't it?"

Baba Yaga's black eyes glinted, her mouth moving into a very pleased smile.

"The Witch in the Wood sends her regards," Raegan told the old woman. "She is quite fond of you."

Baba Yaga beamed. "And I her," the witch replied, clapping a gnarled hand over her heart.

Then Raegan turned to the King, his expression so full of fragile, tentative hope that it almost broke her heart clean in half. Their eyes met, and Raegan tried to find words—she was good at words—but everything that came to mind failed to encompass what she was trying to say.

So instead, Raegan leaned forward, grabbed the front of his sweater, and pulled his mouth to hers. Baba Yaga whistled, ambling for the door as if they were going to tear each other's clothes off while she was still there.

But then Raegan broke the kiss, put her face to the King's chest and wept. She wept for all the sorrow she had known, for her lives that ended in pain and darkness, for her lives that never touched magic—so shallow and distant, she could hardly recall them, even now. She wept for all the misery she had witnessed and known. She wept for the reality she had almost believed was real—caught in her worst nightmare as the

Seal's removal threatened to pull apart all her lives and trap them in separate tiny, gray boxes.

And most of all, she wept for the world—the one that had existed before the Gates and the Protectorate and the Timekeeper. And she wept at the rising, slinking terror that she might not be strong enough to bring that world back.

~

Baba Yaga insisted that Raegan and the King remain in her realm. The Protectorate had stopped sniffing and poking around her door, as she put it, so she could harbor them for a little longer. It would give Raegan time to rest and to begin unspooling her memory. Maintaining herself and her mind seemed to have come at the cost of her magic's immediate return. It was there, Baba Yaga kept saying. Without a doubt, Raegan could feel the difference. She finally possessed all of her pieces. But she had not yet figured out how to put them together. So not *quite* whole—but almost.

"Well," Baba Yaga said the second day after Raegan's Seal had been removed. "You could be raving mad. So what if you can't do magic just yet? It'll come. I can see it." She sat back in her chair, gesturing at the King, who stood before the hearth in her chicken-legged hut. "He can, too," she said, her voice louder, as if purposefully prodding Oberon to agree.

The King turned, taking in the two women. "I do," he said with a regal incline of his head. "As Baba Yaga said, it would be much worse if your abilities came back in full but your mind shattered."

"Then we'd probably have to kill you," Baba Yaga said cheerfully. "But we don't. Lucky, lucky!"

Raegan and the King shot Baba Yaga identical withering glances, but the old witch hardly cared. She just tut-tutted as if they were children— they both had hundreds of years on her—and then set off trying to explain all the ways eggshells were very useful to witches. Raegan took copious notes, to the point that her hand cramped. Of course she was beyond excited to be learning magic from the actual fucking Baba Yaga. And she could feel her power rising up in herself. Sometimes she could bring it to the surface of her skin. But never farther. In all truth, it was

411

more infuriating than anything else, especially because if she focused, Raegan could recall the feeling of working magic. But only the memory.

Before Raegan even voiced anything, Oberon made sure to tell her that he was not disappointed in her and that he'd never expected everything to return immediately. The way he already knew what she might be feeling and took care to address it made butterflies stir in her stomach, aided by the waterfall of memories that often came to her when they were alone together. But it did not stop the sour feeling that arose from Raegan's own disappointment in herself.

Raegan realized she was not paying attention to Baba Yaga and jumped, forcing herself to sit up straight. The witch stopped speaking, eyeing Raegan with her small, dark eyes.

"You seem exhausted," the King said, suddenly beside her. She hadn't heard his footfall, though she did not know why that kept surprising her. "How do you feel?"

Raegan dragged a hand down her face, not understanding how someone that a solid part of the general population would not incorrectly identify as a monster had more emotional intelligence than most of the people she'd dated. "I'm exhausted," she admitted, embarrassed.

It had happened like this the night before, too—she'd hit a wall and she'd hit it hard. She didn't think it was all the information she was trying to absorb—she was good at that—but rather the weight of living with everything she'd seen. Everything she'd done. Everyone she'd been.

"Let's just finish up on the eggshells," Baba Yaga prodded, reaching out toward the mortar and pestle before the King's hand fell on the witch's shoulder.

"She is done, I think, for the day," Oberon said with that quiet authority of his. "You may recall that the years we wear can certainly be an advantage, but sometimes they become a hindrance. It is a lot of weight."

"Sorry," Raegan said to Baba Yaga, whose gaze softened when she heard Oberon's words.

"Yes, yes," the witch said, getting to her feet. "I know your warrior cannot hold the wards forever. I suppose I'm trying to stuff as much into as few days as possible."

"It is appreciated," the King replied, open and sincere.

As Raegan stood, her head went all woozy. Embarrassed, she

expressed that she needed to lie down. Baba Yaga promised the delivery of hot bowls of borscht to the bathhouse, and then Oberon led Raegan out the door. He offered her his arm the same way he had in the beginning of this journey, when he'd needed the physical proximity to glamour them better. But now it seemed to be a reflex, or a desire to feel her warmth. It made sense in a terrible, aching way. Raegan could remember enough to know for certain that the King had spent more time by her graves than walking at her side.

Which made her feel even guiltier about how the past two nights had gone. She would've loved to spend the evenings tangled up with his large, powerful body, forgetting anything else existed. But so far, Raegan had ended her days by weeping in the bath. Oberon had held her, sometimes for hours at a time. He hadn't tried to tell her it would get better, or that he was sorry, or that she needed to calm down. He'd just held her, running fingers through her hair or massaging her hands.

Raegan wasn't stupid. She knew it was partly because he simply did not feel things the way her human heart did. But the space he made for something he did not understand, and the way he always *saw* her, was breathtaking in the best way.

As they walked to the bathhouse, Raegan leaned her head against his arm and realized with a sudden shock—though it should not have been a shock, she supposed—that the King really did love her. Not blindly, not unconditionally. She remembered the lives where he either could not summon it, or could not bear it. But he always loved her when she was like this, when she was herself—a wild, keening howl of river water and magic and rage. His love was as strange and inhuman as he was—intense, deadly, unyielding. Raegan looked up at him, wanting to say something, to acknowledge that she cherished it. But as she did, the King's stride faltered and he stiffened.

A bee had settled onto the bathhouse door. It was larger than any bee Raegan had ever seen, its glassine wings the size of her hand. Instead of a buzzing or otherwise distinctively insectoid noise, the bee called with the low, haunting sound of a mourning dove.

As they approached, it swiveled its head. The bee looked at Raegan and then the King in turn with black eyes before releasing a few more sorrowful coos into the air.

"It appears," the King said, "that the Oracle has returned."

CHAPTER FIFTY-NINE

When the King finished speaking, the bee took off, the fading evening light shining through its stained-glass wings as it rose higher and higher into the sky. He said nothing, and he didn't have to, because now that the Seal was gone, Raegan understood the way of things.

"We must go," she murmured.

"You are exhausted," the King said, turning to look at her appraisingly—not a romantic partner trying to see what their lover needed, but a commander deciding if his warrior was up for battle. "The Protectorate's alarms will sound the moment we walk through Baba Yaga's door. No matter how well I glamour us, the twisted black pine has too much magic behind it."

She closed her eyes, tipping her head back, reminding herself to breathe. She knew she would be a hindrance if anything went wrong. "And that does not even account for Fate," Raegan mumbled. "If She is still angry."

The primordial winged being had not entered Baba Yaga's realm, though She certainly could have if She'd wished it. Oberon tensed at her question, the movement barely visible under the dark wing of dusk outside the bathhouse. A wolf howled in the distance, and Raegan saw the skulls on Baba Yaga's fence begin to glow.

"Fate's fury is often a brief flash," the King replied. "Do not misunderstand me, She will find a way to make us both pay for what you said. But not with physical violence. That is entirely too mundane for Her."

As he spoke, Raegan knew what he said was true in the same way she knew she had two feet and the sun rose in the east. Was her entire recurring, rebirthing existence not some exquisite torture for the way she had dared to defy Fate all those years ago by creating a shield for the changeling when there was only meant to be a sword for the king of men?

"Regardless," the King said, breaking Raegan's thoughts, "the Oracle is not asking for our presence. She is demanding it. A bee maiden's appearance is a summoning, and no doubt it is about the Prophecy."

Prophecies, Raegan understood now, were fickle things—not promises, not assurances, nothing at all but a place where the Threads shimmered, and Fate deemed something important enough to turn Her eye toward it.

"But Oracles are essentially Fate's high priestesses," Raegan said, turning to the King. "Will she want to help us? *Could* she even help? Or is this just another one of Fate's machinations?"

He smiled that low, dangerous smile, the expression of a dark and slippery thing that had survived for a millennium. "Octavia," the King began, reaching forward to open the bathhouse door for Raegan, "has her own plans. And more importantly, she owes me a debt."

She stepped into the bathhouse, not able to contain a smirk. *Of course* the Oracle, the Seer of All Threads, one of the most powerful beings on this side of the Gates—perhaps even both sides—owed the Unseelie King a debt.

Behind her, Oberon began to pack up the few articles of his clothing that had migrated outside of his bag. Raegan supposed this meant they were leaving imminently and began to do the same. Less than ten minutes later, she stood with the King at the edges of Baba Yaga's thorny green realm, the bathhouse and the chicken-legged hut already moving into memory.

"Your work is deeply appreciated," Oberon was saying to Baba Yaga, his tone regal and kingly. "If the Gates fall, it will in many ways be thanks to you."

Baba Yaga stood with her hands on her hips and sniffed at his words.

"The Unseelie Court owes you a debt," the King added, only a little begrudgingly. At that, the witch grinned, pleased. The sight of her smile tugged at Raegan's heart, and she pulled the taller woman into her arms, breathing in her mugwort and smoked-bone scent.

"Try to stop dying all the time, my dear," Baba Yaga said, squeezing Raegan hard for a moment. "You know where to find me if you need me."

"When this is over," Raegan found herself saying, "I'll need you to help untangle the rest of me."

"I know," Baba Yaga said softly, stepping back from Raegan, one hand still on her shoulder. "The twisted black pine will always allow you through." Her eyes snapped to the King, the hard beadiness returning. "Not you, unnatural thing," she added, pointing a thick, curved finger at the Fey being. "Only *born* creatures in my realm from henceforth. No made monstrosities."

"It is your realm," the King said, sweeping into an impossibly elegant bow. "I will respect your wishes as its creatrix."

Baba Yaga stared at the King for a moment longer before her gaze slid to Raegan. "I will admit he is very charming," the witch said. "For an abomination."

Raegan laughed and pulled Baba Yaga into another fierce hug. When she turned away from the witch, who was striding back to the hut, she found Oberon kneeling on the damp earth, speaking an unknown language to a small pond surrounded by mossy rocks.

Raegan listened for a moment longer and found she *did* know the language—or at least, someone she had once been did—and understood he was calling forth a kelpie. Before she had a moment to brace herself for seeing one of those murderous fish-horses again, something came through the puddle, breaking the surface with such force that it shattered water droplets everywhere.

Dark as the ocean and dripping wet, a kelpie now stood beside the pond. It was enormous, easily six and a half feet at the shoulder, its strong neck cresting up and away. It was much, *much* larger than Raegan would have thought from her previous encounters. It was shaped like a horse, more or less, but gills gaped on its stomach and scales adorned its hindquarters. Its mane and tail were more like seaweed than hair, and its skin was shiny—slick and ridged.

When it turned, its dark eyes met hers briefly, and she realized who it was. "Rainer," Raegan said, her heart beginning to thud harder.

"Hello again," the kelpie replied.

"You know he was killing innocent people, right?" Raegan demanded of Oberon, who shot a glance at the kelpie.

"I already told you. It is in my nature," the kelpie said, swinging his massive head away. "Besides, you banished me from your city."

The King looked at Raegan, one dark eyebrow arched, then his gaze slid back to Rainer.

"A human with no training and a Seal on her memory banished the Scourge of the Isles?" the King wanted to know, appearing to be doing his best to suppress a smile.

"She knew the words well enough," Rainer grumbled. He shook his head and neck, much like a dog trying to remove water from its coat.

"I can understand your position," the King said after a beat of silence, looking toward Raegan. "But Rainer taking us through the Rivers is the only way we might escape detection and avoid starting yet another battle when we are trying to win the war."

An older understanding unfolded in the pit of Raegan's stomach as she stood in the kelpie's presence. She didn't like it. It was telling her that even the Rivers were constricted by humanity's encroachment, and there were so few places to be a kelpie these days. Rainer had to hunt. His instincts told him to survive, no matter the cost. A kelpie was ruled by water and shadow and not much else.

"It is in his nature," Raegan said with a sigh, pulling her leather jacket closed across her chest. "But don't kelpies usually murder you if you try to ride them?"

"Yes," Rainer answered. "But you are with the King. The King is my friend." Then the kelpie swung his head back around again and examined her. "You, too, are my friend, Lady Or'Afron. Do you not remember? I thought this time you would remember me, though of course, there are many times you do not."

Raegan looked at the kelpie, puzzled, searching through what felt like miles and miles of thread to find the right spool with the right life. And then she did, for a brief flash. Raegan was aboard the kelpie's broad back, one hand interlaced in his seaweed mane, the other brandishing a sword as they leapt from the sea directly into the thick of a battle on a driftwood-strewn shore.

"Oh," was all she said, looking at Rainer with fresh eyes.

The kelpie kneeled, all slow, elegant tides of movement, bringing his shoulders and back closer to the ground. She understood and strode toward Rainer but found that, though her mind recalled their shared past, her body did not have the muscle memory. What Raegan had intended to be a snappy, skilled mounting of the kelpie was more a desperate scramble, aided by Oberon, who steadied her and then pulled himself up behind her.

He wrapped one arm around Raegan's waist and placed his other hand on the kelpie's dark green shoulder. "Thank you, Rainer."

"Always, my King."

And then before she'd really had a moment to prepare, Rainer plunged forward, moving more like water across glass than a horse. Raegan thought it felt like freedom. She could not be sure how they were traveling—everything was a blur, and she couldn't tell if this was simply the forest or the Rivers. But the wind was in her hair, stinging her cheeks, and she told herself, just for a moment, to feel this temporary joy.

Before she knew it, Rainer had slowed, moving into a lofty trot. All around them, seaweed danced in long ribbons of dark green silk. Kelp forests billowed in the distance. The light came from above, filtered through the brackish waters into glimmering rays of blue-gold. Then the kelpie broke through the surface, and the otherworldly setting was gone.

Instead, Raegan sat astride Rainer beneath an overpass, graffiti climbing its walls. The ground beneath the kelpie's feet was strewn with Styrofoam bits and loose dirt. Somehow, though water dripped from Rainer's mane, she and Oberon were completely dry. Behind her, the King dismounted and then reached his hand up to assist her.

Wordlessly, Raegan climbed down and took in the large, muddy puddle a few feet behind Rainer's back hooves. It was barely an inch in depth, and yet it had opened a yawning mouth to the older, darker places.

"Thank you," the King said to the kelpie, inclining his head toward the ancient creature.

Rainer arched his thick neck, nostrils flaring. "You may repay me," the kelpie said, "by riding me into battle once more."

The King reached one hand out to Rainer's muscled neck, palm flat. The kelpie swung its head around, meeting the King's gaze. Raegan held still as the Unseelie King and the kelpie shared something that was not for her—something of bloodlust and inhumanity and a terrible ache.

"It would be my honor," the King murmured. Then he seemed to remember the world around him all at once. Turning to Raegan, he took a large, almost-running step in her direction. "We must go," Oberon said, catching her by the wrist and striding out of the overpass's shadows and into the low, glinting afternoon sunlight beyond.

As they emerged, Raegan looked back, but Rainer was gone. She held her free hand over her eyes as a shade from the sun, realizing she recognized the neighborhood. The Oracle's temple was nearby. The King moved quickly, sticking to shadows whenever possible. In only a few blocks, Raegan found herself standing on the same sidewalk in front of the same tucked-away strip mall shop that held unimaginable things.

Everything was different from when she had first seen the dusty windows filled with houseplants and winking glass ornaments. When she had originally walked through those doors, she'd known so little—of herself, of the world.

"Are you ready?" the King asked from beside her.

Raegan let out a long breath, her throat tight and choked-off. No, she was not ready. When she'd managed to retain herself after the removal of the Seal, she'd also retained the parts of herself that still ached for Fate's approval. A common thread in nearly all her lives, which Raegan knew was likely no coincidence. But she felt it all the same. In truth, she did not know what she might do if she was no longer chosen and all of this had been for nothing.

"A Prophecy," the King reminded her, "is a fickle thing."

"I know," she murmured. "But there is a part of me that still needs it to be real. That needs all of this to have been for something. For Fate to have had some far-reaching plan, some Thread She had been following all of this time."

Beside her, Oberon said nothing, and Raegan felt that silence like a stone in her stomach. So she set her jaw and reached for the door.

CHAPTER SIXTY

Inside, there was white marble and blue velvet and lush fruits in the abalone shell bowl and the smell of spring rain and far-off thunderstorms and fresh flowers. The long counter still stretched in a soft curve. It distressed Raegan how everything could change with no material reflection to mark the passage—not when she looked in the mirror and not when she moved about the world. It had been the same when her father disappeared. She remembered wondering how the sun could still rise in the same place when nothing was as it had ever been before.

"My liege and my lady," came the Keeper's smooth voice. He appeared at the counter, dressed in a crisp navy-blue suit, his glasses a brown horn-rimmed pair to complement the fabric. "I see you received the Thriae's call."

"We did," Oberon replied, leading the way across the expansive marble floor.

The Keeper inclined his head. "I will inform the Oracle of your arrival," he said, his gaze darting to Raegan for a moment.

They took each other in, Raegan assessing why he had seemed so familiar in the first place, and the Keeper clearly looking for a sign that she was changed, altered, and remade by this Thread of Fate they all walked upon.

Apparently, he found it.

"Welcome back," the Keeper said to Raegan, the words weighted with meaning as they fell from his mouth. Then the tidy, besuited man disappeared behind a long length of velvet curtain into the hallways that Raegan knew snaked around the half-moon of a foyer. The ceiling still towered far above her, cloaked in the colors of a sunset, the constellations moving as she watched. But it all felt smaller, somehow. She had little time to think about it before the Keeper reappeared.

He stepped through the curtain, looking at Oberon and Raegan in turn. Then he cleared his throat. "I present to you the Oracle," the Keeper said, his voice grand, "the last of the original Pythia, anointed and ordained by Fate Herself."

A shape moved in the darkness of the hallway, and Raegan *felt* something, like a tidal wave or a great cloud passing over the sun. Then the Oracle appeared.

She was small, so much smaller than Raegan would have imagined. Her spine curved, one hand resting on a simple wooden cane. Her tiny frame was cloaked in billowing velvet, necklaces of gold and bone adorning her chest. The Oracle's skin was a deep umber, made all the richer by the color she wore: the blue that appeared to be common in this Temple, but deepened and darkened into a shade of blackberry. Her graying locs were gathered in a matching silk scarf.

The Oracle looked at Oberon, and then her eyes slid to Raegan. She moved out from behind the counter, coming to stand before the pair. Up close, the Oracle's features were softly wrinkled with age, making Raegan wonder exactly how impossibly ancient she must be. The immense power that the Oracle radiated almost made it difficult to breathe. She was eternal and absolute—qualities somehow made all the more terrifying by her small stature. Raegan was utterly transfixed. If she'd wanted to move, she was not sure she could've, not with the Oracle's gaze pinning her in place.

"I wish that my Apprentice had not offered you Fatespeak," the Oracle said, her voice melodic and velveted. "When we read Fate's prophecies, it calls Her attention, and then She strums Her fingers along our Threads to hear the sound of us."

Oberon said nothing, so Raegan did not, either. The Oracle reached into the depths of her velvet kaftan and retrieved something. Whatever it was, it was small and fragile, able to fit in her fist. The Oracle released a shuddering breath, her eyes squeezing shut for a moment. Then she opened her fingers.

Within her palm sat torn shreds of paper. For a moment, Raegan understood nothing at all, but then she peered closer and saw the crumpled thing was the Prophecy—the luna moth she had watched take to its paper wings and soar. And now here it was, broken, lifeless. Beside her, Oberon had gone entirely still.

"By going into the Vaults and retrieving the Prophecy, you accepted the path," the Oracle continued, her immense gaze falling upon the broken-winged moth. "You allowed Fate to put Her breath into your sails, to be a guiding wind beneath your wings. And then, from what I understand, you rebuked Her. So She took back what She had given you. Your Prophecy, your shimmering place among the Threads, the path you might've walked. Gone. Its wings are crushed."

The words slammed into Raegan's chest. Grief and fury and sorrow came crashing upon her shores. She felt as if wings had been ripped from her own back, crushed between great, powerful hands, and left hanging by tender shreds of flesh.

"I have exchanged my fair share of words with Aranrhod," the King said, breaking the thick silence that had settled across the foyer. "She has never crushed a Prophecy as punishment."

The Oracle's eyes slid to Oberon's, a knowing expression as sharp as a knife falling across her face. She tucked her hand and the forsaken Prophecy back into the billows of her velvet garment. In the distance, bells chimed, soft as silver water. The smell of lilacs and thunderstorms danced across Raegan's senses, but she felt as cold as the marble beneath her feet.

"You have never wanted what She offered you," the Oracle said, one thin eyebrow rising. "Like a misbehaving child, you were forced to continue accepting what you did not want. But this? You both wanted this. And so, She took it back."

Raegan was still herself, and because of that, anger had begun pounding louder than all her other emotions. She took a step toward the Oracle, her teeth grinding together. Though Raegan had at least a few inches on her, she felt much smaller than the velvet-cloaked being.

"Does She not want the Gates to fall?" Raegan demanded, hot

fury curling around her words. "What is the *point* of any of this? Can't She—can't *you*—see the Threads extending for thousands of years, eternities maybe, and yet there are these constant games? *Why?*"

She found her fists were clenched at her side by the time she finished speaking, nails biting into the flesh of her palms. The Oracle's expression grew darker and darker with each passing word until Raegan felt as though she was attempting to stare down the entire universe. But the Oracle said nothing.

"Go on, then!" Raegan snarled. "Go ahead and tell me Fate has plans that I'm too stupid to understand. Tell me I should trust in Her. That I'm a silly child who is too easily frustrated. Tell me. I dare you."

"I am not your enemy," the Oracle said, at the same time as Raegan heard the King say her name in a softly threatening tone. "And as such, you will not speak to me in this way."

"Oh, I'm so sorry for my *tone*," Raegan snapped, advancing another step on the Oracle. "I'll make *sure* to—"

Her words fell away because two things happened at once. The King's heavy grasp landed on her shoulder and pulled hard, and the Oracle began to levitate. Her velvet robes blew in an invisible wind, thrashing about as if a thunderstorm had appeared in the space of a heartbeat.

"Let us remind you that it is not *our* hands that string your Threads," the Oracle said, her words booming, coming in from all directions, hundreds of other voices joining in chorus. "Fate is a cruel and indifferent mistress. We Oracles—we Called Ones—are not Fate Herself. We see and we know and we advise. And if we are lucky, we get the chance to untangle and unloop. But we are not your enemy."

The Oracle, Raegan could see now, was vast and unbearable in her power. The small-statured woman before her was only one branch of a tree, one root of a plant—a piece of the Oracle visible to Raegan's eyes and understandable on this plane. Raegan cast her gaze at the floor, blood pounding thickly in her veins.

When the air seemed to loosen and the King's grip on her shoulder slackened, Raegan looked back up to find that the Oracle had returned to the ground, a small woman in a flowing velvet garment. But her dark, roving eyes still held the universe in them.

Raegan opened her mouth, but the King made a low sound of disapproval and the Oracle held up one weathered hand, silencing her.

"I do not deny the misery of your path," the Oracle said. "I know it well. You might remember that Oracles are called. We do not choose our fate, either. Instead, *She* chooses us as Her vessels, forces those of us with the gift of foresight to hold Her essence in our bones. I have no fondness for Her, but I certainly will not allow you to come into my Temple and treat me with disrespect, let alone as your enemy."

Silence hovered like a low-lying cloud as Raegan did her best to suffocate her still-smoldering anger.

"Please accept my apologies," the King said, his words uncharacteristically humble. "We had no right to treat you in this manner."

At that, the Oracle's eyes shot to the King, her face pinched. "I do not accept your apology because you have not transgressed," the Oracle said, looking the King up and down. "You have nothing to apologize for."

"I have brought a mortal with a recently Unsealed memory into your space," the King replied. Raegan turned to narrow her eyes at him. "Emotions are close to the surface and difficult to control in the days following a Seal's removal."

Anger coiled hot in Raegan's ribcage, fangs bared.

The Oracle's gaze fell on her, heavy and cool. "Do not infantilize your companion," the Oracle said to the King, her tone moving from righteous anger to flat annoyance. "After a thousand years walking this planet, fragmented as those years may have been, I would hope she has learned to master her emotions."

Raegan waited for the King to defend her. He did not. The fury inside of her threw its head back and hissed. She turned her attention back to the Oracle, feeling her face flush hotter and hotter. But then— something cold and swift, a slip of river water, rose up from a deeper, older place than the anger. It was icy and calculating, packed with all the force of rushing water. At its bottom, like a dragon curled asleep beneath an ancient waterway, was not anger or fury but *rage*. She relaxed her jaw and leaned into it, surprised by how easily the current took her.

"I apologize," Raegan said, meaning it. "I had no right to speak to you as I did. Truth be told, I am so, *so* angry that sometimes I forget who and what I'm actually angry at, and I take it out on whomever is in front of me at that moment."

She heard the King let out a small, low sigh at her shoulder.

The Oracle's face relaxed, the feeling of her gaze not as heavy as it had been before. "Anger is useful when we control it," she said. "But not when it controls us. Come. Sit."

The Oracle turned, moving toward the gorgeous sitting area that Raegan recalled from her previous visit. It simultaneously felt like no time and forever since she had last settled upon the emerald velvet couch and wondered how the world might part itself for her.

Oberon trailed after the Oracle, expecting Raegan to follow, so she did. The fury in her belly felt like someone had thrown a bucket of water over it—cold, indignant—wishing for more than anything to slink away and re-establish some dignity. Instead, she took a seat upon the couch, angling herself to face the Oracle, who had settled into a chair of magnificently twisted willow branches.

"Octavia," the King said, a question tilting his voice upwards as he lowered himself onto the couch beside Raegan. "I am always grateful for your counsel. But what is there to discuss if the Prophecy is broken?"

The Oracle perched on the edge of the willow chair, her hands folded on one knee. She considered both of them before speaking. "You were in possession of spellwork left to you by your father," she said, looking at Raegan. It was not a question. "Do you still maintain it?"

"Of course," Raegan breathed, her heart rate increasing.

"Fate has turned Her eye away from this Thread," the Oracle continued, voice lower now, a sacred sort of hush.

Beside her, Raegan heard Oberon take in a small, sharp breath. "What would you have us do, Oracle of Delphi?" the King breathed, his tone taking on the same reverent stillness.

The Oracle looked down at her hands, as if recalling the sight of the broken-winged Prophecy in her palms—hopeless and crushed, abandoned by the very force that breathed life into it.

"Do the spellcraft anyway," the Oracle said as she looked up, her features now a mask of long-simmering defiance. "Make your own fate."

Chapter Sixty-One

The Oracle's words beat like a war drum inside of Raegan, awakening things sleeping in river muck and lost to bonfires long ago extinguished. All of these lives, all of these years, and so many of them had not meant anything at all because she'd always bent to Fate. The only lives where she had made a dent—Nyneve in the place called Camelot, and Titania during the Uprising in the Otherlands—were when she had spat in Fate's face and pulled her own fortune from the silt.

"Yeah," Raegan breathed. "Okay. I'm in. But how long will it take me to be able to complete such delicate, complicated spellwork? There is an . . . urgency here, isn't there?"

Despite knowing that these events have been in motion for thousands of years, she had the strangest feeling that time was running out. Perhaps because her own clock was always resetting too soon.

"There is an urgency indeed," the Oracle agreed. "There always is with you, Lady of the Rivers. Your blood runs as quickly as a storm-swollen stream. The Prophecy is lost. Follow the spellwork instead."

The formal address made Raegan's mind swim, conjuring images of low firelight and thatched roof cottages and an imposing gray stone citadel. Her vision blurred for a moment.

"Regardless of the Prophecy," the King said, his words pulling her back to the present, "Raegan is the only one who can follow the spell-craft. Her father is an anchor in the Timekeeper's realm, and only those sharing his blood or an oath can work the spell. And she is not ready." At those last words, spoken in a murmur, she felt the King's eyes land on her.

The Oracle sat back, her velvet caftan pooling around her. "Or are *you* not ready to risk losing her again?" she asked, her gaze heavy on the King. "Because you always will. That is the punishment. I had thought you were used to its sting."

Raegan turned to the King, who did not respond to the Oracle, though a muscle leapt in his jaw. "What punishment?" she asked, looking up at the Oracle.

"His creators made him on a day that was not a day, in a time that was outside of time, in a place that was not a place," the Oracle said, answering Raegan evenly and without hesitation. "He has no true name. Decisions such as these are transgressions against the forces that rule our universe. As such, his creators promised that he would assume the fate of the child he replaced to rebalance it all. And yet your bones do not rest on the plains of Camlann, do they, Unseelie King?"

Oberon held the Oracle's gaze and said nothing.

Then her dark, world-devouring eyes fell on Raegan. "Because *you* pulled a shield powerful enough to resist the Pendragon's blade for him from the old places in the river silt," the Oracle continued. "He lives forever and remembers. You die continuously and forget. A punishment that would have crushed the will and resiliency of anyone else, but you two are fools."

To Raegan's surprise, the Oracle's tone bordered on fondness when she called them fools. It did not stop the pain that embedded itself deep in her marrow at what the Oracle had just told them.

Her eyes slid to Oberon. Apparently, it was only a revelation for her, not the King.

He met her gaze. "Even when you remember other things," he began, quite composed for someone speaking of something so horrible, "you forget this part, the nature of what we are trapped in. That we exist within our very own ouroboros, doomed to keep repeating it."

Raegan's mouth was dry, and her throat smarted. Her chest felt hollow, as if something had reached its hands inside and scooped out anything red and alive. Swallowing hard, she fought to put this knowledge into a box that she could bury deep down somewhere. She had no more room for more sorrow, for more ache.

"If it is any consolation regarding the Prophecy," the Oracle said, her words sounding ten miles away, "the 'of thirteen' does not refer to your birthdate, but your age. The Threads *might* have still held the weight of this path, but you were supposed to start this Prophecy when you were thirteen, Raegan. Not now. These nuances are why only anointed Oracles offer Fatespeak."

Another blow to her chest, right where she was already tender, where there were gaps in her armor. "That makes me feel worse, actually," Raegan murmured without thinking.

No one comforted her. The conversation continued as if Raegan had not just discovered that she was not only useless but also an active obstruction. No wonder the King had treated her with such disdain and cruelty at first. Raegan's gaze drifted to him. Would he revert to it now that she could offer him nothing? Was this the most magical her life would ever be, held aloft by a now-abandoned Prophecy? Was everything downhill and mundane and ordinary from here on out?

"I need a minute," Raegan mumbled, getting to her feet and staggering for the door. Thankfully, the Keeper was not at the counter, and she ran across the glimmering marble floors, pushing out through the doors and into the cool autumn evening. Petrichor and fried rice met her nose. The flashing neon light of the pawn shop next door reflected off a puddle in the parking lot. She leaned against the building's wall and buried her head in her hands.

All of her grief and anger and ache was not some pull to a greater destiny or a Fate-touched path. It was meaningless. A punishment she would possibly repeat until the sun exploded and the entire universe was snuffed out. And despite all of it, Raegan knew that deep down, part of her still craved Fate. The remnants of that Fatesong—golden, looping, the most beautiful sound she had ever heard—still rang out in her chest alongside the pain, and she hungered for its splendor. When she had pulled the paper-winged Prophecy from the depths of the Temple's Vaults, it had all felt so clear and lucid. Everything was for a reason, and it had been such an overwhelming *relief*.

She would likely never hear a Fatesong again.

"Raegan." Her name came from beside her, though she had heard no approach. The King drifted across her vision, leaning against the Temple's wall beside her. "The ward only extends till the end of the walkway," he murmured, as if that were the reason he had followed her. She felt the warmth and weight of his arm meet her shoulder, and it broke the levy.

"I'm sorry, Mordred," Raegan sputtered at the King, barely holding back tears. "You bet on a losing dog. I can't offer you anything but more pain."

The King only watched her, eyes hooded by shadow. Raegan dragged the back of her hand across her face, roughly shoving away the tears. A sob caught in her throat, and her cheeks burned with shame.

"You made a mistake," she said, hot tears streaming freely down her face as she drew in ragged grasps. "I'm not what you thought I was."

The King turned to face her, closing her in against the wall. She felt his long, cool fingers on her jaw, a gentle request to lift her chin and look at him.

"I was not sent to Camelot all those years ago to fall in love with a mortal," the King murmured, his dark eyes locked onto hers. "I jeopardized everything for you. I was prepared to betray everyone for you. You woke something within me I did not understand, nor could I bear to extinguish it."

Raegan's entire body braced for impact, though she knew it would come only in words—but those words would cut deeper than any dagger. Refusing to shut her eyes even though every fiber of her being begged for the release, she held the King's gaze.

"When you learned of the Fate I had stepped into, the Prophecy I inherited," he continued, "nothing could dampen your rage. You fought with everything you had to change the ending. And you *did*."

Her mind raced. She knew this already—she did not understand why the King was saying any of it again. Anxiety twisted in her chest.

"We have both, in some ways, accepted an ending," he said, leaning down closer to her. "Magic will die. My people will fade. You will amount to nothing with the Prophecy gone. Both of us will remain trapped in this cycle of grief."

His words lay like broken glass at her feet, and she did not think she could avoid cutting herself upon their edges.

"Instead of your sorrow," the King continued, his gaze boring into hers, "no matter how righteous it may be, I want something else from you. I want your rage."

Woodsmoke and damp stone and wild rain flooded her senses. His hand found hers, and she slid her fingers into his, gripping as hard as a drowning man would a buoy. Raegan took in a long, dangerous breath, pushing aside that artificial longing for Fate, reaching past her sadness and then her anger and then her grief.

Beneath the churning torment that thrashed within her like an inferno, she found the still, placid waters of a river. The current there swept away everything in its path with calculating and nearly endless power. A river provided life, and a river offered death. One in each hand. Always just below a surface that belied the intensity beneath. Cold, surging, unimaginable power.

Raegan dipped her hand into the water. It sang to her, sweeter than she could possibly imagine, a deliciously dark symphony that filled her lungs and fortified her body. A song of the dark, rushing places, where all light is swept away. She tipped her head back and let the cold water and the river's song devour her whole—or perhaps, she devoured the river. Their edges ran together, lapping at the other's shores, because rivers gave life. And sometimes, they took it back.

Raegan opened her eyes to find the King still holding his vigil, their fingers intertwined, his forehead resting against hers. Her tears had dried. Her skin was finally cool, her face no longer flushed.

Something that was not her heart beat inside her chest, a flutter of paper wings that should have been dust in Fate's fist. And yet . . .

The King pulled back and gazed at her, eyes searching and then finding. "What are you going to do, Lady of the Rivers?"

Raegan drew herself up, pushing off the wall to stand straight, looking up at the King of the Unseelie Fey. "I'm going to change the ending."

Chapter Sixty-Two

Back inside the Temple, the Oracle and the Keeper gazed down at the spellcraft Raegan had laid out on the coffee table in the seating area. Oberon stood off to the side, his arms crossed. Raegan watched the Oracle and the Keeper circle the spellwork like sharks, taking in every detail. The Keeper's small mouth moved ever so slightly all the while, as if he were speaking to himself. He kept readjusting his circular, horn-rimmed glasses, and Raegan wondered what enchantments they offered.

Finally, the Oracle reached the large parchment with the illustration of the Gates, lines extending from multiple sections as if intersecting the structure. Then she let out a low whistle.

"I mean no offense," the Keeper said, standing up straight, folding his arms behind his back, "but your mortal, Protectorate-oathed father did not create this."

Raegan shrugged, taking a step toward the coffee table. "I'm not saying he did," she replied. "And for what it's worth, with my Seal removed, I find that nearly impossible to believe, as well."

"It is . . . old," the Oracle said, prowling around the coffee table again, her movement a three-beat gait with her cane. "But it is also new. Your father simply . . . possessed this?"

"I'm sure there's a story," Raegan said, the idea of her father's tales tugging at a tender spot inside of her. "But I don't know it. I think the Timekeeper, or someone working with the Timekeeper, came after him for having it. Just before he came to the States. I've been assuming he was fleeing the Protectorate, but I think it's more complicated than that."

The Oracle nodded, peering closer at one of the spell sheets.

"And you want to perform this craft, my liege?" the Keeper asked, his gaze wide with concern as he looked at Oberon. Raegan's attention snapped to the King, confusion creasing her brow.

"Who else would do it, Anakletos?" the Oracle asked, looking at the Keeper like he was a foolish little boy. "No one on this side of the Gates is powerful enough. No one on this side is . . . unnatural enough."

"Was I not created for situations such as these?" the King asked, only his eyes moving, rising to meet the Keeper. "Andronica will continue to hold the wards. Kamau will command the knights. Raegan and I will follow the spellcraft."

"Wait," Raegan said, holding up a hand and taking a step forward. The zipper pull on the sleeve of her leather jacket clinked, metal against metal. "You said back at the archives that this spell is so different because of an anchor, secured by blood or an oath. How do you share either with my father?"

Silence cloaked the space, the sound of running water slipping into the peripheries of Raegan's hearing. For a long moment, no one made eye contact with her.

"The King and your father do indeed share an oath," the Oracle said finally, leaning on her cane.

Raegan stared at her, dumbfounded. None of it made any sense. She turned to look at the King, expecting some convoluted lecture on the fluid complexities of real magic. Instead, he held her gaze with his ocean eyes. And in that split second she understood, and it threatened to crack her down the middle.

"Love," the King told her, his voice raw, like it was only the two of them in that vast marble room, "is as good an oath as any."

Emotions crashed heavily in Raegan's chest. He smiled at her—how could a smile be so sad, she wondered—and then turned back to the spellcraft laid out on the coffee table. She wanted to jump into his arms or maybe grab him by the hand and leave this place, make a life somewhere quiet and safe. Maybe all they needed—wanted—was each other.

But the Keeper began to speak of further preparations and Raegan remembered that her father and all of magic hung in the balance, and the Fair Folk were on the brink of extinction. She bit down on her tongue and looked at the Oracle, who was shaking her head at the Keeper's words. The paper-winged thing beat harder under Raegan's breastbone. If they were going to do this, it had to be now.

"Keeper," the Oracle finally said, her voice taking on that booming quality. "Any more talk, and you risk Her attention. Let it be done."

Pale beneath his bronze skin, the Keeper exhaled heavily and nodded. He took a few steps toward the back archway to lead Raegan and the King to the ceremony room that the Oracle thought would be the safest place to attempt the spell.

Which was how Raegan came to stand on the edge of a ritual circle's outer ring. The loops were marked with glyphs and symbols that made her brain buzz when she looked at them. Some she could recall, but others remained mysteries, even if she could draw up an impression of what they might do.

The room stood empty save for the circle, Raegan, a small chest of materials, and the King. No Fatesong trilled. None ever would. They made their own destiny now, and the only sound Raegan heard was the pounding of her blood and the whispers of doubt.

She watched the King pace the outer ring, stopping to make adjustments, sometimes in ink, sometimes in blood. Her father's spellwork was laid out on the floor a few feet from the circle, allowing Oberon to reference it as and when he needed.

Breathe. That's what Oberon told her to do while he prepared. Just breathe. A simple enough suggestion, but Raegan was having a very hard time. All of her choices, all the horrible things she knew, wrapped their hands around her throat and squeezed.

She looked around the blank room. High ceiling, marble floor, no windows. The door had essentially disappeared when she had closed it behind her. If she tried, she could perhaps pick out its seam along the wall, somewhere. It didn't matter, though. The room was warded to hell and back. They could only leave if they chose at the last minute to not attempt the spell at all, or if they managed to make it back from wherever it took them. The moment they opened the pathway to wherever the spellwork led, they would have no choice but to go forward.

In a few more days, the eighteenth anniversary of her father's disappearance would go by. And here Raegan was, disappearing herself. But what else could she do? Tell her mother that she was following in her father's footsteps? That she was doing what she needed to do, and to not be sad? To understand that some people are just not meant to be loved and held closely but to disappear into the sky?

There was nothing she could say to her mother or to Henry or to Saanvi or to anybody else that would make them understand. She shoved the heels of her palms into her eyes, trying to suffocate the feelings. When she pulled them away and her vision cleared, Raegan saw Oberon had finished working on the inner ring. She recognized the design immediately. It was depicted on the first sheet of her father's spellwork—she'd laid eyes on it in the bank only a few miles away. It could have been a different life, another timeline, for all she knew. It felt so very distant.

"Are you ready, Nyneve?" the King's voice landed on her like a heavy cloak, devouring her frame in black velvet as he spoke her name from that first life that had changed everything.

Raegan let out a shaky breath. "Honestly," she replied, looking up at him, "no."

Oberon moved toward her, skirting the ritual circle at the center of the room. "It feels almost . . . wrong, does it not?" he asked, tilting his head. "As if Fate is pushing us back onto our correct paths, restringing the Threads to conceal that the Prophecy ever existed."

She looked him up and down. There was no trace of the young knight she remembered loving. Only the Unseelie King stood before her —wolf-like, ravenous, deadly. She had little doubt of what he was focused on: sinking his teeth into Fate and reclaiming his Throne, regardless of the tender oath that made it possible for him to work this magic.

"Hey," Raegan said, reaching out to touch Oberon's arm, bringing his gaze to hers. "If I don't come back from this, it's fine. And maybe, unless you need me for some compelling reason, you should ignore me when I come back. Maybe you don't need all this sorrow. All this ache. Maybe you should find some other people and enjoy your immortality."

The King did not hesitate as he slid one hand along her jaw and up into her hair, his palm pressed flat against her cheek. "I have known many others in the years I have walked this earth," he told her, his gaze a dark inferno, "and yet I have tasted nothing as sweet as the sorrow you bring me, nothing as sacred as your faithless love."

Raegan flinched at his words, though she knew them to be true. He did not speak them with anger or judgment but as simple fact. She left him, always. But she always came back, too.

"You should know," Raegan began, the worlds trembling on her tongue, "that I really do lov—"

"Please," the King whispered, his fingertips passing over her lips. She had known him for so many years, long enough to know that the rough tone in his voice was the closest he ever came to begging. "Please do not say you love me."

Raegan met his eyes, hurt surely spilling over in her expression.

But then he brought his forehead to hers, his hand sliding around to cradle the back of her head. "If you do," the King said, his breath ghosting across her skin, "I think you will break me."

The penned sorrow climbed out of Raegan's chest, and she squeezed her eyes shut. She had cried enough. She had shed enough tears over the things she could not stop, and the people she could not save, and the Fateblessings she did not receive, and the Fatesong that she could no longer hear.

Enough.

"Fine," Raegan murmured against his lips. "To destiny, then."

"Let us make our own fate," the King replied, the steadiness of his tone strengthening Raegan. One last desperate hope. Fragile as a moth in a hurricane.

Then he kissed her in a way that took her breath away—pulling her whole body into his, as if he could slip her beneath his skin and keep her safe, like a secret. Raegan met him with the same red-hot hunger she always did, digging her fingers into his chest because if Fate was going to drag her down into the soil again, at least she would leave a mark. At least someone would know she had been here at all.

They broke apart. Raegan tried to smother the growing tenderness inside her with that cool, calm rage. But the King's mouth on hers after all these years of wanting him, of chasing shadows, of waking up with a name she did not know on her lips, turned her ache exquisite and all-encompassing.

"Maybe," the King breathed, forehead against hers, "in the next life . . ."

He did not need to say more. Raegan nodded, blinking back tears, and reached out her hand. The King placed his palm into hers, and with a soft flex of his other hand, he set the candles ablaze. They exploded into light and fire, starting with the largest candle directly in front of where they stood, moving clockwise until each flame crackled to life. The ancient smell of beeswax filled the room. Outside, the sun might have been rising.

All in all, the scene would almost have been beautiful were it not for the thousand years of pain and sorrow and strife that had led to this moment, this Thread, this slip in Time.

The King led her into the circle, both of them coming to stand in the middle. And then he did not hesitate. He began the rite. As he did, Raegan felt a hum that shook her entire being, threatening to dislodge the very marrow from her bones, sinking deep into her essence with barbed, hooked claws. It was *in* her, all around her, breathing in her ear and shouting in the distance, threatening to swallow her whole.

It was magic, she realized. *Real* magic. Not the small explosions she had mustered, or even the workings of Baba Yaga, and certainly not the battle magic of the Protectorate. This was something else. It was pure and dark and strange, pulled down from the sky as if this reality were just a fabric to be unwoven and restitched into something else.

The magic poured out of a single source: the King. For the first time since the removal of her Seal, Raegan was aware of how steeped he was in the oldest of magics—darkness. For a moment, he was nothing more than slinking shadows.

Then a door opened with the same pop she often felt in her ears when a plane descended. She had no choice but to walk through it, just as she did anytime a door showed itself to her. The door called to her, low and primal and vibrating, and she reached for it in the only way she knew how.

A flicker, and then the ceremony room at the Temple was gone. Instead, she and the King stood in an old train station. It was empty, almost like no one had ever touched it at all. Dark wood paneling along the walls devoured the light. Black iron benches marked the stone floor in severe lines. Raegan could detect no sound, no smell, nothing at all but the cold rage in the pit of her stomach and the hammering fear in her veins. Even the light was strange—colorless, slanted, dust particles swimming through it.

"Where are we?" Raegan asked Oberon. Though she supposed part of her already knew, might have known since she'd first touched the spellcraft in the bank's safe deposit room.

"I do not know," the King replied. "Despite its relatively modern appearance, this place—or plane, perhaps—is old. It has been painted over many, many times."

"Then we go forward into destiny," Raegan said, noticing their hands were still entwined. She stepped forward, and the King followed.

At the other end of the train station was an archway. It had been obscured when they first entered by a large clock tower that speared the middle of the space. The hands of the clock moved, but it made no sound. Raegan and the King stepped past it, eyeing it warily. But it was the archway that commanded attention.

Beyond the archway was nothing but bright unadulterated light. It too was incorrect—all white, coming from no one direction but everywhere all at once. Raegan walked toward it like all roads had always led her here and she was just remembering now that there had never been another escape.

When she approached the threshold, the King barked a warning, but it was too late—hadn't it always been too late for them both, anyhow— and the moment that strange, white light fell on Raegan, she suddenly found herself on the opposite side. A train platform greeted her. Just a square of raised brick, really, with one track and another clock tower. This clock had no hands at all and no numbers, either. Out here, the light twisted sepia, and everything gleamed raw and rust-red in the low light.

Raegan turned back and saw the King in the archway, unable to pass through it. Her heart raced wildly at the sight of a barrier bursting into existence and gleaming like an ax before throwing the King back into the depths of the station.

He said something, but she couldn't hear him, so she just watched, trying to decide what to do. She supposed she had been an idiot to think the universe would allow them to face this together, but she had hoped. Raegan saw his temper flare—rare, she knew—and he threw shadows at the barrier. For a moment, the entire archway was filled with nothing but his darkness, all light suffocated by the loops of black silk. But the barrier held.

Fear spiked deep into her body. What place could this be that a ward held back *him?* Fear escalated to terror, sorrow souring her stomach, and Raegan started to make her way back to the King.

Maybe they each saw different things. Maybe this space could be anything to anyone. But Raegan did not think it was a coincidence that this in-between looked exactly like the train platform in her father's story. The story that had been ringing in her bones since he'd first told it. The story that had kept her up at night and asked her what it meant to be human, and what it might mean if there was nothing else.

And then something shifted in the distance, like pressure popping or maybe an air bubble breaking, and Raegan could see that, down the rail line, far down around a bend, a train was approaching. Her cold, ancient rage slipped its fist around her terror and wrung its neck.

She looked at Mordred, and he looked at her, and maybe he already knew.

The train, despite having been in the distance just moments ago, was already pulling into the station. It slowed, the sound of the screeching brakes the only thing that reached Raegan's ears.

The train shuddered to a stop right in front of her, its sides heaving like an exhausted animal. Again, Raegan looked at the King and then back at the train.

She would never know which way was right.

The door slid open. Gloom loomed beyond it—a dead kind of dimness where even Time curled up and devoured its own tail. The sound of a train whistle split the air.

"All aboard," Raegan murmured under her breath, eyeing the steep set of stairs that led onto the train and then to the place that her father might be.

She looked back at her King. He stood on the other side of the barrier, his darkness sheathed. She almost smiled at that. He had always seen her, even when it hurt. The King held her gaze, his jaw set, spine straight. Raegan just looked at him for a moment, cherishing the slope of his shoulders and the oceanic depths of his eyes.

But a river only flowed in one direction.

The train whistle sounded again, louder this time, insistent, and Raegan turned back to see the gears around the wheels begin to skitter like beetles. A moment later, the train shifted, like it was about to begin moving again.

She took another step toward the train. She looked back at the King.

"Outlive me," she said to him, hoping perhaps the universe would take pity on her just this once and ferry the words to his ears. "Outlive me. I love you too much."

And then Raegan stepped up to the train door, just as her father had, just as her father always had, through every story and every re-telling, in every chance he had ever been given before they all turned to ash. And then, despite herself, she hesitated.

It was just a small pause—

one,

two,

three.

Part Two
Beneath the Buried Sea

Book Two
of the
FATEBOUND
DUOLOGY

BENEATH THE
BURIED SEA

a novel by

VICTORIA MIER

CHAPTER ONE

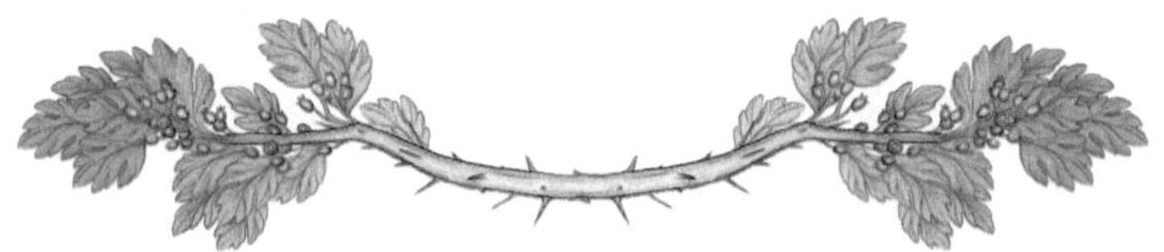

Inside the train car, gloom crouched in every corner. The air smelled of dust and steel and blood. Beyond the tracks, endless miles of vast and hopeless desert stretched out, barren and parched—a scene perfectly set for retribution.

Good. Because Raegan Maeve Overhill was finally going to get her revenge.

She set her jaw, gripping the handrail. The train began to move, scuttling beneath her like a scarab. For a heartbeat, she hesitated—if she looked back now, she might catch a glance of the King, trapped beyond the warded barrier that held him fast.

But it would've only broken her, so Raegan swallowed hard and prepared herself to continue forward instead. She'd clawed her way to the Timekeeper's realm through the ritual her father had left behind for her, but she'd been forced to abandon Oberon. And now she was alone in the mouth of a beast, unable to access the vast majority of her magic. Raegan gritted her teeth, steadying herself as the train rumbled forward. What the fuck had she *done?*

Doom settled onto her shoulders, an unwelcome weight, as panic surged poisonous in her stomach. Her fingers shook on the handrail. But going forward was the only way she might know the truth of her father's fate. The only way she might see the King again. Dry wind tugged at

Raegan's hair, the metal connection beneath her feet writhing as the iron beast crept along the tracks. There was one car to her right—the engine, it seemed. The rest of the dull silver train snaked off in the opposite direction.

Releasing a long, trembling breath, she glanced through the train car's windowed door to her left, finding nothing but rows of empty seats on the other side of the glass. She turned right, pressing her face close to the fogged-up window of the engine's door to peer inside. Also empty. Fear and fury slid hot down her throat, igniting something in her belly. Fuck Fate. Fuck the ouroboros. Fuck the Gates and the Prophecy and her destiny.

She was here to find her father. Magic had already waited hundreds of years. It could wait a few more if it meant she might know what had become of him, if she could finally silence that keening howl in her chest that kept her awake at odd hours. Besides, Raegan's father was the only reason she had gotten this far, thanks to his protective wardings and the spellcraft he had tucked away in that little safe deposit box. She owed it to him.

Raegan plunged into the empty carriage at her left. The door swung shut behind her, entombing her in the deathly quiet, sealing away the clang of machinery as the train picked up speed. She paused at the threshold of the car, wary as she scanned the space. Dread pressed in all around her, thick as a wool blanket on a summer's day. She forced herself to focus, to be sharp and sure like a folktale's heroine. Unease curled in her stomach as she noticed that the light refracted strangely inside the train, coming from the wrong places. No sun was visible through the windows. The car smelled of nothing at all. Rows of brown leather seats crouched beneath handsomely appointed black iron luggage racks.

Narrowing her eyes, Raegan searched the luggage racks but found nothing. All the seats were empty, too, though they bore the signs of past passengers: sagging leather and old ticket stubs, stains and scuffs.

The train car bucked suddenly, and Raegan reached desperately for a luggage rack. Her fingers just caught the edge of it and she steadied herself, though her hip banged roughly into a nearby seat. She ignored the damp clamminess that swept over her body, forcing herself forward. But something held her in place with a firm grip on her jacket. Confused and more terrified than she wanted to admit, she twisted at the waist, expecting to find the mocking smile of the Timekeeper, snatching at her like a kitten grabbed by the scruff of its neck.

Instead, the train car's passenger seat was somehow restraining her. The seat's leather looked utterly normal to her eyes, and yet it held her jacket fast, as though armed with a thousand barbs. She pulled again, her heart thudding noisily, blood beginning to pound in her veins. One more desperate yank, and then the leather released her with a sickly tear, leaving a gash in her jacket.

"What the fuck," she whispered, her voice hoarse. She'd almost grabbed the back of a seat instead of the luggage rack above her for balance—and what could've happened then? Fear swept through her, but a tide of fury beat it back. If she was going to die here, so be it. But she'd save her father first, and then she'd take this entire goddamn place down with her.

Continuing along the aisle, Raegan examined the seats more closely, her feet shoulder-width apart, both hands grappling either side of the luggage rack to keep herself steady. The indentations she'd considered normal looked alarming up close—more like bloated bellies of a beast recently sated, or perhaps one filled to the brim with a ferocious hunger. She ground her teeth, wishing with every shred of her being that the King walked this place beside her. It was all civilized on the outside— orderly platforms, polished rod iron, ticking clocks. Beneath the surface, though, lurked something ancient and predatory.

She picked up her pace, headed for the door to the next car, turning it over in her mind. Oberon had said the Timekeeper was likely behind much mortal folklore about the Devil figure. The god made deals, she suspected. Ten years of all the success you could want, but the rest of your natural life would be spent on this train as the very essence of the place feasted upon everything you were, on any time you had left.

Raegan forced a deep inhale, the exhale coming out as a huff. She'd reached the other end of the car without further incident. A sudden awareness of *something* prickled the back of her neck, and without turning, she fled through the door, across the connection and into the next car. She pulled the door shut behind her, breathing much harder than warranted, her heart running away in her chest. Dread yet again threatened to drown her.

Raegan slid her hand into her pocket, fingers closing around the bundle of meadowsweet from Blodeuwedd. That night at Gossamer felt a thousand miles away as she continued her unsteady trek into the train's belly. She pushed away the thoughts swirling in her head—that she was not equipped for whatever this place held, full of knowledge but no power. Or that, worst of all, she'd perish at the hands of the Timekeeper without even finding her father.

"Steady," she told herself, wishing the word had come from the King's lips instead of her own. But in her gut, she'd known the moment they'd stepped into the station, the brick raw red and gleaming in the low light, that this path was hers alone. Perhaps it always had been. Perhaps everything always led here. Perhaps she was little more than a snake devouring its own tail. She ached tenderly for the King all the same.

Raegan did her best to shut off her racing thoughts. Only her father mattered right now. Was he on this train, the Timekeeper devouring his years? An answer sang out from deep in her marrow, but it tasted sour in her mouth, so she pushed onward instead. She opened the door at the end of the train car, that prickling awareness on the back of her neck growing more intense, needlelike in its insistency.

Outside on the connection, she paused, gripping the handrail hard. An expressionless landscape flashed by her, something maybe like a desert but rendered in shades of gray. On either side of the train tracks, the earth bore jagged cracks, like the soil here had never known rain.

Raegan pushed through into the next car, expecting more dried-out leather with lumps and bloats. Instead, what awaited her stole the breath from her lungs. Horror gripped her stomach with a cold, iron hand. She blinked once, twice, three times, hoping the image before her would vanish.

It did not. People—*remnants* of people, stray limbs and bleached bones—filled the train. At the front of the car, one passenger was only the barest suggestion of a ribcage beneath the seat's smooth surface. Another was little more than the wet rasping of lungs trapped in scuffed leather. Raegan quelled the nausea climbing up her throat. How could she possibly free her dad from trappings such as these? She curled her hands into fists, fingernails biting into the flesh of her palm.

Forcing herself to continue walking down the aisle even though all she wanted to do was flee back into the King's arms, she examined each passenger for as long as she could bear it. The farther she walked, the more that remained of each person—sometimes a full limb or even a head, hair and glasses and moles still in place. By the end of the car, most seats held at least torsos, many clothed in what she thought might've been fashionable seventy years ago.

To find her father, Raegan would have to keep going, no matter how hard doom beat at her, no matter how much she wished she'd never left Oberon's side. Shame burned her face. What a fucking coward she was, and yet she had thought she was strong enough to face down a god.

With no other choice, Raegan let her rage carry her farther into the train, shouldering through door after door, moving carefully to avoid the hungry grasp of this place. She did not know for how long she walked— maybe a second or a moment or a century—that prey's sense of a nearby hunter growing louder and louder with each step. The sharp, searing inevitability of it all roiled in her stomach. She was going to die here. But first, she was going to tear the Timekeeper limb from limb. Either way, Raegan held little hope of seeing Oberon again. Not in this life.

Her eyes burning with tears, she pushed through into yet another car, biting off the urge to peer over her shoulder or hide beneath one of the seats. The door closed behind her with a sigh, the sounds of the train's rumblings falling away, leaving only the soft breaths of the passengers. She scanned the car, finding more modern clothing and intact people, though all of them looked straight ahead, blind to her presence.

Just as she steeled herself to push through another door, to bear the horror of the train's twisted and unnatural passengers, she caught sight of auburn curls. So much like hers. So much like her father's. Forgoing her handholds on the luggage racks, Raegan rushed forward, every beat of her heart heavy with poisonous, stupid hope.

"Dad?"

Chapter Two

Her breathing came in ragged gasps, her mind struggling to comprehend what she saw before her. In the back of the train car in that empty, horrible place sat her father. He wore the same clothes as on the day he'd disappeared: a brown blazer with a hunter-green pocket square, a cream crewneck sweater, and olive corduroy pants. His hazel eyes gazed straight ahead. In the indirect light, Raegan could see more wrinkles than she remembered lining his face, and the tight auburn curls were shot through with gray.

"Dad?" she repeated, her voice hoarse. Remembering the gash in her leather jacket, she shoved her hands in her pockets to stop herself from touching him. God, after all these years, she just wanted to touch him. She swallowed a sob, shoving tears away from her face. She needed to get closer if she wanted to save him. But the idea of actually doing it tore her in half; she was so happy to see him, and she was so devastated it had to be *here*, caught in a bargain with a cruel god.

Raegan forced herself into a crouch at her father's feet, bracing herself on the floor. His hands had melted halfway into the seat, she saw, and there was little way to determine where the back of his neck ended and brown leather began. He seemed smaller, sunken-in, like the Time-keeper had already taken anything good and only a husk remained.

Black spots danced across Raegan's vision, nausea blooming thick in her stomach. She squeezed her eyes shut, trying to regulate her breathing. When she forced herself to look at her father again, nothing had changed. "Dad?" she repeated, desperation unfolding in her tone this time, tears choking off the word. "Daddy?"

Despair wrapped hands around her throat, and she struggled to fill her lungs with enough oxygen. She'd need an entire *army* to save anyone trapped in this forsaken realm, and yet she'd walked in here alone, thinking she would be enough. Thinking she'd be some grand hero, her name sung by the bards for generations to come. But Raegan was so small. Just a half-mad, not-quite-mortal woman who had more rage than real power.

The train rumbled on, the light remained blank and strange, and the person in the seat before her did not move or react. Perhaps she was simply too late. After all, she'd been meant to undertake this path at thirteen years old—not nearly two decades later. Raegan bit into the side of her cheek, forcing herself to her feet.

The car jolted hard to the right, nearly sending her tumbling into her father. At the last possible moment, her leg about to brush the hungry leather of the seat, she caught herself. Her breath rattled in her chest as she wrapped her fingers tightly around the iron luggage racks above her head.

Once she'd somewhat slowed the galloping pace of her heart, Raegan turned to look at her father again. He was practically a corpse—grayish skin, unseeing gaze, a sick, garish imitation of the person she had loved so much. A sob tore at her throat, and she squeezed her eyes shut. All this time, he'd been *here*. Right here, at the end of the spellcraft he'd left for her. And she'd just let him waste away in this horrific realm of death and sun-blistered metal. Raegan didn't know if she could save him —if she could do anything other than curl up on the floor and sob for everything she'd lost, all the ways she'd failed.

In the deluge of her despair, she ached fiercely for the King. She clung to those last few days finally returned to his side, visiting Fey clubs and researching in the archives, traversing pocket realms and hidden doors—

She opened her eyes, her mind seizing on the memory of the way he opened a porticus: that brief touch somewhere in the air, like an acknowledgment and invocation at once. With a shaking exhale, she summoned up all the broken remnants of her power, hoping beyond hope that it would be enough. Her hand trembled as she reached out, careful not to touch her father's unnaturally hued skin. She clenched her jaw hard, tried to remember exactly who she was, and on an exhale, she brought her fingers a hair's breadth from her father's forehead.

Replicating the King's posture—the fore and middle fingers straightened, the thumb activated, the ring and pinky fingers bent downward—she sent everything she was into that single forward dip. Somewhere from within that vast and blank plane came a screech of metal on metal. The train car rattled and bucked, but Raegan held her ground, the muscles in her arms screaming, her heels dug into the floor.

And then her father opened his eyes. She reeled back, her knees almost giving out beneath her. For the first time in almost two decades, Raegan was looking her dad in the eyes. She was staring at one of the people she loved most in the world, returned from the grave by some strange twist of Fate, a flick of the snake's tail. A shriek or maybe a sob gathered in the pit of her stomach, all those years of grief and ache building like a hurricane.

"Raegan?" came a rasp from the lips of what had once been her father.

She stared at him, dumbfounded, her mouth moving to speak, but no sound came. Her throat caught on a thousand unsaid words, her body feeling like it may give out at any moment.

"Raegan?" he asked again, straining toward her, trapped by his own skin and whatever bargain he'd made. "Is that really you?"

She clenched her jaw and shoved down her feelings as best she possibly could, sealing shut the floodgates that penned all her ferocious, tender emotions inside her chest. If she didn't, she'd drown. "Is it really *you*, Dad?" Raegan asked, eyes searching his.

"Yes." He coughed, as if he had to clear dust from his lungs. Beneath the years of disuse, his voice was just as it had always been—mid-toned, soft around the edges, his accent lightened by years in the States. The sound of it made her want to weep for a century.

Then his face suddenly sharpened. "Oh, Raegan. You should never have come here."

Ice slid into her veins, and she shifted away. "You're the reason I'm here," she protested. "You *led* me here."

"How?" her father rasped, his eyes wild, straining against the places where his body was stitched to the leather of the train seat. "I never would've . . . I . . ." The words died in Cormac's throat, and his expression slackened, whatever she'd woken in him fading.

"Dad," Raegan said, loud as she dared. "Dad, I need to know what's going on."

His eyes tracked slowly to meet hers, and then his brow furrowed, as if he was struggling to place his own daughter. "Where are we, Rae-Rae?" he asked in reply, trying to pull himself out of the seat again, only to be held fast.

Hopelessness crashed onto Raegan's shores, and bile flooded her stomach. Every inch of her body was too hot, clammy with sweat, prickly with fear. Her mind raced, but no answers materialized, as if all her cleverness had evaporated in this dry, dead realm.

"Dad, I really need your help," she said, her voice breaking. She clasped her hands in front of her, hoping it would be enough to stop herself from reaching out to touch Cormac. All these years, she'd yearned to pull the pocket square from his jacket once more, to bury her face in the wool of his sweaters, rich with the scent of books and oakmoss and cedar. Here he was, *right* in front of her for the first time in decades, and yet more out of her reach than ever before. Bottomless sorrow threatened to swallow her whole.

Cormac was listless again, and the train car had taken on a deadly, eerie silence—the forest when a predator stalks, all the little soft things gone into burrows and shadowed places to avoid claw and fang. Raegan gritted her teeth. A cold current of rage swelled within her.

"I . . . I left the book and . . . the box," her father said suddenly in a choked voice, his eyes squeezed shut with the effort, "only . . . so y-you .. . would understand. Understand w-why . . . why I h-had to go. The letter, Raegan. If you . . . if you read the letter, why are you here?"

His gaze lifted to meet hers, and suddenly, she saw her father again —a shadow of the man she knew, yes, but still Cormac.

"What letter?" Raegan asked, though as the words left her mouth, she remembered the empty envelope affixed to the book she'd used to summon the kelpie.

"I m-made . . . the deal," Cormac rasped, "to keep you *out* of all this."

She opened her mouth to tell him that she was hopelessly entangled in it, had been for a thousand years, long before Fate had made him her father. Her head throbbed. She felt small and insignificant, a speck of dust to the primordial forces that used her and her dad like chess pieces.

Then, at the other end of the train car, the door swung open. Raegan snapped to attention, all her fear and misery forgotten as a man in a three-piece tweed suit appeared from the gloom. He was of average height, his eyes shadowed by the brim of an old-fashioned hat. If not for his choice of clothing, he was someone Raegan would've barely noticed on the street.

And, of course, if not for the way power emanated from him, pulsing like a million heartbeats, a thousand stolen lifetimes. Her gut twisted, doom raking its claws across her chest.

"Finally," the Timekeeper said, his voice the low, vibrating timbre of a grandfather clock. "The Deathless One comes to meet her fate."

CHAPTER THREE

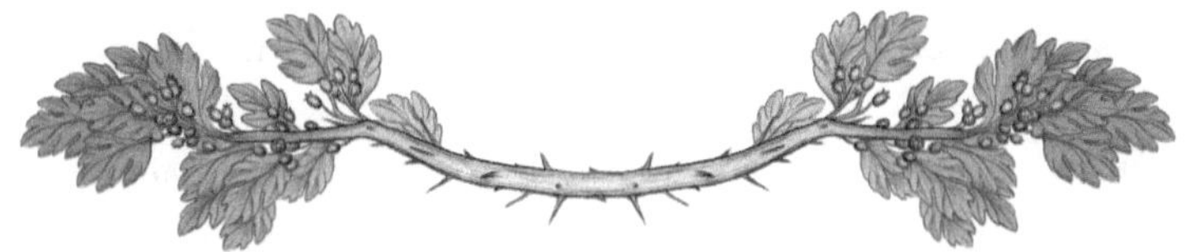

Fury flushed hot against her skin, and beneath its warmth, a cool tide of rage lapped onto her shores. She rose to her feet. "Fate," Raegan spat, "can go fuck Herself."

The Timekeeper laughed, the sound buzzing in the air around her. "Your father is too weak to give you the answers you desire. Shall I offer them instead?" He slunk closer, all his movements so utterly wrong, lacking a single shred of humanity. "If you are to rot here for all eternity, I want you to know *everything*. I want it to haunt you, all the things you could not stop, all the machinations you were too blind to see."

Raegan clenched her jaw, eyeing the average-looking man in the suit. She slid her hand into her pocket on some strange, half-remembered instinct, her fingers searching for the bundle of meadowsweet Blodeuwedd had given her at Gossamer. Horror gripped her spine when she found the lush, soft plant was little more than dust.

"Your father wanted you to shirk your birthright to the Protectorate," the Timekeeper continued when she said nothing, his eyes twin black holes beneath the brim of his hat. "He made a deal. Twelve years and a day with you and your mother, wardings to keep you unseen."

Raegan swallowed. So this, too, had been all her fault. Had she ever done anything but cause pain?

"And then he'd follow the working to wherever it led," the god said, clearly enjoying the way each word tore deeper and deeper into her. "He tried to warn you against following him and completing the spellcraft in full. A letter and a book and a key. And how easy it is to pluck a letter out of existence. Perhaps if he loved you more, he would have tried harder."

The world lurched. It wasn't the train this time, just Raegan, her knees threatening to buckle. "That spellcraft takes two," she said, the words barely audible, her rage drowning beneath the dust storm of despair. "So it was—"

"Oh yes, it was *you* I wanted," the Timekeeper said, prowling another step forward. None of his movements were right, almost like a large, powerful predator had stuffed itself into a suit and stood up on its hind legs. "Fate's little undying dog. All those years. All that *power*. And Fate was willing to trade you for just a little more magic to flow through my Gates."

Raegan stood up straight as an arrow, feeling like the god had driven a dagger right into her heart. *No.* That would mean—

"Enough for Her Seers and Her Oracles and whatever else She holds so dear," the Timekeeper continued. "So She paved the way to ensure you would play your part and the King would not stop you."

Nausea exploded in Raegan's gut, and it took everything in her not to double over and vomit. The entire Prophecy had been a lie. Fate had crafted it all to put a particularly difficult pawn where She wanted it. No one was at fault—not the Keeper nor Cordelia nor the Oracle. If Fate Herself spun a Prophecy, who in the universe would have the power to see it was false?

"What did you do to the King?" Raegan asked, because apparently the Timekeeper liked to talk and that might buy her a few moments. And maybe help her stop thinking about her father, a sickening heap of gray skin and crumbling bones in her peripheral vision.

In response to her question, the god waved a gloved hand in the air lazily, as if shooing away a fly. "Nothing," the Timekeeper replied, taking another slow step down the aisle toward her. "You're Godstouched and just mortal enough to get into my realm. But your Unseelie king? He's Goddess-blessed, which is another thing entirely, and not welcome here." He smiled then, all teeth, no warmth. "I can make this easy, soft, gentle. You can even sit next to your father. I know how much you've missed him."

Raegan's anger took her two furious, lightning-quick steps forward before the river of ice deep within slowed her pace. She steadied herself, fists clenched at her sides. The Timekeeper was assessing her every second; he had to know her Seal had been removed. But what he couldn't know was how much of her power she had gotten back. Raegan would not give him anything to use against her. With all her might, she tried to dip her hand into that cold current and summon what she had back in the café with Maelona.

"Dad," Raegan said, though she didn't—couldn't—take her eyes off the Timekeeper, "I love you and I'll see you again. I promise." It was all she could get out. Because she couldn't save him. She had known that the moment she'd seen him sutured to that train seat by the bargain he'd kept. All for her. He'd done it all for her.

And now, for nothing at all.

The Timekeeper smirked, taking another step forward, drawing parallel with the seat Cormac occupied. "Enough. Have a seat." His spindly fingers, hidden beneath the dark brown leather of his gloves, suddenly clasped her father's shoulder. "He does not have much time left, after all. I've nearly had my fill."

Fear ate at Raegan. Not for herself, but for her father. She didn't know how to get both of them out of this alive. Her heart pounded hard in her chest, anxiety sparking like a flare. The river did not answer her call, unable to reach into this world of death and slow, agonizing decay.

"Sit," the Timekeeper said, more forceful now. "Or I'll take everything he has left."

Raegan's heart froze in her chest. Her mind failed her; she could see the validity of the Timekeeper's threat, the way the ancient thing in a three-piece suit had devoured so many of Cormac's years. That old darkness sang a hymn inside her chest. She'd found her father. Perhaps her quest was complete. Oblivion had always called to her so sweetly, and there was no use denying it—she was, after all, very tired.

"*Cariad*," Cormac wheezed, shattering death's thrall. "I'm sorry. I love you. Run. *Live*."

And still her body did nothing, a deer in the headlights. She'd either spend the rest of eternity hating herself for not saving her father, or she'd die utterly in vain at the hands of a primordial power she detested. It was no choice at all.

As if sensing her thoughts, the Timekeeper laughed. His attention sliced at her skin, a shard of broken glass. "Time's up."

The hand resting on Cormac's shoulder flexed, the fingers spider-like, and then Raegan watched as her father disintegrated. It happened so quickly that for a fleeting moment, she thought—foolishly, hopefully—that it was only a cruel illusion. She stared, helpless and useless, as her father simply fell apart as if he were only made of fresh, powdery snow. Dust particles drifted through the train car like funeral ash.

Raegan choked back the horror that reared in her chest. She'd come so far just for her father to die before her eyes. And he *had*, she knew— the fierce warmth beneath her breastbone that had insisted for all these years he was still alive blinked out, a dead star in a cold, uncaring universe. She looked at the Timekeeper to find his gaze already on her. She screamed.

And then he pounced, moving like the hands of a clock spinning with no care for the rules of its making. In a heartbeat, or less than one, or maybe in an interval so quick it could not be measured at all, he loomed over her. Beneath the brim of his hat, his eyes were bottomless pits—devourers of light, the harvester come reaping.

She clawed at him, eager for revenge, not caring if she didn't live to celebrate it, but the primordial monster slipped out of her hands like smoke. With another snarl, Raegan lunged for him, and the Timekeeper let out a cruel bark of laughter, tripping her. She barely caught her balance, stumbling back a few steps. He was playing with her—had been doing so from the second she walked into this place, and probably long before that, too. If she was going to die, Raegan refused to give him any further satisfaction.

She held her ground as he prowled closer, hot tears of rage spilling down her cheeks. Her fingers closed around the meadowsweet dust in her pocket. With no time to think, she yanked her hand free, held her palm flat before her lips, and blew the dust into the Timekeeper's face.

She expected only a momentary distraction, but instead, the thing in the tweed suit howled, reeling back from her. The train bucked and bristled, screws rattling and metal scraping. The luggage racks shook, one detaching from the wall, landing on the leather seat beneath with a heavy, crushing thud.

"*Run. Live,*" her father had pleaded before he turned to dust before her eyes. Raegan saw no other choice. The promise of revenge burned hot and bright as she turned and took off down the aisle. At the end of the train car, the door flapped madly on its hinges. She caught the handle, throwing herself through the doorway. Outside on the connection, the train seemed to be moving faster, gearing up for another strike. Desperate, she looked to either side, finding only gray, cracked earth. But she could not stay here. She could not share her father's fate, even though part of her wished for it, yearned for oblivion.

Raegan gritted her teeth and wrapped her arms around herself. Then she took a running step toward the edge of the connection platform and threw herself into the air. Dusty ground rushed at her, but she cared little whether it crushed all her bones and split her skin open. As long as it was not those empty, world-devouring eyes of the Timekeeper that took her. That was all that mattered. Perhaps in whatever life came next, she would get to see Oberon again. If that were true, then death could come as quickly as it wanted—as long as it ferried her back to the King.

A hard impact to her left arm, then a sickly roll: gray earth, blank sky, gray earth, blank sky, over and over again. Dirt filled her mouth, and she smelled blood—hers this time, she thought. And then Raegan realized she could only see the expressionless sky. She was still breathing. Her left ribs stung, and the right knee of her pants was torn open, exposing skinned flesh. She raised two shaking hands, finding both heels of her palms bloody and raw. Touching a few fingers to her face, she discovered a gash across one eyebrow.

But Raegan was alive. With a shuddering groan, she pulled herself up to a kneeling position. The fabric of her pants scraped against her skinned knee, and she cried out, trying to bite off the sound at the last moment. Hot, stinging tears rolled down her face.

She wrapped her arms around herself, tucking her chin to her chest. She needed to move, to find a way out. Otherwise everything had been for nothing and she would never see Oberon again or drink cocktails at Gossamer or sit by the fire with Baba Yaga or tell her mom she was sorry.

But despair closed in all the same, a tidal wave of dim gray, and she began to weep. Her father was *gone*, just like that, after so many years of searching. Sobs gripped her shoulders and crushed her ribs. Her throat ached and her lungs cried out for air, but she couldn't stop. The tears were as relentless as that river inside her, swollen with stormwaters. She fed the dry, cracked earth her sorrow, unable to move or think or do anything but cry out for everything that she had lost, and all that she thought she still might lose at the hands of a hungry god and foolish men.

Raegan managed a deep breath, though her lungs hitched and tears still stung the tender flesh of her face. She sat back on her heels, raising her head to look around. The realm had not changed. The tracks lay to her left, the steel spine of a monster fading into the gray horizon. The train was nowhere in sight, though she had little doubt the Timekeeper would come to collect her when he had recovered and she had exhausted herself attempting to find a way out.

Hopelessness crooked a wing over her shoulder, and Raegan hung her head. But then, before her, just a few inches past her skinned knees, she noticed a shimmering pool. It was small—only about two feet in diameter and so shallow she could see the scarred earth beneath. Her tears, she realized. She shoved the despair aside. How many times had she read that the tears of a phoenix held magical properties? And was she not a phoenix of some sort—constantly rising from her own grave?

Tentatively, Raegan reached out a hand and skimmed the top of the puddle. The water was cool, nothing like the feverish tears she had shed. Planting her palms on either side of it, she peered over the edge. There, she found her face reflected—auburn curls hanging down like a curtain on either side, the hazel eyes and freckles and cheekbones, the soft, square shape of her features she'd detested so much as a teen.

She gazed into her own eyes, breathing raggedly. In a rush, she remembered the King holding her gaze outside the Oracle's Temple, his body so close, the heat and intensity and darkness of him surrounding her.

"What are you going to do, Lady of the Rivers?" he'd asked.

Raegan looked at her reflection, settling her shoulders into a firm line.

"I'm going to kill a fucking god."

Chapter Four

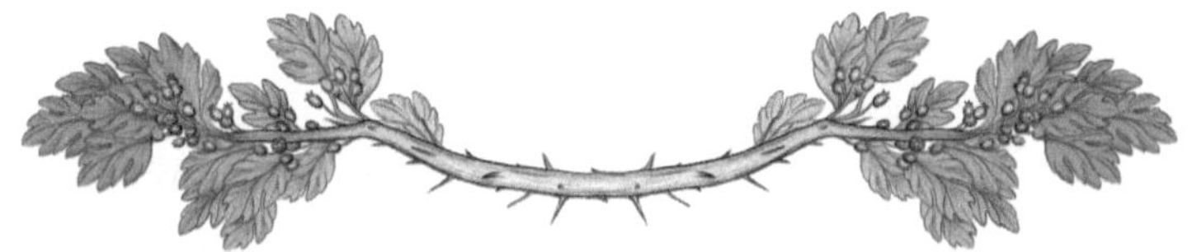

The words tasted like a promise on her tongue, all hellfire and retribution. She pulled herself to her feet, stumbling on unsteady limbs. With her Seal peeled back, she remembered enough of the way of things to know that she'd have to walk through this door without a single shred of disbelief. Certainty had always been the key, strung on a silk ribbon of wild-eyed hope.

Raegan brushed her hands off on her thighs and immediately regretted it, having forgotten the torn-up skin on her palms. She winced, clenching her teeth to fight the wave of pain. But then something else stole her attention entirely: the rumble of a train in the distance, of time devouring its own tail.

She turned to look over her shoulder and saw the train approaching, shaking its mechanical hide like a bull about to charge. A dust storm gathered in its wake, the sand writhing like locusts. Upon a set of steps at the front of the railcar stood the Timekeeper. His tweed coat flapped ferociously in the wind, though his hat stayed firmly in place, casting his devouring eyes in that ever-present shadow. He did not look like Death or even the Devil—he looked, Raegan thought, like something much worse, something mortals had not even dared to name.

She inhaled, dust and blood and steel thick in her nose. This moment would be an extraordinarily bad time to be wrong. But fuck it.

Ignoring the searing pain in her side, Raegan raised both hands to the Timekeeper, displaying two proud middle fingers.

"I'm the rising tide," she shouted, her throat raw and aching, the wind tearing the words from her mouth. "When we meet again, you and everything you've built will drown in my flood." Then she turned back to the pool of tears, brought her palms together above her head, and swan dove into the shimmering surface.

Cool currents greeted her, singing old riversongs, a language she'd learned some thousand years ago when the earth still spoke freely. Relief bloomed so suddenly in her chest that Raegan let out a gasping cry, accidentally inhaling water into her lungs. But she found none of the discomfort or sting this body remembered from weekends down the shore. So she swam on, trusting the dark blue of the dazzling currents to guide her home.

Home was not a place; she had lived too long, seen the borders change a hundred times, watched the soil be cut into by men who knew nothing of honor or stewardship. No—home was *him*. The ocean eyes, the dark waves of raven hair, the low and quiet intensity, the powerful hands and unwavering relentlessness. So she swam toward that shadowy harbor, the place where she knew he waited. Where he always waited for her.

An hour or a year or maybe a millennium passed, and then all at once, Raegan broke the surface. She gasped, pulling air into her lungs on instinct. Her leather jacket and boots were suddenly far too heavy to keep her body buoyant, and she flailed for a handhold. Her fingertips found only slick, cool stone. Fear shot through her as she surfaced again, panic beginning to choke the air in her throat. Had the Timekeeper somehow turned the Rivers against her?

She reached up, desperate, fingers sliding uselessly against the smooth surface. But then a hand grabbed her wrist—a touch she'd know anywhere. Raegan sobbed in relief as she was lifted from the water by the King of the Unseelie Fey. Despite her waterlogged clothing and all her sorrow, he pulled her ashore as if she weighed nothing. He wrapped strong arms around her, and she collapsed into the darkness of him, black pepper and woodsmoke and damp rain.

Shifting back from his kneeling position to sit on his heels, the King clutched her to his chest like he may never let her go again. "Raegan," he murmured in the same tone someone prays for one last time, hoping it might finally work.

"He's gone," she sputtered, her words choked by tears. "My father's gone."

He did not pry as she dissolved into sobs. He only held her close until her shivering slowed, until his black wools and dark eyes and expansive sweep of coiled muscle felt more real to her than any blank plane stitched together by a steel railroad.

And then, gently, he pulled back to examine her, his fingertips trembling as he brought them to her jaw. "Your wounds need tending, but you are back, and you are safe," he said, his voice breaking like a storm upon the shore. "Raegan, I . . . I do not—I do not know what I would do if . . ."

For the first time since she'd lost him in that horrible place, the King's oceanic gaze met hers. She saw a thousand things within the storm of gray, but most of all, she saw that shared oath of unconditional love. The bloom she'd discovered in herself at Gossamer unfolded, petals seeking the dark, dangerous heat of him that she preferred to any sun.

Raegan gripped the front of his shirt with both hands and pulled his mouth to hers—never mind the split skin and wind-worn lips. Oberon met her eagerly, his hands sliding around her waist, crushing their hips together. Despite her exhaustion, his touch reminded her body it was alive after all. That living was revenge in itself.

He broke the kiss gently, long fingers brushing wet hair away from her face. She opened her mouth to speak and then closed it again, the memory of her father's frail body disintegrating into dust choking out the words she'd wanted to say. So she put her head to the King's chest and cried some more instead.

"I promise," he murmured, holding her tightly to him, his powerful grip near-crushing, "you will have your vengeance. My love for you knows no bounds. Neither does the violence I will gladly wreak on your behalf."

Raegan nodded, her hands shaky as she sat up straight, brushing the tears off her cheeks. How many times would she have to grieve the same person? Was there no end to this ouroboros? There were so many different kinds of death. But here was the last, she supposed—the final door through which she could not go questing beyond. For the first time in her entire life, Raegan's father was actually, truly, irreversibly gone.

A cold chill spread across her body suddenly as her mind ground to a halt, as if her survival instincts refused to allow her to contend with such a thought in her current state. In the King's arms, Raegan trembled —with sorrow, with rage, with exhaustion, with things she did not even know how to describe.

"Can you walk?" Oberon asked, straightening. When she tried to move her lips and speak, she found she could not answer. She thought he might pull her up anyway, dragging her along behind him like he had so many times before. Instead, the King stayed put on the cold tile floor beside her. The only move he made was to gently shift her fully into his lap.

"I do not know what awaits us beyond this chamber," Oberon warned her as he tucked the top of her head under his chin, not seeming to mind that her hair was cold and soaked. His words registered slowly; Raegan's mind felt like a blank, white room—not dissimilar to the one currently surrounding them. Oh gods—had she even escaped the Time-keeper at all? Was her mind tumbling through some homecoming fantasy while her body stitched itself to the leather seat of that forsaken train?

"Oberon," she ground out. "What happened to you? After, I mean."

"I waited for you. As I always do," the King explained, gesturing to the space around them; his hands still shook like a storm-ravaged willow. With a start, she realized it was the same room where they'd opened the door to the Timekeeper's realm at the Oracle's Temple, bare but grand with its high ceilings and golden light and expansive creamy marble floors. "I have not left this room in a number of days. Perhaps a week."

She looked up at him as sharply as her frozen muscles would allow. "Why?" Raegan asked, her throat raw, heart pounding as she tried to convince herself the King and the marble and the Temple were real.

"If I left," he continued, his gaze skipping away from hers, the long, dark lashes dipping down, "you would have had no chance of coming back at all. Once the chamber is unsealed, the protection warding burns away any spellwork completed here." The King's voice —that dark, melodic, eternally steady voice—shattered into silence. A moment stretched long and lonely before his eyes met hers again.

"And then nothing would connect this room to the In-Between any longer." A muscle in his jaw leapt, broad chest rising in a quick, sharp inhale.

"Fuck," she whispered, digging her knuckles into her eyes. So much unimaginable power, and the King had been reduced to nothing but breathless waiting and razor-edged hope. She fought to find the right words, her body drooping like a wilted flower from the effort. With a low, pained breath, she decided to say nothing, turning to bury her face in his chest again. The dark heat of him loosened the cold stiffness of her joints, the icy sludge that seemed to grip her thoughts easing.

"I tried," Oberon whispered, hands cradling the back of her head. His voice hitched, tone growing thick and heavy. "Raegan, I need you to know I tried so hard to reach you."

"I know," she replied into the fabric of his shirt. "The Timekeeper *wanted* me there. Fate fucked us over. She made a deal for more magic to flow through the Gates. I was Her fattened calf for Kronos, and I went fucking willingly. Imagine how he could gorge himself on all my endless time. I don't even want to know how long She's been planning this."

Oberon's body went still against hers. She waited to feel that rare tide of rage spill through him, bloodthirsty and wild. But he only let out a long sigh. No words left his mouth. For a long moment, there was nothing but the sound of their breathing echoing against the marble. They stayed like that, a tangle of trembling limbs and damp clothing, until Raegan spoke again.

"It feels like everything is even worse now," she said in a raw, forlorn whisper. "We've tried so hard. We've done so much. And somehow we've only lost more."

Oberon did not deny it. "Can you try to stand?" he asked instead. "Let me care for you. Let me make something better than it was."

Raegan nodded, the corners of her mouth lifting even as tears spilled down her face. Oberon helped her to her feet, bracketing her body against his larger, sturdier one. She tried to take a step toward the door and found she had absolutely nothing left. Her legs shook, ankles and knees screaming in protest, every muscle liquified. Before she could even voice her distress, the King swept Raegan off the floor and into his arms. Her vision pitched, black spots swarming on the edges, until the darkness consumed her entirely.

~

S he opened her eyes to a familiar place: that autumnal meadow, the mountains rising into gray skies, the river snaking low in the grass. Woodsmoke slunk into her senses. Heavy wool draped over her shoulders. Instinctively, she turned to her left. There he was—always, relentlessly, endlessly. Tall and powerful, inhumanly beautiful in the overcast light. He wore his past self well—every inch the mysterious, dangerously charming knight he'd been a thousand years ago.

He turned to face her. That oceanic gaze did not belong to Mordred, she knew; it was the Unseelie king staring back at her. "What is this?" he asked, his younger voice—less husky around the edges, more melodic, the accent thicker—a mismatch for the weight of those eyes.

"I don't know," Raegan—and she was Raegan, not some echo of Nyneve—murmured, looking around. The dreamscape was the same as it always was—except both of them seemed to have autonomy. As if the ouroboros could be broken, as if they could do more than retrace the same patterns in river mud over and over again until it broke them.

Her senses prickled. She turned away from the knight, back toward the rushing waters in the distance, her heart pounding like a wild thing against her ribs.

Just a few paces from her stood something tall and terrifying.

Someone. A woman, perhaps, but only because Raegan lacked more expansive language. Blue tattoos marked cool, pale skin—woad, Raegan recalled. Intricate plaits of raven hair fell around angular shoulders, which were cloaked in a cape of feathers that shifted from black to cobalt in the light. The mouth was thin and serious, the eyes large and bottomless.

"Phantom Queen," Raegan breathed at the same time the faerie king beside her murmured, "Morrigan."

"There is not much time," the goddess said in the voice of a thousand crows cawing into a thunder-swept sky. "You must listen closely."

Raegan's marrow hummed. She nodded because what else was she to do in the presence of the ancient goddess of war and sovereignty she had once trusted with her life? With his life. Because she had, after all, been involved in his creation—alongside Nyx, the Morrigan had torn a wound in the midnight sky and crafted the King from the obsidian jewel it bled.

"You opened a door through the In-Between," the Morrigan said, those ink-black eyes falling on Raegan. "And now, finally, we might have our revenge."

The goddess raised her long arms and then shot forward in a terrifying movement of black braids and crow feathers. She stopped a hair's breadth from them both, fingertips pressed to their foreheads. The moment the Morrigan's divine body touched hers, Raegan's vision went black—the black of congealed blood on a battlefield, the black of war banners, the black of the things that fester when too long denied.

And then, all at once, she saw.

A set of ancient stone steps leading into water.

A sword the color of ocean water during a storm.

The mortal king who had once wielded such a blade.

The blood of the Fair Folk he had spilled with it.

An isle shrouded in mist.

A snake shedding its skin.

The feeling of something winged taking flight in her chest—hope, if she dared.

"Find Avalon. Seek Excalibur." The Morrigan's voice boomed in her head, heavy as death, magnetic as destiny. "All doors that were once open to the deathless witch remain so. If the faerie king can return the faerie blade to its original state, so too might he return the world to what it once was. Together, my children, you could liberate us all."

Chapter Five

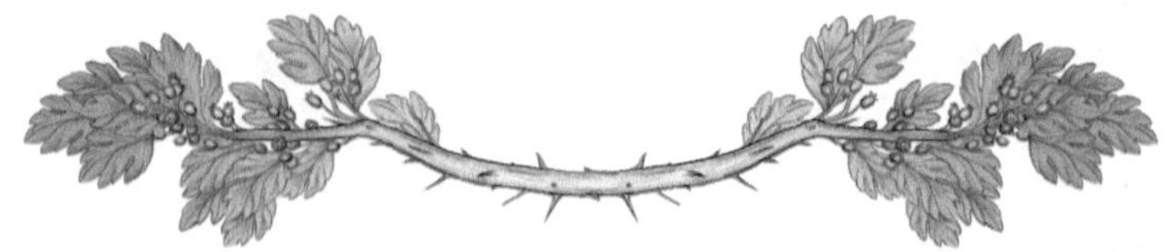

Scent came back first: perfumed waters heavy with spring thunderstorms, chilly vanilla, a soft sprig of lilac, and, beneath it all, something rich, herbal, and slightly medicinal. She breathed in deeply, clearing stagnant air from her lungs. Smooth, silky fabric pressed against her skin, a gentle cocoon from which she might emerge more glorious than she had entered. She opened her eyes—slow, steady—to warm, golden light floating down from somewhere high above her. The space held a downy silence, but just beyond it, she could detect running water and the gentle tinkling of silver bells in the distance.

The Temple of the Oracle, Raegan knew—a familiar place, as familiar as the heavy weight of grief that swept into her body like a homecoming. Her father was dead and she'd watched it happen, unable to save him from the Timekeeper. Nausea shot through her, and she doubled forward, gagging. "No, no, no, *no*," she stammered through a torrent of unshed tears, squeezing her eyes shut, doing anything she could to banish the memory of the worst thing she'd ever witnessed.

Her hands reflexively curled into fists. Raegan hissed as the torn flesh on her palms smarted. She yanked her hands from beneath the blankets to find the heel of each hand wrapped in a thin, spidery gauze—far more organic-looking than any medical gauze she'd ever seen.

And her right hand, it seemed, was not empty. Tucked along the indentation in her palm that some people called a fate line was a crow feather. In the golden light of the Temple, it shimmered like an oil spill. All at once, Raegan remembered the dream—or perhaps the vision—in that meadow she knew so well, the goddess she hadn't seen for a thousand years speaking directly to her.

Speaking of a way they might know revenge. Of an ancient blade and a hidden place and the true nature of things.

Raegan sighed, looking away from the crow feather and all its responsibility. To combat the anxiety swarming her mind, she began to catalog everything in the room. To her right, a side table with a pitcher of water and glasses. Beyond it, dark blue velvet draped from the ceilings in soft swathes. The bed frame was made of twisted willow branches, the sheets and blankets varying shades of porcelain white and rich cream. To her left, a tasseled silk loop caught the wall of heavy velvet in a swoop, exposing a sliver of the hallway. Along the outer edge of the room, a fawn-colored tufted leather chair sat empty, two teacups stacked beside its leg. Raegan forced a long inhale and equal exhale.

Every atom in her body dragged her eyes back to the crow feather waiting in her open palm. She stroked its silky black surface. She wondered if she was strong enough. It would be easier, kinder, to let the grief swallow her whole—to forget about gods and magic and destiny. To mourn. Her father was finally, truly gone. And yet that did not stop the Morrigan from crawling through the tiny door she'd opened and throwing another crucible at her feet.

Shadows stirred beyond the swoop of velvet at the threshold of her room. Raegan glanced up from the feather and met the King's oceanic gaze.

"Hey," she said weakly.

"You are awake," he replied, stepping into the room and pulling the plush blue fabric curtain closed behind him. His expression was wary, guarded, holding hers as if the rest of the world did not exist.

Raegan looked away, swallowing hard and wondering if she should even tell Oberon about what she'd seen. She did not doubt that it was real—and that was exactly the problem. But as her gaze skipped down, she caught sight of the King's powerful hands.

Tucked between long, elegant fingers was a crow feather, gleaming wildly in the diffuse light of the Temple.

"You too?" she asked, holding up her feather.

Oberon nodded, measured and grim. "It would be madness."

"To follow the Morrigan's quest?" Raegan asked, meeting his eyes again.

The King sighed, raking a hand through his hair. "Quite frankly, I do not care much about goddesses and quests. I care about *you*. How are you feeling?"

Raegan moved to sit upright. "I'm okay. Well, no, that's not true. I just watched my father die, felt pretty sure I was going to die, too, and then when I was trying to sleep that off, a fucking goddess showed up in my dreams and told me I have more shit to do."

A sardonic smile ghosted Oberon's lips as he sat down on the edge of her bed. He reached out and gently—far more gently than he should even have been capable of—took her hand into his. As always, the dark spell of the faerie king rolled over her like a heat wave, lighting a spark low in her belly despite all the horrors she'd so recently suffered.

"You look well, all things considered," Oberon said, eyes meeting hers. "You have only slept for about a day. After your ordeal, more rest would be wise."

Raegan was only half-listening. In her head, she was replaying the Timekeeper killing her father over and over, one of the people she loved most in the world dissolving into dust because he'd had the misfortune of caring about her.

"I can't lose anyone else," she said, looking up at the King, tears hemming her words.

For a long moment, he was silent. "I wish I could tell you that you will not."

She raised her free hand—the one that still clutched the crow feather—and pushed her tears away with the back of her palm. "That *was* real, wasn't it?" she asked, hollow, knowing she didn't need to specify.

The King sighed, his fingertips moving in a slow serpentine over her skin. "Yes."

"And Excalibur was a faerie blade?"

"There have always been rumors that Myrddin perverted a Feyrish weapon for the king of men," he replied. "It would not surprise me, no, though I cannot say for certain."

"Even if it isn't," Raegan mused, digging through the recesses of her mind, "Excalibur siphons the power of gods and Fair Folk, right? That's why it's so legendary. The first weapon that could stand against magical beings, using their own power against them. So maybe it *could* actually harm the Timekeeper."

Oberon nodded, his mouth a grim line. But they'd have to actually find Avalon first. Raegan dropped the feather into her blanketed lap, raising her hand to massage her temples. The soft hush of running water and tinkling bells in the background lulled her, the halfway light tempting her with more sleep that would delay all she faced.

"And Avalon . . ." she mumbled, the hopelessness of it all threatening to crush her. "Apparently even the goddamn Morrigan doesn't know where its door lies."

"I would think not. Danu's safe refuge for Her first generation has not been located by anyone in living memory," he replied, something not unlike grief slipping into his words. "That door has been closed for nearly three thousand years. She sealed it behind Her."

Raegan let out a long breath. The Morrigan's vision had been a call to arms screamed from the top of a windswept hill, not a murmured sweet nothing from a honeyed tongue. She might be a fool for it, but Raegan believed she could follow black feathers and the cry of a crow better than she had ever chased windsongs and the soft rustle of white wings.

"The old gods have not been able to reach into this world for centuries," she said, choosing her words slowly as she raised her eyes to Oberon's. "And even though it was all bullshit, the false Prophecy that Fate set up for us created the situation that allowed me to tear open a door—no matter how small—between the realms."

The King said nothing. He only watched her, his eyes restless as the sea, the candlelight-like illumination of the Temple turning the strands of silver in his hair golden. Shadows draped across his angular face. His powerful body was utterly still, more statue than living thing. He looked like destiny. He looked like defiance embodied.

"You want to seek Avalon," he said, his tone tinted with reverence like stained glass. "You want to quest for Excalibur. After everything, you wish to follow the words of a goddess."

She held his gaze, her jaw clenched. She did. She wanted this to be over, once and for all. No more resurrections. No more hopelessness. No more of this. Rage kindled deep within Raegan. All her endless sorrow and grief wove itself into the fabric of her never-ending anger, creating something sharp and shining, chainmail-like.

"My love," the King breathed, closer to her now, the intensity of him like a wildfire, "I know not where you find the resilience to follow another Thread that may well give out from beneath our feet."

Raegan bared her teeth at him in something that was not quite a smile. "Spite's as good a reason as any. Besides, you said I would have my vengeance. Could there possibly be a better revenge than destroying everything the Timekeeper holds dear with the single swipe of a long-lost faerie blade?"

At that, the King smiled back, all nightmare, all predator. "I told you I would follow you to the ends of the Earth." A promise for her, a threat for their enemies.

"Oberon," she said, her tone sharp, "I think we should do this. The Morrigan has never led us astray."

A long moment passed where he said nothing, though he reached up to cup her face in one large, warm hand. "You need to mourn."

She ground her teeth, the truth of his words swelling up in her like stagnant lake water thick with algae. "We all mourn in different ways," she replied, arching an eyebrow.

"And I suppose you have usually mourned by seeking revenge," the King observed wryly. Then his expression went still, serious. "It is possible. We would need a few weeks to prepare, and we should move in secret. Only our most trusted accomplices can know of this vision, this hope. But Andronica could hold the wards once more, Kamau could lead the Court's defenses, and the kelpies would no doubt aid our quest." He paused, cocking his head to one side, examining her. "What do *you* want, truly?"

Raegan let out a long breath, looking down at the creamy fabric that stretched across her lap, at the gauze covering her body, at the bruises developing on her forearms. It was going to take a hell of a lot more than that to keep her down. If she destroyed the Timekeeper, she'd avenge her father—and she'd make his sacrifice worthwhile. What had Cormac wanted more than for people to be free to choose their own paths? Magic could do that.

"I want to find Avalon," she finally replied, meeting his gaze again. She shifted her weight on the bed, moving toward him. "But first, I want you to distract me. Is that fucked up?"

The King's expression didn't change as he leaned in, his fingers sliding between hers. He brought his mouth to the underside of her forearm, trailing soft kisses down her flesh. A thick drumming started up in her core.

"Is this the sort of distraction you were hoping for?" he asked, gaze meeting hers.

"It's nice," Raegan teased. "But maybe something a little more . . . full-bodied?"

Without saying a word, the King gently folded the blankets back, down to her legs. Then he gathered her up in his arms. "As always," he said, his lips moving against the shell of her ear, "your wish is my command."

Tucking her close against his chest, Oberon strode to the opposite wall and parted the shimmering fabric, revealing a square room tiled in a deep, opalescent blue. A stone basin crouched on what appeared to be a giant slab of moonstone, an antiqued silver mirror hanging above it. To the left, roughly cut stone stairs led down into a large bath. The waters sparkled metallic in the light, as if a current danced beneath. The entire space carried the scent of spring thunderstorms and a cool whisper of lilac.

Along the wall, a bench had been carved out of the stone and then covered in soft blue mosaics. There, the King set Raegan down. The tiles were cool through the thin fabric of her long dressing gown. He settled beside her.

"May I see your bandages first?" he asked, gesturing to her palms.

"Fine," Raegan replied, sighing dramatically as she extended her hands to him. Tenderly, Oberon peeled the spiderweb-like gauzing away. She braced herself for bruised, torn skin, but when he finished unwrapping the bandages, there was little more beneath than some pink scrapes.

"Good," he murmured, pulling his hands away from hers. "How do they feel?"

"Okay," Raegan said, realizing it for the first time as she examined the tender pink flesh. Then her eyes slid to Oberon's, her heart beating faster. Nervousness fluttered in her stomach like she was a tween again, experiencing her first crush. "Still hurts a little. A kiss might help."

Amusement slid across his angular features like a mirage, the corners of his sculpted lips lifting. Gaze on hers, the King bowed to bring his mouth to both of her scraped palms in turn. Heat slid through her belly.

"And your knee?" he asked, eyes dropping down to her legs.

Raegan obliged without a second thought, pulling up the hem of the gown. Oberon gently maneuvered her legs to lie across his lap. The knee she'd torn after jumping from the train was bandaged in a similar fabric, and Oberon unwound it with the same care. Much like her hands, the skin was pinkish and scraped, still a little sore, but far more healed than it should have been after one day.

"Hurts a bit more than my hands," Raegan said, not able to stop herself from smiling.

The King returned the expression, and gods, to see playfulness on his face was such a balm for everything. He lowered himself over her legs, brushing her knee with his lips. She bit back the soft sound of pleasure, watching as Oberon trailed his mouth along her thigh, both of his hands sliding up her legs. Then his powerful grip was on her waist and he sat upright with an elegant contraction of predatory muscles.

"Do you think you can stand?" he asked, eyes on hers like no one else existed.

"Don't flatter yourself," Raegan replied, pushing to her feet, though he caught her halfway, bracketing her smaller frame against his. Heat sparked deep in her belly as their bodies met, her soft curves pressed against his hard musculature.

She permitted a brief detour to wash her face and brush her teeth at the sink, noting that it was very much her own reflection looking back at her in the antiqued silver mirror. More or less, she wagered. She'd been a lot of people, after all.

At the edge of the stone bath, the King pulled her dressing gown up and over her head, and thoughts of the past melted away like swollen stormwaters. Beneath the garment, Raegan wore nothing save for another spiderweb gauze pad on her side. With a touch so gentle no one else in the world would believe he was capable of it, Oberon peeled the bandaging away. Beneath, her skin was bruised and scraped, but nothing like she'd imagined—no horrific sights of bones breaking through skin or flesh torn away entirely.

She opened her mouth to make the request, but Oberon was already sinking to one knee, his mouth brushing the sensitive, bruised skin where the gauze had been. Her entire body woke up all at once, a thunderstorm rolling across the horizon, and she gasped his name into the steamy air. The tender place at the apex of her thighs throbbed.

He stood then, like she'd commanded it, cupping either side of her face in his hands. The intensity of the King's gaze threatened to consume her. Good. She'd like to be devoured—by him, and only him. The thought alone sent a spike of desire, lightning-hot, into her chest.

Then his mouth was on hers, the dark intensity of whatever they shared washing over her. Oberon wrapped powerful fingers around her waist, mindful of the bruised rib, his hands sliding down to the generous curves of her ass. Raegan deepened the kiss, something desperate rising within her, every inch of her body aching for his touch.

"I thought I lost you," Oberon murmured against her mouth, his voice low and husky. As he spoke, one of his large, warm hands slipped to her belly, and then lower, finding precisely where she wanted to be touched. Raegan let out a soft moan at the wave of pleasure, arching into him. His other hand moved to cup her breast, teasing until her moan deepened into something full-throated and breathy. Her breath quickened as her heart began to race.

"I thought I had grown accustomed to that pain," the King continued, increasing the pressure of his touch. "I have not. I *will* not. I will destroy anyone who seeks to steal you away from me."

Pleasure uncoiled within her and she gasped, half-strangled by desire. She clung to him, as if the harder she gripped, the more she might prove he would never lose her again. Or maybe she just wanted him to remember this—to remember the heat of her body, her heavy breasts pressed into him, the way she said his name. She left him with little more than memories; they may as well be good ones. With that end in mind, Raegan began to unbutton his shirt with shaking hands. A few moments later, she'd gotten what she wanted—nothing between his skin and hers, only fervent kisses and the sound of her name in his mouth. Desire pounded between her legs, her breath coming in quick gasps.

He coaxed pleasure from her body as if he spoke the same language as her flesh. A powerful sensation mounting in her depths, Raegan rolled her hips harder into his hand, desperate for more. At that exact moment, Oberon pulled his touch away from where she wanted it, sweeping her into his arms instead.

"Fuck you," she panted, limp in his grasp, her chest blushed pink and heaving.

"That is the intention," he replied in a low voice that sent her core curling in on itself.

Raegan met his gaze and rolled her eyes as Oberon carried her into the bath. There, he gently set her on a ledge cut into the stone wall. Hot, silky waters stretched over her, rippling around her collarbones. A soft exhale slipped from her mouth. She closed her eyes and tilted her head back, leaning the base of her skull against the lip of the stone.

"I don't remember asking for a bath," she murmured when a few moments had passed without the King's hands on her—too many to bear, though it embarrassed her to admit it.

"I will have you know I am capable of accomplishing more than one task at once," Oberon said, the weighted warmth of his palms roving to her shoulders, his hands soap-slick, perfumed with honey and oatmeal.

Raegan laughed, and some of the tension and fear slipped away with it. The sound melted in her throat as the King massaged soap into her shoulders, his mouth meeting the sensitive skin just below her ear. His hands traveled lower, powerful fingers working out the tension in her back. But tension flared hot and hungry elsewhere, a torrent of desire building with each breath. Raegan pulled him closer, and in response, Oberon let his hands slip from her collarbones and then to her breasts. His mouth met hers again to capture the resulting moan.

Cupping the heavy flesh, he teased her where she was most sensitive. Need seared through Raegan's body as his touch traveled lower, across her belly and then her lower back, working in more soap as he went. By the time she was feeling thoroughly clean in perhaps the dirtiest way possible, her muscles had finally softened, but the thick, beating desire at her core had only wound tighter.

Oberon began to rinse the soap from her skin, one hand slipping to the damp heat between her legs. Her thighs slid open for him, a thousand years' worth of desire relentless and throbbing. Pleasure pounded her from every angle, the material world melting away, leaving only the curvature of his muscled, scarred body and the softly swaying curls of steam.

"I thought I had lost you," he repeated, deep and breathy, as both of his powerful hands gripped her by the waist, lifting Raegan to the lip of the bath. The temperature of the air was a welcome relief, her hair plastered to her neck, her face red. "And it is only a half-life without you, my witch." Before she could say anything, Oberon slid between her thighs, sinking to his knees.

The Unseelie king kneeling before her usually only meant one thing.

"Permit me to memorize your taste," Oberon asked, right on cue, his gaze sliding to hers.

"What have you done," she murmured, her breathing hard and fast, "to deserve that?"

His mouth moved into something dangerous and feral, and it sent a thrill through her. "I have spilled blood," the King murmured, his lips meeting the inside of her thigh. "Killed legions. Defeated a hundred armies in your name. Toppled kings. Destroyed worlds. All for you. Always you. *Only* you."

His breath moved across her skin with each word, mapping her generous thighs with hot, open-mouthed kisses, his long fingers hooked behind her knees. Her blood pounded.

"I think," she panted, digging her nails into his shoulders, "that will do."

Dark and dangerous amusement simmered like a heat wave across his face, and then his mouth met the yearning heat of her core. Raegan fought to savor the moment, to do everything in her power to never forget, but Oberon knew her body too well and had worked her into a frenzy. She crested the wave of her release a few minutes later, body melting into his as she cried out his name.

He held her against him, one hand splayed across her lower back. Raegan closed her eyes and pressed the side of her face into his chest, her heart still fluttering behind her ribs. They stayed like that, the ancient king of shadows bowed over the witch who refused to die, and for a long moment, even destiny and Fate and ancient goddesses did not dare to disturb their peace.

But their peace never seemed to last.

Chapter Six

Little was visible through the rough hood they'd forced over her head. She closed her eyes, focusing on her other senses instead. Through the fabric, she smelled sunburnt dust and sweat—her own or that of the Protectorate dragging her, she did not know. For a third time, she fought to plant her bare heels into the hard-packed earth, but her body responded with little more than a pathetic jerk. Still, the Protectorate man to her left halted abruptly, taking a handful of her hair and yanking hard.

"It's no use, love," he laughed in her ear, the sour warmth of his breath making her flinch away.

They dragged her forward again, her feet catching on the ground, a stray rock scraping her skin. She hardly even felt the pain. Panic was too thick in her throat now, the hood suffocating, her anxious inhales dampening the fabric. Whatever they'd done during those long, endless hours deep within their stronghold, she had no magic. Her body did not obey her commands. Desperate, she fought to do something as simple as flexing a few fingers. Nothing.

She opened her mouth to scream because at the very least she'd make this as unpleasant as possible, but no sound came out. A few tears, however, did manage to tumble down her face. Her heart still pounded, and a heavy weight still crouched on her chest. Hunger still sat sticky in her stomach and her head still hurt. So she'd feel every last unpleasant thing but have no control. Rage boiled in her, and for a long, skittering moment, she thought she could feel the edges of the Protectorate spellwork.

A harsh pain in her ankles and knees broke her concentration.

"Oh, apologies," the Protectorate on the right mocked. "Stairs."

The pair dragged her to her feet, and she scrambled for dignity, but to no avail. She could see little more than faint outlines through the hood, and the depth or number of the stairs beneath her was a mystery. She tried to put her shoulders back and tilt her chin up as she struggled, but her muscles didn't even seem to hear the instruction.

Then the stairs stopped and the air changed. Woodgrain beneath her bare feet, a dry breeze tickling her arms. She strained to listen—murmurs of a crowd, pennants snapping in the wind, the thump of boots. Peaceful, almost, if not for the sense she was perched at the top of a hill about to give way beneath her.

And it did—the Protectorate men forced her to her knees, the wood biting into her skin. A hard push at her upper back doubled her over, and then a gloved hand grabbed her hair again, positioning her head so the side of her neck rested on cold stone.

Oh. Well, she should've expected that.

The hood came off in a violent flourish, sending stark sunlight streaming into her eyes for the first time in . . . days? Weeks? Her vision was sideways, the platform stretching out before her, banners embroidered with the Protectorate's dragon rampart flying proud and cruel. She strained but could not see beyond the platform, though the sudden jeering told her there was, of course, a crowd.

She squeezed her eyes shut and fumbled for the spellwork that held her fast, trying to find the weave in her Threads. She could feel it, the way it strung her like a puppet, but she could not reach it—vast miles seemed to separate her magic from theirs.

A commotion caught her attention. At the other end of the platform, a group of at least ten Protectorate were climbing the stairs, looking for all the world as though they were trying to drag a wild animal along with them. Her mouth went dry.

She knew immediately what—who—was at the center of that tangle of chainmail and dusty cloth, surrounded by straining magic and anxious *shouts. The rest unfolded like terrible poetry: a large, masked man stepped forward into her vision, his wicked ax glinting in the high sun. At the same moment, the Protectorate group at the other end of the platform split, revealing the High King of the Unseelie Fey.*

Despite the magicked chains that wrapped around almost his entire body, despite the deep cut over one black, swollen eye, he lurched forward and screamed. She'd heard that sound before, once—in the crumbling walls of an old stone building, her body laid out on a rough slab of wood, the life bleeding out of her.

A figure stepped between her and the King: a mountain of a man, his chainmail well-used, his familiar weathered face pulled into a victorious sneer. She summoned every ounce of her rage, her defiance, fighting to dip her hand into that cold, dark current.

"S-see," she sputtered, every movement of her tongue a monumental effort, "you soon."

"No," Bedwyr replied, tucking his hands behind his back, strolling forward on the platform, allowing her to look at the King again. Just once more. "Not this time, I don't think."

Then the sharp glint of sun on steel raised high, followed by nothing at all.

～

Darkness. The manic scream of a banshee. And then someone saying her name, just audible beneath the grating shouts. Raegan's throat hurt, which probably meant that she was not dead and also that she might be the one screaming.

She opened her eyes, panting, but only more darkness greeted her, a few rough outlines visible in the dim light. Panicking, Raegan raised her hands to her face, clawing to remove the hood from her head. But there was nothing there; her nails only scraped skin.

A large, deft hand caught her fingers, gentle but firm. "Raegan," murmured a voice that sounded like dusk over the lake and heather on the hills. "*Cariad*, you are safe."

Golden light fluttered in from no direction in particular, illuminating the foot of the willow-branch bed, blue velvet walls, creamy marble floors, and the familiar face of the King leaning over her. As they made eye contact, he released her hands.

"Fuck," she muttered, dropping her head into her palms, pulling her knees to her chest, bedsheets snagging at her ankles. A shiver wracked her body, the slick sweat on her skin turning cool. "It was the same dream again."

Ever since she'd made it back from the Timekeeper's realm—nearly three weeks ago—Raegan had been haunted by this particular dream. Three weeks of careful planning, intensive training, and relocating Fair Folk to safer places, every bit of it made that much more difficult by the sleep stolen from her each night. As if she needed anything else on top of the horrendous, bone-deep grief that she'd barely had the time to feel, let alone process.

"May I touch you?" Oberon asked, his broad, powerful frame a comforting shadow in her peripheral vision.

"Please," Raegan pleaded, biting down on the tears climbing her throat.

Oberon pulled her into his arms, tucking her head beneath his chin. She buried her face in his chest, woodsmoke and black pepper and damp stone washing over her. Wrapping her arms around his waist, Raegan clutched the fabric of his shirt with all her might.

"Your dream will not repeat itself in the waking world," he murmured, one hand stroking her hair.

"You can't promise that," she whimpered into his chest, misery crashing onto her shores. "What if I doom us all *again*?" The memories pressed in all around Raegan, thick and suffocating. "Why do you still trust me, believe in me?"

The King lowered himself to be eye level with her, cupping her damp face in his hands. "Perhaps I am an old fool," he murmured, his long fingers brushing away her tears, "but I do not believe a love as enormous, as magnetic, as unending as ours could be a path to destruction."

Raegan saw in his dark gaze how much he believed the words tumbling from his mouth, but doubt still sat like tar at the bottom of her stomach. It was too easy to remember the way he'd treated her less than a month ago when they'd first found each other. How he had framed their love not as enormous or magnetic, but as poison that had torn his world apart.

"My liege, are you— Oh," a voice boomed from the doorway. "Apologies."

Raegan raised her head, dragging the back of one hand across her eyes to wipe away the tears. Through blurred vision, she saw Kamau, one of the King's most trusted knights, standing in the doorway, concern etched across their features.

"The Rivers are clear," Oberon said in a low, soft voice, stepping back to look at her.

Raegan forced a shuddering exhale, fighting to pull herself out of the dream and into the present moment. "It's time to go, then," she muttered.

"Yes," he replied, brushing away a fresh tear with the pad of his thumb.

Raegan threw back the sheets and scrambled to her feet, pushing down the thick swell of fear and horror clamoring in her marrow. She reminded herself that they'd been desperately waiting for this moment, holding on to the Philadelphia Temple by the skin of their teeth through an increasingly brutal onslaught by the Protectorate.

She would not destroy this sacred, shimmering chance because of a bad dream. A memory from another life, she knew, but it was so much easier to imagine it as only a nightmare—then she could tell herself it was not a portent, not some horrible omen. That dreaming repeatedly of how she'd destroyed their chance at liberation last time as the Seelie Queen was not some kind of very bad sign.

"Is Rainer ready?" Raegan asked, shedding her sweat-dampened t-shirt with little concern for Kamau's presence. She scrambled into the clothes she'd had neatly folded on the nightstand since they'd decided to follow this path.

"Yes," the King replied, moving aside to give her room to pull on a bra and then a pair of jeans. Thanks to the light seeping from the hall-way, she noticed that he was dressed already—an ink-black suit with a charcoal waistcoat and midnight-dark leather boots, all sharp angles and deadly shadows. His appearance settled her; if she had to walk into the mouth of a beast, at least it would be at his side.

"Is Andronica in position?" the King asked, breaking her thoughts, his question directed at Kamau.

She didn't hear an answer as she pulled her gray wool sweater over her head, so Raegan assumed everything was ready. Anxiety twisted her gut. Only a handful of people knew about the vision from the Morrigan: the Keeper, Andronica, Kamau, and Rainer. This last, mad hope was too precious, too delicate—so they'd opted to pursue it in secret.

Raegan leaned against the bed to pull her boots on, turning to glance at Kamau. The towering knight looked capable and sure, no hint of doubt in their large, expressive brown eyes. Raegan set her jaw and straightened, grabbing her leather jacket—the tear inflicted by the Timekeeper's train since mended—from the willowy bedpost. The King handed her a familiar luggage tag, and she slipped it into her pocket.

Then they moved for the doorway. Kamau held up a hand, glancing back out into the hallway, and then gestured them forward. The three of them fell into stride abreast, Raegan bookended by the much taller statues of the King and Kamau.

"Let us run through it one more time," the knight said in a hushed voice, their fingers rubbing the pommel of the dagger at their waist— something they usually did when they were nervous, Raegan had noticed. "Rainer will take you as far as possible in the Rivers. The Protectorate will almost certainly intercept you at some point. The kelpies can only hold them back so long."

Raegan gritted her teeth, lengthening her stride to keep up, trying to stay mindful of ensuring her footsteps were quiet. The plush blue carpet that ran down the marble hallway helped, and the two Fey beings on either side of her moved like silent shadows despite their size.

"You'll be forced to surface," Kamau continued, holding out a hand, their head whipping to one of the curtained archways. Raegan slammed to a halt, trying her best to not even breathe. The Unseelie Court had been reduced, yet again, to refugees, thanks to the ongoing Protectorate assault. The city crawled with operatives, and apparently, the United States' paramilitary force that governed magical affairs had given the Protectorate much more leeway than they usually did on American soil. Most of the Court was hidden away in the remaining pocket realms, trying to weather the storm—a task only made harder by the way residual magic bled from this half of the world faster and faster every day.

Kamau gestured for them to move forward again. From her left, the

King let out a long, low sigh, raking his hand through his hair. "I hate misleading our people," he muttered.

Kamau's dark brown gaze shot to the King, their heavy brow furrowing. "We have discussed this," the knight said, remembering halfway through the sentence to lower their voice. "It would cause panic. And we still do not know the identity of the turncoat in Blodeuwedd's faction. We cannot take the chance of the Protectorate knowing your intentions."

The King nodded, his jaw clenched. Up ahead, something clattered—metal on marble, Raegan thought as she froze. The three of them held their breath. Her blood thundered in her ears. But then nothing—only the silence of the witching hours.

"When you surface," Kamau continued, moving forward again, "you'll only have the River Wye's protection. Maybe the hawthorn trees, if you can find them. It will be a hard road to Hiraeth."

Raegan's vision tunneled, nothing but blue velvet and marble floor and golden light. Her hands shook at her sides. She didn't know if she was strong enough for this. The Protectorate were at the height of their power on the Isles, both in magic and bureaucracy—they were part of the government in the United Kingdom and enjoyed all the freedoms that came with it. The Americans didn't let them use time magic or most modern weapons—some centuries-old squabble Raegan didn't care to learn about. But where she and the King were headed, the Protectorate had anything and *everything* they wanted at their fingertips.

"And you absolutely must be clear of any Protectorate interference when you cross Hiraeth's walls," Kamau said, the muscle in their sharp jaw working. "It is a risk to allow Hiraeth to host you while you search for Avalon."

More nervousness roiled in Raegan's gut. Her palms were damp. How long was this goddamn fucking hallway? It felt like walking to the gallows.

"The last Fey city on the Isles," the King murmured, the gravity of the situation clear in his tone.

"The Protectorate have hunted it for so long," Kamau replied, something not unlike fear coming across their features. "We cannot hand it to them on a silver platter."

The King reached behind Raegan to grip his knight's shoulder. "I know you have loved ones in the city, Kamau. I would die before I exposed Hiraeth."

The tall, broad knight nodded, biting down on their bottom lip. "I know," they murmured. "Truly, I do. I just . . ."

"This is fucking terrifying," Raegan supplied, wiping her hands off on her jeans. "It's, like, endless risks for a *vision*."

"The Keeper was convinced the vision was true, direct from the Morrigan," Kamau reminded her, their expression softening. "And Octavia, too. I spoke with her before she evacuated with the other Seers. The Keeper and the Oracle herself, both utterly convinced, Raegan. That is not nothing."

She looked away from the knight. The Keeper and the Oracle had *also* been convinced of the false Prophecy. Setting her jaw, Raegan stopped herself from saying just that to Kamau, instead staring at the path ahead. The Fey viewed an Unrequited Prophecy and a vision from a goddess as two very different things, but she—admittedly—did not. At least they moved in the opposite direction of the Vaults—it was almost like a declaration they would do this their way. She reached for Oberon's hand as the corridor's terminus came into view: a large door stained in woad, such a dark blue it was almost black. Carved rivers of abalone shell snaked through it, glimmering in the golden light of the Temple. Its doorknob was shaped like the long, powerful body of a kelpie, rendered in patina-blackened silver.

Beside the door, the Keeper and Andronica stood like silent guardians. Doubt rushed into Raegan's chest. What if they were wrong? *Again?* The stakes felt higher than ever. The King could not hold the protective wards around the pocket realms from where they were headed—across an ocean, on a quest strung upon a few words from the thin, sly lips of a goddess who had been locked on the other side of the Gates for a thousand years.

Raegan steadied herself, attempting to clear her mind of the doubts clustered there, thicket-dark. The King squeezed her hand, sending a memory skittering out of her recesses—another time, another place, but still facing a door, the weight of too many hopes perched on their shoulders with clawed talons.

"My liege and my lady," the Keeper said, the sound of his voice pulling Raegan back to the present. "Everything is prepared."

"Thank you, Anakletos," Oberon replied, reaching to embrace the Keeper. The smaller besuited man returned the King's gesture, gripping for a moment or two like he may not let go at all. Raegan knew the feeling.

To her surprise, the Keeper released the King and immediately swept Raegan into a tight hug. "I feel it in my marrow this time," the ancient thing murmured close to her ear, his words sounding for all the world like prophecy.

Raegan pulled back to look into the Keeper's eyes, where she thought she might have caught a glance of the galaxies turning. He nodded once and then stepped clear of the door, out of her vision. Kamau pulled Raegan and the King into a tight embrace, long, heavily muscled arms easily encircling both of them at once. The knight murmured an old Fey blessing and then stepped aside. Andronica moved forward, reaching for the King first.

The two of them exchanged low, fervent promises in the Old Tongue. Oberon bowed his head, bringing his brow to meet Andronica's —an Unseelie expression of deep mutual admiration and trust, Raegan remembered suddenly. Andronica would once again bear the weight of the wards in the King's absence.

Raegan gathered herself up to offer some kind of parting word to the deadly swordswoman who understandably hated her guts. Before she could say anything, Andronica grabbed her by the shoulders and pulled her into an embrace.

"Don't fuck it up this time, yeah?" Andronica said in a tone that was almost friendly and definitely playful. She pulled away, still gripping Raegan by the shoulders, near-black gaze searching hers. "It's different. *You're* different. I know we only had a few weeks to train together, but I hope it pays off."

Raegan's heart soared; she hated how much she craved the approval of this gorgeous, talented, dangerous Fey version of Lucy Liu. "I'll do my best," she replied, not able to contain a grin. To her delight, Andronica grinned back, as sharp and bright as the edge of a blade. Raegan tried to savor the moment, a dewdrop in a drought, but then she saw the Keeper approach the door, his ornately carved ring of keys flashing in the low light.

The moment her eyes fell on the keys, every door in the Temple sang out to Raegan all at once, a chorus of silver bells. She rooted herself to the spot, fighting the tide—though she didn't have to for long, because then the way of the kelpies swung open before her, and the pull of it was so strong that she didn't hesitate.

Raegan swept into the room with the King at her side, the dark and constant shadow looming beside her frantic, chaotic flame. Inside, the room was blank—creamy marble floors, walls tiled in pearl. It was similar to the ritual room they'd used to complete her father's working, but much smaller, the ceiling a more reasonable height. She did her best not to think about that.

At the chamber's center, Raegan noticed gentle movement—the sway of a large puddle. She took a step closer, the King keeping pace. The door closed behind them, and even though she'd known it was coming, the feeling of being cut off from the world made her stomach flip. Raegan gripped Oberon's hand harder as they approached the dark waters lapping at shores of marble.

There was no summoning this time—no drops of blood or shared whiskey, no precise words or wardings drawn in chalk. Instead, the puddle rippled twice, like a giant walked somewhere in the distance, and then the surface of the water broke into a thousand droplets.

From the shadowy depths rose a massive head and thick, curved neck, a seaweed mane hanging in heavy waves. Backwards hooves rang out on the marble floors, and Raegan's mouth went dry as she yet again took in the kelpie known as Rainer.

"I understand that I am a very impressive sight," the kelpie intoned, lowering his head to look at each of them in turn. "But we must go. *Now.* The Rivers will only remain clear for so long before the Protectorate finds a way to dam them up again."

"Then let us be on our way. The Unseelie Court delights in partnering with the kelpies once again," the King replied as he helped Raegan onto the creature's back. He mounted behind her, sliding one arm around her waist.

Rainer began to move immediately, hooves ringing out against the marble. Raegan took a fistful of slippery, dark green mane into her hands. She reminded herself to breathe.

"I have you," the King murmured in her ear. "I will not lose you again."

Raegan gritted her teeth and nodded, fighting the fear that gnawed at her stomach. Rainer came to a halt a few paces from the puddle, his entire body pointed toward it like an arrow.

"To long-overdue revenge. Let there be blood," the kelpie announced, his voice a thousand rushing rivers. Before Raegan could prepare herself, Rainer gathered himself up and without another word launched into the surface of the water.

CHAPTER SEVEN

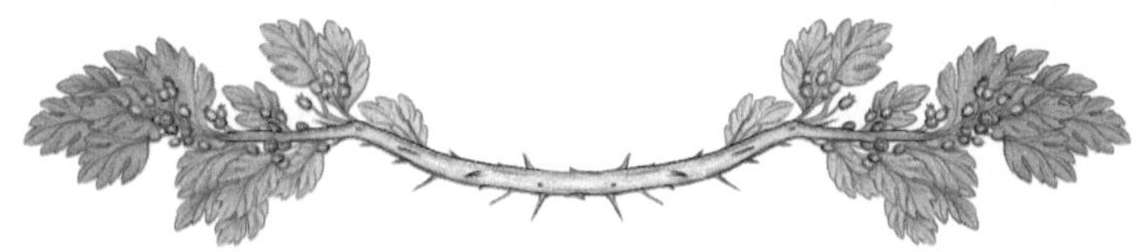

Raegan didn't know if they'd been traveling the half-lit, watery realm on Rainer's back for seconds or days. Time slipped out of her grasp entirely, a snake slithering away through dew-damp grass. It didn't help that even though her eyes told her that they were deep underwater, her breath came easily and her body remained dry as bone.

We shall surface soon. Rainer's voice boomed in Raegan's head so suddenly that she jumped, causing Oberon to tighten his grip around her waist. *Prepare.*

For the hundredth time, Raegan tried to summon a memory of their destination: Hiraeth. The final stronghold of the Fey in the Isles, a city hidden by mist and magic and a wall of hawthorn trees. She'd been there before, she knew, but the magic that concealed it seemed to have stolen her ability to remember it as well. Hiraeth operated on very old, very powerful workings—the kind that could have only been crafted on this half of the world before the Gates existed. She was eager to be within its walls again, though she wished it were for much different reasons.

But for now, only the dim blue-green of the Rivers surrounded her, kelp forests looking more like thick black thunderclouds in the distance. Rainer's hooves did not travel across a sandy floor or river-worn pebble underfoot; instead, he moved through the water like a fish, his back legs transformed into a massive tail covered in glimmering scales. Raegan took a quick look down, not comforted by the vast darkness lying in wait beneath them.

They'd encountered no one else traveling the same section of the Rivers. Beyond the occasional shadow of a horse-like body or watchful, shimmering eyes at the edge of a kelp thicket, it was only the three of them. Or at least, it seemed that way until Rainer spoke.

The Protectorate is near, the kelpie boomed in her mind, a warning. *They cannot enter the Rivers, but they can dam the waterways and attack from the surface. I believe we are about to encounter both.*

As if on cue, Raegan watched a shining silver spear pierce the space just to her right, moving far faster than anything metal should in water this deep. Rainer launched forward, veering toward the open mouth of a kelp forest. The King pulled Raegan back against his chest, his sword—an impossible thing woven from pure shadow—appearing in his free hand.

We may need to take a path through the deep places, Rainer warned, sending a delicate whisper of dread skittering up Raegan's spine. Such places were not for mortals; they were not even for something like the King, not without invitation. Things older and far more terrifying than Rainer lurked in the low places, sunk deep and sleeping in the river silt, kelp woven over them like a thatched roof. It would not do well to wake what slept in the Rivers.

At her back, Raegan felt Oberon tense in response to Rainer's words, and she watched his hand wrap tighter around his sword's pommel. She gritted her teeth, panic fluttering like a moth somewhere in her throat. White-knuckling Rainer's slippery seaweed mane, Raegan tried to focus on staying with the kelpie's quickened movement. She wished she could talk to Oberon in this place, but the only voice she'd hear until they surfaced was Rainer's. It was the way of things, she knew.

Another spear sliced through the murky depths, alarmingly close to Rainer's right shoulder. In response, the kelpie banked left hard and would have unseated Raegan if not for the King's arm around her waist.

They are trying to kettle us, Rainer said, surprising Raegan with his choice of vocabulary. She might've laughed if she weren't deeply afraid for her life, a delicate thing in this game they played. *Fools. I am far older than such tactics.*

Raegan peered ahead through the dim watery light, catching sight of what she instantly knew was one of the dams Rainer spoke of, looking for all the world like a wall of chainmail. Dull, lifeless metal stretched across the path ahead, kelp forests looming on either side. Even from a distance, Raegan felt the way the Rivers could not flow through the Protectorate's dam. The water seemed to rear away from the chainmail entirely, fronds of kelp wilting when the current pulled them too close to the unnatural thing.

A chorus of spears sang through the water just behind them, the King batting most of them away with a slice of his sword. Beneath her, Raegan felt Rainer gather himself, powerful muscles bunching in anticipation of his next move. Head thrown high, he surged forward, as if he intended to run straight into the wall of metal. Oberon ducked lower to the kelpie's neck, sheltering Raegan with his body. She flattened herself against the seaweed mane, heart hammering in her chest.

At the last possible moment, Rainer swung himself to the side, an impossibly elegant pirouette. But the tight turn slowed his pace, and for a second, it felt to Raegan as though they hung dead in the water. Dread danced in her gut, and she looked up, responding to a prickling sensation at the back of her neck.

From above, a net of thick, rusted metal descended on them, diving through the depths at an unnatural speed. Terror slunk low through Raegan's chest—after everything, here she was, about to be captured like a prize, dragged back to a hunting lodge, throat slit.

But she was not prey. Not anymore. No—she was more predator than the Protectorate could even begin to imagine. She was the Lady of the Rivers, and this was *her* domain. Raegan straightened, squaring her shoulders, gaze locked on the descending net. Then she swung one hand above her head, palm-up, fingers clawlike and ravenous. With all her might, she called to water, reaching for that cold, dark current that ran through the very center of her being.

Something serpentine and sharp exploded into existence between Rainer and the Protectorate's net, razor-toothed and keen. A dragon, maybe, Raegan thought, its body slim as a torpedo, its mouth a gaping maw of destruction. To her eyes, it seemed to be made entirely of water and river silt, a darker shade than the space around it, pieces of kelp layered on its body like scales or armor. The water dragon tore into the net with its barely corporeal teeth, a shriek emitting from its empty belly. Without hesitation, it turned and dove for the chainmail wall.

When the dragon's jaws met the chainmail, the metal exploded. Instead of shrapnel, a thick wave of dust plumed from the impact before floating down into the depths of the Rivers below. Rainer righted his course and surged toward the now-open path, the dark shadow of the kelp forests on either side forgotten in favor of the way illuminated by crystalline blue light.

Raegan might've raised a triumphant fist or even let out a soundless battle cry if not for the darkness creeping in from the corners of her vision. She swayed in the King's arms, trying to shake off the intense dizziness that spun her world around. But the shadows slipped in closer and her stomach flipped, and then everything went black.

∾

Raegan blinked her eyes open, expecting the diffuse golden illumination and blue velvet of the Oracle's Temple. Instead, she found the deep oil spill of night. Dead leaves rattled on branches, and everything smelled of damp vegetation and cold mud. She narrowed her eyes, trying to make out the form before her by the light of the moon. With a start, she realized it was Rainer, curled on his side like a regular horse in a farmer's field somewhere in the mundane world. His neck was upright, his head alert, ears swiveling.

"We are safe," the kelpie said, toad-like eyes finding hers easily even in the gloom.

"Right," Raegan replied in a hoarse croak, wondering why her back hurt so much until she realized she was wrapped in a thick woolen blanket and propped up against the base of a hawthorn tree. Its jagged bark bit through her leather jacket.

"We have surfaced," Rainer added, his words almost obscured by the wind humming through the bare trees surrounding them.

"Yeah, I see that," she grumbled in response, rolling her neck. "Figured there wasn't a forest in the middle of the Rivers."

In the wan moonlight, she saw Rainer cock his head. "Well, actually—"

"You are awake," came another voice, deep and low, as the King melted out of the shadows. He moved to crouch by Raegan's side. "How are you feeling?"

"I'm fine," she said, though her heart panged at the urgency in his movements. She wondered what it was to love something so fragile. "Just frustrated that every time I use magic, I lose consciousness."

Oberon glanced at her with one of those knowing, sideways looks. "Perhaps," he began with a wry smile, "you might consider starting smaller than creating a monster from water when you reach for your magic."

"I know," she said, shivering as a cold late autumn wind cut through her. "It's hard to reach past the Protectorate magic. I always have to go farther than I think, and then I end up going . . . *too* deep."

Baba Yaga's removal of Raegan's Seal had restored the potential for her to reliably reach her older powers, but it did not erase this body's birthright. As such, whenever Raegan did any sort of working, she had to evade the Protectorate magic. It was like the ocean, she had thought a few times—right beneath the surface was that mortal, god-granted power. She had to dive deeper to find the Lady of the Rivers or Titania or the Witch of the Wood. And when she found that low place, thick with black currents and heavy with the ages, it was far too easy to drown.

"That, too, will fade with time," the King replied, leaning his shoulder into hers. The contact, even through multiple layers of clothing and quite chaste in nature, sent warmth sweeping through her body.

"Now that our lady has awoken," Rainer said from across the small clearing, his tone dry, "might I suggest we save our discussions for when we are within Hiraeth's walls, not in some unwarded Welsh forest where our enemy may appear at any time?"

Raegan's heart leapt into her throat. "You said we were safe," she hissed at the kelpie, who got to his feet far more elegantly than she'd ever seen a regular horse manage.

Rainer tossed his head, eerily similar to a teenager's eye-roll. "Yes. Relatively speaking. But we could be saf*er*."

The King stood, extending a hand down to her. Raegan unwound the wool blanket from her body and hauled herself to her feet with Oberon's help. Leaves and damp soil clung to the fabric, the smell of late

October heavy in her nose. The King reached for it, and when his fingers brushed it, the woolen textile disappeared from sight.

Rainer eyed him. "The Protectorate's reactivity to magic is much more sensitive here, my liege, as you'll surely recall."

The King slid one arm through Raegan's and gestured to the hawthorn trees with his free hand. "They agreed to harbor us as Raegan recovered. We will lose such protection when we return to the riverbeds, but for now, the hawthorns keep watch."

Rainer acquiesced with an elegant nod as Oberon helped Raegan mount. She settled onto the kelpie's broad back, comforted by the feeling of the King behind her—like a bonfire on a cold winter night. All the world hung still for a moment, and she felt Rainer take a deep breath. Then the kelpie plunged through the trees as if neither he nor his passengers were made of anything but shadow and night air. The exhaustion clinging to Raegan faded away—she sat astride an ancient kelpie with the Unseelie king, and she'd used that old, sleeping thing she'd always known was within her to turn back the Protectorate. The embarrassment she'd felt at needing to rest faded, too—her body was, after all, only mortal.

When Rainer broke the treeline, Raegan saw that dawn clung to the horizon, casting the world in hues of golden gray. The River Wye awaited them up ahead, a wide silver python cutting through the damp browns and muted oranges of late autumn. It was quiet—no birds had begun their morning revelry yet, and the only sound was the soft splash of Rainer's hooves. For a moment, Raegan found herself lost in it—the thick, heavy crest of the kelpie's neck, the faint remains of moonlight sketching a path on the water. It looked like an illustration in a children's book, the rightful princess returning to her realm upon the back of her trusted steed.

If it were a children's book, though, the enemies and the dangers would be surmountable. But the hush with which Rainer moved, not even offering a snarky quip when she dug into his sides too sharply with her knees, indicated their safety balanced on a knife's edge. She felt it, too, with her Seal removed—the river offering all the protection it could, the path wavering as the moon slipped behind the sky.

The sun began to rise in earnest, flipping the power balance back in the favor of their enemies. Thickets of trees huddled on the river's banks, and Raegan had to stop herself from inspecting every shadow for a flash of chainmail. She cast her gaze ahead instead. The large, lichen-covered stones dotting the river were damp with dew, each drop catching the light like a tiny crystal. It should've been a quiet, beautiful, early morning in the Wye Valley. But instead, the hair on the back of Raegan's neck stood on end. The air was wrong—still and dead. Everything around her seemed three shades too light, like the vibrancy had been leached out of the landscape. Behind her, the King tensed, and she watched as shadow-spun armor burst into existence, quickly covering the arm he held around her waist.

"We are very close," Rainer finally said in a low voice. "But so, I fear, is the Protectorate."

Raegan glanced over her shoulder at Oberon to find him scanning the horizon, his head thrown back like he scented his prey's blood on the wind. With a deep breath, she reached out to the river, fighting to do what he'd tried to teach her during their weeks recovering at the Oracle's Temple—imagine a wall between the Protectorate magic of this body and the older, stranger things that had clung to her soul for millennia.

Then words shattered the air and Rainer jerked to a halt.

"I have to say I'm surprised," bellowed a voice that Raegan knew well and liked much less. From behind the wide, dappled trunk of a sycamore tree on the opposite bank stepped an all-too-familiar mountain of a man. Bedwyr. "I never thought you'd dare to walk these lands again. I'm glad you proved me wrong, though—now you get to see how far we've come and how far *you* have fallen."

Raegan did not know if the once-knight of Arthur was addressing her or the King or perhaps even both. All she knew was that behind her, the air exploded with that teeth-rattling magic, and when she called for the river, it did not answer.

Chapter Eight

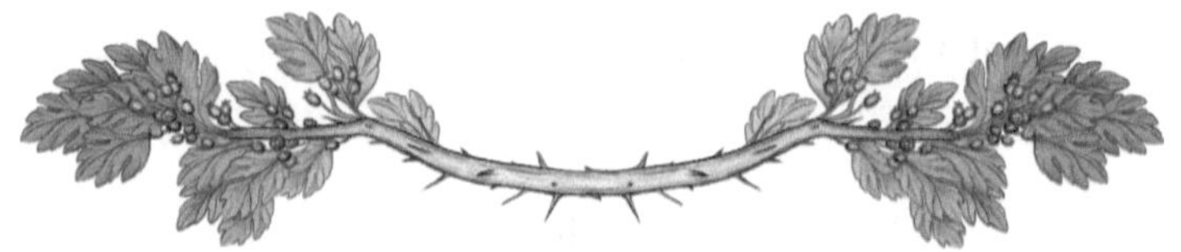

Her heart pounding, tongue sour and acrid in her mouth, Raegan whipped her head around, looking for the source of the attack. But instead of Protectorate operatives, she found herself staring at an eerily beautiful orb of slinking, transparent shadows that now surrounded them. Beyond the veil of gloom, she could just make out a group of figures, predictably dressed in drab suits. Their magic assault landed on the surface of the shadowy shield with a half-hearted boom and then dissipated.

Raegan twisted to face forward again, delighted to discover a willow tree on the opposite bank had wrapped thin, snaking branches around Bedwyr. He hacked at them with his sword, but another of the tree's limbs shot out and plucked the sword from him, promptly chucking it into the river. Beneath her, the kelpie pranced in place, sleek muscles contracting, as if eager to commit his own violence.

"Do not waste energy on anything but keeping him at bay," the King said to Rainer, gesturing to Bedwyr. "The Timekeeper does not allow death to touch him."

No, Kronos certainly did not—the only reason Raegan hadn't killed the fucking monster herself for what he'd done. She blanched, nausea rising in her throat at the memory of being carried like a carcass over the man's shoulders, brought to the crumbling manor where she'd found moments of peace and refuge with the knight she had known then as Mordred. Laid out on a damp, rotting table like a prize or a feast, a trap for her beloved. Her hands curled around Rainer's mane in white-knuckled fists.

But for all her power, she'd been human then. Mortal. She was not any longer—not entirely. Raegan let that thought sink deep into her, into the bones of this vessel and then through her legs to the kelpie and finally into the earth beneath her—the soil that had known her for a thousand years. She felt something stir, dark and deadly.

At that exact moment, the King grabbed her waist with both hands and spoke a single, sharp word. Rainer charged forward, moving down the river like a jousting destrier. She had little choice but to hold on for her life, his long stride and powerful gait dangerously close to unseating her. Up on the banks, more Protectorate were gathering, though they met a hearty resistance from the willows and ash trees.

A blow of attack magic whistled right past Rainer's ears, slipping around him as if the Protectorate's magic could not touch him at all. But the kelpie threw his head back and screamed anyway. The sound was a low and awful thing of ancient folklore and hungry riverbanks.

It stirred something in Raegan, and she almost got her hands around it before she noticed with a jolt that Oberon was trembling. The muscles of his arms were nearly convulsing. She raised one hand to his forearm, laying her palm flat.

"Are you doing *all* of this?" she asked, raising her voice to be heard above the din. "The trees, the shield?"

"Yes," Oberon grunted in her ear, his voice pained, unwinding his sword arm from her waist. "Hold on."

Raegan barely got both hands back into the kelpie's mane before Rainer leapt straight into a gallop, somehow moving even faster than before, the river spraying as his massive hooves struck its surface. Guilt and shame reddened Raegan's face. Oberon was aware she still couldn't defend herself and saw no choice but to fight on the defensive and the offensive at the same time.

"More ahead," Rainer said over the thunderous roar of his gallop.

Raegan felt the King draw a quick inhale against her back, and then his shadow blade appeared in his hand. Rainer galloped through a section of the river where the willow trees grew together closely, their branches hanging low. On the other side, the banks opened up to little more than tall grasses and woodland flowers.

The river was lined with Protectorate. For a long, terrible moment, Raegan's world moved in quarter-time, showing her every single drawn bow in horrifying detail, too many iron-tipped arrows winking in the sunlight. Between the tightly regimented formation, she could see foot soldiers waiting behind the archers, armed with swords and guns and spears and rifles. And then she realized, no, it was *not* adrenaline slowing the world down for her. It was something so much worse.

Rainer's earth-eating strides had nearly halted, too—like they were doing little more than crawling through mud when just moments ago they had been gliding across the surface of the water. The protective shield of shadows surrounding them blinked out. She had a terrible feeling that the Protectorate forces would move in real-time, which was confirmed less than a second later when arrows and bullets drew down upon them, quick and numerous as raindrops. Raegan's heart leapt into her throat as she ducked instinctively, gripping hard with her knees in a way she knew Rainer would scold her for later. If they lived long enough for such things.

Oberon had no choice but to release her waist, throwing his free arm out in a sweeping motion. Darkness rippled above them, like someone had cut a bolt of the night sky and fashioned it into a cloak. The majority of the arrows and bullets pinged off it harmlessly, falling to the ground, but she saw a red slash open on Rainer's shoulder.

All of the warnings when they'd formulated this plan came roaring back to her—that the Protectorate was much stronger here on the Isles, that pursuing this alone meant that it would be three of them against all the Timekeeper's horrors—of which there were many; Kronos and his armies knew much of the old Fair Folk magic still slept in the ancient cairns and beneath grassy hills, and they defended it as fiercely as water in a drought.

But Raegan had thought the river would answer her. She did not think she would sit helplessly on a kelpie while bullets and arrows and magical attacks rained down on her.

Rainer's voice split her concentration, but she couldn't make out his words over the vast thundering of her own blood. She threaded her fingers tighter into the kelpie's dark mane and, despite the danger, squeezed her eyes shut. The King's arm slid back around her waist, for which she was grateful, and a second later, she felt the contraction of his muscles as he cut someone down with his sword. He moved, she thought, faster than Rainer, but his speed was clearly reduced by the Protectorate's time spell.

Raegan bit down on her lip until she tasted blood—a thick rush of warmth, like the river's summer storm surges. Her eyes still closed, she leaned over Rainer's shoulder, hoping the King would keep her astride, letting her fingertips sweep the surface of the water. With all her might, she forced her Protectorate magic into a box—small and dull, a container no one would bother to open. She had not asked for this birthright, and neither had her father nor her aunt nor anyone at all in her line, she wagered, for many hundreds of years.

No more. No more of this. No more of Maelona's endless exhaustion, of her father's wild-eyed and shattered hopes. No more early graves for blood-conscripted soldiers who maybe, like Cormac, had yearned for a different world despite their inheritance.

Her fingers slick with river water, Raegan sat up straight on the back of the kelpie. She remembered that arrows and bullets rained down upon her, iron swords not far behind, and that she rode astride a water-horse whose kind had haunted folklore for a millennium. Her truer, older birthright had always been the water. The river. Life and death given in tides, ebbing and flowing with moon and storm and season. And then delicately, softly, she reached into that cool, dark place inside her, where currents rushed unseen beneath pearly gray waters.

For a heartbreaking moment, Raegan felt nothing except a sureness that she would fail everyone she had ever loved. She gritted her teeth, told the river to go fuck itself, and then plunged her hand into the black water deep within her.

Something *roared.*

Raegan opened her eyes. The water ahead of her rumbled and roiled like a witch's cauldron. Any of the Protectorate soldiers who had made their way down and into the river began to scream, rushing back up the banks, breaking their formation. Some tripped and fell, and Raegan watched with a pleasure she did not even try to deny herself as they were boiled alive. Blistered, bubbling corpses began to dot the surface, and the Protectorate forces closest to the water scrambled to step back and close ranks.

Raegan almost couldn't believe it—the river had answered. Her eyes brimmed with tears that blurred her vision, which would not do on a battlefield, so she raised one hand to wipe them away. Despite the clamor and the chaos, she felt Oberon pull her closer to him, his palm opening on the curve of her hips.

"You are terrifying," he murmured, his lips brushing the delicate shell of her ear. "I find myself jealous of those who are ravaged by your power."

Suddenly, for the first time in her life, Raegan understood the true meaning of bloodlust. She leaned back into him, sliding her fingers through his, and then she steadied herself. The river, she remembered, would give her everything. She need only ask.

What she wanted was for every single Protectorate to die here, on these banks, by her hands, and for whatever haunted these waters to feast upon their bodies. Let this section of the River Wye serve as a monument to magic's return, to defiance of the Timekeeper's reign. Let any Protectorate who survived tell their children to stay away from these banks, lest the old ghosts of war and horror awake in their graves, open-mouthed and bleating like a slain lamb.

Both the King and Rainer seemed to have shaken some of the time spell, or perhaps it had been weakened by Raegan's onslaught. Rainer's pace quickened, though he did not attempt to return to that full-out gallop; instead, his movements were agile and sharp, veering around attacks like a warhorse, snatching at flesh with his teeth as he passed.

Raegan trained her eyes on the formations along the banks. They had broken, she could see, and some Protectorate were still stumbling in the mud at the shore, clutching burned and boiled limbs.

She leaned low over Rainer's thick, arched neck, her muscles somehow no longer in need of constant willpower to keep her astride. With a deep breath, she threw out one hand, letting her fingertips graze the top of the waters again. This time, she heard riversong the moment she touched the surface—ringing in her ears as loudly as if someone were right beside her, singing ballads of teeth and silt and bones picked clean by currents.

"Feast," Raegan murmured, the word coming out long and lilting, like it was a song all on its own. And perhaps it was, because the moment she spoke, the river ahead of them reared up like a snake, every ounce of water leaving the bed entirely. Rainer veered around the neck of the riverbeast, his hooves thudding on wet mud instead of the water's surface. The creature she had summoned, Raegan saw, was not impacted by the time spell in the slightest.

With awe, she watched the river do her bidding. The creature was similar in shape to the water-dragon she'd summoned deep in the Rivers, but so much larger and realer. Currents and vegetation shimmered like scales, and when the beast opened its mouth, sharp stones studded the cavernous maw. Someone screamed, just once, and then the river was upon the entirety of the Protectorate on the left bank.

Throwing his head back, Rainer let out a battle cry that hummed in Raegan's bones as he leapt onto the opposite bank, effortlessly navigating the damp, thick grasses and hidden rocks. Higher up the bank, a red stag appeared, so glorious in the early morning light that it made Raegan's breath catch. For a moment, she wondered what had called the stag to this place—but then it caught sight of the nearest Protectorate, took three running steps, and impaled the man on its antlers. A laugh bubbled in her throat, raw and drenched in violence.

Raegan stretched her arms wide to either side, only her legs gripping Rainer's flanks, her hair flowing behind her like a bloodstained banner. She turned to the left, focusing her energy on the riverbeast that decimated the Protectorate's forces. When she saw only a few remained, she beckoned the beast to her. It reared back and screamed before snaking across the wet black riverbed, its jaws open for more.

The sound of grown men imbued with an unnatural and unearned power screaming at the top of their lungs would live in Raegan's bones forever, she thought, and she would store it carefully. Wrap it in wax paper, bind it with blessed twine, and take it out only to feast in the most hungry and lonesome of times. It was a sacred sound, and it was worship —just as good as any prayer or offering.

The Protectorate had gone against the natural order, the Time-keeper had taken more than he needed while others went hungry, and the woods and the fields and the waters had been razed and polluted and bled dry.

And now they would pay for what they had done.

Chapter Nine

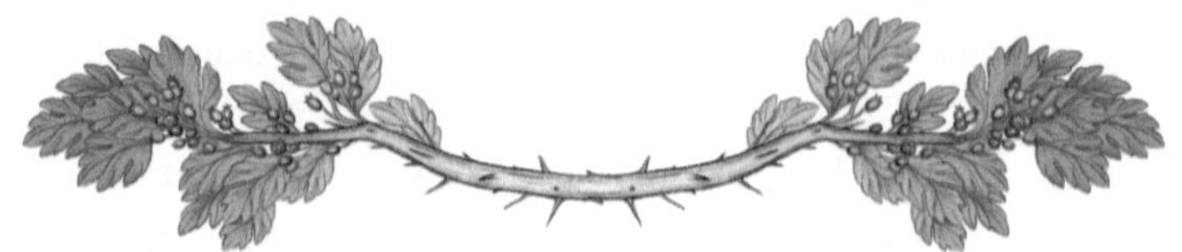

Her river monster tore through the Protectorate's ranks. Anyone who managed to miss the creature's riverstone teeth met the King's blade or Rainer's hooves. In a few minutes, it was all over, leaving Raegan breathing hard and shaking. Light-headed and nauseous, she slid off Rainer, moving to stand at the kelpie's shoulder. She watched the King roam the battlefield, chewing her bottom lip raw in the process.

In the old times, the Morrigan would've appeared with her crows. If neither side of the battle had her favor, she'd feast on the hearts of brave warriors while her crows devoured whatever flesh they could find. But if one army had the Morrigan's allegiance, then the goddess would roam the battlefield with one of her many daggers and dispatch any of the enemy that remained.

With the Gates still standing and the door Raegan had torn long since sealed back up, there was no goddess of war, death, and magic to do this work. Instead, the King took it on, examining each prone body for signs of life and sliding the point of his sword through every heart he could find. Unable to continue watching, she turned away from Rainer and made her way to the banks to give thanks to the river instead. It was necessary, yes, but in truth she could not handle the task Oberon had silently taken up. Fighting in the heat of battle was one thing, but ensuring there were no survivors, ending the lives of those who could not fight back—it turned her stomach. She supposed it was a mercy for some, and she understood the strategic advantage of leaving no one alive. It probably made her a coward that she saw the reasoning but couldn't carry it out herself.

When the river had been properly sated—a long, tumbling prayer Raegan hadn't remembered until now, a lock of her hair, and seven drops of her blood—she felt the King appear at her side. Raegan straightened, dusting the dirt off the front of her jeans. The birdsong had returned a few minutes prior, and the wind danced coyly through the dry leaves. She examined Oberon in the bright morning light. His shadow armor had dissipated. Barely a hair was out of place, his elegantly cut suit unmarred, as if he had wandered in from afternoon tea, not a battle.

Oberon sheathed his sword without saying a word. Then he closed his eyes. Raegan took a step toward him, surprised to find that upon closer inspection, he looked harrowed. An exhausted shadow clung to every sharp angle of his face, sunken and sallow instead of feral.

Movement rustled a few paces down the river, and the King turned, all predator again, his eyes gleaming hungry in the sunshine. A low groan came from behind a willow tree's curtain of limbs. Oberon moved like a panther, nothing but shadow and grace and violence. Before Raegan could fully process the scene before her, the King was dragging something—*someone*—by the scruff of their neck from beneath the willow.

"P-p-please," a voice—young, shrill—sputtered.

Raegan moved to meet the King as he stalked out into the open, pulling the person behind him like they weighed nothing at all. She stood facing the King, peering down into the grass. In Oberon's deadly grasp was a mortal who looked barely out of their teenage years. The sight of their sandy brown curls sent discomfort skittering through her stomach. Hazel eyes peered up at her, wide with horror and brimming with tears. Without a word, the King released his fingers from the back of their armor, sending them slamming into the earth. They let out a long, low hiss, squeezing their eyes shut.

"Oberon," Raegan murmured, reaching out to brush his arm as he went to draw his sword.

He looked down at her, the angle casting a hood of shadow over his eyes. He said nothing, but he didn't have to—her lover was not present. Only the Unseelie king, the faerie rebel who had survived a thousand years of warfare and near-extinction, stood before her now. He had no mercy left, and part of Raegan didn't blame him.

"They're just a kid," she said softly, looking up at him.

Without a word, the King gestured to their chainmail and gray suit, the gun holstered at their waist, the empty scabbard—probably missing a shortsword, Raegan identified reflexively.

"I know how much some of us don't want this," she implored, reaching for his hand. The King allowed her to touch him, but he didn't curl his long fingers around hers in his usual reflexive motion. "We aren't given a choice, Oberon."

The young Protectorate hacked a horrible-sounding cough, and as Raegan looked down, she saw blood bubbling from their mouth. They laid their head back down in the grass, eyes staring up at the sky, roving about like maybe it might be the last thing they ever saw.

"And my people are?" the King wanted to know, his voice low and slinking. "Perhaps you noticed during your time with my Court that there are very few Fey children. Has the removal of your Seal reminded you why that is?"

Raegan flinched. The cruelty of his tone felt unnecessary; she hated the Protectorate, too. For gods' sake, they'd executed her once. In that life, Fate had either played Her most fucked-up trick, or She'd simply made a mistake, and Raegan had lived as the High Seelie Queen. She knew the way the Protectorate would seek out Fey children and slaughter them. She'd held limp and gray faerie babies to her chest and wept. She fucking *knew*.

"They're a kid," she repeated, her voice louder now.

"They are dressed and armed for battle," the King roared in response, his lip curled, his eyes all black, none of that fathomless gray sea she thought she might like to drown in. "If they are indeed a child, that transgression is on the Protectorate for sending their little ones into the fray."

"I–I'm t-twenty," the soldier piped up unexpectedly, their teeth beginning to chatter. Shock, Raegan realized.

"Did you want to fight today?" Raegan asked, placing her palm flat against the King's chest. She knew it was as good as hoping a single strand of silk ribbon might hold back a charging panther. To her surprise, the soldier laughed.

"Do I l-look like I'm having f-fun?" Their voice was clearer now, the accent Irish. "Besides, d-don't think you'd b-believe anything I s-say."

Before the King could stop her, Raegan stooped low, settled her hand on top of those uncomfortably familiar curls, and spoke softly to the river. The waters had fed today; there had been much death. *Allow a little life*, she pleaded. Her fingers warmed, and something effervescent and sparkling bubbled in her chest, golden as an August sunset. She felt the warmth leave her fingertips and rush into the young Protectorate. They gasped, clutching their hands to their chest as their pallor changed from gray to pale sand. Freckles suddenly stood out on their cheekbones, and they blinked, breathing raggedly.

The King let out a long sigh.

"Did you—did you just . . . ?" the soldier asked, their voice trailing off. They groaned, moving stiffly to sit up. Surprisingly, they made no attempt to flee, though Raegan hadn't intended to heal them completely —just stave off immediate death. The soldier took a deep breath and then looked up at Raegan and the King. Their eyes widened as they took Raegan in, but when their gaze fell on Oberon, pure horror shattered their little heart-shaped face.

"May Kronos save me," the soldier whispered reflexively, trying to use their arms to propel them backwards, but the King caught them by their scruff again. At the mention of the Timekeeper, Oberon flinched and then looked at Raegan, as if to prove a point.

"I still say 'Jesus Christ,'" she said before the King could speak, one eyebrow arched at him. "Or 'for god's sake.' I don't actually *believe* in it."

The soldier was struggling hard against the King's grasp, completely ineffectively, like a fish on land, the hook already in its mouth. Raegan walked around their captive, kneeling to face them.

"What's your name?" she asked.

The King let out a long string of curses in High Feyrish, a beyond-ancient language that even most Fair Folk didn't know anymore.

"Reilly," the mortal replied, their eyes never leaving the King's broad figure. "Th-thank you for healing me. For . . . for w-whatever it's worth, no, I didn't much fancy fighting t-today. Or any day, really." Oberon's grip did not slacken. Raegan chewed her lip, examining the soldier. "Makes n-no bloody sense, but, you know—thanks," Reilly added, hasty and nervous.

Wordlessly, the King lifted the soldier from the ground by their collar. Their feet dangled, and their breath came out in panicked gasps as Oberon raised them to eye level. He held them aloft, saying nothing, and Reilly visibly panicked more and more with each passing second they were forced to spend staring down the nightmare they'd been raised to fear beyond all else since birth.

"It was the Lady of the Rivers who spared you today," the King said in such a low, cruel tone that goosebumps prickled Raegan's flesh. "Not I. Not the Unseelie king."

Reilly nodded furiously, like they were in full agreement, though Raegan knew the King could have spouted nonsense and the young soldier would have readily complied.

"Go," the King commanded, barely letting Reilly's feet graze the earth before he released them.

The soldier scrambled for their footing and then stood there, their eyes wide, breathing shallow and quick, completely frozen in place.

"Go," the King repeated in a roar, one powerful hand moving for the pommel of his sword.

At that, Reilly bolted like a deer, taking off along the narrow riverside path, almost invisible beneath the willows. Raegan watched them go, grinding her jaw.

"*That*," the King snarled, suddenly so close that his breath stirred Raegan's hair, "will almost assuredly be a problem later."

She turned back sharply to face the King, away from the direction Reilly had run, her stomach boiling, poisonous words on her tongue. But as she did, she saw that Rainer had joined them.

"There appear to be no reinforcements coming for now," the kelpie said, sticking to the shallows, moving like the shadow of a large fish beneath the waters. "May we depart?"

Raegan bit down on her tongue, unsure if Rainer hadn't seen any of what had just transpired or simply chose to not comment. No, she was sure he hadn't seen anything. When had the kelpie *ever* managed to refrain from commenting?

"Yes," the King agreed, offering his arm to Raegan despite their argument. Unsure, she took it, and he helped her onto Rainer's back. The kelpie moved into a lofty trot, the gash on his shoulder appearing to bother him only a little. Raegan thought she'd have energy to heal it when they found a safe place to rest, though she felt a pang of guilt for helping Reilly first.

Silence sat heavy as they followed the river. None of them spoke, though that storm still brewed between Raegan and the King.

A mile or more had passed when the waters twisted into a copse of ash and alder trees, the branches thatched together to create a roof of gloom. Rainer slowed at the copse's mouth. The King tensed behind her, and Raegan cast her eyes into the dimness, desperately waiting for her vision to adjust from the bright sun of the unsheltered banks.

"I hope you enjoy it, for now," came a voice—a voice Raegan knew so well, had hated before she even remembered who she really was—from up ahead.

Rainer let out a snarling, carnivorous sound and plunged forward. On the right bank, his back against the trunk of a tree, lay Bedwyr. One hand was pressed to his side, and even in the low light, Raegan could see the blood pooling between his fingers. Triumph surged through her before she remembered he could not stay dead—he could bleed and he could die, but the Timekeeper always brought his favorite pet back.

Rainer approached, his footfall heavy and threatening, moving like a cat about to pounce. Bedwyr watched them, heavy-lidded, his breathing uneven. Raegan shuddered with revulsion as she realized Bedwyr might be one of the only other people to ever exist who knew intimately what she went through. Rage flared to life in her chest; how *dare* Fate and the Timekeeper link her to her once-murderer like this?

"How long will you last this time?" Bedwyr asked, his gaze meeting Raegan's. "A year? Maybe two? Time never seems to be kind to the Unseelie king's little whore."

Raegan rolled her eyes at the predictability of men, but behind her, Oberon stiffened. She felt his hand clench tighter around her waist, and some twisted kind of heat pooled between her legs.

"May I?" the King murmured in her ear.

Raegan froze, bloodthirsty desire racing up her throat, open-mouthed and wanting. But why would he *want* to after their disagreement? Why would he still seek to exercise the sharp, violent edges of his devotion—wasn't she too hard to love?

"Be my guest," she managed to reply breathlessly.

With her consent, the King slid down from behind her and stalked toward Bedwyr. As much as she wanted to watch the King's movements —imbued with an impossible predatory grace that set her entire body on fire—Raegan found her eyes falling onto Arthur's fallen knight. The myths remembered Lancelot and Arthur being so close, but by the end of it all, the fabled king had grown to favor Bedwyr more. Arthur had valued Bedwyr's penchant for cruelty—and put it to good use.

Which made it even more satisfying to see that Bedwyr was afraid. She didn't bother holding back her laugh. Didn't she know that feeling so well? Neither of them could melt into the quiet, dark embrace of death, but they could both *die*. Death was soft and lovely. But dying? Raegan found that it usually fucking hurt.

The King lifted Bedwyr from the ground by his throat, pulling his sword from its scabbard with his other hand. He moved languidly, like all of this was a ballroom dance and not a cold-blooded murder. Bedwyr scrambled, reaching for his own sword, but the King batted his hand away, pinning the knight against the trunk of the tree. Then he buried his sword in Bedwyr's existing gut wound, twisting it in slowly. The knight screamed, the sound reverberating through the trees and deep into Raegan's bones.

The limbs of the alder Bedwyr had just been impaled against began to reach for him, sliding through his legs, driving slowly into his flesh.

"It doesn't make a difference," the knight wheezed, trying hard to sound triumphant and failing. "I'll come back."

"When you do," the King said, his voice regal and horrible all at once, fingers still tight around Bedwyr's neck, "stay *far* away from her."

And then the King tilted his head, bared his teeth, and tore out Bedwyr's throat.

CHAPTER TEN

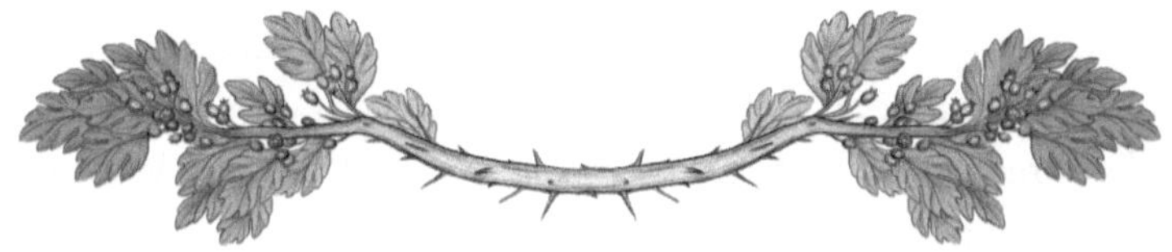

The King let Bedwyr's lifeless body drop to the ground like spoiled fruit at late harvest. Then he turned, sheathed his sword, and met Raegan's eyes. A pulse flared hot and hungry deep in her bones, every part of her igniting, flint-sparked. Blood streaked dark across his full, sculpted lips, a harsh shadow on his ivory skin. Sparing the young Protectorate soldier had deeply angered the King, and yet here he was, looking at her like he'd devour the entire world if only she'd ask. With a deep breath, Raegan tried desperately to center herself, digging half-moons into her palms. She did not even want to think about what the kelpie she sat astride might be able to sense.

But as the King approached, the dark, raw power emanating from him overpowered Raegan entirely. He stopped, standing silent beside her, gaze tipped up toward hers as one powerful hand slid onto her thigh. She thought of nothing—not the kelpie, not their exposed position, not magic nor Fate nor the Protectorate. Nothing at all but *him* as she reached out with both hands, seized the King by the front of his shirt, and brought her mouth to his.

He met her with a palpable hunger, his palms slipping to the curve of her waist. Raegan tangled her fingers in the obsidian waves of his hair, Bedwyr's blood—like iron and ash—mixing with the taste of the King, all woodsmoke and folklore and the endless reach of night. She could've stayed there forever, but Oberon broke away gently, though his hands still roamed her body.

"We must keep moving," he murmured, long fingers brushing back curls that had escaped her braid.

"Thank you," Raegan replied, holding his gaze, wondering why she had ever tried to love anyone else.

"Always," Oberon replied, fingertips brushing her lips—now bruised with Bedwyr's blood, too, she imagined—before steadying himself and swinging onto Rainer's back.

The three were silent as they traveled down the River Wye. Raegan dabbed at her mouth with the sleeve of her sweater, perversely pleased to find the gray fabric darkened with blood. The thrill lasted only a few moments—then her adrenaline crashed entirely, and Raegan realized exactly how exhausted she was. Every muscle in her body ached, particularly her legs, and sleep pawed at her. The temptation to doze off to the gentle sway of Rainer's movements, tucked into Oberon's muscular arms, was thick and sweet as honey. But she knew that for all her exhaustion, the King must be feeling it tenfold. With a sigh, she sat upright in his arms, not wanting to ask him to give anything more than he already had.

The banks ahead seemed clear of Protectorate, and at some point, Rainer broke the silence by relaying that the kelpies thought the soldiers had withdrawn to regroup. That should buy enough time to get to Hiraeth. Raegan ran her fingers through Rainer's thick, wavy mane, hoping beyond hope that they could actually find the door to Avalon. That they could actually turn back the faerie blade. Actually save magic.

Early morning slipped away, the sun rising higher as Rainer ferried his cargo along the river. Raegan watched, fascinated, as the kelpie slipped by hikers and kayakers and fishermen, all completely unaware of their presence. She'd just thought she had a grasp on the magic Rainer was using to render them undetectable when the kelpie spoke.

"Nearly there," he said. "We should be able to cross quickly. The Protectorate is licking their wounds, at least for now."

She straightened, peering around the tight bend of the river. All she saw was a vast meadow nestled in the curve of the river, nearly obscured by the slant of the trees and roll of the hills. She narrowed her eyes, fighting to engage her second sight—something that had once been as easy as breathing in previous lives, but since the Seal's removal in this body, took intense concentration.

For a moment, the kelpie beneath her and the solid mass of the King behind her faded away, and she almost had it—a slide of another lens across her vision, like a lizard's inner eyelid. The meadow disappeared. Or rather, it was no longer empty. An image flickered to life instead: rain-dampened stone and smoke-wreathed chimneys and narrow, twisting pathways. Something in her heart panged, familiarity wrapping around her like an old, worn-in blanket.

But then it was gone, only an empty meadow staring back at her. Frustration simmered in Raegan's body, but then she realized that this time, she hadn't failed. Instead, her sight had been fiercely and definitively rejected.

"What exactly *is* this place again?" she asked Oberon, not stopping the awe from creeping into her tone. As far as she knew, they were still deep in the Welsh countryside, but the village—or small city, perhaps—she'd glimpsed for a heartbeat looked more like photos she'd seen of Edinburgh.

"A hold-out," the King replied. Rainer began to work his way into the shallows as the sun dipped behind a thick coil of incoming rain-clouds, casting the picturesque surroundings into grayscale. "An exception to the Protectorate rule of the Isles. A last defiance, if you will."

"And do you trust it?" Raegan wanted to know.

"I do not trust anything," Oberon replied, an amused laugh leaving his lips when Raegan reacted with an overly dramatic sigh at his predictable answer. "But I trust the people of Hiraeth, and in particular I trust our host more than most. He has done this work for many centuries, never ceding an inch to the Protectorate."

Raegan nodded, anticipation fluttering beneath her breastbone. Another glance through the worn spot in the tapestry, another foray into the world-behind-the-world.

"We won't put them in danger?" she inquired, though she knew the answer from their weeks of preparation: yes.

"We will," Oberon replied, his tone soft and hung heavy with all the weight of a throne. "But it is a necessary danger, and, more importantly, one that the people have accepted. Their wards are strong and have stood for many years."

Raegan nodded, though anxiety still churned in her stomach. A column of wind blew hard across the river, bringing a spray of rain with it. She examined the meadow, eager to be tucked away behind stone walls, no longer out in the open. Through the raindrops, she spied hawthorn trees dotted around the space and smiled. If she thought it was only open land, she wouldn't have given the hawthorns a second thought —but knowing what she did, it was hard not to see a circle of trees sacred to the Fey. It was hard not to see a faerie ring.

The river barely reached Rainer's ankles now, and he carried them up a marshy bank, coming to a halt a few strides from the water's edge. Behind her, the King dismounted, and though the movement itself was full of his usual grace, the landing was unsteady. Concern and a small trickle of fear shot through Raegan. He needed rest as much as she did. She scrambled down from the kelpie's back on her own, not wanting to further tax him, and earned herself a grumble from Rainer about preferring that her flailing elbows stayed away from his ribs.

"Thank you, Rainer," the King murmured, reaching out one hand to rest it on the kelpie's thick, heavy mane. In response, Rainer said nothing but turned to nuzzle the King's shoulder in an alarmingly equine manner given the rest of his personality and tendencies.

"Into battle we shall always go as brothers," the kelpie said eventually, his tone low and sonorous. Oberon nodded, leaning forward to rest his forehead against Rainer's. Raegan settled for reaching out to stroke the kelpie's neck.

"Thanks for not drowning me," she said, preparing herself to follow Oberon as he straightened. Then she noticed the wound on Rainer's shoulder from their clash with the Protectorate. "Oh. Here. I think I can do this again."

Raegan spoke to the water, wondering if it might grant one last boon. The goddess of this river, Gwy, had been slain by the Protectorate during the Uprising, so nothing divine could answer her call. Only the water—the water blackened with blood, the primal and ancient wells of life and silt and death.

When she opened her eyes, the gash on Rainer's shoulder was certainly still visible, but it had gone shiny and pink, a wound at least one week healed.

"I am in your debt, Lady of the Rivers," the kelpie told her, bowing his head. "Now go. Beyond the wards with you both. I doubt such a small act of healing would alert the Protectorate in their current state, but we must move with the utmost caution."

Raegan nodded and took one more look at the kelpie—right now, every single time felt like it could be the last—and then turned toward the meadow. The rain bore down, bringing with it the smell of woodsmoke and beeswax and damp oilskins. Raegan shivered.

Beside her, the King offered his arm, and together they climbed up the slope from the river. Raegan felt a soft pull at her very essence, like the waters bid her to stay, to forget the world above and sleep in the muck, where she would be hidden and safe. But Raegan did not want to be safe and she did not want to sleep. She wanted to fight.

"You should know," Oberon said, glancing over at her, his profile regal, "many years ago, there was a Temple here and, of course, an Oracle. After the Uprising, the Protectorate destroyed the Temple and killed its Oracle."

Disgust simmered in Raegan's gut. An Oracle's Temple was one of the most sacred places on earth, and there were so, *so* few. To destroy one felt profane, even for the Protectorate.

"But our people took what they could back, and the Temple became something else—a teahouse for the city's citizens and a waystation for its visitors. Our host," the King continued, grass underfoot now, something shimmering in the air around them, "was once the Temple's Keeper."

CHAPTER ELEVEN

A door opened in the rain. Despite all she'd seen, Raegan struggled to process it for a long moment—a rectangle cut out of the meadow, drenched in blues and greens, the silhouette of a man standing within it, backlit by the dancing orange glow of a hearth.

"Come inside," said the shadowed man in a clear, strong voice, each letter enunciated. "And welcome to Hiraeth."

The King laced his fingers through Raegan's and pulled her across the threshold. Behind them, the roar of the wind through the meadow abruptly cut off, leaving her ears ringing in the silence. But then different sounds quickly trickled in—low murmurs and the clink of porcelain and the crackle of a fire.

The man who had invited them into Hiraeth stepped back, the light from a nearby lantern illuminating his features. He was tall and distinguished in a casual sort of way, just as easily thirty as fifty or three hundred. His sharp jaw and deeply set monolid eyes revealed wisdom but defied exact age. Round metal glasses perched on his nose, and his hair was black-brown, shot through in some places with shimmering silver, a handsome contrast against his warm, rich skin. His expression was kind but guarded, and his dark eyes held a sharpened sort of intelligence that Raegan liked immediately. Unlike the other Keeper she was familiar with, this man dressed in worn jeans, brown leather boots, a faded chore jacket, and a gray sweater.

Raegan's eyes swept around the narrow room surrounding them—a vestibule, maybe, considering its small footprint and high, vaulted ceilings. Behind the man were beautiful double doors, all glinting leaded glass and carved dark wood; she couldn't make out anything on the other side.

"Merry meet, Emrys," the King greeted, regal as always.

The Keeper inclined his head with a slight smile, his gaze dipping toward Raegan, something that might have been distrust crossing his expression for a moment. "It has been some time, my liege," he replied after a moment's pause. "Please, follow me."

The King moved forward, his hand still in Raegan's, and she went with him. Together, they passed through the grand, heavy doors, which led into a stone-walled antechamber. An iron chandelier hung from the highest point of the vaulted ceiling, the flickering candles upon it casting uneven shadows around the room. At the far end stood another set of large double doors, and through the glass, Raegan thought she saw movement. She strained her ears and caught more of the sounds she'd heard earlier—conversing voices and clinking porcelain. The teahouse, she figured.

"We appreciate your hospitality despite the dangers," the King said, coming to a stop when Emrys did atop a beautiful if threadbare rug. Raegan looked to either side and found a hallway leading off in both directions, cloaked in shadow. It was the kind of room where assailants might slip from the darkness, knives gripped in steady hands, but Raegan found she felt no apprehension.

"It is our honor," Emrys replied with a bow of his head. "As I discussed with the kelpies, I think it is best that no one knows you are here. Every year, the people of Hiraeth have renewed their centuries-old agreement to harbor the Unseelie Court when and if necessary, so understand that you are not imposing on innocent townspeople unaware of the risks. But that does mean you'll be a bit cooped up."

"It is for the best," Oberon replied with that easy authority of his. Raegan, realizing that Emrys was looking to her for agreement as well, nodded.

"Then please, follow me," Emrys said, turning to the hallway on the left. "You'll be staying with me in the old Temple."

The passage was much shorter than she would've expected before entering the shadow-cloaked space—or perhaps it was only brief and painless because Hiraeth had permitted them within her sanctum. There was a soft pop as she passed over the threshold, and then she found herself standing in a large room. At the far end, a fire crackled in a massive stone hearth, engraved with figures and creatures Raegan couldn't make out. To her left, the rain lashed a large bay window that offered a view of a narrow stone street and roving tendrils of mist. Nestled beneath the bay window was a heavy wood table with high-backed chairs.

She moved deeper into the space, Oberon at her side, and noticed two faded tapestries hanging on either side of the fireplace. One depicted a maiden peering into a large, shallow dish of water; the other showed a tall, elegant figure standing before a small fire, arms raised skyward.

Oracles, Raegan realized. Remnants, she imagined, of the Temple that once stood here. The only parts of that place its Keeper could still watch over, kept beside the hearth in a place of honor. Her heart panged. Such was the story of magic—endless losses, a thousand funerals, the few survivors holding tight to the tiny fragments of what once was.

"Have a seat, please," Emrys instructed, gesturing to the table. He shrugged out of his chore jacket and hung it on a much-used iron hook set into the wall. He was more muscular than the Keeper Raegan knew, and a voice at the back of her head whispered that he was likely quite comfortable with sword and bow.

"If what I hear from the kelpies is true, you must be exhausted," Emrys called before ducking through a dark archway on the far side of the bay window, disappearing into another room.

Oberon pulled a chair out for her and then settled into one beside it, his elbow resting on the table's dark, shining surface. "I would never encourage you to be completely without suspicion," he murmured, eyes meeting hers, "but we are safe. We can rest. Emrys has kept the path longer than most."

Raegan nodded, sagging back into the chair. Despite the heat of the fire, she didn't remove her leather jacket yet.

A door creaked open, and Emrys appeared from a shadowed hallway, carrying a black metal tray with swooping, scalloped edges. Upon it was a plate piled high with tea cakes, two large pots of tea, a selection of jams and creams, and three teacups with saucers. The teaware was beautiful—a shining sterling silver pot in the shape of an elegant gourd, a stylized vine curling off the lid. The teacups were pitch-black, gilded with silver around their wide mouths.

"Thank you," Raegan said, reaching for a cup the second the tray hit the table. The three of them prepared their tea in silence. After a few large, perfectly brewed gulps that burned her mouth—she did not mind —Raegan reached for a tea cake. They were perfect: a little sweet with hints of cinnamon, dotted with dried currants.

"Do you have any injuries that need attending to?" Emrys asked after a few minutes of companionable silence. "Any other immediate needs?"

"Only rest for now," the King replied, folding his hands on the table. "Raegan will likely require a larger meal, yes?" He turned to look at her to confirm, and for a moment, she clearly saw the deep exhaustion on his angular face.

"Yes," she said, meeting Emrys's gaze. "Still very much human in that regard."

"I expected as much," the once-Keeper replied. "Should be ready in a few hours, if that's alright."

Raegan nodded, adding a few more biscuits to her plate, this time sampling some of the different jams and jellies.

"I encourage you to rest today," Emrys said, pouring more tea into his cup. "If you have cause to walk the streets of Hiraeth, please use one of the glamoured cloaks by the door. The glamour workings are linked, so wearers of the cloaks are visible to each other, but no one else. Try your best not to speak to anyone. Hiraeth's people will question new faces. Remember, we keep this city safe because those of us who become citizens agree to never again leave its walls."

The jelly's flavors of earl gray and strawberry bursting delightfully on her tongue seemed much at odds with Emrys's grave words. But

Raegan nodded, casting another look out the large bay window to her left.

Across the winding stone street, tall stone rowhomes rose into the mist. Most of the first floors seemed to be occupied by shops—she could make out an apothecary and a stationery store. The path was lit by elegant lamps, dark metal stalks curling from the street, delicate pools of honey-colored light hanging like lily-of-the-valley buds. Her heart ached to explore this place.

"We thank you and Hiraeth's people for providing us a home as we search for Avalon," the King said, his tone mild, long fingers tracing the silver-rimmed mouth of his teacup.

"We should speak of Avalon after you've rested," Emrys replied, expression softening. "No offense, but the two of you look like hell."

Oberon and Raegan laughed in unison, the amusement genuine but the sound itself ragged, torn around the edges.

"There are many places Modron could have buried her door," the King mused. "I look forward to hearing your theories. The Unseelie Court is lucky to have a mind as vast and nimble as yours to call upon."

At that, Emrys beamed, his kind but serious face looking far more human for a few moments. Raegan smiled into her tea; the way so many Fair Folk blossomed under Oberon's praise delighted her and probably, if she was being honest, helped assuage any concerns she felt over possibly choosing the wrong side.

Looking up from her teacup, she examined Emrys's features. He *was* Fey, she was fairly sure, though he lacked the feral angles and his ears were only slightly pointed. Perhaps, like her, he was something alto-gether more complicated, though Raegan did not have the mental energy to tackle that at present.

"Will you actually be safe?" she asked suddenly, looking into Emrys's dark brown eyes, scrutinizing what she found there. Thoughts of the Philadelphia Temple laden with makeshift bedchambers and displaced Fey who didn't know if they'd ever see their homes again filled her mind. "Will your wards hold? I don't want to fuck up your life, too."

Emrys evaluated her, and then his mouth twisted into something arch but not unkind. "Hiraeth's wards have held for more than three hundred years, and nearly a thousand before the attack on the Temple.

And alas, even if they do not, my lady, it is our choice to make the sacrifice."

Raegan held his gaze and said nothing for a long moment. Then she sighed, shrugged, and settled for, "Thank you, Emrys." She took another sip of tea, hoping the weight of so many people's hopes and faith would not crush her.

Once the remaining tea cakes had been polished off—mostly by Raegan, with some support from Emrys—Oberon got to his feet, grimacing when he shifted weight onto his left side. "Emrys," he began, "would you be so kind as to show us to our room?"

"Of course," the distinguished man replied, pushing his chair back. "Follow me, please."

Emrys led them through a passage that branched off from the far end of the room, near the fireplace, and then up a set of grand stone stairs. The stairwell was adorned with portraits, each painting featuring a silver nameplate affixed to the heavy, ornate black frames. A plush rug of deep plum florals softened the landing where Emrys paused for a moment before continuing down a wide hallway lit by Art Nouveau-style lamps.

He opened the third door on the right. Raegan kept close on Oberon's heels, curiosity overpowering her tiredness for a few moments. The room that greeted her was breathtaking. Clad in gray stone and dark wood, the space included an ornately carved fireplace, a four-poster bed with a tapestry-like quilt on it, and a heavy armoire. The far wall was mostly taken up by gabled windows. One deep windowsill was lined with round velvet pillows in moody jewel tones. Raegan eyed the little nook with delight; it was so easy to imagine herself tucked away there with a book, looking down on the twisting, rainy streets of Hiraeth. But then she remembered her path held little room for pleasure and turned away regretfully.

Emrys showed them the narrow door that led to the bathroom. The dark wood continued there, too, accenting the high ceilings with carved crown moldings. The wallpaper depicted a meadow scene not unlike the ones visible in the valley beyond the city's walls. A clawfoot tub, pedestal sink, and separate glass-surround shower—the only modern-looking thing in the room—were arranged beautifully in the space.

Another large bay window of leaded glass invited in the delicious sound of the rain's pitter-patter.

"I have some work to attend to," Emrys said, looking between Raegan and the King. "But help yourself to anything in the old Temple. Take care if you step beyond its walls. You'll know you've neared one of the city's edges when you come across the hawthorn trees. Our wards are strong, and the city moves constantly, shrouded in old workings—which is why you'll find it's always raining in Hiraeth. And that reminds me—I'll need to add your blood to the wards. They are . . . hungrier than most."

At that, Emrys pulled a glass vial from his pocket, along with a sharp sewing needle. Oberon and Raegan pricked their fingers without protest, squeezing a few drops into the vial. At the bottom, Raegan noticed a curl of paper, as well as some dried herbs. Rosemary, maybe, and angelica. In any other situation, she'd pause, refusing to give her blood until all her questions were answered. But as difficult as she normally found it to trust people, she felt no apprehension at following Oberon's lead. She had trusted him—and often *only* him—for more than a thousand years. Besides, truth be told, she just didn't have the energy.

Raegan barely had the bandwidth to run a bath and climb into it, which was exactly what she did after Emrys departed. Once the bath had filled, dosed with some of the lavender-scented salts kept in a lovely glass jar beside the tub, she gleefully shed her blood- and river-mud-streaked clothes and slipped beneath the hot, silky waters. In moments, she was half asleep, and she barely even registered when Oberon entered the bathroom and stepped into the shower. By the time she felt a bit more like a living, breathing person, he'd long since departed and her bathwater had gone cold.

Raegan climbed out, supposing that not everyone spelled their bathtub to stay hot like the King had for the guest rooms in his archives. She toweled off, rubbing condensation from the mirror above the sink with the flat of her forearm. It felt like a hundred years since she'd been in the archives, though in reality, Raegan knew it hadn't been more than a few weeks. She splashed some water on her face, brushed her teeth, and pulled on one of the soft flannel robes that hung on the back of the door.

Then she walked out into the main room, finding Oberon on the bed with his eyes closed, though she very much doubted he was asleep. Just in case, Raegan tip-toed to where she'd left her clothes, digging into her leather jacket pocket for the luggage tag—the spelled object the King had given her back at her apartment in Philadelphia that condensed all her belongings to a slim piece of leather. She found the tag and placed it on the gabled windowsill, waiting for the spell to unfurl and reveal her travel bags.

As she did, Raegan caught a flash of movement outside the window. A Fey toddler and their parent walked down the street, the child stopping at every puddle and jumping into it as hard as they could, splashing rainwater everywhere. A strangled noise escaped Raegan's throat as panic surged in her chest.

"What if the Protectorate find Hiraeth because of us?" she asked, her voice raw.

"We will do what we can to ensure they will not," Oberon reassured her.

Raegan spun, hands clenched into fists. He hadn't moved from the bed, though his eyes were open.

"But they're so much more powerful here," she said, thinking back to the time magic they'd worked at the river, at how taxed Oberon was.

She'd *known* this—it had been discussed in all their planning. The American government had its own shadowy paranormal organization, but they hardly considered the Protectorate their brothers-in-arms. The Protectorate, in their eyes, were superstitious and obsessed with the Fair Folk. Operatives were under strict rules of no gunfire and absolutely no larger workings like time magic while on American soil. Raegan suspected the United States just didn't like to be outgunned; *their* organization certainly didn't have a thousand-year-old pact with a god. But the Protectorate still followed the Americans' rules. Leave it to two imperialist empires to begrudgingly respect each other, if no one else.

"They are indeed more powerful here," Oberon agreed, sounding a bit ragged.

He did not offer any other words of comfort as Raegan grabbed a pair of sweatpants and a t-shirt from her bag. She took one last look at the narrow, winding streets below, which were busier now that the rain had lightened up. When the guilt felt like it might swallow her whole, she gave up with a sigh and walked over to the bed. She'd been planning to get dressed and go make another pot of tea, but the sight of him derailed her thoughts.

She'd never quite seen him like this—barely able to keep his eyes open, but also unable to sleep. His brow was heavy, his jaw clenched, the vast tides of his breathing interrupted by sharp hitches. Hesitating, Raegan stood on the other side of the bed, biting down on her lip.

"Can I do anything?" she asked, the words coming out hoarse, scraping her throat as she spoke. Shame spun a web around her lungs. She could've done more at the river, she knew. Been stronger. Fought harder. Gotten her shit together. And then Oberon wouldn't be suffering like this, laid out like a corpse.

"No, but thank you for offering," he replied, barely more than an exhalation.

Raegan told herself it was just the gray light of Hiraeth's rain that made him look so sallow, so wan. She swallowed hard and gritted her teeth. Her hands went clammy, her insides twisting tight as a hangman's noose. How close, Raegan wondered, her eyes pricking with hot, burning tears, had she come to losing him again this morning?

Trying to shove the thought away, she settled onto the quilt. "Is it okay if I lie down, too?" she asked in a whisper.

At that, Oberon opened his eyes. "Of course," he replied, his gaze sweeping over her, a frown twisting his full mouth. "I will be alright, *cariad*. I am in a great deal of pain, but it will improve with rest."

"Okay," she replied, pushing away a stray tear before he could see. Gods—he was only in so much pain because of her, and here he was, comforting her all the same. Raegan curled onto her side, keeping her back to Oberon so he wouldn't notice her distress. With a long inhale, she tried to stifle her emotion, to drown her shame. Tracing the quilt's pattern with her fingertips, she rooted herself in the vast, defiant warmth of the faerie king beside her. The pitter-patter of the raindrops striking the windows on the other side of the room lulled her into drowsiness.

It might've been peaceful, but then Raegan made the mistake of closing her eyes. In an instant, Oberon and the four-poster bed and the rain and Hiraeth were gone. Instead, that platform creaking beneath her bare feet, the feral cry of her lover, the rough hood over her head, the inescapable doom.

With a stifled gasp, she opened her eyes, fingers fisting the quilt.

Raegan fought to reason with herself. Spiraling would not help. But her thoughts spun out anyway—all her past failures, every moment of this morning's battle played in an endless loop. She wiped her clammy palms on her thighs and then pulled her knees to her chest. What if Reilly *did* become a problem later, just as the King said? She'd have no one to blame but herself. It wouldn't be the first time she made a decision that felt so right in the moment and only brought ruin in the end. The dream of Titania's execution stalked the edges of her waking hours, baring its teeth.

Anxiety and shame and self-doubt pounded in her blood. She turned to look at Oberon—*really* look at him, cataloging the scars and the fierce angles and the full mouth and the dark, silken waves of hair. Fuck—she loved him. Absolutely and completely, madly and irrevocably. Raegan bit down on her lip, choking back tears. In all the fairy tales she'd spent her childhood reading, love was a pure thing. Divine, even.

But in the dim, rain-shook light of the teahouse's room, she worried that *her* love amounted to nothing but destruction and demise.

Chapter Twelve

Raegan awoke to the violet-hued light of late dusk seeping in from the window. She didn't even remember falling asleep, and for a moment, panic enveloped her at the sight of an unfamiliar room. But then she remembered—*Hiraeth.*

She turned to check on Oberon, a knot releasing from somewhere beneath her ribs when she saw he was actually sleeping. A bit of tension had eased out of his brow. For a few moments, Raegan basked in it all— the murmurs of the city outside, the safety of the teahouse, the opportunity to rest. But then all the usual ghosts and bad dreams returned to her conscience, and she knew more rest was out of the question. Even if she managed to fall asleep again with her heart racing like this, she knew where she'd end up: back in that hellish nightmare of her past mistakes.

So she stood, careful not to disturb Oberon, and dressed, pulling on boots and grabbing an oversized sweater from her bag to ward off the evening chill, and then slipped out of the room. She found the kitchen easily enough, returning to the first floor by retracing her steps. As Emrys promised, dinner was indeed in the oven, and the smell of it made Raegan's mouth water. She tasted rich spices, savory broth, and delicious vegetables in the air. Her stomach rumbled. The old-fashioned lemon-shaped timer on the counter indicated there was still a little time to go before the meal was ready, so she wandered through the archway into the main room.

The fire in the hearth had gone out, and the space was colder for it. She walked over, determined to stoke the flame, when the front door opened. Raegan's body tensed, and that dark current deep inside her flexed—but it was only Emrys.

He nodded at her as he pulled the door shut. "I thought you'd still be resting," he told her, unlacing his muddy boots.

"I probably should be," Raegan replied mildly, crouching to position a log in the hearth's hungry mouth. Doubt and shame still gnawed at her, so she looked for a distraction. "Hey, I was wondering. Why do your wards need blood?"

In her years of journalism, she'd found a shocking number of people would answer not-so-pleasant questions if she asked them in a pleasant enough voice, like it hardly mattered to her, anyways. This technique did not work on Emrys.

She glanced up from the hearth to find him already looking at her, eyes glittering in the low-lit gloom. Raegan watched as he considered her, the sensation not unlike staring into one of those endless trick mirrors. She wasn't easy to read, never had been—but all at once, Raegan was overcome with the thought of what it might be like for Emrys to try to get a handle on her. What was it like, she wondered, to look at someone who was not only the person standing before you, but also a thousand others, all beating about like birds caught in a too-small cage?

"When the Temple fell after the Uprising," Emrys said, examining Raegan as she lit a match and held it to the kindling, "my Oracle was murdered and only a handful of my Seers survived."

His use of possessive language was not precisely that—not as if these people had belonged to him but as if they had been his responsibility. Emrys said it the same way someone might say "my child" or "my sister." He paused, moving into the room, his jaw clenched.

"I held on to a scrap of the Temple's realm," he continued, gesturing to the space around them. "We built something out of the ruins our enemies left us with. A place where they could not find us. A place that moved with the rain and the mist. A place that might be a home for our kind."

The fire took, and Raegan leaned low, infusing it with a long whoosh of her own breath, which the flames gobbled up. Then she stood, considering Emrys in the dancing shadow and light of the fire. He stood at the back of the armchair now, hands gripping the rich fabric.

"To create Hiraeth, I set new wards," he continued, meeting her gaze, unwavering. "Ones with more teeth. It's an old working—very old —and like many of the old things, it requires blood. But I had to be sure my Oracle had not died for nothing. I had to be sure nothing like that attack could ever happen again. So I dug deep into the earth here, just at the center of what remained of the realm, and I buried seven Protectorate soldiers alive."

Raegan found she could not read Emrys as well as she could most people, and she respected him for it. That said, she didn't see any remorse in his face as he retold the tale of his actions, but to her judgment, there was no glee, either.

"And once wards have a taste of blood . . ." she replied, her voice trailing off, one eyebrow arched expectantly.

"They begin to require it," Emrys confirmed, standing up straight and folding his arms. "I bleed myself for them, and any visitors must make offerings, as you have."

"And the annual tithe?" Raegan asked, Seal-less and knowing the way of things.

Emrys smiled, dead-eyed, all teeth and no warmth. "You are a witch, my lady. I imagine you know."

Raegan did—the wards would almost certainly require seven more Protectorate lives every year, and if Emrys strengthened or added to the working, the wards would want even more. It explained their power, the way Hiraeth existed in ancestral lands plagued by the Protectorate and remained hidden. It also explained why Oberon felt confident the Protectorate could not cross the wards. Not only would it be an incredibly hard spell to undermine, but the wards already knew the taste of their blood and apparently rather enjoyed the flavor. She briefly wondered how he'd convinced his own working to let her within the city's walls, or how he might procure seven more Protectorate soldiers each year.

But if Emrys wanted surprise or horror from Raegan, he would not get it. Yes, Protectorate blood ran in her veins, but it felt more like a technicality than an immutable element of her existence. Besides, she found it difficult to imagine herself in Emrys's shoes and not doing the same as he had.

"Well," Raegan said, dusting her hands off, "I might actually feel safe enough to sleep through the night here, then."

Emrys smiled again, fox-like and genuine this time, and she smiled back. She liked this Keeper and opened her mouth to say so, but a shrill sound from the kitchen cut her off.

"Ahh," Emrys said, firelight catching the silver in his hair as he moved across the room. "That'll be the ramen."

"Need any help?" Raegan asked, which was how she found herself pulling chipped porcelain bowls from the teahouse's cabinets and setting the table. She ducked back into the kitchen for glasses, only to find the King had arisen and was filling a large pitcher with water from the farm-house-style tap. She took in the sight, amused—three ancient, deadly creatures preparing themselves a little meal that, in appearance at least, would not be unwelcome in a Beatrix Potter scene.

Either the ramen and its accompaniments were perfect, or Raegan was very, very hungry. Perhaps a bit of both. She greedily filled her bowl of broth with Emrys's perfectly cooked noodles, brisket, soft-boiled eggs, bok choy, scallions, and miso paste. With the knowledge of the wards, the setting sun behind the mist, and the fire burning merrily in the hearth, she nearly summoned a shred of peace.

"What are your initial thoughts on our path, Emrys?" Oberon asked, an untouched bowl of broth, noodles, and vegetables before him. Raegan could tell he was still in pain by his careful, deliberate movements and the ever-present crease between his ink-dark eyebrows.

"I have a list," Emrys replied after a long swig from his ale. "Only a few places seem possible when human folklore and Fey texts are cross-referenced. Though, I admit, there are many tales of Modron and Danu, and there is much oral tradition among the Welsh that I may not be accounting for."

"Especially as Modron and Danu are viewed as separate entities by the mortals," the King mused, his gaze a thousand miles away.

Raegan paused in thought, turning over the Irish and Welsh goddesses in her head, the result of two similar but separate cultures interacting with the same expansive, ancient being—the All-Mother, the Creatrix of the Fair Folk, the Maker of the Gods-Touched.

"We knew Her long before anyone called Her Modron or Danu," Emrys said, pausing to consume another mouthful of ramen. "The Druids also came to know Her true history by way of their relationship with the Seelie Court, but of course the Romans destroyed their libraries. So yes, this will be difficult. I think beginning the search at Tintagel, the Sgwd Yr Eira waterfall, and Carn Doedog is the best course, considering you saw water and a mound of earth in the vision from the Morrigan."

Raegan considered, scooping up a piece of egg, the fragrant scent of seasonings and vegetal musk curling into her senses. "None of those places are connected with Danu or Modron. But I guess neither goddess has many associated sites. Which is . . . peculiar, now that I'm thinking about it."

"Or a very intentional obfuscation," the King replied drily, giving her a side glance that would have been mischievous if not for the pain she could clearly read in his features. The events of this morning had taken too much from him. "Those three are an excellent start, Emrys. Thank you."

Raegan decided that, after she'd slept more, she'd ask Emrys for access to his library—she had no doubt in her mind that there *was* a library somewhere in this ancient and magical place—and do a bit of her own digging. Two heads were better than one, and if she was honest, Raegan wasn't capable of entrusting this task to someone she barely knew.

The thrum of the quest and the hunt sang in her, a sharp thrill rolling through her body, as if her tendons were all harp strings to be plucked. Her father had taught her this folklore for a reason, intention-ally filling her head with stories hastily costumed in Christian robes, the thick haze of the past waiting just beneath.

Oh. Her father. All at once, the thrill swept out of her and she aban-doned her spoon with a clang. It was strange how easily she forgot he was dead, gone, lost to her forever despite all she'd suffered to find him. Such a thing should plague the forefront of her mind, destroying any ease or pleasure that rose up inside her. And yet Raegan found she could almost tuck the loss away like a handkerchief. Perhaps because she'd been practicing it for so many years, Cormac good as dead all the while.

And there was her mother, too, undoubtedly losing her mind, the lie of an in-patient stay worn thin nearly a month later. And Henry and Saanvi, who might have taken it upon themselves to hunt for her the way they usually hunted down a source or a lead. Regular, everyday people who—against their better judgment, surely—cared for Raegan, who would be hurt by her choices.

"What's going to happen to mortals when the Gates are opened?" Raegan asked, the words coming out of her before she quite realized what she was saying.

Across the table, Emrys went entirely still. She felt the heavy weight of Oberon's eyes land on her. She lifted her own gaze, somehow finding Emrys's the easiest to meet first. She had to remind herself she did not know this Keeper, and unlike the Temple in Philadelphia, had not known him in another life, either. And yet—she felt so incredibly sure that if the King hadn't been right across the table, Emrys might have shrugged and said, "Who cares?"

Raegan swallowed hard. Why had she never bothered to ask this before? She let out a long breath, flexing her hands. Because she hadn't wanted to know. She'd wanted only magic and questing and to see behind the curtain. She'd leapt without looking because she thought her father would be beyond the door. He had been. Just not for very long.

"I suppose we have not yet had time to discuss this matter," Oberon said, annoyingly diplomatic.

"Yeah, well, it's kind of important, isn't it?" Raegan snapped, though of course she was mad at herself, not him. Who in their right mind would ask a faerie king to put mortals first, to consider their needs above that of his people?

"It is," Oberon replied, turning in his chair to face her, even though she could see the movement pained him. "It is important to me. And also complicated."

Emrys, still silent, stood, collecting his dishes and then reaching for Raegan's nearly empty bowl. She watched him, daring the Keeper to say something she could sink her teeth into, but he only gathered up his napkin and departed for the kitchen. So she turned on Oberon instead.

"Go ahead," Raegan snapped. "I know you want to say it."

The King narrowed his eyes, tilting his head as he examined her. "What do you think I wish to say?"

She threw her hands up in the air, her face reddening. "Why didn't I ask this question before? Why in all our weeks of planning at the Temple did I never once bring up the fate of mortals if we accomplished our task?"

Oberon's mouth parted slightly as he watched her, saying nothing for too long. In the firelight-soaked silence, all Raegan could see was the raw red brick and sepia-colored sunset and her father's fading red curls, trapped forever on that train, beyond her reach.

"No," Oberon replied, leaning forward onto his knees, his clasped hands close enough to Raegan's thighs that she could feel the heat of them. "I wish to know exactly what happened to you in the Timekeeper's realm. You refuse to speak of it, and *cariad*, I am sorry, but the time has come to do so, lest it fester within you."

"Fuck you," Raegan laughed, hoarse and battered, though traitorous tears gathered in her eyes. "Don't turn this around on me, Oberon. Answer my question."

He watched her with such gentleness in the silken gray velvet of his gaze that Raegan wanted to punch him. It was so much easier to be angry, to point fingers and make accusations, especially when Oberon had such an infuriating, unerring ability to be correct, *particularly* when it came to her.

When she held his eyes, refusing to look away, her jaw working, the King sighed and leaned back. "Revolutions are bloody, Raegan," he said in a way that made it sound like he did not enjoy spilling blood when she knew very well that he did. "There is little way around it."

Silence slipped its arms around the remnants of the Temple within the city now called Hiraeth. Raegan let it string itself tight and uncomfortable, all of her attention on the faerie king. He relented, but only because he chose to do so, she knew.

"The world will profoundly shift," Oberon continued, staring out the bay window into the city, dressed in dusky silks and the honeyed cloaks of streetlamps. "Many people—your mother's included, the *Cymry*—speak to gods that can no longer hear them, acting out rituals that are meaningless without a free flow of magic. In my years, I have seen only those who seek conquest and oppression align with the Timekeeper and the Protectorate. If magic is freed and the gods walk the earth once more, power might yet be returned to its rightful places."

Raegan leaned toward him, crowding the King in against the wall and the window. The next question was already falling from her tongue before she even realized she was speaking. "Have you ever helped humans?" she demanded, her fingernails digging into the table as she refused to dive into her own freed memories for the answer. She needed to hear it from *him*. "You've been on this side of the Gates for a while. You've seen a lot of atrocities. But have you actually done anything?"

Her anger surged out, no longer roiling in her stomach but excised like a demon, filling the room with its flame and fury. And she allowed it, knowing that she couldn't hurt him—not like this, at least. Not as badly as she'd hurt herself if she let all this anger and shame and guilt turn inward—and oh, how the tide strained for her harbors.

"You know well that I have spilled my own blood for human rebellions and dispatched monsters before they could make it to the pages of your history books," the King said, reaching for his glass of water, unbothered. "But there is only so much I feel my people should interfere. I will not strip mortals of their agency or their ability to shape their world. No matter their transgressions."

"How noble of you," Raegan sneered, caught between bursting into tears and screaming curses until her throat bled. "I suppose once the Gates open, you'll just sit around the fire with us and we'll all hold hands and imagine a new world together. If you're so generous with us puny mortals, why didn't that happen the first time, before everything went to shit?"

She watched Oberon's jaw clench and reveled in it; how many beings could say they alone could make the Unseelie king lose control? The fire crackled in the background, and Raegan felt her own anger smolder and spit.

"I tried," he said, sounding miserable and weary instead of sharp and cunning like she wanted. "When the Timekeeper made his offer, many of the mortals on the Isles had already forsaken the old gods and turned against the Fair Folk. Christianity promised eternal life, and the Gates offered prosperity and safety until they met their god. The Timekeeper did not require worship—not in a way they understood. So they made the deal without understanding the depth of the cost."

With her Seal peeled back, Raegan remembered most of this history as he said it. The Fair Folk *had* tried to warn mortals of what aligning with the Timekeeper would bring. But men could not bear to see a great, powerful, immortal race walk among them when their own eternal life was more hazy promise than certain inevitability. In their eyes, the Fey had everything and refused to share, whereas the Timekeeper offered all he had and didn't even care if they worshipped another god. But only because the Timekeeper did not want churches or idols or prayers; he hungered for much, much more.

"I know our history," Raegan spat, even though she'd asked the question. "What will happen to mortals? Will you allow the kelpies to lure us into puddles and murder us? Will your court return to kidnapping our children and hunting our loved ones through the woods for fun?"

Oberon's body language changed abruptly. She watched him push aside all his pain as he turned on her, finally giving her what she wanted —the hated and feared Unseelie king who haunted human folklore.

"Your people murder each other for no reason," he snarled, his voice low and impossibly cold. "You war over gods that cannot hear you, or, worse yet, ones you invented entirely. Murder and assault and enslavement were not enough for you—no, you had to colonize and pillage, to oppress those who are different from you, and now you have the audacity to pretend none of it ever happened. Your history is soaked in blood, yet you act as though you are morally superior to the Fey. Spare me this nonsense."

Raegan shot out of her chair, its legs screeching against the stone floor. Her entire body aflame and red with rage, she slammed her fist onto the table, leaning into Oberon's space in a way she knew he loathed. "And does that make it alright to murder us and pile your feast tables with our carcasses?"

Part of her was surprised when the King stood to meet her immediately, rising from his chair like a rogue wave in a quiet sea, tall and fathomless and unspeakably deadly. "Mortals routinely consume intelligent, sentient creatures," he replied, his eyes level with hers, and all of a sudden, she felt like the one pinned in the corner. "What issue could you *possibly* take with my people doing the same?"

Chapter Thirteen

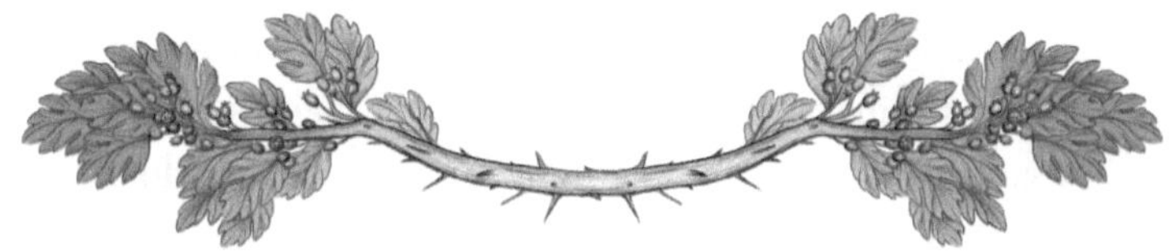

Horror slipped down Raegan's throat, sour and sharp, turning the heated flush of her anger razor-edged. How *dare* he?

"You're a monster," she snarled, knowing it was the thing he feared most, though at this moment, she might've believed it. She waited for the hurt to ease his features, for the feeling of triumph when she won against such a mighty opponent. But the feral angles of the King's face did not soften. He made no attempt to walk his words back or apologize. He did not reach for her. He simply held her gaze, everything about him predatory and ancient. So Raegan, out of any other options, the hungry anger inside her coiling traitorous with a desire to hurt him, did the only thing she could.

She ran away.

She darted for the entryway, where she barely remembered to snatch a glamoured cloak from the pegs before throwing herself through the front door. Raegan tumbled out onto the winding cobblestone streets of the hidden Fey city, tugging the cloak's hood over her head. She abruptly chose a direction and took off, hating herself all the while—for her weakness and her inability to control her anger, her need to express poison because she wasn't immune to her own bite. For being exactly what her ex-girlfriend had said she was: hard to love.

No one looked her way as she plunged through the rain-dampened streets. The gray stones ramped upward, the tall, narrow buildings jutting into the sky like broken teeth. Raegan barely stopped to consider her surroundings; she just continued to run, following the path lit by the honey-hued glow of the streetlights, dodging pedestrians as she went.

Then the angle of the rain-slick cobbles steepened sharply, slowing her pace to a walk. By the time she reached the summit, Raegan was breathless—and then, her remaining breath stole away for another reason entirely. From this vantage point, all of Hiraeth spilled out before her: a thousand pathways spiraling in on each other, a world of rain and mist and stone, a quilt of gray stone and damp green parkland. It was *much* larger than it should be—much larger than the riverside meadow it had appeared to occupy. At the edges of the city, the crown of clouds met the hawthorn trees. From inside Hiraeth, they were towering and unreal, curling in a half-dome around the city, like a hand cupped around a butterfly.

She liked the idea of having something else to focus on, so Raegan pulled her cloak tighter against the wet, dark evening and began to make her way down the hill. Walking helped. It always had. Her dad had taught her that at an early age, taking her for a loop around the neighbor-hood or down to the corner store, or even on the bus to Pennypack Park when a particularly difficult problem arose. What was difficult at eleven years old, of course, paled in comparison to the things she faced now.

But still, Raegan continued through this neighborhood of Hiraeth, pleased to find she didn't even need to bother keeping her head down. She realized upon peering into a shop window and not encountering any reflection of hers at all that Emrys's cloaks were glamoured for full undetectability. The realization pulled her shoulders down her back a few inches, something at the base of her neck loosening. She felt so visi-ble, so central, in this war. It was nice to be no one, nothing, just a stir of the wind.

And at this precise moment, she was just a person hovering outside the raindrop-painted window of a bakery, admiring the pastries on display beneath soft, twinkling lights. Each creation was decadent, sugar-spun, perfectly delicate. Like the happy ending of a fairy tale. At that thought, Raegan felt her heart pang for a reason she refused to investigate. Instead, she sighed and continued walking.

Hiraeth passed gently by in soft blurs of dove gray and storm blue and rain-drenched black. It was the thoughts devouring her from the inside out that felt dagger-sharp and dangerous.

Raegan slipped around a group of shorter, stockier Fey leaving a pub, their expressions a-glitter with faerie wine. She'd really thought that with her Seal removed, she might make better choices—be a better person. Scoffing, she kicked at a pile of wet leaves that had drifted onto the cobblestones from an ancient sycamore in someone's neat front yard. Here she was, still playing the same stupid song. How had her therapist phrased it? That she'd figure out how to provoke people so they would treat her the way she thought she deserved. And then everything was easier with her darkest suspicions proven correct. Raegan could walk away, firm in her belief that she brought out the worst in people. Firm in her belief that she was better off alone. After all, it'd be better if Oberon remembered why he had grown to resent her sooner than later—before she couldn't live without him. Didn't her failures haunt him as much as they did her? And yet he still trusted her, still followed her into the dark.

Up ahead, the cobblestone walkway came to a T, a dark and rambling garden devouring the path she'd been following, the hawthorn walls rising up starkly behind it. To the left, the cobbles widened, leading to taller buildings, broad avenues, busier foot traffic, brighter streetlamps—a commercial corridor, it seemed. To the right, the way turned narrow and winding, bending sharply and then disappearing behind a block of elegant townhomes; she had the sense it wound back up the hill she'd just come down. Raegan wavered, examining the options, the cold, rainy night air making her feel alive and almost fragile in a way she welcomed. It served as a reminder that her next grave could always be her last.

Fuck.

And she'd called him a *monster*. Jaw clenched, she held very still, never mind the nearby pedestrians blind to her presence. "What is wrong with me?" Raegan whispered. "I love him more than I even understand."

Suddenly, the grand charcoal sweeps and Art Nouveau arches and golden lamplight and low murmur of other living creatures became far too much to bear. She needed to be alone, *now*. Raegan barreled forward to the gates of the shadowed garden. The towering metal had been bewitched into the shapes of hawthorn leaves, tiny glittering stones emulating dewdrops. A small silver plaque, green with patina, was set into the low stone wall, indicating it was a public garden—no surprise, given the general Fey sensibilities about how the world should operate. At this hour, night having thrown its velvet skirts over the city, the garden should probably be closed, but the gates opened at Raegan's touch and she slipped inside.

Beyond the ornate metalwork, the garden was damp and hushed. Despite the late autumn season outside Hiraeth's walls, deep purple hellebore clustered around the path, fiddlehead ferns curling just behind, shading the dark shadows a lush green. The graceful furl of the ferns reminded Raegan of Oberon's hands. She ground her teeth and kept moving.

The twisting path was clearly charmed against mud. Despite the mist still pouring down from the skies, the dirt was firmly packed and dry, lined by twinkling willow-o-wisp lights. Amusement stirred inside Raegan; as a child, she never would've thought that willow-o-wisps would be safe to follow. No matter how much she'd wanted it, she had never dared to *actually* think she might not belong to the world she'd been born into, but a stranger, wilder place entirely.

Ash and alder and willow grew denser and tighter for a few moments, barely more than looming shadows despite the blueish-green light lining the path. But as Raegan continued, the garden opened up again, the treeline creeping farther and farther back. In its place, strange ferns in a shimmering shade of pitch, wine-dark tulips, black roses, and deep purple flowers she didn't recognize grew instead, creating an impossibly lovely—and poisonous, she suspected—carpet of midnight foliage.

And in the distance were the hawthorns, looking for all the world like something created by a witch in a fairy tale to trap a sweet princess. Gnarled, reaching limbs twisted and climbed into the evening sky. The hawthorn wall was much closer now; this must be a very old garden, Raegan realized, to back directly up against the wards. All of the newer sections of the city typically had a boulevard for travel and security between any structures and the wall itself. But even by the faint light of the willow-o-wisps studding the edge of the path like phantom jewels, she could see the garden's dark, tumbling flora stretched all the way to the hawthorns.

Something else caught Raegan's eye—a wooden arch, old and sagging, barely standing. If not for the lush vines wrapped around the entire structure, she suspected it might not stand at all. There was something familiar about it, so she walked closer—though familiarity with strange things was beginning to feel normal these days. Gravel crunched under her feet as she approached.

All at once, she understood—the structure was just like the portico from the overgrown community garden back in Philadelphia. The King had still been able to use it for traveling within the city, but *that* was why she'd felt such profound sadness, why the sight of it had stirred her memories. This gate had once connected entire realms, spanning oceans and deadly wards and planes of existence, a relic from the days before the Protectorate's attack on the Temple that had been Hiraeth's epicenter once.

Now it stood ancient and forgotten, a reminder of why the last Fey city had cut itself off from the rest of the world. Raegan let out a long, shuddering breath, raising a reverent hand to brush her fingers against the portico's structure.

Before she could, the hawthorn wards at the end of the path *shivered*. The hair on the back of her neck stood on end. "Okay," she said, taking her hand away from the portico. "Sorry."

But the prickling across her skin did not ease; if anything, it intensified, as if her nearly touching the dead gate hadn't mattered in the first place. An old voice inside Raegan told her that some other disturbance had caused the wards to react—and that she only felt it because whatever had triggered the hawthorns was close. *Very* close.

Instinct took over, and Raegan ducked behind the wide trunk of an ash tree, letting the shadow and mist obscure her form before remembering she wore a glamoured cloak. Her blood pounded. She peered through the gloom, desperately searching the open space beyond the portico where the path curled up at the hawthorns' feet. Emrys and Oberon had both been so confident nothing could cross the wards. If they were wrong, this entire city—this entire way of life the Fey had carved out from the world that had been stolen from them—was at risk because of her. And if anything happened, Raegan didn't think she could survive the guilt.

Seconds trickled by. There was only the soft murmur of the misty rain and a few distant lashes of wet branches. Maybe she was just being paranoid. But then her senses prickled again, and this time, Raegan found her eyes falling on a specific place at the end of the path. A few of the hawthorn branches didn't look quite right. Discomfort perched on her shoulders, sharp and taloned, as she realized there was a strange shape on the wall. And then everything got worse.

In the depths of a tiny, half-forgotten public garden, right at the edges of Hiraeth's wards, crouched a woman in dark clothing. The willow-o-wisps turned the long locs falling over her shoulders to a shadowed blue-black. Raegan watched, her breath dead in her chest. The intruder's hands were moving, and Raegan was terrified to realize they did so with spellwork. One section of the hawthorn roots shimmered like wet blood, a symbol appearing. Raegan narrowed her eyes, craning her neck, desperately wanting as much information as possible before she made a decision. The swoop and the shape of the symbol felt familiar, but she had only faint faerie lights to see by. Before she could inspect further, the woman straightened.

Raegan stood stock-still as the woman looked left and then right. Her heart hammered in her throat; she was sure the trespasser had sighted her, even though she knew it was impossible thanks to the glamoured cloak. But then the woman glanced around and took a tentative step closer to the path, away from the wards, which still hummed like slightly offended bees. As blue-green illumination drenched the trespasser, Raegan noticed two things: the stranger was beautiful, and she was also not really there.

It was the best way to describe what she was seeing: the woman was faintly translucent, a gentle glow tracing the outline of her form. Raegan's mind moved sluggishly. God, she was too tired for this shit. She examined the stranger for a moment longer, noting her strong profile and tall, curvy frame, the perfect obsidian skin and high cheekbones. Beautiful but mortal. The woman moved forward again, looking like a deer on high alert, terrified to make even the tiniest of sounds. Silence bled into the woods, the rain and the wind ceasing all at once, like they'd taken note of an unwelcome guest. The stranger froze, afraid to shatter the quiet.

But Raegan was not, so she stepped from the shadow of the trees onto the path and pushed back the glamoured hood, moving directly into the woman's line of vision. "Shadewalker," she boomed in a voice that was once the Witch of the Wood's. "You don't fucking belong here."

Chapter Fourteen

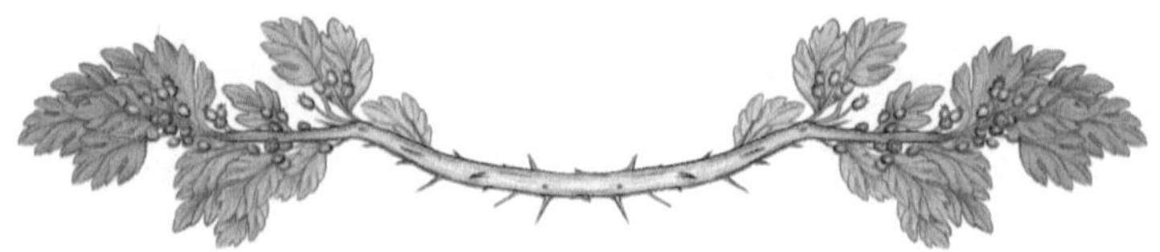

Hiraeth moved constantly across the Isles, so Raegan had no way of knowing how close they were to any river beyond the city's walls—and yet, she heard waters roar somewhere. Good. Anyone capable of shadewalking in a realm leached of magic by the Timekeeper was a formidable creature—so let them make no mistake that Raegan had buried legions beneath silt and tide.

"You know what I am," the trespasser said, her eyes wide, brows furrowed, her chest rising and falling quickly. Her voice was rich, inflected with hints of London and the Caribbean.

"Yeah," Raegan replied, moving toward the woman, who took a backwards step. "Not. Fucking. Invited."

Holding her ground, Raegan called to the water in the core of all things, not knowing if attempting to work such dangerous, difficult magic would be the death of her. But a *shadewalker*? It shouldn't even be possible with the Gates standing—not to mention that the Protectorate had hunted those born with the gift into extinction. Or so she'd thought.

The seconds stretched too long, and Raegan realized a few things all at once: the woman was young, maybe mid-twenties at most, rooted to the ground, absolutely terrified, and, most disconcertingly of all, had Protectorate blood and magic running through her veins.

"How are you even here? And *why*?" Raegan demanded, taking

another step forward, this one more aggressive, which sent the stranger tumbling back two, three steps. She could see in the woman's body that every instinct was pleading with her to flee, to never look back and forget whatever madness had possessed her to follow this path.

And yet the stranger remained, her jaw set, hands curled into fists. "Where . . . where exactly *is* here?"

Raegan blinked. Behind the intruder, the hawthorns curled the tips of their limbs, as if awaiting a command. "What?" she demanded, the word coming out a hoarse shriek that was not exactly intimidating.

The stranger released a long, hitched breath, and Raegan realized exactly how much the unwelcome mortal was trying to rein in her panic. "I don't . . . I don't think I meant to come here," the Protectorate explained weakly, retreating another step. Her back bumped into the hawthorn's outstretched limbs and she jumped, scrambling forward again. "I was just looking for . . . okay, well, I *was* looking for you."

Raegan stared, pushing away a swell of horror. The Protectorate had a terrifyingly useful asset—someone who could stow their body safely away and then wander the land, looking for signatures of magic that only they could see. Wards, pocket realms, protective workings, curses, bindings, blessings—all exposed by a shadewalker's sight. Such a power could allow the Protectorate to track the Fair Folk far too easily, as was terribly clear by this woman's presence inside Hiraeth's wards. A place she should never have been able to locate, let alone enter.

"Looks like you found me," Raegan replied flatly, desperately trying to summon her quickness, her cleverness. Maybe the Protectorate stranger didn't realize she was inside Hiraeth. She pleaded for that to be true and for the ability to ensure the woman did not find out. Gods, only a few hours in Hiraeth's walls and she'd already fucked everything up. "Strange thing for the Protectorate-oathed to be looking for me without being a lot more . . . murder-y."

Good. This was going great. Raegan absolutely sounded terrifying and confident. Silence clung to the garden's branches, thick as a woolen blanket on the first day of winter.

"Yeah, but the thing is," the woman began, her eyes darting away, though her voice grew stronger, "you spared Reilly. And I need to know why."

Raegan's mind wheeled, but the calculations were too slow, too thick with the emotional turmoil of her and Oberon's argument. She'd come here for peace and quiet, for fuck's sake. "So you want me to believe you risked performing outlawed magic and being killed by the Unseelie Court just to . . . ask a fucking *question?*"

A large raindrop plopped down from an outstretched tree limb to land directly on the top of Raegan's head. She gritted her teeth. She could've just not been a bitch for once in her life, and then she'd be tucked in Oberon's arms, probably in front of a fire, maybe with another helping of Emrys's ramen.

A few steps down the path, the stranger wavered, though her body relaxed a little. She swept her long tendrils of hair off one shoulder with a shaking hand. "Yes. Because it doesn't make any sense. When Reilly made it back alive from the fight, rambling some nonsense about being spared by the Lady of the Rivers, the generals took it pretty bloody seriously. They're being kept under surveillance that does not feel friendly, and they're my best friend, and I need to know what happened so I can help them. No one will let me speak with them, so I came to find the only other witness. I didn't track you, by the way. I *couldn't*, actually. I just looked for old wards, starting at the river where everything happened, and then spiraling out." The shadewalker paused, a little out of breath. "If it's not obvious, I'm pretty desperate."

Raegan blinked. The woman's thought process was absolutely fucking insane. Shadewalking involved the practitioner entering a deep trance that left their physical body vulnerable as their shade walked free. How had this woman found anyone trustworthy enough to attend her body while she walked? And why had she been willing to wander through ancient wards on a goddamn hunch?

With a huff, Raegan realized she had done things just as stupid before, and probably would again. So she went for a different angle. "What do you think the Protectorate will do to Reilly?" Raegan asked, tilting her head, scrutinizing the stranger. Fuck, she wished she had better eyesight. She needed to watch every muscle in the woman's face, every twitch of the fingers.

As it turned out, the woman was not that subtle. She let out a harsh, arch laugh, looking at Raegan like *she* was the insane one. "Didn't think I'd need to explain the horrors of the Protectorate to you, of all people," she replied.

Raegan raised a brow. "You don't," she said, sly, taking a slow step toward the trespasser, the gravelly earth crunching under her boots. "It's just a rare opinion for those within their ranks to hold." She waited, eyes sharp, knowing everything about the woman's answer would be extraordinarily telling; she had set it up that way.

"That doesn't matter right now," the woman pleaded, bringing her hands together at her chest, her emotions and reactions all over the place —usually, though not always, a sign of genuine despair. "Why did you do it? Did Reilly make a deal?"

The woman said the last three words in a low, hoarse whisper, as if even speaking them might invite the Unseelie king into her very soul.

"No," Raegan replied, resisting the urge to roll her eyes. "They were just . . . really young. And there's not exactly a choice in the Protectorate, is there? Moment of weakness, I guess. Clearly a mistake, since you're here now."

That stumped the woman. Her brow knitted together tightly, and then her mouth fell open for a second before she found the right words. "You expect me to believe that?"

Raegan threw her hands out in frustration, startling the stranger into another backwards step, but all she did was embed herself between hawthorn branches. The limbs reacted, one sliding across her shoulders as if to hold her in place. "You came to find *me*, and when you crossed wards you had no business crossing, I didn't immediately kill you. But you're going to accuse *me* of lying?" Raegan demanded, incredulous.

The woman gritted her teeth, slapping away the hawthorn branches; they couldn't hold something incorporeal, anyway. "I—I've heard rumors," the stranger stuttered, her hands moving in frenzied gestures. "I mean, more than rumors. A lot from your aunt, actually."

Raegan forced herself not to freeze at the mention of Maelona, to not give away any impression she cared about the fate of her father's sister. She only stared at the trespasser, trying to emulate that cold, dead look she'd seen Oberon use more than once.

"Look," the woman continued, straightening her shoulders, making direct eye contact with Raegan for the first time, "if you spared Reilly and the generals don't want any of us to know, that's . . . suspicious. Particularly considering all of the other things I'm already pretty sure are true."

Raegan clenched her jaw. This woman could be valuable. This woman could possibly take her to her aunt, or at least give her information about where she might be. This woman was also mortal, Protectorate-oathed, and capable of passing through Hiraeth's wards, even if only incorporeally.

"What things," Raegan asked, her tone delicate but sharp-edged, "are you pretty sure are true?"

The woman looked hard at Raegan then, dark eyes flashing with a familiar kind of rage. "That the Protectorate either needs to fundamentally change," she replied, voice firm, "or it needs to be dug up by the roots and burnt alive."

CHAPTER FIFTEEN

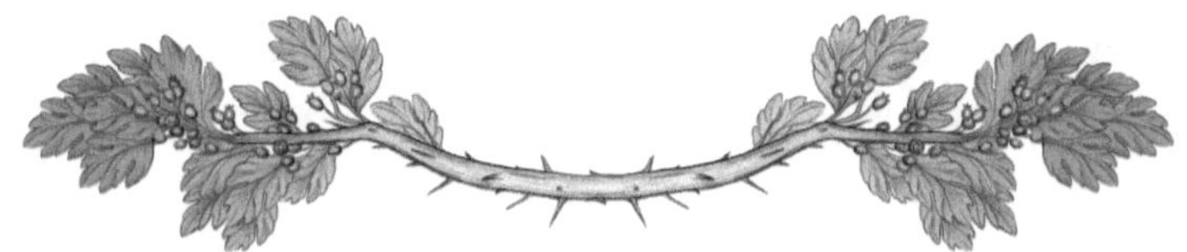

Raegan said nothing, focused on crushing the hope taking flight in her chest, butterfly-winged and shimmering. After everything that she and the Fair Folk and anyone who fought for magic had suffered, she could not find it in herself to believe that Fate would simply hand her this boon. Unless, of course, it was not Fate at all who had brought this about, but rather the stranger's own defiant free will coursing hot and heady through her veins.

"What's your name?" Raegan asked, exhausted and brimming with energy all at once. The mist clung to her hair, pulling a shiver from her body.

The woman looked at her like she was out of her mind. "You're not going to tell me how convenient it is that I've shown up like this or how you'd rather kill every single human with Protectorate blood than trust a single one of us, or something like that?"

Raegan waved a hand tiredly in the air, suddenly feeling quite old. "Sure, I mean, I might get to that. But for now—your name, please?"

The stranger faltered, her full lips pressed into a firm line. The willow-o-wisps pulsed, making her appear opalescent.

"I'm not Fey," Raegan reminded the woman. "I can't do anything with it. It's just—I'm assuming you know mine, so it only feels fair."

"I *do* know yours, Raegan Maeve Overhill," the trespasser replied, considering. She opened her mouth, closed it, and then finally spoke. "Alanna. I'm Alanna."

"Nice to meet you, Alanna," Raegan replied, sidestepping to lean against the defunct portico's side because her body was about ready to give out entirely. The sagging wood structure held her weight. "Though usually I prefer people to stay on their side of the wards."

"I know," Alanna replied, genuine, holding her hands up. "I'm sorry. I didn't see another way. I needed to shield myself from the Protectorate, too."

Raegan had figured as much, and she nodded, but then another implication slipped into her mind. She considered it, breathing in the scent of decaying leaves and damp soil. "They don't know what you are, do they?"

Alanna let out a snort that startled some birds in the undergrowth. The sound of their wings flapping filled the air, and then the garden returned to its nighttime hum. "Of course they don't. If they did, I would be dead."

Raegan rested the back of her head against the portico, crossing her arms. "Nah, they'd find a use for you. They're pragmatic. It would be unpleasant, but you'd be alive. Is anyone attending your body, by the way?"

Alanna looked at her incredulously. "Why would I tell *you* that?"

"So no," Raegan said, hiding her smile, drawing shapes in the gravel path with the toe of her boot. "I can't help you with your friend. What they told you is exactly what happened. The Protectorate won't like that story getting around, so I'm not sure what they'll do to Reilly."

Alanna's countenance darkened, eyes narrowed at Raegan. For the first time, the woman stepped closer, her hands balled into fists at her side, despite the fact that she could enact no violence in her current form. "So *that's* why you did it. Now I understand."

Raegan stood up straight, pushing off the portico, surprised by how much Alanna's accusation stung. "No," she replied, raising her voice. She swallowed, trying to settle the anger digging its claws into her. "No, that's not why. I barely have four brain cells to rub together right now, and I had even less this morning after everything that happened."

She was surprised when it seemed like Alanna believed her. The younger woman studied her hard, looking for any cracks, but relented when Raegan just gazed back at her. Alanna let out a long breath, cradling her forehead in her hands.

"You said you think the Protectorate needs to change," Raegan said tentatively, keeping her hands at her sides, where Alanna could see them. Her words hung in the cold November air, surrounded by the orchestra of a soft breeze stirring damp, rain-heavy leaves in the ancient botanical garden.

Alanna stared at her, expression guarded and distrusting. "Yeah. I did. I'm trying to do my best to change it, but that won't matter if *you* murder us all first."

"No one wants to murder all of you," Raegan said automatically before wincing and leaning back against the portico. "Okay, yeah, some Fey do. But only because they feel they have no other recourse."

"I know," Alanna said softly, to Raegan's absolute bewilderment.

She was off her game, so tired that her bones felt heavy—she was in no place to navigate a conversation like this and come out on top. But not everything comes wrapped in a bow, so Raegan took a deep breath and tried her best. "You do?" she asked, matching Alanna's tone.

"Yeah," Alanna replied, glancing at Raegan for a heartbeat before her gaze drifted away. "I mean, I've seen enough Fair Folk. I'm a researcher, but it requires fieldwork. If they wanted all humans dead, despite everything—despite the Gates and the Timekeeper's boon and the fading residual magic—I think . . . I think we would probably all be dead."

Raegan didn't know what to say to that, so she just nodded grimly. This woman had to be part of some Protectorate trick. Just like she'd said herself—if they knew one of their oathed could shadewalk, they'd find a way to use it.

So why was her gut saying otherwise? Why did that rage in Alanna's eyes feel like a twin flame to her own? She would have grown up with this woman—with Reilly, too—and been like an older sister to them both, if things had been just a little different. If her father hadn't run. That was all that would've needed to change—no complex web of choices and paths. Just one hinge. If her father had stayed, she'd probably know Alanna and Reilly as well as she knew herself.

"Part of why I came here," Alanna said, looking self-conscious, refusing to meet Raegan's gaze, "is because I wanted to see you. I needed to know if you were the monster in the briefings or if you're . . . just a person like anyone else."

Raegan chewed on her lower lip and watched a pale green hellebore petal tumble across the path. "What have you decided?"

"Not sure yet," Alanna replied after a moment's pause.

"Then maybe we have more to talk about, you and I," Raegan hazarded, looking into Alanna's dark brown eyes. If she pulled this off— and if Alanna didn't fuck her over, which was very possible—it could change everything. To have not only a deeply embedded source in the Protectorate but also a shadewalker in a world that thought they were dead and gone? The possibilities hummed in her chest, electric-hot and pulsing with a thousand opportunities.

Alanna hesitated, but she'd stayed for this long, so Raegan knew she probably had her already. "Maybe," the woman replied, but there were more words hanging on her tongue.

"Do you feel safe like this?" Raegan asked, gesturing to Alanna's shade and then the wards. "If you do, just come back and we can talk more. Alanna, I think we might want the same things. Or at least, enough of the same things to warrant further conversation."

"I would be executed as a traitor just for coming here tonight," Alanna replied, her shimmering, incorporeal body still clearly stiff, wracked with tension.

"Well, then you might as well get your money's worth," Raegan said with a smirk.

To her surprise, Alanna smiled, that dangerous flame back in her eyes. "*If* I come back," she replied, moving toward the sigil that marked where she crossed the wards, "it will be in two days' time at sunset."

"Okay, we're making this really dramatic," Raegan replied, knowing the power of humor. "Should I wear a red feather in my hat so you know it's me?"

Alanna held back a laugh, standing within a pace of the wards. "I need to go. If you think of a way to help Reilly, please tell me when we talk again."

"I thought it was *if* you come back," Raegan replied, repeating the woman's words with a playful smile.

"If I come back," Alanna agreed, actually smiling now, her beautiful, young face so different without all the gravity the world had placed upon it. And then, without another word, she slipped through the wards and disappeared.

Raegan stared at the last place Alanna had stood until the interwoven wall of hawthorn trunks and branches nearly burned an afterimage into her retinas. She didn't even know if Hiraeth would be in the same place in two days. If Alanna would ever be able to find her again at all. If she'd just come back with a Protectorate army instead of that glorious rage. Raegan heaved a sigh. Was this delicate, slim chance worth endangering all of Hiraeth? She didn't know.

And worse—would a Protectorate shadewalker crossing the hawthorns for the first time in hundreds of years because of *her* just remind the King why he'd avoided Raegan for all those centuries? The thought choked the air out of her lungs. The last time they'd tried to open the Gates, the last time she'd ruined everything, he had abandoned her to empty half-lives where the memory of him was little more than a distant, blurry dream. Where she'd ached and ached and ached, all alone.

With another sigh, Raegan pulled the glamoured hood back up, turned on her heel, and walked down the path through the botanical garden, out the gates, and up the hill. It was no short walk to return to the old Temple, and now her shoulders sagged even heavier with calculations for the future. But she needed to feel Oberon's arms around her, even if it might not last.

With that thought, she gathered herself up and increased her pace through Hiraeth's winding streets, her heart pulling her back to him the way it always did. Thoughts of all the potential futures spilling out before her should've filled Raegan's mind, and maybe as she walked, she would've untangled them. But it was the King who took up space in her head. The dark-haired, gray-eyed being of impossible power and shocking beauty that she just couldn't stop hurting. Between her repeated deaths and her nearly endless mistakes, she was always clawing at his open wounds. Maybe he always *had* been better off without her. But she was too selfish for that, it seemed.

Raegan crested the top of the hill, the majority of the city behind her now. Her breath was quick, a damp sheen coating her lower back despite the cold evening air. She pushed her tired body into a jog, recognizing the bakery she'd passed on her way out. Finally, she saw the old Temple up ahead, the wide bay window of leaded glass, arched black door, and ornate metal lanterns awaiting her. As she approached, Raegan paused, something not quite right about the slant of the door and the light emanating from the window.

A few moments later—her heart skittering through her chest all the while—she realized the discrepancy came from a tall, broad figure lounging in the shadow of the Temple's stone walls. Raegan would recognize his form anywhere; she'd know him blind and only by touch; she could find him in a strange city a thousand years from now after she'd forgotten her own name.

The Unseelie king waited for her in the darkness, wearing one of Emrys's glamoured cloaks. Good—so they were only visible to each other. Everything else melted away and she ran to him. Her boots thudded on the cobblestones as she threw herself into his arms. He pulled her close without saying a word, the dark heat of him rendering her as senseless and ready to surrender as always. The King rested his chin on the top of her head, wrapping his larger body around hers.

"I'm sorry," Raegan murmured at the same time Oberon spoke. She pulled back and looked up at him, forced to crane her neck back to meet his eyes. "What did you say?"

"I said that I apologize," he told her, amusement glittering in his gaze. "It seems we have both arrived at the same place."

Raegan bit down on her lip to keep the tears she felt brewing behind her eyes at bay. "Can we go inside? It's cold out here."

"Of course," Oberon replied, but not before pulling a wool blanket from the windowsill and draping it over her shoulders. He must've brought it out with him, she realized, while he awaited her return.

Silently, they crossed the threshold. She peeled off her damp glamoured cloak and hung it up to dry. Then they made their way upstairs. As she passed, Raegan noticed the dining table had been cleared and wiped down and the fire in the hearth was cold and quiet. Oberon led the way up the grand stairs, the antique structure sighing under his weight in a way she was quite familiar with herself. The second-floor hallway flickered orange in the dark of the night, all the dark metal sconces along the wall aflame. The effect was both cozy and haunting at once.

They slipped through the doorway to their room together. Raegan was relieved to find the ornately carved fireplace was already crackling away with a bright flame. She wrapped the blanket tighter around her shoulders, breathing in the room's scent of old wood and fresh lavender. It looked larger at night, all the shadows carved out and deepened.

She settled on the edge of the bed, watching Oberon as he came to sit beside her. Raegan let out a long breath, leaning over to rest her cheek on his shoulder. She clutched the moment like a pearl between her teeth. Just a little longer before she brought up Alanna and the garden. Just another moment before he hated her again.

"I apologize for what I said," he murmured, long fingertips stroking her back. "It was unnecessary and cruel, a pattern I find myself falling into all too often."

"I'm sorry, too," Raegan said, meaning it. "You only said what you did because I pushed you. I'm always pushing you. Well, anyone, really."

"Anyone who gets too close," Oberon replied softly, his fingertips still making sweeping, gentle strokes down her frame. She shivered at his touch.

"Yeah," Raegan admitted. "I'm sorry I called you a monster."

At that, the King straightened, moving to cradle Raegan's face in his large hands. For a long moment, he said nothing, only holding her gaze. Then, finally, he spoke. "Do not call me that again. Not, at least, until I am about to cross that line. Until I step into that place from which none return."

"You won't," Raegan said, her brow furrowing with the intensity of her belief, voice firm.

But the King only sighed. "I cannot promise that," he replied, his thumb stroking her cheek. "And you cannot promise to be the only thing holding me back from that ledge."

"But I want to," Raegan said, reaching up to grip both of his wrists with her hands.

"There are many things we want," Oberon said, "that we cannot—or should not—have, my love."

He exhaled and then brought his forehead to hers, hands still against her skin. She closed her eyes, tears gathering on her lashes. The scent of woodsmoke and black pepper settled around her, the familiarity of it reaching deep into the recesses of her memory. Raegan let the scenes roll over her, the current of a cold, thunderstorm-swollen stream in spring.

They pulled apart, only slightly, so he could wrap an arm around her waist. She settled her head onto his chest, tired and spent and knowing at the same time that the battle had only just begun. With a hard swallow, she tried to find the right words.

"I love you," Raegan said with all her might, reaching to slide her fingers into his. "I love you more than I understand. More than I thought I'd ever be capable of loving anyone. It scares me sometimes."

He turned to look at her so fiercely that she lifted her head from his chest, their eyes meeting. She hated the way her words brought no joy to his expression. Instead, Oberon looked haunted. He was, she supposed. She had been his ghost for more years than she'd ever been his lover, and she brought more horror to his doorstep than happiness.

"Not everything is a responsibility for you to take on," Raegan murmured, reaching up to trace the sharp angle of his jaw. He leaned into her touch. "Don't wear my love like a mantle." *Even though it weighs as heavily as one, and I'm about to remind you why,* she did not say.

Oberon took in a deep, jagged breath, closing his eyes. Then he gathered her body against his and kissed her—slowly, deeply, as if they had all the time they could ever want. Raegan drowned herself in his dark tide, a sailor to the siren, moth to flame. His mouth on hers, the feeling of his strong, long-fingered hands roaming her curves—all of it should have torn down her defenses, sent the truth of what had just happened spilling from her lips. But with her father dead and her mortal life forsaken, what else did she even have but Oberon and this quest? So selfishly—as always—she clung to the moment for a little longer.

"Feeling better, I suppose?" Raegan teased, tracing his jawline with her fingers.

"Somewhat," the King said against her collarbone, his voice a low rumble like thunder in the distance. "My pain has eased a little with rest. My desire for you, however, has only grown all the more intense."

He pulled her sweater over her head, bringing his mouth to her neck as he pressed her into the quilt. Raegan let out a soft whisper of a moan, reaching for the hem of his shirt, praying that the deft sweep of his lean, muscular body would pull her from the darkness of her own mind. And it almost did—desire erupted in her at the sight of his moonlight skin, so much power coiled just beneath. Raegan ran her hands down the King's back, wrapping her legs around his hips, her boots long since kicked off somewhere at the edge of the bed.

"I'm sorry I'm such a bitch all the time," she said, the words tumbling out of her, a hundred feelings shouting for dominance inside her chest. Guilt swarmed her like locusts.

Oberon paused, coming up on his elbows, a wave of raven-black hair tumbling across his forehead. Then he examined her, his mouth moving into a frown. "Do not be sorry," he finally said, sitting back on his knees, her thighs still wrapped around him as he reached to undo the zipper of her jeans. "I have always liked that about you."

He wasn't lying, she didn't think; in this position, the evidence of his arousal was hard and straining against the apex of her legs. Raegan studied him, lifting her hips so he could pull her jeans from her body.

"For what it's worth," she replied, breathless now with want as he slid his hands up the bare skin of her legs, "I've always liked that you can be . . . monstrous."

The corner of Oberon's sculpted mouth lifted, but even though he didn't meet her gaze, she could tell the humor didn't reach his eyes. "A pair of angry, broken things," he murmured, lowering himself back over her in a sharp, controlled movement. The heat and weight of him pulled a low, strangled sound of unbridled want from Raegan's mouth. The King reached forward, cradling the back of her head in his hands as he swept her into another all-consuming kiss.

She wanted to let go. Wanted the dark rush of him to consume her, to be devoured by the terrifying faerie king that everyone else had attempted to kill or tame and only she had tried to understand instead. Raegan gasped, the sound half-choked by desire, as Oberon undid the clasp of her bra in an easy, practiced movement.

"Oberon," she murmured, resting an open palm on his bare chest.

With just that light touch and the sound of his name, the King pulled away from her immediately, sitting back to meet her eyes. Concern cut into the languid expression on his angular features.

"How can you love what you know you're going to lose?" she asked, her voice raw, damp desire for him still throbbing between her legs even though her heart felt like it might shatter.

The King's expression hardened for a moment, a faraway gleam in his ocean eyes. But then he seemed to shake it off, parting his lips and taking a long inhale before speaking.

"Like this."

Chapter Sixteen

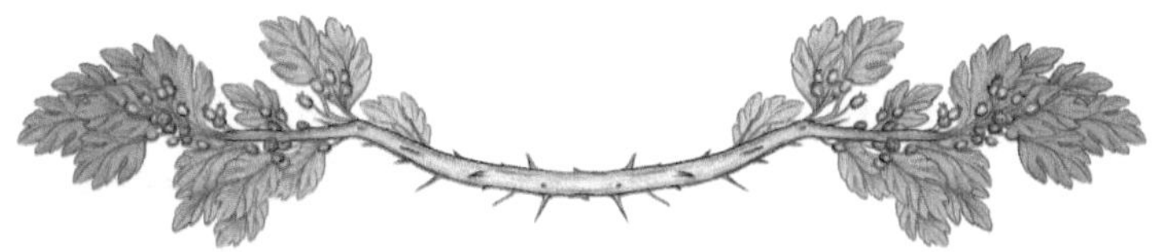

The next morning, Raegan still hadn't managed to tell Oberon about Alanna. She'd tried, but then they'd fought bitterly about something else entirely, and now here she was at the ass-crack of dawn, climbing mist-damp stairs to the mouth of an ancient waterfall looking for a door to Avalon. She felt far too exposed scrambling up the side of the falls, her form clearly outlined by the wide, pearly skies. Down below, the woods surrounding Sgwd Yr Eira were deep and dark, perfectly capable of obscuring gray suits and flashing chainmail. Maybe Oberon was right—maybe she *should've* stayed behind.

Her anger from earlier rekindled in her chest, so Raegan took a deep breath and climbed higher, keeping her attention on the uneven ground and loose soil. At least Hiraeth had its many perks—centuries of Fey history meant its armory was enough to impress even Oberon. They'd left through the city's gate that morning thoroughly decked out in amulets, cloaks, and leather armor bespelled to keep the Protectorate's gaze well away. And then they'd taken a merry, exhausting jaunt around the countryside to see if anyone was following them, but all had been quiet.

Raegan paused, inhaling to prepare for hauling herself up across an absurdly large boulder in the path. The King was only a little ways ahead of her, but it felt like miles stretched between them. She'd awoken this morning and desperately wanted to talk about Alanna—but gods, how the fuck *could* she? Not even one full day within its walls, and she'd endangered all of Hiraeth. Kamau's family. Emrys. The last Fey city, found by a Protectorate shadewalker because Raegan had spared Reilly.

Besides—Oberon hadn't told her that he was planning on searching the possible Avalon sites without her. Raegan had only found out when she'd rolled over, discovered that the bed was empty, and peered through the darkness to find him fully dressed, about to slip out the door. And when she'd pushed him on where exactly the fuck he was going, he'd all but snarled at her that the task would be easier without her in tow. She ground her teeth, searching for a foothold in the rockface. Only a few things made Oberon as upset as he'd been when she hadn't agreed with his plan. One of the top contenders was the prospect of watching her die again.

"Should probably do a better job helping me up this fucking waterfall, then," Raegan muttered, pulling herself up onto the boulder with a groan. After a few seconds of panting, she continued up the path, frustrated at a million things, including the limitations of her body. She was city-fit, not witch-on-a-quest-fit, and her muscles definitely knew the difference. As if on cue, Raegan underestimated the height of the next step and clipped her toes on the edge, losing her balance.

A large hand caught her by the upper arm, steadying her.

"Thanks," Raegan said as she rebalanced herself, peering up through the mist at the King.

"I did not realize you were struggling," Oberon replied, pulling her closer. "I would not have gone ahead." He slipped his arm around her waist, palm open on her hip, and bracketed her body against his taller, harder one.

Despite everything, hunger uncoiled in honeyed spools deep in her stomach. The pull, as always, was so much stronger than the push. "On second thought, it *is* kind of hotter when you're mean to me," she deadpanned.

He glanced down at her, amusement tugging at the corners of his mouth, and helped her up an enormous, rough-hewn stone that served as the next step. "I am happy to make adjustments for your pleasure," Oberon murmured, turning to face her, his fingers digging into the soft flesh of her hips in a way that sent desire snaking up from her core. "Though perhaps not here, climbing the side of the falls."

"Reasonable, I guess." Raegan smiled, sticking close to the King as they made the final ascent.

The sky was still opalescent above them, the sun only just now beginning to think about peering over the horizon. The falls were quiet —no tourists or hikers and hopefully no Protectorate. Only the thunder of the water met her ears, the scents of lichen, damp stone, and rushing currents filling her nose. It might've been beautiful and peaceful if they had been there for any other reason; if the fate of magic and the Fair Folk did not hang in the balance, all their will and energy bent toward the scant words of an ancient goddess.

Raegan stepped out onto the rocky shelf behind the falls, the King at her side. She'd been to this sacred place before in other lives, but awe still fluttered in her chest. To her left was a jagged wall of earth, all dark rock and mossy plants, above her a wide arc of thundering falls, and to her right, the water pitched toward the ground, spraying mist into the air as it hit the pool below. The ledge was wide enough for two or three people to walk abreast. She and the King did just that, falling silent as they searched. They'd chosen the falls—and the other sites they'd search next—based on residual magic. Though it was a resource quickly fading from this half of the world, Sgwd Yr Eira still hummed with a memory of its old power.

"We don't even know what exactly we're looking for," Raegan sighed impatiently a few minutes later, mostly to herself. Maybe if she found Avalon's door first, it would forgive the transgression of Alanna. Or at least soften the blow. She ran her fingertips along the slippery stone, searching for a seam or an inscription or anything that might tell her there was something more here, a door that had known her once and might open for her again. "The Morrigan's vision left a lot to be desired."

"I do not think we will find what we seek in this place," Oberon replied. His tone was so definitive and flat that Raegan glanced over at him. In the mist-shrouded gloom, he looked every bit the vengeful Unseelie king, dressed in black clothing and dark leather armor, a sword sheathed at his side. He tipped his head back as if to scent the air like a wolf. "There is old magic here, yes. But not, I fear, the kind we seek."

Raegan hated to agree, but she did. The waterfall was, on its surface, thick with wonder, looking every inch the place a door to Avalon might exist. It'd been Emrys's top candidate, in fact. But there was no sensation of unfurling, of something long forgotten turning over in its grave to rise again. No matter how much she yearned for it.

Raegan placed two open hands against the fall's rocky spine, trying with all her might to remember. Another thing she'd thought would be different once the Seal was gone. Her memories were there, yes, but accessing them was another thing entirely. It got easier every day, bit by bit, but Raegan had never been a particularly patient person. She wanted all of herself, and she wanted it *now*. Was she not entitled to her own past?

The whisper of the falls suddenly gathered itself up into a symphony, and Raegan's heart lurched, hoping the place would sing to her of doors and salvation. But it was just the wind playing the water like a harp, so she closed her eyes again and focused on the times she'd been to Sgwd Yr Eira before. Snippets of full moon rituals a thousand years in the past came and went, lovely and magical, white blooms floating on the surface and candles lining the pool, but nothing she could use on this quest.

Another memory surfaced, and with a sharp, unwelcome pang, Raegan remembered there used to be nymphs here. She pushed the scene away before she was forced to see the stones stained with blood a second time. Was there any place in this landscape, she wondered, that the Protectorate had not irrevocably altered with their hungry violence?

A hand alighted on her shoulder, jarring Raegan for a moment before she recognized the heavy, weighted warmth of the King's touch. Already deep in her own mind, she lost control of the memory stream and found herself standing in a similar place on the waterfall's ledge. It had been summer then, the air thick with humidity, the forest below like a sea of emeralds. Under the spray of the falls, the air was blessedly cool, smelling of August rain and autumn's promised return.

He'd been there, too—much younger, that beautiful fairy-tale knight she'd once called Mordred. In her mind's eye, she pressed her back to the stone, beckoning him closer, the waterfall feeling so much like a gauzy curtain fluttering around a four-poster bed. He'd looked at her with those ocean eyes, dark with desire, before stalking over with the predatory grace he'd possessed even then.

If these lands were marred by the bloody touch of the Protectorate, she reasoned, what legacy had she and Mordred left behind? Did the all-consuming, revolutionary kind of love that usually only young people were stupid enough to fall into make any difference?

"Sorry," Raegan mumbled, pulling away from the stone. "I was trying to see what I could remember about this place."

"I recall a few things," the King replied in a low, husky voice, his hands sliding around her waist.

Raegan laughed. "I was thinking about that, too." She turned to face him, pressing her back into the stone just like she had all those years ago. Gods, she'd give anything to be young again. A chance to do it all over.

Oberon slid a long, powerful leg between her thighs, bringing his mouth to hers. A lightning strike of need electrified her entire body. Raegan ran her hands down his muscular chest and then fumbled at his waistband. Common sense fled her; the keen sense of danger she'd felt so viscerally since they'd stepped beyond Hiraeth's wards earlier that morning evaporated. Even the heavy sweep of guilt faded. There was only the tumble of water, the soft whisper of the mist, and the undeniable pull of the magnificent, impossible thing before her.

The years and her lives overlapped like a double exposure. It could've been Mordred or the King whose strong hands roamed beneath her garments, whose kiss grew so intense and desperate that she wanted to drown in it. A name escaped her mouth, voice thick with unmet desire. All she wanted was to feel his capable fingers at the apex of her legs, the hard length of him buried deep inside her, the rock wall biting into her exposed skin.

"Raegan," the King murmured against her lips, catching her wrists in his hands. "As much as it will pain me to wait another moment, my plans for you are best enacted within the safety of good wards. After all, you *do* get quite loud."

Raegan rolled her eyes and laughed, coming back to herself. It felt good to laugh. She straightened, pushing off the wall. "If you think about it," she countered, looking up at him, "it's *your* fault I'm loud."

"It is an honor to accept that blame," Oberon told her, a smile dancing across his full lips. Then he sobered, a familiar weight coming back to his brow.

That shared, shadowed heaviness returned to Raegan's chest too, and she sighed. "There's nothing here. Part of me wants to search harder. Due diligence, I guess. But I think I would feel something. And you definitely would."

She considered the King, otherworldly in the misty gloom, looking every bit the last of the Tuatha de Danann. Not Danu's direct prodigy, no, but crafted by divine hands in a similar ritual, infused with the blood of fallen warriors and the bite of sacred swords. Two Fey had not tumbled together beneath sheets and born him. Usually the doors sang to her, but she supposed this one would call to him—the last of his kind, locked out of the paradise that was his due.

"There are other places," Oberon said, reaching out to take her hand. "Imagine how long Emrys's list must be now that we have given him an entire morning alone in his library."

Raegan nodded, sliding her fingers into his as they walked along the slippery ledge back to the stairs at the side of the waterfall. "I didn't think it would be *that* easy—that the first place we tried would be the one."

"It would be nice, though, would it not?" Oberon asked, looking over at her. "For something to be easy for once." The words left his mouth laden with wistfulness.

"Yeah," Raegan agreed, pausing at the top of the stairs, trying to prepare her body for the climb back down. "Easy would be nice."

"I may be able," the King told her, stooping low and sliding his arms around her, "to make *one* thing easier, at least." With that, he swept her off the ground and into his embrace.

"Oberon," she sputtered with concern, "I'm fine to walk. Aren't you still in pain?"

"Yes," he replied without hesitation, his tone even. "The pain never leaves me. You, however, do. So allow me to hold you, and trust me to care for my own body."

Raegan tilted her chin up, meeting his gaze. She swallowed down a wave of jagged guilt and settled for nodding before pressing the side of her face to his chest, desperate to hear his heartbeat. She took a deep inhale. Maybe she could memorize his scent of black pepper and woodsmoke and damp stone. Maybe even if he cast her out again, she could at least remember what she had lost this time.

She opened her eyes when Oberon reached the bottom of the falls and then slid out of his grasp. "Thanks," Raegan said, her heart fluttering.

The King offered her a rare jewel in return—a smile that actually reached his eyes. Her stomach somersaulted. She ached to kiss him again, but then his lips parted, worry creasing his brow.

"My love," Oberon said, reaching for her in a gentle, graceful movement, cupping her face in his large hand. "I worry there are things you are not telling me. You have yet to speak of the Timekeeper's realm, and I feel your secrets have only grown heavier since."

Raegan's instinct was to lean into his touch and tell the faerie king everything. Who wouldn't do the same, faced with his beautiful ferocity and long-fingered hands? He would follow her to the ends of the Earth— he'd said it himself. But Raegan clamped her jaw before the words could tumble out and spill the truth of her father and the conversation with Alanna. If it all came out like this, Oberon would finally see that he'd been right to abandon her. That she was too hard to love.

"I'm not ready," she replied, the lie sour on her tongue, but her defenses snapped down like a bear trap, and even she didn't know how to pry them apart. "I'll let you know when I am."

Oberon held still, saying nothing for a moment longer. Her heart raced, anxiety flooding her veins. "I fear we are not in a position to wait until we are less tender," he murmured, brushing the pad of his thumb across her lips. "I have known you too long. You are keeping something from me. I am concerned."

It didn't matter that the King spoke his feelings with the utmost care or that he was absolutely, unnervingly correct. Raegan's heart rate spiked all the same, her anger flashing as hot as if he'd come for her jugular. "I'm not a member of your Court," she snapped, stepping back, away from his touch. "You can't just command me to do what you want."

The King's hand floated back down to his side, the elegant swoop of a prized bird. For a split second, he looked at her in a way that made Raegan question Baba Yaga's sureness he would never harm her. "Raegan," Oberon said, his tone edged with warning, "that was *not* a command. Not even close."

She crossed her arms, planting her feet wide. "You don't get to decide when I talk about really fucked-up shit that happened to *me*. It didn't happen to you."

The King closed his eyes and raked a hand through his hair, which always made him look more human to her. "But it did," he said, meeting her gaze again. "It very much happened to me, too. I waited and hoped for an entire week in empty chambers. Regardless, there is something else, I think, that you are harboring. Do recall we are not regular people. I am not asking as your lover."

"Oh, so you think you're asking as my king?" Raegan snarled, her fingers winding into fists, the blood pounding in her throat, the anger so much more palatable than the bone-deep shame.

He reeled back so hard that for a second, she thought she'd slapped him without realizing she'd raised a hand at all. "No," Oberon said, his expression an open wound. "No. I am asking as your accomplice. Your co-revolutionary. Make no mistake—this is a war. You cannot leave me in the dark in war. Not again."

Guilt crowded Raegan's lungs, his words validating all her fears. Her old defense mechanisms flared, anger roaring up in a dark wave. "It's not like that," she protested, furious that hot tears were pricking the back of her eyes.

Oberon let out a long breath, holding her gaze all the while. "I cannot know how it is if you do not *tell* me."

Raegan paused, feeling miserable and alone. Some horrible part of her wanted him to throw his power around like he used to in their youth, when his first language was manipulation and threats and violence, all thinly veiled by effortless seduction. She knew how to handle that—how to not be afraid of him, how to bare her teeth in return. She knew how to fuck him into submission, and she knew damn well how skilled he was at doing the same in return.

She did *not* know how to handle what he was doing now—so open, so gentle. It made her nervous, like a panther delicately eating berries from her hand when she knew it craved blood and flesh instead.

"Is that why you brought up some nice old memories and carried me down?" Raegan snapped, making an accusatory gesture toward the stone steps behind her. "Did you think I'd swoon and give you whatever you wanted?"

Now he just stared at her, his eyebrows drawn together, bewilderment moving into his expression. For a long, stretched moment, he said nothing at all. Raegan squirmed but held fast.

"We should depart," Oberon eventually replied, moving toward the waterfall's rock-ringed pool to summon the kelpies. "May we discuss this further later?"

She opened her mouth to tell him no and to fuck off while he was at it, but something stole his attention, expression gone cold. Instinctively, Raegan turned on her heel, following his sightline. On the other side of the pool, about a hundred paces into the forest, movement caught her eye. The world dropped out from under her. Shapes of drab gray snuck through the undergrowth. The smell of metal and gunpowder that suddenly filled her nose could only mean one thing.

Despite all their precautions, the Protectorate had found them.

Chapter Seventeen

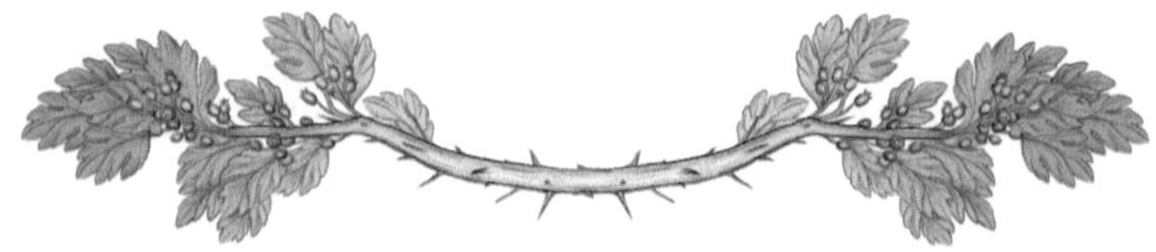

Raegan froze. Her eyes shot to the King. His head was cocked like a predator's, gaze taking in the enemy on the opposite shore. He *wanted* to fight—she could see it in the flex of his long fingers, his muscles spring-loaded. He wanted to tear limb from limb, to find another throat to sink his teeth into. Raegan swallowed back nausea. How many children would he rip through without a second thought? The Protectorate leadership was as cruel and cunning as the Fey they hated; it wouldn't surprise her if this entire squad was filled with round-faced young adults, their curly hair just like Cormac's.

"No," she said, barking out the word, darting forward to grab the King by his wrist. "No. Let's just leave. Save it for a fight that matters."

He watched her, and for a second, Raegan thought she saw suspicion in his expression, which chilled her to the bone. Oberon's centuries-long reign had produced very few traitors, but she remembered what he'd done to the fools who'd dared to cross him. She had no desire to be on the receiving end.

"The kelpies will not reach us in time," the King told her, tone flat, "and there are no porticos left in this land."

"Just get us to the woods behind them," Raegan suggested, her eyes darting to the approaching Protectorate, who admittedly *did* seem very excited to use their guns. "We can lose them and follow the river upstream to call the kelpies. Doing magic now won't matter. They've already found us."

The King did not agree or acquiesce; instead, he reached out and clamped a hand around Raegan's arm. The world spun, the beautiful setting of the falls and the woods turning into a sickening blur that rattled her eyeballs in her skull. When the movement finally stopped, she leaned over and retched onto the damp brown leaves beneath her feet. The King gave her all of two seconds before he tightened his grip on her arm and began to haul her deeper into the woods, away from the river.

"How did they find us?" Oberon muttered under his breath, moving at a pace meant for his legs, not hers. "We used the Rivers and employed no active magic."

Raegan said nothing, her mouth dry, her mind racing. Emrys had triple-checked them for any kind of tracking spells when they'd arrived. They'd been within Hiraeth's wards the entire time, until she and Oberon had left that morning. So how could—

Alanna. Raegan gritted her teeth, trying to keep her footsteps on the forest floor as quiet as possible. She knew a decent amount about shade-walkers, but they were rare and often reclusive or, at the very least, not forthcoming about their abilities. There could certainly be things she didn't know. And that symbol Alanna had conjured on the wards—it hadn't felt like anything much to Raegan at the time. More like a bread-crumb to get back home, a chalked arrow on a tree trunk. But now the events of the night prior returned to her mind as quickly as she tripped through the woods, and her stomach stewed.

"This is why I wanted you to stay with Emrys," the King said in a low whisper, pulling her into his arms as he moved behind a large, rain-slick rock. He pressed his back against it, holding Raegan to his chest, and then lifted his chin, gaze undoubtedly roving the forest.

"You don't know me at all if you think I'm going to sit around while you hunt for Avalon," Raegan replied, whispering despite the anger she felt—and trying to ignore the curl of arousal she felt with her body pressed against his hard, lean form.

"I do not think you will *enjoy* it," the King spat back at her, looking around the side of the rock. The woods had fallen silent, as if all the smaller creatures recognized what hunted within their domain. "I only think it is right."

"Were you even there yesterday morning?" Raegan hissed, trying to keep her balance as he shot around the side of the rock with her body still held against his, a deft movement of shadow and strength. "I made a goddamn river monster eat a bunch of people. I can handle myself."

He said nothing and began to stalk away from the rock, gripping her by the forearm as if she were an obstinate child. Her shoulder pulled painfully, and she broke into a jog to keep up with him. They continued in silence, moving away from the Protectorate and toward the river that fed the waterfalls. It was barely more than a small stream here, but Raegan knew not much water was required to call forth a kelpie—not even for the old-fashioned mortal way she had used when all this began. The King's request for a kelpie was so honed and subtle that even the Protectorate were unlikely to notice it.

"I don't think they're following us," Raegan whispered, just wanting to break the silence, constantly torn between her anger and her yearning.

"No, I think not," Oberon agreed, but he still moved quick and low, a panther hunting. "Your idea was quite sound—the magic I worked would only confuse them, appearing so close to their formation when we were nowhere to be found."

He was trying to mollify her, Raegan knew. She stepped around a large fern, the fronds brushing her leg, leaving her pants striped with dew. He would've thought of the same option in a heartbeat; in fact, he probably had before she'd even said it. But Oberon hadn't wanted to run. He wanted to fight, to maim, to kill.

"Just trying to stop you from murdering people," Raegan muttered, the words harsher than she had really meant.

The King did not even slow down. "Interesting, as you seem to have few qualms about your own actions yesterday."

"I didn't like it," Raegan snapped, yanking her arm from his grasp. "You *like* it."

The King looked at her sideways, his eyes shadowed in the gloom of the November wood. His full lips moved into something cruel. "Yes, you do. Pretending otherwise is a fool's game, and you are no fool."

She opened her mouth to respond, but she was so angry that she didn't think she could say anything without screaming. They seemed to have slipped past the Protectorate, but she wasn't particularly interested in testing that assumption out. So she said nothing, fixing her gaze on the ground ahead of her, anger and frustration boiling in her stomach.

Neither one of them said anything as they moved through the forest, Oberon occasionally pulling her behind a large tree or hulking boulder to double back or check that they had no followers. The silence was not helping. Raegan wanted to have it out—to yell and curse, to make any kind of noise that drowned out her guilt and shame. The King, on the other hand, seemed to relax into the quiet.

Beneath the boughs of a hemlock grove, he finally paused, crouching near the water's edge. Raegan slid as deep as she could into the darkness of the hemlocks, waiting for the kelpies to arrive. When Oberon rose from the stream, he turned back, eyes meeting hers. For some reason, the compassion she saw lingering in those gray depths made her furious, and she didn't know why. Self-loathing sank its fangs into her.

"Nyneve," the King murmured as he approached, saying her first name like she was a goddess and he was only a humble supplicant. She straightened, eagerly awaiting the apology—because when he apologized, she got to pretend she'd done nothing wrong. "You cannot make me love you and then stop me from protecting you."

Raegan's mouth hung open, processing the words he'd said too slowly. "Don't pretend you could love a caged thing," she spat, recovering herself.

He turned away from her, his shoulders sagging. Behind the King, a kelpie's muzzle broke the surface of the stream. Raegan pushed past him, wanting to be back at Hiraeth so she could safely get away from him. As she stepped out from the hemlock grove, she spotted movement on the other side of the stream. But she was already out in the open, and it happened so fast. They'd successfully escaped a close call, she thought, about to return to the old Temple. She'd been about to swing a leg over a kelpie and disappear into the Rivers, hadn't she?

But then there was a man in a pinstripe suit, leather oxfords shining in the light of the now-risen sun, and in his hands there was a gun. He fired, quick as could be, and Raegan called to the water beneath her— and it began to answer, jaws flexing wider. It didn't matter, though, because the King burst from the hemlock grove like an apex predator, sending the bullet curving back toward the man who had fired it with a simple wave of his hand.

The King turned to Raegan, his face a mask of anger and bone-deep fear, and she knew it was only because he loved her so much that he didn't see the other Protectorate man emerging from the shadow of the opposite bank with a shotgun—or something like it, even crueler in design—in his hands. And when he fired, the King wrapped his body around Raegan's and plunged into the stream below. It should've only been a foot or so deep, but the Rivers opened for them.

The shock of the cold water knocked all of the air out of Raegan's lungs, and it took her a few terrifying seconds to remember she'd always been able to breathe in the Rivers. A kelpie—not Rainer—burst out of the dancing river grass to her left, swinging its scaled tail to bank hard. Raegan scrambled onto its back, turning to look for the King. He climbed onto the kelpie behind her, looking no worse for wear until she dragged her eyes down his body, her heart pounding in her throat all the while. Her stomach dropped at the sight of his chest. She urged the kelpie faster.

He'd watched her die, over and over again. That was how it worked, how it had *always* worked, and maybe that was because Fate knew as well as Raegan did that she wasn't strong enough to be the one left behind.

CHAPTER EIGHTEEN

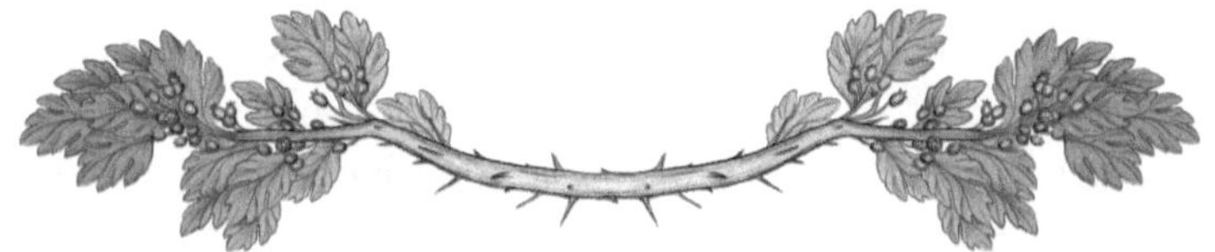

The kelpie didn't hesitate. It broke through the surface of the River Wye and pounded onto the shore, its long, dark legs propelling it up the banks and onto a windswept, forlorn hill. Raegan gripped its slick seaweed mane tighter as she saw a circle of hawthorn trees come into view. And then, a door cut out of the gray morning, the smell of autumn rain and damp cobblestones suddenly thick in her nose.

The kelpie shot through the opening, clattering into a small courtyard Raegan hadn't seen before. It was Hiraeth, though—the old Temple's striking stone façade rose into the deep gray-blue sky, the courtyard abutting what she thought might be the kitchen. Having barely broken its pace through the city's wards, the kelpie came to a sliding stop right by a slim, arched door. It flew open, and Emrys stepped from the gloom, expression tight and drawn. Raegan watched the ex-Keeper register the sight of the King's chest. His ever-present composure promptly shattered. Something about it made her leap into action.

"Shotgun blast," Raegan shouted despite Emrys only being a few feet away, sliding down from the kelpie. "Definitely iron, probably spelled. Left chest and shoulder." She thanked the fickle vaults of her memory for allowing her to reflexively identify the King's wounds.

The kelpie sank to its knees, allowing Oberon to dismount more easily. He did so unaided, though his jaw was clenched hard and he wasn't moving his left arm.

"How bad?" Emrys asked as he yanked the door all the way open before beginning to roll up his sleeves.

"Not sure yet," Raegan replied, wrapping an arm around Oberon's waist to support his injured side. She thanked the kelpie and shooed it back to the river; the younger ones didn't fancy being on dry land for very long.

"I am fine," Oberon said, though he leaned into her. Not very much, of course—he had more than a foot and at least a hundred pounds of pure, heavy muscle on her. But the fact that he leaned into her at all indicated he was probably not fine.

"I have modern medical training and equipment," Emrys told Raegan, coming to the King's free side.

"I can walk quite well," Oberon said, testy now. "They shot my shoulder, not my legs."

"Shut up and let us take care of you," Raegan snapped, trying to match her strides to his.

"She's right," Emrys said from the King's other side as they passed through the door. Emrys kicked it closed behind him. "Not comfortable, I know, but the kitchen table is probably the best place for now."

Raegan nodded and turned on her heel to help the King maneuver toward the large, roughly hewn table. He managed to pull himself up onto it without her or Emrys's help, bringing his right hand to the front of his leather armor. His fingers shook.

"I got it," Raegan said, moving forward to begin unbuckling the breastplate. "Emrys, can you get hot water, rags, and your equipment?"

"Already on it," Emrys called, his voice coming from deep inside the old Temple.

"I will be fine," Oberon told her, catching her gaze, dark hair falling across his forehead, which was covered in a thin sheen of sweat.

"It's my fucking fault," Raegan muttered, trying to get the buckles undone as quickly as possible without yanking on his injuries. She cursed her lack of muscle memory; in other lives, she'd been able to help him remove his armor in a few seconds flat.

"I did not see them," Oberon sighed, trying to sit up straighter, supporting his weight on the flattened palm of his right hand. "So my fault, then. Though I find little use in this exercise. Such things are to be expected. It is war, after all."

"How did they find us, Oberon?" Raegan asked, stooping over to unbuckle the larger straps at the bottom of his breastplate, hoping beyond hope that there was an explanation other than Alanna.

"I intend to find out," he told her, closing his eyes. For a long moment, his breathing was so shallow that Raegan's heart nearly exploded, but he opened his eyes as Emrys burst back into the room. The ex-Keeper's arms were filled with a massive first aid kit, a large bowl of hot water, and a stack of clean towels.

Raegan finally finished undoing the armor's closures and slowly pulled the shredded leather off Oberon's body. It had certainly taken some of the brunt of the blast, but his left chest and shoulder were still a mess of gore, muscle fibers visible beneath torn skin, blood glistening in the low light. She was going to wrap him in fucking Kevlar from here on out. Leaning closer, Raegan caught a sickening glimpse of bone, white-gray and shining. She expected a surge of nausea, but it did not come; she'd been a healer in too many lives, she supposed.

Emrys produced scissors and cut Oberon's shirt down the middle, working with Raegan to peel it away from his skin. "Heart and major arteries look okay," he said, examining the King closely. "This is still bad, though."

Moving automatically, Raegan dipped one of the towels into the steaming bowl of water and began to clear away the blood around the King's grisly wounds. Her hands shook. She'd done this. She'd allowed the Protectorate to track them, and she'd distracted him with her stupid anger and self-loathing. Bile churned in her stomach, and she nearly choked.

But even now, she couldn't make the confession about Alanna come to her lips. A golden opportunity to infiltrate the Protectorate would be ruined, she told herself, even though she knew that deep down, the real reason she couldn't was her own weakness. Because every moment, she wanted to sink to her knees and scream in grief about her father. If she had to contend with the tender sorrow she still bore about the choices she'd made in that life as Titania? If Oberon and Emrys looked at her like she was the cause of all the pain in their world? No. She just *couldn't*, especially not until she knew for sure that Oberon would be okay.

Suddenly the King reached for her, enclosing her fingers in his right hand. She looked up at him, wordless and spiraling.

"I will be fine," he repeated, looking hard into her eyes, "and I will not allow you to blame yourself."

"What happened?" Emrys asked, pulling a pair of unpleasant-looking tweezers from his medical kit. He began to pluck scattered pieces of iron and leather fibers from the back of Oberon's shoulder. Raegan watched as the King didn't even flinch.

"Th-they came out of nowhere," she stammered. "We thought we had lost them and stopped to call for the kelpies. There were two of them, maybe more. Obviously one had a fucking shotgun."

Emrys grimaced. "I want to look you both over again for tracking spells. There's no reason they should've been able to find you so easily, especially in a remote place."

"Perhaps," Oberon said, his voice breathier than usual, his words slowed, "they know we are looking for Avalon."

Raegan paused, holding a bloodied towel in midair, the implications boiling in her gut. Her skin was clammy and hot, but the inside of her chest felt cold, like icicles had slid into her capillaries. Emrys, too, paused, looking at the King with alarm.

"Emrys," the King said, his voice low and dangerous, a predator slinking through the night. "You are one of the only people who know we seek Avalon. Have you betrayed me?"

The destroyed Temple's Keeper straightened like an arrow. "No, Oberon. My liege. You know I want the same things as you."

"I know," Oberon said, twisting to look at Emrys, though it clearly pained him. Somehow, despite being naked to the waist and covered in blood, the King very much still looked like the most dangerous creature in the room.

Raegan didn't move, her throat burning, her heart pumping far too quickly.

"If either a threat or an offer was made to you by our enemies, you would tell me, yes?" the King wanted to know. "I will protect what is yours as fiercely as I protect what is mine." His gaze slid to Raegan, something feral and hungry simmering in those gray depths. "The bullet was meant for *her*, Emrys."

The ex-Keeper froze, tweezers still in his hand, and swallowed hard, his Adam's apple bobbing in his throat. With shaking fingers, he set the tweezers down and moved to stand in front of the King. "Oberon," Emrys implored. "Beyond my loyalty to the Unseelie Court and the old ways and my personal desire for revenge, I also am not particularly interested in you torturing me for three hundred years."

Glancing at him with a heavy-lidded expression, the King's mouth curved into something cruel and dangerous but amused all the same. "Understand I do not doubt you," Oberon murmured, his eyes locked with Emrys's. "But something is awry."

Without another word, the King's eternal, oceanic gaze swung to Raegan. "In a thousand years, you have never outright betrayed me," he said, his breathing heavy, his words sending a spike of fear and hurt and anxiety right into her chest. "Like Emrys, I do not doubt you. Yet I must ask: has your current vessel's Protectorate blood led you astray?"

In that moment, Raegan would've sworn he was a stranger, that they'd never met before, that he'd never torn out someone's throat for her, let alone loved and fucked and fought side-by-side for a millennium. He looked at her with that cold, dead expression he usually reserved for his enemies.

"No," she said hoarsely, for some reason clutching the bloodstained rag to her chest. "Mordred, *no*. Of course not."

With that, the King seemed to shrink, his shoulders collapsing again, that cruel darkness leaving the sharp angles of his face. "Good," he murmured, his spine curving. "I am sorry I had to ask you both."

Emrys shrugged, clearly less affected by this questioning than Raegan, and returned to plucking bits of iron from the King's shoulder. "You had no choice. Let us patch you up, and then we can try to figure out how this happened."

Her hands shaking, Raegan returned to wiping blood from Oberon's skin. He was alive—talking, breathing. He was going to be fine. And yet, with the weight of her mistakes pressing down on her shoulders, Raegan felt like she was going to lose him all the same.

～

By evening, Emrys was no closer to figuring out how the Protectorate had found them, and the secret of Alanna rattled around in Raegan's chest. She stared at the plumes of steam curling up from the two cups of black tea she'd prepared. Her heaved sigh sent ripples dancing across the dark waters. She'd planned to tell Oberon first, because she desperately needed his help to explain it all to Emrys. If he didn't hate her afterwards, of course, which felt like a very real possibility.

Steeling herself, Raegan picked up the tea tray and turned toward the stairs. She knew she had to tell him, and she hated herself for not saying anything to Emrys. They'd spent hours checking the spellwork on Hiraeth's wards together after Oberon's wounds were tended to and they'd gotten him settled upstairs to rest. If the Keeper had clocked how hard her heart had been beating when they'd neared the square leading to the botanical gardens, he'd said nothing. Though perhaps he just planned on going directly to Oberon with the news that the King's lover had, yet again, become his doom.

Beginning to climb the wide, grand stairs, Raegan did her best to banish the thoughts from her mind. Overthinking wasn't going to help. She'd spent too long sitting by the fire, wondering if she was just afraid of punishment or if she hated herself or if she feared nothing quite as much as letting him down. Maybe all three. She didn't know. There was so fucking much she didn't know.

Raegan paused at the partially closed door, taking another long, deep breath. Maybe he'd be asleep. Maybe she could put this off a little longer, refine her words, smooth it over in her own mind.

"Raegan?" the King's voice slipped around the door, as low and dark and melodic as it always was, and despite everything, the sound of it still felt like home. So Raegan walked into the room, her steps slow, her heart thumping louder and louder.

"Hey," she said, her voice shaky, "I brought you some tea. And I wanted to check on you." She set the tea tray down on the windowsill and then turned to face him. Oberon was sitting up in bed, his hands folded over a book that sat in his lap. That Feyrish web-like bandage she'd found on her own body at the Oracle's Temple in Philadelphia wound around his chest and shoulder. Blood seeped through in more places than she would've liked despite the yarrow she'd packed into the dressing. But his color was better and no sheen of sweat glimmered on his brow.

"You and Emrys are quite a formidable pair when it comes to healing," Oberon said, his gaze meeting hers.

She flushed with pride, which the guilt and shame immediately consumed. "I'm glad I had enough in me to at least close up the smaller wounds," she said, stirring sugar into a teacup. Her hands shook, and the spoon clanked loud and sharp against the china. "Emrys got me a Fey anatomy book from his library. I've been studying it to try to close up your larger injuries, but I'm worried about getting all the tendons right."

Healing a superficial tear was one thing, something Raegan could do even this soon after her Seal's removal. But muscle fibers and tendons were another thing entirely, too easy to make worse, particularly on Fey creatures, who she was now remembering were actually built quite a bit differently on the inside than humans.

"They will heal in due time on their own, but it is appreciated," the King replied, watching her every move and making no attempt at hiding it. "My body, despite its pain, still mends quickly."

Raegan nodded, her lips pressed together as she brought him a cup of tea—strongly steeped Assam with just a touch of sugar. She offered it to him, handle-first, the heat searing through to her palms. He took the teacup, fingers brushing hers. As always, her body keened unnaturally for him.

"I need to tell you something," Raegan blurted out, dragging both hands through her hair. Nausea tumbled slick and bloated through her stomach. "But you have to understand. It's not like before. I wasn't planning to do anything on my own, I was just collecting information until I had enough to tell you."

She bit her tongue, cutting herself off from saying more. The King just watched her, his gaze a fathomless pit. No words stirred on his beautiful mouth, the same one that had touched every inch of her a thousand times before. She swallowed hard, beginning to pace at his bedside. The pale green rug of Art Nouveau-stylized leaves that ran alongside the bed was the perfect length of her footsteps, to and fro.

Raegan shook her hands at the wrists, trying to rid herself of the nervous energy. She paused at the end of the rug, her back to Oberon, taking in the brilliant late afternoon sunshine that snuck through

Hiraeth's clouds for a moment, gilding all the carved woods and jewel tones of the room with honey.

And then Raegan turned, her heart pounding painfully against her breastbone, her ribs like a cage containing a wild, traitorous beast. She met his gaze again and opened her mouth. "I think I may have allowed the Protectorate to track us. I think this is all my fault."

Chapter Nineteen

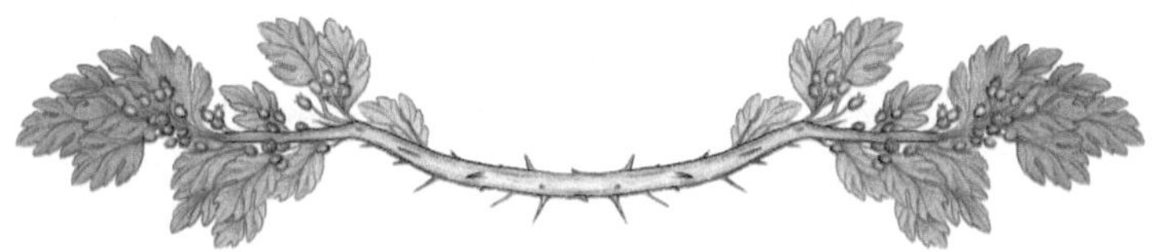

The King said nothing, though she saw his long fingers tighten around the teacup. A bird swept by the window, casting a shadow across his face for a moment. Raegan swallowed again, her throat aching, waiting for him to say something.

But he wouldn't, she knew. She hadn't given him enough information to respond to; instead, he would pin her under his terrifying gaze and wait until the words came tumbling out. Only once he felt he understood would he speak.

"Last night, when I went out, a shadewalker came through the hawthorns," Raegan said, wringing her hands in front of her before she forced herself to stop, stuffing her fingers into her pockets instead. "She's Protectorate."

And then Raegan told him the rest—how Alanna had said she might come back the following night, how she was not interested in what the Protectorate wanted but was afraid of the Fair Folk, too. How Raegan didn't think they could trust her, but they could certainly use her. How she felt so much guilt, so much shame, so much grief, and it was going to break her. Had maybe *already* broken her.

Her heart thrust itself harder and harder against her bones with every word, and she could hear her voice becoming higher, the sentences quickening. Her chest hurt. She shoved hot tears away, pushing her rage down. She had to stop using anger as a defense. She could not scream at the High King of the Unseelie Court until he went away. He was not afraid of her, and she could not cut him deeply enough for it to matter.

"Raegan," Oberon said after what felt like an eternity, setting his teacup down on the nightstand. "I have never heard of a shadewalker able to work tracking spells away from their body. Regardless, if someone intends harm, the hawthorns have their own defenses. Lastly . . . I need to corroborate this with Emrys, but I believe the place you are describing is the Garden of Doors."

He said those last few words with such meaning, such weight, but Raegan didn't recognize the name. Besides, she was mostly focused on the utter relief she felt flushing her body, cool spring water after a long drought. With shaking hands, she pushed a few stray curls away from her face.

"And the Garden . . ." she said, looking at him quizzically.

"Hiraeth is sentient," the King replied. "The Garden of Doors is one of the city's oldest locations, the grit around which Hiraeth was formed. It is an ancient place, and it only appears when it wishes to. There is no precise location it can be found. Its gates open to few. I would hazard that the city *wanted* you to speak with this Protectorate woman."

Raegan's head swam, the meaning of those words undoing her entirely. She closed her eyes, silent tears streaming down her face. What felt like her first deep breath in days filled her lungs.

"But," Oberon continued, a sharp edge coming into his tone that sent her heart hammering away again, "I want to know why you did not tell me what occurred."

"Because . . . you hate the Protectorate," she said, taking a few steps toward him before she thought better of it. "And I get it. I do, too. But in this life, I'm tied to them. And I know from my own family how much a lot of them want no part of it. I've told you everything my dad did to get me away. Why couldn't Alanna be the same?"

The King looked at her, his expression a dagger of frustrated bewilderment. "She very well could be, but that does not explain why you withheld this from me. If you did not know the Garden's true nature, then you were risking all of Hiraeth's people. *Why, Raegan?*"

Shame wrapped around her body, squeezing the fresh air from her lungs. He saw her too clearly, and now there was nothing left but the bare, aching truth. "I . . . I've fucked everything up so much. More than once. Alanna finding Hiraeth was my fault—because I asked you to spare Reilly," she managed, panic and pain clutching at her chest with clawed hands. "I didn't want you to know until I had a handle on the situation, until I was in control. Because I won't be able to bear it if you go back to hating me. Because maybe you *should*."

Silence settled over the room, downy as fresh snow. Raegan squeezed her eyes shut, unable to look at him, to study the expression on his angular face like a palm reader divining the future's bitter truths.

"I have never," the King said, a petal-soft murmur, "hated you. *Could* never. I admit I have tried."

She opened her eyes, reaching forward to grip the bed's footboard, her knuckles white and strained. "Then why did you forsake me for centuries?" Raegan demanded, the hurt of it hollowing out her bones. Shame crept in to fill the empty spaces. "Why is this the first time we've been together again since the Gates closed?"

The King examined her, one powerful hand dug deep into the quilt, his injured arm pressed flat against his torso like a broken wing. "It was not," he said hoarsely, "because I hated you."

Anger took her in one great swell and she slammed an open palm down on the bedframe. "If you love me so much," she hissed, "how could you abandon me for hundreds of years? Maybe I'm not that important to you. And that's why I was so terrified to tell you about Alanna. Because it's just another one of my long fucking litany of mistakes, and you don't handle those very well, do you?"

A muscle in his jaw feathered and he shifted his weight. She paced the side of the bed again, secretly—and shamefully—glad that he was injured. No, not exactly—of course she wished it had never happened. But if it had to happen, she was grateful it was now. Raegan did not know if she could've had this conversation facing down a fully dressed, well-rested Oberon, not when the angles of his face got so raw and feral that he seemed more animal than human.

"I thought," he said, meeting her gaze again with all the gravitational pull of some grand, alien moon, "I was keeping you safe. I thought that was the sacrifice I had to make. Without me, you might live. Without you, my people might endure."

Raegan threw her head back and let out a choked, sardonic laugh, though tears burned her eyes. "What a martyr you are," she spat. "I've never left your side. Being with you has condemned me to early deaths, to pain, to suffering. Have I ever abandoned you?"

"No," the King admitted, holding her gaze, his face gone expressionless.

"Then how do I know, particularly after last night, that you won't be so quick to leave mortals behind, too?" she demanded, prowling closer, a perverse joy racing through her that she'd turned the tables. The guilt quieted to a low hum, though the shame still burrowed deeper beneath her skin. "If they make a few mistakes, or if it just gets too inconvenient. Like I did."

"Is that truly what you think, Raegan?" Oberon demanded, his voice shaking with anger and hurt. She looked away, unable to reconcile that her words had brought such an expression to his face—unfettered sorrow, deep as a wound.

"All I know is how far you're willing to go, how you'll never stop, and right now it feels like the existence of humans is on the line," Raegan replied, tears choking her words, the tides of her rage and guilt and shame and sadness all mixing together to form the brackish water filling her lungs. "And maybe that's a price you're willing to pay."

He looked away from her, his jaw flexing, the lamplight pulling out the threads of silver in his hair. "Rarely are situations so black and white."

"But what if it is?" Raegan demanded, coming to the end of the bed again, gripping the footboard. "You would accept that price, wouldn't you?"

"Complete annihilation of mortals in exchange for the return of magic, continued prosperity and health of my people, and reclamation of my throne?" the King asked, giving her his full attention—normally such an electrifying, sensual thing, but it fell over her instead like the cold slink of heavy fog, treacherous with monsters she could not see. "I tend to make my decisions with more information and nuance. But let us say the situation is so lacking in real-life detail. Yes, Raegan. In that scenario, I might have to accept."

She stared at him, looking for any echo of that complex, yes, but also playful, languid, and fiercely good-hearted knight she'd known so many lifetimes ago. He hadn't smiled enough to reveal the dimples she knew were there in hundreds of years. Mordred's eyes had looked almost blue sometimes, but the King's were undeniably a deep, endless gray.

"Are you happy?" he demanded, his upper lip curling, wolflike. "Are you pleased to have found a way to make me into the monster you for some reason wish to see?"

White-hot anger flared, igniting Raegan's entire body. "You just said you would annihilate mortals in exchange for what you want!"

To her horror, the King laughed. The sound of it was all windswept moor and lonely wood, the shadowed and terrible places where a powerful goddess had once birthed Her children into this world. "Nyneve," he said with a sigh, leaning back against the pillows she'd propped up for him earlier. "You cannot force me into a corner and then be upset to find me there."

Raegan dragged her hands down her face, unsure—not for the first time—if her anger contorted the world around her or if the faerie king had simply just bent her to his will again. Why had Fate crumpled her into this, all distrust and rage and a throat aching with screams she had to exert every ounce of her effort to hold back?

"Nyneve," Oberon repeated, softer. "Come here."

Raegan hesitated, but her body bucked against her like it was its own being, her bones begging to be near him. So she compromised, taking slow, measured steps toward the King's bedside. Her breath hitched the entire time. When she stood beside him, Oberon reached out for her hand, and she gave in. He brought her fingers to his mouth, those perfectly sculpted lips brushing her skin in a way that made her quiver.

"We are not really talking about what will happen to mortals, are we?" he asked, his voice a low murmur that made her bones hum. His gaze searched hers as he looked up at her, the angle sending lamplight cascading into his eyes, pulling out shades of deep ocean blue. "We are talking about *us*. About how I left you."

A sob tore itself free of Raegan's darkest hiding places. "Because maybe I'm just too hard to love," she managed to get out, her chest hitching, tears pouring down her face. "I fuck up too much and all I do is hurt you."

Oberon cupped her jaw in his hand, raw grief in his expression. "Loving you, *cariad*, is the easiest thing I have ever done," he murmured, fingertips soft as ghosts as he tucked an errant curl behind her ear. "Do not ever say you are too hard to love. There have been some, I am sure, too weak to hold the wild, unrestrained wonder of your love in their hands. I am not one of them."

"Then why," she gasped, her knees buckling, "did you leave?"

"Because I was afraid," the Unseelie king told her, his eyes near-black in the lamplight. "Because I was afraid I could not save you. Because I thought losing you was a fit punishment for my own failures. Because I thought you deserved to be free of me."

Raegan let her body go, sliding down into a crumple on the side of the bed. His touch never left her skin and she was grateful for the heat of him, a north star in the darkness of her own heart. "I'm sorry," she said, her voice scraping at the sides of her throat. "I'm so sorry. I just—I couldn't lose you like that. Not again. Not after my dad."

"I am so sorry, Raegan," the King whispered, pausing to swallow hard, his eyes bright with tears. "I am sorry I abandoned you. I am sorry I made that choice for both of us. And most of all, I am sorry I created this situation—that you felt so sure telling me what occurred would leave you with nothing."

She nodded, leaning into his touch. She felt wrung-out, like she'd swallowed broken glass, but there was a weight off her shoulders. A relief so intense she thought she might be able to sleep for a hundred years.

"I love you," the King said, sliding his hand down into her lap and weaving his fingers into hers.

"I love you, too," she responded immediately, the words tasting as rich as late summer and black currant juice. With her free hand, Raegan pushed away the last of her tears.

"Would you like to speak of the future for mortals?" Oberon inquired.

She looked up, taking in the soft coziness of the room, the curls of steam still curling off the teacup on the bedside table. For a long moment, Raegan wanted nothing more than to burrow beneath the heavy, embroidered quilt and never resurface. She chewed on her lower lip, deep in thought.

"Actually," she finally said, raising her eyes to his, "yeah. That would help. I need . . . I need to realize we can just discuss things. Like regular people."

Oberon released a hearty laugh that warmed Raegan to her very core. "Yes," he said, the corners of his eyes creasing with a smile, "I believe we can. Please understand, Raegan. I know that mortals are under the Timekeeper's thumb as much as the Fair Folk. I yearn for liberation, and all liberation is connected at the root. We must do this together—you and I, mortals and Fey—or not at all."

Of course he understood. Of course the dark, powerful king she'd fought beside for a thousand years had always been worthy of her loyalty. She nodded and gripped his hand tighter. "I'm sorry, Oberon."

"I know," he replied, letting go of her hand to cradle the side of her face. "I am, too."

"Would it hurt if I kissed you?" she asked, leaning over, the need for physical assurance all-encompassing.

"Not if you are very careful," he said, his lips moving into something delightfully wicked before she brought her mouth to his.

Her body came alive, the taste of him heavy on her tongue—folklore and smoke and revenge. She had to physically restrain herself from spreading her legs over his hips, hunger drumming beneath her breastbone. Despite his injury, Oberon met her eagerly, sliding his hand around the back of her head.

"Perhaps," Raegan murmured against his mouth, "I could make further apologies for how fucking stupid I am sometimes."

She felt his fingers tighten around her curls, mouth trailing to her jaw. "How do you propose to make these amends?" the King wanted to know, his breath quickening. "You may have noticed a shotgun ripped through me earlier today. I would like to make amends of my own, but the hole in my chest may prevent me."

Raegan sat back, laughing, tracing the waves of his dark hair, then his sharp cheekbones, with her fingertips. "I was thinking," she said, trailing her hand down the right side of his body until she found where he was hard and hot and wanting, "you wouldn't have to do very much. You can make your apologies later, when you have use of both of your talented hands. What do you think?"

His gaze slid to hers, his face a mask of desire. "I suppose I could permit it," Oberon said, his lips curving with that dark, slinking humor she loved so much.

"Thank you for your generosity, my king," Raegan replied, moving the quilt aside gently, her eyes on his bandaged chest and shoulder. She motioned for him to swing his legs over the side of the bed, and he did, albeit with a grunt of pain. "I've been a healer in enough lives to know this is probably a bad idea."

"That," the King replied, watching her with hungry eyes as she shimmied his waistband down, "is precisely the appeal."

She grinned, pushing her hair back and sliding down to her knees between his muscular thighs. Then she brought her tongue to his exposed length. When he let out a low sigh of pleasure, Raegan wrapped her hand around his thick base and took him into her mouth. The sound of her name toppling from his lips sent heat sliding through her core. She glanced up, arousal further igniting at the sight of him—his head tipped back, the elegant expanse of his neck and angular collarbones etched out by the fading light.

Raegan couldn't recall the last time she'd done this in her current life, and she certainly never remembered enjoying it in this body. But with *him*, everything was so different—the way she hungered for him, the way he seemed to seek little but her pleasure whenever they fucked.

Oberon reached for her with his right hand, saying her name like a prayer, fingers slipping around the back of her neck. He met her gaze and held it, setting a wildfire blazing between her legs.

She took him deeper, and he moaned, tipping his head back again. "Good girl," he told her in a low, raw murmur, his fingertips digging into the base of her skull. Desire exploded inside her, and for a moment, Raegan was little more than burning need.

She pulled back a heartbeat later, pressing hot-mouthed kisses along his thighs and hard length, her jaw needing a break. "Don't say that," she panted against his skin, "or I'm going to have no choice but to fuck you, and then your wounds will open back up."

Oberon laughed, the sound of it rough and undone, his fingers massaging the back of her head. His eyes slid to hers, and he was about to say something, but then she took him back into her mouth, and all that fell from his lips was a long, breathy groan.

Some time later, after he came apart for her, he needed help returning to his propped-up position in the bed. Naturally, Raegan pounced. "The faerie king got fucked senseless by a human woman," she said with a playful smirk, adjusting one of the pillows behind his torso.

"Not the first time," Oberon answered, his eyes closed, his words drowsy. "And I pray it is not the last."

Chapter Twenty

A very long soak in the clawfoot tub did Raegan more good than she thought possible. The afternoon had grown unseasonably warm, the rain slowing to a mist, so she'd opened the windows opposite the tub and watched the late autumn breeze stir the tendrils of steam rising from the water. She'd grown blissfully sleepy, the intricate greens and golds and tawny shadows of the meadow scene depicted on the room's wallpaper offering a lush, peaceful backdrop. There'd even been a selection of bath salts—the Fey did not fuck around when it came to toiletries—and Raegan had dropped in a few good handfuls of the arnica-infused soak. After the hard climb at the waterfall this morning, her muscles needed it.

When she emerged from the bathroom, the bedchamber was silent. The King was asleep, she hoped—his eyes were closed, the book he'd been reading set on the nightstand. The space smelled faintly of yarrow and blood, but no sickness or rot. Good, all things considered.

Quietly, she dressed in comfortable clothes, grateful that she'd packed so thoroughly back at her apartment. Raegan gently pulled her damp hair through the neckline of her sweater, scrunching the ends in a practiced motion as her thoughts drifted. It felt like another life. So much had happened since then—in particular, the Timekeeper and her father. She gritted her jaw and sighed, moving to the foot of the bed—an ebony-toned swoop of wood engraved with an ornate triskelion.

Her heart swelled as she took Oberon in; slumber did little to ease his expression. Tension still creased his brow, tight as a bowstring. She studied that nearly imperceptible hitch beneath his eyes that meant he was in a great deal of pain. As she watched, his full lips moved into a grimace. When, she wondered, would he be free?

And then, all at once, the King was awake—no half-aware expression or drowsy in-between, just asleep and then not. "Is everything alright?" he asked.

"Yeah," Raegan said, but her voice came out hoarse and unconvincing. "I was just glad to see you sleeping."

She moved around the end of the bed and came to the empty side— her side; if only she'd known all these years that her preference for the right side of the bed was because he always slept on the left. Then Raegan pulled herself onto the mattress, curling on her side to face the King.

"Is now an okay time . . . to tell you?" she asked, her voice coming out quiet and small enough to ride away on the swirls of mist beyond the windows. "To tell you about what happened? It's okay if it isn't."

The King tried to turn to look at her but stopped with a grunt when his injured muscles protested, so she sat up instead, tucking her legs beneath her and meeting his gaze. "Yes," he told her. "Whenever you are ready, so am I."

His voice was ragged, face a bit gray around the edges. She chewed on the inside of her lip. She didn't want to be unfair, to burden him with more. But she felt vulnerable right now—and, more so, comfortable in that vulnerability. And she didn't trust herself to find this place again.

"Emrys has painkillers," Raegan found herself saying instead of *I traveled into a god's realm just to watch my dad die in front of my eyes.*

"I know," the King replied, his gaze unwavering.

"Right," she said, the vast river of her memories parting, allowing her to see beneath the rushing currents. "You don't trust yourself to stop."

"No," he said, his eyes sliding away. "I do not. Not with the pain my body brings me every day, grave injuries or not."

Raegan dragged her fingertips across the duvet. The air in the room suddenly felt oppressive, the golden lamplight congealed.

"Raegan," the King murmured, moving instinctively to touch her before remembering the sling and the gashes beneath the bandages. "Please. Go on, if you are ready."

She gathered herself up, holding all of the horrors and losses and unyielding pain in her arms, and opened her mouth to show him everything, to catalog her wounds and sharp, aching places. But then instead of words, a hitched sob came out of her mouth, tears tumbling down her face. She tried to stop herself, to banish this ridiculousness and just get on with it, but the sorrow clawed up her throat with defiant talons. Raegan folded in on herself, all the world a blur, a smear of gore where something she loved had once grown tall.

Whether she realized what she was doing or not, she ended up with her head in Oberon's lap, his uninjured hand stroking her hair. The sobs that wracked her body were not the tormented wails of fresh grief or even the frustrated cries of depression; instead, this sorrow was silent in its passing, a rush of mute tears, a fountain of hopelessness.

At some point, Raegan's lips moved and words came out. "Fate used my dad to get me to the Timekeeper. Can you imagine? Reducing someone vibrant, so full of love and life, to bait on a hook. What if all our suffering is for *nothing*? What if everything my dad sacrificed changes nothing in the end?"

She hadn't wanted to admit that, not even to herself, and dark spots skittered across her vision as she said the words. The world closed in around her like a vise. The King said nothing, still stroking her hair, waiting for her to speak again.

"I'm not scared of death," Raegan murmured into the soft, still air. "Just of leaving you, and what you might become after I've made you love me, only to lose me again."

His powerful hand slowed its gentle movements, and Raegan swallowed hard, biting back a fresh rush of tears.

"That is for me to manage," the King said eventually, his words laced with steel. "You have enough worries. I need not add to your burdens."

"Would it be easier," Raegan began, the ache in her chest nearly crowding out her voice, "if I *do* just make you hate me?" Hours ago, there was nothing she feared more, but now she saw the clarity that hatred might offer. It would hurt, of course. But so did everything else.

A pause, heavy as a millstone, the air weighted with the kind of silence that a Fatesong might've filled if there were any fairness or justice left in the world.

"No," he said, the single word so impossibly gentle in its defiance.

"It's easy to love someone enough to be with them," she replied. Raegan pushed herself up shakily to meet the King's gaze again. His gray eyes were misted with the fog of unshed tears, and his face was pinched, knuckles white. "But Oberon—do I love you enough to do the very thing that would hurt the most: destroy what we have? So you aren't forced to carry around an entire mausoleum of all the things we could've been?"

His jaw clenched, and then he closed his eyes, tears spilling from between long, dark lashes. He opened his mouth only to press his lips back together; all the while, Raegan just waited.

She thought she had finally found what could ease her yearning— the truth of her father, the world behind the world, the glory of magic and all that came with it. But now she feared there was part of her that would always, *always* yearn unreasonably for him and for nothing else. And that meant that part of her would always ache. It didn't matter how many times she returned to the soil. It didn't matter if Fate rewove her Threads completely and made her anew. That ache for him would remain lodged in her chest until the world caved in.

"Do you not realize," the King murmured, breaking the silence, his words as fragile as dew upon a spiderweb, "that I love you enough to lose you a thousand times over and still seek you like a moth to flame?"

Raegan let out a shuddering breath, tears obscuring her vision. Her throat constricted. "I think I'm the moth in this allegory," she said with a damp chuckle, shoving away the wetness on her cheeks with the back of her hands.

"No," Oberon said, reaching to take her hand in his, long fingers slipping between hers. "I am the Unseelie King, the Nameless One, the Render of Worlds, and yet I am little more than ash in your flame."

Raegan's breath caught. She gripped his hand between both of her palms. No words came to her tongue, nor her mind—logic and language fled Her entirely, leaving only that bone-deep sense of longing she'd felt for a millennium. And then she raised her eyes to his and saw the truth of what the Unseelie king had spoken in his gaze.

"I love you," the Witch told the King, the words spoken solemnly, like they had the power to dispel prophecies and war.

"And I love you," the King replied in an exhale, as if what he felt for her stole the very air from his lungs.

For a moment, there inside the walls of a hidden city, wrapped in the heavy cloak of mist, she swore the ache buried deep within her ceased its keening. It would return, she knew. But for now . . . for now, there were only the calluses on his powerful hands and the autumnal scent of him and the terrifying vastness of how deeply she cared for someone she could never truly have.

～

When Emrys offered to show Raegan the old Temple's library, she'd been grateful for a distraction. Burying herself in researching any scrap of Avalon left behind was far more appealing than pondering the depths of her sorrows.

For the first hour, she'd genuinely enjoyed the work. The ruined Temple's library was very different from the King's archives—more like a sunken greenhouse than any library she'd ever seen. The entire space sat just below the soil, casting everything in permanent shades of twilight. An enormous Victorian-era solarium glass roof stretched overhead, the towering oak bookcases climbing to the rainy skies above like hungry stalks. Globes and lush plants and orreries and objects she couldn't identify guarded the tops of the shelves.

Beneath her stockinged feet, the gray stone floors were cold, but a fire crackled merrily in the reading area. Antique fainting couches lounged in front of the hearth, covered in moss-green velvet. The parchment-colored rugs were embroidered with scientific-style renderings of local flora. Like every Fey space she had ever entered, it was gorgeous and magical and definitely, fantastically absurd. What charms, she wondered, did it take to stop the sunlight—no matter how diluted by rain —from bleaching all the books on the top shelves? And how were the plants watered without sending damp and rot down to the tomes beneath them?

"You know," Raegan said, leaning against the end of a bookcase, a large potted angel's trumpet brushing her hair, "before I had my Seal removed, I would've asked you a thousand questions trying to figure out how the fuck this place works."

Emrys looked over at her, a faint smile ghosting his lips. He pushed his delicate wire-rimmed glasses up his nose. "Do you not ask now because you can figure it out on your own or because you do not wish to spoil the wonder?"

Raegan paused, running her fingers down the gilded spines of a matching collection on the history of unicorns. "Both, I suppose."

Emrys said nothing, appraising her. For a moment, it looked like he was about to say something in response, but then he seemed to change his mind. "That concludes my tour," he announced. "But I'll be in the dwarvish history section if you need anything."

Her eyebrow rose, but before she could open her mouth to ask, Emrys waved a slim hand in the air. "It's a hunch. If Danu commissioned some kind of a door to Avalon, it's possible they worked on it."

Memory settled onto Raegan's shoulders, and all curiosity fled her. Dwarves were all but gone from the modern world, having retreated far into the earth after the Fall—a common name for the Fair Folk's devastating loss at the Battle of Camlann. The dwarves had little desire to see how man would carve into the hills, or to witness the endless war the Fey would wage to take back what was theirs. A tiny part of Raegan couldn't blame them.

"Thanks," she said, pushing thoughts of the dwarvish people from her mind. "And thanks for letting me into your library."

"Oh, it's not mine," Emrys replied as he began to walk away from her, his tone uncharacteristically light. "It was the last Oracle's."

Before she could inquire further, the ex-Keeper was gone, disappearing around a bend of stone floors and shadowy shelves. She stared at the end of the row where he had just been, but there was only the creeping vine climbing the opposite wall and the tiny, ornate fountain that splashed beneath it.

Reorienting herself to the task at hand, Raegan glanced down at her notebook, scanning her list of the sections Emrys had mentioned that she wanted to explore. For half an hour, she did just that, amassing a pile of books on what looked suspiciously like an overly long potting table, but with banker's lamps and inkwells instead of trowels and shears.

"One more thing to check," she muttered to herself, taking a long sip of lukewarm tea from the mug she'd brought into the library with her. And then she was off, weaving through the shelves, though this time she was seeking a section Emrys had only mentioned, not shown her. She didn't think the Temple's library was that big, but Fey spaces were always larger than they seemed, and in a few minutes, she had gotten a bit turned around.

This part of the library was quite different from the rest. The shelves were empty, moss growing in the crevices, the surface of the wood pock-marked with decay. No fountains burbled, and the solarium roof over-head was covered in muck, as though all Hiraeth's rain hadn't managed to reach it for at least ten years. Raegan almost turned back. Even the floor beneath her feet grew uneven and rough, sections upended like a large creature had burrowed just below the stones.

But something nameless pulled her forward, and before she could stop herself, she heeded the call. Raegan gritted her jaw and hoped it was not Fate's Threads stringing her along yet again. She turned down a narrow hallway, which abruptly dumped her into a stone-walled chamber with a rounded ceiling. Unlit beeswax candles crouched in the corners, looking a bit too much like melted flesh. In the middle of the room, an enormous cabinet stood alone. It was a gorgeous piece of crafts-manship despite the dust coating it—even in the low light, Raegan could make out the shimmer of mother-of-pearl inlaid in its veneer. Jade curls of fiddlehead ferns guarded either side of the double glass doors. A key sat defenseless in the lock, a long tassel of much-worn silk hanging from its loop.

Curious as always, Raegan stepped closer, ignoring the way the walls seemed to press in from all sides. She was treading on a grave of sorts, she knew—but such boundaries did not apply to her. She belonged neither to the land of the living nor the underworld. Only Fate and the Unseelie king could lay any meaningful claim to her.

When her eyes finally adjusted to the gloom and she could make out shapes behind the dusty glass, Raegan regretted her curiosity. Inside the cabinet were Prophecies. Her throat closed off, and grief thundered onto her shores like a hurricane. And yet, she reached her hand up to the key and turned it, springing open the door. Old air, heavy with what could have been, rushed to meet her nose, smelling of ancient paper and melted beeswax and long-dried blood. She told herself not to look, but Raegan was very bad at following anyone's commands, even her own.

A dragonfly the size of her thumb, a pheasant in an enormous glass dome, a stunningly beautiful pegasus, and a falcon with its claws outstretched—all made of paper, all impossibly detailed and so delicate. She shouldn't be moved by them, she thought, not anymore. But longing lurched inside her anyway, and Raegan pressed her forehead to the glass door she'd left closed, like a child left outside in the cold.

It was not for her. It never had been, not really—Fate had chosen her for the sole purpose of offering a fattened calf to the Timekeeper in exchange for Her own desires. Raegan had not been picked for her wit nor her daring nor her unerring ability to read people. She'd been chosen because Fate had already cursed her, and there was little Fate liked more than something She could use more than once.

With a long, wavering sigh, Raegan moved to close the door, but something deeper in the cabinet caught her eye. No. Surely she was mistaken. In the gloom of the catacomb-like room, the weak light slipping in from the hallway providing the only illumination, perched a luna moth inside a slender glass dome.

Her hand reached out of its own accord, but she snatched it back. Surely there were hundreds—if not thousands—of Prophecies in the shape of a luna moth, like hers had been back at the Temple in Philadelphia. Surely it meant nothing at all. This Temple was dead, anyhow —there was probably a very practical reason why a few scant Prophecies lingered in its belly, and why one of them had taken the same shape as the Prophecy that had opened Raegan's life.

She hated that she ached for it, that there was little more she wanted than to place her fingers upon the glass and see the luna moth spring to life. For it to all have been for something, some grand design. For Fate to still be on her side, somehow. An ache bloomed enormous and undeniable in her bones. Biting the inside of her cheek, Raegan followed her yearning, unable to hold it back any longer. Her fingertips brushed the luna moth's glass dome. Time hung still, and then, somehow, against all reason, the glass burst like a bubble. No shattered pieces, no sharp edges to draw blood, just there and then gone.

She drew back, her heart throwing itself against her ribs. The glass cages of the other winged paper things in the cabinet thinned, barely more than a translucent film, and then they too faded from existence, a bubble bursting. With equal parts horror and awe, Raegan watched as the creatures moved for each other, just as hungry and desperate as when she reached for the King. The dragonfly and the luna moth curled around each other in time for the pheasant to devour them both in its paper mouth.

The Prophecies, Raegan realized, were cannibalizing each other, creating a single creature crafted from impossibly thin paper. Her throat closed off. Fuck—all she had to do was just not touch anything, to curb that traitorous hunger for Fate that seemed to live in her marrow.

The winged thing—hooves of a pegasus, wings of a dragonfly decorated with the moons of a luna moth, its head a falcon's—grew in size, moving toward the door of the cabinet. Anger pounded in Raegan's body, and she slammed the door shut. She'd had enough of Fate, enough of these parchment creatures flitting about and ripping her life apart.

"Shit," she muttered beneath her breath, watching words appear like a bloodstain on the dragonfly wings: *all become one, so may the Once and Futur—*

"Emrys," Raegan shouted, desperate to not ruin everything again, to not risk all of Hiraeth again, to not create another monstrous wound of Threads and Fate-kissed paper. She shoved the silk-tassel key in the lock and turned it. And just like that, the creature stilled, words no longer appearing, the Prophecies no longer devouring each other. She let out a long breath, her hands clammy.

When the frantic energy of the catacomb died down, when all felt dead and still, she turned and marched back down the hallway, through the damp, ruined half of the library, until she found the main aisle. Her head down, jaw grinding, Raegan strode for the hall that connected the library to the main section of the Temple. She wanted to throw herself through the front door and back into the winding streets of Hiraeth, where no one would see her and no one knew her name. Where guilt did not gild her shoulders like chainmail, where her mistakes were not lined up like daggers on a belt.

Instead, she nearly slammed into Emrys, who rushed out from around a corner, his eyes wild, the faded chore jacket he always wore sitting askew on his shoulders. Raegan swerved to avoid him, almost losing her balance. Her heart began to thud in her chest. Had Emrys found Avalon? Had the King's injury taken a bad turn? Was the Protectorate upon them like hounds on a fox?

"Raegan," Emrys panted. "An outsider found the edge of our wards."

Her heart climbed into her throat, mind racing.

"She claims," he continued, "that she's your aunt."

CHAPTER TWENTY-ONE

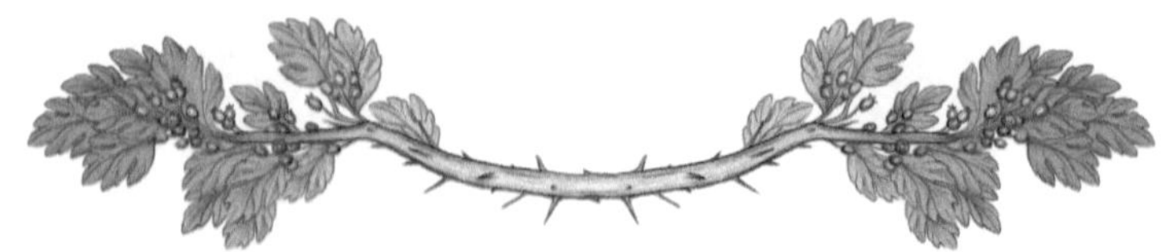

Raegan blinked. "*What?*"

Emrys huffed, gesturing toward the mouth of the library. "Maelona Overhill. That's who she says she is. She found the hawthorns. I have no idea how."

Raegan swallowed, her mouth painfully dry all of a sudden. She hadn't told Emrys yet about Alanna; she'd wanted Oberon to help her with the conversation during dinner, seeing as she hardly knew the ex-Keeper. "Can you take me to her?" she asked.

Emrys stared at her incredulously. "Why? She stinks of Protectorate."

"If it's actually Maelona," Raegan said, slipping past him and beginning to jog down the long passage to the main rooms, "she's not on their side."

"Well, is she on *ours?*" Emrys demanded, keeping pace with her.

"Only one way to find out," was all Raegan said, shouldering through the heavy door to the old Temple. She yanked on a random pair of Wellies from a rack by the front door; this was probably not the kind of situation to walk into without shoes.

"Raegan, how did she find us?" Emrys demanded, blocking her from leaving the small entryway. Though taller, he probably didn't have much of a weight advantage on her, and the only magic she'd seen him do was protective and divinatory. She could probably get past him.

But he was not her enemy, and besides—anyone given the honor of being a Temple's Keeper was formidable, even if they hid it well. "Because a shadewalker found me the other night," she said, her fingertips digging into her temples. "She came through the hawthorns. Into the Garden of Doors. It was a whole thing. I was going to tell you."

"A shadewalker?" Emrys asked, his voice low but eerily calm. He removed his hand from the wall, all his attention falling onto Raegan. "The Garden of Doors opened to you?"

Having known Oberon for more than a thousand years, she never liked when people got quieter when they were angry. It usually meant they had mastered their tempers, wielded their rage like a scalpel—which annoyed Raegan, whose anger was more like a battering ram.

"Yes," she hissed between her teeth, beginning to seriously consider shoving past him to get to her aunt. "And it also opened to the shadewalker, who happens to be Protectorate. Through no fault of her own, I may add. She found us when she searched shade-clad in the general area of our confrontation on the river. Hiraeth's wards are ancient and incredibly powerful. To her, they lit up like faerie lights, if you'll pardon the pun."

Emrys pulled himself up, suddenly much taller than Raegan realized. "And you did not inform me of this immediately?"

"No," she said, tilting her chin to meet his gaze. "And I'm sorry. But right now—"

"Right now, you and I are going to deal with the Protectorate woman gnawing at the hawthorns," Emrys replied, cutting her off, his tone flat and deadly. "And then, we are going to speak about this shadewalker and your questionable decisions."

Raegan ground her teeth together and swallowed her initial reaction, not allowing a sneer to work its way onto her face. "Fine." She buried any thought of mentioning the Prophecy beast deep in the library; besides, she'd sent it back to sleep, hadn't she?

Emrys nodded and then turned, pushing open the heavy wooden double doors to the hallway. It was the same one she and Oberon had entered through originally—long and dark, shadows curled in the corners, the stone floors beneath cold and gray. The ex-Keeper broke into a jog, moving for the vestibule. Her heart clenched, and she quickened her pace to keep up with Emrys. She hadn't allowed herself to imagine Maelona might still be alive. Hope could be a poison. With a huff, she broke into a run, her thighs screaming.

"Emrys, wait," Raegan panted, partially because she really didn't want to fucking run but also because she wasn't sure what he knew of the situation with Maelona. "Let me tell you Maelona's deal."

She watched as he reluctantly slowed his stride, moving from a jog to a quick walk. It was still an exertion for her much shorter legs to keep up with. Why the hell were all these people so tall? Though she'd hardly caught her breath, Raegan told Emrys about Maelona—about how she'd never known her aunt existed, and had just shown up after Raegan summoned the kelpie and shattered Cormac's protective working. How her aunt had wanted to get her out, how she was hardly some fanatic aligned with the Protectorate's goals, and how Raegan hadn't seen her since that day in the café.

"So the shadewalker, who is also considering moving against the organization she was born into, got her here?" Emrys asked, rubbing his forehead furiously.

"I assume, but you know what they say about assumptions," Raegan replied, tripping on the rug that stretched the length of the hallway and cursing profusely. "The shadewalker—Alanna—mentioned Maelona. So I was already aware they knew each other."

Emrys said nothing else, though he looked less than pleased, and Raegan had a very strong feeling his anger was a long, drawn-out thing— that if she somehow managed to survive everything, he'd hold a grudge over this.

Raegan tried to force deep breaths into her lungs, ignoring Emrys for the moment and instead preparing herself to see Maelona. Her mind calculated the reasons and motives her aunt might be here, and she fought to formulate responses to them all. She couldn't let that soft, aching space in her chest dictate how she handled Maelona's appearance. No longer could she be a woman pulled headlong down a velveted hallway by a Seer. There were no Fatewinds in her sails. She charted her own course in these deadly waters.

But then they finally spilled into the large vestibule, the tearoom's doors on one side, the massive, ornate, and undoubtedly ancient gates to

Hiraeth on the other. She hadn't seen them on her way in, not like this—the gates stretched at least twenty feet tall, forged from some kind of long-forgotten metalworking technique. Living hawthorns intertwined with snaking vines of age-blackened silver, creating an impenetrable and foreboding wall—but strikingly beautiful in an alien, inhuman kind of way.

With one hard look in her direction, Emrys reached toward the gates. Instead of opening them in a dramatic whoosh, he instead wrapped his fingers around a small metal latch Raegan hadn't noticed. He pulled, and a section of the hawthorns slid away, revealing a door-within-a-door, a clandestine peek into what waited on the other side of Hiraeth's gates.

Raegan rushed forward, bumping her shoulder into Emrys as she scrambled for a look. And there, standing in what was probably an empty meadow or a windswept moor or some other forgotten place, was Maelona.

Gone was the silver-threaded goddess who looked like she might bring a war ax down on anyone who dared consume another Overhill. In her place was a perilously thin creature propped up against a tree trunk just on the opposite side of the wards.

For a moment, she allowed herself to hope it was just the sunlight dappling her skin, but as Raegan looked closer, she saw that both of Maelona's eyes were blackened—one nearly swollen shut—and a jagged, infected-looking cut ran across her forehead. If Raegan wasn't mistaken —which she rarely was about these sorts of things—Maelona was wearing the same outfit as the last time they'd seen each other, though everything was now covered in grime and blood.

"She can't see or hear us," Emrys told Raegan in a short, even tone.

"Raegan," Maelona rasped suddenly despite the ex-Keeper's words, her eyes hunting but, of course, finding nothing. "Raegan, if you're here, please. If you don't let me in, they will find me. Alanna got me out. Alanna brought me . . ." Maelona's body pitched, one knee buckling, and she skidded down the side of the tree, peeling bark off as she went.

If it was a performance, it was a hell of a job, and better than Raegan thought straight-shooter Maelona would be able to muster. If it *was* Maelona.

"Is it her?" Raegan demanded of Emrys. "Can you tell from across the wards?"

He glanced down at her, his jaw working. Then he pulled his delicate silver glasses from the pocket of his chore jacket and slid them onto his face, like he was about to inspect a particularly lovely flower, not decide if one of Raegan's last living relatives was within their grasp to save.

"I see no glamours," he intoned, clinical, tapping the rim of his lenses. "She is in true medical distress."

Raegan's heart panged, and she turned back to Maelona. Her aunt had slid all the way down to her knees, and her head lolled. Raegan exhaled and then attempted to summon her second sight. For a moment, a lens slid over the world, sending everything into strange hues and shadows. She gritted her teeth and began to examine Maelona, but then the sight slipped out of her grasp.

"Fuck," Raegan snarled, curling her fists and trying again. Sometimes she regretted the Seal's removal, only because now she remembered far too intimately how she'd once worked magic as easily as breathing.

The sight did not come. Instead, instinct rose within her, a wine-dark wave of pure intuition, and she knew without a doubt that the broken form of the woman before her was Maelona Overhill.

"Open the wards," Raegan said. "Let her in."

"Are you out of your mind?" Emrys demanded, wheeling on her. "I am not bringing a Protectorate-oathed mortal within my wards. I'm not even sure if Hiraeth itself would permit such a thing. Your *friend* from the other night only fared so well because she was shade-clad."

And because the ancient, fabled Garden of Doors let Alanna in and had taken Raegan right to her. Ice-cold rage surged in her veins, and she turned to face Emrys, though it pained her to take her eyes off Maelona. "You might recall," she said, lifting her chin, meeting his eyes, "that I am the Queen of the Hill, the Witch of the Wood, and if Fate hadn't been too terrified to allow it, I would have been your High Lady. So open. The. Fucking. Wards."

Somewhere in the back of her mind, Raegan didn't understand why she was suddenly eye-level with the ex-Keeper, who stood at least a head taller than her. But then she watched his gaze widen behind his glasses, and she realized that her feet had left the ground entirely. What a compelling image, her journalist's sense chimed. An ordinary woman, her eyes still puffy with the tears she'd shed, dressed in an oversized wool sweater and loose jeans stuffed into the top of Wellies three sizes too big, levitating above the ground like some kind of vengeful specter.

"If you invite doom into the last Fey city on the Isles, I will hold you accountable," Emrys told her, his tone steady, though she could see all his teeth.

"If you haven't noticed," she snarled in response, "I wear my guilt like chainmail and wield my transgressions like a weapon. So be it, Emrys. If I'm wrong, add it to my fucking armory."

Something like respect might've flitted across the ex-Keeper's angular features, but then his expression smoothed and he inclined his head. "So be it," he echoed.

CHAPTER TWENTY-TWO

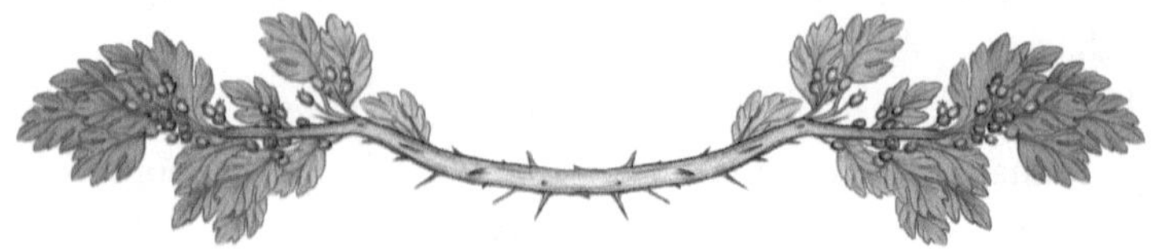

In the end, Emrys and Raegan had to drag Maelona through the gates. Her aunt was barely conscious, flitting in and out, though at some point she seemed to recognize Raegan and relaxed a little. As they pulled her into the vestibule—gently on Raegan's part, not so gently on the ex-Keeper's—the gates closed behind them with a soft sigh.

In that small, square room with impossibly high ceilings and bare stone walls, the entire world seemed to inhale. The space grew restrictive and tight, like all the oxygen had been squeezed out of the air. Raegan tensed, tightening her grip on Maelona. What if Hiraeth wouldn't grant her entrance? Offering a relatively safe meeting place for a shade-clad Protectorate woman to discuss treason was one thing. Permitting a sworn enemy into the city's inner sanctum was another entirely.

Emrys shot Raegan a sharp look over Maelona's lolled head as if to say *I told you so*. Raegan narrowed her eyes at him, trying to look calm, but her hands had long since gone clammy, her heart fluttering like a tiny, trapped bird in her chest. Behind them, the hawthorn branches slithered and tightened.

"Hey," Raegan spat, looking up as if she might find some avatar of Hiraeth floating in the darkness above their heads. "You sorta like me, right? I'm useful to you? Well, I'm only alive because of this woman. So let me help her. Also, see how fucked up she is? The Protectorate did that to her because she's a traitor."

At that, the suffocating air seemed to loosen, the room suddenly feeling a few feet larger. Ahead, the heavy wooden doors into Hiraeth became visible; Raegan hadn't realized until now that they'd disappeared from view. She exhaled, black spots swarming her vision.

"Thanks," she said, unsure where to direct her gratitude, before gathering Maelona up and beginning to walk forward. Emrys grumbled something under his breath but did his part, slinging her aunt's limp arm over his shoulder.

"Even if Hiraeth has allowed her in so far," Emrys said as they trudged down the long hallway, "when we give her blood to the hawthorns, I don't know how they'll react."

"We'll cross that bridge when we get there," Raegan grunted, her muscles despairing at the amount of physical activity she'd done today. She needed to ask Oberon to train her, to maintain the edge she'd started to develop after those weeks working with Andronica. Memories unhelpfully peppered her mind—mages who had met their end on the battlefield because they'd relied too heavily on their magic.

When the door into the ruined Temple finally appeared, Raegan let out a sigh of relief. So far, so good. She hadn't ever thought she'd yearn for the approval and acceptance of an ancient, primordial city, but a lot of weird shit had happened lately.

"Table again, I guess," Emrys said as they shouldered through the door. "Just to check her over for tracking spells."

"And serious injuries," Raegan snapped, trying to be gentle as she lifted Maelona onto the large table. Her aunt looked like skin and bones, but there was a heft to her, a memory of muscle and defiance.

She examined Maelona's right side for life-threatening injuries and found none, though she saw her aunt's thumb had been broken and reset incorrectly a number of times. She winced. Maelona's ankle was swollen too, a more recent sprain, probably in her flight from the Protectorate's dungeons to Hiraeth's hawthorn door.

Working soundlessly, Raegan switched sides with Emrys and repeated her search, discovering a bruised collarbone and a pinky dangling by a few strands of muscle. She swallowed hard and fought to find her extensive knowledge of human anatomy, locked away somewhere in her own mind. To Raegan's surprise and delight, she located it and put it to quick work—reattaching Maelona's pinky, resetting the thumb, completely erasing the black eyes and gash on her face.

"No tracking spells," Emrys confirmed, sounding slightly disappointed. "Let's get her settled. Then you and I are having a long conversation."

"Sure," Raegan said, mostly because her head was swimming and she felt woozy. *Too much too fast*, a voice inside her head chided. She gritted her teeth and blinked rapidly a few times.

"You alright?" Emrys asked, arching a brow at her.

"Fine," she replied, fighting the urge to sneer just for good measure. Clenching her jaw so hard that her teeth ached, Raegan leaned forward to get one of Maelona's arms across her shoulders. Just as she did, the woman stirred, her eyelids fluttering. Then Maelona slapped away Raegan's hands and pulled herself to sit up halfway, a show of sheer will.

Her aunt was surprisingly calm as she took in Raegan and Emrys. "Oh, good," Maelona mumbled. "Got to you before the Protectorate got to me. So, bit of bad news. They know you're looking for Avalon."

Raegan startled a step back, her blood suddenly running cold and thick through her veins while a thousand pins pricked red-hot across her skin. The world tilted dangerously, and her tongue suddenly felt too big for her mouth.

Even Emrys didn't manage to form any useful questions before Maelona slumped back down onto the table. Raegan's mind plodded along sluggishly, offering her nothing at all as Emrys shook her aunt's shoulder, trying to reawaken her. Only when his jostling began to verge on violence did Raegan snap out of whatever trance she'd fallen into, reaching across to shove Emrys's hands away.

"Can we get her somewhere more comfortable?" Raegan asked, the words coming out slow and slurred.

Emrys considered her, an eyebrow arching again, though nothing else changed about his expression. He turned and waved a lazy hand at the two armchairs by the cold hearth. In the space of an instant, a daybed stretched across the space instead, a flame roaring to life in the fireplace.

"Do not ask me to put her upstairs within easy reach of our injured king," he warned as he scooped Maelona up on his own this time.

Raegan blanched, partially due to the nausea, partially due to the accusation lingering in his voice. "Why the fuck do you think I'd want that?"

"Just want to be clear," Emrys replied nonchalantly, arranging Maelona on the daybed. Raegan dragged herself over to remove her aunt's boots and tuck her into the wool blankets Emrys produced.

"Now we wait," the ex-Keeper said, crossing his arms, staring down at Maelona with a frown.

"Thanks for your help," Raegan said, only a little begrudgingly. Emrys just grunted in reply. The dizziness had faded, but she was suddenly very, very tired, barely able to keep her eyes open. She told Emrys she wanted to quickly check on Oberon before they had their little chat, warned him to be nice to Maelona in the meantime, and then made for the stairway. It was unfairly far to walk, all rich fig carpeting and sconces flickering sleepily. She made herself keep going, all the way to the room she and Oberon shared.

"Maelona's here," Raegan announced to the King, who was awake, his nose in a book. She kicked off the borrowed Wellies somewhere near the door and caught only a few seconds of Oberon's startled expression before she collapsed onto the bed. Sleep wrapped itself around her like a cocoon and did not let go.

Raegan awoke to shouting. Not her own this time, to which she felt a bizarre kind of relief. She swallowed, her mouth dry, and then pushed herself to sit up. Oberon was gone. A quilt had been thrown over her legs, but she still wore the jeans and sweater she'd put on earlier. Silence blanketed the Temple for a long moment, and then a muffled, raised voice met her ears.

Not Oberon, she assumed, groaning as she swung her legs over the side of the bed. Her head felt like it had been stuffed with cotton. She should probably do more of the magical exercises the King had suggested to her a few weeks ago. Maybe she'd build up some endurance and stop passing the fuck out constantly.

"She has ruined us before!" someone—oh, Emrys, of course— shouted, closer now, on the landing, maybe. "My liege, I am begging you to see reason. Two Protectorate operatives now know Hiraeth's location. This is madness."

Silence again. Raegan moved to stand, but the world spun. "Okay," she mumbled, sitting back down on the edge of the bed. The hallway outside creaked under someone's weight.

"Emrys," came Oberon's voice, the sound of a dagger burying itself in flesh. "Stop shouting."

It sounded like Emrys offered a strangled kind of huff in response. She didn't even have time to strategize further before the King ducked into the room, a storm brewing on his expression. Emrys followed behind, face red. For a moment, Raegan saw the depths of terror in his eyes—that he might lose everything he'd ever built, let down everyone he'd ever loved. She sighed, pushing down the anger she felt at his distrust.

"Emrys," Raegan began, her head clearing a little. "I'm sorry. This is fucked up. I have caused you so much stress and worry when you've graciously opened your home to us. I need you to know that I may not always make the best choices—I can admit that—but I *always* have the end goal in mind. For magic to return. For our people to be free."

Emrys looked taken aback for a moment before he slid that mask of composure back in place. His gaze flicked to Oberon, who cocked a brow and inclined his head for a reason Raegan didn't understand.

"You don't remember Hiraeth," the ex-Keeper said, fiddling with a button on his chore coat, "because I took your memory of it. You've been here before. With Oberon. You were Titania, the Seelie Queen. You know what happened afterward. We don't need to dig up the past. It is hard for me to not be suspicious of your actions."

Raegan picked a piece of lint from the thigh of her jeans, her hands shaking. How *dare* he? How dare he steal her memories? Why did all of these men think they could reach into her skull and take whatever the fuck they wanted?

When she raised her chin to say exactly that, her gaze met the King's —the placid waves of an ocean under cloudy skies, the tide pulling at that soft, secret place deep inside her chest. She let that blind, seething anger of hers go, a silk ribbon caught in seaside winds.

"Let's not dig up the past," Raegan agreed, laying her hands flat on the duvet beside her legs. "Because I'm kinda touchy about my memories, and it really upsets me that you took them. But I understand you just want to protect Hiraeth. That's what I want, too. Emrys, imagine what a shadewalker would add to our power, one who is still oathed to the Protectorate. And Maelona's extensive knowledge. It could change *everything*."

She paused, the words dying in her throat as she snuck a glance at Emrys. His expression had softened slightly, his jaw no longer working back and forth.

"But I'm so scared I'm wrong," Raegan whispered before she even realized she was speaking. "*Again*."

Emrys inhaled sharply. Beside him, the King was silent, though all his attention was on Raegan. She noticed offhandedly that his color looked better than earlier. It was sort of horrifying that he could take a close-range shotgun blast and be walking around this soon, but it was also kind of hot.

"I'm scared, too," Emrys finally said, his deep brown eyes warmer now, like the soil's first thaw in spring. "Terrified, actually. But you are not wrong. This could change everything. However, we must do it *together*, you understand? You cannot fix a thousand years of history on your own. No one can. Please stop trying."

Something like ease settled into the place between Raegan's shoulder blades. It was tenuous, strung delicately above a chasm, but it was there all the same. She took a deep breath and nodded. "It's different this time," she said, hoping her words were true. "Even the Keeper in Philadelphia said so."

"Perhaps," Emrys said, narrowing his eyes and adjusting the bridge of his glasses, "it is because *we* are all different this time."

The hope of that statement surged in her chest—that finally the resistance had gathered the strength it needed, been transmuted by the past, and shed every skin it no longer needed. Maybe they could do it this time. Particularly with Alanna's—

"Wait," Raegan said, sitting up straight, a feverish chill crawling across her skin. "What time is it?"

"Almost sunset," Oberon said with a start, realizing the same thing she just had. "You need to go."

Raegan slid off the bed, happy to find her legs were shaky but working. She scrambled for the boots she'd kicked off and shoved her feet inside them. "No," she said, looking up at the two impossibly powerful creatures with what was probably a manic grin. "*We* need to go."

Oberon parted his lips to say something, but then he just smiled instead. It reached his eyes, and the sight of that sent warmth tumbling through Raegan's chest.

"I'm sorry, go where?" Emrys asked, folding his glasses back into the pocket of his chore jacket and looking anxiously between the two of them.

"The shadewalker is meant to return," the King replied, moving toward the door behind Raegan. "If the Garden opens for her. For us."

"The Protectorate shadewalker is coming *back*?" Emrys asked, a hint of despair in his tone, but as Raegan slipped out the door and began to run down the hallway, she heard his footsteps following.

"We have more to discuss," Raegan replied, hitting the landing and grabbing the banister to keep her balance as she thudded down the stairs. "Revolution, namely."

"Are you comfortable with this, Emrys?" Oberon wanted to know, his voice coming from higher up the stairs.

"Comfortable?" Emrys demanded, his voice a half-octave higher than usual. "Gods, no. But perhaps . . . perhaps that is good. Perhaps I have gotten too comfortable with the idea that only Hiraeth could survive. That liberation was only a dream."

Raegan hit the stone floor at the bottom of the stairs and pushed her exhausted body through the great room, coming to a halt when she saw Maelona's prone form on the daybed. Her aunt had been tucked into a wool blanket and a quilt, her head propped on a velvet pillow. She was sound asleep, her deep inhales visible even beneath all the layers.

"She will be fine," Oberon murmured, touching Raegan's shoulder. "She made her choices and her sacrifices. Now it is our work to ensure it was worth it."

Raegan turned to look up at him, her throat closing off with emotion. His words echoed the concern she'd had about her father—that everything he'd done had been for nothing. And here was the Unseelie king himself, doing whatever he could to ensure another Overhill would not succumb to such a fate.

She nodded, slipped her fingers through his, and moved for the front door of the Temple. Emrys was already there, slipping one of the glamoured cloaks over his shoulders.

"Oberon should really stay here," the ex-Keeper said in a tone that indicated he did not expect his king to follow the suggestion in the slightest.

"I should," Oberon agreed, but he only unlaced his fingers from Raegan's to reach for a cloak. She smiled to herself at his response, pulling the fabric over her own shoulders. Then the three of them stepped out into the streets of Hiraeth.

At this hour, the cobblestone pathways were thick with Fair Folk, the city gowned in gossamer-thin mist. There were more small children in Hiraeth than Raegan could ever have dared to believe—proof that their people would not fall so easily to the desires of power-hungry gods and misled men. She paused on the Temple's steps, watching the crowds as they slipped by, though she had no need to search the faces in the way she always did. Her heart panged pleasantly.

And then, across the cobblestones, she saw something that she took a long, skittering moment to comprehend, all her assumptions about the Fey of Hiraeth and what the future would look like with the Gates destroyed feeling so incredibly stupid and short-sighted.

"Mortals are accepted in Hiraeth?" Raegan demanded, her throat aching, spinning to face Emrys. She didn't hold the once-Keeper's gaze for long, her heart longing to look back across the street and take in the mortal florist setting out buckets of blood-red peonies.

"Of course," Emrys replied, genuine surprise in his tone. "Humanity has never been our enemy. Many mortals are just as endangered by the Protectorate as the Fey. Magic unites the people of Hiraeth, not race or blood."

Her breath caught in her throat, and she felt Oberon slip his free hand—the other still in a sling—around hers. "I did not realize you were unaware," he murmured, his fingers stroking the underside of her wrist in a way that made Raegan's mind go blank and white and hungry. "I should have, though, knowing Emrys had taken your memories. Hiraeth is a sanctuary to those who need it. Who believe magic is not to be locked away by a ruling class."

"Right," Raegan said, clearing her throat, blinking back the tears that were gathering on her lashes. She didn't know why she hadn't bothered to open her eyes and *look* before—surely she had passed mortals on her walk last night. But gods, her rage had blinded her completely, hadn't it? The words of the Oracle came floating back to her—that anger is a useful tool when we control it but not when it controls us.

"So," Raegan continued, that seed of hope buried deep inside her chest growing large, "it took me a while to find the Garden the other night. We might be in for a walk."

"I think you should lead the way," Emrys said, adjusting his cloak's hood. "It opened for you before. If Hiraeth wants you to continue speaking with Alanna, it'll lead you to her."

Raegan nodded, looking left and then right. Last time, she'd taken the left turn, winding down the hill into the commercial section of the city. But tonight, when she turned the other direction, she caught an improbable thing—the flutter of a moth's wings in the lamplight up ahead. Pale as paper, unless she was only imagining it, twin moons on the delicate curve. She inhaled sharply. Maybe she was Icarus, doomed to plummet just when she thought she'd reached the warmth of the sun for the first time in a thousand years.

Or maybe not. Maybe the story ended differently this time.

"This way," Raegan said, stepping out into the mist, hoping the doors would open for her just once more.

Chapter Twenty-Three

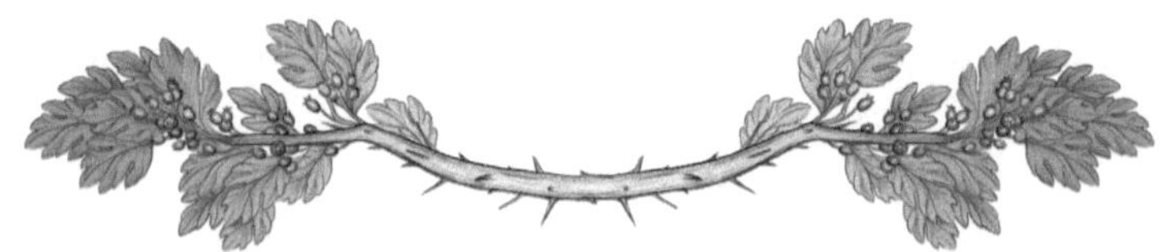

"My gods," Emrys murmured, his words floating on the still, heavy mist. Before the three of them stood the Garden of Doors, willow-o-wisps flickering blue and green and silver through the intricate, stylized gates. "No one has seen the Garden in at least a hundred years."

"Well, here it is," Raegan said with a shrug, swinging one side of the metal gates open. She stepped into the Garden, which was just as awash in dewy aubergine petal and rain-damp bark as the other night. The King stayed close to her side, his cloak arranged to disguise his arm, which was still very much bandaged to his chest. In the faerie lights, the sharp angles of his face were all the more apparent, all the more inhuman. Raegan marveled at his fierce beauty, and then at the even fiercer love she felt for him.

"You said she was near the hawthorns last time, yes?" Emrys asked, walking through the gates and onto the path. His gaze was wide, a sort of childlike wonder overtaking his expression that made Raegan feel like things might just be okay in the end.

"Yeah," she agreed. Up ahead, she saw the path narrow, the thicket of old-growth trees creating a canopy ahead. A vicious wind whipped through the trees, tearing at her clothing. "I still think it's best you hold back. Don't want to terrify her."

Neither the King nor Emrys agreed, but they didn't *disagree* either, which seemed more important to Raegan considering their respective personalities. She moved reverently down the path, her strides constantly alternating between quick and slow—a rush of need to see if Alanna had returned, a deep dread that only horrors awaited them.

But when she arrived at the dead portico, the Garden was quiet. The hawthorns were in the shape they ought to be, no strange shadows draping them, no sashay of Alanna's generous hips or elegant drip of her braids down her back.

"Sunset, she said?" the King asked, his voice low.

"Yeah," Raegan replied, scanning what she could see of the sky, though it was hard to gauge time beneath Hiraeth's crown of mist and rain.

"A few minutes still to go," Emrys said, his voice distant. Raegan turned to find the ex-Keeper turning in a slow circle, looking at the Garden with unabashed wonder. At least she could give him that, Raegan supposed, if everything ended up going to hell. She pushed her hood back, letting the glamour fall away, and watched as Emrys did the same.

She moved to face the hawthorn wall again, running her eyes across the impossible structure. It was something straight out of a fairy tale— her mind almost failed to process the enormity and sweep of it, a tangle of thick, ancient limbs that held the city in the palm of its hand.

At that moment, the air changed, the wind ceasing. Petrichor and damp leaves crushed underfoot filled Raegan's nose, the smoke and warmth of the city streets left far behind. Though groomed and orderly, this was a wild place, she realized. It wore politeness on its face, but its heart was all belladonna flower and hemlock root. Raegan smiled.

Then the hawthorns shimmered, just as they had before. Three ancient things held their breath in a place that was not a place, in a time outside of time. The future felt hinged on this moment, Raegan realized, like all of their Threads might change the weave for the better if they could just make this work. If they could prove themselves worthy. If the Fey put aside centuries-old resentment and bad blood; if the mortals of the Protectorate had finally had enough of aiding their own oppression.

The dead portico at Raegan's side shivered, and then a woman, looking for all the world like she'd been dipped in mercury or draped in silver silk, came through an opening in the hawthorn branches. Raegan held her breath. Emrys stood on the other side of the portico, and the King wisely faded into the shadows of the trees, hidden by his hood's glamour.

"Alanna," Raegan called, her voice trembling only a little.

"Raegan," Alanna called back, taking a few paces forward before she sighted Emrys. She froze, her young face stricken with fear.

"This is Emrys," Raegan said immediately, though she studied Alanna closely. "He's a friend. He wants what we do."

"I thought we'd meet alone," Alanna said cautiously, though she held her ground. Her long braids were bound in an elegant bun this time. Her clothing wasn't exactly visible beneath the shine of her shade, but it struck Raegan as being more casual than before.

"I'm sorry," Raegan said, meaning it. "I can't keep trying to do things all on my own. Hopefully you'll figure that out, too, before you're a thousand goddamn years old."

Alanna smiled, relaxing slightly. "Did Maelona make it to you?"

"Yes," Emrys replied, his tone light. "Thank you. It means a great deal to Raegan."

Alanna inclined her head and took the smallest step forward. "They were going to execute her as a traitor. I have friends in the holding blocks. It should look like an accident—a mistake with the shift change, a lucky opportunity."

"Have you endangered yourself by getting her out?" Raegan wanted to know. Her fingers wound into fists of their own accord. No more of this, the Protectorate devouring whatever it wanted for the sake of enriching itself.

"Probably," Alanna said with a sly smile, one shoulder meeting her ear. "Hard to stage a coup without risking yourself, isn't it? But beyond her being your family, she's useful to our cause. She's lived a lot longer than most field operatives. She knows things."

"Like that the Protectorate is aware we're looking for Avalon," Raegan suggested, shifting her weight. The following silence was so heavy she could hear the gravel crunch beneath her slight movement.

"Not for sure," Alanna replied, her gaze flicking to Emrys. "We have Prophecies, too. Which has always seemed hypocritical to me, but that's the Protectorate for you. It's a firmly held belief that if the King and the Deathless Witch return to these lands, it will be to seek Avalon."

"Does the Protectorate have any ideas about where Avalon may be?" Emrys asked, pulling his glasses out from beneath his cloak.

Alanna narrowed her eyes. "So you *are* looking for Avalon, then?" she asked, a grin taking over her face. The expression was pure oxygen in the depths of blank, dead space. "Why?"

Raegan and Emrys exchanged a glance. Silence hung like the gallows in the darkness, heavy and accusing. "What if we said it was because the Fey are done with this realm and wish to seek safer lands?" Emrys asked.

Alanna looked from one being to the other. A breeze sent pale pink petals tumbling across the path, shaking rain from the tree branches high above the small group gathered in a garden at the end of the world. Raegan held her breath.

"That would be more palatable, I suppose," Alanna finally said, shrewd and sharp. "But I wouldn't believe it."

Raegan bit the inside of her cheek. They'd strategized as they looked for the Garden—of course they had—but all three of them knew so little about what Alanna really wanted.

So then, fuck it, Raegan decided. "What do you want out of this, Alanna?" she asked, stepping toward the younger woman. The willow-o-wisps gleamed brighter for a moment, as if the Garden of Doors approved.

Alanna, to Raegan's surprise, stepped forward to meet her. They stood only a few feet apart now. Alanna was much taller than Raegan, a queenly tilt to her chin. "Revenge," she whispered, her voice hoarse and raw. "They took me from my mother, you know. She'd gotten me out, away from my father—he has the Protectorate lineage. And when they found me, they made my mum forget me. They didn't kill her, because she's good leverage. They always know where she is. Keeps me in line."

Raegan's throat constricted. Beside her, even Emrys inhaled sharply. That was the Protectorate, though—cruelty had *always* been the point. A strange urge rose in her to take Alanna's hands in her own. But she couldn't, because the woman was shade-clad, oathed to the enemy, and not yet in possession of Raegan's trust.

"So many of us do not have a choice," Alanna hissed, her eyes shining with tears in the willow-o-wisp light, even in her incorporeal form. "There needs to be some protection for mortals in a world with Fair Folk in it—of course there does. But *this*? The Protectorate hasn't protected anything but their own interests in hundreds of years. They are conspiring with a god who only brought misery to this world, and they don't care who suffers."

Raegan clung to Alanna's words, the way she spat them out like poisoned seeds. She could help free so many families of the shackles the Overhills had worn since the Battle of Camlann. She ground her teeth together, flexing her fingers. *If* Alanna was telling the truth. But she'd freed Maelona, sent her to Raegan. She hadn't come for them with an army. Maelona was disposable, though, Raegan realized, and the Protectorate might make that calculated move. It was a smart one, admittedly.

"I think I can speak for Raegan and myself both when I say we *want* to believe you," Emrys said, his voice soft and more blanketed in understanding than Raegan had ever heard. "It's just . . . It's hard."

"You think my first option was aligning with the bloody Fair Folk?" Alanna demanded, crossing her arms, looking over Raegan's shoulder to address the ex-Keeper. "I'm not enjoying this either."

Raegan inhaled, shaky and unsteady. This was so different from pursuing her father—it wasn't just about her anymore. Now an entire world was nestled in her hands like a delicate, speckled egg. One wrong move, one stumble, and it would shatter.

"Risk something, Alanna," she suggested, meeting the woman's large brown eyes, which were rimmed lightly in kohl. "Something tangible, something we agree on. Not a random bone to a dog you're thinking about killing anyway."

Anger flitted across Alanna's face, and she drew away from Raegan. "Have I not risked enough?" she demanded, her voice a harsh rasp of disbelief.

Maybe Raegan finally *was* growing as a person, because her own rage did not ignite with the spark of Alanna's. Instead, sadness flooded her chest, the tides leaving salt clinging to her ribs. "You have," she replied, surprised to find tears pricking the backs of her eyes. "My gods, you have. And yet I have to ask you for more."

Alanna shook her head, taking two steps backwards toward the opening in the hawthorns. "What could you possibly even ask of me?" she demanded, but she hadn't left yet.

"Speak with us in your body," Raegan suggested, knowing it was an enormous gamble. "Flesh and blood. Come have tea. Talk. Let me see what Maelona thinks about you in real-time."

Alanna stood up a little straighter, gears turning in her head. Silently, Raegan's hope surged—she just might have the shadewalker. She inhaled. And she might be about to lose her.

"And Alanna, you should meet the King."

The silver-shrouded woman, stately as a vengeful goddess, looked down at Raegan as if she were trying to decide whether to smite her or laugh in her face.

"Have you lost your fucking mind?" Alanna eventually asked, though she held her ground. She could turn to the hawthorns, find that breadcrumb sigil, and disappear back through the twisting limbs. But she did not.

Emrys cleared his throat and opened his mouth to speak, but Raegan held her hand out, shooting the ex-Keeper a look that she hoped he understood. "Actually, yes, I have," she said to the Protectorate shade-walker. "And honestly, I feel much better. I think you might, too."

Alanna's mouth actually fell open, and Raegan understood her youth then—a creature of barely twenty-five summers, maybe less. A girlhood stolen, a Fate rewritten, and now here Raegan was, asking her to meet the living, breathing devil.

The Garden fell into a preternatural hush, the breeze stilling, as if the very place they stood was holding its breath. Raegan found herself holding hers too, her heart a runaway train in her chest. Then Alanna broke the silence, throwing her head back and laughing. It was unbridled and crackling with energy, a wildfire of a sound.

"If only my mother could see this," Alanna began, her eyes coming to meet Raegan's gaze again, the outline of the shadewalker's form against the hawthorns reminding her of a military general painted in victory repose, hung in a museum somewhere.

Deep in the space, a fox or something worse shrieked. A chorus of cries followed, throats raw with defiance and a never-ending ache for justice. A cool breeze drifted up the back of Raegan's neck, making her shiver.

"My mother," Alanna continued, taking a step toward Raegan, mere inches separating them now, "only got me out because she made a deal with the Fey. And they protected us. I don't know the details of the bargain. I just know the Protectorate only found me because they killed the Fey who helped my mother. Whoever they were, they refused to give up our location. And they died for it. The cloaking spellwork died with them, of course. My handlers bragged about it. Called me a changeling. I suppose I am. Just not in the way they think."

Suddenly, like the sacred moment the sun climbs over the horizon and casts the world anew, Raegan understood she was looking an entire revolution in the eye. She understood that for all the efforts of the Unseelie Court and her own father and the people of Hiraeth, nothing would have freed them without this woman. This shade-clad torrent whose voice sounded like the truth.

"The High King of the Unseelie Court humbly extends an invitation to you, Lady Alanna, to discuss what kind of world we might create together," Emrys said from behind Raegan, startling her. His voice rose high on the mist, regal and sure and perfect. She smiled. "Do you accept?"

Alanna grinned, a silvered dagger in the dark. "I do."

Chapter Twenty-Four

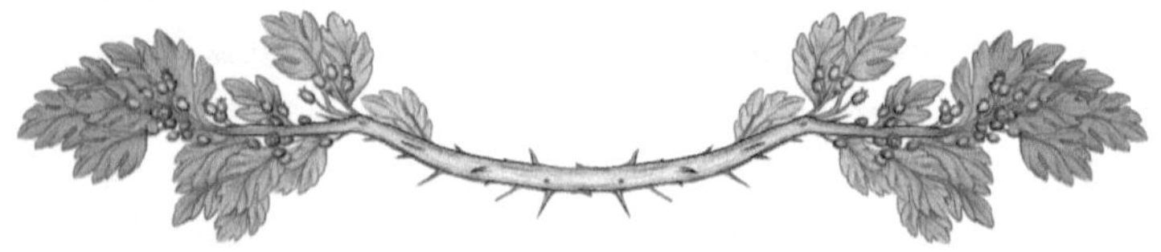

Raegan's left boot sank deep into the mud at the same time the wind turned sharply, buffeting her with rain that felt more like tiny pinpricks. She pulled her borrowed oilskin closer and tried to focus on Oberon's tall form a few steps ahead. Treading the ground where Stonehenge's bluestones had been quarried thousands and thousands of years ago on an epic quest to find a hidden door to Avalon had been very exciting on paper. In reality, she was cold and covered in mud to her knees.

If there was any sign of the Protectorate, any at all, Emrys had made them both promise to leave immediately. Rainer awaited them in the Rivers and could be summoned from a raindrop, the kelpie had sworn, the very moment they needed to flee. For the first time, Raegan felt like there *was* actually something to lose: her aunt who still slept, waking for only brief moments at a time, and the burgeoning alliance with Alanna that could change everything. She closed her eyes against another serrated spray of rain, her gaze falling on Oberon. And *him*. She could lose him, she supposed. Usually it went the other way, but his injury had reminded her there was no guarantee.

When Raegan came to the realization that she wasn't going to be comfortable healing such a complex injury anytime soon, Emrys had pulled a proficient Fey healer from Hiraeth's population. With the promise they'd agree to have the memory taken later, he brought them to the Temple. The damage from the Protectorate's attack was bad—worse than Oberon had been letting on. The healer had done what they could, but it would take months for the King to regain full use of his shoulder and pectoral muscles. Which meant he shouldn't be slogging about in the mud, but he had ignored any assertions of that sort.

"How much farther?" Raegan shouted through the torrent of rain.

Oberon slowed, turning to look back at her, though she couldn't see much beyond his hood. "Only a few paces," he replied as they fell into stride together. Oberon gave her the more manageable path, which forced him to wade through thick, knee-high grass.

Raegan squinted into the gloom surrounding them, finally making out what they were looking for: Carn Goedog. At the top of a slope stood a crown of stones, jutting out from the earth like broken teeth. It was a wild place, she knew immediately, and her bones hummed.

Whether it contained a door to Avalon was another question entirely, and one they could only answer with actual inspection. She threw a glance around, searching for any hint of the Protectorate. Armed with Alanna's information, they'd conspired to stage a few diversions at ancient sites across the Isles. Oberon seemed to think their encounter at the waterfalls might have just been poor luck—that the Protectorate was patrolling the area already. Raegan could only hope that was true.

The path began to incline, and she slogged forward, her knees protesting. And yet, in her heart of hearts, she'd rather be fighting through mud and hill and rain than doing what came next: meeting with Alanna in Hiraeth's old Temple. Raegan didn't think she—or magic itself, for that matter—could suffer losing Alanna. *If* the shadewalker was actually what she made herself out to be, of course.

Raegan slipped on a particularly muddy patch and let out a curse. The King caught her by the elbow and steadied her before they made the final ascent. Hopefully Maelona would wake up before this evening, when Alanna would come to Hiraeth in her own body. She'd requested time to figure out exactly how to disappear for a few hours, and they'd happily granted it to her, needing the three days to strategize and plan. And to check Carn Goedog, the next site on Emrys's list, which clung to more residual magic than should have been possible.

Raegan ground her teeth, holding up an arm to shield her eyes as another sharp gust of wind threw knives their way. Emrys and the healer he'd recruited both thought actively intervening in Maelona's current state was too dangerous. Well, Emrys was not particularly concerned about Maelona herself, but he was very interested in preserving her memories and sanity for future use.

With a huff, Raegan crested a steep section of the hill. She couldn't really blame him. Hundreds of years of war and responsibility had hollowed out the parts of the ex-Keeper that might have been soft once. She wondered, not for the first time, what it was to persist in that endless way, one long line. Maybe dying all the time wasn't such a curse, not in comparison.

And then the slope evened out beneath her, depositing Raegan and the King on a small plateau ringed in giant shards of bluestone. Despite the pounding rain, Raegan pulled one hand out of her dry, warm pocket and extended it toward the nearest stone, laying her palm flat against its surface. She inhaled, closed her eyes, and waited. To her surprise, nothing rose from her depths. That didn't mean the door was not there. With an exhale, Raegan opened her eyes, casting her gaze out wider.

She shook the rain from her fingers and returned her hand to the safety of the oilskin's pocket. The valley opened up in front of them, shrouded in damp blues and sodden grays, the grass browned and wilted with the approach of winter. Bracing herself against the cold, Raegan pulled both hands from the oilskin and began to walk around the bluestone crown, her fingers searching for seams or inscriptions or doors that her eyes might not allow her to perceive.

Time stretched long and thin, though Raegan supposed it couldn't have been more than ten minutes when disappointment began to sing through her body. It was a song she knew well, the movements memorized by heart, all the sweeps and swells as familiar as her own voice. But it still stung. Another wild, fearless place, its teeth firmly sunk into the flesh of history and magic, but utterly lacking a door. Missing the vital way forward that might lead to the end of all this pain.

"Anything?" she asked the King over the rush of the rainstorm. He looked up from the stone he'd been examining, and hope spiked defiantly in Raegan's chest. But then he shook his head all the same.

"Again, I wish to spend more time," Oberon told her, bowing his body around hers to speak close to her ear so she could hear him over the wind. "But it feels unwise to linger."

"I'd really prefer you didn't get shot again," she replied. "Maybe I'm naïve. But if we find the door—even the general area, I think . . ."

"We will know," the King said, his voice firm and faraway at once.

"Yeah," Raegan replied with a nod that sent raindrops cascading down the front of her hood, disappearing into the storm surrounding them. With the weak gray sky behind him, standing atop a broken bluestone crown, Oberon looked forlorn for a moment. She knew how much failure plagued him. They'd lost once, twice—would it be three times?

But then the moment shattered as the King turned, kneeling to brush his fingertips against a puddle of water that had gathered in the soft earth. In the blink of an eye, Rainer's deep green, scalloped ears emerged, and then the kelpie leapt from the puddle, coming to stand between Raegan and the King atop the rocky outcropping.

Rainer swung his head to either side, taking in Carn Goedog. "No door?" he questioned, his sonorous voice effortlessly rising above the thundering rain.

"If it were so simple," the King replied, moving toward the kelpie, "I imagine the Protectorate might have beaten us to it."

Oberon helped Raegan onto Rainer's back. Disappointment held her tongue fast, and so she said nothing. As the King mounted behind Raegan, the kelpie went tense beneath her. Intuition prickled the back of her neck, and she turned in the direction of the wide valley painted in rain.

"Ahh," Rainer said dryly, taking in the five sleek black Land Rovers that had appeared from nowhere and were barreling toward the outcropping. "Our friends join us at last."

"Rainer," Raegan said, leaning forward to lay her hand against the kelpie's neck. "Please. Let's just go. I can't stand to see Oberon hurt again."

The kelpie grumbled something Raegan couldn't make out, but he still turned deftly on his hindquarters, positioning himself to face the puddle from which he'd leapt into this plane of existence. Warily, Raegan eyed the Land Rovers, not liking the progress they were making across the slippery, boggy ground, even if she and the King and the kelpie were seconds from disappearing into the Rivers.

And then she watched something happen that she did not quite understand for a long moment. One of the Range Rovers faltered, like its wheels had caught in the mud. Reasonable, she thought, though her breath was caught fast in her chest. But no—a chasm was opening in the valley, the land splitting itself wide, a hungry maw.

She whipped around to look at Oberon, a confused mangle of emotions bursting to life inside her body.

"I did not ask the valley for anything," the King immediately told her, catching her eye from beneath the gloom of his hood.

Despite the thunder of the rain and the pounding of her own blood and the wretched, gnawing sound of wet earth consuming man-made metal, all the world fell silent to Raegan. The King had not bid the land of his making—the land his ancestors had imbued with their blood and their magic—to do anything at all.

And yet the valley that tumbled out at Carn Goedog's feet bucked and roiled, splitting open like a seam or a door. Not to Avalon, no. Half of Raegan winced, the other yelping in triumph, as a second Land Rover was dragged down into whatever dark, open mouth awaited it.

"The land is awakening," Rainer said, the kelpie sounding in absolute awe—a tone Raegan had almost never heard from him in the years they'd known each other. "How could . . . It is *impossible*. The Protectorate bound the land centuries ago."

The land. There were a thousand stories of where the Twyleth Teg and the Tuatha de Danann of these lands had originated. There were Fair Folk of different kinds all across the globe, but the ones from these Isles were some of the most fabled. Tales were told of how they had long ago walked out of the sea or sailed from an unknown island in the west or arrived from another plane of existence altogether.

But those stories were human. The Fair Folk of this land had been here long before mortals were created, long before they shared their stories around the fire. The Fey were, in many ways, spirits of land made flesh by the gods, guardians of this green and abundant earth. It was why the Protectorate held the Isles so fiercely: to prevent that intimate connection, forged thousands of years ago, from being regained by the Unseelie Court. To stop the old sleeping things in this land from awakening and rattling their chains. The land, in the Protectorate's view, was a thing to be exploited, mined, colonized.

And perhaps Raegan was just being fanciful, gleaning too much from the few seconds of destruction she saw before Rainer plunged back into the Rivers headfirst.

Or perhaps the land—just like the Fey, just like the magical mortals, just like Alanna—had finally had enough. Perhaps that damp, wide mouth in the valley had also tasted revolution. And perhaps it wanted more.

Chapter Twenty-Five

"I wish Emrys could give me back my memories of Hiraeth," Raegan said to Oberon, squeezing water from her hair with a towel from the bathroom. She hadn't even realized so much rain had snuck through the seams of her oilskin, but by the time she'd trudged up the ridiculously grand and increasingly annoying staircase at the old Temple to their quarters, she'd begun to shiver violently.

"Memory spells are difficult on their own," Oberon said from the foot of the bed, pulling his damp sweater over his head. "And Emrys removed your memories of Hiraeth *before* you asked Baba Yaga to place the Seal."

Raegan nodded, padding over to the roaring fireplace to leave her boots to dry on the hearth. "Two separate workings scrambling my brain. So even if he *wanted* to give them back . . ."

"It is unlikely they can be recovered," the King replied as she turned to face him. The dancing light of the fire deepened every dip and curve of his muscular chest and torso, now bare, black pants slung low on his hips. The rest of the world fell away in an instant.

"You'll have to remind me," Raegan said, desire throbbing unhelpfully between her legs; there had been no door at Carn Goedog, and she had a meeting with Alanna this evening, so it hardly seemed the time for such things. "Why Hiraeth? Wouldn't both Fey thrones being in the same place at the same time be an enormous security issue?"

If her mind were not so clouded with thoughts of his porcelain skin and full lips and impossibly sculpted body, she might have realized she'd answered her own question.

"That is precisely why," the King replied, one ink-dark eyebrow raised. "Hiraeth was the most secure location possible, especially considering that we were planning something neither of our advisors or courts would have been particularly supportive of."

Raegan freed her thick auburn curls from her braid, shaking them loose over her shoulders to dry. "Ah," she said, shimmying out of her damp jeans, which clung stubbornly to her skin. "I remember that, at least. We wanted to reunite the Fey courts."

From the other side of the bed, Oberon nodded, something dangerous and delicious playing on the beautifully inhuman planes of his face. His gaze slid down her body to where she was peeling denim from her generous thighs. "We have a meeting with a Protectorate informant in less than three hours," he murmured, but everything about him —the silvered rasp of his tone, the long-fingered hand clutching the bedpost too tightly—told a different story.

"Yeah," Raegan agreed, stepping out of her jeans and moving onto the bed, sitting on her knees as she faced him, clad in only her bra and underwear. "She might bring an army. We might die."

The King reached out, capturing her jaw in his powerful hand. Raegan shivered at his touch, fire roaring through her body. "Yes," he agreed, fingers tracing whisper-light down her neck. "It would be a terrible thing if I died without pleasuring you one last time."

And with that, Oberon was on her, pushing her onto the bed— though his hand cradled the back of her head, just in case she came too close to the headboard. A moan crept out of Raegan's mouth as she wrapped her legs around his hips, meeting his mouth with hers. He caged her between his arms—all coiled muscle and hard-wrought power —deepening the kiss, her name escaping his lips in a long, low groan.

"Shouldn't you be more careful with your shoulder?" Raegan asked breathlessly, tracing the bandage with her fingers. The visit from the healer had left him with only a patch of spiderweb gauze on his chest; the sling and heavier bandaging were gone.

He let out a sigh, and then without another word pulled her against him and rolled. Raegan found herself on top, the High King of the Unseelie Court pinned beneath her on the quilt, his dark waves of hair spilling out onto the embroidered fabric. Despite the deep, rich want humming from the very center of her being, she took a moment to savor him. To memorize the beautiful mouth, the impossibly sharp jawline, the high cheekbones and ocean eyes, the heavy ridge of the collarbone and dusting of black silk across his chest.

And then Raegan could contain the desire no longer, so she brought her body to his, entangling her fingers in his hair. Oberon undid her bra so smoothly she didn't even feel it, and then his hands were roaming her bare back, sweeping around her ribcage to cup her breasts. She rolled her hips against his, all of her electrified and tender and wanting, wanting, *wanting.*

Raegan reached down to undo the closure of his pants at the same time he slid a few fingers beneath her underwear, finding where she was damp and throbbing. Her head fell back, a sigh slipping through her lips. Oberon sat up with a quick contraction of muscle, and she moaned from somewhere deep in her throat as his touch deepened at her center.

"God," she groaned, somehow still surprised at how quickly he ignited the kind of intense pleasure she'd rarely experienced with any other partner.

"Is it a god with his fingers inside you, pulling all these pretty sounds from your mouth?" Oberon asked dryly, his lips moving against her collarbone.

"No," Raegan panted, adding too many syllables to the word. When he brought his tongue to the tip of her breast in just the way she liked, she knew exactly what to say. "*Fuck,* Oberon."

He laughed softly, his body so close she could feel it rumble through his chest. "Better," he said, tilting his chin up to look at her. "I do not remember inviting a god into our bed. Or anyone, for that matter."

Raegan ground her hips into his hand, slipping her fingers down the hard planes of his stomach and beneath his waistband. "You don't share well," she murmured against his mouth, finding his thick, wanting arousal a moment later. A strangled gasp left his lips—the Unseelie king, panting at her touch; what a thing to witness—and she kissed him, swallowing whatever he might have said next.

They tangled themselves in each other, all hungry mouths and ancient longing. When Oberon pinned her against the bed, the sensual heat of him so close to smothering her, Raegan didn't have the selflessness a second time to remind him of his shoulder.

Pleasure sank its teeth into every inch of her, and there was little room left for any other thoughts—only how much she wanted him, how much she had always wanted him, from that very first moment she saw him. Some invisible, undeniable thread was strung between the two of them, burning and endless. Raegan couldn't let him go even if she wanted to. Even if he asked. She dug her nails into his skin, and the King groaned her name. Then he rocked back, sliding out of the embrace of her thighs just enough to slip her underwear off her hips and down her legs.

"You belong to me," the faerie king said, his lips smoldering and insistent against the delicate skin of her thighs. He brought one hand back to her core, playing her like an instrument of flesh and bone. And Raegan sang for him—his name left her lips in a cry so loud she suddenly wondered if the room had silence or privacy wards. Too late now. She certainly wasn't going to stop what was happening to check.

"I belong to you," she agreed feverishly as his mouth drew closer to the apex of her legs.

The King looked up, his dark eyes sliding to meet hers before he placed a soft, delicate kiss where she wanted it most. Her head tipped back of its own will as another wolfish sound tore itself from her lips. When she felt Oberon's tongue dive inside, Raegan's vision went white. Her want for him was all-consuming. She loved him with her entire being, so fiercely that she could barely understand it. The way she had been ripped from him a hundred times over only made every touch sweeter. Pleasure mounted deep inside her belly, growing more and more intense until she could barely stand it.

His fingertips digging into her hips, his mouth barely raised from her core, the King commanded Raegan to come for him. She did, shattering against him, knowing without a doubt that he was the only thing that could make her feel whole. Besides, Oberon could handle her jagged edges, didn't mind that she was more broken glass than woman. He'd still run his tongue along her curves, even if it drew blood.

Moments dripped by, soft and slow as molasses. The only sound in the room was their breathing and the crackle of the fire. Raegan was flushed and still panting when she realized she wanted—*needed*—more of him. She curled deeper into his embrace, sliding her leg against the hard, long evidence of his arousal. Oberon released a breathy sigh into her hair, his arm tightening around her waist.

"Maybe you can remind me," Raegan murmured, lightly raking her nails down his chest, "of my first time?" He said nothing for a long second and she laughed, adding, "In Hiraeth, I mean."

"Oh," Oberon said, a smile that showed those long-lost dimples curving across his lips. "Thank you for clarifying. I would not have been able to fulfill the first request."

"Losing your virginity is extremely overrated," Raegan replied, watching his every movement as he unfolded to stand beside the bed. "Just two people fumbling around and hoping for the best."

"I could not agree more," the King replied, slipping both of his large, powerful hands around her waist and dragging her to the edge of the mattress. "You knew *exactly* what you were doing when we met that first time in Camelot. You did as Titania, too, when we were introduced at your coronation."

She gazed up at him, some distant part of her in complete disbelief that such an impossible, beautiful thing was hers—that she hadn't truly spoiled it, not yet. "Enough to get the Unseelie king to agree to go away in secret with the Seelie Court's High Lady to a hidden Fey city," Raegan teased. She reached forward, trailing a few fingers down his chest and the muscled planes of his stomach, and then lower, to the strong V of his hips, to where he was hard and wanting just below.

But before she could go further, the King slipped one arm around her waist and flipped her onto her stomach, bringing her ass to his hips. She felt the length of him slide against her skin and groaned, grabbing a handful of the quilt above her head.

"I could show you," Oberon said in a barely controlled rasp, his breath dancing across her neck, "what happened the last time we were here, if you ask nicely. Or if you beg. I would prefer, I think, if you begged."

Raegan smiled into the duvet, though the expression quickly morphed into something else when she felt Oberon's capable fingers move against the place she was most sensitive. "Please, Oberon," she moaned, grinding her hips into his hand. "*Fuck.* Please."

He did not reply, though with his other hand, he gathered her hair around his fingers at the nape of her neck, pulling ever so gently, just enough to set a wildfire spreading across her skin. How something as powerful and deadly as him, Raegan thought with a gasp, could know the *exact* pressure to exert on a creature so much more delicate and breakable . . .

"How badly do you desire me?" the King asked, the silken husk of his voice alone driving her close to madness. "Enough to betray your court?"

Despite Emrys's spell, despite the lingering effects of the Seal, despite the hundreds of years that separated her from that life, for a split second, Raegan thought she saw it—her body willingly, achingly bent at the waist over a large writing desk, long golden hair gathered in the hand of the king who could destroy her entire world.

"Yes," she rasped, barely more than damp, desperate need. "*Yes,* Oberon."

"Say it," the King replied, gripping her hair tighter in exactly the way she wanted, crushing her hips with his. "Say you want my cock so badly that you would betray your own throne."

The words tumbled out of her like she'd been born to say them, and all of time condensed for a moment, like everything was happening all at once and nothing had ever ended. And then the faerie king slid himself inside her and Raegan went limp with pleasure, save for her hands desperately clutching the sheets above her head.

"More," she begged, barely able to say anything else as another orgasm threatened to devour her entirely. "More. *Please.* Fuck me as hard as you can, Oberon."

He did what she asked, burying himself inside her. A feral cry thundered out of her chest as the feeling of his hand between her legs and the hard length of him deep within her took Raegan over the edge. She said his name again and again—like an incantation, like maybe if she repeated the sound of it enough, Fate would understand how badly she needed him. Oberon followed behind her, and if Raegan had uttered his name like it was a spell, then he said hers like it was the entire universe contained in only a few syllables.

He pulled her close, and they both tumbled onto the bed, Raegan's head coming to rest on his chest.

"Jesus fucking Christ," she panted.

The King laughed—genuine, deep from his belly—in response, and she clung to that sound, a silvered bell in an autumn meadow.

The rest of the world forgotten, the lovers lounged in each other's arms, their breathing like the tides of two oceans meeting somewhere far from the shore, far from where anyone might know their names.

But that was the thing with the sea. Everything turned up in the shallows at some point, dragged in by the merciless tides.

CHAPTER TWENTY-SIX

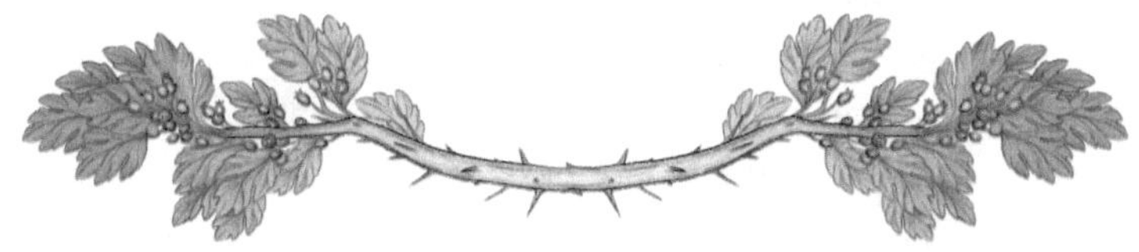

An hour later, Raegan stood at the gates to Hiraeth—the last free Fey city—and hoped with every fiber of her being that the Protectorate-oathed shadewalker would not betray everything she held dear. At her side, Emrys paused before the mystifying structure of hawthorn branches and ancient metal, his body going completely still.

"What?" Raegan hissed, trying very hard not to sound frantic.

"Just this whole godsdamn thing," Emrys replied without looking at her, his gaze locked on the towering gates. She bit down on her tongue, eyes darting between the ex-Keeper and Hiraeth's doors, very much wishing the three of them hadn't agreed for Oberon to stay behind in the old Temple—a reasonable enough decision to not overwhelm Alanna, but Raegan personally would've felt a lot better with the King at her side, especially now.

But then Emrys reached forward and pulled open one of the twin gates as if it weighed nothing. He slipped through into the never-place at Hiraeth's edges. Raegan sucked in a deep breath and followed him into the shadowy chamber where the ancient, sentient city would decide Alanna's fate.

At the far end of the room, silhouetted by the gray light of open moorland, loomed two massive kelpies. Rainwater streamed down their murky green-gray coats, spilling out onto the worn stone floor beneath their hooves. Alanna stood between the two creatures, wrapped in waterproofed wool, a sword strapped to her back. When she pulled back her hood, Raegan saw that her locs were bound in an elegant twist at the nape of her neck and her spine was ramrod straight, shoulders defiant. Again, Raegan felt that tug toward the shadewalker, that preternatural sense she couldn't quite put into words.

Alanna's dark brown gaze met Raegan's, and something passed between the two women, something old and feral and lightning-charged. Raegan understood that they were not alone in Hiraeth's antechamber; she knew Emrys was busy conferring with the kelpies as he checked Alanna over for spellwork, toggling between lenses and spells on his delicate silver glasses. And yet for a long, haunted moment, Raegan felt as though the only thing that existed was the future they might create together—delicate, half-birthed, hung on nothing but a silken thread of hope above a yawning abyss.

Alanna glanced down, and the sensation evaporated. Emrys dismissed the kelpies gratefully and then led the shadewalker into Hiraeth's chamber, explaining it was the space itself that would make the final decision. He was careful not to name Hiraeth or even mention a city at all; it was safer for everyone involved if Alanna remained unaware.

Raegan held her breath as she felt the chamber constrict. As a witness this time, safe enough at the other end of the room, she distinctly felt something very much *alive* turn its all-seeing eyes to the tall wool-clad woman at the ex-Keeper's side. To her surprise—and Emrys's, judging by his expression—Hiraeth did not deliberate long. One heart-beat, two, and then the room released all its tension, the exhale of a beast choosing different prey.

"What the hell was that, exactly?" Alanna inquired as Emrys guided her through the gates, her words aimed at Raegan.

"Some ridiculously old faerie magic," Raegan replied, cocking her head, playing the irreverent mortal card. "Follow me," she added before anyone could have second thoughts about the madness of this situation—a faerie king awaiting a Protectorate turncoat, a real chance that the world could be upended and made anew.

Alanna showed no trepidation. She swept down the hallway at Raegan's side, politely clipping the length of her longer strides. The shadewalker was clearly on high alert, her eyes roving, body poised to react, but there was an ease about her that Raegan deeply envied. A sureness that she would be ready for whatever awaited her. Raegan had never been sure about anything for more than five seconds at a time.

Only when they reached the entrance to the Temple's great room did Alanna pause. "Here?" she asked, gesturing toward the tall, arching door carved out of black wood that gleamed in the low light.

"Yeah," Raegan said, expecting Alanna to hesitate, to ask more questions, to maybe make a threat about what would happen if they fucked her over. The woman did none of those things; she simply held Raegan's gaze for a long moment, tilted her chin up, and stepped through the door of her own accord.

Raegan was so surprised that she just stood there dumbly, the door swinging closed in her face. A few paces behind her, Emrys let out an amused sound. She glanced back to find him shaking his head, though he looked pleased.

"Gods, I hope we're right," he said, pushing his shoulder into the door but not opening it just yet. His gaze met Raegan's. "I like her, I think."

"Didn't know you could actually *like* mortals, Emrys," Raegan teased, following the ex-Keeper as he moved over the threshold. The two of them spilled out into the hearth-lit great room of the ruined Temple. Any items that could possibly hold any information had been removed from the space, and Maelona had been settled into a small room on the other side of the kitchen.

The space was hushed and still. For a few harrowing seconds, Raegan was terrified that neither Alanna nor the King were there—that something had already gone terribly, horribly wrong. But then she told herself to breathe and cast her gaze around the room.

The King, in typical fashion, was leaning against the far wall, where the hallway led around to the grand staircase. Candlelight danced across his exquisite features. The long legs, the crossed arms, the powerful shoulders—all neutral, relaxed, but clearly ready to strike at any time. He said nothing, letting the silence wind itself tighter and tighter.

Alanna was just to Raegan's left. It looked like she'd only taken a step or two into the room before she spotted the Unseelie king awaiting her in the gloom. The shadewalker's body was straight as an arrow, her feet firmly planted. If not for the way her chest fluttered like a bird's wings, Raegan wouldn't have thought the woman was in any distress at all.

The King unfolded from the stone wall, a shadow detaching itself from the night, and prowled a few steps closer. Alanna flinched but held her ground. Good—Raegan knew that Oberon was testing the Protectorate woman as much as Alanna was surely testing them.

The silence strung itself tight as a noose. Raegan's heart thudded painfully against her throat. Each and every one of her veins suddenly felt overfilled, too thick with blood. And then, all at once, movement bled back into the room.

"Why," the King began, unfolding his arms, his voice deep, steady, dangerously alluring, "are you here, Protectorate-oathed?"

"Because," Alanna replied, taking a step toward the King—Raegan hid her smile of approval—and looking up to meet his eyes, "I want liberation."

The King, in that way of his, draped all of his attention over Alanna's shoulders. She did not crumble; she did not even tremble. And then he waited, pinning the shadewalker beneath the weight of his eternal gaze, waiting for her to fill the silence, to speak the words she'd left waiting at the back of her throat.

"And I want to be very clear," Alanna said, crossing her arms, refusing to look away from the King. "I will free this world of the Protectorate's chains with *or* without you, faerie king."

The quiet settled shadowed and heavy, like all the world had turned its many eyes to the stone-walled room. Perhaps in another Thread, a Fatesong would've trilled, long and low and looping.

Instead, the King smiled, a terrible, world-rending thing. "I think my court has been awaiting you for a very, *very* long time."

Hope flared hot and dangerous inside Raegan—the kind of mad, desperate hope that destroyed empires and shook despots from their thrones. A warm, strong hand suddenly grabbed hers, and it took Raegan more than a few skittering heartbeats to understand it was Emrys—the Keeper who had watched his Temple fall and built a haven from its ash.

A thick wave of emotion uncurled in her throat, tears falling down her face like an unrelenting river. She squeezed Emrys's hand so hard she thought he might protest. But when Raegan glanced over, all she saw were the tears gathering on his lashes.

"Then should we sit," Alanna asked, breathless as she gestured toward the beeswax-crowned table beneath the leaded glass window, "and speak of revolution?"

~

A handful of hours was not enough to make a Protectorate shadewalker, Temple-less Keeper, exiled King, and deathless witch into full-fledged allies. Raegan had known that going in. But what they *were* able to agree on—it felt too grandiose to say it out loud, but it seemed like the kinds of things that changed the entire world.

Rain drummed on the window, an orchestra accented by the sound of clinking porcelain. The scents of Ceylon tea and bergamot wafted heavy and rich in the air, a tiny plume of woodsmoke sneaking beneath the Temple's front door. Raegan shifted in her seat, the antique chair creaking.

"So," Alanna began, reaching to refill her teacup. "Would the Unseelie Court be willing to include a reconstruction committee in the formal bargain, with seats split equally between Fey and humans? As well as the formation and continued support of an organization dedicated to balancing the disparity between our peoples?"

Raegan turned to her left, watching the King as he considered. He moved forward in a languid stretch, resting his elbows on the table. For a moment, he examined Alanna, no doubt weighing every word she'd spoken. And then, to her surprise, the King's gaze came to rest on Raegan.

"What do you think?" he wanted to know, eyes searching hers.

"I mean, that'd be necessary, I think," Raegan replied, gaze flicking to Alanna. "I don't know how we'd proceed without these sorts of things already in place. And whatever decisions we come to, the language of the bargains has to be plain. No wiles. No wordplay."

Alanna smirked, though it was good-natured. "Yeah, I mean, that's usually your thing anyway, isn't it? Plain language sounds great to me."

Oberon nodded, hooking one arm over the high back of his chair in a surprisingly casual gesture that highlighted the carved muscle just beneath his suit. "With that understood," he began, his attention falling back onto Alanna, "will we even get so far? Tell me, Alanna: will Protectorate-oathed humans and those mortals whose minds have been poisoned by propaganda ever be willing to work with my people?"

Emrys inhaled sharply across the table, and Raegan resisted the urge to look down at her hands. They'd been dancing around that question for a while, speaking instead of the world they might shape. But that world could never be birthed if there was no bridging the chasm the Protectorate had torn between mortals and Fey.

Alanna puffed up her cheeks with air and then blew it out slowly. The mannerism immediately—and probably irrationally—further endeared the shadewalker to Raegan.

"My cohort is ready for a coup," Alanna replied, tracing the gilded mouth of her teacup with one elegant finger. "And, look, we know overthrowing the Protectorate's leadership is going to put us in a treacherous situation with a terrifying, ancient god that all of us were oathed to against our will." She paused, coiling the end of one loc, a darkly wry expression moving across her features.

"It's a death sentence," Raegan breathed, all at once understanding, the words coming out hoarse. The sorrow sitting deep in her marrow surged, boiling over into rage. How many people would have to die to rid the world of the Protectorate and the Timekeeper? Unbidden, her father's face appeared in her mind, and she bit down hard on the inside of her cheek. There was no room for more grief, more weight.

"Yeah," Alanna said, chewing on her lip as her eyes darted away. "Rough, innit? But gives us good strategic leeway. I can position the Unseelie Court's involvement as a way for us to . . . maybe not all die horrible deaths. My people are practical. And scared of death, like anyone else. But what about *your* people? That's some ancient grudges we're talking about."

"Yes," Emrys replied, turning to look at Alanna, who was seated at his left. "But you have to understand that both Fey courts have always had mortals among them. Most of us can count at least one human we've come to trust, or at least befriended. It's the Protectorate we hold our grudges against, not individual mortals. Besides, do not underestimate our people's loyalty to the King. Where he leads, we will follow."

Raegan sipped on her tea, finding it had gone cold. In her peripheral vision, she saw the King frown. Alanna stared at him expectantly.

"The Seelie Court is in disarray," Oberon said, his eyes narrowing in thought. "My court is powerful but small. There is some number of unaligned Fey hiding in plain sight among mortals, but I doubt any of them will participate in our plans. What I am saying, Alanna, is that I cannot promise you armies."

Alanna straightened as the rain increased its deluge outside, the roar of it deafening for a moment. "I don't want that kind of a war," she replied, sounding wise beyond her years and all the more burdened for it. "I want the singular kind of power that your people—*you*, specifically —can wield. Remember the Protectorate Prophecy about you two returning to these lands I mentioned?" She paused, gesturing between Raegan and the King, one perfectly groomed eyebrow arched. "It's a doomsday Prophecy."

Emrys turned sharply toward the shadewalker with rapt interest. Raegan watched him open his mouth to speak before closing it, setting his elbow onto the table and then his chin upon his palm, watching Alanna closely all the while.

"Go on," Oberon commanded. The air around the four of them sharpened with expectation and revelation.

Alanna exhaled, staring into the dark liquid swirling in her teacup. "The Prophecy says you seek Avalon because there's some ancient weapon hidden there. And that you'll destroy the world with it."

The silence pulled taut as a bowstring. Raegan's heart hammered in her chest, palms gone clammy. The room seemed three times smaller than just a moment ago, the fire in the hearth burning too warm, the air filled with smoke.

"So," the shadewalker continued, raising her eyes from her teacup, examining the three ancient things seated around the table. "Are you *actually* looking for Avalon? I've asked a few times before, but none of you have given me a straight answer yet."

Raegan shot forward in her chair at the exact moment the King leaned back and drawled, "Yes." She whipped her head around to stare at him in disbelief. Across the table, Alanna was fighting to maintain composure. Raegan watched as she picked up a tiny, delicate teaspoon, her hands shaking around the fluted metal.

"For a weapon?" she asked, her eyes meeting the King's, her voice heavy and stilted. But not, Raegan realized all at once, with fear as she'd expected. No, the shadewalker's voice was laden with the treachery of hope.

"Yes," the King replied, holding Alanna's gaze with a simmering intensity.

"Would you say," Alanna asked, leaning forward to rest her elbows on the table, steepling her fingers as she gazed right back at the King as if he were not the avatar of every horror story she'd ever been told, "it's a weapon strong enough to destroy the world that we know? The world we seek to remake? Maybe even a weapon powerful enough to destroy that tweed-suited fuck of a god?"

Hope wrapped its green vines around Raegan then, too, infecting her with the same sweet poison that had led Alanna to do something as reckless and utterly unhinged as attempt to align with the Unseelie king.

"That is our hope," Oberon said, and he was smiling now, dangerous and impossibly beautiful. "We know not for certain, but the weapon we seek could indeed bring about doomsday for the Protectorate."

A feral grin overtook Alanna's features. "That's *exactly* what I was hoping you'd say."

Silence swept through the room again. Something not unlike awe unfolded in Raegan—that maybe after all this time, after all this suffering and pain and darkness, the world had just been waiting for these four people to turn the key and unlock salvation.

"Not to ruin the moment," Emrys said as he rubbed his jaw, indeed ruining the moment, "but I want to be honest with you, Alanna. We don't know where Avalon is. And I'm not sure we're going to find it in time to make a difference."

Even though she knew it was true, Raegan still squeezed her eyes shut, wanting to savor that honeysuckle-sweet drop of hope upon her tongue.

Then the sudden sound of movement rang out behind her, sending the King to his feet. Alanna leapt from her chair a few seconds later, her sword already drawn by the time Raegan scrambled out of her seat and whirled around.

Of all things, there in the long shadow of evening within a ruined Temple, draped in a woolen blanket, stood Maelona Overhill. "Good news," she said, her voice hoarse and wavering, her body unsteadily propped up against the stone wall. "I'm not dead. Also, I might know how to find Avalon."

CHAPTER TWENTY-SEVEN

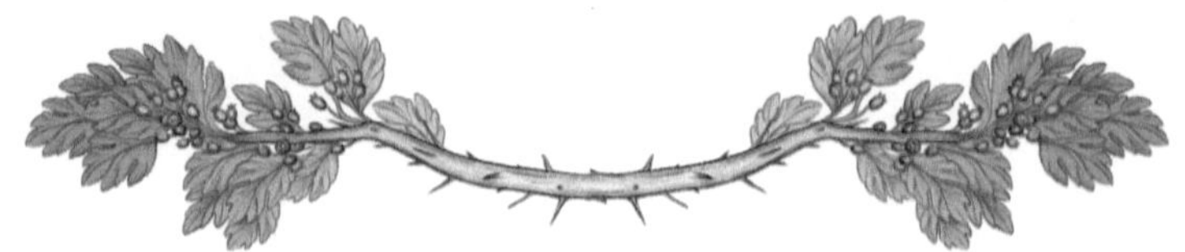

No one knew what to say, so instead, the four of them stared dumbly at the Protectorate woman who had crawled back from the grave.

Maelona scowled in response, eyes narrowing, one still shadowed by a bruise. "If someone gets me a chair," she grumbled, "I'll tell you all about it."

Oberon moved faster than any of them, so by the time Raegan even thought about reacting, he'd pulled his chair to the head of the table and held it out for Maelona. She gathered up the blanket draped around her shoulders and limped over, muttering a "thank you" under her breath. Just when she reached the high-backed antique chair, she looked up at the King.

Really looked at him.

"Are you— Fucking hell, it's *you*," Maelona sputtered, stumbling back a step. Raegan had more or less regained her senses by then and reached out to steady her aunt. "Is it all true?" Maelona asked, her voice low now, gray-green eyes meeting Raegan's.

"That's a very vague question," Raegan replied slowly. "Why don't you sit down? You can barely stand."

Raegan gestured toward the open seat. Oberon had wisely stepped away, crossing his arms. With a huff, Maelona collapsed into the chair, her gaze fixed on the King standing in the dimness of the ruined Temple.

"Do you really know where Avalon is?" Raegan asked, pouring a cup of tea for her aunt, wondering if she should ask Emrys if there was any coffee. But Maelona didn't seem to mind, eagerly curling her hands around the warm teacup.

"Are you really a thousand fucking years old?" Maelona shot back, a harsh set of coughs curtailing the end of her sentence.

Raegan exhaled, sinking down to squat with her forearms on the table, as if she were talking to a small child. "Yeah, sort of," she settled on, her gaze flicking to the King, whose expression was impassive.

"Hmph," Maelona said, reminding Raegan so much of Baba Yaga for a moment that her heart almost burst. "And he's . . ." She trailed off, narrowing her eyes at Oberon.

"The Unseelie king," he supplied, leaning back against the stone wall, the firelight making his features all the more inhuman.

"Oh, I know who you are," Maelona replied with a venom that surprised Raegan. Anxiety fluttered in her stomach. Alanna's fear and distrust of the King was one thing. But open hatred was another, and she knew she could only ask Oberon to tolerate so much. "We've met."

At that, Raegan nearly toppled over. Emrys twisted suddenly in his chair, looking at the King. Only Alanna didn't react, slowly sipping from her tea as if she were watching an afternoon play staged in a botanical garden.

Oberon examined Maelona, his lips parting slightly. And then eventually, he said one word. "Prague?"

"Prague," Maelona confirmed with a sneer, taking a huge—and likely searing—gulp of her tea. She wiped her mouth with the back of her hand and reached forward for the sugar bowl. "You almost killed me."

Oberon exhaled in an exhausted, long-suffering way Raegan recognized immediately. "I am sure it would have felt that way to you," he replied, his voice even. But Maelona only scoffed, digging a spoon deep into the sugar bowl. "In truth, I was trying to help."

"As fascinated as I am by the history between you two," Emrys said after a moment of silence, "you indicated you might know where Avalon lies. Is that true?"

Maelona's gaze briefly darted toward Alanna, who nodded, before drifting to meet Raegan's eyes. "There's a dossier of some kind. Despite being a pretty high-ranking field operative, I'm not even supposed to know about it."

"So then how *do* you know about it?" Raegan asked, folding her hands on the table. Emrys shifted in her peripheral vision; the King was barely more than a large shadow.

"Because when you suddenly reappeared after thirty years, I got pulled into a lot of meetings that I normally wouldn't have been involved in," Maelona replied, sitting back in her chair and pulling the woolen blanket tighter around her shoulders. Despite the warmth of the room, a shiver wracked her body. "I kept my ears and eyes open for Alanna. Anything that might be useful to what she's trying to do: explore ally-ship with the Fey in order to overthrow the Protectorate."

Raegan chewed on her bottom lip. So her aunt, despite being heavily entrenched in the Protectorate, was not necessarily bigoted against the Fair Folk—just Oberon. Just the person Raegan loved more than anyone else in the world and who had been very deep inside her only a few hours ago. Good. That was great.

"I would like to know more about this dossier," the King said, prowling a step closer to the table. Maelona watched him carefully from the corner of her eyes.

"Very interested myself," Alanna said, settling her elbows on the table. "We didn't really get to discuss it yet."

"Didn't really have time to," Maelona replied, pausing for a few concerning coughs. "It came up in a few briefings when I was in the States looking for Raegan. But when I got back, all the beatings and interrogations sort of filled up my schedule."

"Do you have any idea of its purpose or why it was created?" Oberon asked, completely ignoring her aunt's dark humor, something in his tone that Raegan couldn't place. His gaze was magnetic and consuming, pulling even Maelona into his orbit. Raegan studied him, her brow furrowing.

"I assume it's because of the prophecy," Maelona replied, all of her attention on the tall, inhuman being looming in front of her. "Keep possible locations heavily surveilled and guarded, or, better yet, find Avalon, destroy the mother of the Fey, and take the weapon first."

Again, ferocity moved across Oberon's face. Unease stirred in Raegan's stomach; there was clearly something she didn't know, which was not her favorite feeling. She picked at her cuticles under the table, her gaze still on the King even when Maelona said something about feeling absolutely insane that she'd rather the Unseelie Court have the weapon than the Timekeeper.

And then, all at once, his eyes were on hers—haunted, hollowed, filled with that endless pain. She looked away, back toward Maelona, only so Alanna would not catch anything. But she took a few moments to refill her cup of tea, moving slowly while her mind raced.

When the realization hit her, Raegan had to disguise her reaction with a cough, as if she'd choked on her tea. Of course—Avalon. Fucking *Avalon.* Where the Once and Future King slumbered until England needed him to murder any and all living creatures who had made the mistake of being born with magic in their blood again. Where the man who had founded the Protectorate, orchestrated so much of Mordred's misery, launched a war against the Fey, and ordered Nyneve's execution slept peacefully, Excalibur forevermore clutched in his hands.

Because there wasn't a more secure prison on the entire planet than a goddess's realm that had long since faded into the perfect disguise: mere legend.

"Do you know where the dossier is?" Alanna asked, sounding slightly breathless. "Because if Raegan and the King could get there, recover that weapon, then . . ."

"Then our little coup might stand a chance," Maelona said with a tight smile. "But unfortunately, it's kept in the Manor." She said the place's name with no small degree of dread.

Alanna's face fell in response, taking Raegan's hope with it.

"The Manor is basically impenetrable," Oberon said, moving to stand behind Raegan, his fingertips brushing her shoulder for a moment. She knew why he'd done it—because she'd been glancing at him too often and they needed to get through this meeting without raising alarms with Alanna. "I have tried more than once. I imagine this dossier is in the Undercroft, yes?"

"I'm uncomfortable with your knowledge of a highly secure Protectorate building," Maelona said with a narrow-eyed glare. "The only thing I know for sure is that there is a single copy and it's held in the

Manor. The Undercroft would make the most sense, but . . . then I have no fucking idea how we would get our hands on it."

But they *had* to. Raegan fought to maintain her composure. Not just because the dossier could significantly shorten their search for Avalon, but because she was suddenly very sure that the Protectorate wasn't just defending possible locations. They were searching, too. And not just to steal a weapon.

They wanted to *awaken* one. Arthur Pendragon, the Once and Future King, in particular. The thought made Raegan ill. Before she'd known him, Arthur had held ideals, or so people claimed—had been a good king, had pulled the world back together after the apocalypse of Rome's exit. But then he'd given it all up in exchange for power. As if he'd needed more.

Her fingernails bit into her palms as her memories of King Arthur turned in their sour graves. He'd feasted while others starved. He'd barred Nyneve from healing peasants when the plague swept through, wanting her available at all times if any of his favored few developed so much as a cough. He'd used magic for his own gain while executing anyone he suspected of witchcraft with no trial, no chance to prove themselves innocent. He'd treated Guinevere—whom Nyneve had loved dearly—with such casual cruelty over not being able to produce an heir, even though he knew any issues with fertility lay squarely at his feet. Worst of all, he had an infuriating way of making his decrees seem completely and utterly reasonable.

And like every shitty man, she remembered with rising rage, he'd found a way to make himself even more powerful: Excalibur. The blade was not just crafted—or altered, apparently—to kill the Fair Folk more easily. It also siphoned power from the Fey and god blood it spilled, granting its bearer magic and powers that were not meant to coexist within one being. That's why the kelpies had tricked Bedwyr into putting his mortally wounded king and Excalibur onto the coracle with a tale about the Lady of the Lake, spun to match the story Merlin himself had concocted about the blade's origins. Bedwyr and the Protectorate had been trying to wake their liege ever since.

The heat of Oberon's touch brushing the back of her neck returned Raegan to her body. She clenched her jaw. She must've drifted too far into her thoughts. God, she wanted to punch something and then sit in a quiet room with a notebook and untangle all of this shit. But everything would fall apart without Alanna, she reminded herself.

"No, that wouldn't work," the shadewalker was saying to Emrys with a frown, turning to look out the window. And then all at once, Alanna sat up very straight, her pretty eyes blown wide. "The Founder's Gala."

Maelona reacted immediately too, the hand reaching for her teacup stilling as her gaze shot to Alanna's. Raegan exchanged a look with Emrys, who just shrugged.

"Could you please elaborate?" Oberon asked from behind her. "I do not see how the existing wards at the Manor would be anything but thornier during an event with the Protectorate's most powerful."

"Oh, they will be," Alanna said, looking over Raegan to meet the King's gaze, a dangerous expression tugging at her full lips. "But the unfavored are always left working during the gala, tasked with sustaining a particularly nasty series of protection spells while the elite party. It's a long, taxing night that's left me unable to do magic for *days* afterward. I'm sure you wouldn't be surprised to hear the vast majority of people assigned to the holding wards are well within my little faction."

"Could that not all be by design, then?" the King asked, to which Emrys nodded vigorously. "Could your leaders not be counting on you to assume that they will be intoxicated and relaxed at this event, and use any failures with the warding as proof of your suspected treason?"

"I understand where you're coming from," Alanna said, tapping her fingertips on the tabletop as she paused in thought. "But you have to understand how oblivious the Protectorate is to threats from within."

"Really?" Raegan asked. "Because they seem . . . paranoid to me. I mean, they ordered Maelona to kill my dad for desertion."

"Only because Cormac had been a problem since he was about twelve, and they thought his motivation was opening the Gates," Maelona cut in, sounding a little stronger, her face less pale. "To acquire more magic. More power."

She paused, and Raegan shoved away any thought of her father at twelve, the tender place in his breastbone already yearning for what he could not have. Maelona spoke again, her expression wry and sour.

"*That's* how they expect us to be corrupted. Bargains with faerie courts or the few gods left alive, offers from wealthy occultists hungry for the real shit. The Protectorate leadership would never expect something like this," she continued. "All they understand is power. And acquiring more of it. The idea that we would collectively band together to *give up* our power for the sake of the world would never cross their minds."

"If we betray our oath to the Protectorate," Alanna began before Raegan really had a chance to process everything Maelona had said, "the binding spell devours our magic. Not just the Timekeeper's boon—any shred of latent ability within us. Even if the Gates open, we'll never be able to do magic again."

Raegan's heart climbed into her throat as she looked between Alanna and her aunt. She hadn't known. She hadn't realized. She never would've thought they'd be willing to give up so much. With a long, shuddering inhale, she considered what it all meant.

And then, for the second time during this meeting, she had an ill-timed revelation. No wonder her father had been forced into bargaining with agents of the Timekeeper. The second he broke his oath by not offering Raegan up to the Protectorate as a baby, all his magic would be gone. How else would he have gotten them out of the country and successfully hidden away? Of course he wouldn't have been able to see the long game—that he was just delaying the inevitable; that whoever he thought might be his savior was just the Timekeeper in sheep's clothing.

Raegan curled her hands into fists beneath the table. All of her father's aching, that open wound he'd hidden beneath whimsical smiles —he had yearned for the same thing she always had, too. And he'd given it up completely for her.

She realized suddenly that she'd need to tell Maelona about Cormac. But for now, Raegan just cleared her throat. "And you're both willing . . ." She looked between Alanna and Maelona. The two exchanged glances and then nodded.

"The gala is Saturday evening. Tomorrow," Alanna said, sitting up straight and folding her hands on the table. "Let me speak with my collaborators. I might be able to get you in. But that's it. It would be on you to navigate the Manor's inner wards, whatever hellish defensive magic is lurking in the Undercroft, and grab the dossier."

Alanna paused, looking between them, her expression deadly. "And

then, of course," she added, "you'd have to manage to get out alive
without a bloody ounce of the King's magic. You understand that, right?
Any Fey magic will trigger the wards, and then the Protectorate will
have something they desperately want right in their hands—the Deathless Witch and the Unseelie king."

Chapter Twenty-Eight

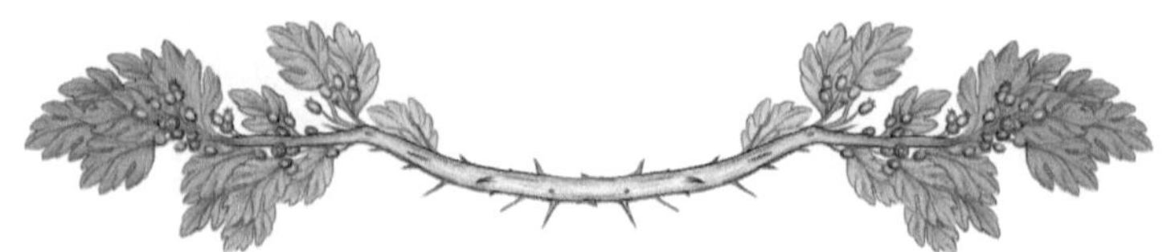

Raegan yanked open a battered steamer trunk that looked like it had survived at least three wars. "Blue velvet box, blue velvet box," she muttered under her breath, reminding herself to be gentle as she sorted through the contents of the trunk.

"Not here," she called, sitting back on her heels. Even though he was far off in the reading room, Emrys's loud curse was still very much audible.

"Nor here," Oberon announced from the other side of the aisle, closing the double doors on a clumsily painted hutch that could have been in any suburban mom's kitchen. He turned to look at her, one eyebrow raised.

"I know," Raegan said, holding up her hands in a peace gesture as she got to her feet. "If we can't find the glamour relics, we won't go."

Oberon opened his mouth to reply, but then Emrys's voice came drifting through the library, shouting directions for another location. "This way," the King said instead, turning on his heel and exiting the aisle. He took a sharp left out of the stacks, leading them deeper into the library. Rain pattered pleasantly on the greenhouse roof, and warm light spilled from the hanging lanterns bolted to the last book-shelf in each row. Emrys had lit a fire in the reading room, and they'd even brought a fresh pot of tea down from the kitchen with them. A perfectly cozy scene in which to desperately search for the one thing that might keep her and Oberon from dying during an ill-advised heist.

Letting out a sigh, the King turned to look at her with an arch, sideways glance. "We should not go at all," he said, slowing as he scanned the shelves on either side of them. "For Modron's sake, Raegan. Will we allow the Protectorate to lure us so easily to our doom? Or perhaps worse, are we willing to locate Avalon *for* them?"

"I know, I know," she muttered in the low light, grabbing the sleeve of his shirt and gesturing to the aisle he'd nearly walked by. "Here, I think."

"Thank you," he replied, stalking into the row of bookshelves and antique display cabinets. "Do you recall what he said?"

"L-142," Raegan replied, gesturing for Oberon to keep going. "Yeah, trust me. This whole thing seems like a really great setup to imprison you and cut off my fucking head again or get us to do their work for them. Probably both. And I'm not ready for something like this, either. I know. I just—"

"You think it is worthwhile," Oberon began, giving her another sideways glance, one eyebrow raised again, "because of your aunt's involvement?"

"Not just that," Raegan huffed, stopping in front of a small metal cabinet. She turned the key that was already in the lock and began hunting, yet again, for a blue velvet box that stored two matching rings. "I think Alanna is being honest with us, too. I mean, did you pick up on anything?"

When the King didn't answer, Raegan looked over her shoulder. In the shadows of the stacks, his eyes were black hollows, the impossibly sharp points of his cheekbones and jaw like daggers beneath the pale skin.

"No," he admitted, though unhappily. "Not anything significant, at least. Truth and intention spellwork is difficult. You know this."

One of the conditions Alanna had for meeting them in the Temple was a bargain promising no harm to either party, including interfering spellwork. She had worded it quite well—at least, for a twenty-something-year-old human with little direct experience with the Fey. But Alanna was dealing with the Unseelie king, and it hadn't taken him long to find a way around the bargain to perform a series of workings intended to gauge her trustworthiness.

"I know," Raegan muttered, holding up a box. "What color is this?"

"Purple," Oberon replied immediately despite the low light.

"If she *thinks* she's telling the truth, the spell counts that as truth," Raegan sighed, putting the box back and pulling out another drawer. "If she doesn't *think* she intends harm, the spell counts that as neutral or positive intentions."

"It would be a clever plan," he murmured, stretching above her to check a top shelf that was well out of her reach. "It is easy to view her actions as incredible risks for a cause she believes in, but if all this was orchestrated by the Protectorate, those risks significantly decrease."

Raegan slammed the drawer with a huff. "Okay, but not really? Like, hello, being around you is a huge risk? No offense."

"The Protectorate, despite their preaching, know I do not kill indiscriminately," he said, pulling out a container before tucking it back into place. "Not typically, anyway."

She rolled her eyes, opening the last drawer. "Even if this *is* all a ruse, the motherfuckers are dumb enough to let us inside the Manor. I think we shouldn't waste that opportunity. Because Oberon, you and I both know that they're . . . they're . . ."

The words caught in Raegan's throat, old memories stirring up like a sudden sandstorm, clouding her vision and stinging her eyes.

"Trying to wake Arthur," he finished for her, stepping back from the cabinet. "Yes, I imagine they are." He met her gaze, and their shared pain stirred between them.

She opened her mouth and then closed it; there was little point in digging up the past. They'd both been there. They'd both been hurt time and time again by Arthur's cruelty, which had grown more ingrained each year. They'd both tried to pull him back from the brink. Arthur hadn't been born evil, but she'd always thought that only made everything worse. They'd both watched a city full of people they loved crumble into despair and war because of one man's choices.

"Why wouldn't Danu or whoever else is on Avalon just kill him? I mean, we're talking about the Mother of the goddamn Fair Folk," she demanded, closing the last drawer—no blue velvet box—and turning to face the King, just in time to see the bitter curve of his mouth.

"He amassed so much power through taking life with Excalibur," he replied, his tone empty. "He would need to be dispatched either by Excalibur itself or something very similar. Another hungry weapon, another blade that siphons the powers of its enemies to its bearer instead. But I do not think there is another."

"And the Fair Folk and gods can't wield Excalibur because it was created to destroy them," Raegan breathed. Then anger surged in her, white-hot. "Jesus fucking Christ."

And sure, she knew a mortal might be able to handle Excalibur like a regular sword, but they wouldn't have the power to actually *wield* it. To open the blade's hungry maw, to take all of Arthur's stolen power back through its tangled web of vicious enchantments.

"Unless you and I can return the faerie blade to its true nature," Oberon sighed. In the orange-hued lantern light, Raegan watched him pinch the bridge of his nose. "Come. Emrys just shouted the next location instead of using any of the multitude of sound projection workings at his disposal."

"Go easy on him," she suggested, following the King out of the row. "He's freaking out."

"I had not noticed," he replied, turning to look over his shoulder, one of those ink-dark eyebrows lifted again, a wry smile on his face. He paused, levity bleeding from his expression. "It does not help that the library's cataloging was Sylvionne's design, which means Emrys is currently searching through a card catalog handwritten by his dead lover."

Raegan paused as the weight of his words caught on her limbs, threatening to drag her down. Though Emrys had devoured her memories of Hiraeth, a series of short but rich images flickered through her mind: blackberry-hued ink, an elegant brown hand dripping in gold jewels, a melodic voice explaining the best way to apply kohl eyeliner.

"Should one of us go through the catalog instead?" she asked in a hushed voice, even though Emrys was far off, breaking into a jog to catch up with Oberon.

"No, I think not," he replied as she drew even with him, gesturing toward the aisle on the right. "It likely allows Emrys to feel close with Sylvionne, which may be needed after he invited the Protectorate into the home they once shared."

Sylvionne's murderers, Oberon did not say. Raegan let out a long breath, her mind still tossing memories she shouldn't even possess onto her shores like the remnants of a shipwreck.

"Why do I feel like I remember him?" she asked, her throat raw, as Oberon led them deeper into the stacks.

At that, the King glanced back, worry creasing his brow in a way that made her heart pang. "You and Sylvionne became quite close in your short time here," he replied, slowing his pace as he began to scan the shelves. Raegan couldn't make out much this deep in the library, the lights dimmer with each row. "He cared for you, and you for him. Strong emotions can tamper with memory spells, no matter how proficient the practitioner. Emrys is the best memory-eater I know, but you feel more intensely than most."

The King came to a halt in front of a slim, towering cabinet. Raegan did her best to shove the unfolding memories of the Temple's murdered Oracle back behind whatever door they'd come tumbling out from. It felt like a dishonor to his memory, but she couldn't carry anything else. No more grief. No more fuel to the fires that already burned too hot in her ribcage.

Oberon ran long-fingered hands down the front of the cabinet in a way that made her irrationally jealous of a piece of furniture. He murmured something under his breath and then conjured a small sphere of light. Déjà vu threatened to devour Raegan—he had done this before, back in the archives when she knew nothing of herself. And another time, somewhere else . . . the memory slipped through her grasp like river water.

"Ahh," the King muttered, pressing a rectangular section of the cabinet, its face heavily carved with stylized berries. A small slot popped open.

Fascinated, Raegan leaned closer, finding a compartment lined with rich blue velvet. She exchanged glances with Oberon, her heart fluttering in her chest. There, nestled in the shimmering fabric, was a key—long and slender, its bow so ornate that Raegan couldn't make out the details in the low light. Oberon gently plucked the key from its resting place, revealing that it was strung on a loop of pale blue silk.

"If this isn't it, I will lose my mind," she announced.

His shoulders shook with a short burst of laughter as he leaned in and unlocked the main compartment. A soft hiss and then two doors fell open, revealing a shallow cabinet shrouded in shadow. Oberon reached in, and time seemed to stand still.

Then he pulled his hands back out, and resting within his palms was a blue velvet box. Like the cabinet itself, it was elegant and slender with a domed lid. Oberon looked over at Raegan, who nodded excitedly. The box opened with only the gentlest touch from the King, revealing two silver rings resting on a bed of silk.

"Fuck," she breathed, leaning closer. Under the faerie light, Raegan could see the rings were indeed silver, but in the same way a chameleon would be silver while crawling in front of a sterling chalice. The edges of the rings bled into the pale silk of the ring box, even pulling in the golden warmth of the King's conjured light in a few places.

"I did not think these still existed," Oberon breathed, one hand hovering, though he did not touch the rings themselves. "Somehow I am not surprised Sylvionne stashed away old Fey relics for safekeeping. The rings are sleeping, and I am unsure if they can be awoken. But if they can—"

"—we might be able to do this." Raegan laughed with wild-eyed glee. Physical glamours—like this set of rings—were impossible to create anymore with so little residual magic left in this half of the world. But that kind of working was the crème de la crème when it came to concealment and espionage.

Physical glamours subverted defensive spellwork because the wearer didn't actually alter their appearance the way most glamour magic worked. Instead, Raegan and Oberon would still look like themselves—nothing would actually change in their physical appearance—but anyone who looked at them would think they were someone else entirely. It was more mind-spellery than anything else, and that was one of the most difficult kinds of magic to detect. And best of all, only the most sensitively attuned wards would read physical glamours like these rings as *active* magic and trigger a response.

The air shifted, the back of her neck prickling as a shiver trailed down her spine. Oberon said something, his long fingers entangling with hers, but Raegan did not hear his words. Something obscured his voice, spiriting it away on bronze wings. All at once, the room filled to the brim with a golden thrum she'd never thought she'd hear again.

Despite the crushed Prophecy she'd seen with her own two eyes in the Oracle's grasp back in Philadelphia, a Fatesong looped through the half-sunken library. Oberon's hand tightened around hers. The hymn was ancient, orchestral, humming with so much want and ache that Raegan wondered if she had not composed the song herself in another life. That tender place in her chest opened wide as if she had never stitched it closed with shaking fingers.

Movement stirred in the corner of her eye, and her mind churned sluggishly, half-expecting Emrys to come barreling around a corner, his eyes wide and wild with the impossibility of it all. But instead, a paper-winged creature floated out of the gloom and down the aisle. It was neither luna moth nor griffin, not falcon nor pegasus, but some terrifyingly beautiful combination of them all. Raegan watched it sail on the looping and lonely notes of the Fatesong, the twin moons at the bottom of its wings blinking in and out of existence.

Her Threads quieted to a low hum as the paper beast landed on the velvet box in the King's hand, perching on the open lid. Its wings beat once, twice, three times. Then the creature floated off into the shadowed gloom of the library, taking the Fatesong with it and ending—as always—with the same haunting note on which it had begun.

Chapter Twenty-Nine

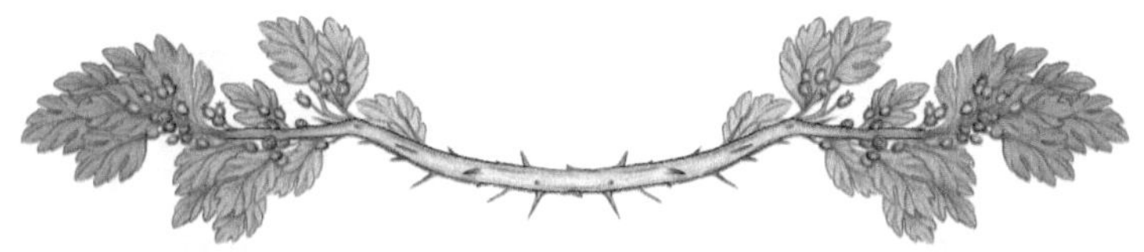

"That is impossible," the King murmured, his head tilted back, the lovely expanse of his neck exposed as he searched the ceilings of the library, like he might find Fate Herself there, held aloft by dove wings.

"How fucking *dare* She," Raegan seethed a heartbeat later, that place in her chest empty now with the Fatesong gone—no, emp*tier* than before. As if each time Fate ran Her fingers along Raegan's threads, the primordial goddess stole something else.

Oberon swung around to face her. Just as Raegan met his eyes, footfalls at the mouth of the stacks rang out and she turned, finding Emrys standing there.

"Did I just hear a Fatesong?" the ex-Keeper shouted, a few card catalogs still clutched in his fist. "There's only dead Prophecies here, tucked away in the drowned halls. I do not understand how this is even—" Emrys cut himself off, his gaze falling on the blue velvet box in Oberon's hands, eyes going wide.

"Yes, you *did* hear a Fatesong," Raegan said, her voice strangled as she remembered the cabinet in the abandoned chamber all at once. "Earlier, when I was researching, I found a cabinet with old Prophecies in it. And—and there was a luna moth, like the Prophecy back in Philadelphia." She paused, looking between Oberon and Emrys, bracing herself for their reactions. "I opened the cabinet because . . . because I'm a piece of shit, I guess, and they all came to life and, like . . . ate each other?"

In the low light of the library, both the King and the ex-Keeper just stared at her, no expression on the ancient planes of their faces. So Raegan took a deep breath and kept going. "I closed and locked the cabinet, and it all stopped. I was coming to tell you, Emrys, but then Maelona was here."

The Keeper's eyes closed and he massaged his temple. "I am no Oracle. The drowned halls of the library can be . . . strange. And if Fate is toying with our Threads, I imagine She *wanted* you there." He shifted his weight, leaning against one of the heavy bookshelves, his metal frames slipping down his nose. "I don't understand it. But I don't think you did any harm. My Temple feels the same as always. And I know my Temple well."

Silence hung heavy in the towering, dark stacks where a Fatesong had just trilled. Raegan swallowed hard, glad that Emrys was not angry. She had no intention of keeping the cabinet and its creatures from him; with all the other bullshit she was busy dealing with, she'd honestly just forgotten until the damn thing had fluttered out in front of them.

"I do not believe we ever will understand," Oberon replied, his voice heavy with exhaustion. "Frankly, I have no interest in cabinets of dead Prophecies or Fate's winged things. Let us see if the glamour relics can be awoken. We will pay no mind to Her abuses."

Raegan set her jaw and, her hand still entwined with Oberon's, began to make her way to the mouth of the aisle. He was right. What point was there in unwinding what this all meant? They had no Oracle, no Seer—they'd left all of that behind in Philadelphia for a quest to end this once and for all. What interest did Fate have in endings? She seemed only to enjoy bringing Raegan back from the grave, waiting just long enough between each life to drive Oberon mad.

"For a million reasons," Emrys said as they reached the main aisle, "I wish Sylvionne were still here."

Raegan reached her free hand out to brush Emrys's shoulder. "I know. Me too. I remember . . . a little. More than I should."

Emrys examined her in the light of the aisle's lanterns, his deep, dark brown eyes glimmering. He opened his mouth and then closed it with a small shake of his head. "I won't entangle your memories further. But I am glad someone else remembers him. He deserves to be carried into the future."

Then the three of them made their way back to the reading room, shoulder-to-shoulder, yet again returning from the deeper, darker places with a sacred jewel in their hands that might just change everything. Maybe this *was* possible—maybe magic could be returned to the world, and maybe it could stitch the earth back together again. Raegan's heart swelled at the thought as she sat in a leather Chesterfield chair at the far end of a large table, watching Oberon's every move as he set the box down.

Across the gleaming surface, their gazes met. Emotion crowded her throat. And maybe one day, she and the faerie king could just *be*. She imagined looking into his eyes over the bursting jewels of their garden, over a candle-laden table surrounded by friends, across a meadow they walked every evening at dusk.

Anything but another battlefield, another graveyard of shattered hope.

Emrys muttered something, breaking the hush of rain and crackling hearth, toggling lenses on the side of his silver glasses. Raegan watched him closely, wondering exactly how the magic worked; there were no visible additions to the frames until Emrys touched his fingertips to metal. She supposed it didn't matter, but that was always how her brain operated—inquisitive, curious, always wanting to understand.

"Yes," the ex-Keeper said, the single word rich with triumph. "Yes, I think there is enough magic to awaken these relics." He pushed his glasses down his nose, looking at Raegan and then the King. "But whether that means we should send you two into the belly of the beast is another thing entirely."

"They want to wake Arthur, Emrys," Oberon replied. "I fear that was always the plan. Put down the initial rebellion, build the Gates, use our resistance as a reason to restrict the flow of magic further and further. Then, once the Gates were closed and all the residual magic gone from this half of the world, they would descend on Avalon to awaken their Once and Future King."

"And I doubt they'll just be interested in this side of the Gates," Raegan said as the realization dawned on her, sending dread creeping through her veins. "With Arthur, they could finally subdue the Other-lands in their entirety."

"Because Arthur was the only thing that came close to destroying the Unseelie Court," Emrys whispered, squeezing his eyes shut. "I mean, we knew this was possible."

"Yes," Oberon replied, placing both palms on the table and then leaning onto the dark, rich surface. "But we did not realize how quickly the residual magic would bleed out."

"I don't think we have a choice," Raegan said, chewing on her bottom lip. "How many sites on your list, Emrys?"

The ex-Keeper shifted uncomfortably, looking down at the glamour relics instead of at Raegan. "Thirty-three on the short list. Almost a hundred on the long list."

Oberon heaved a sigh. "I can go to the Manor alone."

"How the hell would that even work?" Raegan spat, more harshly than she meant. "No magic, Oberon. Fuck, even your aura will have to be rolled up so tightly you'll hardly be able to breathe. How, exactly, are you going to get through the Undercroft's wardings without any Protectorate blood and no magic?"

"You are not oathed," the King reminded her, drawing himself up, his features all the more inhuman in the skittering light of the hearth. "The wards may read you as much of a stranger as me."

"But she's mortal," Emrys chimed in, though he immediately shrank under the intense look Oberon shot him. "The Overhills are an old Protectorate family, Oberon. Even unoathed, she may be able to slip by the wards with a little clever glamouring. But you? Alanna will get you in, and then what?"

Raegan watched as Oberon's jaw clenched, muscles jumping beneath his moonlight skin. His hands gripped the edges of the table too hard, powerful tendons flexing. "I will continue to think it over. I have not made a final decision."

A short rush of fury burned through Raegan, and she slammed an open palm on the table, loud enough to make Emrys jump. "Why do you get the final decision? It's about *me*."

His shadowed, heavy gaze landed on her then, the long column of his body angling toward her. "I have told you before, Overhill," the King snarled, as if they were not lovers, as if she had imagined everything since that night at Gossamer, "a Fey court is *not* a democracy."

She shot out of her chair, a few steps bringing her directly in front of him. The King towered over her, a wall of muscle and ancient power. "And I'm not a member of your fucking court, Oberon! I don't know why I have to keep telling you that. You're not my king. I do not bow to you."

He closed the meager distance between them, a storm brewing on the planes of his face. But Raegan wasn't afraid of him—she never had been. Wasn't that the reason they'd ended up tumbling into each other's beds in the first place? Because the Druid girl sent to Camelot wasn't afraid of the king's bastard son with a heavy Prophecy on his shoulders, who turned out to be something much worse—an embedded Unseelie changeling?

"Why do you *insist* on endangering yourself?" Oberon demanded, his eyes narrowing, though his words were husky around the edges now, soft and raw.

"Why do you think your grief is more important than my agency?" Raegan asked in return, her hands balling into fists at her sides. Anger snaked through her, prodding at the locks of its cage.

At that, the King flinched, his weight shifting away from her, eyes dropping to the boxed rings.

"May I offer an observation?" Emrys asked meekly from the other side of the table.

"No," Raegan and Oberon snapped at the same time. The King dragged a hand through his hair and then pinched the bridge of his nose, eyes closing briefly. Raegan stepped away, straightening the hem of her sweater, the anger cooling inside her. Emotions were bound to run high due to the intensity of their situation, she reminded herself. He wasn't trying to curtail her autonomy; he just loved her more than anyone else ever had, and sometimes that scared the shit out of Raegan.

"I will work on awakening the relics," Oberon said, reaching a hand out, his fingertips brushing the rings for the first time. She palpably felt the relics pulse in return, like an old thing rolling over in its grave to rise again—a sensation she was well familiar with. A glance at Emrys told her that the ex-Keeper felt the same call-and-response of the King's magic to the relics. Raegan let out a long breath.

"I'll see if any couturiers are available last minute," Emrys said, stuffing his hands into the pockets of his chore jacket. "I assume neither of you have evening wear? Maelona said the Founder's Gala is black-tie."

Across the table, Oberon shook his head, the weight of his attention on the slim filigree rings.

Raegan glanced at Emrys. "Nothing black-tie, no. I'm assuming we should limit our glamours beyond the relics, right?"

"Thank you, Emrys," Oberon replied without looking up. "Raegan is correct. Appropriate attire would be helpful, as our appearance should be as unaltered as possible. The relics work best on their own without interference."

For a moment, anger nipped at Raegan's insides—was he trying to make some kind of a sly comment about not needing her for the gala? She opened her mouth and then closed it. She could not push him away by twisting his words and assuming ill intent. She didn't *want* to, not actively—but her survival mechanisms were strange things with a life and bite of their own.

"Emrys," the King added, glancing up. "Could I borrow your glasses for a moment before you go?"

The ex-Keeper nodded, handing Oberon the slim metal frames, briefly explaining how they worked. Raegan grasped at the information, her curiosity sparking, but the second the glasses settled on the King's face, all intelligent thoughts went out of her body. Fuck. Why did he look so *good* in his casual suit, no waistcoat, the white shirt unbuttoned at the collar, and those glasses perched on the end of his aquiline nose?

She chewed on the inside of her cheek. Didn't he realize she didn't want to leave him either? That every time she tangled her body with his, she knew she was only cutting deeper and deeper into his wound? The fierceness with which she desired him was a double-edged sword. Every moment they were together, Raegan was asking the King to love something he knew he was going to lose.

Oberon handed the glasses over the table with a few words of thanks, and then Emrys disappeared down the long hallway that connected the library to the great room and living quarters. A heavy silence descended, squeezing her insides.

"I apologize. I do not seek to curtail your autonomy," the King said just when Raegan felt like she might burst. He looked up from the rings, both palms flat on the table, his hips hinged over the edge. Hunger stirred low in Raegan's belly as she took in the way his suit jacket strained against his broad shoulders.

"I know," she replied in a low, raw whisper. "I'm sorry for saying that."

One of his powerful shoulders moved in a shrug at the same time a smile ghosted his lips. "No need. I admit there is a part of me that enjoys it when you are angry with me."

She leaned away from the table with a grin, crossing her arms. "Is that so?"

"Not when it is serious, of course," the King clarified. Raegan was delighted to see a pale blush blossom on his face. "Only in these minor disagreements. Few dare to argue with me, and there is a certain . . . thrill, I suppose."

"That's good," Raegan said, uncrossing her arms and prowling toward Oberon, chin tilted up to meet his eyes. "Because I'm going to do whatever I want. I don't care what you say. You're not my king."

She raised a hand and flattened her palm on his chest, giving what would've been a solid push to anyone else, but the King did not budge at all. He did, however, gaze down at her, those oceanic eyes all-consuming, the hard lines of his body gone predatory, his breathing rapid.

"I'm not afraid of you," Raegan whispered, curling her fingers into the front of his shirt, holding his gaze all the while. "In fact, you can be as terrifying as you want. I'm not going anywhere."

The words barely felt like they had finished leaving her mouth when the King seized her in his grasp. In one fluid movement, he pulled Raegan against him and lifted her onto the worktable. Woodsmoke and autumn rain surrounded her as desire beat a drum between her legs, faster and faster.

"Still not afraid of you," she breathed, even as she felt the might of his magnificent body, even as his large hands took the back of her sweater in fistfuls.

"No," the King echoed, breathless, "you are not." And then he swooped low and kissed her, the taste of him like folklore and revenge. She wrapped her thighs around his hips, welcoming the way he pressed her into the table, the weight of him sending damp want howling through her core. He kissed her like it might save them both, like he wanted to devour her whole, like his love could hold off her always-waiting grave.

Raegan wound her fingers into his hair, pulling him closer. The hard evidence of his desire pressed against the apex of her legs, and she let out a strangled moan.

"Fate can sing whatever songs She wishes," the King murmured, his mouth trailing down her neck, the heat of his words like a flame against her skin. "You are mine."

"Yes," Raegan gasped as he slid one hand into her hair, his palm cupping her skull, his other arm wrapped around her hips. Then the King dragged her closer, her thighs opening wider for him of their own accord.

In the hush of a forgotten library where a Prophecy had awoken from its grave, he leaned close, a promise falling from his tongue. "And I am yours forevermore, my love."

Chapter Thirty

Raegan sucked in a breath, desperately trying to avoid the cold pinch of steel. She felt like she'd been trapped here for hours, every muscle in her body screaming for release. Her arms trembled from being held at an uncomfortable angle, hovering above her sides like broken wings.

"Okay," the couturier, Monette, said as she stepped back, running her critical gaze over Raegan. "That'll do it. Take a look and tell me what you think."

With a sigh of relief, Raegan let her arms fall against her sides and turned toward the full-length mirror on the opposite wall.

"Well, fuck me," she sputtered, her mouth falling open. The gown that the Fey seamstress had just finished pinning was *glorious*—almost too beautiful for its purpose. She ran her hands across the sumptuous fabric, wishing she could be wearing such a heart-stopping creation to attend a faerie fete instead of infiltrating the Protectorate's Founder's Gala.

Whisper-light storm-gray silk swept across her body, gathering in a tauntingly low neckline before looping over her shoulders, providing plenty of support for her full bust. A dramatic slit displayed one generous thigh, the rest of the long skirt fluttering to the floor in artfully uneven pieces. An ethereal train floated down from her waist, soft as mist. Across the bodice, just under her bust, tiny blood-red jewels dripped down irregularly like a bloodstain. The gown was terrifyingly and impossibly beautiful.

"Do you like it?" the couturier inquired, rearranging the pieces of silk that made up the short train.

"It's incredible," Raegan breathed, turning slightly to take in the low dip of the garment's back. Leave it to the Fey to figure out how to make a dress with a low back *and* deep neckline that somehow still provided enough internal support for a large bust. "You're extraordinarily talented."

The Fey couturier beamed in response. "I wish I could know more about my very beautiful mystery client," Monette said with a sly smile, coming to stand beside Raegan to consider the dress in the mirror. "But you are hardly the first to request such discretion. So, alas, I shall keep quiet about one of the most lovely things I've ever made."

Monette had meant the words playfully, but a pang of guilt still sounded in Raegan's chest. Much like Oberon, she hated hiding from the residents of Hiraeth, even if it was for their own good. She hated the short, sparse missives from Philadelphia that grew more alarming every day. The Protectorate's siege there had only intensified in an attempt to draw the King out of hiding. The Unseelie Court had expected that eventuality and prepared for it, but Raegan hated knowing her friends and comrades were fighting for their lives across the ocean while she languished in relative safety.

Well, at least for the moment.

She turned, pleased with how easy it was to move in the dress, as the couturier spoke an incantation to finalize the stitching on the garment. In just a few hours, Raegan and the King would attempt to steal the dossier on Avalon. Trying to keep her suddenly clammy palms away from the silk, Raegan thanked the designer again and dismissed her. Downstairs, Emrys would pay Monette and then devour her memory.

Raegan allowed herself another moment to take in the way the dress hugged her curves like a lover. She hoped with all her heart that it was not the garment she'd die in.

~

An hour later, thoughts of death still circled her like buzzards. Raegan shifted uncomfortably, rolling her shoulders as she watched her aunt take a seat at the Temple's heavy wood table. She probably should've told Maelona about Cormac already. But when had there been a moment to tell Maelona that any hope she might secretly hold for Cormac was wasted? That Raegan had watched her father dissolve into nothing, the Timekeeper devouring everything he'd ever been? As if he'd never been anything but a corpse ripe for harvesting?

"Your last meal, as requested," Emrys said, jarring Raegan from her thoughts as he slid a beautifully prepared bowl of ramen in front of her. But she just stared blankly, her mouth not quite able to form words. "I suppose that was funnier when you weren't less than an hour from leaving for the Manor."

"Something like that," Raegan replied, picking up a chopstick and poking at a thin slice of beef. "Thank you, Emrys. Seriously. I really appreciate it."

Maelona leaned closer, sniffing like a bloodhound. "Well, if you can't eat it, I certainly will."

"No nerves around your last living relative possibly being murdered tonight?" Raegan asked, looking up at her aunt, who frowned.

"When you put it like that," Maelona began, twisting her mouth, "I suppose my appetite is a bit shit, too."

The side door to the Temple opened, and the King appeared with Alanna at his side. They were so clearly not comfortable with each other, Alanna looking like she was walking beside an enormous predator who hadn't eaten her yet for reasons she could not begin to comprehend, the King trying too hard to hide his inhumanity, lest it send her running. Raegan snorted. It was kind of amusing, actually.

"Alright," Alanna said by way of greeting, coming to stand at the head of the table. She gently pushed aside a plate piled high with bean sprouts and artfully sliced pickled eggs. Maelona snatched up the bowl of ramen Emrys had wordlessly handed her. Then Alanna unfurled a large piece of parchment on the table. Raegan leaned closer, peering at the charcoal lines in the dancing candlelight.

"There are no blueprints of the Manor, for obvious reasons," Alanna said, using a candlestick to pin the sketch down. "So this is what Maelona and I came up with from memory."

Alanna—with interjections from Maelona—walked them through the single entry point for the gala, as well as all the security measures. None of that was particularly of concern. If the Unseelie king and the Queen of the Hill simply wanted to slip into a Protectorate gala to fuck around, it wouldn't be hard, particularly with Alanna's help. But getting into the Undercroft and the secure vaults was another thing entirely.

"Besides the general gist, I can't tell you a ton about it," Alanna said, frowning. "Our wards are complicated. Actually, probably not that different from your own—protective spells added to again and again over the ages to the point they're nearly sentient. They will sense Raegan's bloodline and the intention of any magical acts. You'll need to be clever. But that's all I can tell you."

"I wish I could say I knew much more," Maelona added woefully. "But it's above my pay grade. I'm a special ops soldier, essentially. Commanders tell me to jump, and I ask how high. That's it. Alanna's right about the wards, though. And they're more intense in the Undercroft."

Alanna gestured at a section of harrowingly long and circular corridors that burrowed deep into the earth below the Manor. "There's checkpoints all throughout. Sentient spellwork, glamour-eaters, gods only know what else. My oath would prevent me from going past the research archives—that's on level two—and I think Maelona's would halt her somewhere around level six. You need to get to the very bottom floor of the Underbelly. Level twelve."

"Great," Raegan replied, her mouth dry, the whole thing much more dizzying when sketched out in charcoal and paper, taking up nearly the entire surface of a massive table.

"I still don't think you should go," Maelona said, looking at Raegan.

"On that, we agree," Oberon replied without hesitation. Her aunt and the King exchanged glances of pleasant surprise, naturally bonding over telling Raegan what to do, of all things.

"Too bad," she said through gritted teeth. "Not even the Unseelie king is getting through all of this shit with zero magic. And I'll be able to do *some* magic in there."

Beside her, Oberon let out a long sigh but did not refute her statement.

"My people are in place and know to expect you, though of course most are unaware of the details," Alanna said, stepping back from the table and clasping her hands behind her back. She looked formidable, dangerous, but in the shifting beeswax light, Raegan could see the worry on her too-young brow. "Maelona will be on standby, hidden in the wooded parkland across from the Manor, just in case everything goes to hell. She can help you navigate the compound if it comes to it, but ideally, you'll leave with the kelpies' help through the Rivers. You'll have a few minutes—at most—after triggering the wards to get out. Use them wisely."

The five people bound together by a shared audacity that they might be capable of killing a god sat silently around the table. Raegan's blood thudded in her veins. She picked up her spoon and tried to shovel some broth into her mouth, but her stomach revolted.

"I have attempted to follow much more foolish plans before," Oberon said, looking over the parchment.

"Yeah, well, not all of us were made by goddesses and the night sky or whatever," Maelona grumbled, poking at her ramen. "Mortals are a bit more fragile."

Oberon flinched and then tried to hide his reaction by straightening the collar of his shirt. But Raegan caught it and her heart clenched. He knew precisely how fragile mortals were. He'd watched her die more times than she wanted to count. He knew *exactly* what he was risking. The King looked at Maelona and then Alanna. Raegan recognized that feral, predatory glint in his eyes and opened her mouth to speak, but it was too late.

"Yes, mortals *are* more fragile. Understand that if Raegan is harmed tonight due to either of your actions," the Unseelie king said softly, a palpable chill taking root in the air, "I will tear the flesh from your bones and feed you to the kelpies."

Maelona froze, her jaw grinding as she glanced at Alanna, who had also stiffened. There was a part of Raegan that wanted to placate or make a joke out of Oberon's fierceness, but she couldn't deny the heat unspooling low in her belly. She let out a long, shuddering breath and crossed her legs.

"Trust me, I don't want to see Raegan hurt any more than I want to be fed to kelpies," Alanna said, all business, ignoring the tense hush that had settled over the table. And then she softened, her eyes meeting Raegan's. "We can pull this off. And when we do, we'll have a map to a weapon that can finally take the Timekeeper from his unearned throne."

Raegan smiled and gave Alanna a firm nod, but when the shade-walker turned to leave to make her own preparations, she felt a shred of relief. They needed Alanna's assurance and steadfast fierceness that the world could be changed. But the four left at the table—Emrys, Maelona, Oberon, and Raegan—understood too much of the toll that hope took from her victims. To imagine a newer, better world was a beautiful thing. To have it taken away before it even had a chance to bloom was a gut wound that never quite stopped bleeding.

But time was running out, magic was dying, and there were no better options. So Raegan forced some bok choy and noodles into her mouth before getting to her feet.

"I'm going to get dressed," she said. As she expected, the King stood beside her, forever the shadow to her defiant flame.

"I should as well," he said, slipping his hand around hers. They left Emrys and Maelona at the table and headed for their chambers. A charged silence hung between them as they climbed the stairs, Raegan's mouth dry and her heart racing all the while. The anticipation was the worst part, she repeated to herself. Soon, her mind would be dedicated to real-time calculations, split-second decisions, and nothing else.

But for now, as they entered their quarters, the nature of what Raegan and the King were about to do strung the air tight around them like a spiderweb. The gorgeous room—all dark, gleaming wood, rich velvets, and wide windows—suddenly felt like a coffin as they changed into their gala attire. For a moment, she fussed with her curls as the King awaited her silently, the blue velvet box clasped in one hand.

"I'm ready," Raegan finally said, though she had never felt less ready for anything in her life.

Oberon turned toward her, the moonlight breaking through Hiraeth's clouds dipping him in silver. He was statuesque in an all-black tuxedo, the tailoring of the garment absolute perfection.

"You look magnificent," Raegan breathed, her heart racing.

Oberon offered her a slight smile, the gentlest curve of his shapely mouth. "And you are a vision," he murmured, one hand reaching out to trace her jaw.

"How do these physical glamours work?" Raegan asked instead of saying that maybe they should just disappear and leave the world-saving to someone else for a change.

"Quite well, actually," Oberon replied, lifting the domed lid. He'd been adding to the existing spellwork and testing the rings most of the morning while Raegan attempted to get a few hours of sleep. "They are designed to function as a pair, which is fascinating. It is best if I recite the activation rite for yours and vice versa."

"Sure," Raegan said with a shrug, not really grasping exactly what he meant. She just took another step toward him, clenching her jaw and trying to force her heart to beat slower, calmer, to find that river deep within.

They stood facing each other, heads bowed over the domed box, as Oberon told her the rite. It was short and sweet, though she had to repeat the High Feyrish a few times to make sure she had the pronunciation correct. Then the King went first, reaching for her hand as he recited the words.

And all at once, Raegan realized—here she stood in the most beautiful dress she'd ever worn, Oberon before her in a garment that showed off all his sharp, inhuman angles instead of hiding them away, speaking ancient words and slipping rings onto each other's fingers. A violent flood of sorrow roared through her chest. They'd tried to marry, more than once, but Fate always called Raegan back to the soil before the words could be exchanged, the vows made.

Oberon slid the ring onto her finger—not her left hand, no, but it hardly fucking mattered—and shifted away slightly. She choked on the sorrow, on the ache, her dress suddenly weighing a thousand pounds, as if the silk had been spun from her own heavy grief. Raegan forced herself to look up at him. The King's expression softened the moment he saw the tears brimming on her lashes.

"Oh," he murmured, so much feeling in a single syllable. "Nyneve. I —I did not think—"

"It's fine," she replied in a hoarse whisper, patting the tears away, not wanting to smear her eyeliner. "Let's just finish."

Raegan reached into the blue velvet box—fuck Fate and the gods; it was literally borrowed and blue—and palmed the second ring. She said the incantation, doing her best to remove the actions from any kind of meaning. Just words, just a ring, just a glamour. Not another stinging reminder of what they couldn't have.

When she'd finished, Raegan shrank away from Oberon, stumbling back to sit on the edge of the bed. She forced herself to breathe. "How does it look?" she asked, biting down on her tongue as soon as she finished speaking.

The King only sighed. Silence overtook the room, thick and oppressive. And then, finally: "Excellent. Emrys will be the final test. He knows the diplomats' identities we have chosen to borrow."

"Okay," Raegan said, misery latching hooks into her chest. She couldn't breathe. She couldn't see. She couldn't think. "I just need a minute. I'm sorry. I know that's ridiculous."

"It is not," Oberon murmured, suddenly kneeling before her, the heat of him washing over her like the first rays of spring sun after an endless winter. "Not at all." He took her hand in his, bringing it to his chest, where he cradled her palm as though it was a wounded bird.

She looked at him through watery eyes, and her heart only broke a little more. She'd wormed her way into his heart and created an empty space he could never fill. The Unseelie Court would be so much less compromised, their king more focused, if only all those years ago she hadn't fallen in love with someone who did not think he could be loved.

And yet, Raegan was a selfish creature as much as Oberon was a monstrous one, so the only words that came out of her mouth clung to a future that would never come to pass. "If we survive this—all of it, I mean, not just tonight—if the Gates fall and we live to see that world, would you, High King of the Unseelie Court, do me the honor of marrying me?"

She wanted to take the words back as soon as she said them. God, was there no end to her cruelty? Raegan stuttered through her tears, trying to walk back what she'd said, but the King only held her gaze. Then he let go of her hand and reached up to trace his fingertips over her mouth. The all-consuming sensation of his touch distracted her, and the words died in her throat.

"My love," Oberon murmured, studying her, "do you so fervently wish to make a widower of me?"

A sob gathered like a storm in Raegan's chest, but she forced it down. Her hands shook. "No. Gods, *no*, Oberon, that's—"

"Every part of me aches to say yes," the King said, that inhuman ferocity prowling onto his features. "But you understand the weight of a Fey union. I—I do not know if I am strong enough to endure losing that, Raegan."

"Right," she stuttered, her face bright red and hot as a flame, looking down at her hands. "I know. Fuck, I know. I know it's a bond for life, and I know how horribly it affects the Fair Folk when their spouse dies."

She absolutely did, all of her knowledge deciding just now to release itself from the recesses of her mind. Commitments among the Fey were not unusual, but marriage was. The ceremony was intense and binding for the Fair Folk—much more than a pretty dress and nice dinner and a signed piece of paper.

Raegan exhaled, digging her nails into her palms as she forced herself to look up and meet the King's gaze again. "That was fucking stupid of me. I'm sorry. I didn't— I just mean that I love you with everything that I am."

"I appreciate the sentiment," Oberon murmured, one eyebrow arched. "And I return it threefold. You know that, yes? That all of me belongs to you. That I was not even created with the capacity to love, and yet I love you eternally."

"I know," Raegan said, not managing to raise her voice above a whisper. She roughly shoved tears off one of her cheeks and moved to do the same on the other side before the King caught her wrist. With his free hand, he pulled an inky black handkerchief from his waistcoat pocket and dabbed her tears away in impossibly, absurdly gentle movements. She shivered.

"I'm fine," she said a few moments later, straightening. "We need to go."

"We do," Oberon replied, fingertips brushing the underside of her jaw. "Let your sorrow sharpen you. Let it feed that flame in your belly."

His words danced like a lightning storm across her skin, and Raegan pushed herself to stand. "You're right," she said, as if she were not little more than broken pieces. "If they won't grant me peace, then I'll take my revenge."

Chapter Thirty-One

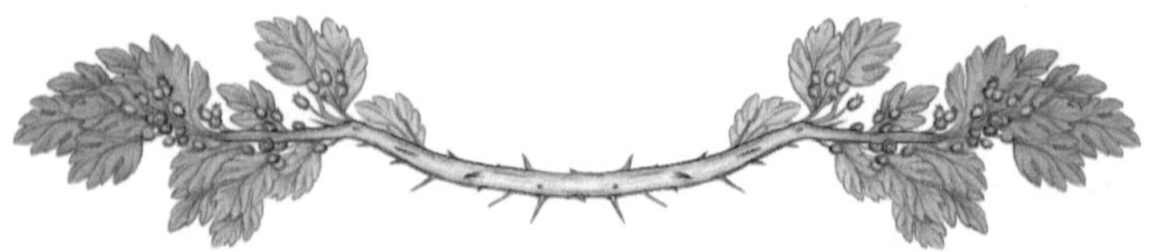

With each heavy, anxious thud of her heart, Raegan reminded herself of the glamours. She and Oberon had made it through the first two checkpoints into the Protectorate compound. In all likelihood, they'd make it through the third. After all, Emrys hadn't recognized them when they came into the great room, even though he'd been expecting the glamours and they still very much looked like themselves. None of that mysterious toggling of his lenses revealed anything—except that the latent magic in the rings had been fully awoken and bent to Oberon's will.

But fuck, every glance from the people milling about sent a spike of fear through Raegan's chest. She bit down on her tongue, wrapping the King's overcoat tighter around her body. November's approach had turned evenings into cold, shivering things, but her leather jacket looked absurd with the dress. A fine wool overcoat about four sizes too large draped over her shoulders, clearly belonging to the beautiful man at her side—now *that* was more acceptable.

"I was having a little more fun last time we dressed up," Raegan murmured, knowing the King's sharp hearing would catch her words. He chuckled and looked at her sideways, something ravenous in his gaze. For a moment, it transported her back to that evening at Gossamer, which felt as though it could've been another life entirely.

"I must agree," Oberon replied dryly, taking a few lazy, long-legged steps forward as the queue of gala attendees moved. The gravel crunched under his feet, pulling Raegan from her memories.

She frowned, staring down at her feet. "Why do rich people always have gravel?" she wondered under her breath.

"There are many things I do not understand about these people," he replied, his voice right in her ear, tone edged in something hard.

She didn't either. The compound was located in the Lake District, a breathtakingly gorgeous area of England. But as she peered around the queue and took in what she could see of the estate, Raegan noticed immediately that the natural beauty of the land was hardly emphasized, let alone respected.

Beyond the courtyard they were standing in, the Manor waited like a camouflaged beast, crouched in the shadow of the mountain behind it. The massive stone building hummed in a way that made her head hurt. The wards, the battle magic surely embedded into the walls and grounds —all of it stolen and twisted. Barely magic at all, really. The entire compound seemed to be made of sweeping, imposing stone and cutthroat angles. A low-lying series of manicured hedges interspersed the gravel, their long, sharp lines creating a labyrinth—or a killing field.

Only the Manor stood tall, its turrets clawing into the night sky. Raegan had a soft spot for antique buildings. But not this one—not even dressed up for festivities with twinkling lights and red banners draped across the boxwoods.

The queue shifted ahead of her, and she was treated to a much more pleasing sight.

"Oh, there's Alanna," Raegan said in a tone that she hoped sounded like someone spotting a work colleague. But gods, what a relief it was to see Alanna—stern-faced, her hair flattened against her skull in a severe braid—at the main security checkpoint. She'd do her part and get them through, glamour intact and undetected. It was also a comfort that Raegan and the Unseelie king were standing in a large crowd of high-ranking Protectorate and no one had given any indication they'd noticed a glamour in their midst. People had hardly looked their way.

Well, no, that wasn't true. More than one man had stared long and hard at Raegan's body, to the point she had become concerned Oberon was going to expose them before they even got inside. The King had plenty of admirers, but they were mostly women and took their pleasures in smaller morsels, sneaking glances at the tall, lithe, dark-haired creature in his perfectly tailored tuxedo. All preferable to someone pointing at them and screaming about enemies infiltrating the Manor.

The queue moved sluggishly, and Raegan took another step forward, catching the scent of expensive perfume on a fur coat. Otherwise, the night air was crisp and cold with late autumn. She chewed on the inside of her lip, tracing the ornate details of the silver ring that took up her entire middle finger on her right hand. It was jointed in the middle and strongly reminiscent of armor, delicately inscribed with ancient spellwork. The rings had been small bands in the box, but once awakened, became something else entirely. She could relate.

"Pity Alanna has to work so hard this evening," the King said into her skin, his mouth moving against her neck, skin exposed by the simple yet elegant hairstyle she'd coaxed her curls into.

Raegan shivered, leaning closer into him. Then the line moved again and they were nearly at the last security checkpoint. So far, so good—unless, of course, they'd already been detected and the Protectorate had decided to let them dig their own grave. Raegan swallowed that thought down.

"A pity indeed," she replied, feeling like that might be how the French ambassador she was impersonating would talk. It didn't actually matter; the physical glamour would change the way everyone perceived her, including her speech patterns and accent.

A large group was waved through ahead of them. And then Raegan and Oberon were standing face to face with a line of heavily armed Protectorate operatives, as well as a few dressed like Alanna who seemed to be doing the inspections for glamour and weapons. *And* holding the wards. No wonder all of them looked a little unsteady on their feet, dark circles stamping their eyes. That was just like the Protectorate, wasn't it? Exhaust the people keeping them safe for the sake of exerting more power.

"Good evening," Alanna greeted, her voice at least an octave higher than usual. "I'm just going to look you over for any unauthorized spellwork while my colleague checks for weapons, alright?"

Oberon nodded his consent, and Raegan did the same, realizing Alanna didn't recognize them—an absolute mindfuck considering their appearance hadn't actually changed. But then Alanna's gaze connected with the glamour ring on Raegan's finger. For the briefest of moments, her eyes widened, but Raegan was sure she only caught it because she was already looking. The rings were the tell they'd agreed on. Alanna had no idea what the rings actually were, though she now certainly understood more about the kind of magic the Fey still had at their disposal.

She watched them a little too intently as she completed her spell-work, but scrutiny of foreign ambassadors from another country's paranormal and magic regulation organization was probably not going to raise any red flags. And then she waved them through. Oberon slipped his arm back into Raegan's and followed the flagstone pathway through severely pruned hedges to the mouth of the Manor.

Raegan found herself digging her fingers into the King's arm. All of her instincts told her to flee. The closer she drew to the building, the more she felt the wrongness of it leach out into the ground—the stolen magic, the god-granted oaths, the perversion, the power. The enormous front doors were thrown open wide. With the cold air nipping at her, Raegan should've wanted to pass over the threshold into the brightly lit and undoubtedly warm foyer. But she'd weather any chill if it meant staying away from this goddamn place.

"I know," the King murmured in her ear. "Steady, love." Then he pulled back and smiled at her as if he'd just offered a flirtation instead. She tried to match his expression but worried it looked too garish, so she settled for what she hoped was a soft smile and not a grimace.

A tangle of black-tie-wearing bodies thronged around the entrance. Despite the chaos, a doorman greeted them and offered to take Oberon's coat. Raegan exchanged words briefly with someone who complimented her dress, and then they were moving through the foyer. The ceilings were absurdly high, a marble staircase snaking around the sides. She squinted in the light of the enormous chandelier and noticed about twenty gunmen lining the staircase, stock-still in the shadows.

"Lovely," she muttered, directing her gaze in front of her instead. The floors were wide, flat stones, worn down over centuries. They moved through a hallway with a few doors—all white with dull gilding—and then followed a length of red rope to a ballroom. As they walked, hopefully long-dead Protectorate men leered down at her from ten-foot-tall portraits. Wall sconces with spindly candles brought their features to life, shifting in the illumination.

"Well, I hate it here," Raegan whispered, her tension easing a little when Oberon laughed, turning to look at her with an amused expression.

"Ahh," he exhaled, pulling her closer against him. "Cannot say I am surprised."

For a moment, Raegan watched him, equally impressed and disturbed by the ease with which he moved about the stronghold of the people who had been trying to kill him for a thousand years. Yes, when she looked closely, she could see the notch between his eyebrows, but she knew him better than anyone and it took even her a moment to find. Otherwise, the King was all fluid grace, drawing appreciative glances, moving about the space as if it belonged to him. She swallowed. His rage had always been different than hers, simmering in his depths, only released when he knew for sure that everyone would drown in his tide.

"Welcome to the Founder's Gala," greeted a woman in a shimmering dress at the double doors that led to the ballroom. She stood behind a small table laden with what appeared to be ribbons. After looking closely at both of their faces, she waved her hand over the table and then handed them a pair of blue ribbons. Brass tags at the top were engraved with the names of the married couple from Contre La Sorcellerie, France's magical enforcement agency, whose identity they were borrowing. The kelpies had promised to ensure the mortal couple "would not be permitted to depart their hotel." Raegan had not taken the time to question by what means.

"Same color system as last year," the woman explained sweetly. "Just so we all know each other's roles! Always so many faces on the night of the gala. Have a great evening!"

Oberon thanked her and affixed the ribbon to his lapel.

"Hold on," Raegan said, struggling to find a good place to pin hers. What a stupid idea—tell people to dress in black tie and then ask them to shove a pin through their garments?

The King swept Raegan to the side of the ballroom, near more of those off-white and dull gold walls. "May I?" he asked, leaning over her in that way she liked so much.

Raegan glanced up at him, briefly distracted by his mouth before nodding. "Thanks." He nodded, sliding the pin around the strap of her dress without actually piercing the silk. "Oh," she muttered. "I guess I should have thought of that."

"You are nervous. I am always happy to serve you," Oberon replied, his gaze hot and intense on hers before he swept his eyes around the ballroom.

Raegan quelled the warmth low in her belly and followed suit, hoping to get a feel for their surroundings beyond what Alanna and Maelona had sketched out in charcoal. A waiter passed by and offered them champagne, which Raegan took mostly so she would have something to do with her hands while she looked around.

Despite the glittering chandeliers and the sashes of blood-red fabric draped everywhere and the rococo moldings and the white tablecloths glimmering with fine silverware, it felt more like a cavern than anything else. Like the deeper she went into this place, the more terrifying the creatures sheltering within its walls would become. She knew the entryway into the Undercroft was farther down the hallway from the ballroom's entrance, and she'd seen the line of soldiers standing stock-still, blocking any passage. For a moment, panic fluttered helplessly between her ribs, nervous sweat pooling on her lower back. Raegan had no idea how they were going to get this done.

"Steady," Oberon reminded her a heartbeat later, his thumb stroking the back of her hand. "Let us get our bearings first. One task at a time."

Raegan nodded, smiling as if he'd said something amusing, taking a swig of her champagne. With a long inhale, she swept her gaze across the room. Maelona's summation of the meanings behind the colors and styles of the ribbons pinned to everyone seemed to track with what Raegan saw.

"It looks like Maelona was right," she said to the King in a low murmur. "Blue for outside but friendly organizations. Red for Protectorate. The small swags are for spouses, the larger ribbons for oathed members. The golden crossed sword ornament is for titled officials. The wide black stripe is for top leadership."

"Seems accurate," Oberon replied, slipping his arm around her waist. The feeling of his fingers splayed across her belly eased a knot of tension in Raegan's chest. She tried to breathe deeper, looking around as if she were enjoying the view and not calculating how to destroy everything this place stood for.

With both relief and a dash of anger, Raegan noticed that only a few women had the gold ornament on their ribbons; none bore the wide black stripe. The majority of the women milling about the room in glittering gowns bore ribbons marking them as spouses or members of other organizations. The few women with the gold swords reminded her of Maelona, actually—not so much in appearance but more so in the way they moved about the space, stiff and alert, eyes darting this way and that. By contrast, the men with similar ribbons laughed and slumped, grabbing a third or fourth champagne flute from a passing tray.

Protectorate guards dressed like Alanna—tactical black clothing, weapons on their belts, combat boots—prowled the ballroom, arms clasped behind their backs. The first time one came near, Raegan thought the pounding of her heart would give her away. But the operative only offered them a nod before moving on.

Even so, Raegan's anxiety didn't cease. This place was well-organized, well-resourced, and remarkably well-fortified. What kind of magic would they have to work to actually get from the ballroom to the Undercroft? Would she even be capable of it? Yes, she was getting stronger every day, but her progress was infuriatingly slow—and she did not want to let Oberon down. Again. Or, worse, get them both killed.

"We talked a lot about getting into the Manor and navigating the Undercroft," Raegan muttered, leaning into Oberon, tilting her chin up so the crown of her head rested on his chest. "Not so much about how we get inside the Undercroft in the first goddamn place. How much magic and spellwork are we talking? Because . . ." She trailed off, embarrassed.

"Oh, *cariad*. Be sensible," Oberon replied with a lazy smile, his expression gone heavy-lidded as he met her gaze. "We are going to seduce our way in."

CHAPTER THIRTY-TWO

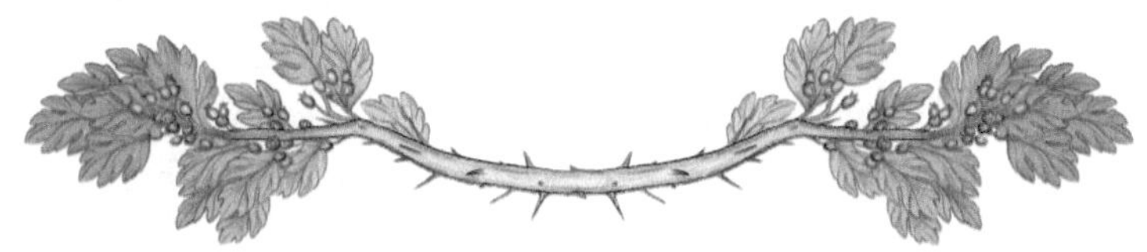

A thrill slunk through Raegan, banishing the anxiety. "Oh," she murmured, raising a brow as she slid out of Oberon's grasp to turn and look up at him. "I'm quite capable of *that*. Why didn't you tell me earlier?"

The King's full mouth parted. The gray of his eyes was all molten heat, amusement rolling across his expression in a way that made her feel light-headed. He reached out a capable hand, cupping her jaw in his palm. Her knees went weak.

"What was there to discuss?" he murmured, closing the distance between them, gazing down at her with the intensity of an inferno. He tilted his head to one side, studying her. A flame ignited in Raegan's core, white-hot. The King—this beautiful, impossible thing—found her so irresistible that the idea of anyone not falling under her spell was absolutely foreign to him.

"Won't you be jealous?" she asked playfully, tugging at his jacket lapels.

Instantly, Oberon's palm flattened against her ass, pulling her hips against his thighs. "Extremely," he replied, his mouth brushing hers.

"Espionage as foreplay," Raegan said, trailing her fingers down his chest. "I'm in." And with that, she disentangled herself from his arms and began to stalk farther into the ballroom.

She moved slowly, like it was a dance, stopping to compliment people on their outfits, asking what *exactly* was in that canapé, greeting other attendees with blue ribbons. And she watched. Raegan cataloged the way people grouped themselves, whose features grew hungry when she passed by, who lingered on the fringes and who stood at the center of adoring circles. The King moved like a shadow, a few paces behind her. Raegan knew all too well what kind of men were in this room; in all probability, they'd love to feel like they'd stolen Raegan from someone who looked like Oberon. But she'd need to play it just right because she also knew men respected another man's property more than anything else.

And despite the Timekeeper's power surging in their veins, the bloodline they'd been born into, the oath they'd been laden with at birth, that's all they were: men. And Raegan could handle some goddamn men.

The ballroom seemed to stretch on forever. She peered into the rafters, eyeing the excessive number of chandeliers, the exposed beams draped in more banners—tasseled, embroidered with Latin phrases she had no desire to translate. And then up ahead, when a large group of people broke apart, she spied something much more interesting.

A tented bower of red fabric loomed in the distance. She imagined it was meant to seem mysterious and elegant, but it looked quite a bit like the top of a circus tent. Raegan prowled closer. The open panel at the tent's front revealed a circular bar in its shadows. The bar was handsome, she could admit—Art-Deco-inspired, which did not match the rest of the atmosphere. But the burl wood veneers on the bartop and the inset fans of glass were nice to look at.

As she and the King drew closer, skirting what looked like an art auction, Raegan noticed the lights were dimmer beneath the tent top. She wavered, pretending to read the sign with information about the artwork offered for sale, but her gaze slid back to the shadowed, red-hued space. She noticed small seating areas dotting the floor around the bar. Tucked into a banquette-style booth was a man wearing a black-striped ribbon, four women draped over him like ornaments.

Raegan glanced to her right, making eye contact with Oberon, who was a few paces away. When he caught up and came to stand beside her, she slipped her arm through his.

"Certainly looks like the place where naughtier things go down," she said, stretching up to speak into his ear, battling the sound of the mediocre jazz band playing somewhere in the ballroom. "Want to see if we can hook ourselves a black stripe? I doubt these guys would be into a threesome with both of us, so we'll have to make it look like I'm sneaking off with him."

"I will be just behind you, even if you do not see me," the King replied, his hand open on the small of her back. "But please take care if you pass through security or warded doors, as that may limit my ability to follow you."

"Of course," Raegan replied with a wink.

As they approached the blood-red tent, a man of middling height moved toward them. He was dressed in a drab but probably expensive suit, his hair slicked back so harshly that it gleamed like a burnished shield. He didn't block their way, not exactly—but he waited expectantly, like there was something they were meant to do or say before slipping into the darker recesses of the evening's offerings.

"Last year was our first Founder's Gala," Oberon added, feigning nervousness that Raegan knew he almost never felt. "We were not aware until afterward that there were additional . . . *activities* to explore."

Raegan shrank back against the King's solid bulk, looking at the ground as she wrung her hands nervously in a pretty little motion that made her bust strain at the neckline of her dress. She glanced up and found the man immediately distracted. Too easy. He managed to drag his eyes away, gaze skipping to the King.

"Of course," he replied with a leer, stepping aside.

Oberon slipped his arm through Raegan's, and they strode into the tent's mouth. Inside, small lamps were scattered throughout the seating area and a few chandeliers dangling down beneath the tent top cast everything in shades of red. Perhaps it was meant to look carnal, seductive—and it probably did, Raegan realized, to the kinds of men who saw women as nothing more than conquests. A bloody, vicious hunt ending with a delicate neck between their teeth.

Oberon led the way now, reading her mind regarding how she thought they should adjust to the tone of this space. In this high-danger, high-pressure situation, she felt so attuned to him, like she could make the slightest suggestion with a shift of her weight or a tug on his hand and he'd respond immediately.

A delicate warmth spread through Raegan. She'd wanted this for so many years—a kind of magical, intuitive understanding between herself and a romantic partner. At a certain point, she had convinced herself it was only the stuff of fairy tales, of myth.

With a smile, she looked over at her faerie king for a moment, realizing she hadn't *exactly* been wrong after all.

As they reached the bar, he pulled her into him, arms sliding possessively around her waist. Good—making her look claimed and untouchable would probably only heighten interest. Raegan glanced around the bar as Oberon ordered drinks, trying to get a read on as many people as possible.

They'd arrived fashionably late to the gala, so it was a bit past nine PM, but she was still surprised by how drunk a lot of attendees seemed. She was *not* surprised to see the way the majority of Protectorate men interacted with women. They either left their spouses behind before striding into the tent or dragged their wives along to look pretty on their arm as they bellowed in laughter at other men's piss-poor jokes.

The bartender slid two drinks onto the bartop, and Raegan scowled into her glass. Maybe she could summon a tidal wave of river water and just drown all of them. She sighed and shifted her weight, turning her mind to more practical forms of action. Should she be meek and demure, like she hadn't realized how hot she was, like her husband had purchased this dress to show her off? Or should she be more herself— coy, sharp, wild? Something already broken or something they could tame and mold into the docile, domestic thing they desired?

Yes, she decided. The latter would probably work. It was the Protectorate, after all—they'd demonstrated a long history of breaking wild, magical things. So she took a long sip from her drink and then reached over, playing with the King's silken black pocket square. He'd wisely struck up a conversation with a middle-aged man next to him, giving Raegan the opportunity to act as though she had to fight for his attention. She did just that, turning to face him, her back arched, tilting her head to look up at him.

Oberon turned and glanced at her, one eyebrow arched, face impassive. "Yes, dear?" he asked in a tone she'd never heard out of him. "The men are talking."

Oh, he was *good*. Not just how quickly he'd picked up on her play, but also the way he said something completely different with his body. The heat of him bled through that fine suit as his fingertips trailed up her thigh, exposed by the slit of her dress.

Raegan pouted, all of her fear and anxiety sweeping out of her on a rushing current, leaving only the dark, slinking thrill. "You've been talking to colleagues *all* night," she whined, pitching her voice higher.

"Just a little longer," Oberon replied distractedly. One hand brushed away one of the curls framing her face as if she were an exasperating child, but the other slipped farther up her thigh. "Be a good girl for me, yes?" He timed the words with a brush against the apex of her legs. Raegan inhaled sharply in response, her chest heaving against his torso. She'd thought a lot of things about how this night would go. At no point did she think she'd be heady with arousal, fear long forgotten in the rush of desire.

"I will," she agreed with a sigh, dipping her lashes. She slid over so she could turn around and face the bar, fiddling with the orange peel on the rim of her glass. Oberon angled his shoulders away from her, but she had the strong sense he was doing the same thing she was—subtly surveying the room, seeing who might take the bait on the hook.

Raegan glanced up, finding that a young blond man's eyes were already on hers. She met his gaze, coy, but when the light shifted, she saw he wore a plain red ribbon. With a huff, she turned away, looking over at Oberon for a long moment.

She took another sip, propping her elbows on the bar, perfectly aware of what it did to the neckline of her dress. Shifting her weight as if impatient, Raegan glanced over her shoulder to her left. Again, someone had already been looking at her—this time, a man probably in his late forties with blunt, severe features. A possessive sort of hunger that she knew too well clung to his expression. The ribbon pinned to his tuxedo had a wide black stripe, accented at the top with golden crossed swords.

Raegan bumped her hip into the King's so he would glance over. He did with an irritated exhale, meeting her eyes before his gaze skipped over her head. When he looked directly at her again, she nodded, ever so slightly. Oberon frowned and then checked his watch, making sure the movement was visible to the man at the other end of the bar.

Oberon swore, just loud enough, and made his apologies to the Protectorate operative he'd struck up a conversation with—who would probably never know who they had actually been talking to. Then he downed his drink and turned back to Raegan. "Late to speak with the chamberlain," he told her, pressing a hasty kiss to her hairline. "You can stay here. Enjoy yourself. See you in a bit."

And then Oberon pulled away, hesitating for almost a moment too long before he turned on his heel and stalked out from under the tent, leaving Raegan alone. She watched him go, twisting her mouth into a mopey expression before collapsing a bit dramatically against the side of the bar.

"From the gentleman across the way," the bartender said, interrupting her thoughts, sliding another drink in front of her as he gestured to the young blond man. That was quick. Raegan raised the glass and smiled prettily at him, hoping it would spur the black-striped ribbon she actually wanted into motion.

It did—like poetry. A minute or two ticked by, and then the severe-featured man appeared at her side. His harsh mouth moved into something like amusement, but she didn't think she was in on the joke. "Your husband?" he asked, gesturing toward the mouth of the tent, where Oberon had gone.

Raegan paused, reading the man before her—the expensive but classic suit, no wedding ring, but also no pretty young thing on his arm. Yes, she surmised. He would do just fine.

"Yes," she replied, turning to face him, her glass in one hand. "Doesn't always keep up with his husbandly duties, though." A test.

The man—Commander W. Rochester, according to the shining brass tag on his ribbon—frowned, but she saw the interest flicker in his gaze.

"Oh my goodness," Raegan amended, covering her mouth with her hand for a moment. "Apparently I've had too much to drink. I can't believe I just said that. And to a stranger!"

That's what he wanted. His body slid closer to hers with an exhale. He wanted her desire to be real, and he wanted her to feel shame for it.

"Would it make it better," he asked, leaning toward her, one elbow on the bar, "if we were no longer strangers?"

Raegan laughed and then took a sip of her drink. "That might help, I suppose."

With that, the commander formally introduced himself, offering her that limp fish handshake that men like him for some reason always gave women. She supplied the French ambassador's name as her own and pulled Rochester into further conversation.

She didn't wait long to start with the delicate, fleeting touches—his forearm, his wrist, and then a swat at his shoulder when he told her how beautiful she looked in her dress. "Do recall I *am* a married woman, Commander," Raegan said, though she shifted another few inches closer to him anyway, running her eyes down the length of his body.

She couldn't make it too easy, so she followed up by immediately leaning away, letting silence build between them for a long moment. "Your compound really is something," Raegan added when she saw just the right amount of tension in the commander's body. "Much nicer than where we work from in Paris. The neighborhood's lovely, but the offices? Terrible little spaces."

Rochester grinned at her for the first time, all teeth, all hunger. Raegan swallowed, missing the feel of Oberon right at her side. She twirled a lock of curls, leveling all of her attention at the commander. He was slim though well-built, likely fit, certainly brimming with the Time-keeper's boon. She had access to some Protectorate magic by virtue of her blood, but she hadn't been inducted as an infant, so she wasn't vested with full power. If she had to fight him, she'd have to maintain the element of surprise, or else she'd probably be fucked.

"You have some time to spare, don't you?" Rochester asked, leaning too close, his breath heavy with alcohol, his gaze devouring her body. "Would you like to see our offices? I could give you a little tour while your husband finishes up his business."

Raegan hesitated, looking over her shoulder as if Oberon might reappear. Then she glanced back at the commander, biting her lower lip. "Oh, I don't know . . ."

Rochester closed the small space between them and plucked a curl from her collarbone, wrapping it around his fingers. She clenched the fist he couldn't see at her side.

"I can see how badly you want to," the commander muttered gruffly, his hand roughly grabbing her hip. "Besides, if he doesn't give you what you need, I'm doing you both a favor, right?"

She forced herself to smile and nod. When Rochester's hand closed like a vise around her wrist, Raegan barely managed to let out a giggle instead of a growl.

CHAPTER THIRTY-THREE

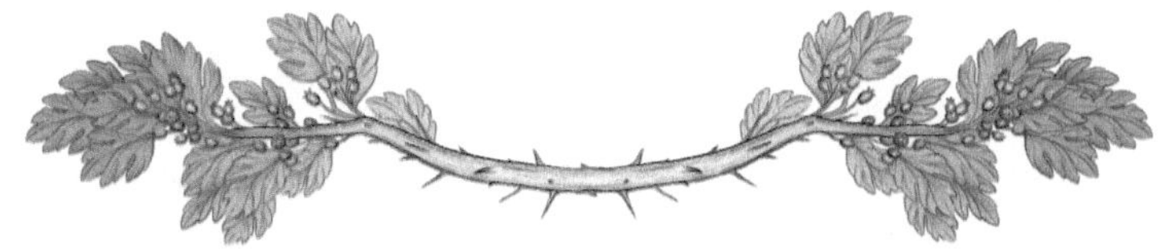

"And don't worry about your husband," Rochester said as he pulled her along, slipping through a side opening in the tent's blood-red fabric. "He's out front. Won't even see us."

"Oh," Raegan cooed. "Done this before, have you?"

"Women are simple creatures. You see the alpha of the pack and can't help yourselves," he said over his shoulder with what he seemed to think was a charming grin. "But lucky for you, I'm generous."

Raegan had been planning to use a sedation spell—it was an old, little-used healer's incantation, so wards and defensive workings almost never registered it—but now she was considering slitting his throat. Surely he'd have some big, phallic letter opener in his office. The thought settled her as she glanced around him, trying to figure out where they might be headed. But the slim opening in the tent seemed to only lead to a dead end a few paces away.

"Commander, perhaps you've been blinded by my beauty," Raegan said when he came to a halt. "But this is a wall."

Rochester winked at her. "Like I said. Simple creatures." And then he laid his hand on the white wall, just between two drab, chipped gold ornamentations. He applied pressure with his fingertips at seemingly random intervals, and then the wall opened into darkness.

"Oh, a secret door?" Raegan asked as if it delighted her, letting her voice drop low and husky.

"Obviously," Rochester scoffed, somehow becoming even less charming—an impressive feat—the closer he came to getting what he wanted. Instead of holding the door open for her, the commander plunged into the darkness, his hand still wrapped around her wrist. His lack of manners was actually good, though, as it gave Raegan the opportunity to shift her weight back and catch the door with her heel. She had no doubt Oberon would've seen where she'd gone, but it would mean nothing if he couldn't get through. So she did her best to ensure the door remained cracked open just a hair, but with Rochester moving quickly down the corridor, she couldn't risk pausing to be sure. That'd only cause him to notice what she'd done.

The shadowed passageway opened up in only a few steps, spilling out into the massive main hallway she'd come down earlier. Raegan tried not to smile with glee when she saw this secret little passageway exited *behind* the line of soldiers that blocked anyone from leaving the ballroom and moving deeper into the Protectorate stronghold.

"See, look at this," she said, keeping her voice low, trotting a few steps to fall in line with Rochester. "Architecture, antiques, art! Much better surroundings than my gray cube."

She and Oberon had memorized information about the French organization whose representatives they were impersonating, but there had only been so much time. Raegan knew for sure that the offices were quite gray and modern, but she wasn't positive that the ambassador she was masquerading as didn't have a nicer, cushier workspace somewhere in the building.

Rochester didn't answer because he obviously didn't think women were people, so Raegan paid careful attention to the space around her, straining her ears. Sounds spilled out from behind the closed doors that lined the imposing stone walls. What she heard gave her two impressions: Protectorate officials using their offices for such dalliances during this gala was not uncommon, and they did not seem interested in the female orgasm. No surprises on either account. She swept her gaze from side to side, counting her footsteps. The entrance to the Undercroft should be visible at any moment.

Rochester muttered something filthy and not even remotely hot into her ear, almost making Raegan miss the gleaming iron door. She barely caught sight of it in the flickering light of the candles, appearing just as Maelona and Alanna had described. The Protectorate thought Fair Folk would have no chance of opening it—on account of it being made of iron and enchanted to throw any Fey magic directed its way back at the user threefold. But the Fey they'd locked on this side of the Gates were more resilient than that. Sure, iron *did* hurt—but pain was fleeting.

The commander, though, would have a swipe card for the estate's outer gates and a set of spelled keys for the more secure parts of the Manor's innards. Raegan would have to get the keys from him without offering something she did not want to give.

"Here we are," Rochester said triumphantly, stopping at a massive oak-hewn door. As if on cue, he pulled a set of antique skeleton keys from his pocket—left side, likely an interior pocket of his waistcoat.

Raegan summoned her strength. It would be too hard to get those keys back out once he stowed them away again; she was no pickpocket. So as Rochester unlocked the door and pulled it open, Raegan grabbed the front of his tux jacket and stretched up to kiss him. In the same moment, she slid her thigh between his, pushing him backwards and off-balance.

It worked. The commander stumbled inside, and Raegan kicked the door closed behind them. She cataloged a quick impression of the office —lavish, stone-walled, a massive antique desk, leather armchairs in a sitting area near a fireplace, locked metal cabinets—before Rochester grabbed her by her hair. Adrenaline exploded in her blood.

"Not so fast," the commander said in an ice-cold tone that didn't really surprise her. Raegan had been expecting something like this; after all, it was always easier to fool the men who had no doubt they were at the top of the food chain. Rochester yanked her to the front of the desk by her hair. Maybe those weeks of training with Andronica had done something, because Raegan *let* him do it as opposed to being over-powered.

Rochester shoved her forward. The edges of the desk bit into her hips. Then he closed in behind her, reaching around to pin her hands to the desk. But he let the keys fall onto a neat pile of folders to do so. With her back to him, she was free to smile with glee.

"Fucking Contre La Sorcellerie," Rochester spat in her ear. "Are you stupid enough to think you can get your hands on that report so easily, just with a bit of whoring?"

Raegan pretended to freeze, going completely still against him, which he seemed to enjoy.

"And also stupid enough," he continued in a snarl, "to follow a man you know to be dangerous into a location where your partner will never find you?"

Raegan rolled her eyes and then realized she should be afraid. Shouldn't she? She knew what men were capable of more intimately than she'd prefer. But she wasn't what Rochester saw when he looked at her—ass and tits, a bitch to conquer, just a girl. She never had been. But particularly not anymore. With an intact Seal, she would've been afraid. Angry but afraid.

But Baba Yaga herself had removed her Seal. Then Raegan had walked the wasteland of a thousand lives and returned not only intact but stronger than ever. So for regular, mortal women everywhere, she decided to make him pay.

"But I hope you're smart enough," Rochester panted, his fingernails digging into her skin, "to not make this harder than it has to be. You're going to be spending the night for some questioning." He paused and she waited, prepared to react. "And don't worry. I won't be taking *advantage* of your precarious situation here. You're lucky I'm a better man than that."

God, she fucking hated this guy. She said nothing, making a series of quick, dagger-sharp calculations. She knew that defensive spellwork or even something as subtle as a disorientation working would trigger the wards, particularly this deep into the Protectorate's compound. Her sedation spell wouldn't help; he'd need to be relaxed for it to take.

"Unfortunately for you," she said, her voice so low and dark she almost didn't recognize it, "I'm not Contre La Sorcellerie. I'm much, *much* worse."

She snapped her head back hard, slamming her skull right into the commander's nose. He barked out a loud curse and stumbled back. Raegan turned, staying low, knowing that he would reach out for her with clawing hands—which is exactly what he did. She slipped under his guard and placed a hand over his heart, digging her fingernails into his chest. Relief and victory flushed through her when the spell took root immediately, rushing out of her memory like whitewater rapids. The wards did not even tremble.

Rochester did, though, when Raegan shoved him. He stumbled back against the wall, rattling a metal cabinet, his hands clutching uselessly at his throat. As if that would save him.

"You know," Raegan said, looking up at the commander with what was probably a manic smile, "I'm familiar with some ancient Druidic medicine practices that most have forgotten. Very advanced for the time, you see. It was men like you that outlawed it as devilry."

Rochester gasped, groping at her forearms for purchase, but in his weakened state, it was easy enough to shrug him off with her free hand. His eyes bulged out of their sockets like fat, ripe grapes she could pluck and devour.

"You might know from modern medicine that sometimes it's necessary to briefly stop the heart so repairs can be made," she continued, laughing now, her head thrown back. "And that's exactly what I'm doing now, you stupid fucking asshole. I'm stopping your heart."

"Th–the—wards," Rochester stuttered, blood draining from his face, "w-won't l-let you—"

"Oh sweetheart," Raegan said with a feral grin. "I'm not *hurting* you. I can see how badly you want it. I'm just being *generous*."

On some level, she recognized that she was taller than him now, her feet leaving the ground in a swell of magic and rage. She leaned in close, as if for a kiss. "After all," Raegan sneered, "why would you go to a secluded place with the Queen of the Hill if not to die?"

Chapter Thirty-Four

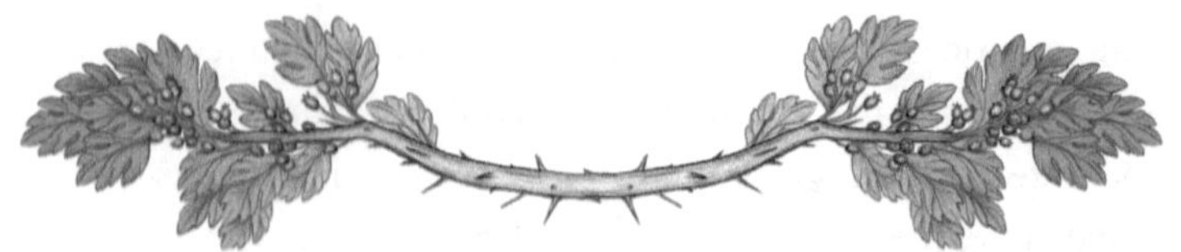

Rochester went slack, sliding down the wall into a gray pile on the floor. Anger and victory coursed through Raegan's veins, heady as ambrosia, but the intensity of the working left her a little woozy. With her feet back on the ground, she staggered to the desk, steadying herself. Black dots danced across her vision. She would feel better in a few moments, she told herself—and besides, she was safe for at least a little while here.

Sheer horror electrified her insides as Raegan watched the heavy wooden door swing open. She shoved herself upright, unsteady in her heels, calling desperately to the rivers that wound long and terrifying within her.

But it was the Unseelie king who slipped into the office, closing the door behind him with a soft click. Despite the headache beginning to drive nails into her head, Raegan couldn't help but notice that he looked ridiculously good. He must've shed the tuxedo jacket at some point, pushing the sleeves of his black dress shirt to his elbow. His waistcoat remained, and *gods*, was it fitted beautifully around his powerful frame.

For a moment, the King's eyes took in Raegan and then tracked to the dead man on the floor. In the next heartbeat, he moved in a sweep of shadow and grace, pulling Raegan off her feet and into his arms.

"My villainous thing," the King murmured, holding her tight against his chest, "are you quite alright?"

"A little woozy," she replied, trying to meet his gaze instead of staring at the curves of his sculptural mouth. "But there's one less asshole in the world. Oh, and the Undercroft keys are on his desk."

Oberon's gaze didn't falter. He looked only at her, not even taking a split second to glance at the spelled keys that might lead to his people's salvation.

"Would you say," Raegan began, giving up and tracing a few fingers along the bow of his full lips, "that I was a good girl tonight, like you asked?"

Amusement shimmered across the inhuman angles of his face. "Yes," he replied, cradling her skull in one large hand. "Even better than I could have expected."

And then Oberon pulled her close for a kiss that made her feel as though perhaps the world had stopped spinning on its axis. Perhaps there was a Thread where he was helping her harvest honey from their bees. A Thread where she was just sitting down next to him by the ocean and nothing had ever been taken from them. It was the kind of kiss that shivered with possibility, that cracked the future open wide and glorious.

When they broke apart, Raegan found the dizziness had dissipated, her limbs feeling more like muscle and bone instead of jelly. "I think I'm okay," she said. "If my knees give out, it's only because you're a hell of a kisser."

With a laugh like an autumnal bell, the King gently set her down. Only then did his gaze wander to the dead commander.

"Oh," Raegan said with a wave of her hand. "Had to be crafty with the wards. I stopped his heart. Archaic Druidic healing spell."

"You are terrifying, my love," he replied, tracing her collarbone with the lightest touch. "Do you need another moment, or are you ready to press onward?"

In response, Raegan snatched the keys from the desk and jingled them. "Let's go steal a dossier or die trying."

The side of his mouth curved upwards, but she saw the anxiety draw his brows together. All for her, Raegan knew. The King had made his peace with dying for freedom centuries ago, but losing her seemed to be something he could not live with.

"Come," Oberon said, his fingers wrapped around hers, pulling Raegan closer to the body of the man she'd killed, not toward the door. In the movies, people usually vomited or had existential crises or passed out after their first kill. As she looked down at the gray, empty corpse, Raegan felt none of those things. Perhaps her soul remained tainted with every new body, each resurrective life, carrying the weight of death always.

Oberon released her hand, kneeling beside Rochester's corpse. "Do you think you would be able to lift some echo of the Protectorate oath from this man and craft it into a glamour?"

Raegan stared at him, her mouth going dry. The exercises Oberon had given her and the spellbooks Emrys had lent her fell firmly in the category of practical magic. It was, of course, nothing like the magic she'd so frequently seen depicted in television and movies growing up in this life. Still, it had a formula, a logic, that made sense to her because she was mortal.

Oberon was suggesting she attempt faerie magic. Humans pulled magic from the world around them with set rituals and incantations charged with will and practice. The Fey *were* magic; they could shape the world as they saw fit.

"It is alright if you cannot," the King said, reading her like a book. "I would do it for you, would it not trigger the wards."

"It's an excellent idea," Raegan said, spreading her hands wide. "I just don't think I'm capable."

"You were born Fey, once," the King murmured.

"Exactly," Raegan scoffed. "Only *once*."

"You taught Baba Yaga witchcraft," he added, one ink-dark eyebrow arching. "Morgana le Fay said you were the most brilliant witch she'd ever worked alongside. You may be human, Nyneve, but you have *always* worked magic like the Fair Folk."

Raegan swiped damp palms on her dress before remembering it was a beautiful, exquisite thing. She sighed, squeezing her eyes shut. If she tried and failed, they'd have wasted time and possibly tripped the wards in the process. Too much time could pass and someone might come looking for Rochester. The French operatives they were impersonating might evade the kelpies and alert the Protectorate. She opened her eyes, watching the King stand in one long, fluid movement.

"How can I do that without upsetting the wardings?" Raegan asked, meeting his gaze. She felt the workings palpably as she spoke, like a hundred spiderwebs stuck to her skin, suddenly aware of her.

Oberon tilted his head, considering. "We do not categorize magic in the way mortals do," he said slowly, "but it would be a . . . transfer of sorts, yes? Neutral magic, as humans sometimes call it."

Raegan tongued the inside of her cheek, picking at her cuticles. "Okay," she said, nodding. And then she crouched down beside Rochester's cooling corpse and the currents surged—a thousand jaws with a million teeth scuttling scavenger-like across the riverbeds.

"Steady," the King murmured, a gentle warning, his voice like a hot cup of tea on a cold, wet day.

Raegan nodded, sinking to her knees beside Rochester, her thighs cramping. She pushed aside the rivers with a firm, gentle hand, fighting to stay within the boundaries of her Protectorate magic instead. Sweat began to pour down the back of her neck as she sent her magic through the commander's body, pulling back on the coursing river of her older power. She put herself in that healer's mindset—like she was searching for what had hurt him, or perhaps what might pull him back from that dark, final place.

Alanna and Maelona had stressed how much the wards sensed intent. Raegan had to believe she was helping Rochester or risk triggering an immediate reaction. She *was* helping him, though—lifting that heavy burden of an oath not asked for, letting his body rest for the first time since he'd been born.

The moment she thought about it that way, something floated to the surface—gossamer-thin, pearl-gray, and lightly iridescent. It was not, Raegan knew, the full oath. Such a thing would be deeply embedded in Rochester's skin, in his heart, chained around his lungs. But this thing she'd conjured was a reflection, a simulacrum of it, almost like a grave etching. If she extracted it correctly, it would look like evidence of the Timekeeper's oath, at least on a magical level.

Raegan let out a long exhale. Best not to think about the complex theory. That was something she enjoyed over dinner with Oberon, tucked in a cozy chair beside a fireplace. Not in the belly of the beast, attempting a spell that mirrored faerie magic in a place where faerie magic was forbidden.

"Holy shit," Raegan whispered, the words leaving her mouth entirely by accident as the gossamer-thin veil drifted toward her on the currents of her power. She snatched it before it could float away and let it settle onto her body. For a horrible moment, she thought it was going to disappear—that her Protectorate blood would betray her, seeking the oath like a moth to a flame—but it just sat on her skin, damp-looking like a newborn thing.

"You clever witch," Oberon breathed, staring at her wide-eyed, the corners of his mouth upturned with wonder.

"It won't last," Raegan said, knowing intrinsically that whatever she had conjured was delicate as a butterfly's wing. "But it should at least get us through a few levels."

"Allow me to field dress your kill," the King said in a low, husky tone, "and then we may be on our way."

"Into the Undercroft," she said, trying to mentally prepare herself.

Oberon's eyes left hers, dragging around the room as he searched for something. "Ahh," he said, moving toward a large bottom drawer of the metal cabinet. He pulled it open, revealing about ten thousand manila folders.

"They should really digitize," Raegan said, wrinkling her nose.

"The Protectorate are paranoid about modern technology," the King replied, grabbing a pile of the folders and moving to the desk, where he yanked open drawers with his free hand. Finding an empty one, he began ferrying folders. Raegan understood a little too late, apparently still recovering from the spellwork. But when she caught on, she moved to the desk drawer, shoving folders in as Oberon handed them to her.

When the large lower cabinet was empty, the King knelt in front of Rochester and wrapped his hands around the corpse's leg. And then he snapped it, bending the limb at an angle it should never be bent. A novel combination of queasiness and arousal bloomed low in Raegan's stomach as Oberon continued to break a grown man's bones as if they were toothpicks. Once he had folded the corpse into a more suitable size —her stomach did roil a bit then—the King stuffed Rochester into the cabinet and closed it.

He turned to look at Raegan. "A bit distasteful, I know."

"I mean, he deserved it," she said with a shrug. "Kinda gross to watch, though."

"Onward, then," Oberon replied, closing the distance between them with a few strides. He took her hand with the same fingers that had just committed so much violence, and yet he touched her with unyielding tenderness.

They slipped out into the hallway, a pair of shadows. Beneath the skittering candlelight, the space was silent. In the distance, the hum of the gala was detectable, but it felt a thousand years away.

"This way," Raegan said, pulling the King toward the door she'd spied on the way in with the commander. She counted her steps again, just to be sure, but she saw it looming and her heart quickened.

"This is dwarven-made," Oberon observed in a low murmur, his tone sour. "Undoubtedly stolen."

"What a surprise," Raegan replied, standing directly in front of the massive iron door, sweeping her eyes across it. "All of the Protectorate's power is stolen."

She took a hesitant step forward, spying a keyhole in the middle of the door, which was curious. Raegan reached for the oath's veil and felt it like threads of silk across her shoulders. Her fingers ghosted the ring of keys in her hands. She didn't need to look; it would be the dull iron key, the one nearly the size of her hand, that would open the Undercroft.

It was a strange thing, she realized, to stand in front of a door that did not call to her with all the sweetness of a lover. This door did not repel her, not precisely, but when one only knows songbirds, a silent winged creature is unsettling.

Raegan took a deep breath and held the enormous skeleton key just above the lock, her body grinding to a halt at the last moment, stiff with hesitancy. But then she remembered something she couldn't believe she had forgotten: hadn't she, all her life, been looking for a door?

So Raegan put the key in the lock and turned it.

CHAPTER THIRTY-FIVE

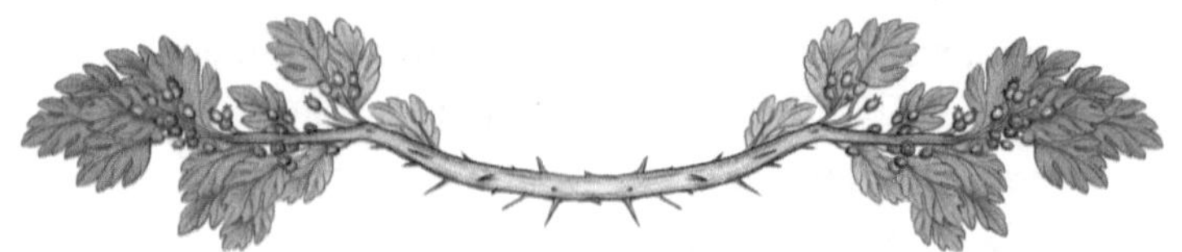

When the twelve-foot-tall iron door opened without a sound, there was no time to celebrate. Raegan and the King disappeared into its mouth. The door sealed shut behind them with the quietest of sighs.

Once her heart no longer felt as though it was going to burst out of her chest, Raegan took a look around. The Undercroft's interior was a cruel space, at least to Raegan's eye. The echo of the rest of the Manor was there, all the old, dark stone and high ceilings, but steel and glass sutured it all together. A blood-red runner stretched down the center of the stone floors, the dragon rampart stamped in yellow every ten feet or so. Conference rooms seemed to make up the majority of the chambers off the main hall. They were dark and empty, their glass pane eyes staring back lifelessly. Sickly fluorescent light poured down from the ceiling.

"I don't understand how this would be *less* creepy if it were some stereotypical dungeon," Raegan hissed as she forced herself to move forward.

"The wards appear to be reading me as your guest," the King said in lieu of a response to her statement, his gaze roving the space. Good. So far, they were neither dead nor captured.

But the space was eerie in its utter silence. Oberon moved forward, his footsteps soundless on the carpet. She trailed behind, her heart still somersaulting. It was not helpful, she kept reminding herself, to think of the Undercroft as a sleeping beast that would awaken the moment they put a foot wrong. They passed by more glass rooms with heavy, immovable tables, then a small space for document storage, though the pigeonholes were empty.

Ahead, shadow devoured the blood-red runner and the hallway curved sharply to the left. In front of the yawning darkness of the corridor stretched a gold-washed gate. It reminded Raegan of old-fashioned accordion elevator doors, except instead of open diamonds of metal, chainmail stretched between the hinges. In the middle of the gate were two enormous scythes, crossed at the middle, a strange-looking keyhole fitted into the place where the weapons met. She palmed the keys she'd stolen from Rochester and walked closer.

"The scythes are glamour-eaters," the King said from a few steps behind her, his footsteps silent on the stone. She nodded, glancing back at him. They'd expected this from Maelona and Alanna's reports, but the magic built into the barrier shouldn't register the physical glamour spells in their rings, let alone devour them.

The metal keys clung to her fingers, which were damp with anxiety and nerves. In the gloom of the dark corridor, Raegan found a key that appeared to be the right size and had a scythe etched into it. She put it into the lock and twisted. For a long and deeply horrible moment, there was nothing but silence and the heavy weight of Oberon at her side, like the electrified rush of an incoming thunderstorm.

But then the scythes hissed like snakes, sliding apart and granting them passage. Raegan let out a breath, her heart still hammering away at her ribs. "So far, so good," she said as she walked through.

"We should probably close them behind us, yes?" Oberon asked, eyeing the tall stretch of golden chainmail. It was a risk to have the literal Unseelie king touch anything here, so Raegan reached forward and pulled the two halves of the accordion gate back together. The scythes slid closed.

"Right," she said in a huff, pushing a curl out of her face. Then she reached for the King's hand, and once their fingers were firmly intertwined, she continued down the corridor. Lights clicked on as they went —like industrial fluorescent bulbs in a warehouse. Up ahead, the corner rounded sharply, creating a blind turn. It would be like this on the approach to every level, Raegan knew, but seeing it in person was unsettling. The Undercroft's structure felt too much like following the trail of a massive serpentine beast that had burrowed beneath the earth. Every step felt as though she might disturb a great sleeping thing.

Oberon moved out ahead of her to round the tight corner, but she kept close, wanting to feel the solidity and security in his bulk. When she saw what was awaiting them around the bend, she regretted her choice. Like a sentinel with its back against the wall, a grandfather clock stood there. It was quiet, no ticking hands, no chiming pendulum, but the aura of the thing was vile. In fact, Raegan realized, it felt very much like the Timekeeper's train platform, the place her father had—

"Steady," Oberon said, slowing to a halt, his bicep brushing her shoulder as he drew close. Though his nearness eased her tumbling thoughts, her body still very much wanted to panic.

"Luckily," the King added, his gaze narrowed as he examined the clock, not drawing any closer, "I believe it sleeps. For now."

Without letting go of his arm, Raegan searched the ground around her uselessly, looking for a rock or something similar she could throw out past the grandfather clock to see if movement would make its teeth appear. But then she realized the workings on this abomination were probably much more sensitive and fine-tuned.

"Guess there's only one way to find out," she sighed, her jaw clenched. At her side, Oberon nodded his agreement, though it was clear from the expression on his face he was not any happier about it than she was.

Together, they stepped forward tentatively. Closer now, more lights clicking on, she saw the clock did not possess simple carved feet made of mundane wood. Instead, tentacles curled at the bottom, gray and fleshy. She swallowed hard, trying not to stare at the thick, slimy-looking appendages.

"We're just going to walk right past it," Raegan said, looking up at Oberon. His mouth moved into a firm line. "It's a fucking *clock*. I'll stomp on its tentacles or something."

Up close, the thing was horribly tall, rivaling Oberon's height, its skin a burnished walnut, its face lacking any kind of numerals, only two spindly arms still on the blank white. In her peripheral vision, she noticed unmoving pendulums hanging down into its hood, something about them not quite right.

Three, two, one—and then they drew even with the awful thing. Raegan shoved down the anxiety boiling in the pit of her stomach, clenching her jaw. She prepared herself to punch a sentient piece of furniture, which would be a new experience, even for her.

But the clock, like the rest of the Undercroft, was silent. Raegan didn't dare release a breath or relax until she and the King were at least ten paces away. Only once her head began to swim with a lack of oxygen did she unclench her jaw and suck in air.

"I do not wish to see one of those awaken," Oberon observed archly.

Nervous laughter bubbled up Raegan's throat. "Absolutely not," she replied, focusing on the dark, narrow hallway ahead.

The corridor turned sharply again ahead. She half-expected something horrible waiting in the gloom of the hallway's sharp turn, but there were only plain stone walls and that plush carpet the color of dried blood stretching down into shadow. It was empty and quiet, save for the humming of the fluorescent lights that cast everything in a pallid shade of gray-green.

When the hallway deposited them into a circular room that looked like it had been dug out of the earth two thousand years ago, Raegan slowed to a halt. Her heart thudded noisily in her throat, her legs trembling. It wasn't exhaustion—it was fear. Something about this place reduced her to prey, a rabbit hopelessly digging deeper into its warren even though a wolf had its hind legs firmly between quickly closing jaws.

"Okay, we made it to the second level," she breathed, sweeping her gaze around the space. This room had stone walls, too, lined with wrought iron benches that were too familiar. They were just like the ones in the In-Between. Raegan gritted her teeth again, refusing to fall into the pit of despair and grief that waited for her with open arms.

"You are a force of nature," the King murmured, pulling her close, fingertips tilting her chin up to face him. "I am in awe of you."

Raegan smiled, that look of admiration on his angular features chasing away the darker feelings clamoring in her chest. "Save it 'til we've got the dossier in hand," she said with a wink. "Then you can properly admire me."

He bent his brow to hers, hand flattening against the small of her back. The endless heat of him rolled across Raegan's skin, banishing the chill of the Undercroft. "I look forward to it," the King said, a gruff rumble that sent anticipation unfurling low in her belly.

Raegan stood on her tiptoes, suddenly grateful for her high heels, and kissed him for good measure. Then she turned, reached for his hand, and snuck deeper into their enemies' burrow deep below the earth. The second level reminded her of a college library, but more evil—more glass and steel, that blood-red carpet running down the stone floors, documents and books piled high on plain shelves. It was frustrating to leave it behind without rifling through to see exactly what the Protectorate knew, what they were putting effort into researching—but with the dossier, none of that would matter, she told herself.

The next few levels passed in much the same fashion. An accordion gate of chainmail with its scythe keyhole, the tentacled grandfather clock waiting at the turn of the corridor. Tight, winding hallways with steep inclines. It was *working*—the physical glamours and the veil she'd made of Rochester's oath. And yet Raegan couldn't relax, feeling as though their lives were hanging on a knife's edge with every step, the Undercroft a living beast watching their every move.

But as they went farther into the dark, she discovered the horrors contained within the Undercroft were so, so much worse than the deep, damp wound in the earth that held them. The Protectorate held far more reserves of sainted iron—metal specifically forged through an intensive, time-consuming ritual to better kill the Fair Folk—than the Unseelie king himself had even known existed. The Fey had thought the ritual no longer possible, the weapons low in number.

"They are preparing," was all Oberon said as they passed another armory filled with shining, yet-to-be-used weapons hungry for Fey blood.

From there, it only got worse as they followed that carpet—too much like a blood trail shining in the fluorescent light—down into the shadows of the Protectorate's most secure holding. An entire library of books bound in human skin. Kelpies in too-small tanks, their eyes plucked from their skulls, a thousand tubes running from their sickly hides. Rarer magical creatures kept like test animals, skin pinned down by vicious hooks—an aged griffin, a tank of water leapers with clipped wings, a cockatrice, a cage of Coblynau. A handful of Fair Folk and magical mortals, some of whom Oberon knew by name. All of them dead to the world, unaware that the Unseelie king himself stood just feet from their enclosures.

Raegan didn't have the strength to look at him directly. She saw the powerful hands curled into fists at his sides, felt the dark rage he kept hidden deep within him begin to stir.

"We could look at the spellwork, see what's keeping them in stasis and whether we can get them out," Raegan murmured, reaching out to sweep a hand down his back.

"There is no need," the King seethed, his eyes flat and black. "I already have. The stasis working is tied to remaining in this level of the Undercroft. I cannot remove it. Only the Protectorate mage who placed it can. I cannot even ask them if they wish to live or die. So instead, I must abandon them. Fail them. Again."

"My love," she replied, though any words died in her throat as she felt her rivers begin to rise, a call-and-response to the faerie king's rage. She gritted her teeth and shoved the currents down, forcing them back under the veil of Protectorate magic.

"We should keep moving," the King said, though his voice broke.

Raegan roughly wiped away the tears that gathered in her own eyes. "That's all we can do," she replied, her tone gruff as she held back the torrents of blackened water and emotion.

They didn't speak as they continued to the next level. In the massive cavern they found there, full skeletons of the Fair Folk were proudly displayed with their names and places of death, shining gold plaques assuring the reader that these Fey had been murdered and skinned like animals, not simply found and harvested. Out of the sixteen skeletons, Oberon had known seven of them when they were alive. Two of the displays were children, the details on the plaque too gruesome for Raegan to manage reading more than a sentence or two.

"Sometimes," the King said, his voice hoarse, breaking the silence that had descended heavy and hot between them, "all you can do is witness."

Raegan didn't know what to say, all the words withering in her throat. What was there to say in the face of such meaningless cruelty?

She reached over and took his hand. "And keep going," she reminded him as they continued down the corridor.

The Undercroft was more than Alanna and Maelona had managed to convey. Their sketches weren't incorrect—there was just no way to conceptualize or prepare for one long hallway winding itself deeper and deeper into the earth like a poison, horrors lining its walls.

Strangely, the Undercroft looked older as they descended; Raegan would've expected the surface level to be the oldest, the Protectorate digging deeper as time went on. But it was the reverse, nearly all traces of metal and glass disappearing, save for antique display cases and more modern enclosures. The majority of the space was ancient, unflinching stone, filled with that rigid, masculine kind of grandeur—marble and gold and animal skins.

Down at this level, the fluorescent lights overhead disappeared. Instead, candelabras burned on plinths, wax dripping down like melted flesh. Another grandfather clock guardian and slinking hallway loomed ahead, but Raegan was more than happy to leave the hall of death behind. At least until the King stiffened. She flattened herself against the wall without a second thought, the position providing her the best sightline in either direction.

"We are no longer alone," Oberon said, his eyes flicking to hers before he turned to face the direction from which they'd come.

Raegan tried to slow her breathing and waited for more information; she knew his hearing was far superior. Time dilated, viscous and rotten as it passed too slowly, those few seconds stretching into an eternity.

And then the King grabbed her hand and moved into an urgent, long-strided walk. "At least twenty people just entered the Undercroft," he explained, his eyes darting to hers, a flash of white in the darkness as they rounded the too-sharp corner. "It does not sound friendly. It is safest to assume we have been discovered."

Raegan nodded, grim panic twisting her stomach. In the scenarios they'd run earlier in the day, this one was the worst: that they'd be in the depths of the Undercroft when the Protectorate came for them. Burrowed deep in the earth where no kelpie could reach them and Oberon's magic was a dangerous liability, not a god-like power among mortals.

"Not to pile on," Raegan said with a steadiness she did not feel, "but the past two levels . . . the wards have been getting tighter. I don't know how else to explain it."

"I feel it as well," Oberon said. "The corridors are becoming narrower, too."

"I thought I was just claustrophobic," she muttered. They rounded the last turn, coming to the opening of level eleven. Just like the other levels, a hallway twisted and opened up into some kind of receiving room. All were the same, though they had become more luxurious the farther down they went—plush cushions lining the wrought iron benches, marble statues of past Protectorate leaders standing tall, chandeliers hanging in the center of rooms.

This room was much the same, except for one significant difference: a massive grandfather clock stood at the far end.

And this one was awake.

Its tentacles were easily the width of her body, already writhing about, twisted in their direction. In the hollowed-out trunk, a mace hung instead of a pendulum, its razor edges winking in the light. She and the King exchanged a long, tense glance. But there was no other choice. No other options. There was only forward into the devourer's mouth where salvation might await if they could just stay alive long enough.

They approached the too-large abomination. Oberon had to tilt his head up to look at the thing, the arms on its face scuttling about like beetles. And then a chime—deep and resonant, a shrill train whistle buried in its depths. Raegan's breath caught in her throat. The filigreed brass handle of the clock's trunk turned, and it swung open.

A slot unfurled from beneath the clock's face, looking too much like the tongue of a python flicking into the air, tasting its prey. Raegan settled her racing heart as best she could and leaned forward, peering at the small, wooden tray that extended from the now-still grandfather clock.

Resting upon the slim slab of wood was a scarab beetle, its thorax etched with a scythe. Every movement of its legs released a ticking sound. The beetle stood on its back legs, its jaws flexing. Anxiety thundered through her body, all her muscles trembling, every good sense buried in her mind screaming at her to run and never look back.

But Raegan just set her jaw and, with a deep breath, extended a finger toward the beetle. As she expected, the insect lurched forward and sank its jaws into her flesh.

CHAPTER THIRTY-SIX

Aprick of the finger, a bead of blood, the drop devoured by the not-living, not-dead thing that emerged from the grandfather clock. The stifled air of the Undercroft hung low and weighted. Raegan stopped breathing, her heart raging against her breastbone. Then the scarab retreated, its jaws closed, and the wooden tongue slipped back into the clock's maw.

Tentacles shifted across the stone floors, the sound sending a shiver down Raegan's spine. The clock swayed to the side, allowing her to pass into the dark hallway that waited beyond. Tentatively, she moved forward, gripping Oberon's hand firmly.

"Raegan," he warned, but he followed her anyway. Disappointment sang through her body when the clock shot between them, blocking the King from following. Raegan's hold on him was broken as she turned, her heart in her throat, watching as the scarab beetle slid expectantly from the dark, waiting mouth open again.

From around the pillar of the clock, Oberon met her gaze, his brows knit together.

"You can't," Raegan whispered, terror slinking through her chest. With the glamoured oath and her very real Protectorate blood, she'd passed the test. But a faerie king? It was a miracle he'd made it this far. Which meant there'd be two floors of the Undercroft's horrors to navigate on her own, the King waiting in the vestibule, caught between the advancing Protectorate and the monstrous mechanical thing.

"How close are they?" she asked, blood thundering through her veins.

The King tilted his head, a wolf homing in on the pack of deer moving through the forest. "Be quick," was all he said, a dangerous smile moving across his inhuman features.

"I—I can't . . ." Raegan's tongue felt too large for her mouth.

"You can," Oberon reassured her, stepping back from the threshold into the vestibule. The clock retracted its tongue, the tentacles ceasing their writhing. "If anyone can, it is you. It has always been you."

Raegan hesitated, knowing she was wasting time but feeling incapable of leaving him behind. How far would her rage alone carry her into this place? Every level down felt more oppressive, the hair crawling on the back of her neck, unease coiling thick in her stomach.

"I am well-accustomed," the King began, his expression gone tender, "to awaiting your return." Raegan's heart broke a little, tears pricking the backs of her eyes. "Go, so you may return to me all the quicker."

"I love you," she said, fierce as an oath, her fingers curling into her palms.

"I love you," Oberon returned immediately, his oceanic eyes locked on hers. Then he nodded, just once, and before she lost the nerve, Raegan turned on her heel and shot down the hallway.

It was the same as the last—a short, curved corridor that deposited her into level eleven. To her surprise, no horrors awaited her in glass tanks. Instead, something not unlike a gentleman's club surrounded her. Carved marble fireplaces, the heads of magical creatures mounted above the mantel, whisky-brown leather armchairs, shining marble floors, a wine cellar.

It had only recently been emptied, she saw—a tumbler with half-melted ice sat on one side table, the condensation spreading in a circle on the wood surface. Raegan swept her gaze through the rest of the space, looking for movement, for a slip of tweed or the dull glint of a gun. But she found nothing, though she stuck to the carpeted runner down the center, wanting as much cover for her footfall as possible.

"Rich-ass fuckers," she grumbled as she passed a second cellar, this one filled with casks and barrels that were probably worth enough to feed a small family for years. Briefly, she toyed with the idea of yanking out the corks and spilling liquor all over the stone floors, but she decided against it. Better for it to seem like no one had been here at all, if possible.

Raegan unlocked the accordion gate and passed through it. No grandfather clock awaited her at the turn of the hallway, which filled her with relief for a moment before the abnormality stirred dread deep in her stomach instead. She tried not to think about what might happen on the way back up, instead plunging forward.

The air was damp but chilly in the corridor, and she noticed in the dancing light of the candelabras that the walls here were earthen instead of gray stone. Single candles lined shallow shelves in the corridor as she turned the corner to the straightaway. It felt more like a mausoleum now, any remnants of the gentleman's-club feel long gone.

The corridor deposited Raegan into a simple room. It was positively ancient—arching walls, well-swept dirt floor, no seating area or fancy chandelier. She turned, expecting another horrible clock monster. But the short hallway was empty. At its end stood an iron door—certainly a sibling to the one at the Undercroft's main entrance. She stepped closer, her heart pounding ceaselessly against her ribs all the while. Raegan was tired and cold, her nerves completely frazzled. But this was the most important part, what *everything* was hinged upon. So she took a deep breath and snatched a candle from one of the built-in shelves on the wall, examining the door.

On its face was some kind of a cipher. Twelve concentric rings of metal, fitted within each other like a Russian doll, sat in the middle of the door. Esoteric etchings covered them in equal increments, absolutely none of them familiar. Unease slid through Raegan's veins. What if she wasn't good enough, smart enough, strong enough to see this through?

She tossed the thought aside angrily, passing the candlelight over the rings. Possibly, she thought, each individual Protectorate member granted access to the twelfth floor had their own combination. Like a particularly brutal high school locker. Raegan bit the inside of her cheek, leaning closer.

But nothing made any sense. There was no dial where the etchings could be lined up to mark a combination, and besides, all the symbols were nonsense, anyway. She found a few almost-alchemical symbols easily enough, but each was altered, rendering it meaningless. Why the whole dog and pony show with the terrifying clock and the scarab beetle if all that could be accessed was a room with nice alcohol and some fireplaces?

"Why would it need a lock at all, then?" Raegan muttered out loud. "And what self-important prick is going to dial in a twelve-symbol code every time they want access?"

She reeled back then, her mind turning. "*Oh.*" Hoping she was right, intimately aware of the wards stretched like cobwebs across the Undercroft, Raegan raised Rochester's key ring and held it up to the middle of the door like a swipe card.

And just like that, a soft click sounded and the door opened. She'd been right—the cipher was a trap. The real way to get through was to hold one of the magicked keys up to the door. Raegan resisted the urge to whoop in triumph and crept forward, peering around foot-thick iron.

On the other side, she saw a setting much like the last floor's. But instead of empty space for entertaining or sacrifices or whatever the fuck the Protectorate did, there were rows and rows of bookcases. She slipped inside, deciding to keep the candlestick in her hand for now.

Raegan's heels clicked loudly on the pristine marble floors, so she set the candlestick down for a moment and pulled them off, shoving the keys into the bodice of her dress while she was at it. Then she padded deeper into the space, finding display cases filled with scrolls and worktables piled with books, as if someone had stopped mid-research. Large corkboards attempted to trace her and the King's whereabouts. Worth a detour from the main aisle, she decided, so Raegan slipped over and examined the papers pinned to the cork. She smiled. It didn't seem the Protectorate knew shit about Hiraeth besides the fact that a hidden Fey city existed somewhere on the Isles. They also seemed to think hanging a cross blessed by a bishop over a doorway could keep Oberon out of a building, which was positively laughable.

The dossier. Letting out a long breath, Raegan strode deeper into the archive, trying to get a sense for its organization. She even doubled back to look for a card catalog at the front of the room, to no avail.

"Of course you motherfuckers don't know how to properly catalog a collection," she grumbled, abandoning another disordered bookshelf. Minutes ticked by. She was undoubtedly aware of them thanks to the grandfather clocks lining the walls every twenty feet, all ticking away, mocking her inability to find the *one* thing she, the King, Emrys, Alanna, and Maelona had risked everything for.

At least she found a light switch. Once flicked on, the archive was illuminated by plain white light bulbs encased in industrial wire cages that studded the ceiling above her head. Much easier to navigate an underground room full of flammable objects by artificial light than the naked flame of a candle.

Finally, at the very back of the archive stood an antique display case —shining ebony and sloping glass. Raegan noted the locks on each compartment, as well as the complicated protection spells that would prevent a simple smash and grab. Elation flitted in her lungs.

She darted toward the case, starting on one end and working her way over. Her entire body stilled when she saw it—a document case labeled "Avalon: Possible Locations & Theories." The case was slim, brown leather with ornamental brass accents on each corner. The label was written in a spidery hand and faded. Her blood hummed, and she fumbled through Rochester's keys, looking for one that might fit the clever little lock on the front of the case.

When she found it, she slid it inside and popped the top of the case. And there it was—the fruit of their labor, one last mad hope. Gently, Raegan flipped the case open, skimming the first few pages. An introduction outlining the Protectorate's search from the early days until the present. Lots of raving about being tricked by the kelpies and how, at the very least, they had the right to bury their lord's body. Raegan scoffed. As if they just wanted to honor their dead, not raise Arthur Pendragon from his grave.

And then, there it was—a page stitched in between two much older ones. "CURRENT LOCATIONS OF INTEREST."

Her hands shook. For a long moment, her eyes refused to comprehend any of the words below the title, as if her mind couldn't fathom actually getting this far. But then it all fell into place, and Raegan found herself looking at seven place names. She scanned hungrily, her limbs still shaking violently—exhaustion or elation or something else entirely, she didn't know.

Carn Goedog
Tintagel Castle
Sgwd Yr Eira
Defynogg Yew
Forest of Borth
Pen Pyrrod
Maes Gwyddno

Raegan's mind swam. Only seven locations—so many less than Emrys's list, making this search almost manageable. She studied each name carefully; something about seeing each location written out in ink tugged at her marrow. She steadied herself against the edge of the glass case. From the depths of the long, ancient tapestry of her mind, she felt a strange, lilting hum—like there was a lost thread she could pull and bring the truth tumbling out.

Raegan considered. They'd been to Carn Goedog and Sgwd Yr Eira already. Tintagel was on Emrys's secondary list, as was Defynogg Yew. Which ones could she remember visiting in other lives? But the tides of her memory stubbornly offered her nothing, so she quickly flipped through the rest of the dossier, finding extensive notes on each location— more fieldwork than they could ever hope to accomplish without dying— as well as transcriptions of interviews with Fair Folk the Protectorate had captured, tortured, and executed. She gritted her teeth. In the back, stamped repeatedly as "TOP SECRET," were timetables and schedules for ongoing patrol at each location.

"Time to think later," she muttered, setting the candle down on the floor. The plan had been to memorize the locations and leave the dossier itself. But there was too much valuable information she couldn't squander, and she certainly couldn't hope to memorize it all. So Raegan steadied herself and tried to slip into her second sight so she could search more thoroughly for any warding that might prevent her from taking it with her or, perhaps worse, any location spells attached to the document case.

"Oh, fuck you," she grumbled at herself more than once, frustrated that she could create a glamour out of a Protectorate commander's oath but still struggled with something so basic.

Ultimately, though, Raegan found nothing. So cautiously, her heart pounding against the inside of her throat, every muscle in her body coiled and ready to spring, she lifted the slim, leather-bound dossier from its glass case.

Time stretched long and thin. Clocks ticked. Raegan's blood raced. A bead of sweat trickled down her brow.

Silence. Nothing.

"Okay," Raegan whispered, her voice hoarse, as she gathered up her shoes, slipping her wrist through the straps, and tucked the dossier under her other arm. She grabbed the candle and moved as quickly as she dared to the front of the archives. None of the grandfather clocks along the wall suddenly sprang to life. The Timekeeper himself did not appear—though that was mostly a given, as he rarely left the In-Between and the Otherlands, the same way no king went into his own vineyard for grapes, so long as his servants kept bringing them directly to his mouth.

Raegan shoved the candle back into the alcove, almost dropping it. She swore, righted the candlestick, and then ran through the vestibule and up through the hallway. Back to the King. Always back to him.

The look on his face as she emerged from the corridor sent tears rushing down her face. Her heart burst into a thousand pieces. How often he had to let her go, expecting her to never come back, but here she was, running out of the darkness barefoot and undone. Only a few paces to go, the one person she had deeply, truly loved waiting for her across all eternity.

Raegan surged forward, eager to touch him, to kiss him, to feel like maybe this time things would be different. But instead of the powerful weight of the King's arms closing around her, something slippery and strong wrapped around her ankle. And then it pulled.

Chapter Thirty-Seven

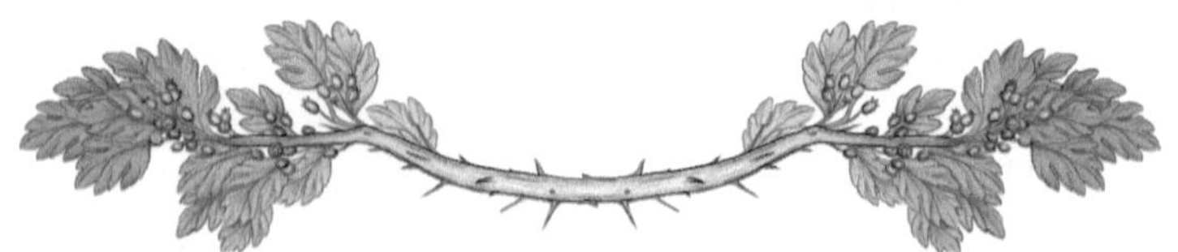

Rough stone floor rushed toward her face. At the last minute, she managed to tuck her arms and roll. Her bare legs banged hard into the wall, but she hardly felt the pain. Not with the tentacle of that massive clock guardian wrapped around her ankle, dragging her toward its writhing nest of limbs.

She struggled for purchase on the floor, unwilling to let go of the dossier, which she imagined was what the creature wanted. Now it came all too clearly into Raegan's mind: it was very likely that nothing from that room was permitted to leave the two lowest levels. The thought would've brought more relief—that it wasn't Oberon's Fey blood or her glamoured oath responsible for enraging the thing—if more tentacles weren't hungrily slithering toward her.

With a grunt, Raegan snatched one of her high-heeled shoes by the vamp and slammed the heel down into the tentacle clutching at her ankle. To her surprise, the clock *screamed*—the sound of universes ending and civilizations falling and a snake eating its own tail. It did, however, let go of her, if only to send a smaller, more agile limb snaking out at her, grabbing the shoe she'd stabbed it with and flinging it to the other side of the hallway.

"Fuck you, I have *two*," Raegan snarled, scrambling to her knees, raising the second shoe in preparation to strike.

It was, however, entirely unnecessary. The Unseelie king was magicless, not defenseless—and he strode right up to the clock, hauled his fist back, and punched the beast in the face. No—more than that, Raegan realized as she struggled to her feet, breathless and covered in scrapes. He'd knocked the monster off-balance with a direct hit, then reached his other fist into its trunk. With a snarl, Oberon drew his hand back, pulling the clock's pendulum and other innards with it. The creature let out a mechanical whine but fought hard against the King's hold, its tentacles still reaching to clutch at Raegan.

"What *is* that?" she demanded, still out of breath, stumbling backwards out of the beast's reach, avoiding the broken glass now scattering the floor. Oberon was clutching what looked like a pocket watch between his fingers, but it was *moving*. Raegan leaned closer, finding a writhing maw of tiny tentacles housing the watch face.

With disgust, Oberon tossed the thing hard at the stone floor, then crushed it beneath his heel. It disintegrated into dust, and a moment later, so did the enormous clock monster. One second, they'd been trapped in a tunnel with an eldritch beast, the next, only silence and ash.

"Raegan," Oberon murmured, moving lithely as a panther and seizing her in his powerful arms.

"I'm fine," she mumbled into his shirt, relishing the feeling of being crushed against his broad chest. For a long moment, neither said anything. The tide of each other's breathing was enough—alive, for now, gloriously alive.

His grip loosened slightly, and Raegan pulled back, smiling up at him. "Look what I got," she said with a grin, pulling the dossier from where she'd had it clamped under her bicep. "There's a lot more in here than just locations."

The King's eyes sharpened with interest for a second but then slid to the pile of ash where the creature had once towered. "I wonder if the rest of the guardians will react similarly to you trying to leave with the dossier in your possession."

"Fair point," Raegan admitted, something reckless and wild and giddy with abandon surging through her. "But I *will* very much enjoy watching you gut them all." She grabbed one of her high heels off the floor and went to maneuver around Oberon to grab the other, which had been thrown across the corridor by the clock.

But he grabbed her, his long fingers devouring her forearm. "Too much broken glass," he said, gazing down at her, the candlelight rendering his face in half-shadow. "Stay here."

And then the heat of his touch faded as the King stalked to the far wall and picked up her shoe in one continuous, elegant movement. He returned to her in a few strides of his powerful legs and lowered himself to one knee before her without a word. When he glanced up to meet her eyes, muscular thighs visible just beneath the fabric of his trousers, desire unfurled at the apex of her legs.

Oberon held out a hand expectantly, wordless, and Raegan took too long to react, happy to drown in the endless gray of his ocean eyes. But then she placed one open hand on his broad shoulder to steady herself before lifting one leg. He curled his fingers around the curve of her ankle and guided her foot to his knee. From there, he slid her shoe back on, his touch a gentle caress as he redid the tiny buckles.

"This shouldn't be so hot," Raegan laughed, a blush warming her cheeks as he repeated the process with her other shoe.

The King glanced up at her again, his full mouth parted, one eyebrow arched, the perfect portrait of playing with fire. "You enjoy this?" he asked, his voice a low thrum in the earthen corridor, fingertips sliding up the back of her calf.

Raegan shivered, clutching at the fabric of his shirt. "Yes," she whimpered.

"Interesting," Oberon replied, his hands gripping her by the waist as he got to his feet. Then, without hesitation, he propelled her back into the wall, his much larger body an unstoppable force that she'd happily be destroyed by. In the candlelit gloom, his fingertips brushed her jaw, tilting her chin upwards. His lips parted as he cocked his head to the side. For a moment, she thought he might say something. But then he just kissed her, fully and completely, stealing the breath from her lungs. Raegan melted against him, not wanting the moment to end but knowing there were miles and miles left to go before this night was over and done.

"Should we face the remaining horrors?" he asked her, lips moving against the delicate skin of her neck in a way that made her entire body tremble.

"You know," she said, hooking a leg around his hips, nails raking down his back, "almost *anything* is foreplay with you."

He laughed then, a sound too crisp and rich for this dead place. "Is that a yes, my villainous thing?"

"Absolutely," Raegan replied, weaving her fingers into his. And then they turned and began the ascent, moving in careful steps up the corridor. Generally, she enjoyed being right, but Raegan was quite dismayed to find their theory about the grandfather clock guardians proved correct when the next one lurched at them, tentacles unfurling.

The King wasted no time, shattering its trunk and yanking the writhing pocket watch from its depths. He threw it at the floor, and Raegan slammed her heel down onto its face. The next moment, there was no proof either the clock or pocket watch had existed except for the dust piled in the middle of the walkway.

The level itself was quiet, and for a moment, Raegan hoped that Oberon had been wrong about hearing a large number of people enter the Undercroft earlier. Or maybe it'd just been for a completely different reason—some kind of fucked-up viewing party of a Fey skeleton or people looking for a good place for an orgy. Any other reason than because the Protectorate knew their secret warren had been raided.

But as they destroyed the next guardian and slipped out onto level nine—an armory, mostly—she realized that hoping was just as worthless as it'd always been. The King paused at the mouth of the corridor, motioning for her to be quiet. Then he pulled her close to him and slunk along the wall, darting behind a rack of axes the moment he had the chance.

Maybe twenty feet away, coming from between them and the corridors to the surface, a voice called, "Clear!"

Raegan nearly jumped out of her skin. She felt Oberon bow around her, his lips nearly at her ear. "Could you work a subtle silencing spell for your footsteps?"

The request sent anxiety pulsing in her blood. With Protectorate soldiers so close, she'd have to be incredibly precise to avoid detection. But the other options were just as poor—carrying her would slow Oberon down and add more bulk to their movements. There wasn't time to try to yank the high heels back off again, and even if there was, the full black-tie outfit was essential if they were discovered. When all else failed, lying just long enough to create an opening could save them.

But Raegan could do this; she'd done about ten much harder things already this evening. Instead of reaching for the older, darker powers deep in her marrow, she skimmed the surface, purposefully playing in the shallows of her Protectorate magic as she worked a common silencing spell. With luck, even if the working was detected, the soldiers in the room would assume it was one of their colleagues.

She felt the charm sink in and looked up to nod at Oberon. He met her gaze, concentration written clear across his features; he was likely tracking every single person in this room by sound alone. Anticipation wrapped itself thickly around Raegan's body, stealing the air from her lungs. And then the King squeezed her hand once, giving her maybe half a second to prepare before slinking around the corner and darting across the aisle. He pulled her behind a row of towering display cases, her heart careening out of her chest. But her spell had worked—she'd been completely soundless even when moving across the stone floors. Small victories, Raegan told herself.

"All the way to the door this time," the King whispered, gathering himself up. Raegan nodded, trying to prepare herself.

"Wait," she replied, barely even speaking the word aloud. Oberon turned to her, his movement sharp as a raptor's. She held up the dossier and motioned for him to tuck it into his waistcoat. Delicately, Oberon took the slim leather document case from her and slid it beneath the rich fabric. It was testament to how stressful the situation was that he hadn't done it himself when she'd first returned with it. For a second, her mind wandered, recalling how the Unseelie king had been most concerned about making sure she didn't step on broken glass.

Raegan's face heated again, just as he closed his fingers around her arm and slid away from the display cases, barely more than a mundane shadow. Together, moving as one animal, they slipped around book-shelves and crouched behind large crates, evading soldiers armed to the teeth. When they darted out of the floor and into the next hallway, Raegan almost fainted from relief.

Shouts echoed through the cavernous space when they were barely a few feet up the corridor. Her body threatened to freeze.

"They do not understand what happened to the guardians," Oberon told her in a low voice. "Which may work in our favor as long as we keep moving."

Raegan steeled herself and pushed onward, sticking close to the King's bulk. As they rounded the corner, she gave him room to disembowel the next clock guardian. Level eight was clear and quiet, the Protectorate soldiers sticking together, hunting like a pack. That was their mistake, wasn't it? They always saw themselves as the predator, not the prey. And yet their warren had already been robbed.

The thought of the dossier tucked into Oberon's waistcoat carried Raegan through the ascent to the surface. Her heart never quite returned to a normal pace, but her thoughts crystallized and her muscles obeyed her without question. It felt good to be stealing through her enemy's stronghold with her faerie king at her side, salvation snug against his skin.

On level three, they paused for Oberon to see what he could hear from the two floors above them. Raegan knew the soldiers had likely reached the bottom archive and were searching to see what had been taken. She had little doubt they'd go for the case the dossier had been in first, and then all hell was going to break loose. So she slowed her breathing and steadied herself as the King took a few steps away, his head cocked to one side.

She watched his brow furrow, tracking his gaze as it slid to a closet off to the left. Unease slid through her, catching at her insides with serrated teeth. This level was fairly bland, appearing to mostly function as a debriefing space for higher-ranked officials. But Oberon moved toward the closet all the same, his footsteps utterly silent despite the weight of his muscle and solid bone. He looked up and motioned for her to stand behind him, putting her out of sight while he opened the door. Raegan inhaled sharply and shot across the hall, glad she had maintained her silencing spell for her high heels.

The King glanced over his shoulder at her, and she nodded. The door was locked from the outside, and he slid the latch over with the barest of sounds. The next moment, he'd pulled the door open before Raegan even processed his movement.

"Sir?" stuttered a voice that she distantly recognized. "Sir Tristan, is that— Oh fuck."

With a look of disbelief, Oberon gestured Raegan over, pushing the door all the way open with a sigh. Trepidation skittering in her veins, she obeyed, coming face to face with Reilly, the soldier she'd spared at the river.

They'd been nearly dead when she'd seen them last, but frankly, they didn't look much better. Their tangle of limbs indicated someone had probably thrown them in the closet. Their hair was matted, caked in blood by the left temple. Dark circles deepened their eye sockets. Their clothing—only an undershirt and sweatpants despite the chill—was stained and torn.

"Reilly?" Raegan asked in surprise, remembering too late to keep her voice low.

"Who are you?" they demanded, scooting farther back in the closet.

Raegan looked at Oberon in confusion.

"The glamours," he explained, gesturing to their rings. "Twist it very lightly to the left. That should dial down the glamour for Reilly to realize who we are without deactivating it."

Raegan did so, glancing over at the King so they could make the movement in unison. She was pretty confident it had worked when poor Reilly barely choked back a scream.

"How are you in the Undercroft?" they demanded, their voice hoarse. "The damn Unseelie king. In the *Undercroft*."

"Reilly," Raegan interrupted, pushing Oberon back gently. "I didn't let him kill you, remember? Can you tell me what happened? Why are you here?"

Reilly looked at her like she'd lost her mind. But then something in them shattered, like everything was just too much, and they opened their mouth to speak. "I—they were transferring me to somewhere else in the Manor w-when one of the lower levels' alarms went o-off," they stuttered, a shiver wracking their body. "Sir T-Tristan threw me in here. Told m-me to wait while they looked."

Raegan and Oberon exchanged a glance.

"Absolutely not," he said, his expression darkening.

She inhaled deeply and let it out slowly before turning back to Reilly. "Wanna get out of here?" Raegan asked, crossing her arms.

"L-like this closet?" Reilly asked, bewildered. "I mean, yeah. It smells weird."

"Like the Protectorate," she replied, amusement tugging at the sides of her mouth when she heard Oberon disguise a laugh at Reilly's reply as a cough. "All of this shit you had no choice in."

Reilly scrambled to their feet, knocking their head on a shelf and cursing. "So Alanna really did it, huh?" they asked, wrapping their arms around their torso, something not unlike hope gleaming in their eyes. "They haven't gotten anything out of me, just so you know. On my honor."

The King sighed, pinching the bridge of his nose. "Are you coming with us or not, little traitor?"

CHAPTER THIRTY-EIGHT

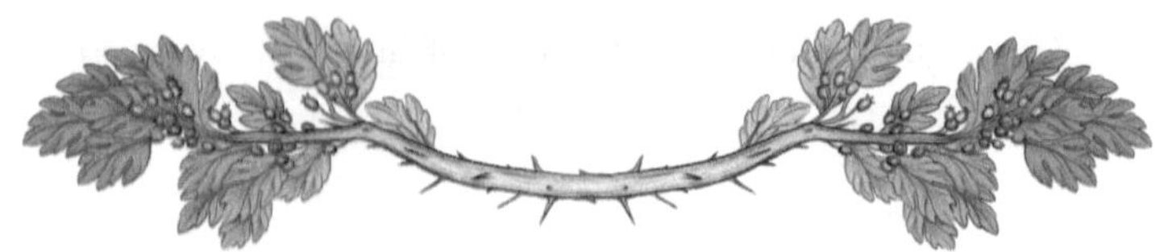

Reilly paled and retched, stumbling back against the wall, clamping one freckled hand over their mouth. "Oh my gods," they choked out. "That's the worst thing I've ever seen."

Oberon let out a scoff as he pulled Rochester's crumpled corpse from the filing cabinet. Raegan pressed her ear back to the office door, listening hard. Outside in the hallway, it was more or less chaos. The three of them had just barely made it out of the Undercroft and into Rochester's office before the regiment of soldiers broke through the upper levels.

Another flurry of shouts and barked orders resounded through the corridor. Raegan's gaze flitted back to the King. He was stripping Rochester's corpse of the expensive tux, now fighting against rigor mortis —not that he was particularly struggling.

"You want me to put that on?" Reilly gasped when Oberon handed over Rochester's jacket.

"Do you want to live?" he shot back, narrowing his eyes at Reilly. When the young Protectorate soldier didn't answer, Oberon flexed his wrist and sent the jacket flying through the air, landing squarely on Reilly's chest. They let out a little shriek but caught the garment and held it, watching Oberon as he pulled the starched white shirt from Rochester next.

"We're not even close to the same size," Reilly sniffed. "And this fabric is hardly appropriate for a late fall event."

To Raegan's surprise, Oberon laughed, shaking his head as he pulled the corpse's legs out straight, which released a horrific tearing sound. But Reilly donned the dress shirt all the same. Raegan watched their hands shake as they did up the buttons.

"We're lucky Rochester wasn't wearing anything more distinctive," she muttered, sagging against the door. She'd already put the commander's keys back on his desk, hoping to make it look like nothing had happened at all. Provided no one opened the cabinet drawer, of course.

Reilly finished dressing, adjusting the waistband on the pants, while Oberon rocked back onto his heels. He took a long look at the corpse, let out a sigh, and then began to fold Rochester's limbs back up again.

"Oh god, that's awful," Reilly sputtered as they turned away from Oberon and the corpse, kneeling to tie up the brogues that were at least one size too small. "Almost as awful as brogues with a *tux*. For Kronos's sake."

Raegan snorted, feeling an immediate sort of warmth toward Reilly —the same way she had with Alanna. It must mean something, she told herself, especially since she usually had difficulty forming attachments. Or maybe she was just grasping at straws, reaching into the dark and hoping for something she could hold on to for more than a moment or two.

"How are we going to just waltz back out there like we had no idea what was going on, anyway? I mean, your glamours are damn good, but still," Reilly asked as Oberon finished with the corpse, pushing the cabinet closed.

Raegan felt the King's gaze on her and looked up to meet his eyes, finding a sliver of that molten heat she knew so well. "Well," she said, taking a step away from the door, drawing the word out, "there's one obvious option. Probably the most effective."

Oberon raised one muscular shoulder to his ear in a shrug. "Agreed." He glanced down at his outfit, untucking his waistcoat, moving to unbutton one of his cuffs. Raegan followed suit, pulling the neckline of her dress to be slightly uneven, sliding one sleeve off her shoulder. Reilly looked at them both like they had lost their minds.

"What are— *Oh*," they said, their heart-shaped face turning red.

"May I?" Raegan asked, approaching them. "And are you okay with our idea?"

"No, no, it's fine. It's smart," they replied. "It's okay with me. Thanks for checking."

Slowly, Regan undid their collar another few buttons and pulled their shirttails out a bit. She chewed on the inside of her cheek, trying to figure out how to use her Protectorate magic to alter their appearance enough to slip out of the Manor. Healing, she decided, figuring that something familiar in her exhausted state was best. She sent her magic to soothe the dark circles, ease the chapped lips, mend the scabbed wound on their temple. But Raegan added a little more meaning beneath that first current, altering the shape and color of their eyes, making the lips thinner, lightening the distinctive freckles—subtle changes were all she could risk. Hopefully it would be enough.

"Okay," she said, standing back. "Oberon, you're sure there's no location spellery on the dossier?"

The King nodded. "I do not believe so. It would be too easy for an enemy to use such a working as a beacon, so the Protectorate seems to rely on preventing entry and theft in the first place."

"Great," Raegan beamed. "Right. So, probably best if we all spill out the door together, acting drunk. Remember, we're in that post-orgasm haze."

Reilly, if possible, turned even redder, the color creeping up into their hairline as Raegan hooked her arm through theirs. Oberon slipped his hand around her waist, throwing his other arm over Reilly's narrow shoulders. With a deep breath, she moved their little convoy to the door, throwing it open without giving herself the chance to hesitate.

They tumbled into the hall. It looked exactly how it sounded—commanders screaming orders, soldiers sprinting up and down the hallways. The wall sconces burned brighter, as if they'd been dialed up to highlight exactly who didn't belong. Raegan plastered a confused look on her face, dropping her mouth open as she looked left and then right.

As a soldier rushed by—so young, *too* young—Oberon called out, "You there. What in the name of Kronos is going on?"

The soldier halted, immediately turning to face the three of them. The King's deep, authoritative voice and towering height no doubt made the soldier square their shoulders and formulate a reply. "Sir. The Undercroft was infiltrated. We are searching for the perpetrators."

"Oh," Raegan said with a giggle, twirling a curl around one finger. "Guess that's why Rochester had to cut out early. A shame."

The soldier turned to her, interest sparking on their long, thin face. "You've seen Rochester? No one can find him."

"He was with us," Reilly piped up, swaying back against Oberon's muscular frame as if they were too drunk to stand. "Maybe, I don't know, twenty minutes ago?"

"More like thirty," Oberon corrected, amusement seeping into his tone. "This one's a bit out of it. Apologies, soldier—Rochester worked a privacy spell on his office, so we did not hear the commotion. We are only visiting diplomats, but we would have offered assistance sooner if we knew the gravity of the situation."

"He just said he had to check on something," Raegan added, stifling a very real yawn, putting her head on Reilly's shoulder. "Can we help at all, though?"

The soldier took in the three of them. "We're asking everyone to head out onto the front lawn for now. There will be officials there with more details."

"Copy that, soldier," Reilly said with a lusty wink.

Oberon, acting as if he were the most sober, shepherded the two of them through the long corridor. No one stopped them. Raegan fought to keep her movements relaxed and loose, her face muscles hurting from the silly girlish smile she kept plastered on her face.

She could hardly believe it when they exited the cavernous foyer onto the front lawn. There was a long queue of guests undergoing careful examination by Protectorate security. It didn't appear that anyone was being permitted to leave. Raegan gritted her jaw and looked over at the King. He met her glance with an equally worried expression. The physical glamours *might* hold, but Reilly would certainly be caught. She doubted Oberon wouldn't set off an alarm, and all they'd need to do was look a little too closely to see he wasn't even human.

"We will not be able to sneak away," the King said to her, his voice low, one hand blatantly sliding to her ass, making the comment seem like a flirtation. He was right—soldiers with large, unnatural-looking dogs were beginning to circle the property. Floodlights burst to life across the gardens.

"Can Rainer get through the wards?" Raegan asked, tilting her head to look up at Oberon, letting her chest heave as she leaned toward him. Ideally, they'd get off the Protectorate compound, or at least out of the highest security zone, before summoning the kelpie.

"Who is Rainer?" Reilly asked, looking a little shaken before they pushed it away, playing up their intoxication.

The gravel crunched under Raegan's heels as she pivoted toward them, cupping their jaw in her hand. "A kelpie," she replied with a forced giggle.

"Probably," Reilly said with faux drowsiness, leaning into her touch. "It's less about getting in and more about getting *out*."

"We will be able to fend off the wards," Oberon said in a low, sonorous tone, running one hand down Reilly's arm. The Protectorate soldier trembled, making Raegan choke back a laugh. No one, it seemed, was immune to the Unseelie king when he turned his attention their way. "It will be a short opening, though. A few moments. There can be no hesitation, no mistakes."

"Still want to come home with us?" Raegan asked Reilly, straightening the lapel on their jacket. They nodded, their expression gone solemn again.

Oberon reached into the pocket of his waistcoat and pulled out a small vial. In the floodlights, the river water contained beneath the glass glimmered viciously. For a moment, her mind wandered—back to that moment in the alley in Philly when Oberon had summoned Cath Palug, the faerie cat who'd kept the Protectorate distracted. She remembered the heat of his body against hers, those brief seconds held to his chest among the weeds and debris. She'd thought that would be all she'd ever get to taste of him. And now she'd had all of him since then, time and time again—yet she still wanted him as fervently and as achingly as she had in that alley. Her yearning, it seemed, was as insatiable as the tides, ebbing in and out but never able to stop reaching for the rugged beauty of his shoreline.

The King held her gaze, something dark and ravenous moving in the ocean of his eyes that made her wonder if he knew exactly what she was thinking.

"Take me home," she murmured, the words barely breaching the real world, intended only for the ears of the faerie king.

His elegant fingers curled around the vial. The glass shattered, sending black water trickling down his hand like tiny tendrils of ink. And then the King called to Rainer—not the summonings Raegan knew but a communion between two inhuman beasts that time could not touch. She felt the wards constrict, a bear trap clamping down, and then she let those winding rivers within her rise to meet it. The glamour she'd created from Rochester's oath fractured and broke, a fine weave of silk to a shard of glass and, finally, to nothing at all.

From deep within the abyss of the Rivers that could not be dammed or denied, a kelpie shimmered into existence, fully formed, at the King's side. Gasps went up from the crowd around them. For a moment, all the world hung still—a handsome guest shedding his humanity, a fabled creature dissolving from thin air. Someone screamed.

And then a hundred Protectorate soldiers were rushing toward them, incantations hurtling through the air. The King tossed Reilly onto Rainer's back as if they were a child, reaching for Raegan next. She summoned the rain that had fallen earlier—river water once, river water again—and soldered it into a shield. The working gleamed like a scythe, stopping that teeth-rattling magic in its tracks. The Protectorate wards howled and tore into the shield, but it held despite the horrific pull Raegan felt on every inch of her flesh.

Then she was astride Rainer's broad back, Reilly in front of her, the King behind, his shadows devouring the weave of the wards, panther-like in their ferocity. Rainer leapt forward, his scalloped ears moving this way and that, as he charged for the opening Oberon had created. It was going to *work*. Elation burst golden in Raegan's ribs, banishing that ever-present doubt.

Oberon had chosen a gap in the Protectorate's guard, lessening their chance of injuries inflicted by more mundane—but just as dangerous—weapons. As the kelpie raced toward the growing fissure in the wards, hurtling around a boxwood sculpture, Raegan saw something that made her heart stop.

Three soldiers—armed to the teeth, their faces covered by helms—violently tackling a tall, beautiful, dark-skinned woman. *Alanna.* A nightstick slammed into the Protectorate woman's stomach, and she doubled over, shouting something Raegan couldn't hear above the thrum of blood in her ears.

"Oberon!" She turned to face him, finding his eyes already trained on Alanna. Their gazes met. The next second, Rainer slammed to a halt, swinging his head around to look at them in frustrated shock. Arrows landed like stones against a window on Raegan's shield.

"Get Reilly out of here," Raegan yelled, sliding off the kelpie in unison with Oberon. "Then come back for us if you can."

Rainer followed the King's gaze beyond the shield of river water and shook his head. "What a terrible time to have honor," he scoffed before he turned, gathered himself up, and leapt into the door the King's shadows had carved into the wards. It closed behind him like a cauterized wound.

And then it was just her and Oberon against the entire might of their oldest enemy, in the very seat of all their horrible power.

CHAPTER THIRTY-NINE

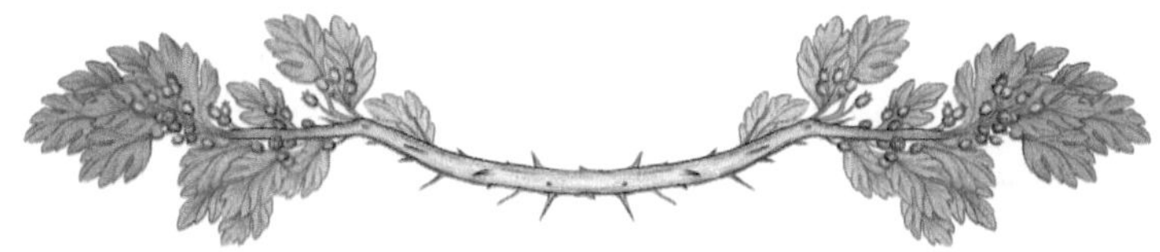

Oberon raised a hand, sending a plume of silver-laced smoke bursting into the air—a signal for Maelona to get out and meet at the rendezvous point. Raegan watched as dull black armor began to slink into existence across his body: arm bracers with elongated, violent edges, blackened chainmail, and, of course, that terrifying blade spun of shadow and unearthly power.

The King gripped her bicep with his gloved fingers, pulling her behind a tall, sculptural hedge as battle magic tore through the air around them. "Do not let them separate us," he told her, his gaze steady. "Hold your shield. Do not stop unless I do."

"I'm with you," Raegan said, offering him a grim smile. She risked a glance out around the side of the hedge maze. The festive—if heavy—atmosphere had been rent in pieces by the appearance of the Unseelie king. The Protectorate's guests were scattered, some cowering behind heavy gray planters as if that might save them. Many, it seemed, had retreated into the Manor; it looked to be mostly soldiers out on the killing field of the front lawn.

"Ready?" the King asked, gazing down at her, mischief pulling at the sides of his mouth as if this were all a game.

"Why not, I guess?" Raegan replied, trying to quell the explosion of anxiety eating away at her insides.

He arched his brow at her, obscenely playful given the battle magic rocketing through the air, and then strode out into the open. He did not slink or sneak or even dart. Instead, the King moved in deliberate, graceful strides. Raegan kept pace with his bold movements though her heart felt like it might burst out of her chest. As attack workings rolled in, she fought to extend the shield, her teeth bared, sweat trickling down her back.

"Hey," she managed, "just wondering, are you fucking insane?"

"Yes," Oberon answered her, batting away a particularly nasty battle spell with the flat edge of his blade. "But you enjoy that, do you not?"

It was absurd that even in the middle of a battlefield, he could reduce her to little more than half-mad need. The way he spoke those words—his tone husky with promise—as he moved in a beeline toward Alanna, the moonlight cascading across his black armor, impossible and deadly and beautiful all at once . . . She'd die for him, Raegan realized, and he'd die for her, and there was something intoxicating about strolling so close to death the way most couples strolled around a leafy park.

Exhilaration shot through Raegan as a small group of soldiers came bursting from a hedgerow, blocking her sightline of Alanna. The Protectorate were armed to the teeth, covered head to toe in dull plated armor that hummed with protective workings. None of it mattered; Oberon summoned a bank of shadows and sent it coiling toward the soldiers, where tendrils of darkness shoved themselves into throats and noses and eyes. They dropped to the ground, gloved hands clutching at throats, and Raegan tried not to feel glee.

Instead, she stepped over the prone Protectorate, the dirtied train of her dress sliding across their bodies like a funeral shroud. Only twenty feet or so left to reach Alanna. Shoulder-to-shoulder with the King like this, adrenaline and fury rushing through her like river waters, Raegan felt like she could do anything.

But the more rational part of her brain recognized that she was drenched in sweat, droplets running into her eyes, her hair plastered to her skull. She didn't know how much longer she could hold her shield so resolutely, not with the intensity of the attack workings increasing with every moment. One slammed into her defensive wall so hard that every bone in her arms rattled. She clenched her teeth, ignoring the pain.

"Hey!" Raegan managed, the word coming out strangled not by pain or fear but by long-suffering rage. "In case you can't see, we're your nightmares made flesh. We're fucking primordial. But we only want the girl. Give her to us, and you live."

Two more steps forward, and the King's blade clashed with a spear of sainted iron someone had expertly lobbed their way. Raegan hadn't seen it. She swallowed hard. They were running out of time. Alanna was still a ways off, the soldiers who had restrained her dragging her backwards for every step she and the King took forward.

Through the chaos, Alanna's eyes met Raegan's. Something sparked in the rebel's brown gaze, hope so fierce it turned furious. Without a moment of hesitation, Alanna spun to face the soldier pinning her arms to her back and headbutted them hard. The two other Protectorate scrambled to restrain her, but they'd been understandably focused on the two eldritch terrors advancing on them. Alanna ducked out of the larger one's grasp, grabbing their nightstick in the same movement and swinging it up to slam into the shorter soldier's jaw.

Then she ran, crossing the open, dangerous space, trusting Raegan and Oberon to keep her alive. Raegan gathered up everything she had, a scream tearing from her throat as she sent the edges of her shield to extend to Alanna. Bullets ripped through the air but found no purchase. The woman tumbled into them, Oberon catching her with one outstretched arm and pulling her between himself and Raegan.

Now for the retreat. Like a soundless orchestra, everything fell into place—the King pivoted to tear a path through the forces that had snuck up behind them, Raegan holding the shield at their backs. Despite the blood pouring down her face, Alanna yanked an impressive number of knives from her belt and threw them with alarming accuracy. There was gore and screaming and the rending of bone. Raegan focused only on her shield and the feel of the King at her back, all of her instincts attuned to chasing the heat of him, just as she always had, across time and space and continents.

And then her vision blurred, the world broken into pieces by black splotches. "No," she grunted, biting down on her tongue. "No. Not yet."

But her shield faltered all the same and someone stole up close to her, all carefully trained movement and calculated attack. The King flipped his hold on the pommel of his sword and swung it in a backwards arc toward the attacker. They just missed being cleaved in two, taking the brunt of the sword's power at their shoulder. But it was enough—they screamed and plummeted to the ground.

Raegan staggered back another step, her mouth painfully dry, only dimly aware of Alanna at her side, who also seemed to be tiring. She risked a glance over her shoulder. The sweat and warmth coating her body chilled, terror slinking down her spine at what she found awaiting her. A well-organized group of thirty or so soldiers blocked the garden's exit in a solid half-moon, pinning them in place to be destroyed by the Protectorate forces advancing from the Manor.

Every step felt like her ankles were breaking. She should've fainted by now, Raegan knew, but it wasn't an option; it couldn't happen, so she clung to consciousness. The King slowed his pace, no doubt calculating what to do about this encroaching net of Protectorate. The Manor's wards dug deeper and deeper into Raegan with every passing second—the worst agony she'd ever endured, like meat hooks had been driven into her joints and now she was being pulled in ten directions at once.

Her shield flickered, and a bullet grazed Alanna's thigh. A gossamer-thin wash of darkness cloaked Raegan's shield—Oberon, lending some of his power to reinforce her working, even though he felt the wards just as she did. No, Raegan realized. He must feel the defensive spells *much* more than she did.

"Isn't it time," a voice called, "to surrender already?"

"Fucking Bedwyr," Raegan spat, knowing she shouldn't expend energy so uselessly but unable to stop herself.

"Aren't you tired of this?" the knight continued, speaking from some-where Raegan couldn't see him—likely at her back, facing the King. "Aren't you—"

Bedwyr's words cut off in a guttural sound, followed by a small commotion.

"What's happening?" she hissed to Alanna, though her words, too, were cut short. Hooves on gravel, she realized—Rainer returning to them. She grinned through the pain, tasting sweat on her tongue, and poured everything she had left into the shield. And then the King's arm was around her waist, Alanna laughing in her ear, the broad, muscular back of a kelpie between her thighs, the wind in her hair. And then, predictably, even though she fought it, nothing but darkness.

Fervently whispered words, a cool hand on her clammy forehead, a bloodcurdling scream, her name in the wind, the scent of fire crackling hot and hungry.

"Raegan," someone said, hoarse and urgent, "you gotta wake up."

"Okay," she grumbled in response, pulling herself from the downy dark of the void. She blinked her eyes open, finding Maelona crouched before her. "You're okay," Raegan gasped, rocking forward to toss her arms around her aunt.

Maelona froze at the contact and then relaxed, gripping Raegan hard in return. "Alive for now," her aunt said with a fierce smile as they broke apart. "We need to go. We all made it to the rendezvous point but with a lot more heat on us than we had planned for. We're in the hawthorns now. But they're . . ."

Raegan understood the thick scent of fire and smoke in her nose. Her heart plummeted to the bottom of her stomach. "They're *burning* them," she whispered. She pulled herself to her feet with a groan, dismayed to see dead leaves and forest debris had marred the storm-gray silk of her dress. The wound on her shoulder had been field-dressed with a strip of starched white fabric—Rochester's shirt that Reilly had been wearing, she realized.

Biting down on her tongue and praying her head would clear, Raegan took in her surroundings. She saw Oberon and Rainer a few paces off, deep in a hushed conversation. A twinge of tension in her chest gave way upon seeing they were both safe. But then her gaze drifted toward the night sky and her stomach twisted again. Smoke billowed in noxious plumes, thick as a stormfront and far too close for comfort.

"We can't go back to Hiraeth," Raegan said in a whisper, meeting Maelona's eyes. "Not with the Protectorate nearby. There's too much risk they might be able to follow us."

"No, we can't," her aunt agreed. She brushed dirt from her palms— she must've been keeping watch over Raegan until she regained consciousness. "There's an old faerie fort not far from here."

"A *Seelie* faerie fort," Alanna chimed in, materializing from the darkness of the hawthorn wood that surrounded them. The blood had been cleaned from her face, the wound on her thigh wrapped in more of that starched white fabric. Oberon, Raegan remembered all at once, did not have the power to heal. Not magically, at least. He'd been created to destroy. Nothing more, nothing less.

"Protectorate's been trying to get into that fort for a while," Reilly said, appearing from Alanna's far side, desiccated leaves crunching underfoot. They pulled Rochester's tux jacket tighter around their body, shivering. Their dress shirt had clearly been sacrificed to tend to wounds. It was sort of a look, though, Raegan thought deliriously.

"They can't breach it," Maelona said, her mouth a grim line. "They've been throwing some of the younger folks—like Alanna and Reilly—at it. The perimeter's secured. We just can't get *inside*."

"And you think I . . ." Raegan pulled on the door in her mind that led to Titania's life—her time as the High Seelie Queen. She wished fiercely and fervently for Blodeuwedd.

"There are few other options," Oberon said, moving closer to her, Rainer at his side. The King's gaze turned skyward, watching the approaching curls of flame.

"Well," Raegan said, coughing, "I suppose we've tried stupider shit tonight."

"Can't argue with that," Maelona grumbled at the same time Rainer tossed his massive head in triumph, sending the heavy waves of his mane rippling in the smoke-choked moonlight.

A few moments later, Raegan and the King were leading the way through the hawthorn woods, mounted on Rainer. The kelpie had been able to call a few of his comrades. Maelona was astride a silvery mare with white crowfoot blossoms wound into her long braids, while Alanna and Reilly rode double on a stocky, stoic kelpie the color of black floodwaters, his mane roached short on his thick neck.

Smoke billowed into Raegan's eyes as Rainer surged through the wood. Tears tumbled down her face—partially because of the fire, but also because this ancient copse of hawthorn trees was burning to the ground. All because they'd needed a safe harbor for a few moments. Hatred boiled low in her gut for the Protectorate, but she hated herself, too—for not being strong enough to end this so many years ago.

Up ahead, the hawthorns grew sparser, giving way to open moorland and lichen-covered rocks just visible in the moonlight. A whisper-thin sphere of shadows blinked into existence around their entourage. Silently, Raegan thanked Oberon. She didn't think she had very much left in her, which sent guilt spiraling up her throat. She forced it away, focusing on the rhythm of the kelpie beneath her and the faerie fort she only hoped she could open.

Forts had once dotted the landscape—underground dwellings with a small cache of rooms and supplies. They'd been essential to the Fair Folk's ability to move about the land unseen and organize against the Protectorate. Most of them had been cracked open like geodes in the past few hundred years, their glimmering insides raided and harvested by the enemy. If someone knew precisely what they were looking for, they might find a skeleton of a fort somewhere in the rural, tucked-away places of the Isles.

But Raegan had no idea one still stood intact. Oberon was going along with an idea formed by three Protectorate-oathed humans, so she assumed he'd had some prior knowledge that a fort might still exist. She took a deep breath as Rainer burst out into the open moorland, nothing but the hawthorn berries they'd all shoved in their pockets offering a shred of protection against the heavy, burning eye of the Protectorate.

The kelpie moved like a shadow, his heavy hooves silent as he galloped. Raegan resisted the urge to hold her breath, scanning the horizon. Instead of a gray-suited soldier or a faerie fort's beacon, she felt the sweep of a river somewhere, her sisters of the water calling out gently, lending their strength.

"Is there a river nearby?" she asked the King.

"The Derwent," he replied, the English name spilling from his tongue.

The night wind whipped through her hair, stinging her face with its cool kisses. Raegan grinned into the pain. "Derwennydd," she whispered into the air.

Somewhere in the distance echoed a rush of tides—a roar, a battle cry. She felt the King go still at her back.

"Around the next bend," Alanna called from Rainer's left, pointing toward a craggy knoll. A cairn crowned the top of its rise—from when mortals had understood the power of the old places and respected them instead of harvesting the guts of what remained.

Rainer swung around a large, flat stone pockmarked by a thousand years of rain, the moorland tilting down beneath his hooves. By the glow of the moon, Raegan took in her surroundings, realizing that the site of the faerie fort was atop the banks of the Derwennydd. She grinned, feral and vicious.

"Stay astride," the King instructed Maelona, Alanna, and Reilly as he dismounted, holding a hand out to assist Raegan. She took it gratefully, sliding down to the peaty soil of the moorland. The faerie hill's knoll rose up before her, the river—barely more than a wide stream this far north—stirring at her presence.

"Do you have any idea how to get inside?" Raegan asked, wading through the knee-high stalks of heather, a difficult exercise in high heels.

Beside her, Oberon shook his head, the wan light of the moon just allowing her to see the movement. "No," he told her, stepping closer to the rise of the knoll. "You never allowed me to watch you open it."

She threw him a sideways glance, just for a moment, before turning her attention to the wide piece of broken shale at the hill's base. The dark stone devoured the moonlight. Raegan squinted, looking closer—was that an etching in the rock? She parted the heather and gorse gently, crouching to examine the rock that was looking more and more like a threshold stone. It was cracked down the middle, but the carving was deep and deliberate. A spray of wheat, maybe? No—feathers.

An owl.

Raegan's mind pulled her beneath the currents with one sharp tug, showing her images of Blodeuwedd at her side, of this grassy hill when it had been young and sweet, of lanterns strung on the earthen walls of its interior, of the river creeping up from the shores and—

A howl of rage from the mouth of a kelpie tore Raegan's attention back to the present. She spun around, the knoll at her back, to find a wall of Protectorate soldiers coming at them from across the moorland. Their chainmail glinted dull and artificial under the moon's gaze, the muzzles of their guns pointed from gloved hands like hunting dogs straining at the leash.

"Do something before they get a time spell finished!" Alanna shouted, drawing a dagger from the top of her boot and throwing it into the night, where it hungrily embedded itself into the neck of a tall woman in a dusty navy suit. Alanna slid off the kelpie's back despite Oberon's request for her to do exactly the opposite. She yanked Reilly down behind her, shoving them toward the mouth of the fort. A few large stones circled the knoll, and Reilly crouched behind one, their face pinched.

Raegan's heart raced. Reilly was in no condition to fight. Maelona and Alanna were only human and had to be tiring. All no longer had magic, their oaths to the Protectorate broken.

She scanned the hills, watching black hounds materialize from the tall grasses. For a moment, Raegan's heart stopped in her chest—until one of the beasts tore into the thigh of a Protectorate soldier. She glanced over at the King, watching a bead of sweat glide down his temple, the muscles in his jaw feathering.

Raegan gritted her teeth. No more. No more iron littering the hillside, no more fingers of hungry men digging into the heather, no more chipping away at the bones of the old world. She curled her hands into fists and called to the river.

Power surged in her, the flame fed by her undying rage, and a shadow rose from the water, taller and taller, taller than even the King. A woman, or something that people might call a woman, a column of river water and ruin, arms like a spider, her fingers long and ravenous.

As Raegan watched, the massive creature unhinged its jaws. A damp, dark maw yawned wide. Then the river-woman's arms shot out into the Protectorate ranks and the screaming began.

CHAPTER FORTY

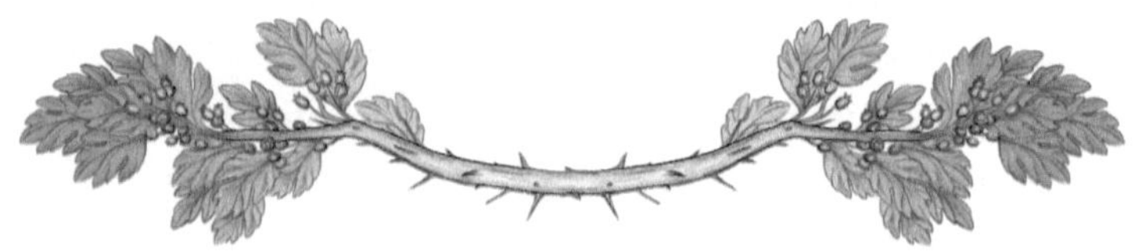

"Y ou will take no more from us," Raegan snarled, advancing into the meadow, little more than the dark river that rushed in her lowest places. There was nothing but that blackness, that cold and endless fury. She threw her head back and shrieked, banshee-like on the moonlit moors, feeding the river-woman all of her anger.

"You have taken my father," Raegan shouted, passing Rainer, who looked on with something like awe in his black toad eyes. She couldn't feel the ground beneath her feet. She should be unsteady, she thought distantly, walking in high heels on peaty ground, navigating clumps of thick grass and moss-covered boulders. But she floated, deity-like, sanctified, across the ancient ground. The woman-shaped column of river tore into the Protectorate ranks, soldiers clutched in her many hands. She drowned shouts and bullets as she drew them into her mouth, devouring and devouring and devouring.

"You have taken my aunt's freedom," Raegan continued, the wide stream at the bottom of the slope swelling into something too large, too thick with dark currents and silver eyes. "Alanna's autonomy. Reilly's choice. *No more.*"

The black hounds crafted from little more than spite and shadow were herding Protectorate soldiers toward the river creature's spindly-fingered hands, tearing apart anyone who fought back. Raegan reached for the Threads that spun all around her—magic, or what was left of it, tattered lines of silk sagging in the air—and stilled the ravenous column of water.

"If you, too, were never given a choice," she said, her voice hushed and yet still singing across the moor like a hymn, "leave now. I won't stop you."

The words had barely left her mouth when a number of soldiers—younger, from what she could see—dropped their guns and maces and spears. Time hung tense and still. And then one took off into the gloom of the moors, the woodsmoke from the burning hawthorns closing like a door behind them. Two more followed, then four, then ten. The force that remained was halved, reduced to rocky-faced mortals clutching tightly the sainted iron and the grips of their guns.

"So be it," Raegan said, and then she let the Threads go—released her hold on them entirely, letting the violence sing out true and unrestrained. The column of river water threw its head back and shrieked, more limbs sprouting from its sides, its jaws unhinging even wider.

"Raegan!" Maelona's voice came on the wind, whipping through her hair.

Raegan turned and found her people at the door of the faerie fort. She watched the river slink toward the knoll, soft and gentle in its movements, so unlike the thing that ate Protectorate men hand over fist at her back.

She blinked, and the next moment, she was standing beside her aunt. "The river will open it," she said, her voice not quite her own, staring down at the owl she'd carved into the threshold hundreds of years ago. It was cracked, yes, but its wings were still spread wide and proud, its beak still half-opened, that vicious cry building at the back of its throat.

Raegan watched, impassive and filled with peace, as the water slowly filled the owl etching. Once the carving had disappeared from view, golden bells rang in the distance like a homecoming. The hill face split down the middle, a seam opening for the first time in centuries, a soft yellow glow spilling out into the gray velvet of the moorland night.

"In you go," Raegan said, ushering Maelona, Alanna, and Reilly into the forgotten faerie fort until only she, the King, and the kelpies remained on the other side of the door.

Rainer said something, long and low, the words from a language long forgotten, and then turned to dive below the surface of the river water, his comrades at his side.

The King stood resolute and still in the shadow, the moonlight tracing silver strands in his midnight hair. Raegan gazed up at him, a thousand feelings tangled in her chest, the love she felt for him so over-powering that she thought she might faint.

"You know," she said instead, gesturing toward the river-woman behind them, "there's a reason I've been called a maneater."

The faerie king swept low, his long, elegant fingers gripping her jaw in a way that made Raegan feverish and half-mad. Those ocean eyes met hers, the tide of him all-consuming. But his body was too far from hers; her skin craved contact, to consume the heat of him, to be consumed in turn.

"A terrible day to be a member of the Fair Folk and not a man," he murmured, his head cocked to one side, a dangerous gleam in his eyes, "for I would gladly be devoured by the likes of you."

Raegan seized the front of his tuxedo jacket and hauled her mouth toward his—no elegance, no whisper-light touches, just the depth of her hunger ruthlessly on display. The Protectorate flesh her river-avatar had devoured would not satiate her. Not the way the faerie king did with his ivory skin and coiled muscle and elegant hands.

He met her with an equal hunger, fingers curling into her hair, drawing her close to his broad frame. A moan escaped Raegan the second his tongue slid into her mouth; there were so many other places to invite him inside, so many other ways he could slip beneath her skin and claim her. The patched dusk quilt of the moor, the rush of the river, the final cries of the Protectorate soldiers, the baying of the King's hounds—it was all swept away on the currents of her desire. Her hands slid down his sides, moving to the front of his hips, fingers splayed across the sharp V of muscle.

"We have houseguests," Oberon reminded her, trailing his lips down her jaw, though his hands cupped her breasts, her body painfully aware she wore no bra beneath the structured silk dress.

"Let's get them settled," Raegan said breathlessly, but her hands also wandered, finding hard and tightly wound proof of the King's desire—though she'd heard it loud and clear in his hitched tone.

"They've had quite the night," Oberon murmured against the shell of her ear, his arm winding around her waist, palm open on the soft slope of her belly.

Raegan looked up at him, amazed that he was still hers and that maybe this time it might stay that way. "Follow me," she said, interlacing her fingers with his. And then, with one last glance at the now-quiet moors behind her, Raegan stepped into the seam of light. Like most old doors, there was a moment in between, a long and skittering heartbeat where nothing was real at all. But then she stepped out into the hall of the faerie hill, the King's hand still in hers.

Memory burst like ripe orchard fruit, the juice running between her fingers, sticky and sweet. The faerie hill's main hall was a large, earthen chamber—the bones of it so much like the Undercroft that for a second, she wondered if they'd even made it out alive at all. But no—this place was different. The Undercroft's design was theft; this forgotten faerie hill the Protectorate could not breach was another thing entirely.

Thickly knotted vines—wisteria, she was quite sure—were latticed across the walls, holding the soil in place. Delicate glass ornaments hung from the bare vines, scattering rainbow kisses this way and that. The ground beneath her feet was a creamy stone shot through with veins of gold. She smiled up at the King and moved forward, headed for the hallway reaching off the entrance room.

Willow-o-wisp lights studded the corridor like strange sapphires, curling around the shadows. Each willow-o-wisp was contained in the metal-worked mouth of a swan, its elegant neck curving away from the wall, beaks open to emit illumination. Despite the cobwebs stretched across the lights, Raegan marveled at them—their cobalt-teal hue, dancing with wild abandon in a way no natural flame should.

At the end of the corridor, three hallways branched off of a small chamber. In the middle of the space stood an elegant round table with three impossibly delicate skeleton keys upon it. The golden metal winked in the light. The air smelled like wisteria and cool spring water and osmanthus, the deep, rich scent of petrichor and dark earth lingering beneath.

Wordlessly, Raegan and the King stepped down the hallway with light spilling from its mouth; the other corridors were silent and dark. They emerged into a great room. Dark carved wood graced the walls, the cream marble joined by deep blue accents that created mesmerizing patterns. At the far end, an enormous marble fireplace drenched the space in a warm orange glow. The hearth was shaped like an owl—stone wings stretching out along the walls, the mantel formed by powerful shoulders, its head and beak just above, another willow-o-wisp glittering in the depths of its open maw.

Sitting in front of the fire, wrapped in woolens likely retrieved from the open cedar chest beside the hearth, were Alanna, Maelona, and Reilly—all safe, their bodies curled around one another. A moth-eaten silk settee had been dragged to the side, its legs broken off to feed the flame. A large table sat in the middle of the room, looking like it had been carved from the same marble as the hearth. Raegan walked past it, running her finger down its side, creating a stark line in the dust that had gathered over the years.

"I cannot believe it's all still here," she murmured, startling Maelona, who turned sharply, worry written clearly across her features.

"We're all alive," her aunt whispered, one brow arching. "I'm astounded." Despite her low tone, Reilly and Alanna stirred, and then Raegan had three sets of wide, mortal eyes staring up at her and the King.

"This faerie fort was mine," Raegan explained, clasping her hands in front of her. "When I was Titania, the Seelie Queen."

"The Queen of the Hill," Alanna murmured, her gaze going even wider.

"Yes," Raegan confirmed, gaze darting toward the King, who watched her with his usual dark intensity. "We are safe here. I don't think they'll have much luck breaching the walls."

"But we will be under siege," Oberon said when she fell silent. "We should rest, but then we need to catalog our supplies and calculate how long we can reasonably stay here."

"This place is, like, hundreds of years old and covered in ten centimeters of dust," Reilly said, a yawn cutting their words in half. "How could there possibly still be edible food or anything of the sort?"

Oberon and Raegan exchanged glances. "There's a lot of magic in this place," she settled for, catching Reilly's yawn—her body still mortal, after all. "I'll explain later. I'm exhausted. Remember the table in the hall? You'll find keys on it. The lights will lead you to your rooms. For now, will the three of you be okay if I go take a bath?"

Alanna and Reilly nodded easily, but Maelona's gaze locked onto hers. "I have questions for you, niece," Maelona said, and Raegan might've thought they pertained only to the workings of the fort had her aunt's eyes not strayed to the King.

"Later, I promise," Raegan replied, offering a smile that took too much energy to muster.

Maelona didn't relent with the steel in her gaze, but then she nodded, waving her niece off. Raegan wavered, watching as Maelona gathered the woolen blanket around her and curled up on her side. Raegan exchanged a long glance with Oberon and then turned to investigate the quarters the fort offered.

She remembered the hill being eerily close to sentient with all the magic she and Blodeuwedd had poured into it—a necessary expenditure considering the political machinations of the Seelie Court. Moving slowly, Raegan took in the tapestries hung on the walls. Their stories were incomplete, half-devoured by moths as the strength of the housekeeping spells she'd woven into the space had weakened over the years with the loss of residual magic. She left the great room, sliding her arm into the King's.

She plucked a key from the center table, gesturing toward the hallway that bloomed with soft, wisteria-toned light the moment her fingers brushed the metal. "Have you been here before?" Raegan asked, parts of her memory still fuzzy.

"Yes," the King replied, moving soundlessly at her side toward the mouth of the corridor. "I think with some rest, you will remember quite vividly."

Raegan frowned, digging for the memory. Then, a beat too late, her brain registered the slinking heat in his tone. "Ah," she replied, leading them to a doorway at the end of a short hallway, sliding the golden filigree key into the lock. "I brought you here for that first discussion about uniting the courts."

Before she could open the door, Oberon reached above her, his open palms against the earthen walls, pinning her in. "And I tasted you for the first time here, too."

Warmth unfurled low in her belly, but Raegan rolled her eyes, reaching over to push the door open. "You were trying to seduce me. You saw an opportunity," she said playfully, ducking beneath his arms to enter the chamber the faerie hill had conjured for them.

The space was, unsurprisingly, breathtaking. More dark wood stretched across the walls, carved with all manner of ornamentation and medallions. The flat panels in between the intricate moldings were painted with breathtaking scenes—a unicorn, decorated in gold leaf, before a verdant meadow; a dragon curled at the bottom of a river, mother-of-pearl shimmering on its scales; a griffin flying low at sunset, the sky studded with amber jewels. In one corner, the floor sloped downward, a spotless clawfoot tub lounging across the creamy marbled floor.

A large canopy bed towered at the far end, its linens thankfully fresh. She and Blodeuwedd had tied a few of the more important housekeeping spells to the river instead of relying on ambient magic. They'd focused on the necessities, like clean bedding, preserved food, and fresh water, though now Raegan wished they'd taken the time and energy to protect things like the tapestries, too.

"Yes, I saw an opportunity," Oberon admitted, his voice a low, deep, sonorous sound just above her ear as he stalked in behind her. He paused, pulling their luggage tags from his pocket and setting them down on a carved wooden chest by the bed's footboard. The dossier followed, retrieved from beneath the fabric of his waistcoat. "But I desired you as well. Much more than I had any right to. Much more than good sense and all my careful plans dictated."

Despite its grandeur and the way it felt like home in a way almost nowhere did, the faerie hill's chamber faded away. The world condensed to the beating, wild-hearted love conjured by the Unseelie king. Raegan turned to face him, ensuring the door was closed. He swooped low, arms encircling her, and kissed her until she felt like the world had stopped turning.

Then Oberon lowered himself to one knee before her again, even though she saw the way his body caught in painful places, and undid the buckles on her high heels. "You did say I could undress you if we survived," he murmured, his hand skimming up the back of her calf to her thigh as he recalled a playful conversation they'd had during one of their many planning sessions. Goosebumps blossomed across her flesh, the ache winding tighter in her core.

"And you said," Raegan panted, curling her fingers into the silken strands of hair at the back of his neck, "if I got the dossier, you'd fuck me with more than your tongue."

"And I," the King replied, helping her out of her shoes and then rising to stand, his large hands spread wide over her hips, "always keep my promises."

"No, you don't, faerie king," Raegan laughed, unbuttoning his waistcoat, delirious and incandescent with belief and joy they were alive.

"For most souls, no, I do not," he agreed, slipping the silk straps from her shoulders and then bringing his mouth to her collarbone. "But for you, my love? *Always.*"

CHAPTER FORTY-ONE

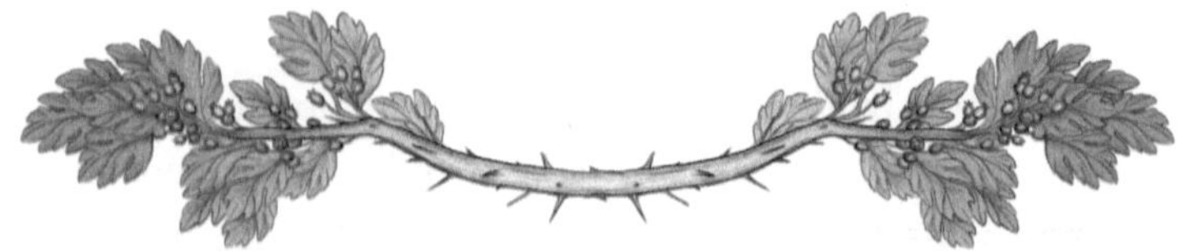

"I told them I was taking a bath," Raegan laughed as Oberon pressed her onto the bed, his body an unrelenting weight she would happily be crushed beneath.

"You will," he replied, tone gruff as he gathered up the floating train of her dress—mostly torn to pieces, a few scattered fragments of dead leaves caught in the silk.

"To be clear," she replied, her voice shooting up three octaves as he ghosted her shoulder with kisses, "I'm not complaining."

She felt the deep rumble of laughter in his chest, their bodies fitted together like a locket. He undid the zipper on the side of her dress, exposing her skin to the warm, humid air of the room. Raegan tipped her head back with a sigh, admiring the patterned canopy top over the bed for about two seconds before the King slid the bodice of her dress down to her waist. The ache between her legs wound tight and pleading as she met his gaze, shimmying her hips so he could pull every stitch of clothing from her body.

For a moment, he stilled, gazing down at her in the same way Raegan had seen people look at art in museums. The King's full mouth parted slightly as he traced the fan of her auburn hair, haloed around her head, his fingertips brushing her jaw and then her collarbone. Both of his capable hands closed around her ribcage, a featherlight touch, sliding down her waist to her hips and then her thighs. His name tumbled out of her mouth, dampness gathering in her core.

"You have all of me," Oberon murmured, his palms at the back of her knees, guiding her thighs around his hips.

Raegan's chest heaved with thick, suffocating desire as she closed her legs around him. "I'll keep coming back," she panted—even though he'd hardly touched her. "Bury me shallow *every* time, Oberon. I'm coming back for you."

An endless sorrow blossomed in the ocean of his eyes, but then he bowed over the edge of the bed and kissed her. She fisted the starched fabric of his dress shirt in one hand, fumbling for the waistband of his trousers with the other. But as much as she wanted his skin against hers, she also loved being exposed to him like this: the King still dressed in his fine, dark clothing, all power and menace, backlit by the willow-o-wisps on the walls, while she ached and panted naked on the silken sheets below his broad, muscular frame.

"I belong to you," Oberon said, his lips moving against her skin, one hand sliding to the apex of her thighs. The other lightly pinched the tip of her breast, sending a moan careening out of Raegan's mouth as her back arched, pushing her chest into his. Even with her head tipped back in pleasure, she felt the heat of him shift as he knelt at the edge of the bed between her thighs.

"You promised," Raegan managed as he kissed the inside of her leg, long fingers caressing her ankle.

"I did," he agreed, eyes sliding to hers, mouth drifting closer to her center. "Burying my face between your thighs is *my* reward for our survival, not yours. Unless you object?" He'd already begun soft, slow circles on her core, his touch unreasonably pleasurable, his precise understanding of her body an absurd, beautiful thing.

"Take what you want, Unseelie king," she murmured, meeting his gaze with one brow arched, opening her thighs wider for him.

Oberon tilted his head back and sighed—a velvet sound, lush and luxurious. "What I want," he said, deepening the pressure of his fingers, pulling a cry from her lips, "is to die like this. *Just* like this." And then his mouth met the wet, wanting heat at her center and Raegan's vision went white. All the tension curled low in her belly exploded. She felt frenzied and wild, rolling her hips against the King, desperate for more. Every time, she knew, could be the last.

She captured one of his long-fingered hands, drawing it to her breast. He obeyed without question, toying with her in the precise way she wanted, bringing Raegan closer and closer to the edge.

"Do you enjoy how I play with you?" Oberon wanted to know, his voice hoarse and husky, barely lifting his mouth from her core.

"Shut up," Raegan panted, gripping a handful of the bed linens in one fist. "Obviously I do. Don't stop."

The King's laugh rang out like a bell, and then his darkness closed all around her—his mouth at her center, hands roaming her body, all of it dedicated to her pleasure, her wants, her cravings. She fell apart for him, crying out his name like a declaration. Distantly, Raegan registered when he slipped out from between her thighs and lifted her into the center of the bed. As her breathing returned to normal, the daze of pleasure morphing into a quiet, satisfied peace, she realized she heard the sound of water running.

"Right," she mumbled, pushing thick curls away from her face as she rolled to her side. "A bath."

At the far end of the room, steam curled in wisps from the mouth of the clawfoot tub. It was large, big enough for two, but somehow not ostentatious, its porcelain a mild-mannered cream, though its feet were darkened silver and decorated in dagger-sharp claws.

The King crossed her vision, reappearing at the end of the bed as he began to unbutton his shirt. She sat up, long hair tumbling across her shoulders. She shimmied onto her knees and moved closer to where Oberon stood. His dark gaze dipped to her—the expanse of her generous thighs as she sat on her knees, the hills of her soft belly, her full, heavy breasts, partially covered by her hair.

"You drive me mad, witch-queen," he whispered, hand stilling on his shirt buttons.

Raegan grinned, tossing a length of hair over her shoulder. "That's the *only* response I'll accept when I take my clothes off," she replied, hungrily eyeing his exposed skin, the dusting of dark, silken hair across his chest visible below his undone collar.

"You drive me equally as mad when you are fully clothed," the King said, his hands sliding into her hair, mouth meeting hers.

Raegan's body keened in response, the ache between her legs returned already, sharp and wanting. He trailed his lips down her neck, taking the tip of one breast into his mouth as he cupped the other, fingertips light across sensitive flesh. She moaned, digging her nails into his back before reaching for the front of his shirt.

She realized he'd been struggling to undo the buttons—the small, mother-of-pearl things were lovely and a gorgeous finish for the fine garment, but not practical for the pain she knew he must be feeling.

"Let me," Raegan said. He pulled away from her slightly, hands returning to her hair. She bit down on the inside of her lip as she worked her way down the buttons, eager to feel his skin against hers. "And if at any point you're in too much pain, please tell me."

A shimmering kind of warmth spread across his angular features in response to her words. Raegan's heart leapt. "I think," the King replied, his voice thick, "you may be able to bring me enough pleasure to override the pain."

"It would be an honor," she said with a laugh, looking at him again. Then she came up on her knees, threw her hands around his neck, and kissed him like it might make up for everything. For all the suffering, all the pain, all the ache. She slid her fingers up the back of his neck, pressing her breasts to his chest, pulling him closer and closer.

"I'm yours," Raegan whispered fervently against his mouth. "Every part of me, every life, every door, every name I've ever had. Yours. Always."

She didn't stop saying it as he pulled her into his arms, his shirt discarded on the floor below, trousers half undone. Not even as he carried her to the bath, not as they both slipped into the silken waters. And though she could barely form words when he buried himself deep inside of her, every ounce of his power and alabaster skin and intricate musculature focused solely on her, she tried to say it again. Again, again, and again.

Just in case.

～

Raegan slipped out through the heavy door, pulling the soft dressing gown tighter around her waist. Her stockinged feet were quiet on the stone floors, the willow-o-wisp lights devouring her shadow in their strange dances.

She'd woken up and hadn't been able to fall back asleep. It should've been peaceful—the high earthen ceilings of the faerie fort, the gentle tide of the King's breathing at her side, that bone-deep ache quiet for the moment. But her thoughts had run wild and sharp-edged, so she'd tried to rummage through her bags as quietly as possible. Oberon had appeared to be in a deep sleep—a rare thing—and she hadn't wanted to wake him.

Part of Raegan was not surprised when she passed through the connective chamber, finding that Alanna and Reilly had taken their key—the fort must've guessed they wanted to room together—but Maelona's still sat on the table, the filigreed gold winking in the cobalt light. Raegan sighed as she passed by, making her way to the great room.

"Hey," Maelona greeted without turning around as Raegan slipped over the threshold. Her aunt was still wrapped in an ancient woolen blanket, seated in front of the fire.

"Hey," Raegan returned. She slowed her pace across the mosaic tile, her heart starting to thud thick and heavy in her chest. It was time—past time, actually—to tell Maelona about Cormac. "Is it okay if I sit down with you?"

"Sure," Maelona said, looking over her shoulder now, her eyes bloodshot and weary.

Raegan took a deep breath and sank down on the cool floor next to her aunt. For a long time—an impossibly long time—she just stared at the grand fireplace. The towering marble, stylized as an owl, made Art Nouveau designs by mortals seem trite. The hearth also made her ache for Blodeuwedd. Like her love with Oberon, her and the owl-woman's friendship transcended time, refuted all the attempts at separation and despair. Raegan yearned for the feeling of talons on her shoulders, to watch Blodeuwedd take off into the golden autumn sunlight. For tables piled high with orchard-fresh fruits to share with her people. She swallowed and blinked back tears. The Seelie Court—at least, what it had been when it was hers—was gone. Like most things she loved.

"Why did my dad know the Unseelie vow?" Raegan asked, her

words barely louder than the crackle of the fire, everything muffled by the sloping ceilings of soil and wisteria vine. "He taught it to me. Why?"

Maelona sighed, dropping her head into her hands. An odd feeling came over Raegan—that she might not even care about the answer. That it might not even matter. She wondered whether it was due to exhaustion, the immensity of everything she had thrown herself into, or maybe a combination of both. She supposed that didn't matter, either.

"When we were young, younger than Alanna and Reilly, even," Maelona began, the words hoarse and thorn-edged, like the bramble at the edge of a meadow before it turned into dark and deep wood, "your father and I handled a small raid of some mortal witches in North Wales. A good operation for us to run, to prove ourselves a little, but without real stakes."

Maelona shifted, the firelight making it so painfully clear she was Cormac's sister. "Ended up with a little more than we could handle. The witches must've been tipped off, because nobody was at the cottage when we seized it. We sent part of our detail to pick up a trail while we went through the place. Wouldn't be unusual to find a secret compartment or a hidden door. Most witches with enough power to attract the Protectorate's attention have prepared for such inevitabilities."

Maelona's tone went dry as she raked one hand through her hair, snagging on a knot and pulling her fingers away with a curse. Raegan fought to stay in her body as she watched a few strands of her aunt's hair drift through the air, silver shimmering in the firelight.

"Cormac touched a divination object without gloves," she continued, still staring straight into the hearth. "We always wear iron-lined gloves when we review the contents of a raid. Don't ask me why he wasn't wearing them. It's protocol. I don't know. He said he thought he had been, but then he heard a voice and went into a back room. The place was all rambling hallways and tight turns. I guess 'cottage' isn't really the right word, but you know, thatched roof, muddy pastures outside, paper-thin walls. Anyway. It was a scrying glass with active old magic, which is rare to stumble upon, even on a raid. Looked like a shitty glass bowl to me, so I gotta admit I might've picked it up to see the spellbook underneath it, too."

Raegan's heart hammered against her ribs. She picked at her cuticles, drawing blood. She dared not say anything to interrupt Maelona's flow of words; she knew too well how easily her aunt could clam up. But, she supposed, that was when Maelona had thought she'd been protecting Raegan. Her aunt had just watched her summon a giant river monster who ate a bunch of people. So maybe Maelona wasn't so concerned about that anymore. Either way, at least for now, they weren't talking about Raegan watching her father die in front of her eyes.

"The light from someone's torch caught the glass, and Cormac saw a vision," Maelona continued after a long pause, saying the words as if they tasted sour in her mouth. "Your father was always sensitive. He either struggled with Protectorate spellwork or nearly killed someone by accident in training. No in-between. But old Feyrish magic? He had a . . . knack for it, I guess. Right before he left, we could bring him a box of objects from a raid and he could tell just by looking which one had Fey magic still active in it. He followed a kelpie through the Brecon Beacons once just based on where he *felt* the magic go."

Raegan chewed on her lip. "That's all very interesting. But, uh, the vision?"

"Sorry," Maelona huffed. "He saw a woman—curly red hair, wearing a black leather jacket, bursting through a door and standing in this shadowy room with dark floral wallpaper. At the other end of the room, he saw a tall, black-haired Fey on a throne. He knew the woman was in danger. He also knew—and even your father didn't understand *how* he knew—that the woman was the daughter he'd not even conceived yet and that the Fey on the throne in the corner was the Unseelie king. And he knew she'd need the right words. He knew that more than his future child's life depended on it. He said, right after he put the glass down and stumbled back to me, that the entire world depended on it."

Maelona paused, the atmosphere winding tight and thick beneath the earth, deep in the faerie hill. "He said that if his daughter said the right words, a secret, unseen Thread could unspool, and it would change everything."

CHAPTER FORTY-TWO

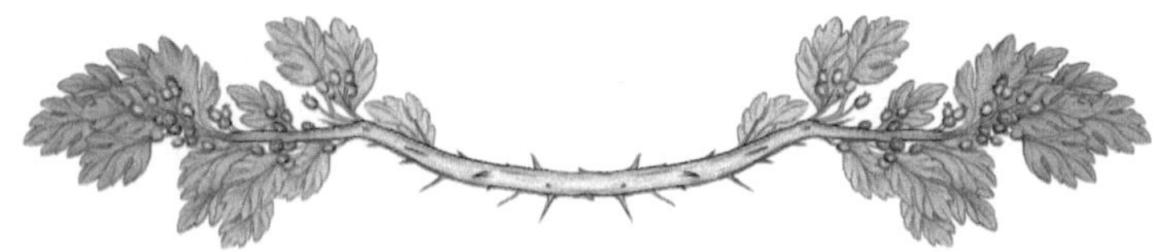

Awe and nausea, then the feeling of Fate's gaze—heavy, dove-winged, treacherous as quicksilver—bloomed in Raegan's body. She shuddered, pulling her dressing robe tighter, and seriously considered throwing one of the folded woolen blankets Alanna and Reilly had left next to the fireplace over her head like a child hiding from a nightmare.

"That's fucking insane," she managed, her lips feeling numb. "You know that, right? That's absolutely fucking insane."

"Well," Maelona said, turning to look at Raegan, pulling her knees to her chin, "was he right?"

She swallowed. "Yeah," Raegan breathed, holding her aunt's gaze. "Yeah, he was. Down to the goddamn wallpaper."

"And now we're here," Maelona replied drily. "In a forgotten faerie fort the best of the Protectorate couldn't open. With the Unseelie king. Trying to find the door to Avalon to retrieve a weapon that could end the world. But, like, in a good way, because fuck the world as it currently stands."

It was definitely the exhaustion that made Raegan throw her head back and laugh, and the same reasoning could probably be given for why laughter bubbled out of Maelona's chest. The last two living Overhills dissolved into a puddle of giggles, wrapped in woolen and antique cloth.

When Raegan caught her breath, she looked up to find Maelona wiping tears from her eyes.

"You met Oberon, you said?" Raegan asked, amusement drying up like a summertime riverbed, all the thoughts spiraling around inside her skull again.

"Oh," Maelona said, waving her hand. "Prague. The seventies. It was a whole thing. I . . . Despite the nightmares I still have, I always . . . I don't know. I got sent to investigate, and while I was away, someone sacked my and Cormac's apartment. He was followed around the compound the whole time I was gone. I won't bore you with what the politics were like back then, but . . . there were worse fates for me than having an admittedly terrifying encounter with the King."

The fire crackled loudly, a log crashing down from the cradle, making both women jump out of their skin. They exchanged sheepish glances and laughed, the vast room swallowing up the sound.

"I think," Maelona said after clearing her throat, "maybe he actually helped me. Made me and Cormac look less suspicious by going after me. And I mean, he didn't hurt me. Just trapped me in some shadowy half-realm for a day or so. If we both live, let's ask him about it."

Raegan agreed with a nod, the words about Cormac still strangled in her throat.

"Speaking of the King . . ." Maelona began, turning to look at Raegan, her brows etched with suspicion.

Anxiety twisted in Raegan's stomach for another reason. "I know," she replied, letting out a long sigh. "Am I being fooled by an immeasurably powerful faerie king? Have I been aiding and abetting the end of mankind for a thousand years?"

"Well," Maelona grumbled, her eyes darting away, "I wasn't gonna start there. But . . . Yeah."

"I can't rule it out, technically," Raegan said with a shrug, settling her chin on her knees, staring at the dancing flames in the hearth. "But no, Maelona. I understand you're looking at me as your niece, the last thing left of your little brother. And I *am* those things, sure. But I'm also a lot more. More than you can comprehend."

"Why would the Timekeeper allow you to be reincarnated into a Protectorate bloodline?" Maelona asked hoarsely, still not looking at Raegan. "Considering all that you are?"

"So I could be raised like a fattened calf to be devoured," she replied with a dark, caustic grin. "Long story. Fate's a cunt. She and the Time-keeper, they're constantly setting up for about a hundred different plays. But they wait until the last second to make their move. To twist the knife."

Maelona finally glanced at her then, eyes wide. "Sure. Fine. But look, could I . . . could I check you over for coercive spellwork? I'm actually really good at this, examining someone's Threads and seeing where they've been rewoven or tweaked."

Anger rose in Raegan like a tide, teeming with sharp-toothed things, all the rage of a storm surge. How *dare* she? This mortal creature of not even a century, thinking she could pick apart Threads stretching across a millennium, believing she could deliver some truth on whether the King's love was true or false?

Raegan sat up straight, poison gathering in the back of her throat. She opened her mouth to spit venomous words at Maelona but then closed it, pressing her lips together. Yes, it was insulting, belittling, and completely absurd. And yet, it would make Maelona feel a lot better, wouldn't it? There was little way for her aunt to look and not see Cormac, not see a young niece who'd been thrown to the wolves. Maelona couldn't possibly look at Raegan and see the Queen of the Hill or the Witch of the Water. She just saw Cormac. Whom she didn't know—not with absolute certainty, at least—was dead.

"Sure," Raegan said with a shrug, settling into a cross-legged position.

"Really?" Maelona asked, looking surprised, pulling her hands out from beneath the blanket. "Alright. Just don't fight me. Apparently it hurts if you do."

"I have felt the brutality of Protectorate magic," Raegan said, the words coming out of her stilted and ancient. "Many times, in fact. Rest assured I am familiar with its bite."

In the low glow of the firelight, Maelona examined her, as if she finally understood something about the woman seated before her. She exhaled and raised her hands—spindly and barely more than bone, the fingers shaking. And then she paused.

"Go ahead," Raegan said once more, relaxing her shoulders. She closed her eyes, not wishing to see Maelona's expression; she wasn't quite sure why.

For a long moment, there was only the warmth of the hearth on her right side and the scent of osmanthus and petrichor. And then there it was; Maelona *was* actually fairly proficient, particularly for a mortal. Her aunt's magic was deft, though far from delicate, as it crept along her Threads. The sensation was still uncomfortable—her chest a filing cabinet that someone was rifling through with cold, sterile hands.

"Okay," Maelona said some time later. When Raegan opened her eyelids, her aunt was slumped, the blanket pulled higher on her shoulders. "Your Thread pattern is intense. You're definitely not mortal, not really. But no coercive spellwork that I can see. Just . . ."

"What?" Raegan asked, faint panic blooming in her chest.

Maelona let out a huff, raking her hand through her hair, leaving the dark locks even more disheveled. "I thought it was a myth," her aunt said, looking up to finally meet her gaze. "This thing called a Godpath. It's a specific kind of knot in people's Threads that indicates some grand entity—Fate, in this case, probably—interfered with the weave of your essence. I've only ever read about them. You . . . you actually *have* Godpaths."

"Godpaths," Raegan repeated, her mouth dry, information racing through her mind from previous lives, though nothing really stuck.

"I mean, it could be something else that we just don't understand," Maelona said with a shrug, looking absolutely exhausted. "Ask the King. Maybe it's just some Fey shit. But yeah. Godpaths. You have a lot of them, Raegan."

She looked away from Maelona, chewing on the inside of her lip. Hadn't she always known? Even with the Seal intact, even before she'd had a shred of evidence besides the books her father had left behind. Her mother had burned them, anyway—likely compelled by Cormac's protective spellwork, though certainly aided by her very real emotions—and left Raegan with only a mad, desperate hope. Some kind of deep-rooted certainty that she was destined for paths unseen.

It had been there all along, knotted deep in the fiber of her very marrow. Godpaths. The touch of the divine, of the grander things that made the universe turn. Raegan hated it and loved it at the same time. She didn't know how to say any of that to Maelona, though, so she just stared into the fire and picked at her cuticles. The memory of her father on the train prowled to the front of her mind, threatening to devour her if she didn't release it.

"I went into the Timekeeper's realm," Raegan blurted out, tears already choking her words. "There were a lot of things I didn't tell you. Thought I *couldn't* tell you. Probably best I didn't, I guess. Anyway, I found him."

Beside her, Maelona straightened, her knuckles going white. "Cormac?" she asked, a ghost in the firelight.

Raegan nodded, looking for the words. "The Timekeeper . . . Dad made a deal to get me out. It had nothing to do with the Gates. He wasn't chasing magic. Maybe he told you that to keep you safe or to keep us safe. I don't know. Maybe that was just easier to believe. He didn't want me in the Protectorate. And I guess . . . I never knew about the vision he had. But that's part of it all, obviously. So he made a deal. It kept me and my mom safe. He had to perform a spell after twelve years and a day. He did, and it set this whole fucking thing into motion because he'd been tricked."

Maelona said nothing, but the way her eyes held Raegan's was feverish, hungry. She'd said more than once she had accepted Cormac was dead, but as Raegan looked at her, it was very clear that even practical, stoic Maelona had held a shred of hope.

And Raegan was about to crush it. "Look, I'm a thousand years old, and so much of this doesn't make sense to me, either, because I'm not a primordial entity beyond comprehension." She fought for her words, for the right way to explain.

"Tell me, Raegan," Maelona rasped, leaning toward her, an arrow nocked.

"He's dead," she replied. "The Timekeeper used my dad like a fucking worm on a hook to get me where he wanted me, to be sure the King wouldn't be a problem. And then he killed him. Just like that. Turned him into dust as I watched."

Silence barreled into the wood-paneled great room, heavy as a freight train. Raegan's breath shortened, her chest hitching, dismayed to find out exactly how desperately she needed Maelona to not hate her.

"But you escaped?" her aunt asked, not a shred of emotion in her expression.

"Barely," Raegan replied. "Dad was caught in the bargain. His skin was . . . it was stitched to a train seat. He'd already been drained of so much. But I—I had meadowsweet in my pocket from Blodeuwedd, and I blew the dust into the Timekeeper's eyes, and then I ran. Because Dad told me to run. Because you have to understand, Maelona, that the only revenge at that point was living long enough to destroy everything the Timekeeper ever built."

Her aunt watched her, those familiar eyes glittering in the gloom. Raegan's heart climbed into her throat, and she thought of ten different things to say, to soften the blow or make herself look better, or maybe to plead with her aunt not to leave her, because everyone always left. Because Raegan was too hard to love.

But despite all the thoughts rattling in Raegan's head, the only thing Maelona did was pitch her body forward and wrap her arms around Raegan. One of them started crying, and the other followed with sobs of their own. Raegan buried her head in her aunt's shoulder and wept. She cried until her throat was sore, until she could barely breathe, and Maelona sobbed like a child, curling her body into Raegan's, tears dripping onto the tiled floor.

Good. Because she'd promised the Timekeeper a flood, hadn't she?

Chapter Forty-Three

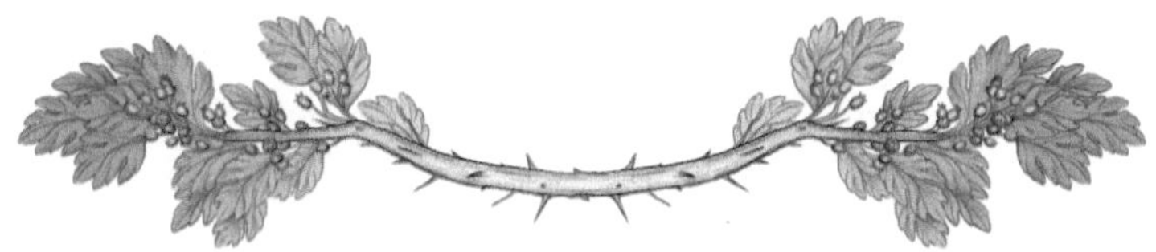

Inside the faerie fort, day was indistinguishable from night. The willow-o-wisps cast the same eerie, pale, blue-lavender light, the earthen ceilings and near-black wood paneling unchanged by the shifting slants of morning sun.

"You saw the ocean, right? Or some body of water?" Maelona demanded, the sound of her exasperated voice pulling Raegan from her thoughts. "So how the fuck could it be the yew trees?"

She chewed on her lip, refocusing on the items spread across the great room's massive table—a thick slab of dark wood settled on ornately carved legs. The end of the table was covered with the fort's foodstuffs— dried mushrooms and salted beef, dusty jars of pickled vegetables, sacks filled with flour, crocks of jam. Enough to last three mortals about a week, maybe more if they rationed conservatively. Raegan thanked the gods she'd listened to Blodeuwedd all those years ago when the owl woman had suggested an eternal food preservation spell, powered by the river, like the housekeeping workings.

The rest of the table's surface was taken up by the pages of the Protectorate's dossier, a map with dried beans marking locations, and Raegan's notes made on delicate parchment Reilly had found in the storeroom. The nib of the pen, which had been tucked inside a roll of parchment, had bitten through the thin paper in multiple places.

"We're talking about a door to fucking *Avalon*, Maelona," Alanna sputtered, spreading her hands wide. "You might be thinking too literally."

"I wish we could just check all of the sites," Reilly offered, scratching their head. Their hair sprang out in unruly directions, sleep transforming their curls into a frizzy halo.

"It's too risky," Maelona snapped, massaging her temple with a few fingers. "They'd be opening themselves up to more battles with Protectorate forces. How many before the Timekeeper decides to leave the In-Between and come have a look for himself?"

"He won't," Raegan said, surprised by the sureness in her voice. "It's the same reason why Fate, in all Her truly terrible power, doesn't just move us around like puppets. Well, not exactly. She and Kronos—they're functions of the universe. She can fuck up my life, he can send all his armies raining down on this faerie hill, but neither can directly interfere with their own hand."

"He is too vulnerable in this realm as well," Oberon added, leaning onto the table, his weight on one palm. "I would not rule it out completely, but it is highly improbable."

Maelona threw her hands in the air. "A year ago, I would've thought it highly improbable I was going to be in a fucking faerie fort with two other traitors and the goddamn Unseelie king. But here I am."

"Why are you so fucking bitchy?" Raegan snapped at her aunt before she could stop herself. "Usually it's endearing, but you're pissing me off right now."

"Oh, my apologies, Your Highness," Maelona replied, sweeping into a mocking bow, the blanket draped over her shoulders fluttering like a cape. "Despite all of your insane magic, the faerie fort that seems alarmingly sentient, and your incredibly powerful faerie king boyfriend, the fact remains that there are no cigarettes and *no goddamn coffee*."

Raegan blinked, absorbing Maelona's words. In her peripheral vision, she saw Alanna and Reilly exchange a glance of amusement. "He's not my *boyfriend*," she settled on, spitting the words out. To her outrage, she heard the rich sound of the King's laugh, followed by Reilly's giggles and a strangled sputter from Alanna.

"Glad to be of amusement," Raegan grumbled as she circled the table, trying her best to ignore the flush of embarrassment creeping across her face. She stubbornly refused to meet the King's gaze. He wasn't her fucking boyfriend. But he wasn't technically her husband, either, though the thought sent butterflies loose in her stomach.

Besides—she wasn't exactly in a laughing mood. She and Oberon had both expended themselves considerably to survive the fallout from the gala the night before. She'd barely been able to heal everyone's wounds without losing consciousness. The King wasn't faring much better—she could see his movements were heavy and stiff, lacking his usual grace. But they didn't have the luxury of rest. The Protectorate might not be able to get inside the faerie fort, but they'd retaliate—likely against whatever vulnerable places they could find in the Philadelphia court. Raegan winced at the thought.

She stared down at the dossier, running her eyes over the list. Frustration bared its teeth and she curled her hands into fists, relishing the sharp pain of her nails biting into her palms. Maybe they had no choice —maybe going to the remaining five locations was their only option. Raegan resisted the urge to fling the dossier across the room.

Instead, she forced herself to go through each page again. From the head of the table, Maelona sighed dramatically. Raegan didn't take the bait; besides, it *was* about the hundredth time this morning that her aunt had watched her do the exact same thing. Feeling the weight of everyone's eyes on her, Raegan tried to pick up her pace, only scanning for things she and the King might not have noticed before—notes in the margin, symbols, a hidden enchantment. With their broken oaths and no magic, there was only so much the three mortals could really do to help.

"Wait," Maelona said, nearly shouting the word, her hoarse voice brightened with excitement. "Alanna, do you have a knife?"

"Sure," the younger Protectorate operative replied, her dark brow furrowed as she plucked a small dagger from her belt and handed it across the table. Raegan's head snapped up to look at her aunt, the sudden bolt of understanding electrifying her entire body.

"Shit," she sputtered, snatching the dagger. Raegan's blood had let her pass the clock sentinel in the Undercroft, so there was at least a chance it might work on the dossier itself. But before she could do anything, a pair of large, powerful hands closed around hers.

"Would you permit me to help you?" Oberon asked, woodsmoke

rolling over her senses as he drew closer. "Your hands have been shaking all morning."

Raegan turned to look at him, the feral angles of his impossibly beautiful face etched out in blue-black by the willow-o-wisps. "Good idea," she said, laying one hand flat on the table, palm up.

Oberon nodded, testing the sharpness of Alanna's dagger against one of his fingertips. Satisfied, he leaned over the table, his eyes meeting hers. Raegan nodded and then, with the heavy weight of the future settled on their shoulders, the King cut a tiny wound into her flesh. With a deep breath, Raegan turned her hand over, squeezing the cut finger. A single glass bead—wine-dark, crimson-jeweled—tumbled toward the dossier.

Time held still, and Raegan might've watched the blood drop's journey for a thousand years, something in the world stretching wide, a forgotten door opening. The paper drank up her blood, the spot disappearing in a heartbeat. Then the pages turned of their own accord, flipping to the back of the folio. Where there had once only been smooth leather, there was now a slim, flat pocket.

Raegan's heart stopped. Holding her breath, she desperately shoved her hand inside the pocket. A piece of heavy, thick parchment met her fingertips and she pulled it free, eliciting a gasp from Reilly.

With shaking hands, Raegan unfolded it, laying it flat on the table. For a moment, her vision swam and she was sure there was nothing but strange, looping symbols. After a few harrowing seconds, she understood that she was looking at magical passkeys to the surveillance spells embedded in all seven possible locations. She inhaled. Helpful, maybe, but not the kind of revelation she was looking for. Exhaling, Raegan turned the paper over, hoping beyond hope. And there, written in faded, old-fashioned calligraphy, she saw:

Those who knew the location of Avalon's door, to the best of our knowledge, both living and dead, contemporary and historical:

- *Danu, Mother of the Fair Folk (beyond our reach)*
- *Nyx, Goddess of Night (slain by Kronos)*
- *Rhyfelwr, leader of the kelpies (slain by Bedwyr)*

- The Witch in/of the Wood, mortal sorceress (dead, natural causes)

- John Dee, mortal magician (slain by the Unseelie king)

Raegan's knees nearly gave out, hands trembling as her mind swam. "In our vision, the Morrigan said all doors once open to me remain open," she sputtered, struggling to find the words. "Fuck. And the Witch in the Wood said that to me when my Seal was removed." She swung to look at Maelona, her eyes wild. "Does the Protectorate *know* I was the Witch of the Wood?"

Her aunt stared at her, mouth falling open, gaze narrowing as she took in her niece. "No," Maelona whispered hoarsely. "The Witch in—*you* evaded the Protectorate almost entirely during your life. We really only understood how dangerous you were after your death. During all the briefings in the States, only Nyneve, a few lesser rabble-rousers, and the Seelie queen were attributed as your identities."

"Why would her blood even work?" Oberon asked, his tone tempered, though Raegan could see the hope glimmering in his eyes. "All the living Overhills are now traitors. Can Protectorate wards not be adjusted in case of defection or betrayal?"

"Of course they can," Maelona said, raising her gaze to meet the King's. "But she was never inducted in the first place, so the workings can't identify her personally. The old wards on the Undercroft, on this dossier—all they're gonna see is one of the oldest Protectorate families. I mean, the Overhills contributed to their *creation*." Maelona paused, looking around the room, the notch between her eyes deepening. "It's hard to lock out a founding bloodline. Trust me, when Cormac deserted, it was all anyone talked about for months. I mean, it's easy enough to designate persona non grata within an existing modern spell, particularly when they're oathed and known. The old workings, though? Too many layers. Much harder to do without breaking the whole damn thing. And in what world would we foresee someone getting past fifteen layers of modern, updated protective wards?"

Silence swept its wings around the great room of the faerie fort. Raegan squeezed her eyes shut, trying to think, to *remember*.

"You killed John Dee? Like, you know, the greatest English magician?" Reilly asked in a small squeak, breaking Raegan's concentration. She opened her eyes and glanced over to find them looking up from the parchment, considering the Unseelie king. A slow, dangerous smile graced the curves of Oberon's mouth.

"Okay," Raegan said frantically, trying to get her thoughts marching in a straight line. "So I just need to remember. It's in me, somewhere."

As she glanced in his direction, concern etched the King's expression. "We discussed this with Baba Yaga. Allowing your memories to resurface on their own is best. Attempting to force anything through spellwork is incredibly dangerous."

"More dangerous than any of the other shit we've done?" she snapped, her frustration with the situation—not so much with him—wearing her patience thin.

The King took a deep breath, and she had the distinct feeling he was counting to ten.

"This is a really stupid idea," Reilly said, fiddling with the blanket they'd swaddled themselves in after retreating to one of the heavy chairs pushed against the wall.

"I'm all ears," Raegan said when no one spoke. "At this point, there's no stupid ideas."

"I wouldn't go that far," Maelona muttered, crossing her arms.

"Reilly, please, if you will," Oberon managed, his gaze dipping toward Raegan. "What was your idea?"

Reilly glanced cautiously around the room, chewing on their lip. "Okay," they began, looking a little sheepish. "So, there were quite a few of us obsessed with civilian stuff as kids. We found all the woo-woo spiritual shit particularly amusing, for obvious reasons. One night, there was some important dinner or whatever, and a couple of us were fucking around on YouTube."

"Oh man," Alanna said, brightening considerably, suddenly looking so young it made Raegan's heart ache. "Those were the days. Before the council realized how expansive the internet was and yanked that away from us, too."

"Yes!" Reilly said, reaching out for Alanna's hand. She tucked their short, freckled fingers into her palm, smiling. Raegan's ache intensified. It was a terrible thing to find Blodeuwedd again only to be yanked apart mere hours later. "Okay, do you remember when we tried the past life regression video?"

Alanna's amusement fled, her eyes darting toward Raegan. "Right, but like, that didn't actually work, Reilly."

"Maybe only because we don't *have* past lives," they replied, looking up at Alanna from their chair. "I think I remember enough of the video. It's worth a shot. It's not spellwork, so it might be safer."

"What," the King began, his hand opening on Raegan's back, "would this entail, exactly?"

CHAPTER FORTY-FOUR

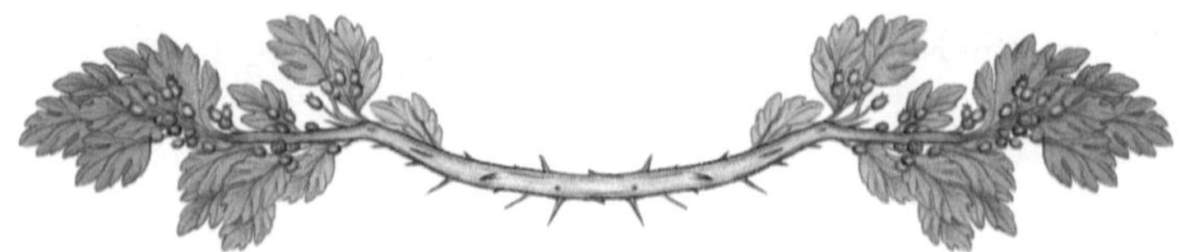

Raegan slipped deeper into the water, adjusting the makeshift blindfold she'd made from a dressing robe's belt. Even though it was confined by the surrounds of the clawfoot tub, this element was still hers. Water was her home. She took comfort in that, spreading her arms out wide.

"I think there's enough salt this time," she said, not sure where to direct her words. "I feel pretty float-y."

"Good," came Reilly's delighted voice from an indistinguishable direction. "Okay, just a reminder that I'm going off a video I saw a few times nearly a decade ago. So temper your expectations."

Words came slinking across the tide of the darkness she floated on, soft and deadly: "Understand that if this harms her in any way—"

"Oberon, leave the kid alone," Raegan snapped, resisting the urge to yank up her blindfold and glare at him. She curled her fists, hearing only the gentle lapping of water for a long moment.

"Thanks, Raegan," Reilly said, their tone significantly meeker than when they'd last spoken. "I'm going to guide you through the meditation. Just listen to my voice."

Raegan nodded, trying to let the feeling of the room around her go; they'd done their best to approximate a deprivation tank. She was wearing only a sports bra and high-waisted underwear, her hair braided tight against her skull. At first, she'd been aware of the tub's edges, of the people standing around her, of the tag at the back of her bra. But now, the setup did seem to be working. There was little more than water and breath.

And then Reilly's voice, opening with a meditation exercise that was standard enough from the smattering of yoga and breathwork classes she'd taken, usually at the behest of a girl she was fucking. Raegan pushed away thoughts of her current life and focused all her energy on Reilly's words—as they instructed—until the time came to "cut the cord," so to speak.

Only water, only breath, the osmanthus and petrichor gone, the slanting cobalt light of the willow-o-wisps a distant memory. But then Raegan's fingers brushed the edge of the tub, and she jolted back into her body. Exhaling, she squeezed her eyes shut—fuck, now she could feel the blindfold again—and tried to relinquish control. Reilly was already trying to guide her through the "rooms of her lives," which might have worked if she wasn't damp and pissed off in lukewarm bathwater.

"Reilly," came Oberon's voice, only lightly edged in steel. "A moment, please."

"Thanks," Raegan said, lifting the blindfold off one eye. She squinted against the sudden light, finding Oberon gazing down at her. "I actually think this could work. The deprivation part of it. But I need to concentrate. Could you three leave? I need Oberon to stay. Baba Yaga said he was my tether. I think if I get lost, he'll help me come back."

Raegan tucked her chin to her chest, looking at Maelona, Alanna, and Reilly in turn. Her aunt's jaw flexed, gaze darting suspiciously to the King. But she relented, nodding, and then the younger Protectorate operatives followed suit. The three of them filed out of the bedchamber, Alanna pulling the door closed behind her.

"Lower, please," Raegan said to the willow-o-wisps, which immediately dimmed. "You, come here."

Oberon closed the distance to the edge of the clawfoot tub with a long, gliding step. Without any further prompting from Raegan, he knelt on the tiled floor beside her, draping his beautiful hands over the porcelain lip. On instinct, she reached out of the water and wrapped her fingers around his.

"Right," she breathed, looking up at him. "I'm going back in." With her free hand, Raegan slid the blindfold back down and let herself sink into the water holding her like a mother. Without Maelona's nervous energy, Alanna's gentle corrections, and Reilly's general anxiety, she found herself able to breathe deeply and float. There was no reassurance like the Unseelie faerie king at her side, fingers interwoven with hers like an ancient thicket. He would not let her stray too far into her own currents. He knew her tides, her ebbs and flows, the drop-offs in her deep waters. He would keep her safe, just like he always did.

And with that thought, she slipped out of her body and into the rivers of her mind. She'd expected something like the room of doors that Reilly had mentioned, or maybe just doors in general, because she'd spent so long aching for one to appear. But instead, she found a thick, rushing current of black water. Raegan moved toward it gently, carefully, seeing how easily it could whisk her away. The currents called to her—here, she could be free and wild, shed her humanity, tangle her hair with the kelp, and sharpen her teeth.

"Thank you," Raegan murmured, wavering at the current's edge. "But I'm looking for a door, actually. From a long time ago, something tucked away for safekeeping. Could you help me find it?"

The currents tumbled around her like a nest of angry hornets, and for a long, tense moment, fear pounded in Raegan's chest. Or no, something much worse—she had no chest, she had no fingers interwoven with the King's, she had no body at all. When she turned, wanting to look over her shoulder or maybe down at the tub below her, she found only dark waters.

"Listen," she said, grateful she at least had her voice, which still sounded like her—accented with Philadelphia, a little rough around the edges, low and rich. "Do you want me to save magic or not?"

But the waters just continued to churn, frothing with silver white-caps. She ground her jaw, or maybe she would've, but she had no jaw of which to speak. Raegan eyed the swift currents, holding her place in the milder tide. And then she realized—she'd have to surrender. She'd have to pitch herself into the blackened waters and let the tides take her where she wanted to go.

Raegan took a deep breath and repeated her request to the waters— the door, the slip in time when Danu had left this realm, the corridor that led to Excalibur. And then she tumbled into the heart of the rushing waters, where the currents twisted vicious and unforgiving, praying she wouldn't drown.

It was not unlike when Baba Yaga peeled her eroded Seal away. Entire lifetimes danced beneath the tides, presenting themselves in no particular order that Raegan could decipher. She wasn't in control, not quite—the currents swept her through this strange world of dark water and glimmering depths, and she could do little to impact their speed or sway. She did, however, have the distinct impression that upon finding the right place, she could choose to dive deeper. There were dangers there, too, she knew—not enough air, too little light, terrible depths in which she wouldn't know which way was up or how to get back.

But she was strong enough. She knew that now. For a moment, she felt something simple, physical—cool, strong fingers between hers, the power lingering just beneath moonlit skin. Raegan smiled and slipped farther down the river, her eyes on the depths below, where the people she'd once been peered up at her like a strange passing cloud.

At a certain point, she stopped trying to move with the current and simply became the water instead. Her Threads eagerly molded into the shape of the river, moving more quickly now. Down below, she saw the life she'd dreamt of back in Philadelphia, of running into the King at a coffee shop in the 1940s in London and feeling like her heart had been broken into a million pieces. Even now, lacking physicality, she still had the sensation of her throat closing, of tears pricking the backs of her eyelids with hot, sharp needles.

Lives she hadn't remembered slipped by on the waters, too. She watched the King—much younger, though he still wore sorrow like a crown—arch his brow at a tall, powerfully built man with thick, sun-bleached hair gathered in a loose braid. For a brief moment, she remembered what it was to have that body—the weight of a battle ax, the sway and creak of a longship beneath her, the tender fierceness with which she tangled with Oberon between sheets—but then it was gone, rushing away like floodwater.

The lives where she hadn't gone looking for doors were barely dull glimmers at the bottom of the river, the scales of a fish long since gutted. But they were terrifyingly numerous, and she found herself averting her eyes, not wanting to know how many she had wasted. Just when she dared to look back, something caught her eye: a woman with a single silvery-blonde plait down her back, hands curled tight around a walking stick as she walked through a meadow.

The Witch of the Wood. Raegan dove deeper, chasing the flash of silver-blonde like a minnow, resisting the current that wanted to pull her forward, forward, always forward, only to come back around and devour her own tail. She strained, reaching for the depths, suddenly aware of the King's hand in hers again. She curled her fingers around his tighter, steadying herself, and then she was tumbling through black-water rapids, falling through space, coming undone.

"Why are you showing me this?" a voice—her voice—asked, clear as spring rain.

No answer came, just the jeweled chorus of a late summer orchestra humming all around her. The light slanted low and golden, as if the afternoon were fading into a balmy evening.

"Because one day, it might matter," came the answer, unsteady, spoken from a voice she recognized but could not place. She strained to find the speaker, but her gaze stayed stubbornly on the soft mound of earth rising from the meadow. It was covered in the green down of moss, and from it grew a tree. She knew she was many, many years in the past—and yet the tree was already ancient, its roots encasing the mound.

"That is hardly an answer," she huffed in reply.

"You should know better than to expect one," came the reply, sharp as mugwort tea.

Her memory-body finally turned, peering into the shade of the towering tree. A woman—no, something much more—stood there, draped in the glory of golden hour. Her face was lined, but her eyes danced with intelligence as swift as a river. A long, thick braid of silver hair fell over her shoulder as she leaned forward, gazing deeply into Raegan's eyes.

Raegan was undoubtedly looking at the Witch of the Wood. But she was the Witch of the Wood, wasn't she? She glanced down, finding rough-spun clothes and worn leather boots. Confused and beginning to panic, she reached for the nape of her neck, finding a braid similar to that of the woman before her, though with less silver and more youth. Raegan stared at the woman, stumbling back a step, thistle and gorse tangling around her ankles.

"Ahh," the witch said, smiling now, reaching up with one hand to shade her eyes from the slanting sun. "You found this little jewel I buried

for safekeeping. For the day when all the Prophecies become one. Well done. Now, tell me—what kind of a tree is this?"

"How is this even possible?" Raegan demanded, her mind reeling, particularly after the thousands of currents she'd tumbled through just to get here. "I—we?—hid a memory in ourselves?"

"Yes," the witch replied, straightening, her expression gone sober. "And we're the only ones who can find it. I did it for a reason. Because no one else could know. And we could only know the truth again if we were strong enough to go looking for Avalon. Which apparently you did."

"Jesus Christ," Raegan groaned, feeling faint. She leaned hard on her walking stick, wondering if she should put her head between her knees. "Sorry. This is a bit of a mindfuck."

"We taught Baba Yaga herself the craft," the witch replied, cocking her head, a vicious grin spreading across her thin, weathered lips. "A bit of complicated memory work is hardly beyond our limits. It's all just Threads, Raegan. And we are quite good with a needle."

Raegan's head spun, but she held the witch's gaze even as the currents began to tug on her again. She dug her staff into the soft earth, scrambling for a foothold.

"Ahh," the witch said, sly and shimmering like a beacon in the late summer light. "No need to tire yourself out. Just have a look at this tree, if you would. Speak its name. Then you may return."

Her head spun hard, and Raegan barely managed to tear her eyes away from the person who was her but not her to look at the tree growing proud and defiant from the soft, vulnerable mound in the earth.

"Oh my god." And then she spoke the name of the tree, the syllables rolling off her tongue like thunder.

She broke the surface, sputtering, her Threads barely returned to her current body. Water droplets spewed in every direction, sapphire-like in the willow-o-wisp light. She yanked the soaked blindfold from her face, twisting to the side of the tub. Resting her elbows on the lip, she reached for the King, pulling both of his hands to her heart. She held them there, ravenous for his heat, for the feeling of his touch to bring her back to this world.

He knew, somehow, because he *always* knew. The King bowed over the clawfoot tub and pulled her from the porcelain pool as if she weighed nothing at all, bringing her close to his body—never mind the rivulets of water running down her shoulders, the way her hair surely soaked his shirt straight through.

But that's how it was—she was forever diving into the deepest, darkest places, and he always awaited her on the shore, always pulling her out when she no longer had the strength to surface. Raegan felt his hand cradle the back of her head and melted into the feeling. Delicately, she searched for words—for the language of this time and place, for the energy to explain. Exhaustion crowded her, sending black splotches dancing across her vision.

"Are you unharmed?" Oberon asked, gently pushing away the curls plastered to her forehead.

"Yew," Raegan gasped, praying she'd found the right language, beginning to shiver.

The King furrowed his brow, cocked his head in that way she always liked, but how she yearned for him was just another depth, and she needed the shallows right now.

"Yew," she repeated, coughing up water. "It's the Defynogg Yew."

CHAPTER FORTY-FIVE

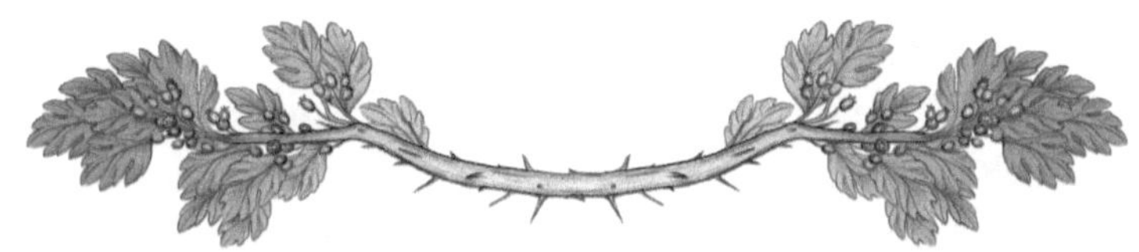

Gray moorlands flashed overhead, and the wind tore ferociously at Raegan's hair, ripping it from the tight braid Maelona had coaxed it into. The mist seemed intent on sinking into her bones. But at least they weren't being followed. Not yet, anyway. The kelpies had agreed to distract the Protectorate, luring them away from the mouth of the faerie fort, while Rainer ferried his cargo in the opposite direction—toward the yew trees in an unassuming church graveyard, on the outskirts of the Brecon Beacons.

Raegan tightened her hold on Rainer's mane as the kelpie's long, powerful legs carried them up the face of a craggy hill, his hooves seeming to just barely skim the ground. Anxiety and terror swarmed her insides, and even the reassurance of Oberon's muscular frame at her back couldn't banish the feeling. What if she was wrong? What if the door wouldn't open to her any longer? What if she failed the entire world the same way she'd failed her father, the same way she'd failed the King a hundred times before?

"Steady," Oberon murmured, his lips brushing her ear, the word just audible over the roar of the wind. For a moment, Raegan smiled into the mist like a fool, marveling at how two syllables spoken from his tongue could settle the tides thrashing inside her. She felt his hand open wider on her waist, fingers splaying. The heat of his touch reached her even through the thick oilskin coat.

It should be carefree, barreling through the moors on the back of an ancient creature born of the same murk and depth she knew so well. But it felt like going to the gallows, taking the train to the last stop on the line. They were out of time, out of options, out of chances. The snake had already taken its own tail into its mouth, Raegan knew, and it was only a matter of time before it began to devour.

"Up ahead," Rainer called, swerving around a rocky outcropping.

Through the mist, Raegan saw the beginnings of a village, the wild, heather-ringed lands giving way to civilization. A power line stretched up into the gray skies, and narrow lanes twisted this way and that, lined in short stone walls draped with vines. And there, farther down the hillside, was a white steeple. It was all a regular kind of pretty, nothing impressive—certainly not a vista that would inspire awe or wonder.

"How could this possibly be the place?" she murmured to herself, eyes searching the landscape. Then she finally found their quarry, tucked into the center of the churchyard between weathered gravestones. The yew trees. They curled in around themselves, an oasis of deep green in a world of smoke and umber.

Maybe it was all going to her head, maybe she just wanted to believe, but Raegan's breath caught in her throat all the same. Even from across the village, power lines and blacktop bisecting her vision, the pull of the yews was undeniable. They pulsed, not unlike a door, but quiet, subtle, a thrum in her blood instead of the soaring loop of a Fatesong.

Rainer tucked his knees and neatly jumped over a low hedge, bringing them closer to the churchyard. Anxiety roiling unpleasantly in her stomach, Raegan looked both ways, eyes sharp for a flash of chainmail or dusty suiting, but she only saw regular people going about their business. Their glamour seemed to be holding, though Oberon had been forced to weave something that wouldn't draw too much attention from the Protectorate. Which meant there was a chance that any mortal more sensitive to the way of things would likely see a kelpie with a deathless woman and a faerie king on its back, careening toward an ancient churchyard as if everything began and ended within its stone walls.

Rainer's hooves clattered over the blacktop, and the world hung so still and slow that for a moment, Raegan panicked, thinking they'd been caught in the web of a time spell. But it was only the dilation of adrenaline, of every moment leading up to this one. Her heart climbed into her throat as Rainer leapt over the wall of the churchyard, carrying them across soft, damp earth to the cluster of yew trees.

Raegan all but flung herself off the kelpie's back, scrambling for the trees; it felt like she was moving through water, or like she was having one of those dreams when all she needed to do was run away but her legs just wouldn't work.

The King hooked his arm through hers, pulling them beneath the dark, soft shadow of the yews. "Keep watch, please, Rainer," he called before letting out a long breath, turning his attention to the trees.

Raegan's attention fell in a similar direction. The yews towered above them, their trunks clustering together at the roots before reaching up toward the sky, interlacing their hands to form a sphere of eternal green. Their trunks were a reddish brown, covered in tiny branches of growth. The mound the yews grew from pulsed, its energy washing over Raegan like ocean waves, leaving her trembling and gowned in salt.

As they stood there, side by side within the yews, something golden and orchestral slipped through the air, delicate as smoke and humming with want. It split her down the middle, digging fishhooks into her intestines, the cruel beauty of it pulling on every fiber of her being. Of all things, a Fatesong looped above them.

Raegan tilted her chin back, looking up into the sky, hating the way she felt like a vine reaching for the sun. The thrum of the song filled up all the empty spaces that stretched wide and aching inside of her. Traitorously, that yearning within her silenced, slipping quietly beneath the mead waves of the Fatesong. With a final trill, the ancient melody ended the same way it had begun, the snake devouring its own tail.

Still in the thrall of the Fatesong, Raegan stepped toward the yews, hand outstretched, reverent as a sinner. The moment her fingertips brushed the bark, the entire churchyard roiled, like something ancient turning over in its grave. Hope keened in her chest, spreading wings as it awaited the headwinds on which it could finally, after so many years, fly home.

But then nothing, not even when she pressed her palm against the trunk. The churchyard silenced, and the yews stood expressionless again. No key appeared in overturned dirt atop the mound. No maw opened with the sound of a half-forgotten lullaby. The hope in her chest turned to ash and nearly choked her.

Despair coiled in her ribs as she looked over her shoulder at the King. As always, he met her gaze evenly, his features all the more feral and inhuman in the deep green gloom. His oceanic eyes held a vastness she still didn't understand, power and prophecy moving like shadows in the depths.

"All the Prophecies become one," she muttered, her mind racing—luna moths and doves and river-conjured swords and crumbling citadels and the skies turning to black and the ground to stone and the mortal king sleeping on the other side of the door in the yews. And most of all, those bloodstained words scrawled across the Prophecy beast she'd awoken in Hiraeth's depths, repeated by the Witch in the Wood.

"Oberon," Raegan said, speaking his name like a vow. "Come here." She held out her free hand, reaching for him as she always did—across time and space, across graves and cradles, endlessly and defiantly.

The King did not hesitate. He placed his hand in hers, the intensity of his attention settling over her shoulders like a mantle. She let out a shaky breath. Then she guided his hand to the yew's trunk, laying his palm flat against the bark. Less than a second later, she layered hers on top, hoping with every fiber of her being that together, they might finally be enough.

The yews shivered. The ground rumbled again. From behind the hush of the trees, Raegan heard gravestones clatter like broken teeth, a great wave of energy rising up like a storm surge, the force of it ringing the church bells. The mound at their feet shuddered and then slid open, revealing a set of stone stairs leading into sparkling waters. Though the sun stood directly overhead, shrouded in clouds, another light source shone from the opening in the mound, spinning the space between the yews with golden thread.

"Welcome home," Raegan said, choking on tears as she turned to face Oberon, "Once and Future King. It's you. It's always been you."

He gazed at her like she might be the sun. "Nyneve," he murmured, expression filled with awe. Despite the door to Avalon—to *salvation*—at his left, the King only had eyes for her. He looked at her with a love so fierce and wild that her heart skipped a beat. "Though two goddesses created me, it is you, I think, who is truly divine."

She laughed, delirious, her entire body shaking. She opened her mouth to say something, but whatever words she might've spoken were devoured by the shrill shriek of a kelpie's war cry. There was barely time to process anything before bullets tore through the air, threatening to snatch this victory right out of her hands. Out in the churchyard, Rainer shrieked again, though this time he was answered by a chorus of shrill, deadly kelpie voices that echoed down the surrounding hillsides.

A gossamer-thin shadow began to encompass the space between the yews, slinking through the air like silk. Before the sphere could close, a spear sailed through the air, tearing the protective working in half. Raegan reached for her power, but they were far from the shores of any river and opening the door to Avalon had taken its toll on her. Beside her, the King pivoted, his back to the door in the mound.

"Stay close to me," he warned, his blade of shadow blinking into existence in his free hand.

Raegan nodded, steadying herself—and then a wall of muscle and cloth knocked her onto the damp earth below, stealing the air from her lungs. She rolled, reaching for the knife on her waistband, but large hands pinned her wrists above her head. With a howl, Raegan struggled, kicking and thrashing, hunting for flesh to sink her teeth into.

The world rolled again, and she took a knee to the stomach, stealing her breath. She gagged, nauseous from the intensity of the blow, only to have her arms yanked behind her back. With horror, she realized the bitter cold of the metal meeting her wrists was of a very specific make— sainted iron. She screamed, the sound bloodcurdling to her own ears, and reached for the water running through her imprisoner's body. But the cuffs had already closed, and the old magics in her quieted. Furious, Raegan reached for the currents within her, but they slipped from her clumsy grasp.

"So close this time, weren't we?" a voice sounded triumphantly in her ear.

Raegan clenched her jaw. *Bedwyr*, yet again carrying on the cruel legacy of his king. She thrashed again, throwing her weight into the body of her murderer and the Timekeeper's favorite pet. But his powerful, mountainous build at her back didn't give an inch. In the thin gray light leaking in from the churchyard, she watched a gloved hand appear in her vision and grip her jaw.

"If you do not release her," the King roared from across the space between the yews, out of Raegan's sight, "I will slit you open from throat to navel and feast upon your intestines."

Bedwyr threw his head back and laughed. "His feelings for you are such a weakness, don't you think?" he purred in her ear. "Oh, and don't stop fighting, Nyneve. I *like* when you fight. You fought so much the first time I killed you. You're prettiest when you're struggling against things too powerful for you to ever come out on top."

Raegan opened her mouth to spit obscenities until she saw something much worse than anything Bedwyr could do or say to her. Just a few paces away, in front of the door to Avalon, the King fought against a net of sainted iron. At least ten heavily armed Protectorate soldiers swarmed him like vultures, battering him with battle magic that rattled Raegan's teeth as it sailed through the air. Her heart stopped.

And then time stopped, too. A powerful working exploded into existence—far too quickly, too easily; those spells were *immense*. It caught the King in its wake, leaving the Protectorate surrounding him to move in real-time as he struggled against air that had turned to molasses.

"We would've never been able to open the door without you," Bedwyr murmured in her ear, the feeling of his lips against her skin vile. "But you led us right to it and cracked it open. Really, I'm in your debt, witch."

Something in the time working bent in on itself, and suddenly, the soldiers surrounding Oberon were moving faster than they had any right to, dealing blows and magical attacks with terrifying speed. Raegan screamed, struggling against Bedwyr. He laughed, dangling a pocket watch—much like the ones inside the grandfather clock guardians in the Undercroft—in front of Raegan tauntingly. Its face was cracked down the center, the arms of the clock trembling.

"I've been saving this for a very special day," Bedwyr said, yanking her arms back at a painful angle. She bit down on her tongue, refusing to give him the pleasure of her pain. "Even in the Otherlands, ambient magic's not what it used to be, so these are hard to come by. But using such a special thing to kill your Fey lover in front of you? Well worth the expenditure."

Raegan's rage knew no words, no languages, only an endless, keening howl as she struggled against her murderer. The King's left shoulder—where he'd already been injured—had torn back open and was bleeding profusely. He'd summoned more of those shadow hounds, but their jaws couldn't snap closed quickly enough around the Protectorate soldiers.

Even if they couldn't kill him here—they *couldn't*, Raegan told herself; they'd tried before and failed—all of it was happening again. She choked on rage and sorrow, her entire body going limp. No matter what they did, no matter how hard they fought, it always ended the same. She'd go to her grave wearing a burial shroud of failure, and the King would face endless torture until maybe they finally figured out how to kill him. A sob tore from her lips, drenched in a thousand years of misery.

"Stop," Raegan begged, fighting against Bedwyr, fighting to gain a hold on the dark river inside of her, the sainted iron dampening her feel of its currents. "Stop."

Her voice hardly broke over the din of baying hounds and shrieking kelpies and battle magic rattling through the space.

"Stop," she said, louder now, something rising in her like a tide. Not the river, not even water at all, but something else entirely, unfamiliar and bitter on her tongue even as she gave into its swell.

Desperate and mad as a wolf, Raegan fought against Bedwyr's iron hold. For a moment, she nearly broke his grasp, but he just shoved her to the ground, the hard-packed damp earth biting into her knees.

"That's more like it," he laughed a moment before she felt a boot on her back, almost pushing her to the ground before fingers caught her by the hair and yanked her back up to her knees. "Careful. Wouldn't want you to miss anything."

Raegan locked eyes with Oberon. There should have been disappointment, there should have been hatred, there should have been the grief that she had once again failed him. But she found none of those things in the ocean of his eyes—just a gleaming, defiant love that would've brought her to her knees if she weren't there already. His face was bleeding now, a gash opened across one of those sharp cheekbones, and he was barely fending off attacks, taking most of the battle magic full-on, swaying under the intensity of the spells.

Something in Raegan broke. "Stop," she commanded, her voice rising above the cacophony this time, a battle cry hemmed in grief.

Did the Protectorate's movements slow, or was she just filled with a chemical hope flooding her brain in the final moments of life? She didn't care—she clung to it, let the tide fill her with the kind of rage she had always thought she needed to keep under control.

Raegan let the anger stampede through her body. It was pure and vicious. It cared not for the sainted iron around her wrists or the immortal abomination that held her fast. A thousand years of fury bled into the air, and the soldiers around the King slowed another half-step.

"What is happening?" Bedwyr barked in the voice of an army commander, though she felt the fear slink through him, and she feasted upon it.

Raegan snarled a response, but even her own words were lost to the flow of boundless rage. No more. No more of this misery, no more watching from her knees in the dirt, no more of this man's hands on hers.

"Stop," Raegan commanded, her voice orchestral and golden like a Fatesong, ringing through the churchyard louder than any bell. "*STOP*."

Silence, yearning wide and endless, and then all the world went still.

Chapter Forty-Six

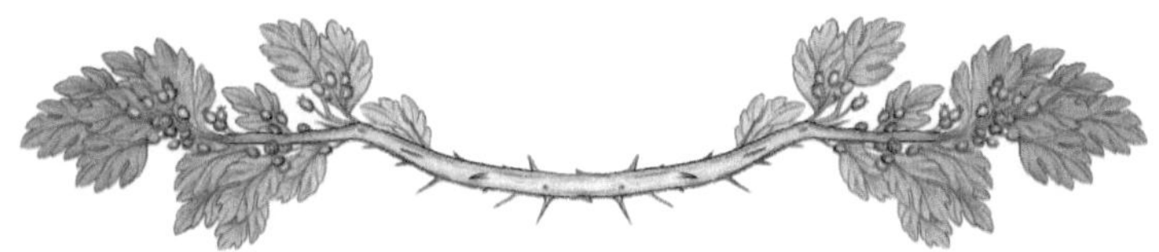

Raegan and the King stared at each other for one, two, three full seconds before she managed to stagger to her feet. Bedwyr was frozen behind her, his mouth open in a snarled shout, hands clasped around where her body had been. A clanging thump broke the silence—Oberon shrugging off the net of sainted iron, letting it fall to the ground below. The soldiers surrounding him were motionless, attack spellery hanging still and powerless in the air.

Raegan dragged herself to him. Despite his injuries, the King pulled her into his arms without hesitation, his mouth meeting hers as if it were the antidote to all he had suffered. She surrendered to the faerie king's kiss, his dark tide rushing to meet her river like brackish water.

"Steady," he murmured as they broke apart, his hands coming to her face, examining her for injuries.

"I'm fine," she protested, running her eyes over the singe marks where the sainted iron had draped over his frame, the blood seeping from his cheekbone, the too-pale ivory of his features. "You're not, though."

But the King was already moving, searching the motionless Bedwyr's pockets for a key to Raegan's cuffs. "We do not know how long this will hold," he said, gaze darting to meet hers, the closest he'd ever come to frantic.

Movement outside the canyon of yews set Raegan's blood on fire. But it was just Rainer, barreling through the small opening, nearly slamming into the King. His bulk filled the minimal space left between the trees, making it feel more like a crowded elevator than a sacred place where the earth's bones showed through.

"How?" the kelpie asked, the weight of his gaze falling onto Raegan like a hundred riverstones.

"I have no fucking idea," she replied, her voice shrill. "Does it matter?"

"Not at this precise moment, I suppose, but in general, yes," the kelpie said.

"Thank the Morrigan," the King muttered, pulling a key ring from Bedwyr's pocket. Without a further word, he strode to Raegan and released her from the cuffs, tossing them onto the ground with a curse. She rubbed her wrists, the skin bruised and smarting from contact with the sainted iron.

"You found the door," Rainer said, his tone filled with awe as he noticed the opening in the mound, sunlight spilling out of it like spun gold. Then he sobered, his flat black eyes looking between Raegan and the King. "Go. You must go."

"She did a time working," the King said, taking a ragged breath as he shifted his weight off his left leg. "None of the Protectorate can return with that information, Rainer."

Raegan did not feel sorry for the soldiers frozen around her, and neither did the kelpie, apparently. The light from the door glimmered, catching Rainer's viciously scalloped ears and ancient eyes. He arched his thickly muscled neck, the long waves of his mane turned iridescent in Avalon's illumination. "That, my friend, can be arranged. After all, I must consume."

His gaze tracked to Raegan at those last few words, and if kelpies could wink, Rainer certainly did.

"That one," she said, pointing to Bedwyr. "Make sure he's awake first."

Rainer bowed his head, his coat shimmering silver-green-black with the movement. "It would be my honor, high lady. Now go. We will ferry the mortals at the faerie fort to Hiraeth as soon as it's safe."

"Thank you, Rainer," the King said, emotion thick in his low, hoarse tone. Then he turned to Raegan, and without hesitation, he swept her into the place beneath the yews where the world opened wide. She felt the door close behind her—a wound stitching itself out of existence, leaving no scar and no trace. The sunlight on her face was warm and soft, the air cool, scented with sea salt and creamy feathers and damp stone.

The stairs led down, just like the vision had shown her, weathered and ancient, disappearing into the lapping waves. The King's hand tightly grasping hers, Raegan looked around, finding nothing but the sea. It seemed to stretch forever, its colors like nothing she'd ever seen—a deep, impossibly rich lapis lazuli turned to sapphire where the sun touched it, whitecaps dusting the tops of waves like chiffon. Dark, drenched stones broke through the surface in a few places, gleaming tide pools pockmarking their surface.

She turned to look over her shoulder, finding a sheer wall of stone so tall that vertigo lurched in her chest. Like the stairs, it looked positively ancient. Beside her, the King swayed, and she reacted in an instant, turning to grab him by the forearms.

"Let me heal you," she said, reaching up to brush a wave of ink-dark hair away from where his temple still bled freely.

"You need not tax yourself further," came a voice from behind Raegan at the same moment an immense presence washed over her.

Slowly, not taking her hands from the King, she looked up to find a goddess floating inches above the ocean's surface, just a few paces from her.

The deity had violet-gray hair rippling down her shoulders, part of it bound in intricate plaits that circled her head like a crown. Her skin was a mossy hue, her features sharp and inhuman—the knifelike cheekbones and sharp jaw that Raegan had come to know so well, the planes of her face feral beneath the kind expression. She was dressed in a diaphanous gown the color of a storm, its hem damp with water, the sleeves billowing about on the breeze. Above the elegant drape of a cowl neckline, the goddess's neck was as long and elegant as a swan's. Her eyes were large, deep-set, a color that was impossible to name. Like a kaleidoscope or a rainbow or perhaps an oil spill, but all of those descriptors were too gaudy for the unyielding beauty upon which Raegan gazed.

"Avalon was a place of healing and knowledge before the rest," the goddess said, her voice like crashing waves and blooming flowers and spring rain. "We can help. Come."

Raegan and the King exchanged glances. He gave the smallest of nods and straightened, brows pulling together in pain. She did her best to support him as together, they sloshed down a few more steps.

"Danu?" Oberon rasped, barely audible over the sway of the sea, but the goddess caught his words all the same.

She smiled, a dangerously lovely thing. "Yes, child," the goddess replied. "I am known as Danu. And Anu. And Modron. And more, I would imagine. I shudder to know what the mortals have attributed to me as of late. Much about motherhood, I am sure, though if they perceived me differently, they might call me a creatrix instead."

Raegan just stared at the divine being in front of them, her body trembling with exhaustion. Had she really spun a time working out of sheer rage? Had Oberon truly survived all those brutal attacks to stand here in the surf and the sun, a goddess making little backhanded quips about gendered human society?

Before she could convince herself that she wasn't still trapped in Bedwyr's arms beneath the shadow of the yews, the water pooling up onto the stairs slipped away. Raegan watched with awe and some degree of unease as the ocean slunk backwards, as if Danu were the mistress of the tides in this place and not the moon. The water's retreat revealed a stone causeway leading through the sea. The goddess turned and began to follow the path, moving in long, elegant strides. Her feet were bare, dainty jewelry around her ankles winking in the sunlight. The back of her dress dipped in a low V, offering a glimpse of the goddess's muscled form, woad tattoos in strange shapes dripping down the line of her spine.

There was nothing to do but follow. So cautiously, her chest tight, her mind still struggling to comprehend everything before her, Raegan held tightly to the King and began the journey. No creatures struggled in the wake of the receded tide—there was only weathered stone and long-dead bones and clumps of glimmering kelp.

"Do you . . . see anything up ahead?" Raegan asked after a long silence. They'd followed the goddess far into the ocean; it would be an easy thing for the tides to sweep them to their death. She didn't dare look behind her—knowing how far away the shoreline of rock and narrow stairs was would offer no reprieve.

"I am hoping that Avalon is glamoured," the King replied in her ear, his voice hitching with pain.

Raegan gritted her teeth. Danu might possibly be their savior, but she was the creator of the Fey—of course she would see little wrong with making one of her own limp along an uneven, rocky causeway. Casual cruelty was not so different between humans and the Fair Folk.

"And that it's not much farther," she replied under her breath. She should be too tired for it, but anger rose in her chest regardless, sparking between her lungs.

"I do so adore your rage, little deathless thing," the goddess in front of them said as she turned to look over her shoulder, coy, though her pace didn't change. "But no magic is permitted in the sea corridor other than the causeway enchantment. Another line of defense. The way is not much longer now."

Raegan held Danu's gaze and then nodded, turning to look up at the King.

"I will be alright," he assured her, though his breathing was still too heavy. "Thanks to you, my brilliant witch, I will be alright."

A different kind of warmth spread across her chest, and she smiled to herself as she continued down the stone path.

She couldn't say how long they walked. The sun never wavered in the sky—too bright to locate, though there *was* a sun, unlike the unnatural light of the In-Between. All she knew was that one moment, she was about to protest, to gesture wildly at Oberon's wounds and demand to know how a creator could be so cruel, and the next, something flickered into existence on the horizon.

An island of mist, just like all the stories said. Ethereal white spires reached into the blue-gray sky, piercing the roving clouds like daggers. When the silvery veil parted, Raegan caught glimpses of rocky cliffs crowned in heather, a half-moon of pearlescent sand beach and dark, thick woods stitched onto the horizon. Sea-drenched stones hemmed the land like sentinels. Her breath caught. That coiled root of yearning deep inside her keened.

"It's really Avalon," Raegan breathed, tears streaming down her face before she even realized she was crying. Wordlessly, the King gripped her hands tighter. She looked up at him, and despite all the pain, she saw

a wild kind of hope in his eyes that made her heart leap. Maybe this time
. . .

"A carriage awaits you on the shore," Danu said, stepping off the causeway and onto the beach, which was suddenly ten times closer than Raegan had dared to imagine. She followed, nearly delirious as the breeze pulled at her braid, bringing with it the scent of mist, black currant, and violet leaf—impossibly green and spellbinding.

A carriage did indeed await, like something out of the fairy tales Raegan had long since forsaken for darker stories with sharper teeth. It looked as though it had been carved out of pewter and mother-of-pearl, fashioned after the ribs of some long-dead creature, glimmering every time the sun broke through the banks of fog. She climbed the delicate, silvery steps, doing her best to help the King along. Once they were settled, she looked up to see Danu lingering before the carriage doorway, though the goddess did not move to join them.

"A visit with the pharmakon first, I think," Danu said, arching a thin brow, her mouth twisting with humor as if she were addressing naughty children. "And then we will speak."

"But Excalibur," Raegan blurted out, her anxiety thudding too loudly in her veins. "It's here, right? And is it true what the Morrigan said—about it being a Fey blade?"

All these years around the Fair Folk—she *knew* the right way to deal with them. But sometimes she just didn't have it in her to cater to their whims. Sometimes the burning question slipped out without a stitch of that stupid Fey-mandated politeness.

"Of course," Danu said, her brows furrowed as if more taken aback by Raegan's doubt than her direct inquiry. "And the Nameless One is the only Fair Folk it could not kill, because he was made in my image but not by my hands. Fey, yes, but different enough that the spellwork imbued in the blade is not as potent against him."

Rage lurched in Raegan's body, her nails digging into the aubergine velvet seat cushions—all this strange and otherworldly beauty be damned if any of it came at *his* expense. She was intimately familiar with the vicious scar on his chest where Excalibur had tried to lay claim to him a thousand years ago. "In other words, you'll heal him just so the sword can harm him again? Because it won't outright kill him like the rest of you, but it'll still really hurt him, won't it?"

Danu's eyes flashed, the universe turning in their depths, anger flattening her expression into something that looked too much like Fate's had back in that forest clearing. "It is just as you said at my door—he is the Once and Future King. Such a glorious destiny comes with pain."

The goddess's gaze slid to the King, who was resting the back of his head against the carriage's mother-of-pearl inlaid interior, the proud line of his shoulders collapsed, his breathing too much like rasping for Raegan's comfort. She reached across the space and took his hand gently in hers, the long fingers and calluses achingly familiar.

"He was spun from the night sky and milked from blood," Danu continued, her voice softer now, a single tear balancing on her silver eyelashes. "His Threads are barely more than grief spooled into yarn. He is a weapon. And all good weapons are crosshatched in scars."

Oberon's heavy breaths filled the carriage, the whisper of the sea distant, Raegan's blood ringing loudly in her ears. She could raise a tsunami, she thought. She was a witch of the water; anything that flowed, that moved in tides and currents, was hers to harness. She could drown this entire island—for the King's older brethren certainly didn't deserve such bliss on the back of his suffering.

"Creatrix," Oberon breathed, his eyes holding Danu's—two oceans meeting in some forgotten place shrouded in mist. "Will we one day, perhaps, linger in the sun?"

That centuries-old ache throbbed in Raegan's chest, and she nearly choked on the grief. She looked away from the King, taking in his shaky exhale, only to notice that tears were streaming down the goddess's face, more gathering in her kaleidoscope eyes. Sorrow spun around the three of them, thick and heavy as a stormfront rolling in.

"My child," Danu murmured, moving as if to reach into the carriage before thinking better of it. "I fear not all of us are meant for the sun."

CHAPTER FORTY-SEVEN

Raegan wrapped her hands tighter around the gilded teacup and stared blankly into the fire. She was going to scream. She was going to throw something. She was going to march down to the pharmakon—a ridiculously beautiful glass solarium bursting with lush foliage—and ask what the fuck was taking so long.

But she had already done all of those things at least once in the past hour, and the kind coordinator had resorted to begging her to wait for an update on Oberon's treatment in their guest quarters. Having a mortal wandering about, the coordinator repeated for the umpteenth time, would draw attention, and Danu would very much prefer to avoid such things. Apparently even a utopia still had politics, and many Avalonians found Danu's desire to interfere with happenings outside of their safe haven alarming at best.

That, at least, Raegan understood. Of course the Fair Folk in their towering spires the color of bone china and their supposedly endless libraries and city center that had been built *with* nature instead of against it didn't care what was happening outside their walls. They were safe. They were happy. Doing anything about the Timekeeper would risk all of that—and besides, hadn't they seen all of this bullshit coming? Wasn't that exactly why Danu had led them away all those years ago? In their eyes, anyone who chose to stay behind got what was coming to them.

She seethed, biting down on her tongue. If not for the sound of the whitewashed double doors opening, she might've bitten all the way through. Instead, Raegan turned in her chair, heart fluttering. And there he was—the Unseelie king, his wounds vanished from existence, his button-down rolled to the elbows, collar open, the blackened remains of his suit jacket slung over his shoulder.

She didn't hesitate. Raegan leapt to her feet and ran to him, slowing herself only at the last moment. "Is it okay if I—"

She didn't manage to get the words out before Oberon wrapped his arms around her so tightly it squeezed the air from her lungs. A sob of relief clawed its way up her throat as she returned his embrace, burying her face in his chest.

"You have been attended to as well, yes?" he asked in a low murmur, tucking her head under his chin.

"Yeah, but I didn't get the shit kicked out of me like you did," Raegan replied, breathing in the scent of him, all damp stone and woodsmoke and black pepper.

"Hmmm. The pharmakons were impressed I was still alive," he observed dryly, fingertips brushing her hair.

"Did you tell them that spite is a very powerful tool?" she asked with a laugh, pulling away to gaze up at him. That notch in his brows said he was still in pain, but his color was no longer that sickly pale hue, his breathing returned to the long, even intakes she'd come to know so well.

He smiled at her, a curve of his beautiful mouth, cupping her jaw in one large, powerful hand. "As are you," he murmured, the pad of his thumb brushing her lower lip. "It is worth staying alive just for you."

Raegan closed her fingers around the collar of his shirt, standing up on her tiptoes. The King met her halfway, kissing her until she was dizzy, until all the horror of the day had been banished for a moment or two. Then she slid her fingers through his before leading him past the hearth and into a narrow side room with high ceilings. Avalonians preferred to do their soaking in large, communal bath spaces, so the washroom only had two showerheads with a low wooden bench, but that worked fine for Raegan's purposes. A thin window of frosted glass at the far end of the room sent sunlight scattering across the stone floors, the shadows of tree limbs dappling the bright, warm space.

"I thought you might need help," Raegan said, her mouth twisting into a smirk as she began to unbutton the King's shirt.

"Very generous of you," he replied in a low, husky tone that made all her nerve endings curl in on themselves, desire unfurling low in her belly.

"Selfless, you might say," she said, bringing her mouth to his exposed collarbone. A deep sound of approval thrummed through his muscular chest, stoking the flames of Raegan's arousal. "If you're in too much pain . . ."

"After everything that occurred today, I . . . I *need* you," he replied, mouth moving roughly against her neck as he bowed around her smaller frame, hands sliding under her sweater. She tilted her head back, giving him more access, a soft gasp escaping her mouth. Everything about him drove her absolutely mad, even a thousand years later.

"I love you," she murmured, pushing his shirt off his shoulders.

He tugged her sweater over her head, powerful palms skimming down her sides, meeting at the zipper of her jeans. Raegan arched into him, begging for more, and he acquiesced. Once all of their clothing was piled unceremoniously in the corner, Oberon caught her mouth in his and pushed her against the wall. The rough stone was delightfully cool on her skin, particularly in contrast with the dark heat of his muscular frame.

The showerhead beside her switched on, water streaming from its sprout raindrop-like, already the perfect temperature. She pulled the King beneath it, marveling at the way water gathered on his ivory skin, how it sluiced down the hard, powerful lines of his body. They kissed each other feverishly, his rough groans mingling with her hitched gasps.

Oberon pulled back, cupping her face in his hands, resting his forehead against hers. Hot water streamed down around them like a rainstorm, soothing Raegan's tired, strained muscles. She could've lived in that moment, nothing but the water and her faerie king.

"The closer we come to the end of this," he murmured, tracing the line of her jaw with his fingertips, "the closer I fear I come to losing you."

Raegan's breath caught in her throat. "I wish I could tell you that wasn't true."

He dropped one hand to her side, curling his fingers possessively around her waist. "But for now," he said in a long exhale, forehead still against hers, his large body blocking out all the rest of the world, "I wish to make you forget we are doomed."

Grief thrashed against her hurricane-glass heart. It was true; they'd been doomed before Cordelia spoke the Prophecy, before the Protectorate closed the Gates, before the Battle of Camlann, before the sword in the stone and before Arthur's birth and before the first Roman ship ever landed on British soil. Doomed, perhaps, since the very first star dared to interrupt the darkness of the primordial night.

"Mordred," she murmured. His breathing stilled, muscles coiled and tense as he traced the curve of her hip. "Please. Make me forget."

He shifted back from her, and she gazed up at him—his black hair flattened by the water, caught in spirals against his skin, long eyelashes framed by tears. An inferno burned in his expression, all the fury and promise of a predator gone too long denied.

The next moment, his mouth was on hers, breathless and insistent, the evidence of his arousal pressed thickly against her belly. Raegan moaned, threading her fingers into his hair, the drenched black strands curling like ink around her fingers.

"Mordred," she gasped, her hands moving to the nape of his neck. "I want to forget everything but you."

For a moment she was lost in the slip of time—just a maiden entangled with a knight, a tale as old as anything. His gaze slid to hers, the angles of his face gone vicious and feral. Then he moved all at once—his hands cupped the generous curve of her ass, pulling her from the ground. Mordred's broad, powerful body pinned her against the cool tile from all angles. She greedily wrapped her legs around his hips, trailing fingertips down his chest, tracing that delicious line of downy, silken hair that bisected the pale expanse of ivory muscle.

Damp with a blistering need, Nyneve rolled her hips against his, digging her fingernails into his shoulders. He caught her lower lip between his teeth, dragging a throaty groan from the depths of her body. Every inch of her skin demanded more of him. One of his long-fingered hands slid between their bodies, teasing at the apex of her thighs. She said his name in a voice that barely sounded like hers, keening with endless ache.

"I would burn the entire world in your name," the faerie knight rasped against her mouth, the pressure of his touch increasing. He shifted her up higher on the wall with one deft movement, bringing his tongue to the tip of her breast. Nyneve couldn't stand it—to feel all of this pleasure, to be surrounded by all his glorious darkness, without him inside of her.

"Mor," she gasped, a nickname she hadn't spoken in a millennium, digging her nails deeper into his skin. He glanced up at her, a dangerous smile gracing his beautiful, full mouth even as he continued his ministrations.

"Is there something in particular," the changeling murmured, his words slow and sweet, "you require of me? As proof of the devotion you seek?" Humor lilted his tone upwards, but his deep voice was still husky with the same desire she felt.

"Fuck me with your cock, you goddamn monster," she managed to get out.

They both broke into laughter, the sound ringing out in the space. She wouldn't have thought it possible, but that sweet look of levity in his expression . . . it filled her with a yearning that might've broken her, were his hands not in all the right places, his hips already lined up with hers.

"As always," Mordred replied, lips ghosting hers, one large hand sliding up to toy with her breast in exactly the way she liked, "your wish is my command."

He buried himself inside of her. He offered none of the gentler movements he typically did to ensure she was prepared for him. Instead, he filled her entirely, completely, ferociously, his teeth grazing the side of her neck. Nyneve let out a sound she was worried all of Avalon might've heard, going near-limp against the wall with the thick, devouring wave of pleasure that rolled over her.

As Mordred drove into her, one hand still working in circles at her core, Nyneve could barely tell where she ended and he began. They moved against each other with wild abandon, as if they only proved how desperately they wanted to be together, Fate may just allow it.

But no such provisions existed in this cruel universe, Nyneve knew, so she told herself to savor every moment of it: the look of ecstasy on his impossibly beautiful face as he slid inside of her, the way he said her name as if it were a wish, the pleasure so thick and sweet that she wasn't sure she could contain it. How he took her like a creature half-starved, how he chased her pleasure like it might save them both.

"Mordred," she begged, the ages and the world outside slipping from her grasp. "Mor. *More.* Fuck, I need more."

With a low, deep sound of acquiescence that rumbled in his chest, the faerie knight increased his pace into something near-punishing. Nyneve moaned his name, her head tilting back against the wall, gaze tracking toward the ceiling. In a movement so quick her pleasure-addled mind could hardly trace it, Mordred lifted one hand from her body, grasping her jaw between his fingers with a steel grip. He lowered her chin, his oceanic gaze meeting hers.

"Eyes on me," he commanded in a tone so darkly devoted that it almost sent her over the edge. She nodded, holding his gaze, her mouth parting to release another strangled cry.

"Just don't stop," she replied, her chest heaving against his.

One of those black brows arched, sending a thrill through her body, though she didn't understand how a sensation so perfect could keep feeling better and *better.* He kept his word, driving into her hard enough to send her heavy breasts bouncing, even with her back pressed against the wall. Through the falling droplets of water and the thick haze of desire, she watched Mordred's gaze drop to the swell of her breasts, his eyes devouring her every curve.

Nyneve didn't hesitate; she let go of his shoulder with one hand and took his sharp jaw between splayed fingers. "Eyes," she began, the word coming out a guttural groan. "On. *Me.*"

Obediently, he raised that fathomless gray gaze of his, water gathering on his long, dark eyelashes as he gave her every single ounce of his attention. With no interruption to the rhythm of their hips coming together, he took one of her wrists above her head and then the other, pinning both her arms against the wall.

"Come for me," he commanded in a voice like dusk, like every shadow sweeping in from the dark and lonely places.

She held his gaze. "Fuck me harder, then."

∿

After, they dried off and stumbled into the large sleigh bed of pale wood, dressed in soft linens and a thick quilt in a sea of blues. Judging by the light—if such things were the same in a place like Avalon—it was only late afternoon. And yet drowsiness pulled at Raegan pleadingly, her eyelids as heavy as her burdens. She curled her smaller frame against the King's, and he tucked her head under his chin, arms encircling her. They weren't safe, she knew. How could they be? Even if they retrieved Excalibur, destroyed the Gates, and vanquished the Timekeeper, their ouroboros would still march on, would it not? She would always slip from his grasp like river water. He would face the centuries ageless and mostly alone.

"Why do you keep returning to me, my queen of lovely rage?" Oberon murmured, fingertips tracing the spiral of curls spilling down her back.

Raegan hesitated, flattening her palm against his chest. "Because it's you," she finally said. "It's always been you. No one else looks at my anger like a sacrament."

His breathing stilled against her, slow as the morning tides. "And yet I can never manage to hold on to you for very long."

"That's not a failure on your part," Raegan protested, lifting her head to look him in the eye. "I'd never ask you to take on that burden."

His smile was wan, awash in the rich golden sunlight streaming in from the large window that overlooked the city. "Good. Take care what you ask of me. I cannot say no."

"You probably should," she replied, raising a brow. "I'm fucking insane."

His resulting laugh rumbled through her body, and she hung on to the sound—sweeter than a Fatesong.

"As you said," he replied as she lowered her head back to his chest, "your madness, your rage, whatever you wish to call it—I would drown in it. Be consumed by it."

"You need to stop saying such incredibly attractive things," Raegan said with a yawn, nestling closer to the hard angles of his body. "I'm not going to be able to walk straight tomorrow as it is." Before he could respond, she patted the long length of his side and added, "That's a joke—you didn't hurt me."

Silence stretched downy wings over the quiet chambers at the center of Avalon. Another impossible city, a place relegated to myth and lore, and yet Raegan had walked within its walls and been greeted as a friend. For all the suffering, it was hard not to feel as though Fate's punishment was in some ways, at least, a gift. An offering. Otherwise she would've gone to the soil a thousand years ago, never to return. Instead, she rose from her grave again and again, searching the wide expanse of the world for her faerie king.

She took a deep breath, his woodsmoke and damp stone scent filling her senses. Not so much a gift for the King, of course. He'd be better off without her, and to pretend otherwise was just fondness on his part.

"I hope you understand," Oberon murmured, his voice soft and quiet in the massive room, "the ways you have mended me. From the first day we met, you have never been afraid of me." His hand slid over hers, and she turned her palm, their fingers interlacing. "I have been feared and loathed and desired. But rarely loved, not truly. I cannot even save you, Raegan. And yet you love me still."

Tears choked her. She wondered if she could raise a tide high enough to wash away all his suffering, to take all his pain out to sea where it could sink into the depths and be forgotten. She could not, she knew.

"This time," the King continued, pulling her tighter against him, "please. I beg you. Outlive me, Nyneve. I love you too much."

CHAPTER FORTY-EIGHT

The sea lashed at the high, rocky cliffs of Avalon. Beneath the mist, the waves roiled in undulations not unlike some ancient sea monster. Raegan swallowed, pushing away a stray curl that the wind had pulled loose from her braid. The path leading down the cliffside was dizzying, barely more than steps carved into the crumbling chalk rock.

"The caves below have served us well," Danu said. Though the goddess did not raise her voice over the wind, Raegan heard her just fine. She turned to examine Danu, who stood at the top of the stairs, her grayed violet hair undisturbed by the same breezes that were currently unbraiding Raegan's curls. Divinity seemed nice. Lots of power, no real responsibility.

"Where in their depths will we find Excalibur?" the King asked, narrowing his eyes at the goddess. It was hard to believe he'd barely been able to limp into the city just the day before. The healing arts at Avalon far exceeded Raegan's thousand years of experience. Part of her itched to stay here, to pore over ancient texts and study every leaf in the greenhouses and wander the permaculture orchards. But as Danu had said, some are not meant for the sun.

"Arthur's chamber is toward the back of the caverns," Danu answered serenely. Both Raegan and the King flinched at the name, even after all these years. "The places below have a mind of their own. Your resolve may be tested."

"Are you fucking kidding me?" Raegan snapped, nearly shouting to be heard over the wind. "What do some goddamn caves know about *resolve*? We've been surviving in a world with no magic."

Danu's otherworldly, impossibly clear eyes met hers. Amusement danced on the goddess's mouth. "I can see how you have vexed Fate so," she said, clasping her hands together in front of her. "Though I find your rage a good match for the last of my children."

"Oh, I'm so glad your deadbeat of a mother who just met you for the first time approves of me," Raegan quipped, looking up at Oberon, whose lips twitched at her words no matter how much he tried to wipe his expression clean.

Danu's mouth pressed into a firm line, but one of her eyebrows arched with something that looked like amusement.

"How might our resolve be tested?" the King asked, crossing his arms. The borrowed overcoat was a little too small for his broad shoulders, pulling the fabric tight in a way that made Raegan think of the previous night.

"Some wander a labyrinth, others confront memories, some see their beloved dead," Danu said with a shrug, as if these were small, simple things.

"Great," Raegan said. "And someone can't just, like . . . go get the sword for us, right?"

Danu's pale silver brow arched again. "The reason the places below may want to taste your intentions is because nothing sealed into those chambers is ever meant to come back out. Thus, the caves must be sure. Besides, I dare say few of us would fare well touching Excalibur."

Raegan eyed the winding stairs, the swelling waves, the entrance to the caves that they wouldn't even see until they reached the bottom of the cliff at exactly low tide, during which they would have approximately two hours to find a half-dead mortal king and his stolen faerie blade.

"You're a goddess," she said, drawing out the words. "So couldn't you—"

"Child," Danu interrupted, her expression unguarded, the crow's feet around her eyes crinkling as she squinted into the sun. "You know there is a way of these things. I can only interfere so much in this Thread. Even here. Even with all my power."

The wind scaled the cliffside in a rough exhale. The heather and gorse around Raegan's feet trembled, the standing stones a few paces off whistling as the wind raced past.

The moment it died down enough to speak, Raegan began, "When, precisely, was anyone aware that Excalibur used to be a faerie blade? And how did the Morrigan know?" Her mind swam as she shoved her hands into the pockets of the wool cape she'd been lent.

"Does it matter?" Danu asked dryly, staring off into the horizon— just ocean, endless swathes of sea in every direction. When neither Raegan nor Oberon responded, she heaved a very un-goddess-like sigh and turned back to face them. "Understand, my information is second-hand. I used to send spies into the Otherlands before it became too dangerous, before I buried the sea-door. Myrddin intended to take Excalibur's secret to his grave, I imagine, but Arthur knew, and at some point, Morgana le Fay learned of it. Arthur executed her for witchcraft to silence her, but as a priestess of the Morrigan, she told her goddess on her funeral pyre."

Wordlessly, Raegan reached out to take Oberon's hand. Morgana— Arthur's half-sister—had been the one to raise the King as a child, teaching him the ways of human nobility. He'd loved her, as had Raegan, and they'd done everything to stop the burning. It had, of course, not been enough. Rarely, it seemed, were they ever enough.

"I conspired with the kelpies to bring Arthur to Avalon so he could not rise again. I knew nothing of the blade's past and have squandered its potential for so many years," Danu continued, something not unlike grief etching her divine features. "When Kronos captured the Morrigan at the Battle of Camlann, the truth of Excalibur was locked away. It stayed that way until she escaped in the Otherlands, but by that point, the Gates had long been sealed in their entirety and the only people who could possibly do anything about it were trapped on the other side. I imagine she has been trying to reach you for hundreds of years. I too was only able to briefly communicate with her because of the temporary door you tore through the worlds with your tears. Avalon exists apart from the realms, yes, but even we cannot access the Otherlands."

Raegan felt exhausted, too much like the cliff at her left, which had spent thousands of years under the ocean's constant assault. She wanted to sleep. She wanted to have tea with Oberon in the mornings and have nowhere to be. Clenching her jaw, she closed her eyes and tried to remind herself of how badly she'd wanted all of this once.

But she'd hardly remembered anything then. Now she carried the weight of the centuries, her spine trembling with the energy to stay upright, to stay alive, at every moment.

"You're right," she said to the goddess. "It doesn't matter. It doesn't matter that the Morrigan has been trying to reach through the Gates for hundreds of years and only because everything went to shit and Fate played me like a fiddle was there even a tiny tear for her to squeeze through at all."

The words had barely left Raegan's mouth when a realization shot like lightning through her body. She jolted to stand ramrod straight, her mouth going dry. She looked at the King, whose wide eyes were already on hers, and then at Danu, who looked significantly coyer.

"Did Fate . . . Was this all . . ." she breathed, resisting the urge to tear her hair out at the root.

"When it comes to the primordial forces, even a being as old as I hesitate to comment," Danu said, staring out at the sea again, her tresses fluttering around her bare arms, which didn't appear to prickle with goosebumps despite the chill of the wind. "But it is possible. Do not trust Her, mind you."

A mass of shadow slunk past Raegan's side. She watched, confused, as the King stalked toward the mouth of the chalk rock stairs, his silhouette slicing into the mist that crowned the island.

"Oberon," she called, breaking into a jog, trying to be mindful of the fog-damp vegetation and loose rock.

"The goddess is right. None of it matters," the King half-shouted, turning on his heel, his eyes dark. "I do not care if Fate is secretly help-ing. I do not care about the machinations by which the knowledge of Excalibur's true nature reached our ears. I care about my people and you, Nyneve. Nothing more, nothing less. So let us go retrieve this gods-forsaken blade."

His eyes slid to Danu and narrowed, his chin tilted arrogantly. "If your island's low places give us undue trouble, know that my witch could drown this place, Old One."

Heat, of all things, slunk through Raegan's core at the way he referred to her. She caught up to him, sheltering from the gnawing wind against his bulk.

Danu grinned, her teeth just a little too sharp. "And if not for the love of my own people, nameless child, I should like to see her try." And then the goddess was gone, only tendrils of mist writhing in the place on the headland where she'd stood just seconds ago.

Raegan looked up at Oberon, and he met her gaze. "The only way, I think, is through," she said, studying his expression. He had just as much rage as she did—Raegan had always known that. He only controlled it better, had a wider and darker chasm within him to imprison it. She was not sure, not even after all these years, which way was actually better.

"Together," he said, bringing his forehead to hers. He planted a kiss against her skin and then turned to make his way down the crumbling stairs. Raegan followed at a safe distance, and they fell into a pattern, relying on the King's agility and quicker reflexes to forge a path ahead. It might've been beautiful, the impossibly sheer cliff face, stretching its white wings before giving way to the roaring gray ocean below, if not for the way all of destiny hung on the shoulders of the two people crawling across its expanse like ants.

By the time about a quarter of the stairs remained, according to Raegan's extremely rough estimation, the tide had begun to retreat, revealing a rocky beach awash with tide pools that shimmered like gems whenever the sun managed to reach through the crown of mist that circled the outer edges of the island. It was pretty, but her ankles and knees hurt. Getting back up would probably be worse, she reminded herself.

"If we come all this way," Raegan began, huffing as she navigated a particularly steep section, "just to die in a fucking cave, I swear to god, Oberon, I'll be so pissed."

He glanced over his shoulder at her, amusement tugging at the corners of his mouth. "I do not think any body of water would force itself into your lungs. And I cannot drown. The Protectorate tried."

Raegan's heart skipped a beat. She had attempted—unsuccessfully—to banish the thoughts of what the Protectorate had done to him following his capture. It had been her fault. They'd tried to kill him for *years*. All that pain and suffering, more than even she could imagine.

And yet here he was, smiling up at her, making a joke of the horrors he'd endured, the wind ruffling his dark waves of hair.

She carefully made her way toward him, stopping on a step that brought her eye level with him. "How we endure," Raegan murmured, reaching out to trace her fingertips down the side of his face. The King leaned into her touch like a love-starved alley cat, closing his eyes as she held his jaw in her hand.

"Forward, then," he said, so softly the wind almost grabbed his words and spirited them away. Upon the chalk-white cliffs of Avalon, Oberon reached for her hand and then brought his mouth to her knuckles, brushing her skin with a delicate kiss, gentle as a butterfly. Raegan's mind reeled, pulling her back to Camelot and the dark-armored knight with a gaze that seemed to see right through all her lies.

"Onward," she agreed, following the King as he turned to continue forging a safe path down the cliffside. The wind, thankfully, died down the lower they trekked, becoming little more than a strong breeze tugging them toward destiny.

At the bottom of the carved staircase, a wide plane of sandy rock breached the surface of the sea like a whale's back. Raegan scrambled onto it with Oberon's help, gripping his forearm tightly. It wasn't fair—nothing about anything was. They were both sufficiently healed, yes, but an exhaustion that no pharmakon could address lingered in their bones. And yet here they were, delving deep into the earth, praying that this place would not be their end.

"Shit," Raegan said as she took in the wide mouth of the sea caves: a door—it was always a door, wasn't it?—of a tall, narrow shape cut into the expanse of the white cliffs. They moved toward it, steps careful and measured. Raegan looked over her shoulder, back toward the ocean, and saw that this location would be woefully inaccessible any other time of the day. Experimentally, she pushed at the seawater with her magic. It did respond, but its answer was sluggish, irritated, unused to this taskmaster with mortal blood in her veins.

"I have a little sway with the ocean," she informed the King as they approached the mouth of the cavern. "Don't count on anything, though. It'd be a Hail Mary."

He looked at her sideways, mouth grim as he nodded. "Better than nothing, I suppose," he replied with a shrug, turning back to gaze into the open maw awaiting them.

The higher tides had left lines on the cave's walls, far above their heads. Raegan eyed them uncomfortably, her heart thudding a bit too hard against her ribs.

"How far does Avalon's sea go?" she wanted to know as they skirted a large tide pool with a lavender-spotted black octopus lingering within its waters.

"Forever, as far as I know," he replied, gazing up at the cavern's ceilings as it closed in on them, the mouth of a predator snapping shut. "From what I've gathered, when Danu pulled this realm out of ours, it did not happen quite right. Avalon should have been, perhaps, a larger, more magically fortified pocket realm. It is not. It is its own place entirely, with its own rules and wonders and terrors."

Raegan swallowed, nodding. It was easy to forget. Avalon was undeniably beautiful, and not terribly different from the Cornish coast, but Raegan was the first mortal to step foot here in thousands of years, if not more, and it would not do well to slip into complacency simply because the environs held some familiarity.

The air stilled farther inside the caverns, smelling of seawater and stones gowned in brine. They continued down the main walkway, silent, eyes roving this way and that, relying on the sputtering torches of lilac flame bracketed to the walls. All at once, the atmosphere changed—there was a deep, bone-rattling hum of terrible, eldritch magic. The awareness of it skittered down Raegan's spine like a chill, and she sharpened her eyes. Some doors, she remembered, are hungry.

But it was hard to keep an eye open for doors as the terrain grew more difficult. She stuck close to the King, scrambling up tight, slippery inclines and shimmying through claustrophobic passages. At one point, they had to descend a sheer drop into the darkness, bringing them into an inner cavern riddled with stalagmites. Neither spoke during their trek; the air filled instead with their footsteps and the drip of seawater, holy as a hymn.

Time, as it does in places such as these, dilated and shrank, passing in an unknown amount, before they saw the first cave. It opened like a mouth in the gray, stretching abyss of the walls. One of those eldritch workings reached over the opening, pale and iridescent in the fading light. The surface of it rippled like a living thing, so similar to the oil-spill surface of a porticus.

Raegan approached it slowly, peering inside as best she could. The space was filled with shelves, laden with plants stored beneath bell jars, seemingly in a form of stasis. It was hard to identify anything in the low light and through the shimmering, spiderweb barrier of the working, but even so, she could see flora that had never grown on Earth in the thousand years she'd been walking it.

"Likely biological stores, in case anything suffers a blight on the island," the King observed, his eyes tracking down farther into the cavern. Where Arthur slept, where Excalibur awaited a faerie king to release its true, feral nature.

Wordlessly, Raegan nodded and continued into the lilac-tinted gloom of the sea caves, aware of the presence that seemed to rove the space. She was growing a bit tired of sentient locations. It felt too much like being surveilled—judged and sentenced by a being she couldn't even *see*, let alone understand or reason with.

They wove deeper into the caves, Raegan worrying about the return of the higher tides, but the clock on her phone had been frozen since they'd entered Avalon. No service, either. Its battery was getting low, and she doubted anyone in the hidden Fey city had a charger. She wasn't sure why it was even still in the pocket of her leather jacket. Habit, maybe, or perhaps guilt about the people she'd left behind.

Farther, farther into the darkness they went, clinging to each other. Fear pounded in Raegan's veins, anxiety spiking at every distant wave crash she heard. But forward she went, because there was little the deathless witch was not capable of with the nameless one at her side. The gossamer-thin, iridescent mouths of more sea caves opened as they journeyed, offering glances at impossible-looking archery bows and strange creatures gone still. Most were empty. She tried not to think about that too much.

"Raegan," Oberon murmured, the heavy silence of the cave carrying his voice right to her ears. She turned on her heel from the cave she'd been examining; it was filled with strange, bloated jars. The hair on the back of her neck prickled.

"You found it, didn't you?" she asked, her voice so small, every fiber of her being aware and terrified and filled with the treachery of hope.

Across the narrow corridor, Oberon nodded. Carefully, like she might be in a trance, like all of the future was balanced on the edge of a knife, Raegan navigated the pockmarked rock and came to stand beside the King.

There, beyond the oil-spill mouth of the door, lay a man on a slab of rock. His eyes were closed, the wrapped leather pommel of an elegant longsword clutched tight between sleeping hands. He was—at least to look at—nothing at all remarkable. A man of middling height and build, of middling pale brown hair, of middling features.

Once, Arthur Pendragon had held the fate of the world in his hands. But it had never belonged to him in the first place, so it was well past time, Raegan thought, to take it back.

CHAPTER FORTY-NINE

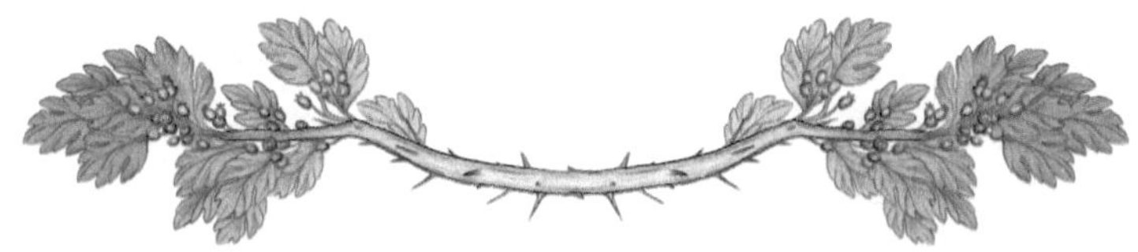

She reached out and brushed the working stretched like spiderweb silk over the mouth of the cave. It gave slightly, bending around her touch. When her skin made contact with it, Raegan's head swam violently.

"I do not think I can disarm it," Oberon told her, pacing in front of the cave's mouth, his dark brow furrowed. He was so far from the young, heartbroken, and outraged knight he'd been the last time he and Arthur Pendragon had walked the same halls, stalked the same fields of war. And yet, an old feeling rose in her chest—she wanted to get him as far away from Arthur as possible. She so badly wanted him to be free of this sword and this man. But like so many things she wished for, it could not be.

"I think it's the test," Raegan said with a sigh, eyeing the eldritch magic. "I think we have to walk through it and let Avalon's low places judge us."

The King's frown deepened, but he did not contradict her. "I wish we had the time to be sure," he sighed, his attention roving back the way they'd come. The lilac fire contained in the simple metal torches dimmed for a second. A warning, probably.

"Together, then," Raegan said, trying not to sound terrified.

Instead of reaching for her hand, Oberon closed the distance between them and wrapped his body around hers, pulling her into a kiss that drove her madder than an ancient spell ever could.

And then, before she could think or hesitate, the King clutched her in his arms and dove into the glimmering maw of Arthur Pendragon's resting place. For a moment, the working stretched against Raegan's weight and almost gave—she was so close to the sword she'd crossed realms for, the King's arms still around her.

And then everything was gone, the cave and the rock-hemmed darkness and the rush of ocean waves blinking out from existence. Instead, there was a nothingness so downy and sweet, as soft as being wrapped in furs by the fireside. But she could not feel her faerie king—could not feel *anything*—so she pushed through it, swimming without sight or hearing. At least she knew the darkness half as well as she knew herself.

Raegan awoke slowly, gently, blinking her eyes open to the molasses-thick light of autumn streaming down all around her. She sat up, finding she was sprawled out on a cozy wool blanket, a book forgotten at her side. The breeze danced across her skin, smelling of woodsmoke and damp stone and fallen leaves. She turned, not understanding, finding herself at the edge of a meadow. Beyond it, a forest grew dark and lovely. In front of her was a stone cottage, smoke curling out of its chimney. A fox roved the far edge of the meadow. Raegan stretched, feeling adrift. A distant buzzing met her ears, and she looked for the source of the sound —beehives, she saw, clustered between the house and the meadow.

Confusion knit thickly on her brow, she stood, finding nothing but mundane tiredness in her limbs. In fact, Raegan felt light—lighter than she had in years. But her body was the same, she saw with a quick glance at her soft flannel pants and oversized wool cardigan. She slid her feet back into the leather boots at the edge of the blanket and walked toward the cottage.

Some voice in the back of her mind warned her to be wary, but that made no sense. She was home, wasn't she? Her bees were busy in their hives, her vegetable garden still offering a few lush herbs even this late in the season. She walked up the moss-lined stone stairs at the back of the house and pushed open the heavy door. The scent of black tea and a hearth fire immediately greeted her, wrapping around her body like a blanket. Moving through the entryway lined with coats she recognized as her own, Raegan found herself in a small kitchen.

The cabinets curved in a half-moon with a large sink set below the garden window that looked out into the backyard. Less hardy herbs grew there in thick, colorful clumps, filling the cozy space with a deep green perfume. And there, at the stove, turning to face her with a kettle in hand, was the person she had loved through the ages.

"Oberon," Raegan murmured, enjoying the way his expression brightened when he saw her.

"I was about to come check on you," he replied in his deep, husky voice that she adored so much, that she had chased across the world. "Did you fall asleep?"

"I must've," Raegan laughed, her heart bursting with a joy so fragile she worried one wrong move might crack it down the center. "Is the water hot?"

Oberon nodded, gesturing with an elegant hand to the pair of teacups on the counter, already garnished with sugar and loose leaves of a dark, malty blend. "I planned to gently awaken you with a cup of hot tea," he said, one eyebrow arched as he poured hot water into both mugs.

"I think you just wanted to fuck out in the meadow again," she replied teasingly, memories flooding her mind of the day before—no, maybe not the day before. Hadn't they been somewhere else? She shook the thought from her head, instead lingering in the scene her mind offered up: autumn sun silhouetting his ivory skin, gilding his black hair with gold; how he'd moved above her, the weight of him pinning her to the blanket; the cool breeze caressing her bare skin.

His eyes slid to hers, all molten heat, the ocean turned to an inferno. "You question my honorable intentions?" he asked, placing the kettle back on the stove.

Raegan laughed, picking up her mug and wrapping her hands around the steeping tea, warding off the chill from being outside. "I had a weird dream," she said, fighting to recall. "We were somewhere dark. A cave, I think? Looking for someone."

The King sighed and leaned his forearms on the counter, the muscles of his chest and shoulder standing out beneath the thin shirt. "We have lived a long time, my love," he murmured, stirring his tea. "I have no doubt we were there, once."

"But we're here now, yes?" Raegan asked, suddenly doubtful, feeling like a rabbit in a snare. "We've been here?"

Any amusement in Oberon's face fled, and he reached for her, wrapping his larger hand around hers. "For six years," he said, his brow pulling tight in concern. "Sometimes you slip backwards in time. There is no danger in doing so, but it distresses you."

"Oh," Raegan said, relief bubbling up in her, though she didn't feel convinced, not with the remnants of the dream still clinging to her. "Right. I'm sorry."

"There is nothing to be sorry for," he replied without hesitation. "As long as you are alright."

"I think so," she promised, looking around the kitchen. The open cabinets were piled with mismatched dishes and bowls that felt like hers. She knew the utensils were in the top drawer of the counter, remembered cutting the fabric for the gingham tea towels by the sink. Trying to let go of the strange anxiety pulling at her, Raegan released a long breath and looked up at the King.

He was hers. The lines around his eyes, the silver threaded through his hair—just a little more than there had been in the strange dream—the full, sculpted mouth, the knifelike cheekbones, the notched scar bisecting the outer corner of his left eye. Yes. This was her love, and this was her life.

"We made it," she realized, tears brimming in her eyes. "Through all of it. You didn't lose me, and we made this little life. The Jersey cow in the pasture is named Acorn. I saw that big fox in the meadow again. We should name him, too, I think."

Oberon watched her, his gaze so full of endless love—love that finally had somewhere to go, to stay and grow—and she resisted the urge to weep. They'd fucking done it.

"We can cancel our dinner plans if you need more rest," he said to her gently. "The weight of your mind is heavy, and some days you find yourself tumbling out of time."

"Dinner?" she echoed, distracted as a crow landed on a tree outside the garden window, its feathers turned blue-black in the rays of the sun.

"Reilly, Alanna, and Maelona are coming by," Oberon told her, gesturing to the backyard. "You wanted to drag the long table out there and decorate it with apple blossoms. And then I believe you wanted to, and I quote, 'become blisteringly and stupidly drunk.'"

Raegan laughed, so much sweet, wondrous joy bursting in her

chest, though unease bloomed sour somewhere in her stomach. "That's right," she said, half-remembering it. "I think I'll be okay if it's just them."

"You can always change your mind," he reassured her. The crow at the garden window suddenly pecked the glass hard, startling Raegan. Oberon glanced over his shoulder, frowning. "Perhaps we are feeding them a bit *too* much."

The crow drove its beak hard into the glass again, louder now. The King stalked the three steps to the window and waved his hands to shoo the crow off. It only pecked harder, almost ferocious enough to break the glass. That tendril of unease coiled around Raegan's gut.

"I'll go give it a talking to," she said, trying to maintain her light tone.

"I am sure it will leave soon," Oberon replied, knocking hard on the inside of the glass. The crow pecked back in return, not stopping now, jackhammering its beak into the window.

Without another word, Raegan turned and fled out the back door, coming around the corner to face the large black bird.

"Could you stop, please?" she demanded, waving her arms. "Glass costs money. I don't think crows have capitalism, but we do, unfortunately."

Raegan paused, suspended in the murky light of late autumn that stretched across the meadow like honey. *Did* they have capitalism? Or had they changed all of that, too? Why couldn't she remember? Her hands curled into fists, fingernails biting into the flesh of her palm as she bit down on her tongue. She had to focus. What had she done this morning? Nothing but blankness arose in her mind, and she looked at the crow. It spread its wings and took off in flight. For a moment, her heart unclenched—maybe that was it, maybe its pecking meant nothing at all, maybe this really was her home and everything had worked out perfectly.

Raegan glanced around the space—the brown cow and speckled goat in the large, rolling pasture, the apple trees rooted in the forest, the swaying grasses of the meadow, the perfect little cottage, the King now standing in the open doorframe. All hers. And yet fear clutched at her, a sob tearing its way up the back of her throat.

"Nyneve," Oberon called, stepping down into the yard. "It is alright. I promise."

Instead of taking off for the trees in the distance, the crow began to circle her with desperate caws, its wings nearly brushing her shoulders.

The seed of doubt broke open beneath her breastbone, taking root. Tears spilled out from her eyes as she drank in the dreamscape, wanting to believe so badly, so desperately. But nothing this sweet and simple would ever be hers, she knew.

The darkness of the crow grew wider around her, the yawning mouth of a cave. She watched it, dizzy, her heart breaking into a thousand pieces. Not only was none of this hers, she knew, but there was the real King and a faerie blade and the future of magic awaiting her somewhere else.

"Stay here," the not-King pleaded, walking toward her with all the predatory grace she knew so well, his hands spread wide. "We could stay here, Raegan."

She gazed at him, eyes wide, brimming with tears, and wondered if this *was* Oberon. Was he trapped in this same working, and was he encouraging her to lay it all down? No, it might not be real—their bodies would rot at the entrance to the king of men's resting place.

But it would *feel* real. Did anything else even matter? She could have the thing she'd always craved: a future with the people she loved, bright and sweet as a honeycrisp apple. Yearning unspooled from the caverns of her body, thick with ache and unyielding in desire. She wanted this. She did not care, maybe, how she got it.

"No," Raegan gasped, tears streaming down her face. "Fuck, I want to. I can't even tell you how much I want all of this. The cottage and the apple blossoms and the afternoon cups of tea and, most of all, you. You without Fate's Threads gouging lines in our skin. You without the rest of it. But we can't. Not yet. Maybe never."

The flap of the crow's midnight wings began to rip wounds in the world around her. Raegan could nearly feel the welts opening inside her own body. She would've rather not tasted this fantasy at all. She didn't want to know what it could be, what it could feel like—she wanted no part in something that she knew deep down she could never have. Some people, like Danu said, are not meant for the sun.

"I love you," she whispered to the King, the words choking her. And then she gave into the darkness forming around her, the shadow that devoured this beautiful little dream. Raegan squeezed her eyes shut, clenching her jaw to stem the sobs building like a storm in her chest.

Nothingness threw its arms around her, quiet and void of anything at all. Part of her thought about staying in the dark, but it was where she'd always return—ready or not—so she pushed through it, seeking the dampness of Avalon's caves and the heat of the person she loved with everything she was.

Chapter Fifty

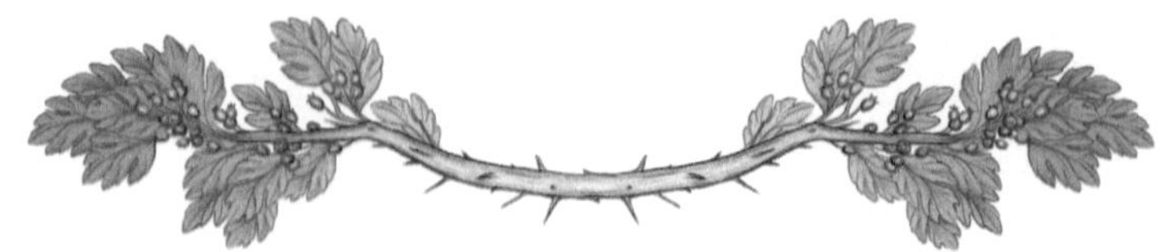

"Raegan." Someone spoke her name, their voice like heather on the hills and dusk over the lake. She stirred, stiff and cold, the wool cape wrapped around her not enough to ward off the chill of the damp stone beneath her. With a start, she bolted upright, nearly smashing her forehead into the King's.

"Are you alright?" he asked, worry curled around his voice. He was on his knees at her side, one hand interlaced with hers.

"Yeah," she muttered, a tide of sorrow still lapping at her being, threatening to pull her back into that daydream. "Did you . . . the cottage?"

The way his angular features collapsed told her everything she needed to know. "I . . . I thought about remaining there."

Her heart clenched. "So was it really you?"

He tilted his head, eyes searching hers. "I do not know. I worry I cannot dwell on it, lest the gravity of it pull me back into its orbit." His gaze slid away from hers, coming to rest on something at her back—the mortal king wrapped in a thousand years of sleep, she realized.

Raegan took a deep breath and, with the exhale, did her best to expel the rest of that beautiful vision she'd almost happily allowed herself to be trapped in forever. Instead, she pushed to her feet, aided by the King, and took a few trembling strides to stand beside Arthur.

The man looked much as he had all those years ago. Raegan's stomach churned with distaste. Arthur had held ideals, once. He'd had honor, once. And all of it had been twisted and leached away by the taste for power and—she realized now in retrospect—probably Excalibur, too.

"Caledfwlch," Oberon breathed, his eyes ghosting the length of the blade, speaking its older name in his native tongue. Something ancient and aching stirred in Raegan as she stared down at the sleeping king, at the tunic she'd watched a servant mend, at the once-broken right ring finger she'd healed. Bittersweet memories rose up from her depths, playing across her vision with a biting clarity.

She spun to look at the King, words tumbling from her mouth. "Why didn't you let me take you away from there?" she choked out. "I offered. I would've done it, Mordred. I would've left my people behind. What difference did it make that we stayed? Camelot still fell. The Druids of old are still gone, their traditions with them. The Gates still rose. The Timekeeper still happened to all of us."

He gazed at her, the Unseelie regent melting away entirely. Suddenly, in the dim glow of the torches, watered down even further by the working at the cave's mouth, Mordred stood in front of her. He was too young for the worry that sat on his brow, heavy as a crown.

"If you wanted it," Nyneve said, tears cutting into her words, "I would've saved you."

All of the faerie knight's attention fell onto her, heavy as the sweep of night, delicate as a moth's wings. He turned from Arthur's plinth— from the last chance at salvation they might have—to take her face between his hands.

"Nyneve, you fool," Mordred murmured, his gaze little more than an ocean of grief, "you *did* save me." His mouth met hers, hot and demanding, hands sliding into her hair, fingers weaving into her curls.

Grief and regret and ache exploded in her chest. She clung to him like a lifeboat in a terrible storm, tears still running down her face as she returned the intense need of his kiss.

"You did save me," he repeated, his breath ghosting her cheek, forehead resting against hers.

Despite all of her instincts, despite the way a voice told her it would make everything else hurt too much in the end, Raegan let herself lean against the comforting, solid bulk of his muscular mass. She buried her face in his coat, inhaling the black pepper and woodsmoke that would surely haunt whomever she came back as next.

With a deep breath, she righted herself, aided by the powerful arm slung around her waist. She dragged the back of her hands across her face, shoving away the tears; it was not the tide she needed now. Instead, she looked past the King and at the sword.

"It used to hurt you to be in the same room," she said, her heart panging with the weight of memory.

"It still does," he reported, bitterness creeping into his voice. "But pain is an old companion now."

A flash of fury tore through Raegan. Why should he suffer more? Why did it always have to be *him*, the person she loved more than anything in the world?

"You're not going near it," Raegan declared, swallowing hard as she curled her hands into fists. Oberon looked at her in clear surprise, his brow knitting in confusion and then concern.

"Who else but a faerie king to turn a faerie blade back?" he demanded in a scoff, his voice thick with that easy, casual arrogance she knew damn well was just a bluff.

Raegan paced in front of the plinth, her thoughts running too fast for her to keep up with them all. "Exactly. You're only supposed to turn it back," she pointed out, raising her gaze to him. Defiant, she held her body between the King and the blade. His dark eyes tracked her like a predator, clearly aware of what she was doing. "The Morrigan didn't say anything about you being the one to steal it out of a damn cave."

His brow arched, the angles of his face growing sharp and danger-ous. "Nor did she say anything about *you* doing it. Raegan, be sensible. We have no idea what Excalibur will do to a mortal vessel like yours."

She ground her teeth, shifting to the left as the King did, again blocking him from moving closer to the plinth. "You know that I have never been sensible a day in my goddamn life," she snapped, throwing up one hand. "Why the fuck would I start now, in an undersea cave with an evil sword?"

He said nothing, so Raegan took a step backwards, closer to Arthur's plinth—a test. Oberon closed the distance as she thought he might. She watched him carefully, noticing the catch in his movements, the furrowing of his brow. Even a single step closer pained him. She wasn't surprised. The power that radiated from Excalibur was immense. If not for those strange, glimmering workings stretching over the caves' mouths, Raegan surely would have felt the blade's presence at the entrance to Avalon's low places. Or possibly on the headland itself, the ancient, twisted magic reaching tendrils up the sheer cliffs.

"Raegan, my love," the King pleaded, that feral glint leaving his eyes. "Please. Let me do this. I cannot bear to see you injured."

"But that's not even *why* you want to do this!" Raegan replied, surprising herself by shouting. The words rang out in the cavern, and for a moment, she was terrified Arthur would somehow awaken. A quick glance over her shoulder told her that the king of men's sleep continued with more peace than he deserved. "You think you earned the pain. As punishment. For failing. You think this is some kind of fucked-up penance."

Oberon stilled, his chin moving in an arrogant lift, the words to deny her statement undoubtedly brewing, eloquent and cutting, at the back of his throat. But when he opened his mouth, he only closed it again, squeezing his eyes shut, too.

"You don't," Raegan protested, her voice rough with the tears she found herself holding back. "You don't deserve to be punished."

"And neither do you!" Oberon replied in a desperate, strangled tone, opening his eyes to meet her gaze.

Her nails bit half-moons into her palms, frustration and long-simmering rage threatening to boil over in this small cavern. Holding his gaze, she began to reply, but then a sound met her ears that filled her with horror.

Heart in her throat, Raegan looked toward the corridor running through the cave system and found seawater. The tide was returning, already ankle-deep and rich with swirling currents. The protective workings kept the ocean out of the cavern, at least, it seemed.

"Oberon," she said, nervousness spilling into her tone. "We can't get trapped down here. But I'm not letting you do this. I'm *not*. It will literally feed on your magic and use that to hurt you. We both know that."

The King's gaze averted from hers, falling to the king and the sword at her back. His full lips pressed into a firm line, a dangerous determination in the ridge of his shoulders.

"And it's already tasted your blood," Raegan reminded him, trying to ignore the water rushing through the corridor just beyond the cavern's seal. "At Camlann. It is much harder, Oberon, to hold back a wolf once it's scented you. Let me do this."

"No," the King said, the words hoarse, his jaw clenched. "I cannot ask that of you. We can make better plans with the information we have gleaned and return with the next tide."

Despair seeped into Raegan. She glanced back at the corridor to find the water had come to knee-level, rushing fast and hard past the mouth of Arthur's cave. The lilac torches pulsed again, a few seconds of frantic fluttering similar to what she felt in her own chest.

"The cave is only accessible *one* day under the new moon," Raegan replied, fingernails biting into her palms. "We got stupid lucky with arriving right before it, but we'd be forced to wait another entire month to come back. And god only knows how fucking long that would be in our world."

"I know," he murmured, looking back at her.

Bile churned in her stomach. She hated to see that look on his face—to see that such a magnificent creature, carved from shadow and blessed in blood, the most breathtaking thing she'd ever seen in her entire life, would be made to feel small and useless in the swell of Fate and destiny.

Water rushed mercilessly at his back. When Raegan pulled on it experimentally, it answered reluctantly, acknowledging what she was but not her authority. She wanted to scream. She wanted to slip back in time and kill Arthur before he could do all the horrible things that had landed them in this underwater cavern, desperate and running out of time. Always running out of time.

Even if Avalon's sea did not answer her, Raegan's rage still rose in her like a tide. She turned to look down at Arthur, and all the memories came surging to her shores: the meaningless cruelty, the rough way he had treated Guinevere, and the iron fist that had defined the last few years of his rule. All because some Gods-touched sorcerer had given him a sword that could rend the world in two.

"Fuck it," Raegan said, reaching for the plinth. The pain Excalibur caused the King slowed his reaction, so when her hand wrapped around the sword's pommel, he had only just grabbed her shoulder.

Time hung still. Even the sea rushing in outside faded away.

Raegan's entire world condensed to the slab of rock, the sleeping king, and the blade in her hand. She let out one breath. Two. Three.

Nothing at all was happening.

Perhaps her rage wrapped around her like a shield. Perhaps her anger was its own sacred thing—a sacrament, like the King had said. With a shaking exhale, Raegan pulled Excalibur from Arthur's grip. His pale, sleeping fingers slipped away much more easily than she would've thought. She turned, the most legendary sword in the entire world gripped between her palms. It was heavy—much heavier than it looked—and she felt it reaching for her, searching for a way inside to feast.

Oberon stared at Raegan like nothing else had ever mattered to him and nothing would. Then he threw his head back and laughed, feral and glorious, the baying of a hound with its teeth bared. "It knows not what to do with you," he explained, a light shining in his eyes that she hadn't seen in so many years. "You are both mortal and magic, dead and living. Your contradictions seem to be rerouting its power, turning the sword back in on itself."

Raegan hefted the blade with both hands, nearly dropping the heavy object. "A snake eats its own tail," she observed in a soft murmur, chills cascading across her skin.

"You are a miracle," the King said, his grip on her shoulder tightening. "And we should take our leave. Can you carry it?"

"I'll do my best," Raegan replied with a grunt, her biceps and forearms protesting as she lifted the tip of the blade from the ground again. The only reason she could lift it at all, Raegan knew, was because of Andronica's training back at the Philadelphia Temple.

Oberon kept his eyes on hers, moving toward the cave's mouth. Fuck, she hoped that Avalon's low places didn't insist on testing those who walked its depths on the way in *and* out.

Raegan had almost made it to the veil stretched over the cave's maw when she remembered. Excalibur could kill the sleeping yet not-fully-mortal king. She froze. But surely it wouldn't let her wield it. The blade would never open its mouth for the likes of her, would never unleash its enchantments on the man who had borne it for so many years. But the sword was—like her—hungry. How long had they both languished in the shadows, away from the heat and light of the world they knew, dreaming of what they used to be? Perhaps Excalibur's loyalty had waned in the dark, damp dimness beneath the buried sea.

With a snarl that didn't even sound like her own voice, Raegan turned on her heel. She raised the sword, and the weapon registered her intent to wield it. The spellwork closed around her like a vise, but her magic—that wild, keening thing embedded in her ribs—was neither Fey nor mortal nor god-granted. And she was neither living nor dead. Excalibur's power reached for Raegan, tearing at her insides, but it found no purchase. There are, after all, no handholds in a river. And what is a river if not a devourer?

So with a feral cry, the pain lancing through her, Raegan scrambled onto the slab, scraping her knees on the sharp, rocky edges. And then, straddling Arthur Pendragon's waist, she raised Excalibur high. In a way she would never be able to find the words for, the not-quite-mortal, half-mad woman felt the ancient, storied sword's mouth open wide, its teeth sharp and long and so, so hungry.

"Fuck you," she snarled, her spittle flecking the face of the king of men. "This is for Morgana. For Guinevere. For Mordred. For *me*."

And then she plunged Excalibur into Arthur's heart.

CHAPTER FIFTY-ONE

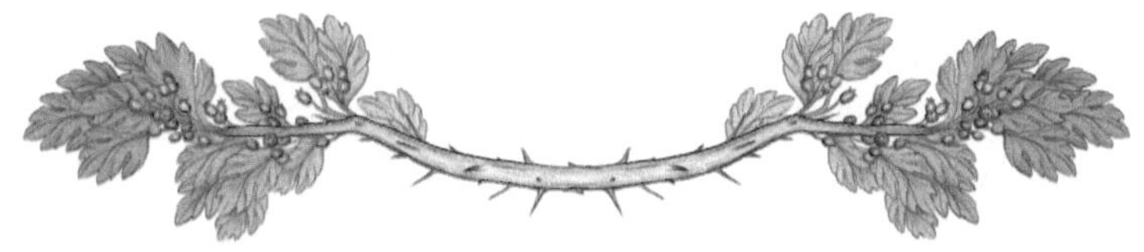

"Do you need to trade off?" Raegan called down to the King as they scrambled back up the chalk cliffs, the ocean closing in behind them. On the way to the sea caves, neither of them had noticed the darkened horizontal lines across the sheer drop, marking how far the tide reached. The ocean appeared to be fighting to beat its highest record, and Raegan thought that *might* have something to do with the fact she had killed one of Avalon's sleeping wards.

The protective working across the mouth of the cavern had all but exploded the moment she drove Excalibur into King Arthur's heart. Somehow, despite the pain and the power it took to combat the blade's hunger, Oberon had thrown a protective spell around them both. They were battered and bruised, but the spellery had fought off the worst of it.

And then, of course, the ocean had surged in anger, the water suddenly writhing and steaming. Raegan had barely coaxed it into parting just enough for her and Oberon to run through the caverns. The wide plain of rock and sand that connected the sea caves to the stairs had diminished to a tiny spit of land, but it was enough.

She huffed, steadying herself with one hand on the side of the cliff. There hadn't been time to examine precisely how or why, but something about feeding Arthur's blood to Excalibur had altered the sword. He hadn't tried to wield it, but Oberon could carry it now, albeit wrapped up in Raegan's salt-soaked wool cape. Surely all the ageless knowledge in Avalon would be of use, if they could just make it to the top of the sea stairs in time.

"I am fine for now," Oberon replied, a few steps behind her, the word tugging at his voice. As if in response to his statement, the sea roared beneath them, crawling up the cliff with open, white-capped fingers. "Hold on."

Raegan felt the King grip the back of her sweater, and she turned in surprise, panic crowding out the air in her lungs. "We need to *go*," she protested, trying not to look at the boiling ocean below.

"Precisely," Oberon replied, his eyes sliding shut, body going still.

She briefly considered screaming, but then she watched as the scant shadows on the sheer drop of the chalk-white cliffs slunk toward his hands. The darkness curled around his arms like snakes, reaching up for the back of his broad shoulders. Her heart in her throat, Raegan watched —with one eye on the alarming progression of the sea's surge—as the shadows stitched themselves into an impressive set of wings at the King's back.

"That's kind of hot," she said, taking him in, the contrast of his pale skin and dark hair all the more intensified by the backdrop of the cliffs. His shadow-wings were too wide to open fully on the cramped space of the stairs.

"Come," he murmured, reaching out a hand, the curve to his beautiful mouth telling her he knew exactly what he was doing. Desire thrummed between her legs, and she obeyed, stepping into his arms. He handed her the wool-wrapped sword, which she clutched to her chest, before sweeping her off her feet.

"Ready?" Oberon asked, shifting to face the sea, his back against the cliffs.

"Oh, absolutely not," Raegan replied cheerfully.

In reply, the King pitched them both off the cliff. For a long, horrible moment, there was nothing but the sea rushing up to meet her and fear clamoring loudly in her chest.

But then his shadow-wings caught the air and they soared higher, leaving the angry ocean to crawl up the sea stairs in pursuit of them. Oberon banked to return to the island, fighting the competing headwinds that buffeted them, trying to tear Excalibur from Raegan's grasp.

All she had to do was hold on, she told herself—he was doing the real work. The heat leaking from his body spoke of the pain he must be feeling. Raegan's heart panged, and then her stomach flipped when she saw the quickly approaching ground.

But the King landed on the rocky, heather-hemmed land with a featherlight agility that should not be possible for bipeds, no matter how many goddesses created them or what kind of magic ran in their veins.

"Jesus fucking Christ," Raegan said weakly, lowering herself to the sweet, blessed ground. She didn't care that the gorse was still damp with dew or that uneven edges of stones bit into her thighs.

Oberon heaved an exhale, leaning against a tall boulder next to Raegan. "I have not done that in hundreds of years," he told her, his breathing quick.

"You look absolutely *delicious* with wings," she told him, gazing up at him from the ground, "but I hated the actual flying bit."

He let out a laugh like a silver bell, languid and free, and Raegan found herself joining in, laughing until her stomach hurt. They'd actually done it. Excalibur lay next to her leg, wrapped up in woolens. She stared at it, half-delirious. Hope soared in her chest, an unwelcome brush of dove wings against her insides. She squashed it, grinding her jaw. It was too dangerous to hope, to think *maybe this time . . .*

"You have done it," came a voice to Raegan's left.

She startled, scrambling to a seated position, finding that Danu had returned. Despite the damp chill of the fog bank that crowned Avalon, she was still dressed in one of her diaphanous gowns, a tiny garter snake curling around her bicep like a jewelry cuff. The wind barely tugged at her waist-length violet-gray hair.

"Yeah," Raegan agreed weakly, reaching over to pat the bundle of wool. "If this is the part where you betray us or take the sword for yourself or whatever, could you give me a second? That was exhausting."

Oberon laughed again, crisp as an orchard-fresh apple, and butterflies fluttered in her stomach. God, all these years later, and just the sound of his laugh had her blushing like a schoolgirl.

"Can you wield it?" Danu asked the King, and only then did Raegan register how grave the goddess's voice was. In her peripheral vision, she watched Oberon stiffen, drawing himself up to his full height.

"No," he replied, his expression growing wary, "but Raegan has shown much promise."

Danu's strange, too-light eyes sharpened as she glanced Raegan's way for a moment. Her lips formed something quick and sly, and Raegan might've said the goddess looked pleased. But then a heaviness came over her expression and she crossed her slender, muscular arms. "I have received word that your Philadelphia court is under quite a brutal attack, worse than what it has already been facing. Much worse, I fear."

The air stilled in Raegan's lungs, any levity or triumph seeping out of her in only a heartbeat or two. She pulled herself to her feet, her joints catching. "How do you know this?" she demanded, watching the goddess suspiciously. "You're locked away from the world, aren't you?" She was suddenly very aware of how still Oberon had gone at her side.

Danu's mouth twisted. "I keep a few choice scrying glasses. They are old, formidable things, and their eyes rove only in one direction."

The words were barely out of her mouth before the King was moving, striding across the gorse-dappled earth as if his body had not nearly failed him just moments ago. He was standing before Danu in an instant, and though they were roughly the same height, the fury on his face and the midmorning shadows spooling at his feet made him look twice the goddess's size.

"How long," he began roughly, "have you watched, *Mother*, and done nothing at all?"

"Child," Danu replied, tears falling down her face as she clutched her hands at her heart, "for too long. It is my greatest shame."

Raegan and Oberon both stared at the goddess wordlessly, unsure what to make of her response. Was it simply a ploy? Or was it the truth? Was Danu's great and powerful magic held back in ways they could not understand? The wind rattled through the clearing, the hem of the goddess's dress flowing out behind her.

"Tearing Avalon from the fabric of reality and creating a new realm to house our people took nearly everything from me," Danu explained, her eyes tracing the horizon, as if in every stitch of this place she could see her blood staining the seams. "I slept for a long time. When I awoke, I was not the same. Other leaders had moved forward, and they hold more sway than I do. I am a sacred relic at best, a forgotten and useless deity at worst."

Something flashed in Danu's eyes that made Raegan believe her—that kind of unhedged fury that only came with mistreatment. The King seemed to read the goddess's response in much the same way; he retreated back a step, the angles of his face suddenly no longer so sharp and feral.

"Can you get me to my court, Danu?" Oberon breathed, barely audible over the orchestra of the wind. He reached for the goddess's hand, timid as a child, but she closed the distance immediately, gripping his fingers in hers.

"There is only one door left in Avalon," she said, her gaze skipping to Raegan. A fierceness lingered there that felt like looking in a mirror, no matter how primordial the goddess was. "It is only meant to open in one place."

The wind stood still, the fog banks parting for a moment so the sun could flood down upon the three of them, rendering the faerie king, the deathless witch, and the ancient goddess into something out of myth.

"But," Danu said, that arrogant tilt to her raised chin a clear hallmark she'd handed down to her children, "it is *my* door and I am no relic. Not just yet."

"We'll follow you, goddess," Raegan said, stepping closer to the two of them, her arms wrapped around the wool-cloaked sword. "Take us to your door."

The goddess nodded and turned on her heel, striding off across the headland. Raegan watched in awe as the island folded itself like an accordion, shortening the long trek to the beach, supplicant beneath Danu's feet. With a sideways glance at Oberon, Raegan hefted the sword against her shoulder and took off after the goddess. The land allowed her and the King to cross it in the same way, but they stayed close at Danu's heels, just in case.

In moments, they stood on the beach, the rise of the fog-crowned cliffs behind them, the otherworldly spires and lush solariums already moving into Raegan's memory. She'd hoped they might have more time here, that perhaps someone could help her sift through her mind. Or better yet—though she didn't dare voice the desire out loud—to see if anyone upon this grand and sacred isle had discovered how to extend a mortal life. So that perhaps she might know peace at the King's side and he wouldn't need to dig a grave or light a funeral pyre twice a century.

But for now, there was only the crash of the foam-tipped waves and the far horizon that she knew held a door, though she certainly couldn't see it from here; at this distance, it didn't call to her, either. The ocean wind whipped her hair into a wild frenzy of auburn as Danu turned to face them.

"If you cannot wield it, I fear you may not be able to turn the Protectorate forces back," the goddess warned.

Obediently, Raegan laid the sword on the ground and unwrapped it from the woolen cloth. Oberon approached, his mouth in a firm, grim line. She didn't think it hurt him as much to be near the blade, but then again, he was excellent at pretending.

"It *is* altered," Danu said from her position about ten paces away. She craned her neck, peering down at the unremarkable-looking sword lying on its bed of gray fabric. With an inhale, she walked closer, her bare feet carrying her to stand beside Oberon. There, she peered down at it, her eyes narrowed. "How did you accomplish this?" she asked, something not unlike awe seeping into her expression when she looked back up, her gaze landing on Raegan.

Nervous energy coiled in her gut. She didn't know what the goddess would think of what she'd done, and when she glanced at Oberon, she saw he wasn't sure either. Before he could take the blame or try to slip out of the conversation, she settled her shoulders back and met Danu's eyes.

"I killed him," she said, finding herself savoring the words. "I killed Arthur Pendragon, son of Uther Pendragon, the once-king of Camelot, while he slept. For what he did. For *all* the things he did."

Danu's lips parted, and she regarded Raegan, her head cocked to one side, one pale braid sliding off her shoulder. "You killed the Bear?"

"Yep," Raegan agreed, though her palms were clammy now, her blood pounding in the veins of her neck. Regardless of how diminished Danu's power supposedly was, Raegan had no interest in being on the receiving end of the goddess's wrath. "He had it coming."

"I suppose he did," Danu said, sounding the words out slowly. "Raegan, you do understand he is nearly impossible to kill? It is why we have kept him in a sleep stasis all these years, unable to disentangle the mortal king from the blade."

"So I heard," Raegan said, not sure she understood the goddess's point.

"There are no worlds in which you should have been able to wield Excalibur to take Arthur's life," Danu said, her tone calm, definitive. "And you, child," she continued, turning her attention to the King, whose mouth curved into something dangerous that sent heat diving low in Raegan's body, "are meant to be the only one who can change the faerie blade back into what it once was."

"Perhaps it is her," Oberon replied, though he looked at Raegan as if no one else was standing on the beach. "Perhaps it has always been her."

Something about his tone—deep and regal, like the decree of a king—made her reach down for Excalibur. She didn't pause this time as her fingers wrapped around the leather pommel. She felt the sword respond to her, its power sweeping through her, looking for a place to exploit. When that didn't work, the blade changed tactics, offering up some of its stolen, blood-soaked power to her, sly as a bribe. Raegan scoffed.

"Unfortunately," she said to the sword, which she suspected could understand her in one way or another, "I am none of the things you were taught to devour. I'm too vast and terrifying to fit between your jaws."

She hefted the storied blade from the ground, some part of her not surprised to find the weight of it was no longer a strain. The wind whipped around the beach, scattering sand like ash, the ocean roaring at her back.

And then, reaching down from the heavens, thick as honey, rich as mead, came a Fatesong, looping around the woman who refused to die, the sound of it like a snake devouring its own tail.

CHAPTER FIFTY-TWO

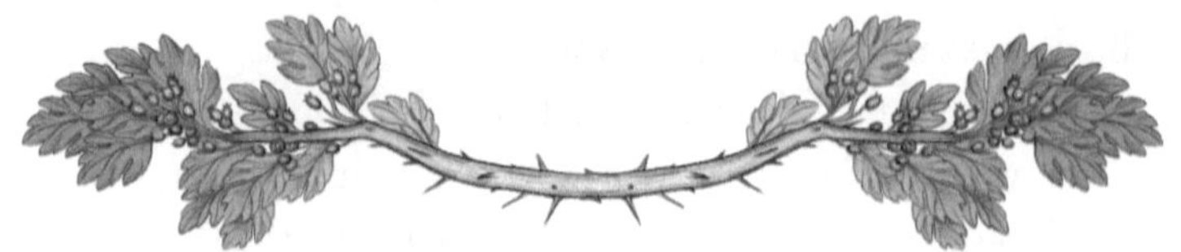

On the other side of the causeway that stretched across the shimmering sea, Danu began to open a door. It might've sung to Raegan the way doors always did if she were not so tired, so terribly aware of how far they still had to go. The path to Avalon had been long.

As Danu whipped the ocean mist into a frenzy with an ancient working that made Raegan's head hurt, she pushed down the rising panic. Would she and the King even survive a winding, arduous journey back to Philadelphia?

But then Avalon's mists settled at their goddess's command, revealing a door in the towering cliff face. Raegan barely choked back a gasp. Instead of ancient yew trees and the white church spire, she found herself face-to-face with the Keeper of the Philadelphia Temple. His pinstripe navy suit was as immaculate as always, glasses tucked into his breast pocket as he peered through Danu's door. Behind him, the long, blue-velveted hallway of the Temple stretched wide and empty.

"Keeper," Raegan breathed, her body frozen in disbelief.

"My liege and my lady," the Keeper replied, clearly startled. Suspicion settled onto his expression. "It should not be possible to open this door. Not like this."

"At ease, my child," Danu said, coming to stand at Raegan's side. In her peripheral vision, she saw the flutter of the goddess's gown, the way her long, violet-gray braids floated around her shoulders instead of lying flat the way physics dictated.

A hundred emotions swam across the Keeper's features at the sight of his long-lost creatrix: awe, terror, the sweetest sorrow. His dark eyes darted back and forth between the goddess and her two charges before settling on the sword in Raegan's grasp.

"You— Did you . . ." the Keeper began before tears choked off his words.

"Yeah," was all Raegan could manage, holding Excalibur aloft. Her forearms strained, but she steadied the shaking muscles. "We got it." She averted her gaze from the Keeper's, tears pricking her eyes, instead watching Avalon's mists curl around the world's most storied blade.

"This cannot be," the Keeper protested softly, one hand clasped to his chest. "We . . . we never know such kindness from either the gods or the universe." His words landed like a storm on Raegan's shores, pulling a sob filled with as much sorrow as anger from deep within her. She gritted her teeth, shoving the knuckles of her free hand into her eyes.

"Anakletos," Oberon said, his voice rich as the wind grabbed for his words with greedy fingers. "I understand your doubt. I assure you we are quite real. Otherwise, how would I know that you keep the best whiskey in the false drawer of your desk? Please, let us pass. We hear you are in great need."

Raegan pulled her hand away from her eyes to find the Keeper looking faint with relief. With a nod, he stepped to the side, opening one arm to offer entrance to the Temple. Raegan turned to Danu, unsure what parting words would suffice. In the end, she let Excalibur's point rest on the rocky ground and threw her free arm around the goddess. A bittersweet vine tangled in her throat, chest burning with the effort to hold back tears.

"You are more my child, I think, than any other creator's," Danu murmured into her hair, clutching Raegan's much shorter frame in return. "Should you ever wish to rest, know Avalon is as open to you as it is to your faerie king."

Raegan pulled back, stunned. Danu only smiled that faint, sad smile of hers and reached forward to brush a single escaped tear from Raegan's face.

"Thank you," Raegan said to the goddess, her throat tight, unable to summon any further words. Perhaps—Raegan dared not hope too fervently—Danu's offer meant one day she and Oberon might linger in the sun.

The goddess released Raegan and turned toward the King. The two ancient beings examined each other, Oberon's chin raised at that haughty angle, his jaw feathering. Danu seemed at a loss for words.

Then, like a stalemate broken, the King sighed. "There is little sense," he offered, his tone measured, "in sowing discord among those of us who nurture the same fruit in the same orchard."

Raegan watched a thousand pounds of weight release from Danu's shoulders. "I appreciate your understanding," the goddess said. "In turn, I will try to better tend the entire orchard, not just the sections I can see."

The King reached for Raegan's hands, his fingers slipping between hers. "Thank you, creatrix," he said, bowing his head. Then, before either of them could hesitate, the deathless witch and the faerie king stepped through the goddess's impossible door.

Raegan looked back just once. Danu's tall, willowy frame was still there, shrouded in mist, and then she faded out of existence as if the goddess and her hidden realm had never really existed.

Instead, the familiarity of the Temple flooded Raegan's senses with marble floors and running water and the scent of cool vanilla laced with lilac. She wanted to feel relief, or perhaps some kind of tender home-coming. But she noticed too quickly that many of the blue velvet wall hangings were torn, others blackened and scorched. Something that looked too much like dried blood stained a section of marble behind the Keeper. Her stomach churned.

"The Morrigan was right," the Keeper whispered, though in the quiet of the corridor, his words nearly echoed. Raegan tore her eyes from the wounded Temple to examine the Keeper. The small besuited man's gaze was locked on Excalibur. His hands shook at his sides.

"She was right about most of it," the King said, his tone dry. "Raegan, it seems, is the one who wields the sword."

The Keeper's attention snapped to her, head cocked to one side as he examined her. "Well," he began, pulling his glasses from his pocket,

"I believe the Morrigan's vision did indicate it was the *two* of you who might accomplish this task."

Raegan frowned, looking down at the sword, its length reflecting the deep blues of the Temple. "I don't think we really turned it back," she said, even though she wanted it to be her, wanted it to have always been her. "It's just . . . confused by me. For now."

A muffled shout echoed from somewhere down the hall. Alarm snaked across the Keeper's face, sending Raegan's heart thudding against the cage of her ribs. "While you were gone, half the Temple was destroyed," he told them. "The kelpie gate, which you used to safely enter the Rivers, is gone. We are far past the capacity that this pocket realm can handle. We cannot feed everyone. We need to evacuate our people who cannot fight, but there is nowhere to go."

"The archives?" the King asked.

"I will not risk it," the Keeper replied immediately, standing up straighter. "Too much of who and what we are is held there. Keep it safe. Our people that remain need to know who they are. What it means to be Tylwyth Teg."

"Anakletos," Oberon said, his tone soft in the heavy stillness of the corridor, "the archives will not matter if there are no Fair Folk left to enjoy them."

Raegan chewed on the inside of her cheek, her mind racing. "So we could safely evacuate to another pocket realm?" she asked, looking at the Keeper and then Oberon.

"Yes," the King replied, his head tilted to one side. "What are you thinking?"

Raegan grinned. "Keeper, can you get me a scrying glass? Sometimes it helps to have friends in low, strange places."

Beside her, Oberon's sculpted mouth curved up at one side, his dark gaze glimmering with a kind of admiration that set Raegan's entire body on fire.

"Of course," the Keeper replied, looking between the two of them like they were a riddle he could not quite parse. "Follow me."

The Keeper turned on his heel and began to walk down the cavernous corridor. Raegan moved to follow him, the King at her side. She had taken a few steps when a thought prickled across her skin, breathing down the back of her neck. Without breaking her stride, she turned to look at the place Danu had opened her door—the place in a well-fortified Oracle's Temple that had parted at the touch of a goddess.

There, in the dim, diffuse glow, stood the door to the Vaults. Its ornate ironwork was precisely the same, its frame humming with something that could not quite be attributed to an inanimate object. The last time Raegan had walked through that door, she'd returned with a delicate Prophecy encased in glass, cradled between her shaking hands.

This time, a sword that might topple a god from his throne.

∼

"Is Baba Yaga ready for that kind of onslaught?" Andronica asked, her face pinched as she examined the plans laid out across the large table.

A muffled boom erupted in the distance. Raegan jumped, but Andronica hardly reacted.

"It's fine," the Unseelie knight said with a wave of her hand, responding to Raegan's startled look. "The Protectorate's not getting through that way and they know it, so they make a lot of noise hoping it'll draw us away from their true entry point. Anyway. Can she withstand what they're going to throw at her?"

"She seems to think she can," Raegan said, looking across the table at the King. He should have been resting, but instead, he'd called an emergency war council. The sleeves of his button-down were rolled up, a shining ink-black lock of hair untucked from its usual place. Both large hands were palm-down on the table, the corded muscles in his forearms standing out like those of a marble statue.

"Baba Yaga and I have historically disagreed on a few things," Oberon said, straightening, one hand raking through his hair. "But if the witch says she can hold her pocket realm, she can hold. She wouldn't agree to house those of our court who cannot fight otherwise."

"I agree," Raegan said, looking toward Andronica. The Fey woman's thin eyebrows were pinched tight, her mouth screwed up in concentration.

"Okay," she said, looking up at the both of them, her gaze skipping to Kamau, who stood at the other end of the table. "Kamau, can you start the evacuation? Orderly, please. Calm. If everyone was out of the Temple by tonight, that would be ideal."

The Keeper exhaled long and low, cradling his forehead in his hands. Raegan glanced over at him, sympathy blooming in her chest. He'd all but collapsed into the chair at the head of the table when Andronica had relayed her idea.

"We're really going to do this, then?" he asked, looking around at all of them, those nebula-brown eyes brimming with tears.

Kamau reached over and tenderly took the Keeper's hand in their much larger one. "Is there another way?" Kamau asked, their booming voice impossibly gentle.

"Not one that I can see," the Keeper replied after a few moments of silence that threatened to choke the air out of Raegan's lungs. "We sacrifice the High Temple of Pythia, home of the Oracle Octavia. For our people."

"For our people," Kamau echoed, crouching before the seated Keeper and cupping his small face in their hands. "We will mourn with you, friend. You are never alone."

"Never alone," the Keeper managed, his voice hitching, before Kamau brought their brow to his.

"For all of this to be worth it," Andronica said, her head tipped back as she examined the domed ceiling above them, covered with those celestial blue illustrations Raegan had admired so much her first time in the Temple—at this hour, the constellations had gone shimmery, more mother-of-pearl than gilt, the background a deep midnight, "Oberon must wield the blade. I see no other way. Raegan, it's not as if we had even six months to train you for combat. We had, what, fifteen sessions together before you left for the Isles, if that? Besides, the Morrigan said it is a faerie blade to be returned to its true nature. A changeling."

Raegan took a deep breath and nodded. "I know," she said simply, glancing at the King. "You're right. I'll try. We'll both try again to revert it with whatever time we have left." For a moment, she sank into her own mind. When she'd first started on this path back to herself, Andronica's words would've infuriated her. But only because of her insecurities, the constant voices that told her there would never be anywhere she belonged, that her true place in the world had slipped past her like a comet.

Not any longer. Because she'd found where she belonged. And she'd found who she belonged *to*—the dark-eyed faerie king who wore ferocity like armor, the owl-winged woman whose smile felt like a summer evening. And the Unseelie Court. She hadn't seen it before, but the Fair Folk accepted her for all her rage and sorrow and yearning. And that meant they'd challenge her, bare their teeth, because they knew their anger was safe with her, too. It was a terrible thing, a lovely thing, to call her own.

And she refused to let it all die on the edge of a sainted iron spear.

CHAPTER FIFTY-THREE

Sweat poured down Raegan's brow, and her entire body felt faint, but she kept going. She pulled on the long, red thread of her fury that rushed through her body like a river. And for the first time she could ever remember, she felt it threaten to snap.

She let go with a gasp, shoulders sagging as she staggered back.

Maelona caught her by the forearm, surprisingly strong despite her wiry frame. "Raegan," her aunt warned, alarm seeping into her tone.

"I'm fine," Raegan sputtered, her chest heaving. She gritted her jaw, staring down at Excalibur. The blade was submerged in one of the remaining divinatory fonts in the Temple. Maybe the shallow, marble-lipped pool in the small chamber wasn't enough water. Maybe she needed to put the sword in an actual river to gather enough energy to break the hellish working.

"I don't think I can do this, Maelona," she admitted miserably, looking up at her aunt, who had arrived with Rainer a few hours before they'd returned from Avalon. Apparently, she'd demanded the kelpie take her to her niece and wouldn't take no for an answer. Since her arrival, Maelona had adjusted absurdly well to being surrounded by the Unseelie Court. Raegan was pretty sure her aunt had even flirted with Andronica.

"You may not need to," Maelona replied, letting go of Raegan to cross her arms. "I mean, the plan is good. Lure the Protectorate sieging the Temple into its walls and then collapse the pocket realm on their heads once everyone's evacuated. Meanwhile, you'll be drawing the Timekeeper's attention by battering down his front door with Excalibur, which at the very least he'll be deeply unhappy to see in your possession. Any of his remaining soldiers will be sent to deal with you and the King, leaving the Manor vulnerable for Alanna and her people to secure it."

Raegan wiped her damp hands on the front of her jeans. "Yeah," she said hoarsely. "But what if everything works perfectly until we're face-to-face with the Timekeeper and then we can't actually kill him, even with Excalibur? Or what if it's worse? What if I hand-deliver the only thing that can kill Oberon right to our greatest enemy?"

"One step at a time," Maelona said, her dark eyes glittering in the Temple's golden light. "It's very possible the King can handle the Time-keeper on his own, Excalibur or not. I mean, there's got to be a reason Kronos has tried so hard to keep the King out of the In-Between. And don't forget that you can apparently work time magic now, too."

Raegan scoffed, putting her hands on her hips. "I have no idea if I'll be able to do that again," she said, letting out a sigh. "It's just . . . *So* much is hanging in the balance, Maelona."

Raegan's gaze slid to Excalibur. The ever-present tide in all of the Temple's waters dappled the dull metal blade with gold. For the first time since she'd taken it from Avalon's low places, it actually looked magical. World-changing. God-destroying. Fate-altering.

Suddenly and fiercely, Raegan wished she could talk to the Oracle. But Octavia had long since been evacuated. As much as Raegan wanted to speak with the powerful diviner who had encouraged her to craft her own destiny, she knew safeguarding the Fey community's matriarch was more important. Cordelia—the Seer who had spoken the Prophecy to life—was safe as well, probably having tea with Baba Yaga by now. It was too dangerous to contact either of them by magical means and risk exposing their location, no matter how much she craved their guidance.

"Hey," came Maelona's voice, cutting through her thoughts. "I don't think spiraling inside your own head is gonna do shit for anybody, you included."

Raegan looked up at her aunt, a wry smile pulling at the corners of her mouth. "You're right," she replied, crouching down beside the font again.

The marble was cold against her knees even through her jeans. She inhaled deeply, steeling herself, and then plunged her hands beneath the surface. Summoning the tides within her, Raegan wrapped her fingers around Excalibur's pommel. The spell woven into the sword barreled at her hungrily. She felt it reach for her, looking for a weak spot. But Raegan was half-mad, barely mortal, and nothing if not ferocious. Her magic sank its teeth into the working, and then she was yet again tumbling through the currents, locked in a battle of wills with whatever Myrddin had done to the faerie blade all those years ago.

The deeper she dove, the more Raegan could feel an impression of the famed sorcerer. The sensation crawled across her skin like an unwelcome touch. She grounded herself in the cold marble, the t-shirt sticking to her damp skin. She'd always fucking hated Myrddin. Hated his constant scheming, never-ending backstabbing, the way everyone fawned over him when it was so clear to her that he'd been using them all for some grand plan only he knew about. Even Arthur himself had only ever been a pawn.

"Guess I ruined whatever you were planning," Raegan spat, tightening her grip on the pommel, her eyes screwed shut, "by locking you in a goddamn tree, asshole." She poured more of herself against the fabric of the spell, her blackened waters and ancient silt seeping through gaps in chainmail. A few threads of the working snapped like old, fraying rope.

Raegan rocked back on her heels, exhausted, nearly toppling over. "Shit," she said, shaking the water droplets from her hands. "This would take me *months* under the right conditions."

"And we only have a few days, if we're very lucky," Maelona sighed, extending a hand to Raegan.

She took it, grappling her aunt's forearm and pulling herself to her feet. With a sigh, she looked back at the sword. Sweat gathered uncomfortably on the base of her spine, and her legs felt unsteady. Even if they had all the time in the world, she didn't know how long she could keep this up.

"Raegan."

The sound of her name slipped around her neck like a silk scarf. She followed the feel of it, a moth to flame, to find the King leaning against the doorframe. Though he still looked exhausted, he was dressed in a clean suit. One of her favorites, actually—the deep, shimmering green he'd worn to Gossamer. She drank in the sight of him, all towering height and raven-dark waves.

"Hey," she returned, some of the tension leaving her shoulders, though another kind sparked low in her belly. Woodsmoke and black pepper slipped into her senses, as intoxicating as ever.

"Maelona," the King said, his gaze falling away from Raegan and taking all that blessed heat with it, "may I have a word with Raegan?"

Maelona looked between her niece and the Unseelie lord she'd dedicated most of her life to hunting down. Surprisingly, that deep furrow between her brows softened. She reached out and brushed Raegan's shoulder with one hand, nodded, and then slipped out into the velveted hallway.

"Is everything okay?" Raegan asked, hoping to delay revealing that she'd gotten barely anywhere with Excalibur—that she'd failed everyone again, just as she always had.

"There are no new developments in the horrors," Oberon told her, his long strides carrying him across the creamy marble to stand before her. The moving surface of the water dappled his cool, pale skin with gold. "I do have a question for you, though."

Raegan bit the inside of her cheek, anxiety somersaulting in her stomach. "Oberon, I'm sorry. The spell on this sword . . . it's fucked. Even if I could get to a real river, it would take me a long time to make it safe for you to wield."

Oberon tilted his head in that way she liked, his eyes sliding to her mouth before returning to meet her gaze. "You have nothing to apologize for," he told her, his voice wrapping around her like a cloak that could keep her safe, keep the doubt and self-loathing at bay. "I am here for another reason entirely."

Raegan stared at him in confusion, her mind too tired to unravel whatever was going on. She opened her mouth to tell him that, but the King was already sinking down onto one knee before her. Startled and still feeling adrift, she took a step back, though her heart began to beat faster, something like anticipation careening through her veins.

"This is how mortals perform such a ritual, I am told," he said, looking up at her. His expression was all molten desire, an inferno of never-ending devotion that made the blood between her legs drum furiously. "Raegan Maeve Overhill, Nyneve Or'Afron, High Queen Titania, Witch of the Wood, and all the others—I am hopelessly in love with you."

Raegan's throat closed off, the soft light and tumbling waters of the Temple disappearing around her. Instead, she was surrounded by his dark tides, his autumnal meadow, his heathered hills at dusk. She wanted to live here forever, wanted to be buried in the rich soil of him even if it meant she'd never see the light of day again.

"I am yours," the King murmured, intense and ferocious even in this act of love. "In every life, Raegan. *Yours.* No matter the form you return to me in, I belong to you. You are the only person who has ever been mad enough and brave enough to love me."

Raegan drew a shaking inhale, choking back a wave of tears that crashed upon her shores. A soft, downy flower bloomed somewhere in her chest, the petals caressing all of her hidden, aching places until her entire body trembled.

"Though I question whether I am good enough to deserve the fierceness of your love," Oberon continued, the melody of his deep voice broken by emotion, though his eyes never left hers, "my heart cannot rest until I ask. Will you marry me?"

She bit down on her lip, but the hot tears escaped anyway, some clinging to her lashes, others falling to the marble below. Every part of her yearned to say yes without a second thought. "Oberon," she murmured, reaching out for him with unsteady hands. "You know I would. But a Feyrish marriage? That bond is . . . eternal. And when you lose me, because you *will*, it'll be your destruction."

The King smiled, as soft and sad as anything Raegan had ever seen. He took her outstretched hand in his, leaning forward to brush his lips over her knuckles. It was only the gentlest of touches, but her body keened madly for him all the same. "And yet," the faerie king told her, the ocean of his eyes fathomless, "here I am on my knees, begging you to destroy me."

Raegan choked back a sob, sinking down to the floor. She shook her head, a curl pulling loose from her braid. "Oberon," she repeated, her voice barely more than a hoarse whisper, "think of the pain you'll feel every moment. More pain, more than what you already suffer. It'll be like someone ripped out your insides. The bond mark will turn black on your finger and poison you."

"If I cannot have you," the King replied, pulling her into his world of damp stone and autumnal rain and sweeping shadow, "I shall have the pain. Never again will I grow numb to this wild, eternal thing that grows between us."

"Your court," Raegan stammered, the words tumbling out high-pitched. She was running out of the strength to protest; she wanted him just as badly as she ever had. With his arms around her, all she wanted to do was surrender. "They'll be so angry. They'll hate me even more. They'll question your judgment."

One of Oberon's ink-dark eyebrows arched. "My court," he drawled in response, "awaits us in a chamber they have spent half a day deco-rating for our ceremony. If, of course, you still wish to have me in that way."

Her heart leapt. "Yes," she whispered, the word bittersweet on her tongue. "I'll have you any and every way I can."

He grinned at her—a rare, shimmering jewel—and then dove forward to kiss her, powerful hands sliding around her waist. She pressed herself tightly against his muscular mass as his thigh slid between her legs, fervently memorizing every place his hard angles met her soft curves. With all her might, Raegan tried to drown herself in his kiss. If it were up to her, she'd never surface.

When they broke apart, Oberon swept her into his arms, sending her into the kind of girlish laughter she didn't think had left her mouth in ages. She tucked herself into his chest as he carried her from the divina-tory chamber, striding into the hallway. In so many other relationships, she'd always felt so heavy in her partner's arms, like she was asking them to carry too much weight.

But in the Unseelie king's embrace, Raegan felt light as a feather. She lifted her head from his chest to tell him so, but the words died on her tongue as she momentarily lost herself in his feral, unearthly beauty. She raised a hand, tracing the sharp slash of his collarbone and then the knifelike jaw.

The King leaned into her touch. "My bride," he murmured, his tone gowned in something husky and only half-restrained. Damp heat unspooled low in her belly, and she dug her fingernails into his shoulder, the other hand sliding beneath his open collar, desperate to feel more of him.

But then he ducked out of the hallway, bringing her to a room filled with flowers, beeswax candles, and people. Still in the King's arms, Raegan looked around with awe, joy filling up the places in her chest that normally burned with emptiness. Somehow, an expanse of tiny violets covered the marble floor, just as rich and thick as if it were early spring. At the far end of the room, curls of otherworldly vines crept along a wooden archway—the shape of it like a portico, like a door. At the arch's base were clusters of large pillar candles of varying heights, their flames dancing. Intricately carved ornaments hung from the walls, tiny tea lights glittering from their depths.

It was beneath the glow of the beeswax flames that Raegan caught the shine of white-blonde hair. "Blodeuwedd," she cried, any lingering homesickness for a place that didn't exist leaving her body at the sight of her dearest friend.

The owl-woman turned away from the Keeper, her entire face lighting up as she sighted Raegan. With a low rumble of pleased laughter, Oberon set Raegan down just in time for Blodeuwedd to barrel into her, wrapping the shorter woman up in a tight embrace.

"You're here," she exclaimed, the words muffled by Blodeuwedd's shoulder.

"Couldn't miss two of my favorite souls getting married," the owl-woman replied, pulling back to wink at Raegan. Then her expression fell serious, eyes darting to the King. "If anything happens, know that I will watch over him."

"Thank you," Raegan choked out, squeezing Blodeuwedd's hand. "Am I cruel for doing this?"

The owl-woman smiled, considering. Raegan drew in a deep, shaking breath, the scent of the King mingling with the dark leaf and purple petal underfoot.

"It would be crueler, I think, to deny him," Blodeuwedd replied, her expression sharp. "To deny yourself. The truest of loves often blooms in the darkest of places."

Raegan looked back at Oberon, who was talking to Andronica, and reached across the space between them for his hand. The moment their fingers interlaced—like the final weave of a tapestry—the room fell silent, a tender kind of hush that made Raegan think of angel's wings, of all things. And then, like it was Fated, like there had never been any other path, the deathless witch and the nameless king walked together toward that all-too-familiar arch.

Raegan had always thought that if she ever married, she might panic at the last moment. She might stand at the altar in a pretty dress or well-tailored suit and realize she was not worthy of this love. That she was dooming the person she claimed to love most of all to misery.

And yet, despite the fact she was dooming the King more than she ever could've with a mortal lover, Raegan felt nothing but peace. A peace she probably didn't deserve, she knew, not amidst the chaos and death and suffering that she'd had no small hand in creating.

But Oberon looked at her with that monstrous, sharp-fanged kind of love, and all she could do was offer up the few soft, tender places she had left. She wanted to be devoured. She wanted to belong to him, for him to belong to her, for there to be no question a thousand years from now that the witch and the king had loved each other with a fierceness that toppled a god.

She might've said all of that if not for the Keeper moving into her vision, asking if they were both ready for the Feyrish ritual. And then all Raegan could do was nod and cling to this moment, the last ripe berry on the vine.

The small besuited man wound a length of silver cord around their hands, speaking in the Old Tongue. Though she only understood a little, Raegan could feel the oath taking hold. She let it in without reservation, inviting it to make a nest between her bones, to lodge itself deep and true so no matter what, she would never forget him.

All the while, Oberon looked at her as if she were his beginning and not his end. She clutched his hands tighter, savoring the feel of his touch, the joy of his presence. And then, because both of them stood beneath the arch of their own free will, and because the old rite recognized the truth of their love, a silver line appeared around Raegan's ring finger. She marveled at it, how it was inked into her skin instead of sitting on the surface, how looking at it made her heart swell.

"Oberon," she told him, half-choked by the enormity of everything she felt for him. "In this life, I'd given up on love. I thought it was nothing more than a fairy tale, meant for children and adults desperate enough to keep hoping."

Raegan paused, glancing out toward the small group of people who she'd do anything for, who'd taken precious time and energy during a terrifying time to make something beautiful for her and Oberon. Then she turned back to the King, tears pouring down her face.

"I was sort of right, though," she replied, smiling through her tears. "Love *is* a fairy tale, and after so much searching, after so many nights of half-remembered dreams, of aching for something I didn't think I could ever have, I finally found you. My faerie king."

CHAPTER FIFTY-FOUR

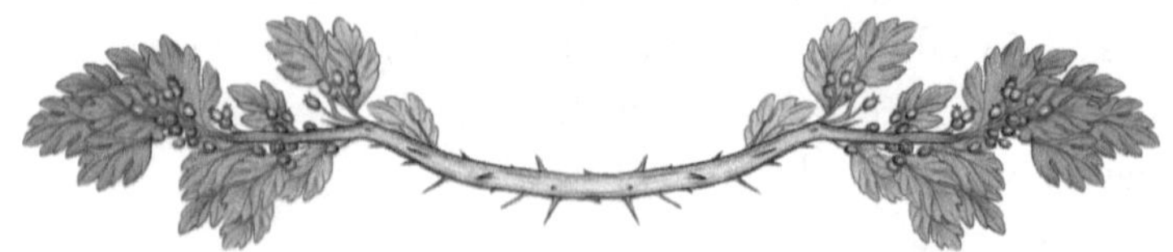

With the oath completed, Raegan reached for the King, gripping him by the lapels of his suit jacket as his large hands slipped around her waist. And then she lost herself in the ocean of his kiss, the sensation she'd wandered the fields of time and space to return to again and again.

She'd barely resurfaced from the thrall of the Unseelie king when she realized the walls of the Temple were shaking. Some of the tiny hand-cut ornaments tumbled from their places, crumpling against the floor. Raegan gripped Oberon's hands as their gazes met. Her throat closed off, and she squeezed her eyes shut. *One more moment*, she begged a universe that had never answered her pleas. *Just one more.*

"They've breached," came a shout from the hallway.

Forcing her eyes back open, Raegan watched as Kamau ran to meet the knight in the doorway, the two conferring in hushed tones she couldn't catch from across the room.

The King disentangled his hands from hers to cup her jaw in his palms. "I am yours," he breathed, those three words somehow so intense that Raegan felt like she was staring down all of the primordial darkness, the vastness of the shadowed universe before the light began. And then the King wrapped his larger hand around hers, turned, and led them to the center of the room where the rest of his court—plus Maelona—was gathering.

"I thought we had bought a few more hours at least," Andronica said miserably, her gaze flitting between Raegan and her liege. And then, louder, she called to Kamau, "What happened?"

"There's a large force too close to Hiraeth," Kamau replied, making their way over from the doorway. "Many of the kelpies were forced to retreat from our defenses to ensure the last free Fey city does not fall."

Raegan's stomach sank, nausea boiling as the lovely room crowned in beeswax light and soft petals blurred. If the Protectorate suddenly knew the location of Hiraeth right after Alanna and Reilly—whom she'd vouched for—arrived there . . .

"Don't despair," Kamau said, meeting Raegan's gaze as if reading her mind. "If—and by all the names of the gods, I hope it is not—Hiraeth is exposed, the kelpies do not think it was your people's doing. Likely the tracking spells the Protectorate's been scattering around the countryside, or just dumb luck. Regardless, we cannot be concerned about that now. They've broken through the Temple's defenses. It's time."

Andronica spat something in Old Feyrish, drawing the sword at her waist and rushing past Kamau. Maelona reached over and gripped Raegan's shoulder.

"Don't die," her aunt said. "Also, I love you." And then Maelona was gone, following two Unseelie knights into the fray.

At Raegan's side, Blodeuwedd went still, gaze finding hers. *Out of time*, Raegan thought. Always out of goddamn time.

"If the Protectorate's here, I have to go," Raegan said, reaching over to grasp Blodeuwedd's hand in her own. "Go to Baba Yaga's realm. Please."

The owl woman smiled at her, slow and creeping, a menacing thing wrapped in the prettiest of flowers. "It has been too long since we graced a battlefield together, sister," Blodeuwedd said, the angles of her face sharp and feral, "too long since I cut down the sort of men who were foolish enough to form me from the meadowsweet and the oak flowers. I wanted only to bloom toward the sun, and they made me into something that unfurls talons at dusk. Of course I must hunt."

Raegan's entire body tensed, her refusals already gathering on the back of her tongue. She couldn't lose anyone else, but certainly not Blodeuwedd.

"Besides," the owl-woman continued, seeming to sense Raegan's hesitancy, "haven't you learned to stop trying to do everything on your own yet?"

Raegan swallowed, opening her mouth and then closing it again. If she had to walk back into the Timekeeper's realm, gods, doing it with the familiar weight of owl talons on her shoulder would make all the difference. She reached up, placing both hands on either side of Blodeuwedd's face, trying to formulate the right words.

But then shouts of warning came racing down the hallway, followed by that ear-splitting battle magic she wished she'd never heard.

"If you die," Raegan said, staring into Blodeuwedd's eyes, "I'm gonna be really mad at you."

With a dangerous grin, Blodeuwedd shook off Raegan's touch and took a few steps backwards. One moment, a woman, tall and sharp-featured, and then an owl, preternaturally large, its yellow eyes too vast. It opened its wings and lifted from the ground with a few strong beats, coming to land on Raegan's shoulder. The familiarity of the sensation pulled a long, slender thread of longing from somewhere deep inside her body. She grasped it, needing all of herself, even the most painful parts.

Andronica sprinted back into the room, her ballerina-like grace intact despite all the chaos, carrying something wrapped in a woolen blanket. The Fey warrior approached Raegan, holding the object out like an offering. She furrowed her brow, not understanding.

Not, at least, until she did. "Oh," Raegan murmured, parting the woolens to find Excalibur's worn leather pommel, though the sword had been tucked into a new leather scabbard with an attached belt. With a start, her memory turned over—the design was an old Unseelie make, crafted to conceal the power of magical weapons from keen eyes.

Steeling herself, Raegan reached forward and wrapped her fingers around the pommel. For a moment, she wrestled with the power of the sword before it quieted, though still it tempted her, a snake in the grass. It was an option, she knew. But if Raegan chose to drink from Excalibur's poisoned well of stolen power, it would only be at the last possible second—right before she drove the sword into the Timekeeper's chest.

"Thank you," Raegan said, meeting Andronica's gaze as she buckled the length of leather around her waist.

"Remember what I taught you," the Fey knight replied, almost looking at Raegan as if she thought the half-mortal woman might be capable of this impossible thing.

"I will," Raegan promised, tears pricking the backs of her eyes. "Don't die. I was just starting to like you."

Andronica folded the woolens with a dagger-sharp grin. "Right back at you." Then the faerie knight turned and marched out of the room and back down the hallway, her spine straight as an arrow.

Raegan tested the weight of the blade, wanting to know how it felt with Blodeuwedd on her shoulders. It felt like destiny, she found. Like all her rage had been building to this moment, like all the ache had been worthwhile.

Setting her jaw, she turned, looking for the King—always searching for him on the horizon, for the fairy-tale ending she never managed to get right. "Ready?" she asked as he turned toward her.

"No," he murmured, his eyes drinking her in. "But it matters not, I fear." In the space of a heartbeat, the shadows around the room pooled at his feet, slinking across his body to form hard planes of otherworldly armor. For a moment, the breath left Raegan's lungs. He was so beautiful in his violence, in his darkness, in the fury that burned low and fierce inside him.

"You are sure about this?" Kamau asked from the door, hesitating on the threshold, their words stilted.

"All the doors that I've opened," Raegan said, moving for the corridor, clutching the words like a life raft in a hurricane, "remain open to a thing like me. This will work, Kamau."

The Unseelie knight looked at her and then the King for a long moment before nodding and turning on their heel, rushing toward the front of the Temple, where the Protectorate had breached the pocket realm.

"Come," Oberon said, holding out a hand for her.

She took it, something in her soothed by the trifecta of his touch, owl talons on her shoulder, and the pommel of a heavy sword between her fingers. "The Protectorate still thinks you're injured, yes?" Raegan asked as they stepped into the hallway, moving deeper into the depths of the Temple, away from the fighting—at least for now.

"We can hope," the King replied, his eyes roving the corridor as more Fey warriors rushed down it, headed in the opposite direction. "But the moment they see Excalibur, that will be called into question."

"Right," she said, sheathing the blade.

Blodeuwedd pushed off her shoulder with taloned claws, spreading her wings to soar down the corridor. Seeing the owl fly ahead brought memories rushing to Raegan's mind. She clamped down on them. If they won, if they freed this world, she would have time to sort through it all. To feel it all, maybe.

Oberon took a hard turn, leading them down a side hallway toward the ritual room. It was the same they'd used to follow Cormac's spell-craft, which felt as though it had happened hundreds of years ago, not a month. Uneasiness squirmed low in Raegan's belly, but she squashed it, keeping her eyes on the steady stroke of the owl's wings, focusing on the feeling of the Unseelie king at her side. Time dilated—a cruel joke—and the walk to that room felt longer than all of the moments Raegan had spent tumbling beneath sheets with Oberon or feeling the sun on her face or waking up knowing who she really was.

But then the door yawned wide and open, the marble expanse of the room cold and waiting beyond it. Beneath the filtered, golden light of the Temple, a regiment of Unseelie knights was gathered—maybe fifty at most. Raegan glanced at their faces, trying to memorize their features, in case they followed her into the Timekeeper's realm just for the god to unwind their Threads, spin them back into nothingness.

The gathered attention of the knights fell onto Raegan's shoulders, heavy and demanding, with more bite than even Blodeuwedd's claws.

"Just as we discussed," the King said, addressing the knights as Raegan walked to the center of the ritual circle. "Only come through the door if you see our signal. If not, wait until the door closes. Another will immediately open in its place, leading to Baba Yaga's realm. Get as many through as you can and then leave. Live. That is what we are fighting for. Not conquest, not riches. Only to live."

Despite knowing every step of the plan, Raegan found herself some-what disbelieving that, after everything, she was back here in this room, standing at the center of a chalk-and-blood circle. She cast her eyes about the space and swallowed hard. Blodeuwedd completed a lap around the room, returning to land on Raegan's shoulders. She leaned her cheek against her friend's downy feathers.

The King was beside her, helping to dress her in chainmail and armor that seemed like it had been made for her. It was much lighter than what she'd worn in practice with Andronica, Raegan noticed distantly.

Dressed for war, an ancient blade in her hand and a small army at her back, Raegan understood there was nothing to do but begin the rite. It flowed to her like water. It shouldn't have; the Timekeeper had surely destroyed the pathway they'd walked last time. But she felt her magic take root, felt her rivers close in around that parched desert realm and its hungry god, felt the door yawn wide. She opened her eyes.

All at once, where there should have only been a smooth expanse of marble, there was instead a door—which meant there was only one choice. Had only ever been one choice.

Raegan took a deep breath and walked through it.

CHAPTER FIFTY-FIVE

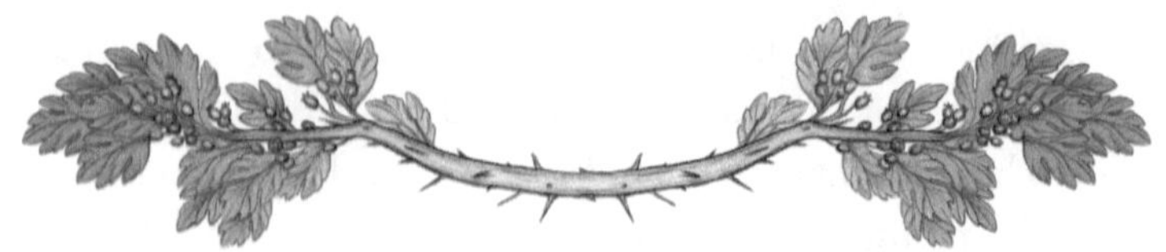

The door bucked. The Timekeeper knew she was here now and he wrenched the opening from her grasp. But Raegan just smiled, tightening her snare. She'd spent her life learning how to hold running water in her open hands. Did this thing of dust and metal think it could twist away from her jaws now that she had closed them tight?

Nothing existed to Raegan but the door. Blodeuwedd, the King, the fabled sword on her waist, even her own body—all gone. There was only a god to be wrestled with, bested in the halls of his own home. Raegan gritted her teeth hard enough to make her jaw crack in complaint. Every fiber of her being protested, her magic stretched to its breaking point. She held on with all of her might.

It was not enough. Had she ever once been enough? With a cry that burrowed up from the depths of her being, Raegan lost control of the door. There was no longer a single stride over the threshold; instead, the long expanse of time snaked around her. The door slithered out of Raegan's grasp, and she was cast into a freefall. Dust filled her mouth, her head throbbing with shrill and sudden metallic clangs. An ancient dread swelled in her chest. When the tumbling and plummeting finally stopped, she found the stillness no less terrible.

Terror turned her palms slick. With a shudder, Raegan opened her eyes to watery light. Her breath hitched. "No," she whispered, her throat constricting around the word. "*No.*"

In front of Raegan stretched the interior of a train car. Brown leather seats lined up like soldiers, empty luggage racks looking more like prison bars. She fought for her breath, shoving away the panic. Her entire body felt limp and wrung dry from attempting to control the passage. Just standing up, she knew, would take a monumental amount of strength.

She tried anyway, biting down on her tongue, hoping a different pain might restart her body. Fear settled onto her skin like white-hot pinpricks when she realized it was not exhaustion keeping her down. It was much worse than that.

She was trapped in one of the brown leather train seats she knew far too well. Her heart hammering, nausea rising, Raegan glanced down. Her armor was gone, her thighs sutured to the leather. Panic exploded in her chest as she glanced to her left, eyes hunting for Excalibur.

It was still there, hanging from her belt, tucked safely into its scabbard. She hoped the spelled scabbard was enough to hide the blade's nature from the Timekeeper, though she wasn't sure it would matter—her arms were stuck fast to the seat as well. He'd probably only left her armed as a tease, a cruel taunt. When Raegan pulled experimentally, a searing pain swept through her, so brutal and fierce that she cried out in surprise. Straining, she looked toward Excalibur again, trying to gauge the distance between her hand and its pommel.

And that was when she saw that she was not alone in the leather seat. By the window was a weathered corpse, little more than bleached bone and piles of ash. The skull splintered down the middle, slumped onto a collapsed chest. Only a few fingerbones remained, the majority turned to flakes of dull gray. Worst of all, Raegan saw, was the all-too-familiar outfit, left untouched by whatever had scavenged the corpse: brown blazer, hunter-green pocket square, cream crewneck sweater marred with dirt.

"Dad," Raegan choked out through dry, cracked lips. Her father's corpse sat beside her on the Timekeeper's train. Had she even left this realm at all? Had she actually watched her father be reduced to ash? She recalled the bone-deep gnawing anxiety she'd felt after surfacing from the Rivers into the Temple—a horrible sense that none of it was real. Had she been right all along?

Despair swept through Raegan, powerful as an angry tide, drowning her defiance and rage in one massive rush. She hardly realized she was crying until she tasted the salt on her lips. So this was how it was to end—all her lives, every ounce of her spite, transmuted into power the Timekeeper could use to subjugate mortals and the Fair Folk alike.

Oberon was a fool to have believed in her. From that very first day in Camelot, he'd been a fool to think a half-mad, not-quite-mortal witch would ever be anything but his undoing. Not to mention her father and Maelona—all they'd endured so things might be better for her, for the future. She'd squandered every last bit, thinking she was fighting some incredible battle the bards would sing about one day. But she was just a rabbit in a snare. Always had been.

Eyes blurred with tears, Raegan looked over at the crumpled remains of her father. A sob wracked her chest, pulling on her body hard enough that her skin cried out in protest. As if a girl could ever topple a god. As if liberation wasn't little more than a daydream. As if the people of both realms were not destined to devour each other whole in a constant bid for more, more, *more*.

"At least I'm with you," Raegan whispered to her father, wishing she could hold his pocket square between her fingers, a small comfort in the face of a long and agonizing death. Maybe this was what she deserved. Her actions had caused so much suffering—for Oberon, for the Fair Folk, for Blodeuwedd, for Maelona. Her chest felt like it might be caving in, and she welcomed the pain.

Time tucked its tail into its own mouth and devoured the yielding flesh. Raegan waited for death to come, yearned feverishly for that old friend to pull her into the senseless void once more. At least there she might not feel like guilt and shame were boiling her alive. At least there, maybe one day, she might see her faerie king again. But no such relief appeared in the long, narrow aisle of the train car. Just harsh, unnatural light and the rattling of her breath in her chest.

The Timekeeper did not show himself, not even to gloat. He'd wait, Raegan realized, until she was closer to death. He'd twist the knife. He always did. Maybe he'd parade in Oberon or Blodeuwedd, or simply toss the remaining funeral ash at her feet so she could spend her years wasting away thinking about everyone she'd failed.

Raegan turned her head as best she could, the train car's seat already biting deeply into the back of her neck. She looked at her father's familiar jacket again, her gaze skipping out the window. Flat plains of dust stretched endlessly in all directions, the land as dry and parched as her own tongue. The train didn't appear to be moving, though Raegan couldn't see the station from her vantage point.

Not that it mattered. The only reason she'd been looking, she knew, was because she thought the King might come save her. One last time. But no one was coming. She had only herself, and Raegan was smart enough to know when it was over. She glanced past her father's corpse and out the window again, selfishly wishing she might get to look at the sea or a rainstorm or a damp, dark, autumnal forest once again.

A flash of shadow caught her eye. Hope soared defiantly in her chest, cutting through the thickly rooted despair. Raegan squashed it; she couldn't see salvation in every shadow just because the shadows were his. Her throat closed off. When the low places of Avalon had tested her with that dream-spun realm, she should've stayed. Regret surged through her body, and more useless, stupid tears blurred her eyes. It wouldn't have been real, no, but it would've been better than this. Her body would've rotted in the caves of an ancient, magical place, her mind wrapped in the comfort of all the things she knew deep down she could never have.

A shadow of movement again. Raegan strained her eyes, realizing that if anything, it was the Timekeeper coming for her. That at least she could face—an enemy to spit venom at, a reason to summon her bravado. Let him come. She'd sink her teeth into him one last time.

But it was not the Timekeeper casting shadows on the long, wide plain. Raegan's heart pounded. No—either her grasp on reality had well and truly failed, or there on the horizon, there was an army.

An army of tattered black flags and wickedly sharp swords, an endless wellspring of defiance and power. An Unseelie army mounted on kelpies, the shadows of their King slinking into the dead world, claws experimentally flexed. The door had held just long enough for them to make it through. Suddenly, Raegan didn't care if it was all delusion or madness or if maybe she was already dead, devoured by the Timekeeper's oblivion eyes.

She was going to see him one last time. No matter the cost.

With a snarl, Raegan fought to tear her right arm from the leather.

The sound morphed into a raw scream halfway through; the pain was too much. It wasn't a matter of risking large sections of torn skin, she realized. This place—this horrible, wretched place—would tear her limb from limb before it let her go.

"Fine," she snapped, a bead of sweat running down her temple. "There are other ways." She cast her gaze toward the army—it had to be real, the way it blotted out the Timekeeper's false sun, so rich and dark and lovely. Which meant her door had held. She was not powerless, not even here. Not this time.

Raegan set her jaw. She'd called to the water on this very train before, just steps from where she was currently trapped, and it had not answered—not, at least, within the Timekeeper's metal confines.

"My rivers," she murmured, squeezing her eyes shut, "please. Come to me, my waters, my currents, my tides. I bid you to rise like the blood of a warrior, like the drums of war. Rise and free us from this hell of twisted magic and endless oppression. It is finally time. *Rise.*"

In all her lives, Raegan wasn't sure she'd ever said anything with so much meaning behind it, with every word so drenched in intention and blind rage. Her command bloomed crystalline and wild in the train car. She hoped and hoped and *hoped.* Her heart thudded against her chest. And then, somewhere in the distance, a roar rumbled through the Timekeeper's realm. At the exact same moment, she felt her magic churn inside of her, electrified by the words she'd uttered—the call-and-response of powers beyond even her understanding.

The door at the end of the train car flew open. An unremarkable man in a tweed suit and hat sitting low on his brow prowled down the aisle. Only his mouth was visible beneath the shadowed brim, curled into a cruel sneer.

"What have you done?" the Timekeeper demanded, haughty and mocking. "And why are you still stupid enough to think it will make any difference, you little bitch?"

Raegan grinned at him, all teeth. She felt the ebb of the tide rush through her, euphoric and vicious. The rumbling grew louder as the dam of this gray and lifeless realm shattered beneath the weight of her rage.

"I told you," she replied, surprised by the tone of her voice—low and soft, just as eternal as the god before her, "that I would flood your world."

The Timekeeper shot toward her, those devouring eyes suddenly visible from beneath the brim of his hat, gloved hands reaching for her. But then the train lurched and kicked up, almost as if the hulking piece of god-made metal had been lifted from its tracks by the sweep of a river.

"Not so stupid, am I, Kronos?" Raegan shouted as the door at the end of the train car burst open, silver currents shoving through, open-mouthed and starving for violence. She threw her head back and laughed, the sound unraveled and mad to her own ears. "And I'm so much worse than a bitch. I'm a motherfucking cunt, and you are going to *drown.*"

CHAPTER FIFTY-SIX

The water took Raegan into its arms, gentle as a lover, the bonds that held her fast dissolving beneath the immutable weight of the current. She gave herself up to the tumble of the tides, trusting the river as she always had—completely. Since that first life spent on its banks, finding solace and peace in a cruel world, she had belonged to the way of the water. It would not fail her now.

The crest of the wave broke somewhere above her head, and then Raegan found herself pulling air into her lungs. Like the ocean depositing driftwood onto the shore, the rivers set her gently upon the train platform. She scrambled to her feet, completely dry despite the dampness of her surroundings, glimmering wefts of kelp draped over rod iron benches. The clocktower's hands spun around madly, furiously.

And then, looking beyond the platform, Raegan beheld a beautiful thing. Maybe two hundred paces away, the King was mounted on Rainer, formidable and deathless in his black shadow armor. His sword was raised high as the Unseelie Court rushed a force of Protectorate and clock guardians on the empty plains. For a moment, all she could do was stare at him: impossibly regal, undeniably glorious, a beautiful apocalypse.

Digging her nails into her palms, Raegan tore her gaze away from her beloved, gathering herself as she searched the platform for the Timekeeper. He was nowhere to be seen. His train lay in a crumpled heap, long sections of the tracks torn up in the river's rage.

"But what about the Gates?" Raegan murmured to herself. She glanced over her shoulder.

The Timekeeper's line of soldiers held fast, even against the force of the Unseelie Court. She chewed on her lip, her heart pounding as she sent her magic out into the space around her. Breaking the front of the Protectorate army would mean nothing if she and the King couldn't go straight for the Gates. They knew this; they'd talked this through a hundred times. If they could not find the Gates, the Timekeeper could reorganize and flank them, or do much, much worse. This was, after all, his realm.

A strange gleam caught her eye. The place where the waters had torn up the tracks shimmered slightly. Raegan stalked to the end of the empty train platform, her entire body pounding with fear and anxiety. Time was precious. She knew that better than most. She gazed down at the flickering section of tracks, eyes sharp, the rivers ready at her fingertips.

And there, beneath that metal spine, beneath the dead soil and the gray dust, was something far grander. Raegan's blood thrummed. The tracks *were* the Gates, disguised by a complex and extremely powerful glamour. With a shuddering breath, she understood that the poor souls trapped on these train cars no doubt fed the vast, endless maw of the Gates as much as they did the Timekeeper's own power.

Raegan leaned over the edge for a closer look, but then a section of damp brick crumbled beneath her weight. With a curse, she righted herself, turning on her heel to scan the platform. Nothing. Nothing but the Unseelie army in the distance, fighting hard, actually gaining ground. Her heart fluttered, beating shallowly somewhere near her throat.

Raegan turned back to the tracks. She released a long exhale, preparing herself, and then bit down on her tongue until her eyes watered with the pain. Good. She needed to be present, to be sharp. And then, despite the unfathomable exhaustion and all-consuming despair she'd almost given into, Raegan called to the waters again. She raised her hands high, like some forgotten saint on a wind-buffeted hill, and commanded the tides to wash away the Timekeeper's glamour. To do as all rivers did—wear away at the surface and reveal what slept beneath.

Power coursed through her, the seams of her mortal body almost bursting, every inch of flesh screaming with pain and spite and fury. The ground trembled beneath her feet, and then the river came rushing, its mouth open, its tide unstoppable. The rivers ripped metal from the earth like sutures from a wound, tearing at the fabricated face of the Timekeeper's realm to find the darker truth that lurked beneath.

Raegan swayed, stumbling away from the edge and catching herself on the back of a bench. Dark spots swarmed her vision, but it didn't matter. Neither did the agonizing pain gnawing at her sides. Just beyond the train platform, reaching high into the blank sky, washed clean by the rivers, stood the Gates.

They were just as beautiful as her father's spellcraft papers had indicated. The metalwork looped in intricate patterns, ancient sigils and symbols of power worked into the design. Looking directly at them made Raegan feel ill. Without the glamour, she could see where the power of the Gates leached into the In-Between, the soil a burnt black, reaching out through the gray plains with greedy fingers.

Dizziness dragged Raegan to one side. She swayed hard, trying to regain control of her own body. A clammy sweat coated her skin, and her breathing was ragged, like her lungs had been torn in two. She gasped desperately for air, feeling so alone.

But then in the distance, a clamor went up from the battlefield. No— a *cheer*, she realized. Triumph climbed up her throat like a glorious, golden vine bursting with budding blooms. They saw the Gates. Blodeuwedd appeared in the sky, rising out of the army on snow-white wings, a furious victory cry spiraling from her beak.

Raegan had finally made good on a promise. Maybe—just maybe— she and Oberon could find a little stone cottage once the world was mended. Maybe one day, people might forget their names. Maybe one day, there would be no need to call on the rivers with fury or raise a sword with the intent to destroy.

With that thought clutched to her chest, fragile as glass, Raegan stumbled away from the Gates, her legs fighting to carry her back to him. Always back to him.

She'd reached the far side of the train platform when she caught a dull glint of chainmail in her peripheral vision. Raegan turned, reaching for Excalibur's pommel, but it was too late. Always too late.

Bedwyr slammed into Raegan, taking her to the ground. The air tumbled out of her body, her chin hitting the train platform hard. She tasted blood and fought to right herself. Black flies swarmed her vision, pain piercing her abdomen.

"Your little kelpie tried to kill me," Bedwyr snarled.

Raegan ignored him, struggling to orient herself, her mind a thick, blank haze. With a pang of dread, she realized she was flat on her back. Arthur's knight straddled her waist, delivering blows to her stomach with a speed and precision that seemed unfair for someone so large and strong to possess.

"Should've tried harder," Bedwyr said, panting as he paused the barrage of his heavy fists just long enough for her to realize how much it hurt and how little energy she had left.

Raegan curled one fist, calling for the rivers. They answered her in a rushing tide, but she couldn't contain them, couldn't direct them.

For a long moment, all Raegan saw was the wide expanse of gray sky. If she was going to die, she thought, it should at least be in her king's arms. Not in the grasp of this man-turned-beast, the Timekeeper's most loyal monster. She stoked the fires of her fury, shoving the pain aside. But Bedwyr just laughed—the laugh of every man who has underestimated a woman—and gripped her throat between his large hands.

Raegan sputtered, driving a knee into his groin. But the knight was faster, shifting his weight away, pressing down harder on her windpipe.

"Fuck you," she spat, finally summoning the energy to lift one hand. With a raw cry, Raegan slashed at Bedwyr's face. Her nails grazed skin, and the knight spat a curse at her. She fought to press the advantage, to drive her knee into his stomach, but Bedwyr recovered too quickly. In a heartbeat, his hands were back around her throat, pressing down harder than before. Her vision blinked in and out as she realized with a bolt of terror that she'd lost sensation in her limbs.

Not like this. Not again. She was meant to tear away the glamour concealing the Gates and then be swept into the shadow of the Unseelie army. She'd ride double on Rainer with the King, and they'd hunt down Kronos. Then she'd drive Excalibur into the god's heart and it would all be over. Couldn't Fate see how perfect it would've been that way—the kind of story that fit neatly in the mouth of a bard, that swelled and hummed in all the right places on the page?

Her fury turned bittersweet, more wound than blade. The despair found her again, hooking barbs into her skin, just as sharp and sure as the leather seats of the train car. Her heart felt strange, like it might either barrel right out of her chest or cease beating altogether. Dust coated her tongue, and the platform beneath her was rough and unyielding. At least, Raegan told herself, it might be over soon.

And then somehow, beyond all reason, the crushing weight was gone. She gasped, pulling fresh air into her lungs, her throat burning. Forcing her body to move, Raegan rolled to the side and grappled desperately for Excalibur with trembling, ice-cold fingers. Desperation clawed at her throat the way Bedwyr had, sending adrenaline skittering through her veins. Death had come for her twice a century. She knew what an ending felt like. Hers would *not* be here, not on this train platform.

With another feral shriek that tore at her bruised throat, Raegan drew Excalibur and used the blade to pull herself to her knees. She swayed, her body already feeling like a bloated corpse. For a long moment, there was nothing but the wide gray plains and the furious tick of the clock tower as she looked with disbelief at the scene before her. Her mind, she thought, might not be understanding. It might be offering prettier images, a softer door into death, a passage she had long since perfected.

If her mind was to be believed, then just a few feet away from her, the King was slamming Bedwyr into the ground. The viciously sharp points of his arm bracers glimmered in the strange light. Just as the knight had done to Raegan, Oberon loomed over Bedwyr. She swallowed, her thoughts keening, her vision split by tears.

The King was a creature of control, she knew. Two goddesses had torn a wound in the night sky and crafted an impossible weapon from the obsidian jewel it bled. The sheer amount of power gathered in one body was incomprehensible. The King could not pull the pin. He could not detonate.

And yet, as Raegan watched, Oberon was more beast than Fair Folk, his shadows devouring Bedwyr from all angles. The sky above them turned black. The magnitude of his rage shook the platform as if the darkness boiling deep in his marrow might be capable of tearing this entire place apart.

"I told you," her faerie king snarled, his voice ringing out like he was the realm's true god, "to *stay away* from my wife."

Despite all the pain and terror and the sinking feeling in the pit of her stomach that told Raegan her body was broken beyond repair, she threw her head back and laughed. Even if they lost this battle, if the Timekeeper consumed them all in his rampage for more power, at least she'd gotten to hear Oberon say those two words: *my wife.*

The King's head snapped toward her. The rest of his body went still as a panther on the hunt, only his eyes sliding to meet hers. "Nyneve," he rasped.

"My husband," she said, the sight of him suffusing her with a strength she wouldn't have thought possible even a few moments ago. Biting down on her cheek, Raegan used Excalibur to pull herself to her feet. Without looking away from her, the King violently shook Bedwyr by his neck—something she might've seen a big jungle cat do in a documentary—and then straightened, like he was going to move toward her.

"No," Raegan said, barely biting out the word. Leaning on Excalibur as if it were a cane and not a mythic blade, she gathered her strength and limped the three paces to where the King pinned Bedwyr to the platform. The knight was the one choking now, blood dribbling from his lips. "Hold him down for me."

"It doesn't matter," Bedwyr heaved. "I'll just come back."

With his free hand, Oberon reached up and steadied Raegan, bracketing her at the waist. His gaze landed heavy on her, the weight of his full attention heady and silken. She almost opened her mouth to explain, but of course her faerie king knew what she was going to do. Raegan watched as his fingers tightened around Bedwyr's throat, the shadows under his command holding the knight to the ground.

With the last reserves of her strength, Raegan hefted Excalibur from the ground. Bedwyr forced out another laugh, but it was hedged in desperation, the same sound she'd heard leave his lips along the River Wye.

"I will," the knight choked out against the strength of the King's long, powerful fingers, "come back."

With an unsteady lurch, Raegan slotted Excalibur against Bedwyr's

chainmail, right where his heart should be. She watched with satisfaction as the knight's eyes went wide, fear flooding his expression as he
recognized the sword. A wolfish laugh tore its way up from her chest,
and then the deathless witch drove the mythic blade into his chest.

"Not this time."

CHAPTER FIFTY-SEVEN

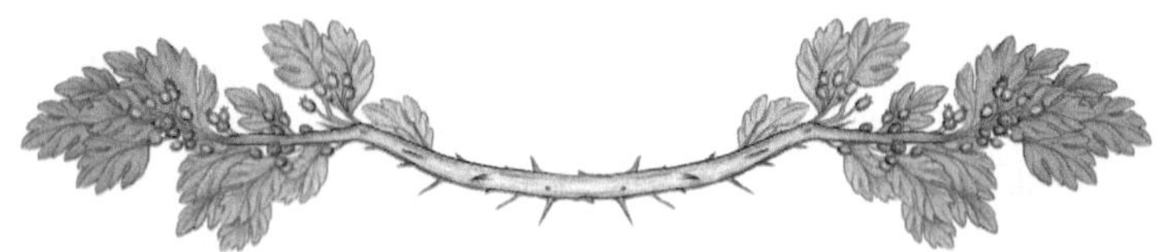

Raegan expected blood, maybe. For some kind of twisted, demonic thing to fling itself from the chest of the knight, screeching and wailing. But Bedwyr's death was quiet, unremarkable. The once-mortal man who had watched a millennium pass him by simply collapsed into dust. Raegan watched, her tongue feeling too thick for her mouth, as ash drifted across the train platform.

"Raegan," the King said, pulling her into his arms.

With a sigh, she let go of Excalibur, barely registering the clatter as the blade hit the ground. All that mattered in this moment was tumbling into his expanse of autumnal meadow and dark rain and black pepper. She breathed in the scent of him, letting the King shift her in his arms so the harsh, hungry points of his armor did not pierce her.

"The Gates," she said. "Get me to the Gates." When Oberon said nothing, she forced her eyes open, tilting her head back to look at him. The expression on his otherworldly features was feral, dark eyes glinting with something mad and unrestrained.

"No," he replied, his words a low growl that thrummed low in his chest. "I refuse to save a world that you will not live to see."

Emotions warred in Raegan's chest. She reached up for the King, brushing his jawline with her knuckles. "Oberon," she managed, her voice sounding so small, so worn out. "You can't."

"I am the High King of the Unseelie Court," he told her, teeth bared, his face a mask of inhuman cruelty. "I will do as I please." He stood, gathering her in his arms as he turned away from the Gates.

Raegan heaved a cough that left her lips bloody. She realized all at once, her mind addled and her body broken, that the King hadn't even tried to pick up Excalibur. That he was going to let the entire world burn if it meant he could have her.

She should resist. She should yell at him. She should summon whatever strength she had left and tell him he could *not* do this. But Raegan was so tired. She was so tired of fighting for so long and so hard against the same things. She was tired of funerals, of the feast table growing shorter every year. Perhaps it was kinder to let things end. Perhaps mortals needed to find their own way out.

"Oberon," she managed, one hand curling tight as a rosebud against his chest. "I—"

Something hit the King hard from the side, sending Raegan sprawling onto the platform. He curled his larger body around hers protectively, but she was torn viciously from his grasp.

She lolled to the side, trying to make her body do anything at all that might mean survival. Rising onto her hands and knees, she dragged herself across the platform, trying to get Excalibur's pommel back into her hand. The rough surface of the platform bit into her palms, the dust stinging her eyes. With a desperate lurch, Raegan grabbed the sword and looked up, only to find something that sent a chill skittering through her blood.

Her faerie king was locked in combat with the Timekeeper. She coughed hard, splattering her fingers with blood, and pulled herself up on one knee. No wonder Kronos had fortified his realm so carefully against Oberon. With one hand, those viciously edged arm bracers glimmering like an oil spill, the King threw the Timekeeper bodily against the wall of the train station.

Gritting her teeth, Raegan tried to get to her feet. Excalibur was the only thing that might kill Kronos, might tear down the Gates. She had to get to the King, *had* to walk those ten paces. Begging her body to obey, she watched as the King stalked toward the crumpled pile of tweed, his shadow-blade drawn.

Raegan swallowed, her throat like broken glass. She managed to stand, leaning on Excalibur. The world spun and her vision played funny tricks—two Kings reaching for the mess of tweed, one Timekeeper suddenly in front of her, his eyes like the harvest, the end of all things.

Kronos drove one gloved hand straight through Raegan's chest, his hungry fingers clutching for her heart. She gasped, the pain unbelievable, unable to move until the god shoved her back onto her knees. In the distance, she heard a guttural, shattered shout from Oberon as the Timekeeper feasted on whatever time was still hers to claim. Around her, the world reduced to little more than blinding, endless pain and the gnashing of teeth.

Raegan felt her limbs grow cold and heavy even as she fought to lift them; only Excalibur's point driven into the platform kept her aloft. The Timekeeper made a meal of whatever lurked in her chest cavity, and the power there was not like the rivers. She could not bid it to flow backwards or to devour that which hemmed it in.

Right as Raegan thought she might succumb to the grayness creeping in from all angles, something protruded from the Timekeeper's chest. A sharpened point of pure black, she saw, glinting madly in the raw red light. Feral elation howled low in Raegan's belly. *The King.*

Death might take her in Their arms once again, sing her a sweet song she only half-remembered and usher her into that wide, vast dark. But the Timekeeper would rot, too, and all his structures would fall, buried by the silt. Raegan's mind exploded with memories, surely some final burst of her consciousness, but she fought to stay in the moment, to at least see the god she hated more than anything in the entire world dissolve into the same kind of ash to which he'd reduced her father.

Instead, Kronos threw his head back and laughed. "It hurts, your power, your blade, Nameless One," the god choked out, ichor dripping from the side of his mouth, "but it will not vanquish me."

Fury flared in Raegan like a bonfire. He would not take her from her faerie king again. Damn the world and the Gates. Damn it all. None of it mattered; Oberon would *not* watch her die. Not again. Never again. The ancient blade in her hand whispered its poisonous promise—the promise that had broken Arthur Pendragon—and this time, Raegan accepted. Just a little. Just enough.

Determination swept her body and she grappled for the Timekeeper. He ignored her, having taken what he wanted, gleeful to leave another husk in his wake, and moved to face the King. Before he could, Raegan saw something gold glimmer in the pocket of his waistcoat.

She shouldn't even still be alive, she knew, but spite and magic were strange things, and she lurched forward, pulling on the short length of chain tucked away in the god's tweed vest. An ornate pocket watch with lush filigree pulled free into Raegan's bloodied fist. A howl burst out of her chest as she threw it onto the ground in front of her. Glass shattered and the Timekeeper screamed, all of his attention returned to the witch who refused to die.

With what she realized was the last ounce of strength this body would ever exert, Raegan grabbed Excalibur somewhere near its deadly point, not caring that the blade sliced into her palm with little mercy. Strangely, it was suddenly light as air, as if the sword's balance had always been crafted for this one particular Fated moment.

Despite the way life seeped from her body, sticky as molasses, Raegan slammed the blade's tip into the pocket watch. It burst into a hundred pieces, scattering like scarab beetles across the platform.

Before her, the Timekeeper fell to his knees, clutching at his throat with those hands that had taken so much from her, from the world. She watched, death's arrival rattling in her lungs, as the god's gloved fingers began to crumble. Then his hands, wrists, arms, legs—all collapsing into nothing more than lifeless gray ash. With everything she had left in her, Raegan held his eyes, tracing the path of the wound that would finally unmake this foul thing.

As the soot-stained marks of Excalibur's bite traveled up the god's chest, the King came into view behind the Timekeeper. Blood seeped from his hairline, and the armor covering one shoulder had been torn away, revealing a deep, heavily bleeding puncture wound. His eyes were wild as he raised his sword and swung in a downward arc. The Time-keeper's head toppled from his body. Only a heartbeat, only an entire eternity, and then there was nothing left but ash, dancing in unseen currents.

Oberon took Raegan into his arms, one hand cupping her chin. "No," he whispered, his voice raw, laden with the kind of grief that destroyed most people. "*No. I refuse to lose you again.*"

Raegan let herself sink into his arms, breathing in the scent of woodsmoke, black pepper, damp stone, and the torrential kind of rain that only ever came in autumn. Her attention narrowed to just the faerie king; she pushed away Excalibur's offers of the Timekeeper's power, knowing what the cursed blade would twist her into. The world had quite enough tyrants already, didn't it?

"Nyneve," Oberon wept, bowing his form around her, as if he might pull her back from the brink of death with nothing but the fearsome inferno of his monstrous love. "Outlive me. *Please.* I love you too much."

How she wanted to say yes, to agree, to swear she'd do exactly as he asked. But it was beyond even her power now and despite its fevered promises, beyond Excalibur's, too. The currents inside her had gone still and dark, and there was nothing to do now but sink beneath the tides.

"I love you," she managed weakly. It was a gift to die in his arms. Hadn't she always wished to drown in the fathomless depths of his impossibly beautiful gray eyes? "But I think it's time to go."

Mordred choked back a sob, his powerful shoulders wracked with grief. But he held her gaze without question, his fingertips on her jaw. "If you must go," he murmured, tears gathering on those long, dark lashes, "go now, so you may return to me all the quicker."

Nyneve smiled at him, savoring the last few moments in the arms of her faerie king. "Bury me shallow," she told him as the darkness closed in all around her. "I'll be back."

CHAPTER FIFTY-EIGHT

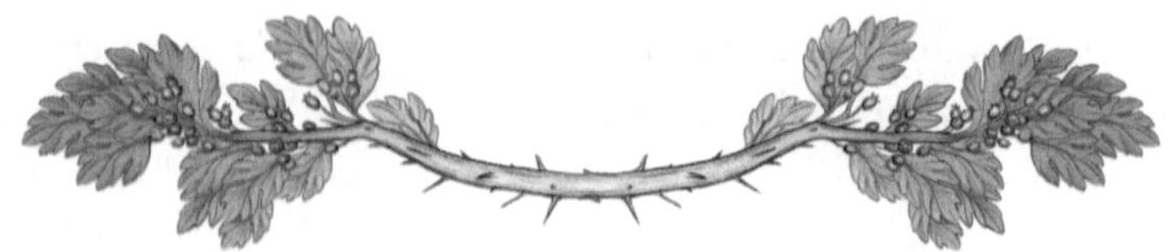

Sunlight poured in, dappled and soft, dancing across the waters like faerie lights. She blinked three or four times, failing to understand her surroundings: a tiled room of some kind, though there was no roof. Trees and vines climbed over the tops of the shimmering white walls, their limbs trailing down. Clear water filled the room, its tiny little waves lapping at her knees.

"Child," came a voice like stars falling.

Raegan snapped her head up from the water to find a magnificent thing standing before her—a woman with quicksilver eyes, the wings of a dove rising from behind her slim, narrow shoulders.

"You may still be a bit disorientated," the being said, her voice gentle despite the feral planes of her face.

Raegan stared at the creature, familiarity rising in her like a soft ache —a yearning she knew better than her name. The heavy tides of memory swept in behind the ache.

"Fuck you," Raegan snapped at Fate, charging forward through the knee-high water, ignoring the way she was suddenly aware of her wet, heavy boots dragging her down. Fate held up a hand, and Raegan's body halted, as if it no longer answered to her.

"I want to speak with you," the primordial goddess said, clasping Her long-fingered hands together.

"We all want shit, you motherfucker," Raegan spat, curling her hands into fists that she ached to sink into Fate's perfect, inhuman face. "I'm very used to wanting things I can't have. Maybe *you* should try it some time."

Fate's expression tightened but didn't darken, more like a parent disappointed with their child's choice of language than an enraged power beyond Raegan's understanding. "I want," the goddess said, letting Her hands fall to Her sides, "to apologize."

Raegan's body stilled, her mind going utterly blank. "What?" she demanded weakly.

"Though I cannot say I am truly sorry for punishing you and the Nameless One as I did all those years ago," Fate said, Her tone strangely soft, the warm, dappled light dancing across the downy, creamy feathers of Her wings, "I was young then, too, and I think you know how deeply you broke the fragile rules of our universe."

Raegan crossed her arms and inhaled, the scent of tarnished silver filling her nose. How fervently she wished instead for black pepper and a curl of woodsmoke. "This is a shit apology so far."

Fate's features did darken then, that flash of primordial rage seeping into Her star-fall eyes. But the goddess's chest only rose with a long, deep inhale, and then She continued. "I am sorry for how I used you to trick the Timekeeper, for the way I moved you about the chessboard. There was no other choice. I have obscured this Thread from him for so long, hoping it might be enough. I have schemed for a millennium, child."

Raegan just stared at the goddess, the water gently lapping at her legs, a bright red leaf floating down from one of the trees overhead. It landed on the surface of the water, sailing on the currents like a tiny boat. So her Protectorate birthright, the false Prophecy, the deal with the Timekeeper—all of it orchestrated by Fate, and not for the reasons she thought.

"I am sorry," Fate said, "for the way the world's destiny has depended upon your suffering. Since Camelot fell, I have been on your side. Always. I know it has rarely felt so."

Raegan narrowed her eyes at the goddess in disbelief. "Wait," she said, digging her fingers into her hair. "Does . . . does all of this mean we actually won?" Hope surged wild in her chest, an untamed thing, and she dared not breathe until Fate answered the question.

"Yes," the goddess said, Her voice impossibly gentle. "Yes, child. After you killed the Timekeeper, the King dismantled the Gates. But first, he held you as you died, Excalibur still clutched in your hand. Something about your death changed the blade, turned it back to its true nature."

Raegan stared at the goddess, opening her mouth to speak but finding no words that sufficed.

Fate glided closer, Her large eyes strangely soft. "Something, I imagine," She continued, words heavy with meaning, "about unconditional love. After all, there is a reason the power of true love has been said to break spells."

Raegan's throat closed off, and tears streamed down her face, falling like rain to the clear water below. "Love," she managed, "is as good an oath as any." She said nothing else, unable to do so without bursting into sobs. She thought about the way her tears had once torn a door into the Timekeeper's realm. How that had allowed the Morrigan to slip through with her visions. How being lured to Kronos like a lamb to slaughter had made all of it possible.

Raegan looked up at Fate, considering. "Normally," she started, her voice hitching with tears, "an apology doesn't mean much without an effort to make amends."

One of the goddess's silvery eyebrows arched. "What do you seek, child? Do you want me to send you back to the world you just left? To the King's arms?"

Yearning unspooled in Raegan's chest, pulling at her heart, straining against her ribcage. Time stretched endless. More leaves traipsed down onto the water, coloring the room like stained glass.

"No," she replied, the single word taking all her might, all her willpower. "No. I don't want him to look at me and only see death. He needs time." Her voice broke again, fresh tears pouring down her face, nearly drowning her words. "I think the world needs him more than I do right now. And if I'm honest, I'm tired. I'm so fucking tired."

Fate watched Raegan soundlessly. Her elegant, thin lips parted, but She said nothing, only watched. Unreasonably, Raegan felt as though every divine thing in this entire universe turned its attention toward her at once.

"But I want to see my dad," she continued, pushing tears from her cheeks. "And I want to know my mom is okay. And then, at the right time, yes, please send me back."

"You wish to flit between the realms of the living and the dead as if they have no bearing on you?" Fate demanded, a hard, glinting edge in Her voice.

In response, Raegan arched her brow, a sly smile creeping onto her face despite the tears. "I am neither mortal nor magic, neither living nor dead," she replied, meeting Fate's gaze. "Such things *never* had any bearing on me, goddess."

Fate's eyes bored into hers, threaded with silver, the pupils barely more than a shining coin. Raegan held her ground. A single second or a thousand years could have passed before Fate's shoulders drooped and the primordial being nodded in acquiescence. Then She turned, the waters barely rippling around Her movements. On the far wall, there was—quite suddenly—a door. It was plain and simple, a rectangle of white wood, but it called to Raegan with all the power and might of doors encased in ironwork or inlaid with precious gems. She walked toward it, the waters parting for her.

"Wait," Raegan said, coming to a halt. A few paces ahead, Fate turned, Her impossible silver eyes sharpening. "When I go back . . . I want to be Fey. So I can actually stay with him. So he won't just be waiting for the day to come that he watches me die again. I deserve it. *We* deserve it, after you've used us like pawns for a thousand years."

The atmosphere pressed down on her all at once, like a thunderstorm appearing out of nowhere on a muggy summer day.

"Have you gone quite mad?" Fate demanded, Her voice sending a tremor through the room.

Raegan grinned. "Oh, absolutely."

EPILOGUE
FIFTEEN YEARS LATER

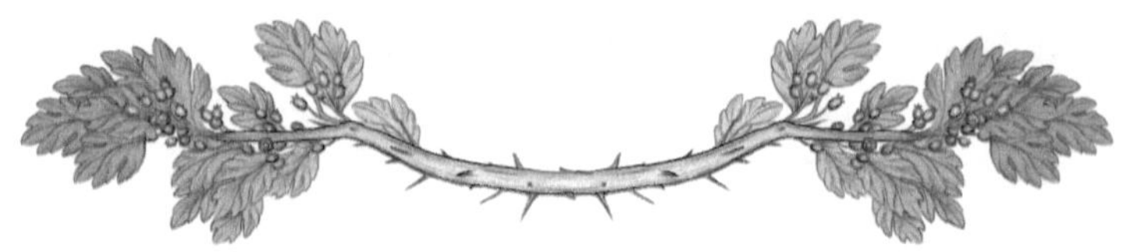

The new pub atop the hill was charming. Too charming, frankly, with its stone terrace overlooking Hiraeth in the valley below. The mature oak trees hemming the south-facing side were lovely, as were the dried husks of fiddlehead ferns clustered around their roots.

From the cobblestone pathway, the King glared at all of it with some measure of contempt. So much cheering, singing, mingling, and drinking under the glorious sweep of golden hour, all in honor of Liberation Day. For the first time in fifteen years, he was supposed to be attempting to celebrate this godsdamn day like everyone else in Hiraeth.

The King leaned on his cane. He considered turning around and going home. He ground his jaw, drawing in a deep breath, the air heavy with autumn sunshine, woodsmoke, and damp leaves. Like a black storm cloud hunched over the pathway, Oberon deliberated. He could admit that something about the busy pub pulled at his aching places—the throb of mortals and Fair Folk alike, the shared mirth, the deep sense of being *alive*. That is what he had fought for, was it not? For his people to *live*.

"Perhaps," he grumbled to himself, eyeing the building and its lush grounds, "the interior will hold less appeal." There was, of course, only one way to find out. So with a harsh exhale, Oberon pulled his wool overcoat closer to fend off the chill and then continued down the winding stone path.

Autumn winds rattled leaves loose from the trees surrounding the stone building, showering his broad shoulders with a gold and burgundy garland fit for a king. He slowed his pace, brushing the leaves from his overcoat with one elegant, long-fingered hand. And then, swatting aside a group of drunk young people with his cane, Oberon slipped through the tall arched door and into the pub.

He groaned as he took in the dark rafters bisecting tall ceilings and lime-washed walls studded with sconces blackened in patina. Fat beeswax pillars crowded every available windowsill and corner, throwing warm golden light into the space. Faded velvet couches lounged in the corners, where the shadows were deeper, thicker. A few long, farmhouse-style tables were tucked against the walls to accommodate larger parties. The space brimmed with joy, the air scented with fermented apples, beeswax, and damp wool.

The King dug his fingertips into the handle of his cane and tried desperately not to think about how much she would have liked this place. How she would have held her drink in one hand, his heart in the other, and led him to one of those dark corners. His ring finger throbbed, throat tightening. If he closed his eyes right now, he would see her—those full thighs draped across his lap, that wide, feral grin on her lovely mouth.

Instead, the King kept his eyes open and walked straight to the bar. Over the years, he had learned to stop indulging his phantom ache for her. It only ever made the chasm of his loss grow wider, large enough to swallow him whole. He was glad he had decided to come to the pub early—time to gather himself before the others arrived. It hurt them all, he knew, to see him shattered like this, so he would down a few drinks and cover up the ache.

He slid onto a tall stool, his knee catching painfully, though his face remained impassive. *She* might have read the slight notch in his brow, the tension around the corners of his eyes. But Raegan was gone, he reminded himself, and it seemed unlikely she was coming back. He sighed, digging into his coat pocket for coins.

Someone at Oberon's left jostled his elbow. With a low grunt, he switched his cane to his right side, collecting the coins in his other hand as the bartender finally approached. "Cider, please," he said, handing over payment.

And then his breath caught in his chest. Distracted by his grief, Oberon had not only used his left hand, but also neglected to put gloves on before walking inside the pub. The King glanced down, tightening his jaw, as both he and the barkeep looked at the corrupted bond mark on his finger in unison.

The thin silver circle that had once inked his finger had long since turned soot-black. Midnight-colored despair leaked up his forearm, coloring his veins an unpleasant shade of blue-black.

Oberon sighed. *This* was precisely why he did not socialize in public. He should have turned around, should have disappeared back down the hill and into Hiraeth's mist-damp, winding streets when he had the chance. Better yet, he should have insisted on the usual private gathering in the first place—not this nonsense at the Black Hare Pub.

The barkeep glanced up at him, eyes dragging across the King's broad, muscular shoulders, then the scar that nicked the outside of his left eye. They shook their head. "Would never dream of charging you in my establishment, particularly today of all days," the barkeep replied, pushing the coins back across the polished wood.

Oberon paused, his eyes narrowing. "Appreciated," he said eventually, taking a long pull of the cider. "Though I am planning to drown my sorrows this evening, so I suggest you consider taking my coin at some point."

The barkeep offered a ghost of a smile, like they knew the taste of such sorrows, and moved to mop up a spill farther down the counter. "Alright, only one little tithe. One drink. It's a small show of gratitude for everything you've done, my liege."

Oberon inclined his head in thanks. To his relief, the bartender turned away, striding to the other side of the bar, leaving him alone again. He exhaled, some of the tension in his shoulders releasing. The barkeep's gesture had been kind, and the cider was fine—earthy and musky, only a little sweet. But there was no need for these little tithes. He had fought for all those years, sacrificed everything he had, precisely so this barkeep could open a pub on a Feyrish city's lovely outskirts. So mortals and Fair Folk could live amongst each other. So magic could thrive. So Hiraeth no longer needed to hide—though after all those years, much of the mist and rain still clung to the city. So people could spend a fine autumn day like today dancing instead of weeping.

Across the bar, a couple laughed, leaning their foreheads together before sharing a tender kiss. Oberon tore his gaze away, staring down at the polished wood counter. Fifteen years later, and yet he could barely handle the sight of someone else with their lover. His longing was too thickly wrapped around his lungs, squeezing the air out of his chest whenever he thought of her.

The cider stung his throat, or perhaps that was just the tears he was holding back. Oberon had never stopped wanting her, never stopped craving her at every hour of every day. It was the Feyrish union, yes, but it was more than that, and he knew it. She was the furious flame to his steady shadow. She was the only person who had made him believe there was nothing wrong with being a monster.

Damn the barkeep for recognizing him. Damn this pub for being something she might have loved, a place they might have gone together when the cottage they should have shared grew too quiet, too lonely. Damn the memories awakening in his depths, twisting and turning in the cages where he had locked them away. Damn the eternal heaviness of his grief, an iron chain wrapped around his ankles.

He scowled into the golden cider. It should not hurt so much; after all, he had gotten almost everything he wanted. They had saved the world. Magic had been restored. The Fair Folk and mortals lived in relative peace. No one had too much. No one had too little. Except for him, of course. He had too little because he did not have her, and it turned out she was all he had ever really wanted.

The room was growing warmer, filled with even more people now. He glanced across the room at the dial for the time. People were, understandably, not very fond of clocks any longer, and it continued to bring him a little delight to see everyone trying to reinvent the physical appearance of the devices. Still a few minutes to go before the others were due to arrive.

He could go sit out on the terrace and wait for them, but being out there alone might actually be worse. So the King stayed put, even when someone recognized him and started up a humiliating chant in his honor. Like the final battle of the Great War had been a sports match and he had scored the winning goal, not lost the love of his life in a gods-forsaken realm of dust and death.

Despite the small, false smile on his face, Oberon's hand curled into a fist and stayed like that, even as the chant faded away and the barkeep shooed the young people off. He desperately wanted to take amusement in their joy, to share it with them—he had fought for this, had he not?

But his grief had grown so heavy. He took another long drink of his cider, the bartop in front of him now littered with offerings of alcohol from the Black Hare's patrons. The King exhaled. At least he rarely had time to wallow in the depths of his sorrow. His hands were full with an actual, restored court and the construction of an entirely new society where humans and Fey could live side-by-side. Nearly everything he had dreamed of for so many years. Some days, it was enough to keep him going.

But what truly drove the King—if he was honest—was the half-mad, foolish idea that he might get to see her again. Setting his jaw, Oberon stared down at his hands, his eyes tracing the corrupted bond mark. For all the might of the Unseelie Throne, all the unfathomable power restored to him with the opening of the Gates, he was reduced to wait-ing. To sleeping in an empty bed, awakening with her name on his lips. Fate refused to speak to him, and any of the Morrigan's attempts to inter-cede on his behalf only seemed to make matters worse. The King had begged, offered to share his seemingly endless lifeforce, or even give it up entirely. He just wanted her—as long as she still wanted him, of course. With a long, shuddering exhale, he reminded himself he had chosen the pain. Chased it, even. Because the pain was still better than forgetting her. Because the pain, at the very least, made him feel closer to her than anything else could.

The King's cider was empty and the pub was thick with people. He sighed. Someone at his side brushed his shirt sleeve, offering some kind of flirtation. Oberon felt exhausted and immeasurably old. When he turned to decline, he wondered if the young mortal even knew who he was. If they saw eternity stretch in his ocean eyes, the way she always had. Probably not.

Oberon slid from the stool and unfolded to his full height with the help of his cane. He narrowed his eyes, searching the throngs of people, telling himself all the while it was only to thank the barkeep again. But that would of course be a lie, and apparently the Fair Folk could not lie. He put his hands into his pockets, preparing to turn for the door, when he saw a flash of red on the other side of the room.

His heart stopped in his chest, that long thread of yearning uncurling, open-mouthed and treacherous in its unrelenting desire. He fervently told himself that it was not her. It had not been her the first thousand times, so it would certainly not be her now. But all good reason seemed to flee the King when it came to his witch. He ground his jaw and told himself to leave, but his body refused, the weight and breadth of his ache rooting him to the spot. His eyes followed the tumble of dark auburn curls like nothing else had ever mattered. That thorny tangle of emotions in his chest keened with a desperation that made him feel weak and foolish.

Oberon squeezed his eyes shut, trying to stem the tears that were gathering like a thunderstorm. When he opened them, there were no deep red waves to be found in the crowd. He heaved an exhale. Not in relief—something else. He did not possess the words for whatever it was —and did not need them, because he *knew* she was not coming back. The Timekeeper had unmade Raegan, and no one—not even someone like her—came back from such a thing.

Oberon turned on his heel toward the door, pausing when he found someone blocking his path. He glanced down, his vision blurred by the tears still clinging to his eyelashes, to find a freckled face looking up at him, framed by curls the color of the leaves at the end of autumn.

"Hey," came a voice above the din—low, slightly hoarse around the edges, sweet as sin. "I've been looking for you."

His lungs pressed too tight against his ribs, his heart breaking under the heavy burden of hope. Oberon blinked the tears away. And there she was. Soft golden skin, freckles scattered across her nose and cheekbones like constellations, eyes the color of a late summer meadow. Her dress dipped low, exposing collarbones and the swell of her full bust, flaring out slightly around her ample hips, the long sleeves sensible for the chill. Good. He would not want her to be cold, not with the first frost well on its way.

Words gathered somewhere in the back of his throat, but his tongue tangled around them, half-choked by a tide of ache that nearly swept him off his feet.

"Oberon," Raegan said, arching one brow. She wrapped a few curls around the end of her finger, and his heart followed the motion, twisting into knots. "Do you want to get out of here?"

"With you?" Oberon replied, his voice so heavy with need he thought she might mock him, that pretty little mouth landing barbs despite his thick skin. "Yes. How far do you want to go?" His body moved of its own accord as if all these long and lonely years had not passed. In an elegant swoop, the King held his arm out for her.

"With you?" Raegan echoed, her voice husky with enough desire to unmake him. "To the ends of it all, I think." The deathless witch took his arm in that way she always did, sidling so close that he—quite suddenly—remembered what it was to be alive.

Together, they slipped through the door. He wanted to say a thousand things to her. He wanted to announce to every person in the pub that his beloved had at long last returned to him, like the tide to the shore, the heather to the hills, the dusk to the lake.

But they had barely made it a few steps down the stone walkway when Raegan unwound her arm from his. The King faltered, needing the blistering heat of her, knowing that he had always loved the pain, but then she wrapped her hand around his wrist and pulled him into the shadow of the oak trees.

"My husband," she murmured, her hands sliding up his chest to grip either side of his overcoat.

"My wife," he replied with so much feeling in a few scant syllables. He set his cane against one of the tree's wide trunks and slid his hands around her waist. His large palms fit in the divot of her generous curves, just so—like they had been made for each other from the primordial dark of the universe. "Is it really you?" the King asked, one hand moving to cup the side of her face.

She gazed up at him, her meadow eyes glimmering in the sunset. In response, she stood on her tiptoes and pulled him toward her by his lapels. Oberon met her with too much eagerness, too much hunger, and the second he tasted her, he knew without a doubt that his deathless witch had returned to him. Tears tumbled down his angular face, but she did not seem to mind—if anything, she pulled him closer, deepening the kiss.

Someone lingering outside the pub spotted them and yelled a good-natured joke. They pulled apart, laughing, and Oberon found Raegan's face was damp with tears, too. He traced the line of her cheekbones, the soft curve of her hairline. He wanted to stare at her until the sun tumbled from the sky. He wanted to bury his face between her thighs until time collapsed and he did not remember what it was to be without her.

The King opened his mouth to tell her so, fingertips diving into her curls to hold her face in his hands. With a start, he found her ears were no longer softly rounded—instead, they came to a sharp, deadly curve. She must have seen the look on his face because she grinned at him, so feral and unbroken and beautiful that he had no idea how he had ever managed to deserve her.

"Would you do it again, if you knew?" Raegan murmured, drawing closer, her thighs opening for him just as they always had. His body keened with desire, hard and aching. "If you knew how much it would hurt?"

"Yes," Oberon replied in a whisper, the word spoken like a vow. "I would do it all again."

She smiled up at him, tears streaming down her face. "I love you, my faerie king," she said, just as fierce.

"I would have waited another thousand years," Oberon replied, his voice raw and breaking. "I love you, my villainous thing."

She pulled his left hand into the golden sweep of the setting sun, turning it over in her smaller palms. The seeping poison of heartbreak that had been slinking farther and farther up his forearm all these years was gone, replaced with a slender, shining silver band.

Oberon tangled his fingers into hers and pulled her out of the oak grove, around the side of the pub toward the stone terrace. For good measure, he kissed her again, the kind of kiss that she always said made the rest of the world stop existing. All around them, autumn shimmered in its unbroken bronzen glory.

"Follow me," the King murmured as he retrieved his cane and then pulled away. "I think this will make you happy." Raegan looked up at him, arching her brow in a way that made his stomach flutter. Pressing his lips together, he just smiled, leading the way down the flagstone path.

At its end was a lovely stone terrace, currently occupied by one long, lone table. Its surface was dressed in beeswax candles, all matter of twinkling lights and snaking vines and aubergine petals. In the far corner of the terrace, a bonfire crackled merrily. The hill dropped off on one side, the mist-veiled vista of Hiraeth sitting at the bottom of the valley like a shining gray jewel.

Oberon led Raegan to the edge of the terrace, taking in the sight before him—desperately trying to memorize the feeling, to tuck it deep inside his marrow and never let it go. On the left of the table sat Reilly and Alanna, giggling infectiously about something. Andronica and Maelona were standing by the table's head, the Unseelie knight brushing the ex-Protectorate woman's knuckles with a delicate kiss. Baba Yaga, looking all the more feral when plucked from her pocket realm, crouched by the fire with a stick, Blodeuwedd laughing on the other side of its dancing flames. And at the far edge of the terrace, his black toad eyes locked on Raegan in utter disbelief, was Rainer. Apparently unable to summon actual words, the kelpie instead began to violently scrape his front hoof against the stone to get everyone's attention.

His heart fuller than he dared to believe he deserved, the King turned back toward Raegan and cupped her face in his hands. For a moment, he said nothing, marveling at the way the sunlight made emeralds out of her eyes. And then, finally, he managed to ask, "Would you like to join us?"

Raegan's lips pressed together as tears spilled down her face. "More than anything," she whispered, her voice choked with emotion as she fought to maintain a casual tone. As if she had only been gone on a short trip somewhere quiet.

His vision blurred, Oberon turned to look at their loved ones. Maelona, with both hands clamped against her mouth, tears running down her face. Blodeuwedd, her sobs taking her halfway to her knees. Reilly, a tangle of long limbs as they tried to help the owl woman stay on her feet. Alanna, standing now, her hands pressed to her heart, eyes shining. Andronica, her arms around Maelona, her lower lip quivering. Baba Yaga, barely more than a shadow at the edge of the terrace, the bonfire catching on her sharp, feral smile.

"What did you have planned for the evening?" Raegan asked, her voice rising in the breeze, the sound of it sweeter than anything else the

King had ever known. That bone-deep ache he thought he would never be rid of, that kept him awake at all hours, that pulled at his Threads with unrelenting fingers, slipped out of existence as if it had never really been there at all.

"We were planning," Oberon replied, his voice breaking, fresh tears running down his face, "to linger in the sun."

And then the witch and the King stepped out of the pub's shadow and into the glimmering light of golden hour. Whatever happened next was theirs alone. There are no more ballads, no more tales, and though a Fatesong swooped low and lovely through the late afternoon, aching and swollen, for the first time in a millennium, it did not loop.

About the Author

Victoria Mier is the queer, disabled author of *Beyond the Aching Door* and a suspected changeling. *Holy Wrath* is her third novel. When she's not writing, you can find her wandering the aisles of a thrift store, deep in the Wissahickon woods, in a field with a horse named Castle, or on the couch with her partner Jordon and their perfect cat, Calliope. Learn more at **victoriamier.com** and follow along on Instagram at **@by_victoriamier**.